GODSTEED

Book 1

Night of Wolves

B.J. Hobbsen

Copyright © BJ Hobbsen 2014

The Author asserts the moral right to be identified as the author of this work.

All rights reserved. No part of this publication may be reproduced, stored in a retrieval system, or transmitted, in any form or by any means, electronic, mechanical, photocopying, recording or otherwise, without prior permission of the author.

This book is sold subject to the condition that it shall not, by way of trade or otherwise, be lent, re-sold, hired out or otherwise circulated without the author's prior consent in any form of binding or cover other than in which it is published and without a similar condition including this condition being imposed on the subsequent purchaser.

ISBN-13: 978-1500737160

ISBN-10: 150073716X

The Author

BJ Hobbsen dedicates her life to the rescue of animals. All funds raised by the Godsteed series are donated to animal rescue projects worldwide. Her writing reflects her passion for horses, swordplay and all things medieval.

Winner 2003 Blue Fringe Arts Festival Literature Award

"Extraordinarily powerful. Told with a great depth of imagination, a broad canvas and written with a great love of her subject. Huge and expansive plot and well handled work of fantasy." Judge: Ann Beveridge (Editor and author)

Finalist 2004 Varuna Awards

"This work has beauty and energy. I find this a challenging and exceptional fantasy work." Judge: Peter Bishop

"It's no secret I love this book. Beautifully imagined. I've never read a story as richly detailed. This book soars in terms of being a fully-imagined fantasy. The theme of the unicorn, with its full complement of mystical associations (the moon, the virgin, the blood) is woven intriguingly throughout the story. This is a fully-real, fully-developed work of art." Linda Steele – author of IBIS (DAW)

Reviewer comments:

"This is the sort of story that readers crave." Karen Mayer – (Winner of SF/F/H category of the 2005 ArcheBooks Publishing Co. novel contest.)

"This is the type of book readers hope they'll find when they go to a bookstore."

"I'm so glad I read this. It left me feeling like a good piece of writing should. You made each scene real. Thanks for the privilege."

"It is exceptionally written with wonderful descriptions and an interest catching story."

Acknowledgments

Thank you to BJ Alexander, friend and fellow author, who did not live to see her wonderful words in print. Your generosity and insight inspired both my life, and this book to see the light of day.

For Strawberry and all those voiceless forgotten ones, abandoned, cold, hungry and alone. May you be found, may you be loved, may you find peace and eternal rest.

Hast thou given the horse his might? Hast thou clothed his neck with thunder?

He paweth in the valley, and rejoiceth in his strength: he goeth out to meet the clash of arms.

He mocketh at fear, and is not affrighted; neither turneth he back from the sword.

The quiver rattleth against him, the flame of spear and javelin.

He swalloweth the ground with storm and rage.

He smelleth the battle afar off, the thunder of the captains and the war cry.

Job 39:21

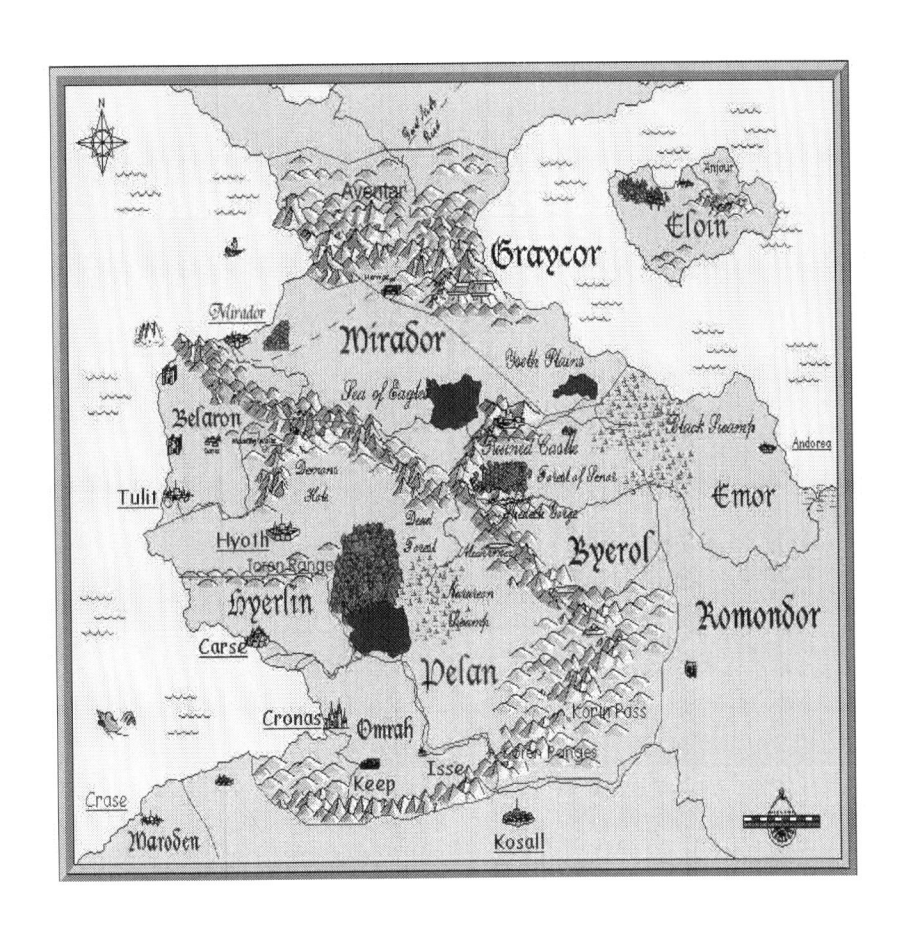

Kingdom of Mirador

Prologue

Eyes . . . watching eyes . . . Sihan twisted in the saddle, fingers closing on the hilt of his dagger, heart beating swift and hard. Nothing met his searching stare; only cloud and snow-clotted wind filled the trail behind. No unusual sound caught his ear, just the muffled crunch and squeak of a multitude of hooves on packed snow.

Cold shivered up and down his spine. He pushed back his cowl, peering at the riders ahead. Neither his father nor any other horseman gave sign they noticed anything odd.

Still, Sihan's skin prickled.

Falling flakes thickened, plastering every man's cloak to his back. At the van of the column of horsemen, Sihan's father set his horse into a resolved trot. Senfari stewards followed suit, mounts kicking up flurries in the race to reach home before the blizzard blocked the trail.

Snowflakes bore down, matting Sihan's eyelashes. He pulled his cowl over his face, sweeping stray brown strands of hair beneath it. Trees, ridges, bushes, everything merged into a blank white canvas.

For a flashed moment, a pale shadow glimmered between trunks flanking the trail, then disappeared, leaving naught but swirling mist. Sihan shook his head. His imagination was roving wild. Leagues spun out behind – the long trek from the Yseth plains to his beloved mountains. It was just exhaustion clouding his senses. In the whiteout, even the other riders resembled ghosts.

Then, close by, a hoof scraped rock. Kheran, the only other youth allowed to ride rearguard, was right beside Sihan, riding knee to knee, so it was not him. The sound definitely came from the snow-veiled trees.

Who or what was following them?

Responsive to the feather-caress signalled by Sihan's hands on the reins, his stallion halted. Another movement, just at the verge of sight. Sihan edged his horse toward the pale shimmer. In the few heartbeats he tarried, a solid wall of cloud obliterated the other riders. Sihan counted another ten heartbeats. When nothing else moved, he urged his horse on.

'What are you doing?' asked Kheran, examining Sihan closely as he rode up alongside.

'There's something back there.'

Kheran pushed his limp wet fringe out of his eyes as he squinted over his shoulder. 'What?'

'There's a horse following us.'

'Bollocks.' Kheran's bloodless lips drew down at the corners. 'Snow's playing you.'

'No,' said Sihan, certain something loomed beyond the pall of white. 'I heard it. You go on with the others. I'll hang back a bit.'

'Don't be stupid. You'll lose us.'

'I'll find you. It's not far to home.' Graycor horsemen had ridden this ancient trail for longer than he had been alive. He had ridden here most of his twelve winters. He would know these mountains sightless. Their streams ran through his veins. Cliffs, ravines, crevasses, wove into the fabric of his being.

'But your father–' Kheran began, wariness edging his voice.

'Won't even know I'm gone.' Denying his friend another objection, Sihan guided his horse to the side of the trail, letting the others vanish, becoming one with the immense whiteness shifting on the wind. Fog shrouding him, he waited.

A branch swished. Whoever – whatever – was coming.

Sihan's stallion snorted and shied as though something passed nearby. But what? Nothing took form. A ghost might have wafted past. Hooves thudded softly ahead, but the blizzard hid the beast completely.

Sihan urged his stallion to a trot. Swift slashing hooves cut into snow. Branches tugged at Sihan's cloak, trunks scraped his knees as his horse dodged between trees.

Again something drifted on the edge of vision, more than just wind-tossed branches. Between silver trunks ahead, an apparition glimmered, so faint, an outline could not frame it. Was that a wind-swept tail, the curve of rump? Did an eye glisten dark beneath a sweep of forelock? Absolute certainty filled him. He tracked a riderless horse through the storm.

Suddenly his stallion propped. For a heartbeat, the flakes thinned. Sihan sucked in a hard breath.

Not ten strides ahead stood the insubstantial silhouette of a moon-pale mare. More shadow than substance, a transparent ghost, yet no denying her existence. With a violent snort, she shook her head, rattling tendrils of ice hanging from her ragged whiskers like a beard. Her ears pricked forward, flickered back, listening. She knew she was being pursued. She stamped a hoof.

And disappeared.

Sihan's mind spun. What he had seen could not possibly be real. Surely it was as Kheran had said, some trick of the weather. The mare could not possibly exist. Not that colour. Not here.

Still, he set his horse into a canter, determined to find her, refusing to accept he had only imagined her. Scanning the ground, he cursed. Any tracks had already been obliterated. Cloud hazed between trees. Had she been an illusion or had there really been a spirit in the form of a mare? Where did truth begin and dreams caused by fatigue end?

With each stride, snow frothed like sea-foam around his stallion's legs. Wet mist swirled against Sihan's face. He peered into the distance, unable to distinguish anything. Candlewoods screaved and creaked, cream branches ghostlike.

Again, his stallion baulked. Sihan watched its flickering ears, searching for a sign of where to look. Wind began to rush, howling through the trees. Further up the mountains, a tempest roared over the topmost peaks, a glacial, killing storm set to sweep down the slopes. They would need to reach shelter before it hit.

The stallion's ears speared forward. Snowflakes hardened, beat in Sihan's eyes. Ahead, weaving in and out of shadowed trunks, the pale mare took form, faded, reappeared, vanished once more.

Sihan pushed his stallion hard through deepening drifts and the wild weather that transformed the mare into a phantom. The press of trees fell away.

Even without any familiar marker, Sihan sensed where they were. It was within him, a mind-map of the mountains, an inborn knowledge guiding him without the need to see.

His horse stood on the edge of a clearing guarded by candlewoods. To his left, dark shapes arose from the spiralling snow – squat timbered structures, stinking of smoke and men. With spring thaw, those barns would house the finest colts in the kingdom, weaned from northern dams that ranged from the rugged mountains of Graycor to the desert plains of Yseth, bred for stamina, swift as arrows. Pride of the Graycor bloodhorse range, they would be destined for the king's horse markets where all would find service as mounts in the army. But no colts lived here now, and the mares would not be brought to the high ranges for another moon's cycle.

So how was this mare here? And not of Graycor blood?

Wind battered Sihan broadside, blotting out the rude dwellings. Shrieking, it hurled stinging pellets against his skin. Every sucked-in breath pierced his lungs like a shard of ice. Then, for a brief unclouded heartbeat, the storm parted, revealing the mare. Her head jerked from side to side, looking, searching.

A weird noise wailed across the clearing. The mare swung toward it. Sihan followed her gaze. From time unknown, a peculiar tor had stood at the centre of that clearing, a rock spire. A singing stone, his mother had styled it, for the wild music it made when winter winds blew over the smooth surface polished by long years of wind and rain.

But this day its song was different: louder, more strident, as though it sought to outcry the gale. The strange iced melody surged, lilted, pulsed. Clear, aching notes flowed through Sihan like heart's blood, as though they were a part of him, within him.

The mare threw her head high, black eyes rimmed white. Fear flowed around her, through the branches of candlewood and ash.

Sihan knew immediately another pair of eyes watched them. Something else stalked the storm.

A wolf howl quavered, near, raw, a soul-devouring tremble against the wind. Heart drumming, Sihan swung his horse about, whirled it again. His leather-gloved hand drew his hunting blade from its sheath. Every sense alert, he scanned the blinding maelstrom through icicle-fringed lashes.

Another eerie cry of bloodlust rang out, flung toward

absent stars.

Sihan's horse leapt. Muzzle, teeth, a heavy shoulder crashed against Sihan. Unbalanced, he fell, sprawling on the ground. Winded, he gasped at breath, struggling to haul himself upright and avoid the stallion's pivoting legs. The horse battered the wolf with its hind legs.

Across the clearing, the mare bolted, floundering in gut-deep drifts, sweat streaked dark across her flank. The wolf, head sunk between jutting shoulders, bounded after her.

Sihan's thoughts jerked every which way. For a lone wolf to hunt near night in such a squall, it must be badly hungered, and desperation fed savagery. Sihan could not take it alone.

He slapped the stallion hard on the rump, yelling, 'Home! Go home!' And prayed as the stallion took off that it would do just that.

The mare lurched toward the rock. The wolf leapt. With a convulsive effort, the mare reared and struck. Hooves thudded flesh. The wolf rolled, bunched, leapt again. Fangs raked flank. Lashing hooves met empty air. Incisors seared her throat. She bit down on the wolf's exposed back, caught fur and skin between her teeth. Crushed.

Writhing, wailing, the wolf shook free from her grip. She whirled, booted with her heels, staggered helplessly. Blood pulsed from her slashed throat. A dark cascading river streamed through the thick hair of her chest, down both forelegs, splashing over her hooves. She threw a desperate neigh, useless because there was no one to hear it but Sihan and he was just a boy.

Leaning into the wind, he pushed through the smothering white, boots slipping every stride. Fingers closed tight on the dagger's hilt, he tried to pick out the glow of blue eyes in the whirling snow. As if in answer, a long, unearthly screech rent the air, a triumphant exultation of blood, singing death into the teeth of the storm.

The wolf lunged at the mare again. Dagger-edged fangs sliced a strip of hide from her withers. The beast clung to the base of her crest. Its weight sent her skittering sidewise. Blood dripped down her belly.

As the singing stone moaned, she drew herself up by force of will, wheeled, shook the wolf away, and drummed it in the gut. Then, fast as it had come, strength melted from her. Head drooped, swinging heavily from side to side, blood-drained and exhausted, she collapsed against the boulder, legs thrust out at an angle.

Keening filled the air, growing louder and louder till it ripped through the trees.

Disoriented, Sihan fought the urge to clap his hands over his ears. He had to be ready to fight. Mountain wolves were fast, crafty beasts, quick to attack and sneaky with it.

A snarl on its lips, the wolf cocked its ears to the song of the stone, padding back and forth as though it dared not come closer.

Forelegs buckling, the mare slid down in a series of jolting spasms, snow crunching under her settling weight. The tide of life ebbed.

The wolf sprang, fangs shredding the hide at her belly. Slashing. Tearing. A final shudder, then the mare lay unmoving, blood melting and freezing about her. There was not even strength for a last grunt of pain.

The stone began to sing in earnest, driving the wolf back. Desolate, aching tones swept over ancient bones. Slowly, so slowly, death crept along each note. Then, in a swift, rising crescendo, the stone erupted in a burst of song so intense it might shake even spirits free from the Shadow Realm.

Whiteness swirled around Sihan, and in the space of a heartbeat, the wolf vanished. *Gods, Gods.* The stone's song screeched so loud now, Sihan doubted he could hear the wolf even if it walked right up to him and howled in his face.

A dark mass struck him hard. Gasping, he hit the ground, senses swimming. Above him, blue orbs glowed, suspended in space. Fangs drove for his eyes. Sihan flung up an arm, rolled, too slow, trapped in a tangle of grey, matted fur. Terror tore from his throat. 'Kheran!' His cry speared through the jumble of claw and fang. 'Father!'

Teeth slashed at his cloak. Fangs scraped his cheek, hot, stinging. Sihan gagged on foul, putrid breath, nostrils filled with stink and hair. In the melee of fur and teeth, the knife flashed.

Hammering at the muzzle, Sihan slammed the dagger with all the force he could muster. Blade grated against bone.

Then the wolf was on top, heavy, crushing. In the grey light, Sihan stared into a gaping maw framed by a big, grey-haired head. Raw-edged steel stuck from the half-cleaved face.

The world rippled. The wolf's eyes held his, no longer glowing, but staring at him with the glass-eyed stare of something undead. Chills coursed through Sihan. Cold, deeper than any he had ever known, crept up his arms, down his throat. Time seemed to slow.

He shuddered, his grip on the dagger's hilt failing as ice settled in his gut. The beast's stare stayed locked with his. It was not dead. Its lips snarled. Its face pressed nearer, a stretching of skin over bone, cadaverous, matching the stare of relentless hatred in its eyes.

Another shudder washed across the storm. Everything became motionless. Even the windsong of the stone stilled to a whisper. Light rippled through the snowbarks as if the moon had broken through.

Something dark arose before Sihan, a faint form in the haze. Something brushed his cheek, a breeze, a shadow thickening into a hand. Ribbons of mist wound about him, undulating like uncoiled snakes, then coalesced, slowly taking the form of a face. A boy's face. Smooth, soft fingers caressed Sihan's brow.

Join with me, the boy said. His lips did not move, yet the silken words flowed into Sihan's mind. *Speak my name, and I will cast this abomination from you.*

Sihan's heart beat loud in his ears as he stared up into a gentle, green gaze.

Join with me. Call my name to your lips and we shall be one. Come.

Black foreboding spread within Sihan, choking thought. 'Who are you?' he whispered, certain he was caught in a dream, in imagination, a child's world of shadows. He was asleep, tucked up in bed, living a nightmare of wolves and storms and ghosts.

The boy answered, *You draw a distinction where none exists. All the world is a dream.* He stiffened. Back braced, shoulders squared, he raised his hand. *My name has passed into the shadowlands. Only you may call it back.*

Sihan groped the darkness in his mind, but found nothing he could offer. 'I don't know your name.'

You know, insisted the boy, voice a shadow-whisper. *We are one. My name is yours. Speak it and call me back to the world.* He held out a hand, ghost-grey fingers tightening upon Sihan's. *Come, join with me.*

Sihan stared at the boy. Pain, deep agony, tore his senses. He knew the blinding torture of a lance driven through his gut. He stared through broken vision, cried out an agony of wordless incoherence.

Speak our name! The boy's voice was command. *Hurry!*

The words slashed at Sihan, but he had no name to offer this half-formed being carrying the bleakness of the world of non-existence. He forced a response past dry lips. 'My name is Sihan. I don't know yours.'

You are not Sihan!

Sihan tried to free himself, but the spirit-grip was unforgiving. Ice and emptiness.

Sihan's heart drummed in his throat. He wanted to wake up from this dual horror of wolves and ghosts, but the weight pinning him down held the sense of reality, the snow stinging the wounds in his face taunted him this impossibility was real. He yearned to crawl away, to run, but the beast held him fast. And all the while the onslaught of demand swirled around him.

You are not Sihan. We are one! Speak our name! Join with me!

Then the world shivered out of horrified stillness.

A roar broke over Sihan. A white horse burst from the whirling darkness, dissolving the image of the boy, bringing with it the storm howl. Hooves crashed down on either side of Sihan's head.

Outlined in moon-bright radiance, a massive stallion reared, towering out of mist and raging snow. Every line bespoke power and strength, and great age – as though it had lived a thousand winters, maybe more – hollowed flanks, face a stark mask whittled to bone, coat lashed with battle scars over hard, knotted muscle. Its eyes ringed white, glowed silver, then flattened to a dead stare matching the wolf's.

Hooves fell. One struck the wolf from Sihan, tearing from the brute a screeching whine. The other glanced off Sihan's chest, the impact powerful as a blacksmith's hammer.

The wolf sprung to a crouch beside the singing stone. Its unnatural shadow, four times the beast's size, spilled against the boulder, black and menacing, rippling as though it might come alive and leap. The wolf put back its head and let loose a howl.

Ears pressed back, head, nose and neck all one snaking line, the stallion bared its teeth, lunged, caught the wolf and crushed within its maw skin and flesh. With a sharp crack, like a snapping branch, it broke the wolf's backbone.

Muscles knotting the great white neck, the horse hurled the wolf through the air, flinging it as though it weighed nothing. Bounding after, in one stride it reached the fallen carcass, reared once, twice, again, smashing the wolf to pulp with each downward stroke of hoof.

Sihan scrabbled back. The stallion stilled over its victim. Standing immobile above the cadaver, the horse raised its head to stare long at Sihan, a haunting, knowing look. Then it pricked its ears as if listening to some distant call.

Something pointed and silver glimmered above black eyes burning fire. Did a horn protrude from its head? Before Sihan could be sure, the silver light faded around the horse, the squall closing about it.

Shivering, Sihan blinked, trying to clear madness from his eyes. Emptiness: nothing but white, and a dark mass of broken flesh. He groaned, trying to rise, then froze, as a shadow moved where the wolf had fallen. Fogged vapour formed upon the air. Threads of mist spun into a sphere, glimmering light at the edge of dark, white-gold, silver, the blinding white of midsummer sun.

Wind blew falling snow apart. A silhouette appeared. Silent and unmoving, a girl clad in a white gown stood there, hands held up to her face, skin luminescent as though cast in moonlight. Ebony hair flowed like a river over her shoulders. Through her fingers she stared at him, from black, accusing eyes, so dark they devoured night in their setting of pale skin. One hand fell away from her left cheek.

Sihan choked.

A dagger stuck in the flesh beneath her left eye. Sihan's dagger. With one swift gesture, she tore it free, leaving a raw, gaping wound. She threw the blade into the ground at his feet before clutching once more at a face streaming blood.

Lifetimes passed as they stared at one another, he in dread and horror, her eyes dark and condemning. Another ripple passed across the world, then she also disappeared, dissolving into an aftertaste of something fluid and evil. Time seemed to rush back to speed.

Sihan's pounding heart threatened to tear a hole in his chest. A haze enveloped his senses, dizziness as though he had sat up too fast. Black mist, white mist, wreathed about him. Fear spider-crawled down his back. He stared into the blizzard, half-afraid to acknowledge what he had seen, but nothing appeared, no girl, no boy, no horse. Just the wolf's battered corpse.

He tried to rise and almost fell over something hard and solid at his feet.

The faint scent of horse filled his nostrils. The mare. Quickly, he knelt and pushed aside snow, shivering anew as it worked its way inside his glove and melted against his skin. Warmth radiated through his glove. He scraped and scraped, reached hair, hide – so pale it was indistinguishable from the snow, and blood, sticky and congealing.

He dug in earnest, grunting as he pulled the mare's head onto his lap. Seizing the pointed ears, he tried to rouse her. Icicled lashes flickered. 'Alive, by all that is merciful!' he cried. If he could get her to the stable . . .

The hope was futile. He knew it. He needed help, but his father was home by now, and the rest of the Senfari stewards were encamped on the lower ranges, guarding the herd.

Sihan pushed back the hair on the shoulder, peering at it closely. There was no brand. He ran his hand over the distended belly, scraped away more snow. White turned to black. Oozing blood froze on his gloves. He probed further, into torn flesh. The wolf's work. What hope there might have been, fled. Then a lifebeat pounded against Sihan's fingers. He started, stared hard, pushed down his hand with force. The beat drummed firmly through the leather glove. 'Gods' mercy,' muttered Sihan.

Tiny hooves drummed an answer within, the mare's foal

seeking liberty.

'By all the seven hells,' Sihan swore. 'It's too early. Too early.'

A sharp kick from the life within roused the mare. For a heartbeat a dark strength seemed to flood into her bones. She raised her head, found Sihan's eyes, almost willing him to understand. A neigh gurgled between her lips.

A swift, angry kick replied, as though the foal readied for war.

The mare's head fell back. Her chest heaved with one last effort, then stilled. A long sigh trembled through her limbs and she was gone.

'Gods . . . Gods . . .' muttered Sihan.

It was a moon's cycle until spring, when the main herd would return to the mountain pastures from the lowlands, grass-fat mares to drop their new crop of foals. Had one slipped past the herders, returned early? Mares ready to foal often hid themselves far from the herd for solitary birthing. But to come here, now, was beyond reason.

He grabbed his dagger. Running a hand over the mare's bloated, torn side, he traced the foal's outline before driving the blade into the riven flesh of soft grey underbelly. A rush of blood poured forth, steam carrying the raw odour of meat. As freezing wind turned the dark tide of leaking life to a film of black ice, he pulled forth a sanguinary mass. Snow melted against the heat of the body, freezing rapidly again to a thin crust of crackling ice. For a moment the foal lay unmoving except for a faint rise and fall of its flank, then tremors coursed across it in waves.

Sihan ran rough hands over the body, the long, spindly legs, pushing away blood and muck. Pale, like its dam, the foal was barely visible. He untied a skin from his belt, then wrapped clumsy gloved hands around milk-taut udders. Still stretched and dilated, the teats hung from the cooling, blood-smeared sac. He tried to trickle life-giving warmth into the skin. All the while he kept glancing about as though another wolf might leap upon him. But nothing moved except swirling white, dancing to the stone's wild song.

His mother's words came to him. She had called the stone's music the voice of the world, said it spoke in ancient tongues men no longer had the will to hear and understand. She had pretended the stone was a gateway to other places, and Sihan had often imagined himself transported to far off destinations. But right now, as blood thickened around his gloves, dying warmth seeping through the leather, all he longed for was to reach the dark barns across the clearing.

The foal lay still, just blood and hide and hooves, a tiny skeleton barely holding his skin apart. Sihan had to hurry. He had to get the foal to shelter.

The teats slackened. Sihan wiped his brow. It was not much but it would have to do until he could get home and milk a goat. He tied off the skin's mouth and hooked it to his belt. His hands were so cold, nothing melted against them anymore. He hoisted the foal into his arms, a dead weight, and began the struggle back to the buildings. The never-ending tempest descending upon them was the most lethal danger now.

Stormblasts roared off mountain peaks, leached heat from aching bones. Clouds of steam puffed from nostrils flared wide. Snow slithered down his back, burrowed beneath his cloak.

Every step dragged against grudging drifts. Air froze in Sihan's throat, and his open, gasping mouth. Legs cramped with strain. Cold bit, deep and fierce, an aching, living hurt. Ice stabbed his lungs with a thousand tiny spear points. The heavy dark of onrushing night weighed him down. Each lift of his legs grew heavier, the gap between each stride a lifetime.

Exhausted, he stumbled. Eyelids half-closed, he could not see the buildings. Surely they must be close. The foal sagged, lead in his arms. His thighs burned. He staggered again, energy draining from him like the light bleeding from the day. He heaved himself upright, faltered once more.

He collapsed, knees crashing to the ground. His chest heaved, iced air slicing his throat. Face buried in the foal's neck, he could barely move. All he could manage was to curl himself close round the bloodslimed foal.

The grey wash of snow faded into black. Blasting gusts battered his back, numbing him till he felt nothing. Snow built up around him, a blanket covering his cowl, his face. The world grew quiet, not even wind-wail to disturb him.

An enchanting sensation of sleep drifted over him. Every

moment he faded further from the world, sinking into oblivion's welcome embrace.

Distant whispers. He sensed his mother calling from the spirit world. One eyelid fluttered open a hairsbreadth. The squall shaped into blurred outlines, spun and remoulded into phantom forms of horses moving in silence. Spectral spirits, a flash of white, then another, until a score massed together, appearing, vanishing, racing swiftly to the heart of the clearing. He blinked away the pellets needling his eyes.

A neigh, shredded by the storm, or the cry of the gale driving through the trees? Or something more – a stallion's call to its mate?

Blood pounded behind his eyes; distorting all to shifting images, he was unable to distinguish truth from dream. Spirit horses galloped with the wind, wild, free. Lightning tore the air above the singing stone. In a blinding blaze, a whirl of snow coiled upward. And there she stood. The pale mare. Floating on air. Beside her, the stallion, high-kneed pride. Both glimmered as though fashioned from starglow. She was young again, her mate stood beside her – light and glory.

The mare looked back to where her body lay, then, mane and tail streaming, she launched into the air, hooves skimming above the ground and crossed the bridge between worlds.

The stallion reared again, looked straight at Sihan, bent one knee in a slow, reverential bow, reared once more, white sculpture against the night, then faded, contours merging with the storm till it was impossible to tell horse from snow.

Sihan wanted to follow them, follow the soundless calls of those long gone. Shadow horses.

The slightest shift of air stirred across the clearing. Then . . . emptiness. The spirit horses that had galloped across the night vanished. Ice music ceased. Absolute silence covered the world.

A cry, borne on the wind, touched Sihan's ear. A broken cry, somewhere on the edge of memory, far away, where a blanket of white covered an abandoned body. Were the spirit horses still there, calling him from beyond? Sihan imagined his father calling. Snow fell, swathing the world, blanketing his body.

Again, a cry. Close. Deep.

It really did sound like his father. Sihan's lips parted, but only a rasp of breath escaped.

Soon the wind filled with voices.

Voices.

A hand reached for him from the fog. Fear filled him. He tried to struggle. He must not let the spirit-boy's hand grab him. Something pushed down on his shoulder. He would have screamed but he could not find the strength. Mind tumbling with a myriad of images, Sihan half-turned his head to find a hand grasping at his cloak. A dark figure loomed over him.

A face formed. His father's face.

'What's happened to you, boy?' shouted Armindras, wind snatching words away the moment they left his mouth.

With a last vestige of will, Sihan lifted his head, but darkness swamped his mind, and his head fell back. Gloved hands rubbed his face, his arms, his legs, pushing back the covering of snow. His father knelt beside him, running hands over his head, roughly rubbing warmth back into his body.

Then there were others, prodding him, ordering him to rise, but it all seemed so far away. Every muscle in agony, Sihan doubted he would ever move again.

Something hard pressed to his lips. Fire scorched his throat with choking heat. He burst into a fit of coughing, rolled to one side and retched.

'That's it, lad,' muttered his father. 'That's it.'

Strange warmth rushed through his veins, bringing life with it. Sihan struggled to his knees. He clutched his father's coat and hauled himself to sit upright. 'Wolf,' he croaked, pointing to where it lay.

Armindras spun, dagger ready. Another man approached the huddle of fur slowly, firebrand raised, ready to smite the beast. He bent down, poked the carcass with the brand. 'Dead,' he called.

Beside Sihan, Kheran appeared. Kneeling, he wrapped another cloak around Sihan's shoulders. 'So there really *was* a horse.' He half-smiled through a frown of concern, face lit by a guttering lantern he held in shaking hands.

Armindras wiped the back of his hand across Sihan's brow, blood staining his gloves as he drew it away. 'Some fight,' he said. 'Looks like you killed the wolf ten times over.'

Unease clawed at Sihan's gut. 'I didn't kill it,' he groaned, staring out from one swelling eye at the corpse. He wanted to say more, but his father was already clambering to his feet, holding out a hand.

'Don't tell me this foal killed it,' Armindras said. 'Or was it the mare you were following?'

Trembling fingers enclosed in his father's grip, Sihan shook his head, trying to clear it. Should he tell of the things he had seen? When the wind's wail echoed in the distance, almost a girl's cry, terror robbed him of voice. He tore his hand from his father's and groped for the knife.

'Whoa! Whoa!' said Armindras. 'Steady, lad. Let's get you and this youngster inside.' He picked up the foal with arms thickened from hard living in the mountains and lumbered toward an assart to the right of the barn.

Joints stiff with cold, Sihan lurched after him, leaning heavy on Kheran's arm, another man taking half his weight on the other side. Armindras thrust his bulk at the assart door, heaving it open. Once inside, Sihan willed him to slam the door shut and brace his back against it, block out the world of shadows and imagination. There were things out there that were neither horse, nor wolf, nor blizzard.

Kicking snow from his boots, Armindras glanced at him in concern. 'What is it?' He eyed the stinging cuts on Sihan's cheek. 'Are you hurt bad?'

'No, I–' Sihan clenched his fist. 'It's nothing.'

Kheran yanked woollen blankets from a chest by a bunk and spread them in an untidy heap by the hearth. While Armindras laid the foal upon them, Sihan dropped in a crumpled heap beside it on the rough stone floor. Kheran set about sparking a fire. Soon a little warmth pricked Sihan's skin, set his fingers athrob. He pulled closer his rugged greatcloak, wet streaks of blood on his face and hands – some the wolf's, most the dead mare's.

More men shouldered the door open and entered the assart. Wind gusts swirled ash from the fringe of the hearth.

Outside, bedlam roared.

Breathing heavily, an elder steward by the name of Yonnad, hauled the door bar in place, then shook off his cloak, releasing smells of hot wool and sweating skin. He pulled off his pelt-edged hat and shook it, snow flying off in a little cloud to melt in puddles on the wood floor. Eyes sullen under lowering brows, he stared disapproval at Sihan. 'Well, you've certainly led us all a merry dance.' Then his gaze fell on the foal. 'Gods! It's whiter than a pureblood swan.'

Armindras hunkered down, examining every knobbly inch of the foal, rubbing the rough coat clean with a burlap sack he scrounged from a chest in the back of the assart. Massaging and warming the foal, he said, 'Should be deeper than black, just out of the womb. Never seen the like.' He looked at Sihan. 'Which of our mares was it?'

'Not ours.' Yonnad's stern voice filled the assart as he pulled on his hat. 'Not Graycor blood. So that half-breed won't last the night, let alone the end of winter. Best end it now.'

Stretched silence wound around the horsemen, while white flecks hissed as they landed in the open fire. No one spoke. Nothing concealed the moan of the wind and tapping of snow against the window.

At last a quiet voice said:

'The horse is the gift of the gods,
'First gift of the dawn of the ages.
'Revere it above your life, your children, your wife.'

Kheran's prayer, soft words, drifted up the chimney with smoke and sparks from the fire. The image of the dying mare's pleading eyes filled Sihan's mind. Eyes . . . watching eyes. Wind wailed beyond the walls, but the white mare seemed to be in the shadows of the assart . . . watching.

As Sihan's mind crowded with images of blood that kept transforming into a girl with a bleeding face, a boy, a stallion, he focused upon the foal as though it was a lifeline to the world, wanting to pray for it, and himself. The prayer of enlightenment, spoken by all horsemen at the altar of the horse god, Senfar, came unbidden.

'Take not its life save in mercy.
'Its soul will soar to the Heavens.
'As that of every man who holds it sacred.

'He who tastes of its flesh shall be damned.
'Hereafter and always to the underworld.
'And their soul shall not take flight among the stars of the Heavens.'

'It's mercy, boy,' said Yonnad. 'You want it to suffer more than it has already?'

'No one's killing it,' said Armindras. 'Not after all this bother. If Senfar wants it, Senfar will take it. His will alone.'

Sihan ignored Yonnad's scowl and tried to turn all thoughts from the foal. 'Will the wolf's soul be damned for eating a horse?'

'If such creatures have souls,' said his father, 'they don't deserve them.'

Sihan hesitated, regretting his words before they were half out of his mouth. 'I didn't kill the wolf. There was another horse out there. A stallion.'

Yonnad hoisted an eyebrow. 'Don't be daft. You must have hit your head when you fell.'

'I saw it,' Sihan insisted, tasting fear like iron at the back of his throat.

Armindras straightened, threw him a levelled glance. 'Nonsense.' He huffed with finality. 'Mares leave their herds to drop their foals alone. You know that, boy. You've tracked enough of ours. No stallion will abandon a herd to chase after one mare.'

Sihan bit his lip, said no more. What use to spill the other things he had seen? He shifted his weight, wincing as pain lanced through his body, certain by the morrow he would have a purpling hoof print on his chest from the ghost horse's blow. Then maybe his father would believe.

In the meantime, he ran his fingers through the foal's fine hair, determined to clutch to the reality of living flesh, something real and tangible. Although the colt's eyes were closed, a strong heartbeat thudded beneath his hand. The legs shook, but they were long, promising speed and height.

'Where did the mare come from?' Sihan asked. 'There're no grey horses on our range.' He did not say white, but he knew she was. By the morrow they would all know.

Armindras shrugged. 'Maybe escaped. Maybe wild. We'll dig her out come daylight, see if there's anything to identify her.'

Sihan's heart thudded hard. His father would dig out the wolf, too. See the evidence of the stallion's wrath.

As if he had read his thoughts, Kheran glanced at Sihan, the edge of a teasing smile in his voice as he said, 'Or maybe she and her foal are like those beasts in your mother's stories.'

Threads of memory wound through Sihan's mind, dim, half-formed. He remembered sitting upon his mother's lap, leaning into her warmth while she wove fine tales. Dream stories, his father called them, of the bitter northern mountains and horsemen who dwelt there. Ghost riders, mist riders, who lived and died in the saddle. Sihan imagined a host of ethereal horsemen emerging from roiling cloudbanks, their horses, strong, swift, beauteous. White stallions, shimmering like feather falls of down. White stallions like the one he had seen this night.

He shivered.

His mother had named the horses sacred – Godsteeds – bound by mysterious ties to their riders and the gods. When he had asked as a child why none of the kingdom colts were white, she had laughed low, fingers tousling his hair away from its natural fall over his brow. 'Godsteeds belong to the gods, not ordinary men.'

'But their riders–'

'Phantoms bound to the divine, shadow riders belonging not to this world. No Godsteed would consent to bear a mere man.'

'Not even if he was the king?'

'Just one, at the birth of the world. The first true king, consecrated by the gods. The legitimate king.' Something darkened her words and he had pressed no further. Now he wished he had.

Glancing at his father, Sihan asked, 'Is the king's horse white?'

Armindras shook his head. 'Celestion is grey. Born black, lad, or close to it. Still has a hint of dapple even now, though he's growing whiter by the year.' A hint of a smile touched his lips. 'Finest horse I ever rode.' His gaze grew distant, and Sihan needed no more words. He had heard the tale from birth, of the king's stallion, born on the volcanic slopes of the island of Eloin, ridden by his father to victory in a great race. The Lady of Eloin had presented the stallion to her liege-lord, declaring none but a king should be borne by a white horse, in honour of the legends of old. The king in his turn had sworn a vow never to ride another horse, honouring her, declaring her his chosen bride.

But Celestion was not white; therefore he could not be a Godsteed. Sihan stroked the foal and wondered. Could his mother's stories have been true? He had seen the white stallion, had he not? This foal was not imagination. Impossible dreams sparked in his mind. What if it *was* a Godsteed? He imagined emulating his father, and presenting the king with a *real* Godsteed.

A shudder ran through the foal, and Sihan smiled ruefully. Would a Godsteed have been corpse-born? Could its dam have been slain by a mere wolf?

He unhooked the skin of mare's milk from his belt and eased himself closer to the foal, careful of his stiffening muscles. He shrugged deep into Kheran's woollen cloak as he huddled close to the grate. Buttocks flattened against hard wood, knees drawn up to his chest, he pushed his back to rough timber. The cottage wall trembled with every booming gust. One storm wave after another, thunderous blasts of air rolled over the roof like vast combers, setting loose slats clattering.

A shudder ran through the foal, tremulous snuffling vibrating from its nostrils.

'Poor little fellow.' Sihan kept his voice low as he dipped his fingers in the milk and placed them between the foal's lips. For many moments nothing happened, then a rough, warm tongue flicked against his fingers. At first, the foal barely had strength enough to suckle, but with every drop, he grew stronger.

A grin split his father's face, like ice cracking in the sun.

As night wore on, the foal's head rested heavy against Sihan's thigh. Sometimes the legs thrashed, as though he was galloping from some nightmare terror.

A burnt shell of sallee in the hearth crumbled in a shower of sparks. Sihan's chin sank low on his shoulder. His eyes closed. Shadows fused into dark, elongating and swallowing him. One shadow distended into the shape of a girl. She stood atop a barren peak, alone, head bowed with grief.

Time drifted by in disturbed half-sleep.

A wind arose, carrying the ring of chimes. The girl danced . . . steps and gestures matching a melody he could not hear, dancing as if her life depended on her executing such exquisite patterns as the world had never witnessed. She danced . . . an eerie and beautiful dance – of courage and oblation, a dance for the gods themselves, weaving spells into a design, evoking . . . what?

Like the spirit horses, she faded, but not into air. Instead her essence seemed to form part of the mountains, the peak on which she danced, the granite tors, the grass, the crystal water of streams. Her soul infused the mountain world he held sacred in his blood.

Her voice slid into Sihan's mind, dark and sweet as molasses. *We will know one another, now and always, in the bitter dark of night, in rain, in fire, for all eternity, as long as life and death endures.*

A wolf howled beyond the Shadow Realm, a cry of blood floating across the rippling blackness of the void.

Then a whisper came upon the night.

You are not Sihan.

Sihan shifted, restless, more asleep than awake. 'Who am I, then?' he mumbled.

You are me. We are one. We are death.

Half-rousing, Sihan muttered, 'Whose death?'

The steed of the dead. The one whose name is War.

Sihan started full awake, staring around in confusion. In the last light of the fire's dying embers, a small white shadow stood before him, wobbling on tiny hooves, switched tail flicking back and forth. Dark eyes watched him beneath a fringe of white eyelashes.

The voice came again, far distant. *You are not Sihan.*

All thought of the foal stilled within him. Sihan clasped his arms round his knees, sat tense and motionless. An image filled his mind – a hand reaching for him from the mist, a boy, and a wolf shrouded in falling snow.

Chilled and empty, he felt as if something was trying to rip the soul from his body. He sensed once more eyes . . . watching eyes, staring at him from out of the darkness. Even the heat of the fire could not ward off the ice in his veins. With savage swiftness, he uncurled, hoisted the hem of his tunic.

Thick layers of leather cloak had warded the fury of the wolf's attack, leaving only faint fang grazes, but the bruise below his ribs, a mixture of dark blue and black, told a truth he could not deny. The mark of the ghost-horse, pressed over a puckered pink-white scar he had held since birth – a blemish akin to a wound caused by a javelin thrust.

He recalled the vision of the boy, the feeling of a lance driven through his gut. As he traced the jagged line, pain speared through him, deep, crimson fire. He stifled a cry, huddled on the floor, shaking.

If the stallion was real, then so was the boy who owned the haunting voice. The voice denying his name. Sihan folded his hands into fists. The stallion was not real. Neither was the boy. Or the girl. None of it. He rocked back and forth. 'My name is Sihan.' The words grated through clenched teeth. 'I am Sihan, son of Armindras.'

At his side, Armindras blinked awake, put a hand on Sihan's arm. 'What's this about a name?'

Sihan's breath came loud, harsh.

'What's wrong?' demanded his father.

Sihan forced a choked sound between tight lips. 'Nothing.' He glanced away to the foal, wary his father might read the lie in his eyes. The foal stretched out its nose, snuffled his face once more, lips lightly caressing his cheeks, his hair.

'You must have been dreaming of names for the colt.' Armindras's stern features softened. 'Well, what is it?'

Aurion, whispered a voice, dry and brittle, the rustle of lifeless leaves, long dead. *Its name is Aurion.*

Cold shivered across Sihan's skin, his heart, as he rolled the name unspoken on his tongue. Aurion. The Fire Star. The star attributed to the god of war. Foreboding clawed at him, half-remembrances of . . . what? He hesitated, stroked the little white colt. Refused to answer.

'Well?' prompted Armindras.

Name him and you call the world to war.

'Well?' demanded his father.

Sihan could not refuse. His voice came out as a thread of a whisper. 'Aurion.'

Armindras remained silent for a long while, then finally said, 'Aurion, the Fire Star.' He paused again. 'There's not much call for white warhorses. Not since the king's edict declaring none save he should be borne by one. But a warrior's name it should be all the same.' He reached out and fondled the frail figure, repeating the name once more as though he bestowed a benediction. 'Aurion. Our little winter warrior.'

Questioning burnt-black eyes returned his gaze.

Sihan stared at the foal in silence, dread settling in his gut. The foal was corpse-born – a steed of the dead. And now its name was War.

And he would be its death.

Chapter 1

Six years later . . .

Mirador

Blackened heads marred the arch over the main fortress gate, no longer human, just peeling flaps of skin clothed in crawling blankets of flies. Jaien shut his eyes, but only succeeded in recalling it all with greater clarity – bone-handled daggers spearing hollowed sockets – King Callinor's death marks.

Shame flooded his veins like poison, fouled his mind, constricted his throat like the putrid stink of rotting flesh. He fought the urge to utter black curses against his king, and wondered, not for the first time, why he had obeyed his liege's summons to return to the fortified sea fortress of Mirador.

Callinor.

Jaien spat. How had he come to serve such a man – one capable of murdering his greatest ally, and greatest friend, the Duke of Romondor? A man who thought nothing of destroying Romondor's people and laying waste their lands. All at the behest of his whore wife because she secretly desired the duke and he had rejected her. No such infamy in the history of the world.

Yet, here he was, an obedient puppy obeying his master's tug upon the leash. Jaien forced himself to look again upon lipless grins of yellowed teeth, pits that were no longer mouths, but black holes screaming silent accusation. His fingers tautened on the reins, sending his mount side-stepping, tension in every high-kneed stride.

'Steady, Falcon,' Jaien murmured, lightening his hold a fraction. He shot a glance at his second, riding half-a-stride behind.

Gerein's face kept rigid and cold as stone, but his eyes darted every which way, measuring, assessing. A horse-length distant, Camar's careless, ever-present grin had fled. The archer rubbed his stubbled jaw, feigned a yawn, then drew back his right hand to sweep a tangled lock of fox-red hair over his shoulder. The movement was studied, deliberate, and placed his fingers within easy reach of the arrows in the gorytos strapped to his back.

Behind Jaien, his company of one hundred archers and ten knights, one-tenth of his full command, kept gazes locked ahead, alert for orders, riders tightening up into two files, as if they sought to keep at bay the unease sweeping the column by closing into battle formation. Some shifted their grey cloaks behind their thighs, revealing the gold falcon of Pelan emblazoned against their black tabards, freeing access to swords. Their warsteeds snorted, tossing heads and shaking manes, sensing their riders' disquiet.

A ripple of movement in deep shadow beneath the gate set Jaien's gloved fingers to beating a rhythm against his sword hilt. Safe from the skulls sightless stares, a score of the king's guard watched the soldiers pass, covered voices muted beneath the jingle of bits and scrape of hooves on cobbles. Royal badges adorned every tabard, the red firefalcon of Mirador stark against white wool. Jaien's swift gaze flickered from one rigid face to another, noting a new hardness and remoteness in each. A few men he knew nodded acknowledgement, most did not, gazes sliding away from his, even those soldiers with whom he had fought side by side.

Alarm engulfed him. What could set such men on edge?

Gerein angled his horse near and muttered from the side of his mouth, 'A hard welcome.'

Something told Jaien it would get harder.
As the column rode into the outer bailey, sharp chills shivered down his spine. The very air seemed heavy with darkness and grief. A few passing onlookers offered quick glances at the cavalcade of horsemen, then swiftly looked elsewhere, fear glinting in every eye as they crept away down darkened alleys like rodents.

Jaien cast a quick look over his shoulder. Heads also adorned the gate's southern façade. Gall rose in his throat. How many more disfigured the other twelve fortress gates? What crime had these men committed? Urging his warhorse toward the stable court, he determined to fathom the meaning of this corpse-welcome.

The company rode down the main thoroughfare, the stench of burned oil wafting from cookhouses and stalls preparing evening meals of roasting pork, venison and beef, and flat fried bread for the fortress populace. Fewer traders than expected at sundown.

Fortress traffic was spare, ringing cries absent. No jongleurs entertained children with whirling firesticks. No cobra-whisperers charmed adults. No sword dancers thrilled the ladies. No acrobats, bards, jugglers or seers, or any of the fleecing throng of followers that gathered like vultures at the first whiff of merriment and gold.

There was nothing to celebrate here, that much was certain.

Gerein spurred his horse nose to nose with Falcon, and tossed an imperceptible nod to the battlements. Squinting against the dying sun, at first Jaien spied only hazed spires of temple minarets. Slowly, shapes took ominous form, guardwalks thick with archers and men-at-arms. Their watchful stillness called to mind eagles set to swoop on prey. He had seen men on the brink of a charge look less threatening.

The column of riders crossed a small bridge overhanging a canal. Scattered vendors in the court ahead kept their heads low, rarely looking up except to serve a patron.

'King's murderers, stop dragging us into your false war!' came a sudden shout from a dark alley to the right.

Absolute quiet fell over the court, bar the scrape of hooves on stone. Shock rippled through Jaien. The words were close to treason, insolent beyond daring. Given the mood of the fortress soldiers, the speaker risked hanging to voice such. But more appalling was the implication behind the words.

Jaien's command had been called away from a long campaign against marauding tribes of Hyerlin who had been laying waste to villages on the border of the duchy of Pelan. A bloody affair; many a soldier had died over the past seven seasons, men from Pelan, and its neighbouring kingdom duchies, Belaron, Maroden, and Omrah. Jaien had earned his knighthood in the third winter, then the command in a savage battle at Tulit where he had led a score of men-at-arms to rescue two units under siege. No kingdom man would dare call it a false war. And no other war raged in the kingdom, not since the Great War over a decade past.

Jaien closed his mind against his darkest fear, knowing with every swinging stride of his horse, he was riding toward a future steeped in more blood than ever he had seen. Every man of the fortress bore the signs of soldiers on the eve of war. He caught in the corners of his eyes even more people scurrying down alleys, pulling hoods close to hide grim countenances, shoulders hunched, sinking into themselves like skulking cats. What by all the hells was going on? By slow degrees Jaien's body braced for a blow.

'Jackals!' a bodiless voice cried out.

'Vermin!' shouted another.

Gerein's eyes narrowed to a cold-metal stare. 'Should I stick an arrow in those over-loose traps?'

The insults weighed upon Jaien, but duty dictated he not react. 'Ignore them.'

The twin files of cavalry rode on, faces blank.

Sunset flowed over blue slate roofs, seeping down stone walls, shrouding the castle Jaien loathed in a lurid haze of gold. High above the ribbed palace dome, gulls swooped, wings crimson as the torchlights flaring to life about the fortress walls.

Through the growing dark, Jaien oriented his way by spires marking fortress temples. Joined by stone walls, arches and bridges, temple towers bounded the whole sprawling complex of buildings making up the inner ward of the fortress. The troop turned toward the stable quarter, threading their way through a warren of alleys running alongside stores, armouries and barracks. These lanes also stood bare, stripped of stalls and stands, awnings of wicker rolled up over empty earth.

They entered a massive courtyard bordered by pillars. In the centre, a fountain spewed water into a circular trough before which a few stable boys held horses. More lads dragged rank burlap sacks stuffed with soiled straw and manure from stables behind the pillars, dodging out of the horsemens' path as Jaien's company filled the courtyard.

Jaien and his men had ridden hard and long across four duchies. Fatigued enough to sleep a moon's cycle, they had earned the right to an early billet, but now, at their destination, none made haste to dismount, all waiting on Jaien.

Gerein eyed his commander. 'Do I stand the men down?'

Jaien did not answer.

Nearby, chanting voices drifted across the stable court – lilting tenors and bold baritones mixed with the deep rumble of bass. Jaien's jaw tightened as he eyed the torchlit prayer hall of a temple at the corner of the courtyard. One of many in the fortress, it would be filled with knights gathered for the sundown prayer – men who could give him answers to the questions lurking in his mind.

Sudden trumpets rang, wild braying in the muted evening. Jaien swung his horse in the direction of the palace. There was no reason for trumpets to sound so late in the day. Without a word to his men, he spurred Falcon toward the dome.

Soft and scattered at first, faint cries warned of peril, but nothing prepared him for the sight greeting his arrival at the palace court. Crowds of people massed. Butchers with burly arms and blood-spattered aprons pressed tight against court ladies reeking of spikenard. Fisherman and dockers, stinking of fish and brine, heads wrapped in scarves, stood shoulder to shoulder with nobles in dagged chaperons. Cobblers in chaps, shepherds in fleeced vests, women clinging tight to children, artisans and sculptors in flowing ivory robes, stall holders and goat herders thronged the court – everyone, in fact, that should have been going about their usual business elsewhere.

Jaien studied the crowd. Many women huddled, crying. A few men turned to regard him, returning his scrutiny with frank contempt. Other eyes betrayed savage, hopeless desperation. Sensing hostility, Falcon tensed beneath Jaien, ready to spring forward at the slightest urging.

'Knight Commander Jaien!' hailed a voice with a marked Pelanese accent. A man pushed his way to the edge of the crowd, a peasant, stinking of beeves, boots caked in cow dung, brown woollen cloak dirt-stained. He reached Falcon's shoulder and pawed at Jaien's cloak. 'You are Knight Commander Jaien?' he asked, reeling to clutch at Falcon's breastplate for support as the crowd jostled him.

'I am,' Jaien answered, body tautening. 'You know me?'

'I know you. You're not like the others. You have honour. You fight for justice. For us. You're not like *them*.' He nodded to the fortress soldiers. Gripping Jaien's sword hand tight, the man glanced back over his shoulder. 'Please, please come . . .'

Jaien urged Falcon after the man, every moment certain he wove a hazardous course through a pit of tiger snakes. The crowd parted in fits and starts, more and more eyes lit with the empty chill of predators. There was a hatred he had never seen before – all directed at the king's command. What had happened? What had they done?

Among the reptilian horde, a few called his name, soft, as though frightened it might reach hostile ears. But as more peasants recognised him, his name became a chant. 'Knight Commander Jaien!' they cried, swarming about him, countless hands stretched out.

The peasant stopped before a woman. She huddled into him, crying, burying her face in the man's cloak.

'What is it?' demanded Jaien. 'What has happened here?'

She stared up at Jaien, eyes wet with pleading, and reached out trembling fingers. 'Please . . . my son. Please, save him.'

'From what? Where is he?'

As if in answer, shouts presaged the marching tramp of boots and the relentless strike of a drum. Agitated, the crowd stirred, heads craning toward the source of the beat.

Prisoners, bound leg to leg by chains, stumbled into the palace court in one long, ragged line, guards on either side. Against the blood-crimson and crisp white of the soldiers' tabards, the prisoners in their stained brown rags appeared dull as sparrows beside rosellas.

One, a young lad no older than sixteen winters, with a faint dusting of stubble upon his cheeks, stared wild about him, pale eyes like the woman's. Darkness clung to him like shadow; awareness of his impending fate tightened the sallow skin of his face. He was doomed, and he knew it.

At Jaien's side, the woman convulsed, moaning like a beast in agony. 'Liamas, Liamas. My son, my son!'

Jaien kept his voice steady. 'Of what crime stands he accused?'

The peasant answered, 'Evading the king's commission.'

Jaien's eyes speared the man. 'A deserter?'

The peasant spat. 'You cannot desert if you've never sworn the oath.'

Farther on, a man bellowed, 'Stop stealing our sons!'

A taut silence gripped the crowd.

Jaien snapped, 'Not a deserter, but charged with evasion. Account for that.'

'Soldiers came a moon's cycle past, dragged our boys from the fields, forced them into service at sword point. Liamas was herding far out on the sheep folds. Not his error they missed him.' The man spat. 'They came for him in the night, accused him of evasion.' The peasant's eyes glittered wrath. 'My boy's no coward, but they're taking his head, just the same.'

A wail tore from the woman, so full of grief, her son might already be dead.

In silent fury, Jaien considered what he had heard. All the while the prisoners approached to the accompaniment of the dull song of chains and the slow beat of drums. They were beasts, prodded toward the abattoir by the sharp jab of spear points. The procession of defeat came to a stop, men with straggle beards and boys with hollow, fearful eyes, crouching and awaiting their masters' will. The stubbled youth began to sob.

Jaien nodded to the boys flanking Liamas. 'Same story?'

The man nodded, eyes granite. 'I don't hold with cowards, but they're as guiltless as my son. Not one would have run from the conscripting.'

Shock followed shock, like rippling tremors in the wake of an earthquake. 'Conscripting?'

The man's eyes lit with surprise edged by wariness. 'Have you not heard? The princess is to wed the Duke of Romondor.'

The words jerked Jaien from his cold contemplation of the prisoners. He could not have heard aright. 'Romondor? What madness are you speaking?'

The peasant stared up at him. 'No madness, Sir. The fortress heralds have been proclaiming it in earnest. The king is wedding his daughter to that vulture. To Valoren.'

'Doom to us all!' The wayward cry echoed the thoughts crashing into Jaien's mind.

'They'll kill her.' The words were out before Jaien could rein them in.

The peasant went on. 'And now they have taken my son, for war must surely come upon us. Someone must tell the king we will not have it!' The man looked to Jaien, as if he held the power to alter the will of monarchs.

The world turned in a circle about Jaien: the deeds of old men – seeds sown a generation before – now bearing fruit in the new dawn. He had buried dark secrets in his heart, of a cuckolded king, of a whore's wrath against a man of honour, of murder and regicide. His disillusion in his king, his loathing for a dead queen, grew by every heartbeat. A decade past, the king had taken the kingdom to the brink of annihilation. Would he finish what he had started by throwing even his heir to the slaughter?

Shouts rose about Jaien, dragging him back to the world at hand. 'Murderers! Murderers of innocents!'

Outraged cries flung up to the darkening sky as a score of soldiers marched through the crowd. The rider at their head – Knight Captain Hessarde – stared straight before him as if the rabble either side was unworthy of a single glance.

'Wolves! Blood-sucking hyenas!' Curses rose to a colossal swell.

Hessarde's pale stallion cavorted sidewise, coat glowing beneath the torches, hooves beating counterpoint to the drum, gaping jaw battling the bit. Butting their way through the crowd, Hessarde's escort of foot soldiers shoved aside peasants and nobles pressing too near.

Within Jaien, rage smouldered. He knew the knight and those with him. They were Shaheden, the king's field command, born predators who acted as if murder was their Gods-given right. Like all kingdom soldiers, he despised these men who cared not they sullied their hands carrying out the king's death marks.

Behind Jaien, a multitude of hoof beats clattered loud on stone. Jaien did not need to look to know Gerein had ridden up with Camar and the entire company in tow. The archer had guarded his back for four full years, would not shirk his duty now.

'What nonsense is Hessarde about?' questioned Gerein, moving alongside and eyeing the advancing knight with ill-disguised contempt.

'No nonsense,' muttered Jaien. He nodded toward the prisoners. 'He's executing that lot.'

The Shaheden spat curses as the crowd continued to push against them, hindering their advance.

'Back away! Back away!' ordered Hessarde with the casual authority of one used to being obeyed. 'Make way for the king's justice!'

'Justice! Ha!' muttered Gerein.

'Free them!' Shouts vaulted over each other in rising crescendo. The mob pressed forward, forcing Hessarde to halt. The woman dashed forth and clutched at Hessarde's boot with one hand, reaching up with the other, begging, 'Mercy, please, I beg you!'

Hessarde eyed her with distaste, as though she was a cockroach floating in his mead.

'Have mercy!' the woman cried once more.

The scar breaking the smooth line of Hessarde's cheek whitened against flushed skin as he leaned forward. 'I *will* have mercy.' His voice slid soft from his tongue like an adder's hiss. 'I'll make his end swift.' He kicked her aside and spurred his horse, raising his voice to shout harshly, 'The next petitioner will feel the point of my sword!'

Outrage bore the murderous threat apace. But men and women, peasant and noble alike, took up the woman's plea, chanting in unison, 'Free them! Free them!' Every moment the urgency increased, taking on a dark quality. Hessarde's second, Sedor, wasted no time in rounding on the most vocal troublemakers, striking them to the ground with the hilt of his drawn sword. His men shouted and cursed, kicking the fallen.

Enraged, the rest of the crowd hurled abuse, curses becoming a tumultuous roar, battering the sky with the angry beat of protest. Soldiers and petitioners faced each other, both spoiling for a fight. A black cloud of looming catastrophe engulfed the fortress, ready to unleash a storm of fury.

'Skulking bastards!' Gerein spat the words.

Jaien spun round to find the king's archer with his head raised, a hound scenting quarry. Camar, likewise, looked up, face set, eyes sharpened to spear points.

Jaien tracked the archer's gaze, up the long palace pillars, to the golden dome of the palace roof. Along the balustrade, dark shadows crept, a hundred or more bowmen with arrows nocked. A further detachment from the ranks of archers stationed on the battlement spread along guardwalks encircling the palace court. Poised above the crowd like vultures over prey, they trained weapons upon the agitated masses below, preparing to shoot.

An arrow tore into the heart of the crowd. Missing everyone. Whether by design or error, it mattered not. The effect was the same.

Screams split the night. Terror dropped the multitude to their knees like a collapsing floor, arms raised in futile efforts to ward against the expected volley. Somewhere in the horde, hapless victims slipped beneath the cloaking ocean of people. Women tried to silence children's cries with hands splayed across open mouths.

Jaien's men spurred their horses through the back edges of the crowd, fanning out to cover ground, all eyes on Jaien, on the archers above them, watching, waiting.

Panic and a sense of wretchedness surged through Jaien. His men were looking to him for orders he could not give. Oaths bound him, strong as blood. Oaths held a man till death.

'Help us! Help us!' People reached to him, pulled at Falcon's bridle. The world reeled, pitching wildly like a ship adrift in a storm sea. Oath warred against oath – to protect the people of the kingdom, to defend his fellow soldiers with his life. Which outweighed the other?

'Help us!' men and women pleaded.

Jaien wanted to slam his ears shut, to shutter his heart. But shame slithered past every attempt at obstruction, a wriggling, slimy thing, forcing him to acknowledge what he could no longer deny – he served corruption.

'Mercy!' Begging voices jolted him. Thoughts rushed in of the siege in Tulit where he had been hailed a hero for destroying the murderous Hyerlin. If he let this night take its course, if he let king's men do this thing, he would be no better than Hyerlin scum. A flame of light ignited the soul-destroying darkness within him, fuelled by fierce-burning rage.

Gerein's eyes flashed to his, bright with expectation.

Jaien nodded. 'Do it.' Within a heartbeat, bows creaked under strain as Gerein's unit of archers readied weapons. They rode forward, aiming at their counterparts on the battlements.

Gerein's shout was clear and in earnest, 'You shoot, you die.'

Confusion swept every terrified face. Men on the guardwalk shouted orders, at each other, at Jaien's archers. On the fringes of the masses, men and women arose and ran, fleeing for their lives, rushing down alleys into darkness. More and more tried to follow; a torrent trying to rush down narrow holes; they banked up in a crush, crawling over each other to get away.

'Hold! Hold!' bellowed Jaien, spinning Falcon sharply about, mind whirling, crammed with panic and rash, unshaped plans. 'Push them back!' he yelled to his knights. The last thing he needed was for people to die in their haste to escape.

His men beat the crowd back, trying to not trample the fallen, or bring down those still standing. King's soldiers rushed from their posts, faces grim, trying to restore order. But the terrified mob could not be quieted. Men grabbed crooks, staffs, pulled timber slats from carts, anything they could use as a weapon. Violence broke out between men-at-arms and the populace, eddies of resistance rippling through the swollen tide of people.

At a swift nod from Jaien, his knights, swords drawn, battered weapons from peasant and farmer alike. They formed a protective barricade of horseflesh and steel between them and the king's men. Jaien faced Hessarde, their eyes locked and murderous. Battle-hardened muscles tensed; Jaien's fingers itched to draw sword.

'Shaheden!' he called against the fearful shouting and wailing of the crowd, rage adding unnatural power to his voice. 'Release the prisoners.'

The challenge spurred an approving roar from the people. They hollered, 'Jaien! Jaien!' hurling his name into the faces of the king's soldiers like a war cry.

Unmoved by the crashing wave of protest around him, Hessarde ignored the order. Instead, he addressed his guards. 'Start the execution.' Dismounting, he tossed his reins to a squire and pointed to the peasant's son. 'Him first.'

The boy struggled to free himself, arms flailing as he tumbled to the ground, legs tangled in chains. Soldiers grabbed him by the wrists. While he thrashed, one unlocked his manacles, then they dragged him to the block.

At his back, the other prisoners formed an ugly sight of inhuman cruelty at odds with the stately grace of the palace. Most looked groundward, while some gazed sightlessly at nothing with the glassy stare of dying carp. Only a few dared to look at the block upon which their heads were to be severed.

The boy, at the edge of death, stilled. Head raised, he scanned the crowd, searching faces grief-struck and hostile. He found his mother, locked wide, fear-filled eyes to hers, pleading for comfort and safety she could no longer offer.

She tore from her child's gaze, to stare up at Jaien, begging silently. The fierce hurt in her face broke loose the bolts on the past. Revulsion engulfed Jaien. Tattered shreds of honour forbade more madness in a dishonourable king's name. He allowed no thought of consequences as he said, 'I give my word. Your son will not die this day.'

Tears rained down the woman's blotched cheeks. Jaien's men stared at him, some, like Camar, with stupefaction registering on their faces, others with the fanatic fervour of battle-lust shining in their eyes.

Gerein reined his mount close and caught at Jaien's arm. 'Have you gone mad? Remember where you are!'

Jaien wrenched himself free. 'I prefer to remember *what* I am.'

'In Senfar's name, it's one thing to protect innocents, but these are prisoners condemned by the king. If you do this, the king's guard will kill you.'

'They'll try.'

'Oh, hells.' Gerein grimaced. 'Then they'll have to kill me, too.'

Jaien ran his hand along Falcon's shoulder, tracing veins in the hot, thin skin, the mark of all quality bloodhorses. Drained of all feeling, he spurred his horse toward Hessarde. Grand palace columns towered before him. Strange irony, the majesty of it, a facade promising nobility while hiding a rotten heart. The lucid calm of a soldier at battle's edge filled him as he halted Falcon before Hessarde.

Derision marred Hessarde's face, scorn accenting the deliberate slow march of his approach. 'My thanks, *Sir*, for your assistance in subduing this rabble.' Mockery slid from his lips with a rapier's deadly smoothness.

A moment stretched into heartbeats of fraught, perilous silence. Jaien's fingers tightened on his sword hilt. His every thought fixated on the fight he knew must come. 'Release them,' he commanded, drawing on the authority of rank to restrain Hessarde.

Murder lit Hessarde's eyes, but he damped it down swiftly. Shaking his head and tapping his ear, he said, 'I'm sure I keep mishearing you.'

'You hear well enough,' snapped Jaien. 'Obey.'

The depths of Hessarde's eyes darkened with disgust. 'You want me to release these cowards?'

'You're the coward, not them!' shouted the boy's father.

'You are snakepiss!' shouted another voice from the crowd. 'Nightsoil!'

Amid torrents of insults, the lifeless eyes of the prisoners brightened, but the boy kept his face closed, gaze fixed rigidly ahead.

Hessarde faced Jaien squarely, cheeks flushing crimson, eyes black with rage. With obvious effort, he schooled his expression to boredom, masking wrath with a chill, ever so slight upturning of thin lips as he said, 'My actions are sanctioned by the king himself. Now, if you please, I've work to do, if you have naught. Be gone and leave me to it.'

Jaien kept his voice even, likewise leashing fury. 'If you touch that boy, I'll kill you.'

Wintry eyes raked over Jaien, then Hessarde sniffed with mock diffidence, nose creasing into folds of distaste as if he scented an offensive stink. He turned his back on Jaien and pointed to the boy. 'Put him on his knees!'

The boy's mother screamed, fell weeping to the cobbles, eyes clenched, hands clamped together. Jaien drew steel. At a shout from one bearded youth, the prisoners behind Liamas bent and lifted their chains. Rushing forth in unwieldy formation, they crashed into the backs of the line of guards set to separate the crowd from the prisoners. Chains wrapped around throats, strangling curses.

For a heartbeat, shock transfixed everyone, then a multitude of swords hissed from scabbards, glinting in torchlight. Tumult exploded into outright chaos. The crowd lost all fear of the archers, surging forth, shouting, 'Free them!' Guards swarmed to block any rescue as the rampaging throng overran the barricade created by Jaien's horsemen. Roars for order from knights on the battlement went unheard.

Battle bellows warred with clash of arms, angered clang of steel against iron, the staccato beat of staff and spear. In an instant, everyone in the palace court was dragged into the fighting. Warring factions swirled together in one massive fracas, horsemen and foot, peasant and noble, crushed together in a storm of motion.

A rift dragged Jaien into the churning onslaught. Steel struck hard against his sword. He turned the assailant's blade, deflecting a strike aimed at his horse. Horns blared over the riot of noise and ringing steel. Jaien parried blow after blow, trying to reach the prisoners.

The doomed men snarled like starving wolves squabbling over a carcass. One kicked a soldier hard in the back of a knee, brought him down. In the scuffle of bodies a dagger flashed, once, twice, stabbing flesh. A torn-off scream ended in fountaining blood as the victim toppled over the block.

'Push them back!' bellowed Hessarde. His swordsmen hacked at bodies clawing for freedom. Hammering blows cracked bones, points gutting, edges slicing open slab thighs like meat on a butcher's bench. Soon all the prisoners' garb and bodies ran red with blood.

'Liamas!' the woman screamed above the din.

Jaien searched for the boy. Tangled torsos and flailing arms and legs made it almost impossible to distinguish prisoner from peasant from soldier. He spurred Falcon, trying to break up the combatants. On edge from the stink of slaughter, the stallion charged into the fray in a maddened rush, knocking aside all comers, slamming soldiers into pillars.

Sparks flew as Jaien struck aside shields, battered iron helms. Crossed spears fouled Falcon's legs, slowing his advance. Jaien slashed arms grasping at Falcon's bridle, hacking through mail into flesh to free his horse. Fighters flowed around him in a frenzy.

A score of voices shouted warnings. Jaien snapped his head round to see Hessarde dragging Liamas up the palace steps by the hair. A savage fist blow to the head put paid to the boy's struggles. Liamas sank to the ground. Hessarde unsheathed his sword with the practised grace of a soldier at home on a battlefield.

Jaien lashed the reins at Falcon's neck, sending the stallion into a lurching gallop up the steps. A unit of Hessarde's men-at-arms formed a hasty line, swords ready, faces unmoved at the sight of the chestnut flying at them. Somewhere in the melee, Gerein shouted, 'To me! To me!' An instant later, Jaien's archers were pacing him, bursting through the crowd, galloping in ragged formation at Hessarde's men. The two forces collided.

The shattering impact broke the line, spinning men apart, bones crushed by the blow, splintered beneath drumming hooves. Jaien rode at Hessarde.

The king's knight did not hesitate. One sweeping stroke of Hessarde's blade cleaved the boy's neck.

A woman's shriek of utter desolation gutted Jaien like a lance.

Hessarde released the boy's hair. Liamas's head splattered on the ground, rolled to rest, eyes blank. His body swayed drunkenly, collapsed chest down, blood pulsing in spurts from the neck in a crimson waterfall down the palace steps.

Jaien's breath choked as he reined Falcon to a halt. Like a beast caught in a rock fall, suffocating, he struggled for air.

'Liamas!' The mother staggered, staring uncomprehending at the pieces of her child. Then she turned to Jaien, and cried in a pathetic whimper, 'You promised.' Her voice, her eyes, her soul screamed betrayal. 'You promised.'

Her words burned like brands on torn flesh, stripping him of honour, of pride, of every shred of self-respect. He had failed her, the people. What use his command, his title, the glory of Tulit when in the heart of the safest fortress in the kingdom, he could not save one innocent boy?

An inhuman screech rent the air, piercing the mayhem about them. The woman launched herself at Hessarde. She flailed wildly, blindly, screaming, 'Murderer! Murderer!' scratching at Hessarde's face like a cat, clawing and gouging streaks of blood into his scarred cheek.

Hessarde's men dragged her off, and forced her to her knees, arms twisted behind her back. Hessarde calmly drew back his sword arm, ready to run her through. The woman spat.

The very air seemed to rush from Jaien, but somehow he found voice to hiss, 'In the name of Senfar, I command you, put up your sword.'

Hessarde's eyes shimmered like a night wolf's, humanity traded for something cold and bestial.

'Release her!' Jaien roared.

Hessarde's lips curled into a malevolent smile. With callous indifference, he drove his sword through the woman's breast.

Her eyes bulged; her body caved, wrapping around the steel. Hessarde jerked the blade free, past protesting ribs, a grating rasp, muted by sucking gore. The woman's eyes drifted to Jaien, a plea, an accusation, so fluid the dying thoughts they leaked into each other. She sank to the palace steps, folding in to herself like a draining skin of wine.

Pitiless, Hessarde wiped the blood from his blade, offhandedly drawing it across the woman's cloak.

Jaien flung himself forward on Falcon's neck, sword aimed to plunge through Hessarde's throat. Hessarde lurched back, the sword point scraping across mail. He tripped over the boy's corpse. Jaien's sword crashed down, a hammer on an anvil.

Hessarde slipped his blade aside, rolled, escaping by inches another blow aimed to shatter his collarbone.

Jumping Falcon over the boy's body, Jaien severed all emotion, disregarding the corpse with the cold detachment of a soldier ignoring a fallen comrade on a battlefield. Air whistled, torn by Jaien's blade. Hessarde scrambled and dodged each strike, boots skidding in gore. Steel slashed past his face a half-dozen times. Then a blow powered down, the full force of Jaien's weight behind it, knocking Hessarde's sword from his hand. Steel rang across marble, sliding down the steps.

'Here, Hess!' shouted Sedor, Hessarde's man. The bearded knight tossed a sword. Triumphantly, Hessarde caught it, and scrabbled to his feet, grabbing at a shield as he did.

Jaien swiped at him, urging Falcon forward in sliding, clattering bounds. Hessarde deflected a sweeping cut, just. The backstroke caught his shield, hurling him to his knees. Like an animal, he paused on all fours, staring up at Jaien. As Jaien prepared the death blow, Falcon suddenly lurched beneath him.

Hessarde's men clawed at the stallion, fists closed on the horse's reins, pulling the stallion off-balance, attempting to topple him. Falcon reared, maw gaping, trying to bite, hooves cutting at air, body twisting. Someone grabbed Jaien, trying to heave him from the war saddle. Shouts filled his ears.

Clattering hooves and yelling heralded aid, Gerein and Camar fighting their way to his side. Their sword strikes never let up.

More and more of Hessarde's men closed round, crowding the horses. A half-yelp of surprise and pain tore from Gerein's throat as his mount lost its footing, crashing to the marble. The archer disappeared beneath the churn of soldiers, swords closing upon him like a line of shark's teeth.

'Gerein!' Jaien screamed.

Camar charged blindly into Hessarde's men, warding off blow after blow set to finish his comrade. Guards surged, a wall of brawn pushing against his stallion. The horse braced, resisting, hooves planted wide, scraping hard against cobbles. Then, he, too, fell amid a mad scramble of thrashing legs. A dozen men threw themselves at Camar, holding him down while others struggled to wrench his sword from his grasp.

Half-freed by the havoc his men had caused, Jaien fought toward them.

Camar shouted at him, 'Leave us! Get the bastard!'

Jaien refused to abandon his men. A sharp prick of spur sent Falcon leaping high, battering the soldiers at Jaien's back with a shattering strike of hind legs mid-flight. A savage down-cut of Jaien's blade splintered a pike set to gut Falcon. Leaping from the stallion's back, Jaien hammered his way through Hessarde's men, rage lending strength to each blow.

More of his men battled to his side – Seth, copper hair awry, sweat streaming down his face. White sparks rained down in fiery hail as sword crashed to sword. Amid the storm, several guards backed away, dragging a struggling man between them. Gerein, stripped of weaponry, eyes wild, screamed curses into unyielding faces.

Then a line of guards closed on the sight of Jaien's second being hauled away. Hessarde stood at their head, waiting for Jaien. The stink of cruelty clung to him.

'Take him!' shouted Seth. 'We'll hold the rest.' With a roar, he led Jaien's men against Hessarde's.

Jaien gripped his sword with a double-hand hold, determined to finish this man in whom all the darkness of the world seemed to have concentrated. They crashed together with brutal force, sword smashing sword. Jaien drove Hessarde back, his blade an extension of himself, infused with a deep feral fury that only increased speed and precision. Every movement took on the cadence of a dance, steel whipping in clean, precise rhythms, legacy of a thousand sword drills. Jaien refused Hessarde room to manoeuvre, crowding him, pressing him hard against the guards arrayed at his back.

Every blow pummelled the knight, a brutish assault. Step by step, Hessarde gave back beneath the onslaught. Swift, ruthless cut followed cut, in rapid unrelenting sequences. Then Jaien's sword point slid past Hessarde's guard, stabbing hard into his upper arm.

Crimson marred Jaien's blade. He readied to follow through. In that instant, Hessarde's eyes ignited in a swift shimmer, flaring blue to molten silver. Shocked, Jaien faltered, staring into pools of intense light resembling reflections of the moon's bright radiance in predator's gaze.

A growl of wrath tore from Hessarde. He lunged, a savage sweep of sword intended to sever Jaien's head from his torso. Jaien only just managed to deflect it, the impact shuddering up his arm. He parried two more swift strikes.

Cuts and hits battered him, with such increasing speed and force, Jaien could barely untangle one incoming blur of steel from the other. He blocked a low ground stroke set to cut his legs from under him, only to next be faced by a sweep aimed at his helm.

He thrust his sword up in wild defence. The shock of impact threw him down. Muscle, bone and sinew strained to breaking. Steel crashed against his blade, a complex interweave of strokes he fought to unravel. He felt like a greenstick, pummelled at his first sword drill. He tried to lunge, but Hessarde parried the blow with careless ease.

There was nothing in the knight's face now but chilled ferocity. He answered Jaien's failed attack with a deep slash at his side. Jaien turned the steel a fraction, so only the flat slammed against him. Agony speared through him as ribs gave, breath rushing out on a wordless cry. Hessarde backed up with whip-crack swiftness.

Blocking and parrying, turning each incoming strike to a shattering glancing blow, Jaien gave back, step by awkward step. Sweat stung his eyes, pain gouged his lungs.

The pace of Hessarde's assault never slowed, increasing, if anything, into a blinding succession of strokes. Jaien caught each a hair's-breadth late. When he tried to counter, Hessarde was ready for the attack before it began, or slipped away entirely, like mist curling around a tree, leaving Jaien's sword to gut air.

Jaien retreated, trying to find ground, a space to breathe, to find some way to turn the tide in his favour. But Hessarde was in no mind to give up vantage, pursuing him mercilessly, the torn flesh of his sword arm giving no trouble at all, though it should have rendered that arm useless. Jaien backed and dodged, sword flailing ineffectually. Then Hessarde's sword slammed him, a crushing blow cracking what was left of his ribcage.

Jaien crashed to his knees, wheezing on sharp gasps of pain. Hessarde advanced, blade raised. Jaien barely blocked the down strike. Strength flowed from him. Ice ran through his veins. The next blow would finish him.

Jaien.

The whisper of his name shivered through Jaien.

Heed me!

Jaien heaved at air, sucking between teeth, certain the words were his misshaped breath. The courtyard rippled, all motion dissolving into a grey haze, distant and slowed as if the very beat of the world were being dragged to an unwilling stop. Jaien blinked, wondering if he were dead already and the world slipping away before his dying eyes.

Again a voice whispered in his ear, a boy's voice, chilled. *Call me unto you and I shall destroy him.*

Bewildered, Jaien shot a glance over his shoulder. No one stood near enough to own that voice. A peculiar, thick silence compassed him about. Battle sounds no longer fell upon his ears, the ring of steel, the clash of weapons, the cry of children, the roars of rage. Confused, Jaien tried to rise.

Your strength has fled. The voice gusted about him, a cooling, welcome breeze. *Call me back unto the world!*

Jaien clutched tight to his sword, his sanity. Was this how death claimed a man, fear ripping the mind to shreds of madness?

No madness here but that men inspire. The voice battered him. *Release me from my chains.*

Jaien closed his ears.

A rising wind tore at his cloak. *Call me back. I will save you. Release me from my chains.*

Jaien reeled. Death. Chains. Could it be the boy, Liamas, calling to him from beyond the veil? Men spoke such tales in weirding hours of the night, of dead that walked if left unavenged. Was this the boy?

Jaien found voice to croak, 'I call you back.'

Whispered words crowded his mind. *We are one.* The voice dragged him back to the massacre, the blood, the horror, the darkness.

Motion returned to the world with brutal swiftness. Hessarde's sword swung down. Fleet as lightning strike, Jaien's sword flashed upward. Blank surprise lit Hessarde's face as he twisted to evade the blow. It slid past his ribs. He spun away, a puzzled frown creasing his brow.

Jaien leapt to his feet, pain a vague distraction on the horizon of his mind. His body no longer felt his own, closing upon Hessarde as if of its own volition and Jaien just a spectator.

He whipped his blade upward, flinging every ounce of power into a driving thrust at Hessarde's chest. Hessarde blocked it, following-up with a sweep of his sword.

Counter strike followed hard on the heels of strike, a lashing of swordplay almost too swift to follow. The surrounding conflict swept past unnoticed as Jaien flowed into step with his opponent, the clash of steel, the drumbeat of stamping feet round a fire, dancers giving and taking ground in an arrhythmic sequence of movements long practised and consigned to memory. For a heartbeat, Jaien knew the world as he knew himself, all its scars and all its beauty.

He knew in some corner of his mind, every stroke he parried, every blow he delivered, were not of his making. But somehow he felt not repulsed by this joining of a dead spirit to his, but comforted, as though a missing part of him had returned after long absence. Perhaps it was his lost innocence, stripped from him by degrees over years of serving his undeserving king; perhaps it was innocence borrowed from the boy. Whatever the reason, he welcomed the clean purity of it, enveloping him with warmth.

Jaien thrust aside Hessarde's blade, slashed down, striving to drive Hessarde's sword to the cobbles. The knight's face contorted as he fought to free his blade. Jaien released it, sending Hessarde toppling backwards, flailing. Fury enraged Hessarde to a foolhardy counter strike. Their swords locked. Jaien pushed the knight back. A well-placed boot entangled Hessarde's legs, sending him sprawling. Jaien kicked Hessarde's sword beyond reach, spinning across cobbles to be lost among hundreds of tramping feet.

Finish him, the arid whisper rasped, dry and shapeless like long-dead leaves. *We were made to destroy the destroyers. Finish him.*

No refusing that voice. Jaien raised his blade.

'Put up your sword!'

The strident order slammed through Jaien with the force of a lance. Confounded, he stared down at Hessarde, that waiting breast, wondering what he was doing.

Then the dead voice came again, overriding thought and will. *We are one. Destroy him.*

Jaien swung.

Something clobbered his sword with the ferocity of a charger's hoof strike. The jolt shuddered through every bone in his body. His knees gave. Another wallop sent his sword flying in a spinning arc through the air.

The deadly point of a blade pricked Jaien's throat. Dazed, he followed the naked steel to its hilt, thence to its master, a tall, stark man booted for riding with a flowing grey cloak draped over his shoulders. Ensilvered eyes speared Jaien – hot, liquid quicksilver with darker shadows at the back – the emptiness within them haunting, not even tempered with a mote of life. Amid the confusion of onrushing pain, the crowd running amok, the commanding otherworldly voice inciting him to murder, Jaien stared up at Knight Commander Areme – Hessarde's commander – a man he considered worse than Hessarde and all his men put together.

A sense of death clung to Areme like the fetid stink of a tannery. Dark pressed close around him, deepening the shades beneath the jutting bones of his cheeks to match the leather-corded plait of ebon hair falling over one shoulder.

Areme's mouth tightened in a scowl before he growled, 'On your feet.' Every muted syllable slid from his lips like a dagger caressing the pelt of a beast about to be slaughtered.

Jaien stared up at that hard, closed mask of a face giving nothing away except the gulf of barrenness underneath.

'Get up,' Areme repeated, sheathing his sword. 'My blade is not so drunk for Kingdom blood as yours.' He kicked Hessarde. 'You, too.'

Hessarde, who wore the expression of a man already confirmed on his journey out of the world, shook his head as though baffled. An acid glance from Areme had him peeling himself from the cobbles to finish in a half-drunken sway on his feet. He rallied enough to cast a final challenge at Jaien who still knelt at Areme's boots. 'You should have killed me.'

Rage had Jaien halfway to his feet, hand unsheathing a dagger at his belt. He threw himself at Hessarde, dragging him back to the ground. He fought to thrust the dagger through Hessarde's throat only to meet again the resistance of Areme's blade, his dagger arm pinned beneath a grey calf-length boot.

Stunned, he could only gape. There had been no sound of drawing steel, yet Areme had done so with such swiftness the motion passed unnoticed until the blade came to rest. Ice slithered over Jaien, a cold deeper than when he had thought a ghost had crossed over from the dead. Such speed was unnatural, such skill, like a gift stolen from the gods themselves.

Areme's voice deepened with anger straining at its bond. 'Drop that dagger or I'll swear I'll gut you with it.'

Jaien's hand shook with the effort it took to unlock his fingers. His dagger dropped to the blood-slick cobbles, nothing left to threaten but words sharpened to barbs. He speared Hessarde with his glare and hissed, 'I swear, next time we fight, you die.'

He never saw the blow that felled him.

Chapter 2

The Fall of Heroes

Awareness dragged Jaien into a dark twisting of shadow and flame. Cobbles iced his back, jagged breath rasped his throat. A man took shape against fallen night. Condemning face lit by a ring of torches, hooded eyes trapping Jaien in an unflinching stare, Travall, King's Champion and knight commander of the king's guard, loomed over him, snarling, 'Have you lost your mind!' Corded muscles strained against leather as the knight pressed a sword point against Jaien's throat.

Dazed, Jaien stared up at him. Where was Areme? Last he recalled, it had been Areme's sword at his throat.

Hurled threats reverberated around the court. Jaien turned his head. Lines of king's guardsmen, shields locked, slammed a path through warring combatants, shoving aside Jaien's men, forcing back Hessarde's, herding peasants like sheep.

Areme stood at a distance, glowering at all and sundry, ignoring Jaien completely. Hessarde stood cowed at his side like a beaten spaniel. As the brawling wore down, the riot of noise likewise, soldiers and peasants disengaged from the fracas. Both Shaheden strode into the crowd, barking orders at their men. Adversaries flowed to either side of the court like water draining from a flooded field into flanking dikes, leaving behind a storm-scum of corpses and wounded amid upturned merchant carts.

With a grunt of distaste, Travall sheathed his sword. 'You've lost your command.'

Jaien scowled, the taste of blood on his lips. He groaned through pain clawing at his side, 'Better my command than my honour.'

Travall's reply came with the force of unleashed savagery. 'Your honour is bound to your vows. You are sworn to serve and obey your liege-lord. You think you can toss fealty aside like an ill-fitting cloak?'

Jaien raised his chin. 'Like every man here, I swore my allegiance in all faithfulness, never knowing what darkness lay behind the throne I served.'

Travall hauled Jaien to his feet, sending spurts of pain along every sinew. To a man at his shoulder, the knight snapped, 'Take him away.'

Giermont, Travall's second, stepped forward.

Jaien doubled-over the moment Travall released him, fire tearing through him. Giermont seized his arm, yanking him upright.

From amid the wreckage of the court, one blood-spattered man staggered to Jaien's aid – Seth, barely recognisable beneath a face masked in gore. He growled, trying to tear Jaien free from Giermont's grip. Pulled in opposite directions, Jaien fought the stab of shattered ribs stretched between the anchor of Giermont and Seth's dragging weight.

'Leave off!' yelled Giermont. 'Unless you want to join him in the dungeon.'

'By all that is merciful,' swore Travall. 'All his men are for the dungeon. If they want to go along willingly, so much the better.'

To Seth, Jaien wheezed, 'Enough. It's over.'

Seth hoisted his commander's arm over his shoulder. Half-lifting, half-carrying Jaien, whose trembling legs would scarcely support him, Seth glared at Giermont. 'I'll carry him.'

Giermont, back stiff, refused to release Jaien, firmly grasping his other arm. He nodded to an escort of guardsmen who formed a cordon around the two prisoners.

The last things Jaien saw as Giermont pushed him inside the dungeon doors, was Liamas's corpse, a sad bundle of rags among the ruin of bodies. And nearby, Liamas's mother, face down, hair fanning her shoulders like a mourning veil of sheer black silk.

Every faltering step along the warren of damp underground passageways, his mind reeled with images – the boy, the mother, his failure to protect them and his own men.

Deep into the bowels of the fortress, boots echoed dully on uneven flagged floors. They might have been descending into the nether pits of the world. Torches cast wayward, tottering light, silhouetting guards stationed along walls. Fetid stink of rot thickened in Jaien's nostrils, congealing swiftly into something rank and vile, an unspeakable squalor of excrement and piss, vomit and bile.

A thin stretched cry cut through the murk ahead, rising in pitch till it cracked and broke. In the shards of silence following, Jaien's senses picked out shuffling of feet. On either side, hands reached through barred doors, mute appeals for aid. Another tremulous thread of a cry sharpened to an inhuman shriek.

'In there.' A guard swung a door open.

With a brutal thrust, Giermont shoved Jaien past a smoking brazier toward a dark narrow slit.

'Not him,' said Giermont, nodding at Seth. A guard grabbed Seth's arms, pulling him back.

Jaien groaned, half-falling. Giermont hauled him to the back of a cell the width of a sow's pen. He shook Jaien's arm off, letting him slide in a graceless heap to ground strewn with mildewed straw. Rib flesh tore on sharp bone edges. Thorns of pain pierced Jaien's innards. His own cries now mingled with those beyond the door. Chains rattled, and someone encircled his wrists and ankles in chilled iron. All images wavered with torchlight, outlines of his tormentors, the doorway, then whirling darkness closed with a crash.

Unable to rise, or even move, Jaien lay still. His breast heaved in rapid shallow gasps of molten breath. Slowly, the spinning dark settled. Timid and faltering, small sounds touched his ears, rustling of straw, or roughened hemp against rock. Rats or human, Jaien could not tell. No light crept into the windowless cell; no gusts of air moved the gloom.

A scream shattered the dark. Another. Just beyond the door. Jaien listened hard, tried to identify the voice, but nothing in that cry remained human, more an animal's squeal of terror.

His hands clawed into fists. They had lodged him within earshot of the torturer's chamber, so he could hear his men beg for mercy. Screams grated on his ears, the crack of bones, interspersed with the stink of frying flesh struck by a brand, the stench creeping through the slit beneath the door. With an explosion of breath, Jaien slammed his fist against the wall.

Orders barked along the corridor beyond his cell, followed by more wailing and screams. Only in the witching hours did the torturers cease their work. Quiet was no more forgiving, darkness inviting only fitful sleep and nightmares.

He awoke sweating, lying in filth. Jaien guessed it must be dawn as screams began in earnest. He tried to count guard changes, marked by shouted orders and tramping boots, but too often lapsed in and out of pain-fogged drowsing. The drum beat on, every strike on hide flaying Jaien like a whip. It had long ceased beating when they came for him.

Boots stamped outside. Moments later, the cell door scraped open. The unforgiving light of a torch drove out the dark.

Jaien did not know if it was night or day as soldiers dragged him along a short passage thick with guards. The corridor widened abruptly to a large chamber. On one side stood a wide barred door to a holding cell crammed with prisoners. Eyes watering in a draft of hot, foul smoke from a forge, Jaien squinted. A grim line of faces returned his gaze. His men.

None spoke. Masked fear glowed in the depths of every dulled, sleep-starved eye. They had been held in the torture chamber, watching the horrors of the fate awaiting them. Jaien looked from one face to another, not daring to ask the question. Who had already fallen?

Mute, they stared back, neither accusing nor relieved. Not broken, yet, but near as he had ever seen it, minds trapped in terror. The cord of the noose might well hang round each neck.

There could be no appeal. They had defied the king's will. They were dead men.

Jaien's entire body shook with the need to rend the king limb from limb. For the barest moment he caught sight of Gerein, standing amid the others, chin raised, defiant still. Their eyes locked. Gerein's narrowed a fraction, a question awaiting an order. Jaien gave him the only answer he could, the barest shake of head, a warning not to act. While they lived, there was hope, if only a glimmer. Jaien would give the last drop of his blood to save them.

Guards dragged Jaien to the other side of the chamber.

Whips hung from hooks on walls, weighted with jagged strips of steel. Metal implements for crushing teeth, fingers and bones, gleamed in the eerie glow cast from brands glowing white on the forge. The rotten stench of blood battled with the stink of vomit and decaying shreds of flesh in the gutter running the length of the chamber.

A prisoner hung from chains, head swinging loose on his shoulders, muscles and sinews lay raw, frayed and crusted black, more meat than man. On a rack, a lad whimpered, ribs staring with every wheeze. Vicious carnelian fissures wept sap down his arms.

Two guards dragged the chained man down. He sank to the cobbles, sliding through the guards' hands, a broken mass of bleeding flesh. One guard kicked him in disgust. 'He's done.'

A man, tall and angular, separated from the thick gloom at the edges of the chamber. He examined the prisoner. Dead eyes closed to suffering, he gave a muted grunt and a sharp gesture of his head. The guards grabbed the limp arms and dragged the prisoner out like a dead animal.

The torturer motioned to Jaien. 'Strip him.'

Two soldiers tore off Jaien's tunic and leggings. Guards shackled him to the metal ring hanging from a chain on the ceiling. Breath ripped from him as cracked ribs stretched and tore further. The torturer's gaze ran over the pale raised lines running unpatterned across Jaien's chest, thighs, back, the legacy of scores of duels with enemy swords. Without a word, he turned to the wall. He took up a thrice-thonged lash, steel weights clanking loudly in the chamber. Turning, he surveyed Jaien's body once more.

Jaien tensed, every muscle braced for the blow. Fire ripped across his chest as the lash tore across the open sword wound, embedded spikes sticking like fish hooks, taking flesh and blood with them on the arcing return flight. Jaien barely had time to grunt with pain before the lash struck more agony through him. His head flung back, then forward, body writhing with every assault. One by one, fresh ragged slits opened across his chest. His fists tightened into balls, wrists jerking against immovable steel. Blood ran in rivulets down his naked, clenched thighs. No wound he had taken in battle rent his flesh so mercilessly. By the tenth strike, his flesh resembled mince, down to bone. His throat choked down screams. The sixteenth stroke robbed him of every mote of pride. 'What do you want?' he cried.

The torturer's voice came cold and disinterested. 'You're the hero of Tulit. We want you cowed. We want you obedient.' He struck again.

'Gods! Mercy!' The plea was more groan than words.

There are no gods here. The words wove into Jaien's mind from nowhere.

He stared wildly around, but only the torturer stood near, guards at his back. Panic seized Jaien. Had the pain sent him so quickly to madness?

The world rippled, smoky faces in the gloom growing dim. Against his ear, a voice of air brushed softly. *Banish fear. I come to your aid.*

Pride fled, a disjointed, limping thing. The agony of hurt forbid he question his sanity. Jaien groped for the words. 'Please, help me.'

The voice rustled like dead leaves. *First, I would have a promise. Your obedience.*

To Jaien's alarm, the voice vanished. Heat scorched his face. A guard stood before him, full flesh and bone, not a voiceless void. The guard thrust a brand against Jaien's thigh.

'Gods! Gods!' Raw voice scraped from Jaien's constricted throat. Agony blinded him, devoured all thought, tore his soul. He screamed in a voice no longer his, 'I promise! I'll obey! Anything!'

A sigh caressed Jaien. *I take your hurt upon myself.*

Jaien slid into the welcome dark of unconsciousness.

Hard, grudging awareness dragged Jaien up through a quagmire of blood and dark. He had fought hard to feel nothing, to block the pain in his body, his heart. It took long moments to even remember what he had been fighting.

He found himself chained once more to the cobbles of his cell, blocks of damp stone pressed against his cheek, chest and stomach, cold eating through naked skin.

By contrast every muscle burned. Air stabbed fire into his lungs. A river of flame pulsed through him. His chest blazed, every heartbeat marked by laboured breaths.

Something brushed against his ear, a hint of air. A voice emanated from the black abyss which held Jaien fast. *I have come to claim what is mine.*

Jaien tensed. A sharp twist of his head spasmed every muscle. Something pushed against his cheek, cold like bleached bones in winter.

Be at rest.

Whispering wind lifted his hair.

Set your heart at peace. There is naught here but wisdom.

Jaien struggled to rise. Breath came in shallow gasps. Sweat dripped from his forehead. What was this witchery? 'Who are you? Show yourself.'

Do not your heart and blood know me? I am you. We are one.

The strange words stalked the hidden corners of Jaien's mind, slipping in and out of shadows like elusive spirits. Every limb grew heavy, as though his bones were weighted down. Dread consumed him, darker than any battle-terror he had ever faced, more fearsome than the torture chamber.

The wielder of the words was darkness itself, so far beyond his understanding, he tried to close his mind to it.

Thought-words teemed into his brain.

You have promised, and I hold you to your word. Together, we are set on a course from which there is no turning.

Jaien dug like a dog in the mud of his brain for a protest, but came up only with a rotten carcass of an excuse. 'I am unworthy. I have broken one vow already.'

An oath to an unworthy king is no oath at all. To what has your vow led you but shame? You made knightly vows to an unconsecrated king. The gods do not recognise them. They are dust, as your king is dust, unseen by the Heavens. I oathe you now to supreme authority, a power beyond stars, untold in your most ancient texts, power above your counterfeit king.

In the silence descending over the cell, Jaien's unsteady breathing grew loud. Only one power held dominion over kings. He shuddered. 'I am unworthy.'

Your worth is mine alone to judge. The insistent susurration wafted through the cell, sweet, cloying, impossible to resist. *I lay before you two paths. One descends to the Shadow*

Realm. The other leads to the destruction of evil and will free you from the stain of dishonour.

Jaien cursed. 'You think I care about my honour when an innocent boy and his family lie dead? When my men are imprisoned and awaiting the block?'

I offer a way out of darkness.

'What way?'

Save another from the fate of him you could not spare.

'Who?'

Your feet already tread the path to his door.

Shouts reverberated in the passage beyond the cell.

The voice became insistent. *I demand obedience. Without my help, you die, and all you hold dear with you. Bow to my will and all is saved.*

The voice disappeared, leaving cold silence in its wake. Jaien lay unmoving, wondering if a god had truly spoken to him, or if he had lost his wits. He closed his eyes, wanting to pray, to cry, to scream, to die.

The cell door was thrown open, and two men entered.

Jaien tried to turn his head, but even that slight movement resulted in manifold explosions of pain.

'Don't move,' ordered one man. 'This'll hurt a lot less if you stay still.' A hard, callused hand cuffed Jaien's calf. 'Though you deserve every bit of pain that's come to you, you stupid, half-witted bastard.'

A heartbeat later a scream tore from Jaien as fire raced across his shredded back. His body lurched against the chains, tearing open lacerations. Agony, a thousand brands of white flame struck against him.

'Silence,' snapped the unseen man. 'It's just salt and water. It won't kill you.' Unrepentant, he poured more on Jaien's back.

Jaien's clenched eyes leaked tears, weeping like his abused flesh. Then the hellish world slid back into a dark mire of nothingness.

Uncounted days passed in a numbing haze of pain and dark. The man went about his work with the ruthless efficiency of the torturer, uncaring of Jaien's groans, dousing whip gouges with watered salt, as though curing meat, a daily ritual of burning flame prodded deep into flesh. Myrrh resin bit into wounds with sharp, ravenous teeth, devouring him. Neither safflower nor wine softened the bite, the bitter tang giving him no more reassurance than the lash. It was not unknown for prisoners to be healed, only to have their flesh split asunder again.

The door grated open once more. Boots tramped around him. Fingers between his teeth forced his mouth open. He choked. Acid cut into his tongue. Poison, maybe. If he was lucky.

Tension corded Jaien's flayed muscles. Pain ran in spasms across his body. He tried to spit out the taste.

Resist not.

'They're t–trying to kill me,' Jaien spluttered.

Not yet. But their crude ministrations will avail you not.

As if to reinforce the voice's words, white fire blazed across Jaien's back, his chest. The boots receded, the door closing upon them.

The silent voice caressed Jaien's ears. *Give me your pain and I shall heal your hurts.*

'Take it,' muttered Jaien, past all resistance.

Breathe, taste, give yourself over to me.

Jaien heaved at stale, mould-thick air, overhung with wild citrus. A strange tang formed upon his tongue, stronger than tears, but no less bitter.

He knew that taste, that forbidden scent – granine – used by healers, it sent men to madness. Jaien wept at the irony – he had long passed into lunacy, needed no more help.

Agony crept along every muscle, flowed along Jaien's veins. His senses stretched taut. His back spasmed, wounds a cauldron as though flesh split to the bone. Broken ribs shot jolts of pain through his chest, robbing him of the ability to scream. He gasped, body shaking, croaked a groan, throat scorched.

'By all that is merciful,' he cried. 'Let me die.'

Your death is mine.

Time crawled and stretched like his flayed flesh. Fractures knit; excruciating pain tore along mending bones. Weals closed slow over raw meat.

He did not know when the gouging agony of torn flesh blunted. Pain dissolved into numbness and utter, utter cold. For the longest time, Jaien felt he drifted in clouds, floating. The creak of hinges spurred his mind back to the world.

'Awake at last,' muttered a low voice.

'His wounds . . . Look at them.' Another, deeper voice did not mask surprise. 'They're healed. How is that possible?'

The first voice ordered, 'Get him to his feet.'

Voiceless men unlocked his shackles. Hands clasped his arms, and hauled Jaien up in a staggering jerk. Torch smoke wafted around him as a skin of wine pressed against his mouth.

'Drink,' came the order.

Half-recognising the rough timbre, Jaien obeyed. He wrestled to focus, trying to make out faces weaving in smoke-thick gloom. Slowly his vision cleared. A semblance of strength returned. The men holding him stepped away. Jaien blinked, swaying drunkenly, staring at them. His chest no longer burned. Where there had been broken bones, no pain, his wounds from the riot and the torture chamber, completely healed.

Travall leaned against the wall of the cell, fingers beating a rhythm against the rock, matching the impatient tapping of his boot. 'The use of granine is forbidden by king's edict.'

Jaien found strength to laugh. 'Granine? How in Senfar's name do you think I could get granine in here?'

Travall grunted. 'Give me enough time, I'll work it out.'

'Does it matter?' Giermont yawned, then rubbed his hands together, cupped them, blew fogged breath against his fingers. 'Against his other misdeeds, it hardly rates.' Giermont's green eyes focused on Travall. 'And while we are discussing misdeeds, remind me again why I'm in this dungeon freezing my arse off and doing something that's bound to get me thrown in here myself?'

'Shut up,' snapped Travall. To Jaien, he said, 'Move,' indicating the open door.

Jaien refused, instead nodding to Travall's sword. 'Why don't you just end it now?'

Travall's eyes hardened. 'That's just what I'm doing, you fool. Now get out before I change my mind.' He tossed a cloak around Jaien's shoulders, tugged the cowl over Jaien's head, then shoved him into the corridor and marched him, in slow, lumbering steps through the torch dark until they emerged from the dungeons into grey dawn.

Jaien's light-starved eyes burned.

Travall led him into long shadows beneath a wall at the northern edge of the palace forecourt. Crows half way up the wall took flight at their approach.

A shifting flurry of wind carried a frightful stench. Jaien stopped, gut heaving. In the murk, nailed to the wall, faces drooped, half-stripped by ravenous beaks, crawling with flies feasting on flesh. Jaien did not need to be told who they were. Travall had brought him here by design, not accident. He turned away, a veil of darkness falling in his mind to block the sight of the boy and his mother.

In the court, long lines of saddled horses stood before the great hall, snorting and tossing heads, hooves scraping sharp against cobbles, woollen blankets shifting with every swing of hindquarter. Eyes rolled back, ears flickering nervously toward the corpse-heads. None of the horse attendants cast the wall's murderous decorations more than a frightened glance.

Jaien stood still, hollow, unable to reconcile the cold apathy of these men with his own burning need for justice. His eyes narrowed as he examined the waiting steeds. Courier's mounts, small, swift and ribby, built for endurance.

Jaien cast a long, sideways look at Travall, wanting to ask what orders the king's couriers were receiving in the hall. The closed face told him he would get no answer.

From a nearby temple, chanting voices drifted on the air, reciting the dawn prayer. Jaien sent his own prayer to the Heavens, for his men.

Travall clamped a hand on Jaien's arm, a band of iron pressing him onward as liveried guards pushed open the wide doors of the great hall. A tide of couriers surged down marble steps into the palace forecourt, faces morose and taciturn. Royal badges adorned every tabard, the red firefalcon of Mirador stark against white wool.

Jaien's eyes darted over each man in the assemblage, examining the dour faces amid the bustle of loading and saddling. Whatever the orders were, they were hard.

'Go,' said Travall between gritted teeth, pushing Jaien ahead of him. Travall and Giermont eased past the muttering press of couriers, flanking their prisoner like a pair of sheep hounds, shouldering him into the westernmost corner of the court.

No one looked their way, couriers too busy strapping saddlebags to saddles and talking in low voices to guards or stable boys holding their mounts. Travall shoved Jaien up the steps to the armoury. 'In there.'

Inside, pale sparks of lambent light glinted along the walls of a large open space. Boots echoed dully on the armoury floor, crushing discarded fletching feathers as men took station at every door. Giermont hauled Jaien past ranks of bows and swords toward the middle of the room. Long rows of hauberks and helms gleamed as if new, enough weaponry for a full command. When they reached a long wooden table covered in ragged cloths and pots of oil and beeswax, Giermont shoved Jaien into a chair.

A ripple of movement in the dark nearby caught Jaien's attention. A man stepped forth, grey cloak billowing around his calves. Jaien held himself rigid as Horsemaster Gerhas marched toward him. Stocky and powerful, the old man's vigour belied his greying hair. Wisps straggled over the weathered face, doing little to mask the deep furrows carving a scowl.

Gerhas cleared his throat, gnarled skin flushing red, then said without greeting, eyes ablaze with fury, 'For the trouble you've caused, I should kill you right now.' Refusing Jaien even the chance of replying, he continued in clipped tones, 'I won't prolong this. You're charged with treason, refusal to uphold your knightly vows, violation of the king's command, inciting civil unrest, and failure of duty. All hanging offences.' He paused to let the charges sink in. 'The same charges hold against your men.'

Jaien bit back an obscenity. 'They followed my orders. The fault lies with me.'

Gerhas cut through the protest with a raised hand. 'All will be held to account. The kingdom is on the brink of war, and you abetted a revolt in the king's fortress. Callinor has ordered an example be made of you and your men.'

Back stiffened, Jaien jutted his jaw and spoke from between clenched teeth. 'Like he made an example of an innocent boy?'

Gerhas's face stayed granite, his quiet voice laced with venom. 'Curb your tongue before I still it for you.'

With nothing to lose, Jaien ignored the warning. 'What oath did *you* murder when you allowed an innocent mother to fall while protecting her child?'

Travall shifted slightly, lips tightening in a frown, warning him to say no more.

Gerhas's unnerving eyes fixed on Jaien, glittering with murderous light. 'My oaths bend with the will of my king.'

Jaien spat.

'The king is also calling your father to account.' Gerhas's words were so soft, the killing edge took moments to sink in.

Jaien's body lost all feeling. 'He wouldn't dare.'

Gerhas pulled a dagger from beneath his cloak, thin steel with a silver hilt.

Bitterness bled into Jaien's heart as he recognised the king's death mark. Denial was an animal sound in his throat. 'No . . .'

Gerhas's voice became silken persuasion. 'It lies with you to amend this.'

A weight of darkness settled about Jaien, heavy with the expectant, calculating stares of every man in the room. Standing as though trapped in the path of a charge, he barely found voice to croak, 'How?'

Grim satisfaction etched across Gerhas's face. The horsemaster nodded to guards at the door. Moments later two soldiers entered with a courier.

Travall pointed at the courier's saddlebags and said, 'Spill them.'

The courier's face ashened as his eyes darted from horsemaster to knight commander and back again. 'Yes, *Sir*,' He dumped the bags on the table, unbuckled the straps of the saddlebags and tipped out the contents – rolled scrolls of vellum fastened with the king's seal.

Jaien could not move, every muscle frozen as though his body sensed the truth his mind wanted to deny. Icy horror gnawed deep at the very marrow of his bones. Blood pounded at his temples. There were over twenty commissions. He did a quick calculation. Each courier delivering twenty, meant well over two thousand commissions all told. Two thousand conscripts.

He bowed his head. Behind closed eyes, he envisioned boy after boy ripped from their families. How many would end up dying on a gibbet, slaughtered like beasts long before the coming slaughters on the battlefield? How many like the boy he had failed to save? He shuddered.

Travall turned to the youth. 'Where's the list?'

The courier fumbled inside his tunic, pulled out a single scroll and unrolled it, hands shaking.

Gerhas snatched it from the youth's trembling fingers and broke the seal. Unrolling the vellum on the table, he ran a hard, callused finger down a list of names.

Jaien read quickly the title – *conscripts from Hermas to Graycor* – beneath it a long list of names, the chicken-scratch scrawl evidencing haste.

Gerhas matched the symbols beside the names to those on the scrolls on the table. When he found the one he wanted, he swept the rest back into the saddlebag and handed the list back to the courier. 'You can mark off the last name on your list as delivered.' His voice came soft, chilled. 'And none of this ever happened. Now go.'

The young man grabbed his bags and dashed for the door, boots beating staccato over a soft-muffled curse. Giermont brought him to a halt by raising one booted foot to the opposite frame of the doorway. He slapped the wooden shaft of an arrow against his hand. 'Do you know the range of an arrow, boy?'

Fear crawled in the courier's wide eyes. 'Two hundred yards, sir.'

Giermont's lips pressed to a tight line. 'If you squawk, it's the length and breadth of the kingdom.'

'I won't squawk. I swear it.' The young man's voice came out thin.

'Let him go,' said Gerhas. As the courier scampered off, the horsemaster turned to Jaien, his countenance steel and distant. 'You know the price of disobedience. There exists just one will here – the king's.' He held the scroll out to Jaien. 'As an earnest of your goodwill, you shall bring in this boy.'

A blast of wind tore open a door and screamed into the room, a voice riding upon it only Jaien could hear. *Touch it not! Touch it not!*

The world swayed for an instant as though the flags beneath his feet shifted. Every sense alerted, Jaien knew then. This was the one he was meant to save.

Ignoring the voice's command, Jaien took the scroll, read quickly the name beneath the seal – *Sihan, son of Armindras, Keeper of Graycor. Service in the king's command.* Why he should save Sihan above so many others, he did not know. A dead boy spoke to him with a god's voice, determined to hold his will in bondage. It must be a prodigy of Senfar, god of horses; the god Jaien revered above all others.

Sihan was the son of a keeper of bloodhorses. Senfar would protect his own. The god had saved Jaien. Jaien would not refuse the price.

Gerhas held out a blade, wrapping it in the scroll. Hair streaming behind him, he said, 'You will deliver this yourself, personally.' Aggression lit his eyes. 'Disobey, and every man under you will spend the rest of their sorry days festering in the black swamps of Emor.' He thrust the hilt into Jaien's hand. 'Either a dagger gets delivered to the boy's father, or to yours. Your choice.' He turned and walked away. The soldiers at the door backed away, nodding in deference.

Fire burned as Jaien's fingers clenched cold steel. The voice in his head became a screech.

Release it! Let go your worldly vows! Deliver the boy not up to his enemies!

Waves of fire and ice swept over Jaien. Flurries of brown-blotched leaves swirled around his bare legs in gusting wind sweeping through the door.

You must not let them have him. That voice again, threatening his sanity. He felt as though two sides of a vice closed in on him.

Jaien turned to Travall, probing that austere face. 'Is this what you saved me for?'

Travall did not answer, but something shifted in his face, a vague unease, as though he approved not of his own actions.

Jaien clamped a hand on Travall's arm, determined to claw something from this slight show of sympathy. 'My men, what will happen to them?'

For a long while, Travall remained stone-silent, gaze locked on a corner of the armoury. Finally, he said, 'What you do now will decide their fate. They'll remain prisoners for the interim, officers under house arrest. Later . . . if you don't . . .' Travall coughed. 'If you don't add to your gross idiocy, I'll petition their release.' He looked Jaien square in the eye. 'Even if I manage that, you won't get them back. Your command will be disbanded. Your men will be split among the other commands–'

'The seven hells they will!'

'You've no longer any say in matters.'

Cold silence stretched between them.

'You could have stopped it,' said Jaien.

Travall's eyes lost their unswerving clarity of purpose, grew mired in defeat. 'Nobody can stop this.' He began to pace the room. Restrained violence in every step, he resembled a wildcat poised to pounce, only to find itself caught, feet tangled in an inescapable net. When he turned back to Jaien, anger and despair flickered in his eyes. 'By all that is merciful, just do this thing. Pelan is already on the road to war with Byerol over stolen bloodhorses. You'd think you'd want–'

'I want to serve justice!' hissed Jaien. 'The same as any man. Not this . . . this farce we all live with, and hide.'

Travall averted his gaze, staring out the door, as if he, too, wanted to escape the lie of their existence. Again Jaien sensed a beast trapped, struggling futilely against bonds it could not break.

Travall's penetrating gaze fixed upon Jaien. 'The old man means it. The king wants you dead. It took all I had to talk them into giving you this one chance.' His voice hardened. 'I don't want to be the one to give the order to murder your father. He'll be on his way to Mirador already. A despatch was sent soon after the riot, announcing a King's Tournament as part of the Fire Rituals horse fair.'

'A tournament!' Jaien stared at him incredulously.

'Callinor wants to put this awkwardness aside.'

'Awkwardness!'

Travall looked away. 'He wants to turn the minds of the populace from what has passed. By next moon's cycle the couriers will have proclaimed it far and wide and this riot will be nothing but a bad aftertaste in the mouth.' He turned his eyes back upon Jaien. 'Every bloodhorse Keeper has been ordered to attend, bringing their best horses with them. Your father won't leave this fortress alive if you disobey. Now, what are you going to do?'

Jaien's fingers white-knuckled upon the king's dagger. Could he allow his father to be the price of disobedience? Whatever course he took, death was inevitable. An unequal choice. A boy weighed against his father, his men, himself. One life stolen so others might live.

'I'm waiting,' said Travall, eyes solemn pools with lightless depths churning far below the shadowed surface.

Sudden certain knowledge weighed Jaien's heart down with boulders. Travall had been ordered to kill him for the wrong answer.

In the gloom of the armoury, Jaien's gaze scraped discreetly the weaponry arrayed before him. Torchlight glittered along keen-edged steel. The chance was there. Travall would not kill him like a dog.

Within like without, Jaien became mutilated flesh, a body flayed of skin, to which the lightest contact brought unbearable agony. Fate again forced him to fight himself, duty warring against morality, his father's life, his men's lives, set against an innocent boy's. No way out. No way to protect the boy and remain a servant of the throne.

Jaien closed his eyes, recalling the long list of names of boys other men would destroy, the thousands of commissions. It was more than one life against the others. Duty and morality became one. His duty was to serve the people of the kingdom. There had to be some way to stop this madness. A god spoke to him. Surely Senfar would help him find the way.

'Well,' prompted Travall. 'What are you going to do?'

Jaien dodged the knight's gaze as he replied, 'The only thing I can.'

Chapter 3

Senfari

Sihan braced one worn boot on the lowest rail of the yard, deep-held breath escaping his lips as he eyed the white stallion. A statue of matchless power, Aurion cocked his ears to spear points. Nostrils flared, red lining distending with every grunting snort, signalling annoyance at curtailed freedom. Not quite rage, not yet.

Wet pooled in Sihan's armpits, ran under his patched tunic and down his sides. He bent, risked a hand through the rails, running it down the stallion's long forelegs, noting the straight clean lines. Would that they might remain so after the coming battle.

Sihan rubbed a sweating palm across his chin, calluses thick and rough against a day's stubble. The drifting heat of the Yseth lowlands sapped energy, made focussing difficult, and he needed all his reflexes lightswift to impress the Senfari.

Another breath, heavy with horse sweat, plains-dirt and well-oiled leather. Sihan stole a glance across the stallion's great expanse of haunch, the dazzling white coat shining and rippling silk. His gaze met narrowed eyes of waiting men. Some ignored him entirely, speaking low, or simply shaking heads, disapproving lips stretched tight.

Only two youths flanking Sihan paid him any heed, Kheran and Tejas, grooms from Yseth, both clad in threadbare tunics, whips tucked into their belts, tan boots running knee-length over leggings. Kheran dug an elbow into Sihan's ribs. 'They're here.'

No need to ask who.

A line of elders approached, wiry, hard muscle over bone. His mentors. His judges. Ruthless, unforgiving. Eyes raked over him, cold, killing, taloned glares, missing not one flaw.

Sihan's blood quickened. Rat-trapped thoughts scurried around his mind. Was he really ready for this? His heart slammed against his chest. He could not fail. Not after he had argued all night for this chance and risked everything. He pushed aside the sudden fear. This day he would prove his manhood, take his rightful place alongside his peers – the Senfari horsemasters: tough men who led proud, meagre lives, sleeping beneath stars, their only seat the hollow of a saddle. Leather peeled from their boots. Their tunics were frayed, chaps worn. Everything about them stank of wood smoke and horses, yet none rode the kingdom with greater dignity or worth, not knight nor lord. They were the horse god Senfar's chosen, the only men truly free in the kingdom, free to choose their lives, beholden to none but the horses in their charge.

Without care for the fate of one youth, they strode past, heedless of the wishing eyes following their every movement – stable lads and grooms – all wanting to be, needing to be among those exalted ranks.

Gaze fixed on the short fur caps edged with wolf pelt, which each Senfari wore to mark their standing, Kheran muttered, 'If it kills me, I want one of those.'

Hatless himself, Sihan raked his hand through his unbound hair, feeling naked because it signified his lack of status. This day must change that.

The gate of the yard behind Sihan rasped open.

'Ready?' asked an age-rough voice.

Stroking one hand down Aurion's massive arched crest, drawing strength from the powerful muscles, Sihan took time turning to face the man set to test him.

Above a blunted nose, Yonnad's pitiless clear-eyed stare met his. The oldest of the Senfari, Yonnad's flesh and bones bore marks of a lifetime's struggles: scars interwoven with wrinkles. Fingers twisted, knees bowed-out, no tougher horseman rode the ranges.

Undaunted, Sihan nodded.

'Best get on your pony, then.' Yonnad smiled, a stretching of skin easily passing for a grimace.

Sihan clenched his teeth, ready to spit back an insult. The old man had all but called Aurion an Emor pony, the most worthless measure of a horse in the kingdom.

Kheran's hand closed on his shoulder. 'Don't.'

'If he calls Aurion that again–'

'You'll beat him on the field,' finished Kheran, glaring after Yonnad.

'He wants to rankle you,' said the other groom, soft-spoken Tejas, crowding closer. 'Don't let him beat you before you're even mounted.'

'You know how he hates Aurion,' added Kheran.

'I know,' muttered Sihan, unappeased. It killed him, having to bow before the masked slur. Why, just because Aurion was of untraceable origin, did everyone consider his blood as muddied as the mongrel half-bred ponies roaming the dead swampland on the southernmost regions of Yseth?

'If you beat him, I'll get my ma to sew a pedigree for Aurion,' Tejas joshed, trying to lighten Sihan's mood. 'You know, like those fancy ones we seen for the foundation sires they keep in the vaults at Mirador.'

A smile teased Sihan's lips. 'Tell her to start sewing, then. But remember, it's got to be silk.'

'Silk, right,' laughed Tejas.

'Andorean silk,' stressed Sihan. 'Like Celestion's pedigree.'

Tejas swept into a bow. 'Only the best for the king's horse.'

Laughter bubbled from Sihan's tense lips. All the lads knew the legends of old, of the white northern Godsteeds, of the right of a king to ride the greatest. For a heartbeat, the tightness in Sihan broke. He was no king, consecrated by the gods, and chosen by a Godsteed to be its bonded rider. The truth, he hoped, was better. He had heard the half-hidden whispers since he had first sat a horse. *He's gifted, sits a bareback horse like he was born on it. See how the horses all pay him mind. He's a prodigy of Senfar.*

This day must prove them right.

Sihan noted the lash in Yonnad's right hand, threads of lead swaying at its tip. The old man meant business this day, intended to take it out on the only horse that had ever bested him.

Yonnad had been the first in a long line of Senfari who had sought to test themselves against this white freak of a horse taunting them with elusive God-promised glory. But Aurion defeated every one. Even staked and blindfolded as a colt, he had thrashed every man approaching within striking distance. A demon possessed, he refused to be ridden except by Sihan. Bruises and scars were Senfari badges of honour. Aurion had added to these immeasurably with hooves and teeth, especially Yonnad's count. The old Senfari had lost the use of his right arm for a moon's cycle after Aurion had caught it between his teeth and crushed like a vice. Yonnad would never forget. Never forgive.

Kheran's knowing eyes met Sihan's. 'Don't worry. Yonnad'll never touch him. Aurion'll make his pureblood look slow as a mule.'

As if impatient for the coming battle, Aurion lifted a big hoof and pawed, stirring up red dust from the baked ground. Beneath the forelock, black eyes hedged by dark lashes, stared out from a long fierce face. In those shadowed depths, something indomitable blazed, a will like the black heart of a storm.

Sihan slipped through the rails, pulled on his gloves.

Tejas's voice rang out, 'Watch it! Watch it!'

Aurion's hindquarters swung, tail switching, back humping as the cinch tightened.

'Stop it!' Sihan hissed, minding Aurion's dancing hooves. The horse would trample all over him if he gave it a chance.

The great black orbs swivelled to glare. It was not quite hatred filling the stallion's eyes, more point-blank refusal to accept Sihan's authority.

Kheran drew his whip from his belt and held it out.

Sihan shook his head. 'It'll just make him worse.'

'Use it on Yonnad, then.'

Sihan grimaced a smile, tightening his hands into fists. No use waiting. He unbuckled the rope halter, letting it swing from the tie-lead like a tangled snake. Aurion's haunches trembled as Sihan grabbed a fistful of mane. Vaulting smoothly into the saddle, he tossed a quick nod to Kheran who flung open the gate. Sihan spurred the stallion from the yard and down through the desert hamlet of Hermas.

Dogs, panting in lines of shadow, growled. The white stallion rolled his eyes, threatening back at them, wanting to strike, to bite. Unforgiving hands restrained him. Aurion swung his head around to nip at Sihan's boot. Sihan kicked him on, past the line of broken fences bordering a huddle of ruins marking the outskirts of the village. The last buildings crumbled into the sere plain as though drought had sucked moisture from the mud-and-straw blocks.

Beyond the ramshackle jumble of hovels stretched the horizon, the baking Yseth plain, testing ground for colts trained for war, for lads wanting greatness. It might have been the kingdom's end, pastures eroded to dirt after the long hot summer.

Sweat stung Sihan's eyes, trickled down the nape of his neck. It was difficult to imagine this same sun crisping Yseth to a dry, burnt-out shell, at the same time sparked vast snow fields in Graycor to the burning white of diamonds. How Sihan wanted to be there, somewhere past the horizon, where mountains towered, tier upon tier, peaks floating among clouds, glaciers in their flanks. How he longed for forests bursting with birdsong, fresh rain upon his face, and snow, snow, snow.

If the choice were his, he would never leave his beloved mountains. If he passed this test, he could go wherever he pleased: a Senfari's right.

He rode to where the judges awaited him, a ring of mounted men, tunics and faces gritted by dust. Sihan breathed deep, of earth, of heat, of horses. His fingers tightened on the rein as he halted before his father, their glances not quite meeting.

Tension corded both their bodies. They had argued all night. Armindras had offered him the best of the Graycor colts for the testing, the most tractable, willing, talented, the most courageous, a strapping bay named Spirit, marked to be the future King stallion. Sihan had refused. He wanted no favours and above all to be seen to be given no favours.

It was bad enough that as Keeper of the Graycor Bloodhorses, it was his father's role as Prime Senfari to sit in judgment on every aspiring Senfari. Sihan could not demand Armindras withdraw from the panel of judges. So he had done the next best thing.

He had chosen Aurion. This way no one could accuse his father of bias. Sihan would earn his rank fairly, and with duress if need be.

The choice had hurt, for the Graycor bloodhorses were his father's pride. That wound bled between them now. Only one way to heal it. He had to pass this test.

Displeasure marred the judges' faces as they eyed Aurion. The riding of a white horse was forbidden to all but kings. The penalty for riding such was death. But they had sanctioned the choice. How could they not when over the years they had all tried? Besides, no man of Graycor would spread word of Aurion and the youth who rode him to unfriendly ears. Not even Yonnad, who despised the stallion. Senfari codes were sacred, loyalty and honour beyond price.

Face closed, Armindras stepped his mount near. 'Ready, boy?' His gravel voice gave naught away.

'I'm ready,' replied Sihan, voice deep and firm – a youthful copy of his father's.

Sun catching every glint in his grey hair, slashing across his drawn, leathered face, Armindras spoke low, shielding his eyes. 'Don't let that horse beat you.'

Sihan smiled briefly. 'I won't.'

'Go, then.' Armindras motioned toward the plain.

Cut adrift, with only himself to rely on, Sihan cast his eyes to the Heavens, straining to see past the sun's white blaze, hoping Senfar was watching and approved of what he saw.

Kheran and Tejas rode up on their mounts, forced smiles pasted to their faces, and wished him luck before joining the group of onlookers ranked behind the judges.

Tension tightened Sihan's gut. What trial would the Senfari place before him? Every testing was different, with only one exception. The judges perversely always chose a horseman's weakest skill, demanding he overcome his failing if he wanted to succeed. But Sihan was uniformly sound in every skill; they would not find him wanting. He listed the tests in his mind, archery and lance, sword and staff, dagger and spear.

Spear.

His gut wrenched.

Yonnad would not spare him. He knew in Sihan he would find no easy weakness. So instead he would exploit Aurion's flaws. If there was one weapon guaranteed to make Aurion fail, it was the spear. Aurion hated the spear, fearing it like a tiger snake slithering between his hooves. Nothing could set him to a fit of bucking faster.

'Declare the test,' demanded Armindras of Yonnad.

The old man, unsmiling, circled before the judges on his horse. Chirot sweated freely, but all horses did on such a heat-heavy day when even the air had stilled to motionless death. When Yonnad nodded to a groom holding two spears, Sihan bit down a grimace, refusing to cede vantage in any form. Yonnad must not see him rattled before they had even begun.

Yonnad took the spears from the groom and thrust one in the direction of the plain. Innards twisting, Sihan followed the line of the shaft to where a circle of white stones surrounded a patch of dark. Left and right, two cairns stood equal distances from the stone circle, a half league distant in either direction. The wolf's test. A trial of blood, played throughout the kingdom, usually by a horde of horsemen.

A black wolf's gutted carcass lay in the centre of the ring of stones. Sihan had to fight Yonnad for it, then ride with the pelt around his designated cairn, then return it to the circle. A task of battles and chase. His mind filled with visions of trampling hooves, torn hide wrenched from hand to hand, horseflesh smashing against horseflesh.

But why the spears? They were not part of the wolf test.

Reading the question in Sihan's eyes, Yonnad indicated a tree stump rising from the barren ground beyond the stone circle. 'Only after you strike the stump can you claim the wolf.'

Sihan's teeth ground on a curse.

Armindras yelled, 'Begin!'

Yonnad tossed Sihan the other spear. Aurion shrank beneath him as the weapon met his reaching hand. The stallion shuddered, plunged away. In an instant he flung his head down and arched his back. Sihan slammed his feet into the stirrups, crushed his calves to the stallion's belly. Haunches came up in a wild, free kick, wrenching him backwards. Then the hump again, a solid ball of muscle with no give in it. Sihan's body whipped every way, head snapping back and forth. Caught in the middle of the bucking storm, Sihan knew Yonnad was already making his run toward the stump.

Fury welled – at Yonnad, at Aurion, at his father, at himself. He could ride as well as any Senfari, and one poor choice was not going to rob him of this chance. He raised the spear and smashed the flat of the blade on the stallion's quarters. If Aurion wanted war, he would have it. Aurion bounded into the air. Another wallop, muscles strained to burst. Sihan wrenched the reins, jabbed Aurion's head up. Spurs gouged.

Aurion reared, striking the air. When he planted his feet, Sihan jerked the reins with a pitiless hand, readying the spear for another blow. The stallion stamped his hooves. Eyes rolling white and back, fixed upon the spear.

'Go on, you bastard!' Sihan shouted. Muscles curved and hardened beneath him, power coiled within white gleaming hide like a volcano waiting to erupt. Grabbing the bit between his teeth, Aurion burst into a gallop of such mind-numbing, bone-jarring roughness he might have been dragging Sihan over a riverbed of boulders. Only by providence had he lit after Yonnad's fleeing bay.

Ahead, Yonnad steadied Chirot. His spear arced from his hand, twisting in unerring flight to bite violently into the stump. He wheeled his horse, galloping headlong to the wolf circle.

Sihan rode the fighting gallop, the weight of Aurion's head an anchor in his left hand. His right hand clutched the spear, shifting it, balancing it, willing strength into muscles racked to shreds.

The stump spiked from the ground, a straggle of twisted wood. Sihan raised the spear. Swift as a striking viper, Aurion shied. No time to think. No time to correct if he wanted to catch Yonnad. Off balance, half-hanging from the saddle, Sihan cast the weapon. It wavered through the air, the arc too high. Floated, floated, flight dying until it dropped with a dull thud, shuddering, into the base of the stump.

Sihan clawed back into the saddle, and stared unbelieving. He had done it . . . just.

Voices shouted from afar, his friends urging him on. 'Go on, Sihan! Go on!'

Sihan wheeled Aurion. He had to catch Yonnad.

Chirot raced toward the stone circle. Left foot in the stirrup, right knee bent round the saddle horn, the old Senfari leaned far out on the left side of his galloping bay, body suspended over empty air. One big-wristed hand snatched up the wolf pelt. With the strength and agility of a man of far younger years, Yonnad swung back into the saddle. His spurs ripped Chirot's sides. His whip lashed them. In a whirl of dust he took off for the southern cairn.

Sihan had two choices – stop Yonnad from gaining the cairn, or wait and block Yonnad on the return journey. With Aurion's unpredictability, Sihan could ill-afford the risk of Yonnad making the cairn, leaving only Aurion and Sihan between him and the goal. He had ridden against Yonnad many times. The man had over fifty years of skill. He had slipped through many a cordon of tested riders to claim victory. What was one untried youth on a fractious horse?

With a sharp kick of his boot, Sihan set Aurion after Yonnad. The stallion sprung away, every inch of him transformed into speed. Muscles bunched and stretched, rippling and flowing beneath sweat-darkening hide. Legs reached and struck the ground, hooves digging deep into parched earth. The plain dissolved into a blur of ochre. Sihan clamped a hand upon the whipping mane. Wind rushed through his hair, streamed tears from his eyes.

Speed. Such speed. Faster, faster, as though the stallion sought to outstrip the world. Ahead, the churning hindquarters of Yonnad's mount grew closer. Aurion bore on the bit, wanting to charge through the biting metal, demanding his head. Sihan kept strict pressure on the reins, a tenuous link to obedience. If he lost control of Aurion again, it was all over.

The distance between the racing stallions shrank. He would catch Yonnad before the cairn. Aurion's blood was aflame, his power and speed beyond anything Sihan had ever ridden. He fought the bit, pressing his charge. Ahead, the bay's hooves spattered Sihan's face with stones and grit. Sihan crouched tight over Aurion's stretched neck, eyes squinting, face and arms flecked with foam, the quarry within grasp.

Chirot tensed, ears flattening. Yonnad glanced back. Surprise flickered across his straining face, quashed quickly by a look of grim determination.

Sihan clenched his teeth. Taking a risk, he eased his grip on the reins. Aurion surged, shooting forward like an arrow from the bowstring.

Yonnad shifted his weight from side to side in a bid to keep Aurion from ranging abreast. His bay, experienced and sensitive to every movement of his rider's body, swung right or left at the merest hint of lean, the feather touch of rein against neck.

Closer. Closer. Yonnad flicked his whip back, striking Aurion's muzzle, trying to force him back and break his bay free of the hounding pursuit. Aurion tossed his head and broke stride for a moment. Flecks of blood flew back, speckling Sihan's arms.

It was fair play, but that did not mean Sihan had to like it. He sat up a fraction, tightened the rein, holding Aurion back, making Yonnad think he had given up the chase. No use to run up alongside, Yonnad might lash Aurion blind to stop him.

Using his weight, thighs and calves, Sihan sent Aurion wide of the bay. Once again, he rode low, the stallion's hot, sweat-slick neck rising and falling with each measured stride. Knees easy on the saddle, Sihan increased the pressure of his calves. 'Go!' he demanded, no longer satisfied with just the wolf but wanting to repay Yonnad in kind for spilling Aurion's blood. The stallion's hooves drove into the ground, Aurion outpacing the bay. Despite the extra ground he had to cover, he recovered all he had lost, ranging up level with the bay in less than a furlong. For a few strides the two horses galloped furiously, ten or so man-lengths between them, then Sihan set Aurion in a curve, angling into the bay.

This unexpected manoeuvre, coupled with Aurion's startling pace, caught Yonnad by surprise. He spurred his mount with a merciless lash. Chirot lengthened his stride. The cairn was just ahead.

Sihan braced, clamping his thighs, slammed Aurion into Chirot, pitching the bay to its knees. Yonnad fell forward, clinging to Chirot's neck like a leech.

Amid the confusion of two masses of entangled, struggling horseflesh, stink-sweat of unwashed bodies, Sihan grabbed the saddle horn with his left hand, tightening fingers clenching warm leather. Throwing his weight to the right, he crooked his left knee around the horn, jammed his right foot deep in the stirrup, hung out precariously over the bulk of Yonnad's bay, straining for the wolf pelt clasped beneath Yonnad's thigh.

Strips of lead from Yonnad's whip hissed in flight. A blistering path of agony shot across Sihan's brow. Hot blood spurted, slid down his cheek. Vision clouded in one eye.

Yonnad hammered his grasping fingers with the handle of his whip. Clawed fingers yanked Sihan's hair and belt. Sihan tore the wolf pelt from Yonnad's desperate grasp, warm greasy fur encrusted with dirt.

Desire and fury blazed hot in Yonnad's gawping, wretched eyes. His mouth twisted in a scowl so fierce it rendered his features inhuman.

Sihan dragged himself back into the saddle, pulled Aurion's head round so hard the stallion reared and twisted, forelegs clearing Yonnad's back by mere inches. Pelt wedged beneath his thigh, Sihan dug spurs into Aurion's ribs, racing toward the northern cairn.

Somewhere toward the village, voices cheered. Kheran? Tejas? No way of telling. Sihan paid them little mind. The pelt was his; he had to get away from Yonnad before the Senfari recovered.

Aurion tore across the plain, no longer fighting for control. A feeling of unity flowed through Sihan, of horse and rider as one. He swayed with the rhythm, enjoying the sensation of flight without wings. Beneath him, Aurion snorted as he galloped across the plain, stretched out to the full, white mane streaming, hooves skimming the ground.

Sihan shot a glance over his shoulder. Yonnad cantered well back, not pushing his bay though Chirot looked uninjured. To race after Sihan would be futile. Sihan had to return after rounding the southern cairn, and Yonnad would be waiting. Sihan had but to put pressure on the reins, to curb Aurion. No need to spend *his* strength either. He would need everything he had to get past Yonnad on the way back to the stone circle.

But he did not. Aurion felt as fresh as when they had started, racing like he did in the mountains the few times when he had the inclination to obey. Sure hooves reached out, struck the ground. A slashing cut. Rebound. Rushing wind buffeted Sihan, whipped tears from his eyes, whistled past his ears. He leaned forward, shouting, 'Go! Go! Go!' and Aurion surged to the spur of his voice. Faster. Faster. Every stride lengthening. Power and glory and so much more.

Ahead, a long split in the earth stretched in a jagged line across his path, a horse's height deep, an equal width across. Aurion bunched and gathered, leapt high in the air. Soared, soared as though he might never come down. Landed so lightly Sihan never shifted in his seat.

Rider and horse melded. Sihan did not want to lose this feeling, so rare, so beautiful it raised a knot in his throat. Aurion submitting to his will – no effort, no struggle. Just two beings fused into one. A Godsteed and its bonded rider. Ethereal and divine.

At the cairn, Sihan turned Aurion, waving the wolf pelt above his head like a pennon to signal the judges he had fulfilled that part of the trial. Before him, a wide open plain, and the waiting stone circle in which to fling the pelt and claim victory. He possessed the trophy. If he had strength enough, skill enough, and a half ounce of luck, he would claim the title Senfari by sunfall. Only Yonnad stood between him and his goal.

Sihan eased Aurion to a canter, measuring Yonnad's intentions by the springing steps of his mount. The Senfari could not outpace Aurion, so he had to charge him. In no way could Yonnad allow Aurion to pass. Sihan ran the back of his hand across his face. It came away sticky with drying, congealing blood gritted with plains-dust. He shifted his weight, knowing Yonnad would be reading him also, every lean of body, to judge which way he would try to pass.

Often Sihan had played this game. He knew how to charge, to feint, to slip this way and that, to evade, to chase, to rush headlong and turn on the sharp edge of a dagger. He waited, waited. Set Aurion forth to the right.

The Senfari charged to cut Sihan off, the bay's long muscled legs reaching further with each stride, hooves ramming dirt. On the verge of collision, Sihan reined Aurion the slightest degree to the left. Yonnad somehow guessed. A jab of spur, a crack of whip, and Chirot swung sharply into Aurion's path. The

Senfari drove the hard-galloping horse shoulder first into the white stallion.

Thrown forward in the wake of the terrific blow, Sihan grabbed at Aurion's mane. Strong hands wrenched the wolf pelt from beneath his thigh. Yonnad swung the prize over the bay's withers, out of reach.

Lurching back into the saddle, Sihan threw his weight over, driving Aurion into the bay's hindquarters. Chirot stumbled, barely, enough time for a single lunge. Sihan slid his foot from the stirrup, shifting his weight to the left. Aurion bore harder in that direction. They raced abreast of Yonnad. Sihan leaned out, grappled for the pelt. His fingers clutched fur. Yonnad tore it away. Another desperate grasp. Sihan snatched it back.

The limp, blood-slick prize clutched between his fingers was all of life to him. He threw all he had into keeping it from Yonnad, this dead, reeking carcass, shredded fur over muscle slime and guts.

Then it fell. Fell. Into churned earth and dust.

Sihan swung Aurion round. Throwing himself to the side, he clung by one stirrup, dangling upside down, Aurion's hooves pounding near his head. His nails tore on stones, his clenched teeth gritted dust. Grasping fingers closed on wet, matted fur. The prize was his.

Sihan dragged himself upright, crushed warm hair and flesh beneath one gripping thigh. 'Go!' he cried, but before Aurion could burst away, Yonnad was there, snatching, clawing. Sihan flattened himself against Aurion's right flank, turned the horse, used the stallion as a shield, protecting him from Yonnad's grasping fingers.

The circle of stones lay ahead, catching the bright light of the sun. The goal was within reach. Mens' shouts became a maddening din.

Somewhere over the thundering hooves came the hiss of lash.

Aurion's gait altered, grew ugly and stiff, the same raging gallop he employed to fight the bit. Shaken, Sihan hung on, barely, the transformation from obedience to madness so swift he had no chance to ready for it.

Another hiss. Aurion lurched, throwing Sihan to the side. As tight as he could, muscles tearing from the unnatural effort of hanging on, Sihan held the wolf pelt.

Lead thudded against flesh. Aurion baulked, turned, ramming sideways into Chirot, then reared, roared a stallion's scream of rage. Sihan dangled momentarily like a doll from Aurion's side, then crashed to the ground in a flurry of red dust.

He lay staring up at four white-pillared legs, the bulk of white flesh, his ankle caught in the stirrup. Astonishment slowed his senses. How had he fallen? How was he not astride? Screaming cut across his wayward thoughts.

Above him, through a haze of dust, Aurion's neck snaked. Within his maw – Yonnad's lash hand – being crushed, crushed, crushed. Screaming. Such inhuman screaming, high-pitched, ringing with pain and terror.

Aurion spat out the bloodied hand, tossed his head. Then he reared once more, dragging Sihan like a sack, tunic shredding on stones, ankle wrenching. If the stallion took to flight there could be only one end. Sihan's fingers released their merciless grip on the pelt. He tried to kick, to jounce his ankle loose. He caught sight of Yonnad clinging to the neck of his horse.

A storm of shouts assailed his ears, Kheran's wild, high-pitched cry. Hoofbeats battered inside his skull. His father's voice, sharp enough to draw blood, cut above savage stallion cries. 'Hold! Hold!'

Something big fell to the earth close by. Sihan could not tell what it was among all the choking, whirling dust. Bodies flung themselves on the white horse. Hooves pounded in rage, eyes white-ringed wild, every inch of the stallion refusing to yield. In the tumult, a dagger flashed. One jerk and Sihan's foot fell free.

He clawed back, palms scraping hot, churned earth, out of range of striking hooves. Aurion squealed and bit and seemed to have a dozen thrashing legs. He reared, then drove down, pummelling a dark lump beneath his hooves. Chirot, riderless, kicked a drumming blow at Aurion's chest, fury matching fury.

A hand caught Sihan by the belt, dragging him back further. His father's face swam into view. 'Get back, get back!'

Sihan scrabbled to his feet, half swaying, sweat pouring down him, flecks of foam and blood splattering his tunic. Two warring horses reared and collided over a crumpled form. Only then, did Sihan realise Yonnad, too, had fallen.

'Aurion!' yelled Sihan. 'Stand! Stand!' But the stallion was beyond guidance, gone utterly mad, determined to trample Yonnad to mince.

Aurion crashed into Chirot, the bay horse valiantly standing its ground, trying to protect its fallen rider as was its training. Knocking Chirot aside, Aurion turned and kicked the bay a solid blow to the ribs. A harsh, grunting breath followed the crack of bone. Chirot floundered, nostrils heaving, flanks distended.

Now there was nothing between Aurion and Yonnad. The stallion charged. A demon's roar broke from Aurion; savage fury fired his eyes. Blows rained down, a raging storm breaking over the fallen Senfari.

'Drive him back!' Armindras's voice drowned the uproar.

Lashes flailed, hissing snakes of lead-weighted leather as a mass of riders and horses surrounded Sihan and his mad, mad horse. Whips tore at Aurion. Blood spurted from neck and muzzle. But still he fought, vicious eyes fixed on Yonnad like the man was a wolf he had to stamp into the ground. Horses collided, surging and ebbing like a tide, rearing high, striking, striking, trying to beat the maddened beast back, but their hooves broke like water against the immovable bulk of the white stallion.

Dust clogged the air in thick red clouds. Lost in the tangle of bodies and limbs, Sihan stared hopelessly at the enraged horse and the doomed Senfari – Yonnad's twisted, terror-racked, torn face – a blood-slicked plea for help.

Sihan had to do something, but before he could even move, a wild ululation split the air, a battle-cry like no other, piercing like a trumpet blast. Sihan swung round. A chestnut stallion drove through the dust, a battering ram forcing its way straight through the melee to its heart. The rider leaned forward, grabbed Yonnad's tunic as he raced by, wrenched the body from the ground, carrying the Senfari away as though he weighed no more than an empty cloak.

Aurion reared and swung to follow, trying to slash a path through a tangled, blood-stained throng of men and horses, biting, kicking, screaming. But everywhere Senfari cut off the route, trapping him in a whirl of colliding horseflesh and jostling men.

Retreating, advancing, the battle between horse and Senfari waged. Aurion surged once more, biting and kicking on every side. He fought free of the churning pack, plunging to a rearing halt a few strides before Sihan. Eyes aflame with hate, vicious, he charged. Sihan just stared at blood-red nostrils, the brutish, frenzied beast rushing at him.

Not one Senfari could cut him off. The wall of oncoming flesh filled Sihan's vision, and eyes, eyes, eyes afire, scorching him with their infernal will to destroy. Reflexes dulled by pain and shock, Sihan stumbled back. Something hard struck his boot. The stump embedded by the two spears.

There was just one hope of stopping the stallion. The weapon Aurion detested without reason.

A striking hoof brushed through Sihan's hair, clipped his ear. His world became a blur of pain. Muscles gave. He fell, became nothing more than a slab of flesh to be pulped by Aurion's pounding hoofs.

He stared into intense black eyes, wild with fury. There was a deadly beauty in that rage. There was death.

Sihan had no idea how, but he seized the spear, fingers grasping coarse wood.

The last dregs of strength surged into his body. He yanked it from the stump, held the point at Aurion, ready to strike. 'Back! Back!' he commanded, forcing words from his parched, gulping throat.

Aurion plunged away, snorting, eyeing the spear as though it was a writhing serpent about to strike.

'Back!' rasped Sihan.

Aurion wheeled and thundered away across the plain.

Strength leached from Sihan. The spear fell impotently from his hand. He barely had the will to open his eyes when a hand touched his cheek. His father's eyes were fixed upon his, tears of weakness and wrath filling them, like the words spilling from trembling lips. 'I'll kill that horse if it ever comes back.'

Sihan shivered, and somehow found voice enough to whisper, 'No. That's my task.'

The bright sunlight across his father's face faded into dark.

Chapter 4

The Dagger and the Vow

Sihan did not know how long he had been lying on the sun-blistered plain. All he knew when darkness unpeeled from his mind was hurt. Every breath hurt. Every movement. All his world.

Muffled voices mixed with beating hooves. Shade interspersed light, moving, shifting, never still, melding, separating, before once more coalescing into a block of pure black. Sihan had a sense of being hoisted upright, shaken. A faraway voice, dark with worry, said, 'Are you all right, lad? Answer me, are you all right?'

Sihan blinked, blinded instantly by bursts of light in one eye, the other eye swollen closed. His father's burdened face swam into focus. Armindras hunkered down before him, shadows filling creases around eyes masking fear. 'Anything broken?'

Pride, dreams. A man.

Gutted, devoid of feeling, mouth dry dust, Sihan just shook his head.

Armindras stared in the direction Aurion had flown. 'Bastard horse must be half way to Graycor.' He stood and held out a gloved hand.

Sihan took it, glad of the strength it offered his trembling body. Pain spiked everywhere as he forced himself up – his neck, shoulders, back. Focussing his one good eye he looked down at his arms and thighs, engraved by the lead weights of Yonnad's lash. Kheran offered a shoulder. Face pale and anxious, Tejas held both grooms' horses a half-stride away.

An eerie stillness settled over the plain, where not long before had been a frenzy of noise and movement. Yonnad lay on the ground, motionless, a lump of battered flesh, every inch swathed in blood, lips stretched back in a soundless, gaping scream. Nearby, Chirot stood, neck and flanks caked in foam and blood.

Surrounded by a group of Senfari, Sihan stumbled with leaden steps to Yonnad's broken body. Bubbles frothed from Yonnad's mouth, popping on sharp, hissing bursts of breath. The Senfari reached toward Armindras. The old man knelt, ear pressed close to Yonnad's lips. Cords tightened in Yonnad's neck, sweat rolled down his brow, fingers white-clenched upon Armindras's wrist. 'I . . . d–die on my horse . . . you hear me? On my horse . . .'

Armindras's face darkened as he stood. He threw a questioning glance at Senfari surrounding Chirot.

'Busted rib,' said Tanai, an elder, face sullen. 'Maybe more. Can't bear weight.'

Armindras motioned to a groom holding his horse. 'Yonnad will ride my horse.' Bending down, he slowly wrapped his arms around Yonnad, then hefted the wounded Senfari on to the bay's back before swinging up behind. Holding the man securely, Armindras muttered into the Senfari's ear in a voice worn ragged, 'Chirot can't be ridden, but if you're going to die, you'll die on a horse. I swear it.'

'My horse . . .' rasped Yonnad.

Sihan stammered as though his voice sought to match his shivering body, 'I–I'll lead him in.'

'You're hurt, too,' protested Kheran.

'I'll lead him in,' repeated Sihan, shaking off Kheran's supporting shoulder. Armindras cast Sihan a hard glance before urging his horse back to the hamlet.

Back rigid, Sihan limped slowly to the wounded bay, through the ring of Senfari, shrinking beneath the crushing weight of censorious eyes. He took up Chirot's dangling reins. The horse's harsh, wheezing grunts loud in his ear, the drying blood matching the plain's sun-dried scarlet, redoubled his sense of shame. 'I'm sorry,' he whispered, 'I'm sorry.'

'You should be,' said Tanai.

Tejas said with a quiet, cracking voice, 'If Yonnad hadn't hit Aurion . . .'

'Wouldn't have made a difference,' Tanai bit back, rubbing his thumb against a scar running along the leathered line of his cheek. 'There's a demon in that beast. He turned on Sihan, too.'

'I lashed him.' Why did he look for excuses for the inexcusable?

'That beast is finished. You heard your father. If he comes back, he dies.'

The words crashed waves of hot and cold through Sihan, but it was Tejas who cried, aghast, 'You can't!'

Tanai shot him a swift look as hard as a mallet striking a wolf skull. 'It should have been done years ago. We've all seen it happen too many times. That beast has no respect for anyone. That's never going to change. He's rising six, long enough for any horse to learn sense. There's enough chance of death in this business without courting it, and that beast wants to hurt. You just have to face it, there's no one can ride him. Just as well, given the king's edict.'

'But–'

'Enough!' Tanai's voice, sharp as a whip crack, lashed Tejas to obedience. 'Armindras is the Keeper of Graycor. His word is law.'

A low rumble of acknowledgment answered.

Tanai said to Sihan, 'Walk Chirot back, tend him. If Yonnad dies, he's yours, in remembrance of this day.'

Sihan shivered. He did not want the horse. He did not want to remember. He wanted to crawl away and cower like a cur, but there was no choice but to obey.

All the Senfari parted for him as he started the long trek back to the village. Not one met his eyes. This was his fault. They would never let him forget.

Only Tejas and Kheran walked with him, looking down at the ground where brittle spikes of grass struggled through the dirt, parched as their hopes. Slow, drudging, the journey dragged at Sihan, every wheezing grunt of the bay horse a condemnation. Sihan's hand tangled in the stallion's mane, a poor consolation, helping it not a whit. He had to get it to a place of rest, ease it as best he could. The bay was lucky. Broken ribs healed in time. Aurion would not have such fortune.

Tejas said, 'I don't care what Aurion did. They can't kill him.'

Sihan's dry tongue chafed over his lips. '*They* won't,' he said, hardly able to breathe the words, feeling like he was crushing his heart beneath his boot heel with every step. '*I* will.'

'*You* can't,' protested Tejas. 'The prayer of enlightenment forbids it except in mercy.'

'After what he did, there's no other choice.'

'Leave him free, then,' argued Tejas.

'And let him breed Graycor mares?'

'Geld him,' offered Kheran. 'That might even curb his will so he *can* be ridden.'

'I doubt it,' said Sihan. 'And even if it did, no one but farmers ride geldings. He would end up as a drudge. That's worse than death.' He imagined Aurion harnessed to a plough or a cart, all that wonderful speed, wasted and useless, a deep collar groove cut into the base of his neck, all fire spent, bright eyes dull and lifeless, the bannered tail limp. 'Death *is* a mercy.' He did not know who he was trying to convince, Tejas, Kheran or himself.

Tejas gave a ghost of a nod, shoulders drooping, all argument spent. Kheran, likewise, studied the barren ground with a matching downcast look.

The thick, suffocating heat diminished with the sun's afternoon crawl. Dusk crept along the plain, transforming brown and gold to deeper hues of purple and blue, softening the land's harsh contours. But nothing could soften the spiked thoughts needling Sihan's mind. He had thrown away the title of Senfari and all it entailed, and with it, possibly a man's life and the life of the colt he had raised from birth.

Sihan now saw the dream of becoming Senfari in clear light. He had imagined them the freest of men. But freedom cost. Every horseman's life was measured in death, loss and sorrow. Look at Yonnad.

Stars crowded the sky when the sorry entourage reached the jumble of yards and fence lines on the outskirts of Hermas. Wind, raw and cold, wrenched at stunted trees, twisting their shadows upon sagging, broken walls. Smoke rose in shredded tendrils from crumbling chimneys and open cook fires.

Sihan's gut tightened, and despite the cold, his hands began to sweat. He wanted to avoid the main street and village buildings, reach his father's barn without notice, but his duty to Chirot overrode pride. All the way down the street, dogs slunk away at his approach, as if they knew death and shame stalked his heels. Men, rough faces aglow over fires, shifted their eyes from him. Stable boys, lurking in shadowed barn doorways, did not call out their usual welcomes. Sideways glances and whispers dogged him.

A flurry of wings beat loud against the muted disapproval. A currawong perched upon the splintered roof of the main barn, pecked once, twice, then with a raucous shriek, took off into the night.

Dread leaned hard on Sihan's chest. Was the bird of death an omen? Had Yonnad died already? His failure and Aurion's death sentence ranked as naught compared with that.

He paused, forced himself to breathe, steadying himself for the inevitable news. Kheran paused. 'Who's that?' he asked, pointing at the barn.

Sihan squinted through masking night to where a man stood silhouetted in the doorway, leaning against the door jamb. A stranger, by his long grey cloak, but somehow familiar, too.

'No idea.' Sihan turned and met Kheran's worried eyes outright for the first time since the fall. 'I'll see to Chirot myself.'

Kheran opened his mouth to protest, gaze darting over Sihan's torn tunic, the bruises and dried blood, but then he nodded and said, 'Come eat with us when you're done.'

Tejas hesitated, then said, 'I'm sorry, Sihan.'

Sihan caught the stricken look on Tejas's face. 'It's not your fault.'

In spite of Sihan's reassurance, the groom looked desolate and small, a reflection of how Sihan himself felt. Tejas reached out, clutched a handful of Sihan's tunic. 'You remember, Sihan, you're gifted. This day doesn't change that. Next year . . .'

Sihan's eyes slid away. Gifted. Next year. Empty words. Forcing a crooked smile to cracked lips, he said, 'Yes, Tej, next year.'

Looking forlorn, and not quite convinced, Tejas followed Kheran to their own barn.

Sihan urged Chirot the last few lethargic, hobbling steps

to the door where the stranger stood. Flickering lantern light cast over the man in waves of gold, illuminating a strong, square-jawed profile, a straight nose, and full lips downturned in a grimace. Sandy hair hung straight over his shoulders, a long fringe swept haphazardly to one side. His lean face had a weather-beaten look to it. The man stared with unwavering intensity at Sihan, expression earnest and grave.

The nagging sense of familiarity gave way to certain knowledge. Sihan *did* know this man. This stranger had pulled Yonnad's wrecked body from beneath Aurion's hooves. A quick glance into the stable confirmed it. A chestnut stood tethered in a stall among the Graycor bays – the horse in the melee.

Without words, the man pushed open the door, waited for Sihan to enter with Chirot, then closed the door after them. He followed Sihan, sword clanging against the metal greaves on his leg. Beneath the thick grey cloak trailing wisps of strewn straw in its wake, a gold falcon rippled against the black of the tabard – the emblazon of Pelan.

Through the clouded confusion of thoughts over Yonnad's fate, his own future, and Aurion's, Sihan recognised the man's calling – a knight. What was a knight of Pelan doing in Yseth?

Sihan led Chirot between a double row of stalls, aged timber railings that might have been laced together by cobwebs rather than twine. Horses poked their noses over stall doors, nickering. A pungent stink of fresh manure and horse piss mingled with the oily smoke of a lantern and musty smell of hay and down. Light threw wild shadows up to the rafters where white-faced pigeons perched. Fat on stolen beads of barley, they tucked their heads into fluffed grey feathers.

'There's an empty stall over there.' The knight motioned down the row.

Sihan said nothing. There was something disarming about the man, the way he watched Sihan, the tone of his voice.

As he neared the end of the row, colts stamped and whinnied, moving restlessly around their stalls, tails switching, ears flickering back and forth. One bay yearling, a mirror-image of its sire, shoved its head over the thick planks of its stable door, eyes wild, ears pricked toward the furthest stall. A wind gust shoved thin lines of hay across the ground. Chirot dropped his nose to snuffle a few wisps when a white shadow lunged at the door of the end stall.

Eyes white-ringed and rolling, the injured bay threw up his head and pulled back. Sihan backed a half-step, snatching his limb away from grasping teeth. From the end stall, Aurion snaked again for Sihan's arm.

'Whoa there,' soothed the knight, quickly striding down the lane and putting himself between Aurion and Chirot, seemingly oblivious to the threat of mauling.

Sihan stared incredulously at the stranger. 'How is he here?'

'I brought him in.'

'But he just tried to kill everyone!'

A patient smile lit the knight's eyes. 'I'm Senfari. He's a horse. A tired, hurt horse, who has had a hard day. Like his rider.' There was no derision in his eyes, no malice on his tongue, almost a tinge of tenderness.

Sihan just stared at Aurion, not seeing the flayed forehead, the neck and shoulders and haunches raw with opened wounds, but rather Yonnad, his staring eyes, the blood pooling in the hollow of his collarbone.

He had to do it now. Numb, stomach knotting, Sihan looped Chirot's reins over a hitching rail, then held out an unsteady hand to the knight. 'I need your dagger.'

The man's eyes narrowed. 'Why?'

'I have to kill him.'

Surprise lit the knight's face, followed fast by dismay. 'Killing a horse is forbidden.'

Sihan shook his head. 'He killed Yonnad. He's not a bloodhorse. He's a fiend. He's unrideable . . .' He listed every reason he should, as if that made it easier, or would make it right. He knew every tracking vein like it was his own. He knew the words of a dark, storm-swept night; the promise this day would come. He would be Aurion's death. His heart pounded double its regular rate. Breath came short, shallow, aching. 'I have to end it. Now.'

The man did not move, neither did he reach for his dagger. 'I won't allow it.'

Sihan tried to shove past. 'You don't understand.'

The knight caught Sihan's arm, restraining him. 'I understand you have two hurt horses and your duty is to tend them, not kill them. And that rider you think is dead, isn't, not yet, or they'd be building a pyre for him. So you can do him the courtesy of paying mind to his horse while he's still in this world.'

Releasing Sihan, the man took Chirot's reins and led him into an empty stall several horse lengths from Aurion, slipped off the bridle, then the saddle. He slung both over a rail where chickens squawked in protest, fluttering from their perch to the ground. Every action he performed slowly, deliberately, calming the injured animal. His hands ran down the bay's blood-caked neck, strong, horseman's hands.

Sihan's eyes swept down to the straggling hay between his boots. Yonnad was still fighting for his life, Chirot was hurting because of Sihan's poor choices, and he was more worried about *his* hurt. Pricked by the knight's spur to his conscience, he grabbed a pouch from a wooden bench, rummaging through it to pull out a thick green corm. Granine – a healing tuber. His mother had used it to tend all manner of ills, saved many a sick horse, and many an injured man others had given up as beyond death's door. Another search revealed no more, where the last time Sihan had looked there had been three. His father must be using the other two corms on Yonnad.

Pressing into its soft, giving flesh, Sihan released a paste. It oozed over his fingers, sharp citrus tang blocking all other scents. He walked to the bay and ducked between the stall rails, his own torn muscles protesting. Pausing, he held out a hand to Chirot. The stallion sniffed and snorted, once, twice. Red-lined nostrils flared, trembling. Sihan placed one hand on the horse's warm, whiskered nose, breathing in hot horse and sweat, the sweetest perfume for a horseman. His fingers trailed upward, across summer-thin hair, to pull gently at one ear.

Aurion neighed from his stall. The bay swung to face the stallion, every inch tense and quivering. Sihan laid a gentling hand on the bay's neck, rubbing thick crested muscles. As the animal settled, he smeared the green paste over each wound, then, easing back the horse's lips, he squeezed a liberal dollop into the side of its mouth. The bay pulled back, then stuck its head out, top lip curled back, nostrils crinkled. Sihan gave one last pat before turning to find the knight staring at him quizzically.

'What?' Sihan challenged.

The knight nodded to the corm. 'That's granine.'

'So?'

The man smiled briefly, skin creasing at the edge of his eyes. 'First I find you riding a white horse, then you plan on killing the same horse, now you're using granine like it's the most usual practice in the kingdom. Surely even out here you know all these are forbidden. Are you planning on breaking any more king's edicts this day?'

Sihan glared at the knight. 'A man is close to dead because of me. You think I care about king's edicts?'

'Violating those edicts is a hanging offence.'

'And killing a man isn't?' Sihan's hands trembled. 'You want to hang me for something, at least make it the right thing.'

'I'm not here to hang you.' Despite the words, the knight's voice lowered, cautioned, and warning burned behind his eyes.

'So why *are* you here?' Sihan did not care enough to take heed or be courteous. Right now, he did not care much about anything. 'And who the hells are you, anyway?'

For a long while the man did not answer. He swiped at a cobweb, setting a hairy black spider scuttling up a post into the rafters where more cobwebs fluttered. 'I'm a friend,' he said finally, but his gaze shifted from Sihan's challenging eyes.

Shivers coursed up and down Sihan's back. The man was hiding something. Eyes met and held when truth was spoken, unless a man was skilled in deception. Though he did not know his name even, Sihan felt he had a part measure of the knight. He was lying, but not born to it.

Again, Sihan courted wrath. 'Friends have names they're not afraid to share.'

Calm and motionless, the knight examined him for another long, uncomfortable silence, then slowly unclipped the clasp of his cloak, casually slinging it over a rail. 'My name is

Jaien. You'll do well to remember it and not incite enemies with such carefree abandon.'

Shock rilled through Sihan. He knew the name. Knight Commander Jaien, a hero of the realm. One of the greatest of the Senfari, having defeated all comers in trials in every duchy of the kingdom. Few finer horsemen had ever put hand to rein. A quick glance at the chestnut confirmed it. Like all Pelanese bloodhorses, its face was white-striped. Falcon, pride of Pelan. He wondered less how Jaien had been able to bring in Aurion.

But how had he not recognised him? He stared hard at the knight. There was deep weariness written into the lines of his face. Age beyond his years. Sihan knew of the riots in Mirador, that Jaien had tried to protect the people. The rumours said he had been jailed, yet here he was. Worn down, no doubt, but not beaten.

Everything inside Sihan dropped. How could he have insulted such a man? He kicked a worn boot at a rotting, splintered post. 'Forgive me, I–'

Jaien waved away the apology. 'You've another horse to tend.'

Sihan glanced at Aurion. 'I told you–'

'I told *you*. There won't be any deaths this night. Neither man nor horse.' Something troubled and hurt ran beneath the words, glossed over by the veneer of command.

Unable to refuse, mind muffled by pain and a myriad of conflicting emotions, Sihan fell into obedience, but as he approached Aurion, the stallion pinned his ears. Sihan's fists clenched and unclenched.

'What are you waiting for?'

Jaien's censure sliced through Sihan's thoughts. 'Nothing . . . I . . .' He scrabbled for an excuse for his delay. 'He needs salt.' Horses died fast without salt, especially after racing as Aurion had in the heat of the day.

'Here.' Jaien upturned a pouch at his belt, shook salt into his hand. He leaned close to Aurion, tempting wrath. Gentling for just a heartbeat, Aurion licked at Jaien's hand. Jaien ran his other hand to the poll, down smooth glistening muscle, knotted and rigid. Aurion drew his muzzle in to his chest, bulging the crest into a tight arch so strained Sihan felt certain the curve must burst or break.

'Go on,' said Jaien. 'Get on with it.'

Sihan stared at man and beast. Aurion had morphed into a lamb. How did Jaien hold such sway over him?

Alert for any sudden movement, Sihan tended Aurion's wounds, many as deep and staring as Chirot's. His fingers tensed, knowing he should end it now, obey his father, but somehow unable. Sihan rested his head against Aurion's neck, surprised to feel no fear.

Silence rode the night. Then, suddenly, as though pricked by another invisible spur, Sihan blurted, 'Did you ever see a horse go mad like that, try to kill someone like that?' No answer would strip away the guilt, but here, now, he had to know.

Jaien did not hesitate. 'Warhorses. It's part of their battle training, to protect their rider, to attack. Like Chirot did for Yonnad.'

'Aurion's never been trained to do that.'

Jaien raised an eyebrow. 'Aurion?'

'He's named after the God of War.'

Jaien snorted. 'He wears it well.'

'I never trained him to kill,' said Sihan, voice shivering. 'And he went after me as well.'

'Not all horses bow to men.'

'It was more than that. I saw it in his eyes, like a demon inside. Like he wanted to tear us all limb from limb.' His mind became a muddled mess of teeth and hooves and dust and screams. 'He's always been intractable, but never like that. If I'd known, I never–'

'Sihan,' Jaien laid one steady, warm hand on Sihan's shoulder. 'You can't change what happened.'

'I can kill him.'

'I told you. No.' Jaien smiled. 'Violating a king's edict is one thing. Violating a god's law is something else entirely. I'm a knight, but before that I am Senfari. I uphold the laws of Senfar. You'll be Senfari, too, if the skills I saw in you today were anything to go by. If you kill Aurion, you'll never truly own that title.'

Sihan glued his gaze to the ground though he was not really looking at it. 'Maybe I don't want to be Senfari.'

'The lad I saw out there wanted it. The same lad I see before me.'

Sihan met Jaien's eyes. 'A Senfari must be able to ride any horse, and to judge horseflesh and know when a horse is beyond him. I might have earned the rank if my choice had been sounder. I had the pick of the finest horseflesh in Graycor, and I chose a half-breed demon.'

'Yonnad knew the horse? Knew its faults?'

'Yes.'

'Then the fault is equally his. He could have refused the match. The judges could have ordered you better mounted. So they, too, share the blame. And Yonnad chose to rile your horse.' Jaien's fingers pressed into Sihan's shoulder. 'A lot of bad decisions were made this day. Own only the part that is yours. Accept this failure for what it is. A chance to avoid future error.' Jaien hesitated, looked like he wanted to say more, so serious his tone, so profound his eyes, holding a warning, a plea. But then Jaien turned away, leaving Sihan's shoulder cold where warmth had been.

A strange feeling of abandonment swept across Sihan, a feeling as though he had lost a part of himself. He stared after Jaien, but the knight busied himself divesting his tabard and mail, then stripping down to his leggings. The smell of sweat mingled with the scent of straw as he pitchforked bedding into Falcon's stall. Sihan squinted through the gloom. In the half-light there was something odd about the knight, vague patterns on his flesh he could not quite discern.

Sihan took down a wooden box from a shelf and grabbed a candle. Sparking light, he pressed a fresh candle in the congealed wax of another lantern, which he hung by a hook on the wall. As the flame stretched tall, he cast another glance at Jaien.

The knight's muscles bunched and rippled over broad shoulders, down his lean body to his narrow hips. Several puckered scars ran down the length of his arms. But his back . . . Sihan tensed.

Deep, deep scars, so deep Jaien's back might have been shredded by a thousand shark hooks. Everyone knew of Jaien's exploits. But in what sort of battle had he earned such wounds?

Oblivious to Sihan's scrutiny, Jaien walked to a bucket and splashed water over his arms and chest, pale skin glinting. Water-soaked grey leggings stretched over muscled thighs. He turned.

A jagged scar disfigured the skin of Jaien's flat stomach. Shock upon shock piled on each other. It was nothing compared to those on Jaien's back, but it captured Sihan's attention like a beacon. It was an exact likeness of a scar marring Sihan's own flesh from birth. And except for the fact Sihan's own hair was brown like his eyes, he might have been staring at his reflection in some distorted mirror. Despite the almost seven year difference in age, Jaien and he were the same, like brothers who had shared a womb.

Sudden burning clawed at Sihan's gut, flaring into a spike of flame. He clutched at a railing, held tight to splintered wood. A haze clouded his senses. Chill numbness spread though his body. He stared at Jaien. Saw a boy with a lanced spear through his gut. The same boy he had imagined the night of Aurion's birth.

Fighting nausea, head spinning, Sihan leant on the rail. How could this be? He had banished those thoughts of weirding ghosts, locked them away in a corner of his mind, never to be revisited. Why had the vision returned?

As suddenly as it had come, it faded, and it was just Jaien standing before him, the apparition merely a cloud on the horizon of his mind. In the dim lantern light, the knight stared at Sihan, face haunted and pale, gaze unwavering. They stood, eyes locked, silence stretching across the darkness, something tremulous binding them together.

Then the faintest of smiles crept across Jaien's lips. 'See something you like?'

Losing all threads of the vision entirely, Sihan blushed and stammered, 'No. I–' He stopped, not knowing what to say.

Jaien's expression darkened and he turned away, donned his under tunic and began to wisp the chestnut. As silence fell once more, Sihan bit his lip, strangely bereft, unable to account why. He eyed Jaien's broad back for a moment, the brown wool pulled tight across it. Wondered again at those scars.

What was it to be a soldier? To endure such hurt. Why had Jaien chosen such a life when he was Senfari? Then Sihan thought of Yonnad. All life ended in death, even a Senfari's. What did it matter?

Not wanting to think, he concentrated on chores, mindlessly sloshing water into a bucket of barley, scooping handfuls of wet grain into troughs. Every muscle tightened with each moment, the wooden grain bucket heavy as a boulder by the time he finished making his way around the barn. By dawn he knew he would struggle even to move. He finished by throwing an armful of hay into Aurion's stall. Drained, muscles grating and locking, he shuffled back down the aisle to find Jaien standing mute, staring into the darkness beyond the barn door, head cocked to one side.

A low rumble caught Sihan's ear. Inside the barn, a horse whinnied, then another. Sihan hurried to the door, pushing it open. Outside, a drum of hooves signalled the arrival of a multitude of horsemen. They thundered round, more sound than shape.

'Who are they?' asked Sihan.

'Never mind them,' said Jaien, face grim. He picked up a saddlebag and pushed Sihan out the door. 'Get me to your father, now.'

Confused, unable to get a clear view of the riders, Sihan obeyed. Together they ran down the line of barns, Sihan forcing his muscles to work.

Kheran hissed loudly from a doorway, 'What's going on?'

Jaien paused, eyeing the groom standing in the shadows of a barn. 'You're Sihan's friend?'

'Of course,' muttered Kheran.

'If you want him to ever have another chance of riding the Senfari test, do what I ask.'

Lines deepening between his brows, Kheran nodded.

'Those men will want remounts,' said Jaien. 'They are king's couriers. You can't refuse them king's bloodhorses. Slow them down with finding suitable horses. Tell them the wells are almost drained if they want water for their horses. Take your time drawing the water. If they ask you questions, act mute, act dumb, act any way you need, but don't let on where they can find us. If you value Sihan, tell all his friends, hold those men off as long as you can.' Then Jaien shoved Sihan in front of him. 'Go on.'

'What's happening?' demanded Sihan, 'And what have king's men to do with me?'

'You'll understand soon enough,' hissed Jaien. 'Just get me to Armindras.'

Sihan led Jaien to a building tucked at the rear of the warren of barns. Cobbled together with weathered logs and thick plaits of twine, daub crumbling away in places, it hung off the side of a leaning barn like a hastily shucked on afterthought.

A sharp shove on the door forced it open. Air, clogged with smoke and noise and the thick aroma of roasting beeves, rushed out of a room crowded with booted, weather-worn men. Some clustered round cook fires heaped with logs crackling in stone hearths. Others sat with legs stretched out at a long wooden table, chewing grits-soaked naan.

Somewhere among the hubbub Armindras's deep, harsh timbre rose above all other voices. 'Bastard horse broke the leg.'

Sihan snuck a glance across the room, firelight strong in his one good eye. At the far end, his father stood with a group of men, one clad in a thick wool tunic splattered with blood – a Senfari healer. All of them hovered over a prostrate man on a slat pallet cushioned with straw stuffed under a coarse cloak. Sihan glimpsed Yonnad's pale face. Grey, sweat-damp hair, straggling from his bandaged head, plastered brow and cheek. Snatches of conversation rose and fell amid crests and troughs in the general tide of conversation.

'Broken in two places . . .'
'Tore him like a shark . . .'
'Laid up till winter . . .'

'Beyond the foaling season,' corrected the healer, bending over Yonnad and pressing a mug to the man's trembling lips. Yonnad spluttered and gasped, brown liquid oozing down his chin, eyes glazed. 'Drink,' ordered the healer. He waited till Yonnad downed the draught, then put the mug back on a small bench beside the pallet laden with an assortment of vials and pouches.

A hard hand pressed into Sihan's shoulder. 'You're going to have to face them sooner or later,' Jaien said.

Nodding, but unable to meet accusing eyes, Sihan sank his head to his chest as he entered the room. When Jaien followed, saddlebag slung over his shoulder, he brought silence with him. All the Senfari turned to stare, those seated rising from their benches.

Stroking his grey beard, the elder Graycor steward, Tanai, strode to meet the knight. He lifted his hand and said, 'Greetings of peace, Jaien, son of Cenriin.'

'Greetings,' answered Jaien. 'May Senfar bless all within.'

The old man continued, 'Grace us your favour by partaking of what little we can offer.'

'My thanks upon you all.' Jaien continued respectfully, yet firmly, 'I would have words with the Keeper of Graycor.'

Everyone made way for him, frowning thoughts hidden beneath courteous shallow smiles. Sihan preceded Jaien, edging with trepidation through the horsemen to his father's side.

Yonnad's battered body filled his vision. Leggings, ripped from ankle to hip, exposed flesh. Bruises blossomed the entire hairy length of leg and arm. The mangled lash hand lay swollen with mottled skin, distorted bones. Yonnad's wiry arms were one huge bruise from wrist to collarbone, lacerations puncturing muscle and sinew to bone. The tang of granine hung strong around the pallet.

The healer bumped the bed a fraction as he reached for a bucket of steaming water. Yonnad bit his lip, groaning, 'Mongrel beast . . . tried to kill me.'

'Shut up and lie still,' said the healer, dabbing at wounds with dampened cloth, sprinkling pinches of crushed herbs from a pouch onto cleaned gashes.

Armindras stepped away from Yonnad and nodded to the knight, the barest hint of a smile on his lips. 'Welcome, friend.'

No answering smile met the greeting. Even the rose blush of the fires failed to bring warmth to Jaien's face. Sihan shivered, remembering his certainty the knight was hiding something.

Darkness lurked deep at the back of the knight's eyes. And danger.

Tension pulled tight the corners of his father's smile, but his voice was calm. 'You're a long way from Pelan. What business would you have with me?'

The knight dropped the saddlebag onto a wooden bench, then drew something wrapped in cloth from one pouch. His every movement jerked and slowed, as though forced upon him by some invisible puppet master. His voice matched the lifeless look in his eyes. 'From the Horsemaster.'

Fear crawled up Sihan's spine as he craned his neck to see.

Armindras quirked an eyebrow as he took the package. 'Since when do knights act as couriers?'

Jaien's gaze slid past him to Sihan, his words likewise, running straight past the question. 'There's bad business on the other ranges. Bloodhorses missing.'

'Stolen?'

'That's the fear. Mainly Pelan so far, but Mirador and Belaron have reported losses as well.'

'Zingars?' Armindras made no move to unwrap the cloth.

'Unlikely,' said the knight. 'We'd have tracked them trading.'

Everything about the man's evasive answers sent warning after warning through Sihan.

'What's Gerhas's opinion?' asked Armindras.

'He's still gathering facts before he puts in an official report to the king. But I can tell you this: Pelan is close to declaring war on Byerol.'

The last had come with a ring of truth, but beneath it lay some lie.

'Makes sense,' Armindras said, his old soldier's eyes hardening as he considered Jaien's words. 'Byerol borders all three countries, and Emor. What news from there?'

'None I've heard,' said Jaien.

Sihan hesitated, unwilling to draw attention. But a desire to bring light where some form of hidden anguish held sway, made up his mind. He forced a laugh. 'Can't imagine anyone stealing an Emor pony.'

Jaien's eyes glinted in the firelight. 'Neither can I.' He smiled, and for an instant the history of laughter showed in the lines around his face.

Blushing, Sihan looked down, wondering why he had spoken.

Jaien's features deadened, and he returned his attention to Armindras. 'There's more. There's talk of the princess marrying Valoren, Duke of Romondor.'

'Romondor!' Armindras spat, danger punctuating every syllable in the name of that hated country. Anger stung a crimson flush to his cheeks. 'That will never happen!'

Men in the room shifted uneasily, boots scraping rough against the splintered floor, all eyeing each other, eyeing Jaien. Sihan's gut knotted with distaste.

Now they were getting to it, the reason for Jaien's presence.

Sihan noted Jaien, his father, the other men, the set, strained faces. They rarely spoke of Romondor, and the Great War of the realm, and then only in hushed whispers, leaving the war two decades earlier a dim, distant darkness. The Duke of Romondor had caused the war. His treason, his declaration of war upon Mirador had wrought the death of thousands. But what had that to do with him?

Jaien motioned to the parcel. 'You'd best open that.'

Armindras pulled aside the cloth, tore the seal on a scroll. As he unrolled the thick piece of vellum, something glinted sharp in the light. Colour drained from Armindras's face and his hands began to shake. 'This can't be,' he said, voice a harsh croak of denial.

'What?' Sihan pushed forward, flanking his father.

'He's just a boy,' Armindras whispered, as if he had not heard him.

'He's seventeen winters,' said Jaien, voice cold. 'Every lad of age is being called to service.'

'Service!' The word erupted like a curse from Armindras's lips. 'Sending boys to die in another futile war?' He threw the scroll to the ground. 'Take this message back to the Horsemaster. He'll not have my son.'

A wall of men closed around Armindras and Sihan. From Senfari to Senfari spread a powerful, animalistic rage transforming the mass of horsemen into something akin to a clenched muscle straining for release.

They had all heard about the riots and the deaths in Mirador – such news had wings – but no one had dared speak openly of what had happened, not even here, on the outskirts of the kingdom. Now the horror stood in the room with them.

Heart pounding against his ribs, Sihan stooped to pick up the vellum. A dagger rolled out and fell with a clatter to the table, thin, sharp-edged steel with a silver hilt. Even with only one good eye he knew immediately what it was. A king's blade. The kingdom death mark. He had seen men who had received death marks. They had ended as rotten corpses nailed to trees. Bewildered and chary, he said, 'My father hasn't done anything wrong.'

'It's not for anything he's done,' said Jaien, stone-faced. 'It's a warning against anything foolish he *might* do. For what it's worth, I'm sorry.'

'How soon do I have to go?'

'You're going nowhere.' Armindras and Jaien stood facing each other, both braced, Armindras's face flushed, temple working, the vein on his forehead gorged and pulsing fury.

The silence descending upon everyone was torn by rough, harsh shouts outside, clattering hooves and strident neighs. Moments later, the door slammed open, shuddering on its hinges as men marched into the room, every one of them with the same assured, casual air of threat. Booted for hard riding, carrying saddlebags over their shoulders, they did not need to say who they were.

The shortened tabard alone marked them as king's couriers. They barged through the crowd, knocking aside anyone who got in their way. One by one they slung saddlebags on the wooden table. Hand on sword hilt, prepared for trouble, their spokesman announced, 'By order of the king, all those whose names are here listed are called to service. The penalty for refusal is summary execution.'

Not one Senfari moved, but the set of their bodies bespoke men ready to kill.

Armindras snarled, 'Not my boy, not any, will take service beyond their will.'

The courier's jaw set. 'Think carefully on your words, Master Keeper. Even in these wilds the king's word is law.' He turned and snapped, 'Atheias. Present your declaration, then let us be on our way.'

The youngest of the couriers, cheeks dusted with down-soft stubble, drew a scroll from his bag, unrolled it and said in a faltering voice, 'By order of the king, a Royal Tournament to be held in Mirador fortress as part of the Fire Rituals. The winning horse to be claimed by Her Royal Highness, the Princess of Mirador. The winning rider to be granted any boon the king may grant. Open to all comers.'

'King's tournament? All comers?' snarled a Senfari. 'Is this some sort of sick jest?'

Another Senfari growled. 'They think we're all dullards, out here on the frontier.' His hand traced the hilt of his dagger as he confronted the courier. 'Think you can fool us with tricks and false promises? Get our lads to walk into your snare freely?'

The young courier took a step back, knuckles whitening upon the scroll.

Jaien waved an arm to the door. 'You've said your piece. Now, all of you, outside.'

The elder courier blanched upon noticing Jaien. He opened his mouth, went to say something, stopped, then just simply nodded. Turning on his heel, he stalked from the room, the others hurrying out in his wake. Shouted orders filled the night air beyond the door.

Armindras rounded on Jaien. 'You knew they were coming for all our lads.'

'I knew.' Jaien's eyes held Armindras's gaze for the first time. 'King's soldiers are pulling in lads from across the kingdom.'

Senfari crowded round Armindras. 'What do we do?'

'Kill them,' said a fragile voice carrying across the room. Everyone turned to Yonnad who continued with pale lips, 'Kill them and run.'

'Don't be daft,' said Tannai. 'You know what happened in Mirador.'

The shock of those words reverberated through every man.

'Don't listen to him,' said the healer. 'Mind's so far gone, doesn't know what he's saying.'

Jaien said, 'It's not certain we'll be going to war. Bolstering the army is just a precaution.' The unconvincing words came out as though Jaien had been rehearsing this speech for the longest of times, and they fell flat upon unlistening ears.

'The king is sending the princess to Romondor,' growled Armindras. 'Of course we're going to war.' He reached for the king's blade. 'The king has sent his message. Let's send him one of our own.'

Murmurs of grumbled assent from all the Senfari answered him.

'Out of my way,' Armindras ordered, shouldering past the knight and shepherding Sihan to the door.

As they strode to the barn, they passed the couriers. King's men stood stiff-backed, watering their horses before they rode on to their next post, muttering to each other in soft tones. Armindras spat, and Sihan shivered at his blatant disrespect. What was he thinking?

In the barn, Armindras ripped harness from nails on the wall, tossing bridles and halters on the floor, stacking bulging pouches on the table, dumping saddlebags with something hanging from every loop onto the ground. Then he was on his knees, rummaging through boxes and sacks.

'What are you looking for?' asked Sihan.

Armindras barely paused to say, 'Never you mind.'

The sudden tramp of boots beyond the barn door sent alarm through Sihan. He hurried to the door, opened it a crack. Relief was a welcome visitor as he spied Kheran and Tejas. They drew back a little to make room for him as he slipped outside.

'The couriers have gone,' said Kheran, but he kept his voice low.

Tejas whispered, 'Is it true? About the service?'

'Seems like.' Sihan rubbed his palm over his face. 'It's all a mess. Everything.'

Both lads looked away, faces shadows in the dark.

'I can't believe it,' said Kheran after a while.

Tejas stared out into the night. 'I'm no coward. But . . . Gods!' Then he said rapidly as if he was afraid he would change his mind if he said it any slower, 'I really thought we'd all be Senfari, us three. You know?'

'I know,' said Sihan. He sensed they were looking to him for a way forward, and he knew only one. He drew a deep breath, stood straight, and said, 'Go tell the others. We all go together to Mirador, try to get in the same companies, watch each other's backs.'

Both lads nodded. Like two shadows, they melted into the night.

Sihan did not know how long he had stood there when another shadow detached itself from the night and Jaien slid into the light.

'Your day's not getting any easier.'

Sihan shook his head wearily.

Jaien stared at him hard, as though he wanted to read his very soul. 'If you were offered the chance to run, would you take it?'

'Are you calling me a coward? Do you think I'd let my father take a dagger in the back?'

The knight's lips tightened. 'No.'

Sihan's mind raced with churning thoughts. There was a chance. Maybe only for one of them, but that was better than for none. The rider of the winning horse in the tournament could claim any boon. The finest horses in the kingdom were Graycor bloodhorses. If they took all the trained colts to the Fire Ritual horse fair, the Graycor and Yseth Senfari could enter the tournament, ride for their sons, their brothers. The lads could ride for themselves.

Then he remembered the age old dream, how as a child he had longed to show off Aurion, take him to the Mirador horse market, ride him in the trials. Present him to the king. Despite everything, the dream still ate his mind, like it had since childhood, never quite letting itself be locked away, bolts slammed closed.

Now the chance was there. The courier had said it. "The king's tournament. Open to all-comers." It was a sign, as if Senfar himself had planned it.

Every obstacle – Aurion being a foundling, with no breeding, and Sihan not being Senfari – had vanished. Hells, because Aurion was white, Sihan could not have ridden him if he had been a pureblood and Sihan had been Senfari. But now . . .

Could Aurion truly be a horse of legend?

What boon would the king not grant to be united with his bonded Godsteed? The thought was crazy, but it was all he had.

His gaze met Jaien's. 'I've an idea. It's utter madness. Just follow my lead.' Sihan walked back in to the barn, Jaien at his back. He strode down the line of stalls, leaned over the rail of the white stallion's stall.

The knight looked at him, then Aurion, then back again. 'You're not serious.'

'Deadly.'

'Then at least let me wear the blame.' As if he could read Sihan's very thoughts Jaien said loudly, 'You know, the answer to our problem is staring us right in the face.'

Armindras, roused from his search, said, 'What?'

Jaien ducked beneath the stall rail. He stroked Aurion's neck, then the black-muzzled nose, letting the whiskers tickle his palm. 'Didn't you get your title as Keeper of the Graycor bloodhorses when you rode Celestion in the warhorse trials? You need a new first steward. Sihan could claim that post by winning the king's tournament. On Aurion.' Jaien roughed the white stallion's shoulder.

Armindras glared at Jaien. 'How can a knight advocate breaking an edict?'

'The rules say "all-comers"', interjected Sihan, not believing he was having a second argument for riding Aurion in as many days, especially after what had happened, but nothing would let him be swayed. 'The king will want Aurion the moment he sees him.'

Armindras's glare intensified. 'You know the king swore on the queen's deathbed he would never ride any horse but Celestion.'

'Celestion is close on twenty winters,' argued Jaien. 'He should have been sent to stud long ago.'

Armindras cut through the knight's comeback with an angry wave of his hand. 'You might as well put a noose around Sihan's neck right now.'

Sihan stared from one to the other, two massive tides sweeping his future hither and thither like a bobbing cork caught in a churning maelstrom of whitewater. He braced his feet. It was time to take control of his own path. Jutting his chin, he said to his father, 'I'm riding in the tournament.' With their attention sharp upon him, he moved to stand beside the knight. 'And I'm riding Aurion.'

Armindras seemed almost ready for his recalcitrance. 'You won't have to ride if I declare you Senfari. No one will naysay it. Jaien's right. I'm going to need a new first steward until Yonnad recovers.'

'I didn't pass the test.'

'You made a poor choice of horse. If you'd chosen wisely, you'd be Senfari, and the king's will could not touch you.'

'This is as poor a choice as mine.' Sihan waved a hand expansively. 'You heard the soldiers. You saw the scrolls. They're taking all the lads. Will you make all of them Senfari?'

Armindras's face set. 'If I have to.'

Sihan sucked in a harsh breath. 'You'll erode the very meaning of what it means to be Senfari. If you do this, they'll have no respect for me, the others, or you. And I won't save my scalp if they can't try to save theirs. Let us go to Mirador. Let us all ride. Let Senfar decide.'

Armindras slapped his hands together, knuckles against palm. 'The horse is mad. You saw him today. He'll kill you.'

'It's a moon's cycle to Mirador. I'll work him into the ground if I have to. He'll obey.'

'That horse has turned your wits.' Armindras stabbed a finger at Aurion. 'If you think he's a Godsteed, if you think anything is going to fix him, you're more out of your mind than if you'd taken granine.' He raked his hand over his head, tearing off the Senfari hat. His weathered face was almost pleading now. 'Aurion has no master. He doesn't want to do anything unless it is on his terms. I won't have you throwing away your life by relying on him. And what if he does win? The courier said the princess will claim him. Do you think *she* could ride him? Do you want to risk hurting an innocent girl?'

Jaien leaned over the rail. 'Aurion doesn't have to win. And even if he did, the princess won't get him. When the king sees him, he'll claim him. Not because he's the best bit of horseflesh in the kingdom. But because he's white. You think the king doesn't know the histories and legends? He'll want him. Callinor's vain enough to want to emulate the immortal kings of old.'

'Aurion's more likely to kill the king than let him ride him.'

Jaien's face grew dark and thoughtful. 'Then your problems will be over, won't they?'

Time condensed into an endless, spinning measure as the implication behind the words settled over all three.

Armindras stared at Jaien. 'What are you saying?

Jaien's face grew cold, calculating. 'I'm saying nothing more than it's Callinor's own lookout if his chosen horse kills him.'

Armindras dropped his voice to a whisper. 'You're talking regicide!'

The barest hint of a smile flitted across Jaien's lips. 'No one could be accused of regicide if the king is a fool and has an accident on his own horse.'

Sihan stared from one man to another, unable to reconcile what he was hearing. Was Jaien really advocating the murder of the king?

'No,' said Armindras. 'It's too big a risk. I know Callinor. He might choose Aurion and still order Sihan's death out of spite for riding him.'

'Then present Aurion at the warhorse market. Gerhas can't possibly pass Aurion over. You'll be the toast of the kingdom, presenting the king with such a horse. Trials or no, if you flatter the king with so mighty a gift, you're sure to be able to ask any boon. Let the lad take his chance with the horse.'

Armindras's voice came low. 'I give the orders here.'

Jaien spread his hands. 'A suggestion, from one Senfari to another.'

Suspicion slitted Armindras's eyes. 'Why are you helping my son?'

The question hung in the air.

Jaien slipped under the rail, and his face turned cold. 'I have my reasons. But know this.' He patted the hilt of his sword. 'However you see your duty, I have mine to perform. Either you go to Mirador of your own accord and try your luck with Aurion, or I'll take Sihan with me, slung over Falcon's backside, if need be.'

Armindras's face wavered between decision and indecision.

Sihan tugged at his sleeve. 'I trust Jaien.' He did not know why, but he did.

Armindras spat. 'His promises are empty air, and he threatens steel. What is there to trust?'

'Aurion, then.'

'Aurion,' Armindras breathed the word. He stared at the stallion, eyes raking over every sleek line. 'If Gerhas rejects him–'

'The warhorse trials,' said Jaien.

Armindras stood in silence.

'*Please*,' begged Sihan. 'For all of us. You know how good Aurion could be. If I can just get him to obey, I won't lose. You *know* it.'

'You lost today.' Armindras's face, hard as nails, looked from Sihan to the horse to Jaien and back again. Black brows drawn close and thin, finally he said, 'I want all the men to be ready to ride by sun-up. I want every broken colt yarded.' Then he turned and walked away.

Sihan stared after him.

'What do you think?' asked Jaien.

'I don't know.' Not knowing what else to do, Sihan slipped out of the barn and sought out Kheran and the other grooms. They eyed him uneasily, not certain how to take his message, and he could offer them no assurances.

As night wore down, he straightened the mess of tack in the barn and packed their bags. Only one thing was certain, they were going to Mirador, to what end, no one knew. Alone in a tiny room tacked on to the barn, he ate in silence on his pallet.

Cold rabbit stew slid down his throat untasted. When he settled back on his bunk, with only the faint glow of coals from a dying fire lighting the room, he nursed his pains, wanting them as penance, and brooded on the uncertain future.

He did not know how he slept, or even if he did. Before he knew it, the canvas over a gap in the boards flapped wildly in blustering morning wind, letting in dim light. Sihan rolled to his feet, every muscle stabbing sharp. He pulled his cloak about his shoulders, glancing quickly out the lone window at rising dawn.

Floorboards creaked when he walked to the door. Horses nickered as he entered the main barn. His hip and back were so sore it was difficult to disguise a limp as he moved from stall to stall. He had spent a season every year on the Yseth range, this ramshackle barn his sometime home. It was ancient, crumbling to dust. But it was just as much home as the mountains. His gut churned at leaving it. Leaving everything he had known.

A candle flared sidelong, borne along by a gust of wind sneaking into the barn through a crack in the timbered wall. Light illuminated Jaien kneeling in the corner of the barn. Mail gleamed dull beneath a black tabard emblazoned with a golden falcon. At his belt, a worn leather scabbard for sword lay empty, no arms permitted while in prayer. A grey cloak spilled across flagstones beside him, cast off while he made obeisance to ancient gods.

Sihan stood silent, waiting in deference until Jaien turned and met his gaze. 'Pray for us,' Sihan said, then. He pulled the cowl down low over his brow and limped to the barn door. As he edged outside the narrow opening, he pulled the cowl folds across his mouth and jaw, pinning them with a clasp, trying to keep the dust-filled wind at bay. He passed rows of stunted trees from which wind tore away the last clinging ragged leaves. Men filled alleys, lying in jumbled heaps or squatting in the thin cover of worn stone walls.

As cocks crowed, they slowly unfurled from sleepless dozing, stretched and walked, one, two, a dozen, a score, a hundred, all unspeaking as they made stern-faced progress to the meeting place. Some Sihan recognised, others he did not, but all were his brothers.

Horse yards stood beyond the huddle of mud and daub village walls. Stallions by the score stood nose to tail, heads hung low to avoid the biting, swirling dust. Tails switched at flies. Bay after bay, they were all throwbacks to the Graycor king stallion, some with stars on their foreheads, others with white socks; all strong and swift with mettlesome manners.

In long aisles between yards, horsemen in their hundreds stood cloak to cloak, whip handles poking from their boots.

The Senfari who had sat in judgment of Sihan stood at the centre of the clustered men. Even villagers, men who had never sat a horse in their lives, scurried up from their cottages, determined to learn what was afoot. Sihan breathed deep, steadying himself on a rail.

Steps scuffed behind him. He glanced over his shoulder. A young man he barely knew offered a cautious smile.

'Asher,' the youth offered his name, hand on his breastbone, greeting of the Yseth plains folk.

Sihan smiled in return. 'Have you been here long?'

'Arrived last night.'

A disturbance heralded the arrival of more grooms. Young men dodged through the crowd, all jostling elbows, craning their necks to look above the multitude of heads. Angered shouts dogged them, but they rushed on, unheedful. Kheran, tallest of the group, caught Sihan's eye and waved.

'What news?' he asked breathlessly, sliding to a stop beside Sihan.

Asher and the other lads leaned their faces close to Sihan's, eyes livened with curiosity.

Sihan said in as even a tone as he could muster, 'I know as little as you.'

They all fixed their eyes greedily on the Senfari.

As a hard line of crimson flared on the horizon, roosters heralded a blood dawn. Armindras approached, cloak flapping, a long shadow following him like a spectre of impending doom. Sihan straightened, grimacing. Tightened, torn muscles with no give in them warred with the raw ache of open cuts.

With his one, clear, open eye, he tried to read his father's face but its inscrutable facade defied his best efforts to pierce it.

Scraps of argument broke out among the Senfari, sharp, angered. The stain of discontent spread among the assembled horsemen like wet dung on moving water. Armindras halted before the Senfari elders, standing silent and motionless for such a time he might have turned to rock. Finally he faced the gathering.

Sihan shifted his weight, every muscle tense with anticipation. Armindras never spared him a single glance when he said in a brusque voice carrying across the wind, 'You have all heard a tournament has been announced. A King's Tournament at Mirador. The king has invited the best horsemen mounted on the best bloodhorses to meet in tourney at the Fire Rituals.'

Above the cry of the wind the word carried from mouth to mouth, ear to ear – 'tourney, tourney' . . . It speared throughout the crowd, travelling to the farthest stragglers of the gathering, not missing one of its intended targets.

Armindras continued, 'You all know its purpose.'

His belief was upheld as all the men, including Senfari who had stood in great dignity at his back, lost all control. Fists punched the air. With strident voices, men cried, 'A deception! A ruse! To steal our sons!'

When the noise of fury died back, Armindras proclaimed, 'We are Senfari.' His deliberate gaze fixed long upon Jaien who stood far back at the edge of the gathering, then moved on, slowly, resting at length upon each of the faces of men his age or older. 'Many of us are no strangers to war, are no cowards. Many of us fought in the Great War.' He paused, fist clenching. 'Now another war is upon us, and we must choose, here, now, our answer to this call to arms.' His hard gaze impaled faces in the crowd. 'Those who were there, know. Those who fought the Black Duke.' His voice grated now, shaking with emotion. 'You know the slaughter, the endless killing fields of ash.' He took a deep rasping breath as though choking on a fire's leavings. 'You know to what our sons are condemned.'

Another forest of angry fists struck the air, all the men shouting in unison, 'They'll not have them!'

Sihan shivered at the violence barely held in check, the fierce fury in every eye, the terror of things about which he knew nothing. What did these men fear with so much dread? What had his father seen? And why did none of them ever speak of it?

Armindras waited for the hullabaloo to abate. He met eye after eye, every man hanging on his words. 'We will go to Mirador and take part in this farce of a tournament, and hope this oath breaker keeps his word to grant a boon. If one of us wins, we might win freedom for all our sons.'

Armindras looked at the uneasy faces of the horsemen and said, 'I choose to confront the oath breaker and cast his treachery into his face.'

Incredulity plunged the gathering into silence. Sihan met Kheran's wide eyes. There was no doubting Armindras referred to the king, and now Sihan almost wished he had chosen to run. Certain death lay in Mirador if his father intended to confront the king. He opened his mouth, intending to speak against the decision, but the chance was lost, his protest drowned by a tidal-wash of voices.

Tejas whistled between his teeth. 'Gods. If there wasn't a war looming already, there'll certainly be one now.'

Armindras said, 'I have made my choice. I leave each of you free to make yours. I hold no one in oath to me.'

Kheran leaned down, picking at a cord of loose binding on the heel of one boot. 'Your father knows the way the wind shifts. Not one of our fathers will break oath with him.'

Confirming his words, arguments broke out among the men. 'What horses will we take?'

'The best,' shouted another. 'Naught but the best for our lads.'

'I'll give up all I own, down to the last clasp to buy a horse fit to save my boy.'

At this last, Armindras held up one wide hand. 'Not one of you buys a horse.' He walked toward the horse yards. 'We have here the best. King's bloodhorses. Graycor horses. Callinor wants our lads so badly, he'll have them, all mounted on his own horses.'

Sihan knew then why Armindras had assembled all the horses and all the men. Boots tramped cracked wind-stirred dirt as men filed down the narrow alleys between the yards, eyeing every full-harnessed stallion.

Deep brown eyes stared back from beneath long black forelocks. Ebon manes streamed over thick, powerful arched crests to broad, deep shoulders tapering into long, straight legs. Hindquarters bunched, muscles rippling beneath coats shimmering like wild silk.

Armindras's probing eyes settled on each man and each horse, evaluating. Harmonizing virtues against flaws, he sought to meld horseman to steed, so the union might reach as near the pinnacle of excellence Senfar would demand.

Not one of the horsemen in Armindras's wake uttered a word. They trusted his judgement, would abide by it. He knew their merits and failings as well as those of the horses he raised. None would leave Hermas poorly mounted.

No one stirred, not a breath of sound but the wind carrying Armindras's voice as he coupled each Senfari, groom and stable lad, to a horse. At last he finished.

Sihan's entire body trembled. His name had not been called. He had not been paired to a horse.

As all the horsemen led away their appointed mounts, Sihan waited in apprehension, nails digging into his palms. Was he not to ride?

Voicing his own troubled thoughts, Tanai, the elder judge of the Senfari, said to Armindras, 'You have denied your son a horse. Will you not allow him to ride at Mirador?'

'He will ride,' said Armindras.

'On what horse?' demanded the Senfari. 'You have given the best to others.'

Armindras's gloved fist clamped down on the Senfari's shoulder, pulling the old man close. With a deep growl he said, 'Snow covers your roof, yet you are still to learn a Keeper's business is his alone.' He thrust Tanai away. 'Attend me,' he snapped at Sihan. Face heavy with burden, Armindras led Sihan to the barn.

Bile surging up in his chest, Sihan whispered, 'I'm not running.'

'Then stop repeating worthless words.' Armindras shoved the barn door open, strode down the aisle to where Aurion stood. Coming to a halt before the white stallion, he said, '*I* won't waste words either.' He stretched his hand toward the stallion's dark muzzle, a motion Aurion cut short by snapping. 'This horse is a rogue. You know it.'

Sihan refused to confirm or deny the fact.

Armindras locked stone-cold eyes with Sihan's. 'When you ride, you will be riding for your life.'

Sihan shivered. 'I won't fail this time.'

'Your life, Sihan,' growled Armindras. 'Are you prepared to trust this horse with your life?'

Bracing his back, Sihan said, 'Yes.'

Armindras drew a deep, shuddering breath. 'You shall have him as your mount.' Without another word he walked away. What he had said would not be unsaid.

Sihan swayed for a moment, as though he had stepped from sure ground onto a coracle. So swift the turn of events. So uncertain his fate. Then he steadied himself. His course was set. No changing it now.

Chapter 5

Whispers from the Past

Sihan lay on his back on thick leaf pulp, head pillowed on a saddle, bright glitter of cold stars high above. Tattered clouds stretched across the moon, torn by ice-tanged wind veering down from the northern mountains. With fall on the doorstep, night was as cheerless as the fragmented thoughts crisscrossing his mind – the future, past errors, what his father might do when he confronted the king. Restive, body aching as though stretched on a rack, he shifted, instinctively making a sweep of his surroundings like every man mountain born, measuring the sky, the ground and everything in between.

Jagged pines swayed, tree tops roaring like breakers at full tide. Horses, tethered to pickets by short ropes, sheared deep swards of grass. Bleached tan by daylight, it was welcome fare after the bleak Yseth desert. By the time they had crossed the border into Mirador, the desert dust storms were long behind them, the country no longer scarred, gaping and cracked, but black tillable soil promising lush harvests.

Throughout the camp, the usual scramble of talk remained muted, men mostly gazing into distance with eyes looking within rather than without, cloaks pulled close. A few men roasted strips of beeves or boiled pheasant they had shot that day. Their faces shone from steam drifting skyward from charred pans set on crude grills.

Kheran lay with eyes closed, chest sinking and rising, legs crossed one over the other, muttering low replies to Tejas's questions about Mirador and the tournament. Like Sihan, he had been there in other years, had trained horses over the tournament courses with his father and other Senfari.

Armindras sat a way off, foreswearing Sihan's company and the others. He, too, remained silent, hands in his lap, staring at nothing. No one slept this last night before journey's end.

Even Jaien, who had no stake in their fortunes, paced alone among the trees, striking fist to palm, every movement troubled.

Sihan frowned, wondering. What could disturb such a man? Jaien had spoken little to him of anything but horses, the tournament course, schooling him and the others in tactics, in every facet needed for the trials. But always, always, Sihan felt currents running beneath his words, something hidden in every guarded look.

But now, it was his father concerned him most.

Sihan rolled to his feet. He approached Armindras quietly, boots squishing down rotted leaves. His father failed to acknowledge him till he stood very close, and then only with a brief, unseeing glance as though Sihan was not really there at all. Close to, Armindras's face was grey with fatigue. Sihan touched one knee to the ground, closed his right hand over his father's shoulder. 'Get some rest. You've not slept a full night since we left Hermas.'

Armindras shrugged him off. 'I'm well enough, lad. Don't fret without cause.' He bent his neck, chin tucked to chest.

Sihan shivered, folding his arms tight around his body as if warding off the night's chill.

What was his father planning, this strong, uncompromising man who had told him to forget Aurion and his childhood dreams of riding a Godsteed? The man who for years had made every decision on the range, which stallion would cover which mare, which would be raised in stables, which fattened on mountain pasture. Armindras had held absolute dominion over everything, nursed injuries and broken bones, overseen the training of every horseman from groom to Senfari. But now . . . Could he defy the king and live to tell of it?

The moon had slid long into shadow and the wind had died before Armindras settled to sleep out the night. Eyes closed, the old man lay beneath his cloak on rough, cold ground, firelight spilling across half his face.

In sleep, his face softened, diminished somehow, stripped bare of strength, of pride.

The last of childhood slipped from Sihan as he recognised age in the deep lines.

Something half-hidden beneath his father's cloak caught Sihan's eye. He bent down. A corner of a small box stuck out beneath a grey fold of cloth. A sudden gust of wind cast the material back completely, revealing a candlewood casket.

Echoes of the past crowded about Sihan. Years melted away like spring thaw, and a small dark woman seemed to glide like shadow through the night, black eyes smiling, fingers trailing down Sihan's cheek in a gentle caress.

Staring at the casket, Sihan wrung his hands, not knowing what to do. This was their family treasure, all they had of Sihan's mother. Armindras carried it everywhere with him.

Sihan glanced back at his father, thought he understood for a heartbeat the fragility inside, so masked, so damped down behind the rough exterior. He knew it like he knew himself, the boy standing beside a pyre, watching his mother burn, her spirit rising in black ash to the Heavens and him crying inside.

He picked up the casket, reliving the echoes of hidden memories, a face the details of which eluded him the older he grew. But here, now, with the casket in his hands, it was easy to summon her image behind his eyelids, her long black hair shaken free about her shoulders, the smouldering glow of her eyes in the soft radiant moon-white setting of her face.

Sihan opened the lid. Within the box rested a book, no larger than his hand. He gnawed his lip. He knew this book. His mother had filled it with her stories, recited them to him in dark winter nights, his cheek resting on the warm softness of her thigh as he sat at her feet before the hearth.

The first leaf rose slightly, caught by the wind, quivered, folded back, then the next and the next, as though the very air were turning the pages with invisible fingers. One by one they fluttered, cautiously at first, but then the wind picked up. A flurry of pages rattled past. Sihan went to snap the book closed, fearing the brisk flapping would awaken his father, but as soon as it had sprung up, the blustering wind died, falling into a gentle zephyr, caressing the remaining leaves of vellum, slow, hesitant, coaxing each to turn. All breath of air died, but still the pages lifted, hung suspended, fell back, flattened. One, by one, by one. Until the last revealed itself, a loose leaf inserted within the book, opened to Sihan's eyes.

Careful curved letters flowed across sheer calfskin, words he had last seen as a child, when he understood little of their meaning.

Hast thou seen the fires of the Heavens, O dearest son of mine heart? Look thence when thine heart is empty. Bend thy will to just cause, and let none place sword within thine hand. Look to night's glittering torch, the Fire Star, for it leads ever homeward.

He stared into the words till his eyes burned from strain, somehow unable to let go. With every breath, pain filled him, a deep, aching hurt.

A sudden draft caught the thin piece of vellum, tore it from its fellows, sent it spiralling into the air. Sihan started, caught it. With great care he laid it flat on his thigh, pressing it gently between his forefinger and thumb, stroking the vellum as though it might scorch him, staring through the words at nothing but memories. Numbness leached into Sihan's bones, a strange lethargy.

A horse neighed.

Sihan's mind snapped back to where he was. Beside him, Armindras breathed heavily, salt and pepper hair falling over his face. Sihan closed the book, pressed down the casket lid on the last fragile remnants of a life long lost. All except one. That he kept for himself, that one page, written for him.

He stood, walked slowly to where Aurion stood.

The Fire Star. He had named Aurion for it. And now his mother seemed to reach for him beyond the veil.

He approached the stallion with an outstretched hand. Aurion trembled, shifting his bulk away without moving one hoof. His eyes rolled back.

'Sihan?' Jaien moved like liquid shadow out of the dark. Waves of firelight rolled across his face and shoulders. Sihan met his gaze for a long moment.

'How fares your father?' Jaien kept his voice low, pitched only for Sihan's ear.

Drained, Sihan did not hide his thoughts. 'I never saw him old till now.'

'The threat of war wearies all.'

Sihan picked up the tether, twisting hardened leather in his fingers. Aurion lowered his head, snatched another tuft of grass. Jaien stood in silence, a lean, immobile, intent presence. Around them, horses shuffled, the only sound their steady chewing, but for all that they might have been alone, the knight and himself. A bittersweet quietness overlaid the dark, and the smell of grass and horses. And for a while there was no threat of war, or death, just camaraderie between two horsemen.

A grunting whinny was answered by others nearby. Sihan shivered. Many of those horses he had trained. He knew their power, the inextinguishable strength, endurance and courage of each horse. He never tired of them. Never forgot them even when they were taken away to the horse fairs to be sold to knights and archers and men at arms. War was their only purpose, a life from which few ever returned, and those only the best, sanctioned as breeding stallions.

They had no choice as to their fate. They were horses bound for war, like him. The thought had hardly taken root, so swift its arrival. It had left no time for fear, only sharp regret. Images formed in his mind of arrows in flesh, lances buried deep, swords hacking at flanks. Would he see horses with their hides pierced with arrows or slashed by steel? Steeds he had raised from foals?

Despite the knight's mission, Sihan found himself drawn to the man whose background matched his own, and curiosity overruled tact. 'You're Senfari but you chose war.'

'Yes.'

'Aren't you scared for Falcon? That he'll get hurt?'

'Sometimes.'

'I say the prayer to horses every night. How could Senfar allow horses in war?'

'War is the one exception to Senfar's rule. We live in the world, and we must protect it. Horses must play their part.'

'I wouldn't have made that choice'

Jaien sighed. 'You're not Senfari. You have no choice.'

No choice, and he had made such poor choices of late. It gave him little comfort to know the next one had been taken from him. Sihan stared out in to the night, to the north, toward home and the mountains.

He clenched his fist. No choice.

Sihan glanced once more at Aurion. His mother's words ran through his mind. Could she have foreseen Aurion? Of Jaien, he asked, 'Do you believe in messages from beyond the veil?'

Jaien's head reared erect, his eyes taking on a distant expression, haunted. 'What sort of messages?'

Unsure of himself, feeling half-foolish, Sihan fumbled with the vellum before handing it to Jaien.

The knight turned the page to the light of a nearby campfire and regarded the writing. All the while, Sihan searched Jaien's eyes for clues as to his thinking. 'Well,' he finally prompted, 'What do you make of it?'

Jaien said without turning his head, 'Whose writing is this?'

'My mother's.'

Jaien gave him a hard sideways look. 'She's passed beyond?'

'Many years ago.'

The knight swallowed, and remained quiet for a time before saying softly, 'Mine also.' Then came in the same hushed manner, 'Where did you get this?'

'Father. He keeps her writing in a box he carries wherever he goes. It's his way of holding to her.'

Stillness hung between their mutually measuring eyes, in which Sihan sensed they both appeared to be feeling each other out. Then finally Jaien said, 'I read it thus: your mother writes you're never to take up a sword.'

'Which means her will was that I never enter the king's service as a soldier.'

'That intent can be drawn from it.'

Sihan breathed out slowly. 'It's almost like she knew. About the conscription. About Aurion.'

Jaien handed the vellum back to Sihan, then said with a voice shaded to a tone almost frightening, 'Never doubt the hold the dead can have over the living.' His eyes grew dark and impenetrable. 'She mentions the Fire Star. Aurion is named for it. If your mother could somehow foresee your fate and seek to allay it, so might she have nudged you with her stories, seeding in your mind the idea of Godsteeds. I judge much owed here to a dead woman's foresight, just as I hold the gods must hold the greater credit, for naught could be done without their sanction.'

'You truly believe in the gods?'

'I believe.' A smile touched Jaien's lips. 'So get to your rest, and keep up your heart, for all is before us, and the gods it seems are with us.'

Sihan looked back down at the vellum. For a long while he studied it, thinking of the morrow, of the past, and how his mother might have read his future so clearly. Then he shivered. The night was half-gone, camp fires dead and Jaien retired to his own camp, but Sihan still contemplated his mother's writing, the messages from beyond the veil. Half-hoping she was there, somewhere, just out of reach, watching over him, he whispered into the dark, 'I won't fail you, Mother.'

As he tucked the vellum into a pouch at his belt, a soft breeze sprang up. In the deepening night, he imagined upon the zephyr he heard a whisper from a longed-for voice. A whisper that said, *I know*.

Chapter 6

Mirador

Dawn forced back the darkness, revealing a cobbled road. Sihan pressed his heels to his horse's sides, frowning at the gravity the future might bring. Though he had a good mount beneath him, riding to Mirador with his father was not the pleasure he had known in previous years. Never had he been so aware his back was to his home.

Heart heavy, he ran gloved fingers through the mane of the bay colt he rode. Riding knee to knee beside him, Jaien also sat his chestnut in moody silence, face darkening with every stride the stallion took. Sihan missed his companions; even Tejas's downcast expression brought more cheer than Jaien's stern countenance. But the others – Kheran, Tejas, and Asher, made their own way now along with all the other lads and Senfari, a feint to avert speculation they came in force with thoughts other than king's service. How long before one of them broke, and stuck steel through a king's man was anyone's guess.

Jaien checked his horse as they came to a rise. Ahead, set on a hill sloping to the ocean on its eastern flank, stood Mirador fortress, grey walls and round towers, white standards emblazoned with the firefalcon fluttering from every turret. A river wound through the open plain before it, gleaming with sombre leaden light, smooth gray wash spilling into the sea.

Sihan glanced over his shoulder. Armindras drove the mule with a click and a hiss, the clattering of hooves and rumbling of the cart failing to mask his mutterings about things he had forgotten to tell the Graycor stewards before he had left Yseth, and his constant cursing of the king.

Tied to the cart, a string of blood-bay colts followed on the end of lead ropes. Beneath their barding, they were all reflections of the Graycor king stallion, all bound for the warhorse market. A ruse. For in among them, also blanketed with Graycor barding head to hoof to disguise him from prying eyes, Aurion walked with ears pricked.

Jaien urged Falcon on. Fields bound the road, some fallow, others swaying gold. On either side, peasants bent their backs tilling soil, methodically digging over bed after bed. Sihan breathed deep the aroma of dewed earth mixed with the sweet scent of everlastings, so different to Yseth, but in the current circumstances not nearly as welcome as dust and tumbleweeds.

Shouts of shepherds herding flocks of muddy goats and sheep to market drifted on the breeze. One man cursed a goat which had taken flight up a tree and refused to come down. He shook an angry staff at it, the sleeves of his corded tunic rolling back to reveal the thick brawn of muscle.

Any other time, Sihan would have laughed, but instead he slumped further into melancholy at the sight of lines of soldiers shepherding bands of youths like beasts along the roadside muck. Both Jaien and Armindras watched them, faces set in tight lines of tension.

As they rode closer to the fortress, a confusion of movement reigned – flocks of sheep, herds of goats and mules and a myriad of other domesticated beasts. Among them strode shepherds, herders, muleteers and guards. Occasionally, an oblique ray of sunlight glinted off steel; swords and daggers, brass greaves and harness rings.

Jaien muttered as he stared at the turmoil, 'There are king's soldiers everywhere. Watch yourselves.'

Armindras set the mule upon the wide ribbon of worn stony ground that testified to centuries of horses' hooves and mens' boots. There was no turning back.

Sihan urged his mount into the deluge of people and animals. His bay thrust forth its broad chest, ears pinned and warning, dashing to nip the heels of sheep, side-stepping to avoid stabbing horns. The air reeked with sweat stink and shit. Submerged in the thick haze, they followed the broken road till the herds thinned.

The river bounded one side of the fortress, a flowing mass of turbid sludge, surface clogged with floating dung. On the opposite bank, clusters of tents crammed the flat plain below the fortress, each sporting pennons of kingdom lords and knights. Standards cracked and hissed, streaming in the brisk breeze.

Jaien nodded at peasants. 'Probably every villager from leagues around.'

Sihan squinted through the dust. Soldiers patrolled everywhere, grey cloaks swept back to display steel. Guards inspected every load, every face. Archers stalked guardwalks high above the walls, peering between crenels. Gate guards eyed everyone.

'There're so many soldiers,' said Sihan. 'Why does the king need us?'

Jaien did not answer.

When they reached the bridge crossing the river, it became impossible to move. Beyond the broad gates of the fortress's battlemented curtain wall, the forecourt quivered with bright colour, flapping tents, rushing merchants. But most men strode purposefully, heads down, disquiet dogging their hurried steps as they sought to distance themselves from the fortress. Armindras drew himself upright, sitting braced, eyes smouldering. 'I'll not set foot inside that place, not without steel at my throat.'

Dread ate into Sihan's bones at the outburst.

Jaien drew close to Armindras's shoulder. 'You'll have all the steel you want, if you don't curb your tongue.'

Sihan pitched his voice low for his father's ears alone. 'We should camp outside the fortress.' He pointed to long lines of horses tethered along the battlements. 'We're pretending to sell horses. That's the place for us.'

Jaien cast a sweeping glance over the horse market. 'It's as best to keep Aurion away from that lot. The less he's seen, the better our chances.'

'You know as well as I our chances in this venture,' snapped Armindras, eyes alive with raw scorn.

Jaien fixed his gaze first on Sihan's taut face, then on Armindras's. With a set to his smooth jaw, he said, 'Be patient and do my bidding.' He nodded beyond the horse lines to a stand of willows. 'Keep Aurion out of sight in the trees as best you can, but on your way, try to make a show of trading.'

Like twin points of daggers, Armindras's eyes impaled Jaien's face. 'I'll do your bidding so long as you keep your word.' Then he lashed the reins, jolting the cart into motion.

Jaien met Sihan's eyes.

Sihan leaned forward on his horse and ventured in a whisper, 'He's out to court trouble.'

'Trouble will find him whether he courts it or not.'

Sihan noted the tightness along Jaien's jaw, knew he was in grave earnest. Before he had time to say more, Jaien led them off the road to where tents filled a large field surrounded by a wooden palisade. They rode past temporary abodes of knights and men-at-arms from across the kingdom, and those of common men and lads, country folk by their attire. Everywhere, air quaked with desperation. Smiles, if any, were forced.

Jaien identified foreign heraldry and exchanged courtesies with some men from Pelan. Sihan eyed every horse he passed, knowing their breeding from their distinctive features – mouse-grey, undersized ponies of Emor, fiery, high-stepping stallions of Belaron, parrot-mouthed, but sought after for their agility, prized above all others by the kingdom's horse archers. None matched the Graycor colts or Aurion. A sense of anticipation raised Sihan's spirits, made the possibility of success seem more likely.

Amid the lively bustle in the horse lines, squires unsaddled horses and unloaded baggage. Others led stallions with bannered tails held aloft like pennons. Nervous and high-strung, they baulked at tents, shied at vendors hawking wares. Sihan raised his chin, proud the Graycor colts walked with calm. Ears flickered, eyes stared alertly, but otherwise the colts remained uncaring of the noisy milieu surrounding them. Several knights pointed, and words drifted on the air, 'Graycor bloodhorses.'

Within a few moments of their arrival, squires were tagging along behind Armindras, throwing him questions about ages and prices and opportunities for purchase before the main market.

A smile finally touched Jaien's lips. 'They'll be sold before Gerhas even gets to put in a bid.'

Sihan did not smile. 'They want them for the trials. They know our horses are the best. They'll be as frantic as us to win.'

'Be thankful then they don't know these are your worst horses.'

Sihan patted his bay. 'Not this one.' Despite the plan, his father had kept back his best colt as insurance, the colt Sihan should have chosen for the Senfari trial. And even their worst horses were better than most in the kingdom.

Armindras pulled the mule under the spreading gold of a willow tree near a small stream, an offshoot from the main river. Sihan halted his bay and dismounted.

Jaien leaned down from Falcon and pressed his hand to Sihan's shoulder. 'I must report I'm back, and it's best no one suspects I'm aiding you.' He smiled briefly. 'Look to yourself, and keep your father from trouble. I'll watch for you at the horse lines.'

Eyes meeting on the promise, Sihan straightened. They were all caught in the trap. But now they had a chance, and the only way forward would be by fighting through the obstacles and emerging the other side. Forcing his lips to curve into a reluctant bow, he said, 'I'll look out for the old man.'

As Jaien rode away, Sihan led his mount to the side of the cart. He untied straps holding down the canvas and rummaged among saddles and sacks for a tether. From beneath a worn leather bridle, a gleam of metal caught his eye. Pushing tack aside, he stared down at the hilt of a sword. For a long, long moment his entire world tilted toward death's embrace. It took forever for him to touch it, to pull the scabbard out by its tail. Both it and the hilt were worn, old leather, unoiled and cracked with age. Sihan drew the sword part way from the sheath. The blade, too, showed signs of misuse, chinks missing from the dull steel.

A shiver shot through him. He had not seen his father's war sword since he had found it hidden in the loft above the barn years ago. He glanced toward his father.

Men haggling over horses still tied to the back of the cart surrounded Armindras. Sihan pushed the sword back, buried it beneath a sack of helbut tubers before joining his father.

'Name your price!' shouted one man from the rear of the crowd, waving his arm in the air. 'For the colt your lad was riding!'

Armindras folded his arms. 'One thousand falcons. And I'll throw the saddle in as well.'

'Better throw the boy in, too, at that price!' shouted another.

Muted laughter rippled through the crowd. Fraught laughter. They all wanted the Graycor horses.

The buyer at the back shook his head, thonged brown hair spilling over one shoulder. 'My limit is fifty falcons, and that's the best price you'll get anywhere.'

'No sale, then,' said Armindras. 'And not one of these other colts goes anywhere for less than one hundred falcons.'

Grumbling met this declaration, but the men did not disperse. Sihan bit his lip. The price was steep, far steeper than he had ever heard his father set. But it was a seller's market. The buyers would go to their limits.

'If you'll make way so I can pass . . .' The curt but gracious request parted the crowding hagglers and let through the buyer from the back. Compact and lean-built, a cloak slung casually over one shoulder, hazel eyes glittering below hair drawn back in a leather thong, he strode with assurance up to Armindras and stopped before him, nose to nose. 'Your price is too rich, Master Keeper.'

'Then what are you still doing here?' Armindras turned away and untied a colt. 'You think I haven't heard about Byerol, or Romondor? I'll wager by spring you'll be reckoning one hundred falcons a bargain and ruing lost opportunities to purchase the best bloodhorses in the kingdom.'

Sihan joined in the sport, determined to make the play of horse trading look real. 'And by then he'll be paying twice as much for an Emor pony!'

'Ha!' laughed a squire in the crowd. 'Twice the price for half the horse! That's rich!'

Guffaws met the ribbing, with each man trying to top the other with an Emor joke, in a strange, failing denial of the axe hovering over every neck.

The buyer flushed, but his hazel eyes revealed determination as he reached for the pouch at his belt. 'I'll put fifty down on the second bay you have there, if you'll hold it – saddled – while I fetch the rest.'

'Done!' said Armindras. 'What name?'

'Gerein.' With a scowl touching his lips, the young man strode away toward the fortress.

Within moments, a flurry of bids resulted in the sale of two other colts. Then a man tried to pull back the barding covering Aurion, earning a savage nip. Jumping away, he cried, 'What's this wild beast?'

Armindras frowned and snapped his fingers at Sihan. 'This one's not on the market. Just here to keep the mule company.'

Sihan hurried to lead Aurion away to the far side of the willow, but some of the men followed.

'Fancy company for a mule,' said one. 'Barded up like that.'

'Gods!' cried another, staring at the prancing legs. 'Is it white?'

'White, and not gelded,' said another, bending over to examine the stallion's testicles, only to jump back when Aurion squealed and kicked out. Recovering his composure the man said, 'What are you hiding, Armindras? Another Celestion?'

Muttering speculation met the question, but Armindras refused to be drawn, repeating the story he and Jaien had concocted to conceal Aurion's presence in Mirador. 'It's not a Graycor horse. Just a hack we picked up at Hermas. It's to be gelded soon enough and sold as a workhorse.'

Despite the unflattering description, the men continued to cluster round Aurion, trying to get a clearer look. For once, Sihan was glad of Aurion's bared teeth and swinging quarters, keeping the men from examining him too carefully. He muttered thanks to Senfar when horns blared from the battlement. The men stirred, scattering like leaves on the wind, preparing for the real haggling at the warhorse lines.

Sihan tied the two remaining colts next to his bay before returning to the cart. He waited while his father unharnessed the mule. Only when Armindras walked back to the cart after tethering the mule, did Sihan challenge him. He pulled back the helbut sack and rested his hand on the scabbard. 'What's this?'

Armindras averted his eyes. 'In case we ran into trouble on the road.'

Sihan set his jaw. 'We have a plan. It doesn't call for steel.' He shoved the sword under the canvas.

'As you will.' Armindras's eyes flickered with something hidden in their shadowed depths, something hard, cold, dangerous, brooking no resistance.

Sihan examined his father closely, searching for some hidden weapon cunningly disguised. Trumpets squealed nearby, and Aurion threw up his head, wet grass and thistles dangling from his jaw.

Armindras refused Sihan more time for scrutiny. 'Let's go.'

Dread stalking every step, Sihan followed his father, but whether to find salvation, or grief, it no longer signified. Whatever the outcome of this uncertain venture, they would face it together.

Chapter 7

Broken Bonds

Jaien rode into the fortress feeling soiled. Though blackened heads no longer marred the gates, he sensed their presence, smelt the blood stench that would never wash away.

Unlike the last time he had entered Mirador, a steady stream of wagons and mule caravans passed him, farmers wending their way from homesteads in the outlying regions of the fortress demesne to spend the day haggling in the market squares. Jaien reined Falcon past spruiking vendors battling for every inch of ground to display their wares. They wrangled with every buyer, amid a throng of fly-by-night peddlers and assorted charlatans that feasted on crowds.

Threads of gaiety – jongleurs plying their trade just inside the gate – were a travesty of bad taste given what had passed not two moon's cycles hence. They left a sick taste in Jaien's mouth, and did naught to mask the coiled tension within every man entering and exiting the fortress.

Shrieked laughter of children seemed elevated to a pitch aimed to cloak those other screams from the dungeons beneath the earth; the veils the woman wore, styled to conceal crying eyes.

As well they might.

All around Jaien, wronged spirits crowded the air. Behind his eyelids he saw a dead boy's decapitated head wrapped in his mother's arms, limitless dread in both faces. Blood, so much blood. Jaien nodded a curt salute to guards manning the battlements. They stared back, unseeing. Like the corpse-eyes of the innocent boy who refused to be forgotten.

Jaien's heart soured further.

Among the crowd, a man dragging a hand cart paused, giving way to Falcon. Jostled every which way by the crowd, he held his ground, staring quizzically at Jaien. Scratching the base of his scalp beneath his hat, he screwed up his thin face in puzzlement, peering closely. 'Don't I know you?' His squinted eyes widened in recognition, mouth gaping to splutter, 'You're that knight from Pelan. The one who fought for us.' He pushed the folds of his chaperon back from his head, and clenched one wiry hand over his heart. 'May the gods grant you grace.'

His words cast Jaien into a fouler mood. He did not want this man's adulation. He wanted no one to look to him for hope, no one to believe he could defend them. He could not save one boy from slaughter. What would they say if they knew he had dragged another to his doom? He rode Falcon past without even a nod.

Hushed whispers followed him. 'Knight Commander Jaien, I tell you! Returned from the dead!'

Whispers flew past on their own wings. People ahead paused to regard him. Fear crossed their faces, and they pulled their cowls close. Others clustered in tavern doorways, fingers tight round tankards of mead, staring at him. Those who staggered drunk from doorways had sense enough at least not to spout perilous opinions.

Jaien rode into the inner ward of the fortress. No one there cast him an eye as he dismounted, but he knew soldiers were observing his every move. He handed Falcon's reins to a stable boy, then walked to the door of the barracks once housing his officers. On the threshold, Jaien brushed at his tabard, dusty from the roads. He delayed, not quite wanting to face what he feared. As Falcon's hoof falls receded slowly toward the stables, he braced his back, opened the door, and walked inside. Along long rows of bunks, men leapt to their feet, smoothing down black and gold tabards, casting quick glances at each other.

No one spoke. Jaien kept control of his countenance, eyes sweeping the room, tallying numbers and faces. Only Camar and Gerein were missing, his closest comrades. No surprise. But where were they? Dead? Prisoners still? Ill at the very thought, Jaien took the initiative to release the rest of his officers from the momentary strain. 'I assume you're all ailing since you aren't at prayer?'

One red-haired knight captain stepped forward – Seth. 'Yes, sir,' he said, half-smile more a grimace. 'Sick to our stomachs.'

'What has Gerhas done?' Jaien demanded, fearing the worst.

'Disbanded our units.'

Jaien's fist clenched. 'And you?'

Seth's lips turned down in a scowl. 'Gerhas tried to put us under Areme's command. We told him to go to hell. He confined us to barracks for defying orders, insubordination, and threatened to re-arrest us for treason.'

Jaien shook his head, and considered his next words with care. 'If the choice were yours, what knight would you serve?'

'You, Sir.' The answer came sharp, without hesitation.

Jaien fought down a smile. 'And if I refuse?'

The next response was less resounding. 'Any knight our Lord Duke commands.'

Jaien wondered if their duke would hold any esteem for them if the king had naught. But he had to take the risk. 'Very well,' he said. 'I'll send word to Pelan. In the meantime, make yourselves presentable. We're already late enough for prayer.'

Men grabbed their cloaks and pulled on their boots, but left all weaponry behind. With his officers at his back, Jaien strode to the prayer hall. As they passed by the king's troops, they attracted every kind of expression from the soldiers, from grudging respect to astonishment, to fear of what they might do.

All voices in the prayer hall ceased upon Jaien's entrance. Throughout the dimmed interior, the curse "oath breaker" shouted from grieved eyes as his men jostled among the other knights to kneel in rows before the candlelit altar. Everywhere backs stiffened.

Jaien took comfort in the fact he had discomposed even Areme, who broke off the prayer to stare daggers through him. Jaien smiled grimly, aware he had not bathed in over a moon's cycle, and the grime of journeying lay heavy upon his skin and garments. Fitting: a perfect match for how he felt.

As Jaien strode across the hall, Areme's strong, expressive voice rose once more, reciting the dawn prayer. Even during worship there was an aura of danger about Areme, cold and calculation.

Jaien sought out Travall, who glared steel-eyed from the dimness where rushlights barely reached. Jaien picked up an unlit candle from the altar, then knelt beside the tall knight, whispering sidewise, 'Has anyone told you you're a horse's arse?'

'Frequently,' came the muted response.

Jaien lit the offering to Senfar from the wavering flame of Travall's candle, then fixed it to the altar with two drops of wax. 'How many of my men are under Areme?'

'I think you know the answer.'

'Where are they?'

'Some with me. Some with Balfere. All mutinous. Gerhas sent for Atiarin. He wasn't risking one thousand men deserting. And we can't afford to execute you treasonous bastards. You'll be with Atiarin, too, once he gets here.'

A sigh escaped Jaien's lips. His old commander. Not so bad, then.

'The price is Gerein,' continued Travall, raising his voice as if to enforce the point. 'He's now a King's Archer. He belongs to the king's guard.'

Jaien's men stirred, hinting steel would have been drawn if all weaponry had not been banned inside the temple. Jaien shot a warning glance, and they resumed their indifferent study of the altar.

'Is he in the dungeon?'

Travall snorted. 'If he was, there'd be blood in the streets. Since the orders were yours, the penalty is yours. We talked Gerhas into pardoning Gerein and laying the fault squarely at your door.'

'And Camar?'

'Same deal. Balfere wants him, the Heavens know why.'

'Same reason you want Gerein. They're better archers than anyone in either of your commands.'

'Deal?'

After careful thought, Jaien replied, 'Deal.' He leaned closer to Travall. 'Where's Gerhas?'

'Inspecting the new stock being offered by the bloodhorse keepers.' Travall shifted slightly. 'Your father's here, too.'

Jaien tensed, fear and anger flooding through him. 'You're holding him hostage?'

'He came of his own accord.' Travall turned to face Jaien. 'Best go see him. He doesn't know you've lost your command. It'll be better coming from you.'

Pain spiked Jaien's gut like bitter fruit. He stood, interrupting the prayer for the second time. Once more, a murderous glint sparked the depths of Areme's eyes.

Jaien inclined his head to the knight. 'I beg forgiveness. I must withdraw.' He drew back among the ranks of his men, making his way past them to the door.

Gerein was waiting for him in the stable square, a grin stretching across his face. 'I saw you ride in,' he said. 'With the lad. I nabbed one of his colts. Can you lend me fifty falcons?'

Imitating Gerein's rapid-fire monotone, Jaien said, 'I'll give you two hundred. Call it penance. I've traded you to Travall.'

Gerein's grin widened. 'Was there a choice? You know, a lot of men from the other commands took bets you wouldn't come back.'

'What odds?'

'The best.'

'Tell me again why I'm lending you gold?'

'I need a horse. Mine's still recovering from the fight. And you're *giving*, not lending,' corrected Gerein, taking Jaien's purse. 'Penance, remember? Besides, I haven't had a chance to collect my winnings yet.' He spat upon the cobbles. 'Bloody exorbitant price for a horse.'

'Fifty falcons sounds fair.'

'One hundred,' Gerein said.

Jaien smiled. 'Armindras fleeced you.'

Gerein shrugged. 'With the falcons I'm about to rake in, I can afford to be shorn ten times over.' He fell into step with Jaien as they walked back to the barracks to collect their swords. From a cautious distance, soldiers eyed them both in silence. Only when they were safe within the barracks did Gerein lean close, handing Jaien a clean tunic and saying almost soundlessly, 'I've news. Wait till we're clear of sharp ears.'

Jaien nodded, pulling the woollen garment over his head and adjusting his sword belt over its cream folds. Bathing and a full change would have to wait.

On their way to the main gate, the crowds in the inner court parted before them, respectful of the swords they carried at their sides. Many hid troubled looks, and some throttled cries of alarm. Veiled women lowered their eyes.

Gerein sighed. 'That's the one thing I really hate about the Fire Rituals. I can't tell whether the girls are comely or not under layers and layers of cloth.'

Jaien forced himself to join in Gerein's game. 'It's one layer of gauze, and it's mainly noble women who wear them. They're beyond your reach no matter how many falcons you've got stuffed in your pouches.'

Gerein smirked. 'The girls I'm after are only interested in one pouch, and it's not stuffed with falcons.'

Jaien snorted. 'Believe that if you want. You know my view of women. They lie, they're deceitful, stupid, greedy, impure, and wicked.'

Gerein's grin widened. 'You sound jealous.'

'Have you seen my father?' asked Jaien, broaching a topic of far more interest to him than women.

'He's in his usual spot, as far away from Emor ponies as he can get.'

Jaien smiled to himself, imagining his father's words. *'Won't have my horses within spitting distance of diseased runts like that! Might catch something!'*

When they reached the narrow confines of the market alleys, crowds of peasants jostled against them. A tide swept them along, past minarets and flat-roofed houses. The smell of roasting meat and too-sweet incense pervaded the air.

Vendors spruiked from bazaars, shops ten foot square set in stone walls. Jaien ignored the beckoning calls, not even flicking quick disinterest at leather goods hanging on hooks round the walls or silversmiths etching fancy designs on vases. He stepped over pots sprawled right out onto the street where proprietors squatted in the middle of heaps of copperware.

It was all so . . . normal, a far cry from what he had ridden into more than two moon's cycles past.

Though coloured awnings fluttered overhead, giving respite from spearing shafts of morning light, sweat prickled

Jaien's back. He wished for his horse and was well pleased when they reached the outer gate.

Beside him, Gerein whistled, nodding and smiling at every girl who sashayed past. They crossed the bridge, then strode along the tents and stalls to the horse lines. Jaien stayed silent while Gerein warbled on about girls – in particular, his plans for a blonde-haired beauty he had been courting of late.

Forever passed until they were clear of king's soldiers and Gerein said under his breath, 'Your father doesn't know what happened. He knows nothing of the death mark.' He met Jaien's eyes directly. 'The men are with you, whatever you do.' He broke off abruptly as several king's soldiers advanced within earshot. Mouth ajar, eyes fixed on a merchant's daughter farther along the line, Gerein cried, 'There she is,' and dashed off.

Jaien continued down the horse lines. How could he tell his father he had lost his commission? What reason could he give? Cenriin would think him mad if he told him it was because of voices in his head. And his father thought ill enough of him already.

Thankfully, the voices had receded to shadow murmurs of whispered breath since he had found the lad. He did not understand it. Sihan was in more danger now than ever, nothing certain in their proposed course. But the voices gave him no clue as to what he must do next.

'Jaien!' Pitched low, yet with a distinct, cutting edge to it, a voice all too familiar startled him from his reverie. Air rushed out of his lungs as he was pulled into a back-breaking embrace.

'My boy!' Cenriin cried, and Jaien closed his eyes.

'Father,' he said, pulling back to regard the old man when he finally escaped his grip. Almost fifty winters, Cenriin bore his age well, strength in his broad shoulders and straight back, belying the grey laced through his russet hair. He stood upright and solid, wide-girthed, but tall in plain tunic and leggings.

'I heard you were in Mirador.' Jaien did not trust himself to speak further.

His father frowned. 'As I heard *you* were not.' His fingers dug into Jaien's forearm as he pulled him toward a line of chestnut horses. 'Two days I've been here. Two days!' He held up two fingers to emphasise the point. 'And all anyone could say was you'd been called away. Called away!' His voice rose. 'And an old man risking life and limb to reach you. Three lands I went through. Three!' He raised three fingers as if his words were not quite enough to convey the meaning.

Jaien smiled, though his gut churned at the irony. He had disobeyed voices that had threatened to tear his mind apart to prevent a dagger in his father's back, while the old man had been courting arrow shafts and swords just as lethal. With both thoughts constricting his chest, he pressed his trembling lips to his father's cheek. 'It's wonderful to see you.'

Cenriin returned the kiss of kin, a quick, gruff brush of lips to cheek, then stood apart, hands on hips, feet square as he regarded Jaien through narrowed eyes. 'Well? Where have you been that you can leave your father mouldering?'

Jaien skirted the truth. 'I went to fetch a lad. He's been called to service.'

'Lad?' His father's lips pressed into a frown. His voice came raised and honed like a dagger. 'Are you still chasing lads? I'd hoped you'd grow out of that once you made Knight Commander.'

Jaien clenched his fists, refusing to enter into the tired, still bleeding, argument. 'I regret none of my choices, Father.' He thought of the loyalty of his men. 'Men stand constant, ask no price but love, respect, and honour. Women can be bought for the price of gold.'

A slap burned his cheek, and his father's eyes flared. 'You insult all women with such fool talk. Would you thus describe your mother, may her bones rest in the sacred sea?'

Jaien thrust back with his own daggered words. 'The days of women of honour died with the Great War.'

The high colour stinging Cenriin's cheeks moments before drained away to leave him grey. The rigid cords of his throat battled to squeeze out sound, the words a strangled hiss when they emerged. 'You still brand all women because of one?'

'Women brand themselves.'

His father turned away. 'I see. As always, the protest is pointless. Who is this lad, then?'

'Armindras's son, Sihan.' Jaien sighed, weary suddenly beyond measure. He had saved his father. Naught else mattered. Best left to the future to salvage good opinion.

His father regarded him closely. 'You value him?'

The question tore through Jaien's mind, and the answer spilled before the thoughts forming it took shape, surprising even him. 'No man's blood is dearer to me. I hold him closer than kin. Yes, I value him.' And with that, he walked away, anger coursing through him. Let his father make of his words what he would.

Their meetings were always like this; driven together by bonds of love, torn apart by the same, never to find a common ground of acceptance. It surprised him it still hurt so sharp, a twisting knife driven deep within, this old wound that had melded over time into a familiar dark ache without respite.

He was halfway down the horse lines before he realised he had forgotten to break the other bad news.

Chapter 8

Veiled Secrets

Vexed, Orlanda rested her chin on the back of her hands, gaze drifting to the northern mountains beyond the window, their peaks a smudge of grey in the morning light. She chewed her bottom lip and leant further over the sill. In the garden below her balcony, rose bushes straggled, thorned and gangly, tipped by tight cold buds doomed never to blossom.

Like her.

Not even the heady fragrance of vanilla from the incense sticks burning around the room could sweeten her mood. Behind her, the rustle of parchment and the sharp, restless scratching of a quill told of another woman filled with equal annoyance but spending her time more profitably. Orlanda heaved a sigh. With her father's strict regimen, the pre-dawn tasks were well over: ablutions, dressing, first meal, all done with brisk efficiency by maids who kept their faces down and lips closed in tight lines even before they had donned their festival veils.

Beneath lowered lids, Orlanda snuck a glance sidewise at her chaperone – her guard – summoned from Belaron to set some fool example of propriety. She bit down a smile. It played to her purpose others thought her wayward. No use for them to think otherwise. No use at all.

She had been practicing waywardness as long as she had been studying Common. Common speech, Common dress, Common customs. Nothing missed her attention. Soon, very soon, all her practice and study and pretence would pay off.

Determined to resume the act, Orlanda huffed, 'I'm bored.'

'Boredom is a virtue,' came the instant retort.

'Then I must be the most virtuous woman in the kingdom!'

The Duchess of Belaron paused in her writing and glanced up, candlelight sparking an angry glitter to the green depths of her eyes. 'I seriously doubt that.'

Orlanda raised her chin. 'You blame me for being summoned here.'

'No,' said Irawan, regarding her with a disdainful stare. 'I blame your father.' She returned to her writing, making it clear the conversation was over. Regal and elegant, she could lay claim to beauty even at forty winters, but that face beneath hair of rich auburn remained marble cold.

Orlanda turned back to the window, twisting her long, blonde hair into knots. She traced the path of the river to the sea, past the city fortress with its jumble of grey-blue tiles and slate-grey walls. The river held a hypnotic glimmer of silver-blue hope, leading to . . . where? What harbours lay over the horizon? Orlanda stifled another sigh. Too many times those aching questions had crossed her mind.

Sun turned the fortress walls to a jewelled wash of silver grey, cobwebs to glittering pearls of beaded dew. She stared intently at the cobbled road leading to the world beyond her home: her trap. In the fields outside the fortress, the last of the unharvested grain belt stretched, rich gold, a graceful swell of oats and barley. Farther still, yellow-speckled pastures swooped to meet forests of candlewood, snowbark, and ash. Sunstreaks touched the crowns, a shifting blaze of light trapped in a ripple of olive-green.

As if to echo the rising sun, a voice rose upon the air, quiet at first, then growing in volume, exquisite, drifting through the opposite window; a male voice reciting the prayer of dawn. 'O, rise in peace and forgiveness, for you wake to the dawning of the age of wisdom.'

'Who is that praying?' asked Orlanda, already knowing the answer but wanting to hear the name, speak of the man.

Irawan set down her quill. 'When will you give up this obsession for a man you can never have?' The admonition came in a staccato rush, laced with exasperation.

Determined to annoy, Orlanda sighed his name with deliberate exaggeration, 'Ah-re-may.' The name slid over her tongue, silken, with none of the rough edges of wear clinging to other men's names. It lingered, untarnished, vibrant. Like the man.

Her heart beat with increasing strength.

Areme.

Her champion, her knight. And if she had her way, her lover.

From the first moment she had seen him, kneeling at her father's feet, swearing the oath of fealty, she had wanted him. Longed for him, as though they had been parted a millennium and he a lost part of herself. She knew it in her soul. He was hers, meant for her, for all eternity. Only Areme and the entire court seemed to think otherwise.

She imagined that gaunt but suave face close to hers, broad-browed with straight nose, lips set in a scowl. He had served her father in the Great War, yet his features remained those of a man more than ten winters younger.

She dreamed his scowl melting as she unrobed for him. Long lashes set over silvered eyes – eyes darkening with need, shadows catching at the hollows of his cheeks, face framed by flowing midnight hair. And his body . . . Dangerous. Forbidden.

In her mind, her fingers trailed down his sun-gilded cheeks, over broad shoulders, on down his chest, down further. Warmth spread to her loins.

She forced the image away, instead picturing him in grey leather, fencing in the courtyard with one of his command, a rapid dance of thudding feet and moonlit blades. Orlanda turned to the duchess. 'Why does he always train by moonlight?'

Irawan scowled. 'Because he likes to keep the court awake at night. Damned inconsiderate. Your father should put a stop to it.'

Orlanda's lips turned down at the corners. At every turn, Irawan seemed determined to bring the conversation around to the one topic Orlanda did not want to discuss. Where Areme was the sun rising in the morning, her father was no more than a shadow, still grieving over a wife who was nothing but a memory.

Orlanda padded across soft rugs spread over flagstones to another window. The attempt to catch sight of her champion was futile, but she resolved to lessen the distance between them in any manner possible. As if to pour salt on an open wound, his voice drifted to silence. Orlanda craned to look down. In the stable courtyard, far below, a procession of hooded knights in grey cloaks formed in a circle. At the centre knelt a man beside a fountain, head bent. Always, always, that tired ritual; her father, still grieving his long-dead queen.

With no way of identifying Areme from the others, Orlanda turned away. 'How long are we going to have to wear veils this time?' she demanded, trying to keep shrillness from her voice.

'It's not an edict,' responded the duchess, tying a ribbon round the parchment.

'It may as well be.' Orlanda stamped her foot, a Common trait she had down to an art. 'All the women of the court toady about him, playing the game, hoping he'll notice them.'

'Like you hope he'll notice you?'

The remark cut home like a sword thrust through the heart, but this time Orlanda refused to back away. 'You know as well as I the reason he encourages the veils. It's because he doesn't want to see *me*.' Her voice broke. 'That's why he's sending me away, isn't it?'

The duchess shrugged. 'That's part of the reason. The better part is politics.' She patted the rolled parchment. 'Like this.' Standing, she smoothed down her dress. 'I must go meet the messenger to Belaron.'

Orlanda brightened. 'I'll come with you!'

'There's no need.'

'But–' Orlanda scrabbled to think of an excuse to leave her rooms. 'I feel faint, Irawan. I need to take some air.'

The duchess waved to the window. 'Plenty of air there.'

Orlanda set her lips in a moue. 'I want to see the horses. Father said I could have the winner of the warhorse trials, and I want to see the horses before then.'

'By all the Gods, you are impossible! Why don't you just ask if you can visit Areme's bed?'

Orlanda screwed up her face. 'Because I know you'll forbid it.'

'Nothing escapes you.' The duchess drew her cloak about her shoulders.

Orlanda pointed to the window, and ground out in a rising crescendo, 'Areme's down there, with Father. Who's p–praying to a ghost. G–Go, see for yourself.' Hot tears stung behind her eyes. Not part of her act. What were they for? Her father? Areme? She balled her hands into fists and stared defiance at the duchess.

Irawan's eyes softened, ever so slightly. After a long moment, she said, 'Very well, you may come, but no farther than the postern. You'll be satisfied with what you can see of the horse lines from there. Understood?'

Orlanda examined her closely for a sign she had been teasing. Seeing none, she let out an oft-practiced girlish squeal, grabbed a pair of leather boots from a stand near the hearth and sat at the writing desk to tug them on. When she stood, the hem of her brocade dress fell back to the floor with a heavy swish. She shrugged into a grey cloak, pulled the cowl over her face, then twirled before the duchess.

Irawan grimaced and walked over to the canopied bed to pick up a silk headscarf. Without a word, she handed it to Orlanda.

Frowning, Orlanda pulled back her cowl and stalked to the mirror. Blue eyes stared back at her from a face pale with excitement. Wishing she looked older than her sixteen winters and less like her corpse mother, she adjusted the scarf into a veil revealing only eyes and kohled eyebrows, then pulled on her gloves.

Her father's words, uttered when she was too young to understand their import, filled her mind. 'You wear her face, so you must wear the veil.'

Even then, Orlanda had not needed to ask to know it was her mother to whom the king referred. Loss was there in her father's voice, as ever when he spoke of her mother. And hate – fearful hate. And grief. And despised love. Wyndarra lived in a deep, dark, private place within him no one else could reach. Always present. And always, always, when he thought himself alone, he sunk into an abyss of darkness and there existed in a living death willing her by his side once more.

Orlanda had not known what to say then or since. In truth, her memories of her mother were vague, and faded more with each passing year. Wyndarra had died when Orlanda was a child, and here she was on the cusp of womanhood. For her father, the remembrances were fresh as morning, but somehow Orlanda blackened those memories to a pitch darker than a starless night.

Shaking off these troubled thoughts, she turned back to the duchess, who nodded her approval.

They strode the palace halls, ignoring guards who stood at almost every door. Irawan patted Orlanda's back. 'You should choose a dark horse, black, to match Valoren's standard.'

'Fuck Valoren.'

The duchess cuffed her shoulder. 'Language!'

Orlanda lowered her head submissively, doing her best to adopt the demure walk of a handmaiden. All the while she repeated the coarse Common curse under her breath as she trailed after the older woman. Coarse Common had its uses. Soon, very soon, she planned to make full use of it.

Her mind turned back to Areme and the big grey stallion he rode – Seroyen – rippling muscles beneath a coat of steel grey. She would find a horse to match. She fought down the urge to laugh. Who cared what the horse looked like? She would ride an Emor pony if it would help her escape this place and foil her father's plans.

While the duchess waited at the postern for her messenger, Orlanda scanned the thick market crowds beyond the gate. A world of confusion teemed outside the fortress, stinking of rising heat, dung and sweat. Pennants floated above tents, and courtiers in resplendent liveries rode toward the fortress gates. Peasants clogged the road, their garish tents making the fields around the fortress look like a camp of soldiers. Leaves were dying on trees, twisted yellow and withered like old dry skin over veins run dry. Gusts stripped them from branches to die churned into urine and mud by a host of boots and hooves. Through the multitude of men and beasts, there was no hope of seeing the horses at the warhorse fair.

The courier strode from the direction of the stables, war mount in tow, splendidly apparelled in the cobalt-blue tabard of Belaron with the white griffin emblazon. With her chaperone distracted, the duchess whispering at length her instructions to the messenger, Orlanda took one sidling step toward the postern. Another.

The duchess's courier vaulted onto his steed. Liveried gate guards drew aside and uncrossed their halberds to grant passage to the horseman. His mount surged into a gallop, sending people scurrying. Curses hounded the rider's wake.

The gate stood clear before Orlanda. Within a heartbeat she was running, past the guards, losing herself in the throng of merchants and guild men all toiling to show skills and goods to advantage. They shouted for customers, competing for the eyes of well-heeled knights and their retinues. All around her, sharp eager faces anticipated trade and profit. Orlanda dodged past them all, cloak drawn close to conceal her identity, shoving her way through the bustle.

Wafting breezes carried snorts, whinnies, and the heady odour of horses across a field of trampled sun daisies. Long rows of mounts held by their attendants stood in ranks as though on parade, awaiting Horsemaster Gerhas and his entourage of knights and followers. Orlanda wove her way through the close-packed horses in the tether lines, scanning the crowd more than the steeds, searching, searching. Areme would be here as soon as her father dismissed him. He was the finest horseman in the kingdom. Gerhas would demand his attendance. Orlanda hid between two men, hoping they might mask her from pursuit.

A skinny page beside her pointed at a chestnut stallion with a white blaze and said, 'Looks like the winning horse from the trials last year.'

Orlanda peered at the stallion with an assessing stare. 'Ought to, he's from the same bloodline.'

A merchant to her right, keen eyes slitted beneath his chaperon, asked, 'How can you tell?'

Orlanda, who had made a close study of all things horse in order to impress Areme, though it did not appear to have endeared her to him as yet, pointed at the brand of a falcon on the horse's offside shoulder. 'The symbol of Pelan.'

An elderly man with eyes matching the duchess's piercing green, stepped forward from the horse's side, a smile carved into his worn face. 'Well-noticed, my Lady.'

Orlanda inclined her head and reached out to pat the stallion. 'What's his name?'

'Wedge,' answered the man. 'After the wedge-tailed eagle. Full brother to Falcon.'

The pride in his voice alerted Orlanda. 'Falcon? Knight Commander Jaien's horse?'

The man puffed up. 'The very same. Jaien is my son.'

Orlanda shivered. She had heard all about Jaien, his attempted mutiny, his flogging. The palace hierarchy thought they could prevent such unsavoury news reaching her ear, cloistered as she was, but in reality, few goings on in the fortress escaped her. She clamped her lips in the presence of those she trusted not, and played the fool they believed her to be. To appear clever could not aid her endeavours.

For a moment, Jaien usurped Areme in her thoughts. The fact he was out of favour with the king earned him merit in her eyes. And such a man could be of use, perhaps. 'Is Jaien here?' she asked.

Jaien's father pointed farther along the horse lines to where a sandy-haired knight stood beside a tall youth. The old man's face clouded over a fraction. 'He's watching over some lad.'

Orlanda narrowed her eyes. Like most of the court, she was aware of Jaien's reputation, and his tastes. Everything about his father's tone suggested disapproval. Probing further, she asked, 'Is the lad a thief he needs watching by a knight?'

'He's been called to service, unwillingly.'

'Service?' Alarm struck her in the gut. Jaien had been flogged for trying to save such a lad.

The man lowered his voice. 'The king's ordered all boys of age to be enlisted in the army. In case there's a war over the princess going to Romondor. The lad thinks he can escape service by selling the king his horse.'

Orlanda closed her eyes, wondering exactly how many lives her father intended to destroy on the back of hers. Nails digging in to her hands, she grated, 'There'll be no war, I swear it.'

The man laughed. 'Only the king can make that vow.' Then he winked at her, taking her by the elbow and steering her around a steaming pile of dung. 'You have spirit, my Lady. If you're not spoken for, perhaps I could introduce you to my son?'

Anger flared in Orlanda's heart, and still further sympathy for Jaien. 'I think all men and women should be left to follow their own hearts, not everyone else's wishes. Being frere isn't a crime. If it was, half the kingdom's army would be adorning the scaffolds!'

Mouth agape at her outburst, the horse trader just stared at her.

Before Orlanda could say more, strong fingers clamped on her arm. She whipped her head round and groaned at finding the duchess's furious face inches from her own. Irawan dragged her bodily away from the open-mouthed man, hissing in her ear, 'Stupid brat. Not enough air in the courtyard, I take it?' She started to march Orlanda back to the fortress, her voice moderating slightly as she glanced back at Jaien's father. 'Poor man. I see nobody has told him.'

Orlanda glowered at the duchess's selective sympathy. 'Told him what?'

The duchess's voice lowered to a whisper. 'About Jaien. He's been demoted to knight captain.' She paused, shutters coming down behind her eyes as she darted a glance at Orlanda. Her words became familiarly vague. 'Something to do with some lad by all accounts.'

Orlanda took the cue to play her game of feigned ignorance. 'A lad? They demoted him because he fancies a lad?' At the curious looks of bystanders, Orlanda forced herself to lower her voice. 'That's unheard of!'

The duchess looked evasive. 'Don't worry your pretty little head about it.'

Sudden rage gave tongue to thoughts Orlanda could no longer hide. 'Like I shouldn't worry about my forthcoming travesty of a marriage to Valoren?' Beyond caring of the consequences, Orlanda ripped her arm away from the duchess and stomped down the horse line, determined to give Jaien the support she would never get. She had almost reached him, when a stronger grip than anything the duchess could produce crushed her shoulder. A menacing voice growled, 'What the seven hells do you think you're doing out here?'

Orlanda twisted, and found herself staring into the intense blue eyes of Areme's second, Knight Captain Hessarde. She scowled. Like all Areme's men, Hessarde was a bloodhound, able to track her down no matter what escapade she contrived. Small wonder he recognised her despite her veil when no one else seemed sensible of her identity.

Then joy eclipsed chagrin. If Hessarde was here, Areme could not be far away. She glanced over Hessarde's shoulder. 'Where's your master?' she asked breathlessly, not caring what liberties Hessarde took as long as it got her to her goal.

The knight grimaced. 'Staying well clear of you.' He turned to the duchess who had caught up with her wayward charge. 'Are you quite mad?' he demanded. 'Don't you know Areme could be exiled if the king gets wind of this . . . this . . .'

'Adulterous liaison,' supplied Orlanda, wishing the reality matched the words. The duchess spluttered a gasping cough beneath her veil, and Orlanda's lips twitched in satisfaction.

The white scar on Hessarde's cheek paled even further in his flushed face. 'If Areme hears of this—'

'He'll what?' challenged Orlanda. 'Ignore me? He's already doing that. He hasn't spoken to me in almost a moon's cycle.'

Clenching his teeth, Hessarde growled, 'He's a knight commander. He has other duties than looking after a spoilt princess.'

Orlanda bristled. 'He's my champion. Looking after me is his primary duty.'

'You don't need looking after,' said Hessarde, voice laced with silken spite. 'You need a bloody good beating. And you're sure to get one if the king finds you outside the palace.' He glared at the duchess. 'And you. What were you thinking? Don't you know the king could strip you of your title for this?'

Irawan fumed. 'You try controlling an unmanageable brat.'

Her words spurred Orlanda. Perhaps she could still turn this unsuccessful venture to her advantage, force Areme into making an appearance. If she caused enough trouble, he was certain to come. Even a harsh word from him was better than no word at all. All his scowls were smiles to her. Throwing off every shackle of grace and courtesy, determined to play the commoner with all her acquired skill, she raised her voice to a shrill whine. 'Release me, you sorry excuse for an ass!'

Hessarde's eyes narrowed. 'If you insist on behaving like a common wench, complain not of the consequences.'

The warning in his tone only served to goad her further. She yanked free of his grip. As he went to grab her arm again, she dodged away. Cloak billowing in her wake, she ran down the horse lines. Behind her, Hessarde's voice cut through the air like a battleground bellow. 'Stop! Thief!'

Orlanda skidded to a halt in front of the lad beside whom Jaien stood. He turned to her, face tight with tension. He was not yet a man, but all he would be was clear, burning through the youthful curve of cheek, the direct, candid eyes.

Shocked to stillness, Orlanda could only stare. With brown eyes instead of silver, brown hair instead of black, the lad still somehow managed to look like an unfinished copy of Areme. Orlanda shook her head, trying to clear it. If she was not careful, she would soon be seeing Areme's features in the face of every man.

With Hessarde bearing down on her, she wasted no time. She reached out and took Jaien's hand in hers. 'Follow your heart, no matter the cost.' Then she turned to the young man, struck again by his looks. 'You, too,' she squealed, as Hessarde clamped his arm around her waist, blunt nails digging hard into flesh.

The young man's eyes widened and he stammered, 'B– By your will, my Lady.'

Hessarde's low voice snarled in Orlanda's ear. 'You play it well. But I trust I can match you.' He raised his voice as he began to propel her toward the fortress, arms holding her in a vice. 'Give back! Give back! Make way for the prisoner!'

Orlanda beat her fists against him and yelled, 'I'm innocent! Innocent! Let me go, you jackass!' She knew full well the outcome. It would take little for Jaien to come to her aid, anything to spite Hessarde. The enmity between the two men must be beyond wrath.

As expected, Jaien stepped forward, frowning. 'Halt!' he demanded, with the steel authority of a man used to command.

Hessarde's face convulsed into a visage of absolute loathing and rage, teeth bared like a baited bear. 'Don't you interfere in my business again, or I swear you'll pay the full cost this time.'

'And you know what I swore last we crossed swords.' Jaien's sword hand moved to the hilt of his weapon.

Men all around the two knights backed away with furtive, stealth-slow steps, wishing to escape notice, giving ground inch by inch, not wanting to be caught in the brewing battle.

'Present your evidence of this girl's crime, Shaheden.' Jaien spat the epithet like an insult, face a study of savage serenity, threat barely hidden below the smooth surface.

'Leave off,' Hessarde demanded, eyes sparking caution. 'This *girl,* as you call her . . .'

'This girl,' cut in Orlanda, pitching her voice for Hessarde's ears alone, 'will make sure she gets hurt just enough to make the king tear every strip of skin from your hide if you start another massacre.' She sweetened her voice to sickly cream. 'He won't want his sacrifice bruised and cut and bleeding when it's presented at Valoren's altar.' Her fingers slipped Hessarde's dagger from its sheath. 'I'll do it myself if I have to.'

The struggle in his eyes was clear, the mind churning behind them, weighing probabilities. He knew her well enough to know she would carry out her threat.

Everywhere now, a swirl of motion disturbed the rear lines of the assembled horsemen, shouts and orders, soldiers emerging into the empty circle around Hessarde and Jaien with marked expressions of distaste and reluctance.

Orlanda advanced her case. 'They don't want it either. Just let me look at this lad's horse, let me see Areme, and we can all save our hides.'

'This lad's horse . . .' began Hessarde, sweeping his gaze past her. And then everything about him became still. Even his words drifted to silence. Face growing paler with every passing moment, Hessarde stared beyond her, past Jaien, his immobility slowly taking on the form of calculation, a hound marking quarry.

His hands fell away from Orlanda. She stepped away, flummoxed, then turned to follow the knight's gaze. Her eyes fixed on the horse Jaien's lad held. Head flung high, tense, it met her gaze with intense black eyes. Head to hoof in barding, still the ridges of muscle bunched and rippled clearly in the strong crested neck, the powerful quarters. But one feature stood out more than any other. Orlanda's surprise mirrored Hessarde's shocked expression as she exclaimed, staring at its nose peeking out from the hood, 'Is that horse white?'

Behind her, the duchess gasped as if she had been holding her breath beneath water. Orlanda half-turned to catch that usually impassive countenance shattered into shards of dismay mingled with wonder, the duchess opening and closing her mouth like a beached catfish.

Just as swiftly the duchess regained control, her eyes becoming impenetrable. She fixed her gaze on Hessarde. 'The girl wants Areme here. I think that might be wise.'

Orlanda's sharpened ears pricked to attention. A darkness in the duchess's voice conveyed a great deal more than she had said. Everyone knew the king's edict about white horses. But this was something more. What? Irawan had done everything to keep Areme away, had cried foul, invoked the edicts, unleashed the hunt, and now she *wanted* him here?

Unease shivered over Orlanda's skin. Had she erred? The enormity of what she had done crashed down upon her shoulders. Had she earned Jaien's lad a death sentence? And Jaien a worse fate than he had already suffered? Suddenly her longing for Areme's presence became the taste of ash.

No. She shook her head. Jaien might be many things, but he was no fool. He would not willingly stand by such foolishness without cause. Let Areme come.

But Hessarde stood motionless, staring at the white horse as though he had not heard a word. The duchess fronted him, eyes levelled to his so fixedly it seemed she determined to pierce the most inner recesses of his mind. 'Go. Get. Areme,' she repeated.

Hessarde still looked shaken and shocked, but he found the words to mumble, 'Forgive my error, mistress.'

Orlanda was not quite sure of whom he begged forgiveness, herself or the duchess, and Hessarde was of no mind to tell before he took off at a dead run toward the fortress.

Orlanda stared after him, nonplussed, then lowered her eyes discreetly, and inclined her head to Jaien, hoping he would not recognise her. Unlike Hessarde, who was part of her guard, Jaien was usually on duty in Pelan, serving on the southern borders. And given his tastes, hardly likely to take more than a passing interest in her. She recaptured his attention, saying, 'I thank you, Sir.'

Jaien nodded curtly, half an eye still on Hessarde's retreating figure. 'That man is a brute. If you wish to bring a charge–'

'No matter,' Orlanda said quickly, knowing full well who would win that round of cards if the case came before the king. 'I'm sure he regrets his error.' She averted her gaze, focusing her attention once more on the white horse. White. The opposite of black. The opposite of Valoren. The perfect choice. And how it would irk her father, to see her riding a Godsteed. For why else would the lad have risked bringing the horse here if not to invoke the legends of old? Callinor would *have* to notice her if she stole a Godsteed from under his very nose. She moved closer to examine the stallion for any flaws. Tall, of a height matching Areme's steel-grey, with a mettlesome bearing and proud eye. When she reached out her hand to its muzzle, the youth holding the horse stepped forth, forehead creased with concern. 'I wouldn't, my Lady. He's a biter.'

'Is he?' Orlanda examined the horse again, looking deep into the eyes. Nothing but gentleness stared back. She gave a tentative tap of a nail to the horse's nose. 'You wouldn't hurt me, would you?'

The stallion snorted, lowering his head.

'I didn't think so.' She trailed her fingers down to the soft, velvet nose, then up the face to stroke the silken forelock peeking from the top of the hood. The youth stared at her like she was stroking a viper, Jaien likewise. She walked around the horse, lifting the barding, earning whispers from men all round craning to see. 'Godsteed, Godsteed.' Shifting restively, they ogled the horse with wide-eyed awe.

Orlanda turned to Jaien. 'Do you think he would make a good match with Knight Commander Areme's horse?'

'Seroyen?' Jaien frowned. 'He's a better match for Celestion.'

Orlanda looked at him sharply. Yes – she had judged aright. The lad wanted to sell the horse to the king and Jaien was helping him. She looked again at the youth. 'Is that *your* wish? That the king buys him?'

The brightness in his eyes spoke frantic urgency, sparking again that flash of sympathy within her. She knew why Jaien had lost his commission, and understood why he was helping this lad. The youth needed to earn a boon, to be kept out of service. What better way than flattering the king with a Godsteed? But his cause was lost without her help, and she was suddenly of a mind to help all she could, sensing yet another way to settle the score with her father.

The duchess cut in to her thoughts. 'Gerhas will be here any moment. And you know what that means.'

Orlanda shuddered. Gerhas was sure to recognise her, and he would not hesitate to haul her before her father. With freedom rushing to an end, she looked at the young man again, then the horse. Giving a slight tug on Jaien's sleeve, she drew him aside.

'I repay the favour with a favour. I will send my squire to you with a gift.'

'It's not necessary, my Lady.'

'You'll find it may advantage your cause, and his.' Orlanda pulled the glove from her hand, revealing the ring of the heir-apparent, a firefalcon set in white crystals.

Jaien's face paled. 'You should not be here.'

'Favour for a favour.' She pressed a finger to his lips, shaking her head.

The duchess called, 'Guards! Guards!'

Within moments, a brace of guardsmen answered the call, surrounded the two women and escorted Orlanda away from the horse lines. Orlanda glanced back at the lad beside Jaien, but the youth's gaze was fixed on the approaching figure of the horsemaster. She smiled, even as she was marched away, and yet another way to irk her father sprang to mind.

Chapter 9

Godsteed

Wishing for unnatural speed, Hessarde barged through the crowd along the horse lines. Stallions threw heads high, eyes wild, skittering back, tugging at tethers. Shouts and curses dogged Hessarde's heels as keepers and stable boys raised angry fists, but only one thing mattered. He had to find Areme.

Who would have thought that worthless twit of a princess would lead him straight to the unicorn?

Shivers coursed up and down his spine. Breath sobbed in his throat. Had iced-fire really glowed about the white stallion? Not in any of his eight reincarnations had power pooled with such overwhelming strength in one place. It had been a millennium since he had first sensed such forces. Eight lifetimes since he had seen a god walk the world and do the impossible.

Could it be? Could this horse be the one they had been awaiting, searched for in vain for so long?

Areme would know for certain.

Bloodwords, Godwords ran through Hessarde's mind, pounding at his skull. The words of the avatar of Senfar, Lord-God of Horses, bidding men to walk into immortal fire for redemption.

Hessarde knew the dread, the glory, when it had come his turn to walk the fire. Flesh splitting and bursting. White agony. A mass of sweat, blood and foam, melting into each other, burning, burning. And then his first reincarnation. He had held power of which common men could only dream. Power over death, and strength beyond equal. Power lost to the world for a millennium.

Until now.

At the postern, one warning glare was all Hessarde needed before guards uncrossed halberds and allowed him to race into the inner courtyard. A group of men lounged near a fountain set into the wall of the battlement, all clad in grey, morning bright on sword hilts and spurs. Areme's men, out of favour since the massacre, forced to keep a low profile. Hessarde had been singled out for the most onerous duty of watching over the princess for his zealousness in carrying out the king's orders. Orders he had neither liked nor agreed with, but which he could not refuse. Areme needed the king's favour, and made certain his men earned it.

Not for much longer.

Areme would not need anyone's favour soon.

Hessarde slid to a stop, scattering pebbles with his boots. 'Where's Areme?' he demanded.

Sedor looked up from his bench and yawned, teeth stark white against the black of his beard. 'What's your hurry, Hess?'

Hessarde dragged the soldier to his feet. 'I said, where in all the seven hells is Areme?'

Sedor's look of non-interest evaporated, replaced with a hard, searching glance. 'What is it?'

The others formed a loose knot around him, awaiting his answer.

Hessarde lowered his voice to a whispered hiss. 'I think I've found the unicorn.'

Every face became still, muscles taut in lines of tension. In an instant, the soldiers had become predators, ready for the kill.

'Where's Areme?' Hessarde whispered once more.

Sedor hooked his thumb over his shoulder.

A quick glance revealed a figure in the lee of a flame tree, grey cloak gathering shade from the heavy boughs above. Hessarde pushed Sedor aside and strode toward his master.

Areme sat with his back against the trunk, eyes closed. Hessarde coughed. When the knight failed to stir, Hessarde tapped Areme's boots with one booted toe. 'Lord Master?'

Areme drew his blade with a hiss and a glitter of dim light on steel, naked point coming to rest hard against Hessarde's throat. 'Do that again, and you're a corpse.'

Backing away, Hessarde gulped. 'But I've got such news, Lord Master.'

The knight's sun-browned face held no trace of expression. 'Worth a death sentence?'

'A thousand years' worth, Lord Master.'

Areme flowed to his feet to lean over Hessarde. His eyes transfixed his second. 'Where's the princess?' he demanded.

'Safe. With Knight Captain Jaien.' The mere mention of the knight's name twisted Hessarde's gut. He hated Jaien. Because Jaien had honour and could afford to keep it, even if it had almost cost him his life.

Even after a millennium of kings' service, the black stain of dishonour still clung to Hessarde and all of Areme's men. They had always been something less, always the dirt beneath men's boot heels; bandits and cutthroats could not be disguised by fine garments. They were the men kings called upon when unsavoury work was required. Men whose lives were so steeped in blood another boy's life hardly mattered.

But it did matter. It mattered to Hessarde. However callous he kept his facade. He had not wanted to kill the boy, or the mother. If only Jaien had ridden in a day later. Now they were all out of favour, reviled, and the king all fury. Callinor had wanted to make a point, but it had gone well beyond that, and now he wore the stain of dishonour, of despotism, the hatred of his kingdom. And he blamed Areme and his men even though he had given the order. And Areme blamed Hessarde, even though he would have done the same.

Hessarde had never had the luxury of honour. He had lived in the hope that in one of his lifetimes he would. But so far his lifetimes had been grim and bleak, awash with blood and infamy.

But this one, now – Gods – the hope was so close he could taste it.

He had found the unicorn. He would be forgiven. They all would be. And maybe, just maybe, when this was all over, Hessarde, Areme, all of them might finally become heroes instead of the black villains everyone thought them.

Emboldened now he had Areme's full attention, he clutched at the knight's arm. 'It's not about her. It's about the unicorn!'

Areme's face set in rigid lines of pain. 'Don't fuck with me, Hess.'

Hessarde kept his voice low. 'It's out there in the horse lines. White as blazing snow!'

'White?' Areme's brow creased. 'Someone brought a white horse to the king's market?'

'It's in the Graycor line.'

'Armindras.'

'I think it's his son holding the horse.'

Areme shook his head. 'Armindras must be trying to buy the king's favour by repeating his trick with Celestion. His lad's been called to service.'

'It's the horse, I tell you!'

'The unicorn could be any colour. What makes you think it's *this* horse?'

Hessarde glanced quickly around, met Sedor's pale eyes, the rest of Areme's men – all spirit beings, Shaheden – martyrs of the fire – men caught in an endless cycle of reincarnation, living unknown among mortals.

He bit his lip as he looked back at Areme. 'I felt it. Power. And I swear it's coming from that horse.'

Areme's gaze held his, timeless, like the man – an almost-god to the men who served him.

Please believe me. Hessarde fell to one knee. 'I swear, Lord Master, I'm not mistaken.' He clutched at Areme's hand, and kissed the ring upon it. 'By this ring I swear it.'

In Hessarde's mind the singing stone at the ancient fortress of Cacrlon stood, its heart shattered by a spear, and the god Senfar held the lifeblood of the world within his hands. Senfar had sealed Hessarde's fate, and thousands of men with him, doomed them to walk through infernal fire to meet their destiny.

From blood upon a crystal, blood of an innocent, blood of an immortal and blood of the world, the Lord-God of horses, Senfar, had forged the rings, the rings of the Horse Lords and granted them to those men he deemed worthy.

Men like Areme. Hessarde stared up at his master. A Horse Lord of Senfar.

The knight's silver eyes fixed Hessarde with all their ancient authority, weighed him. Measured his words. Then Areme stripped off his cloak to reveal the white surcoat emblazoned with the firefalcon of Mirador. 'Show me.'

'What about the men?'

Areme sheathed his sword. 'I want no one with me but you. If you're right, another massacre won't help.'

Chapter 10

Blood of the World

Irawan wasted little time ensconcing the princess in her rooms. With as much haste as decorum allowed, she strode to her own quarters, boots beating urgency upon flags, hem of her brocade dress swishing against grey stone walls. Soldiers drew themselves to attention along guarded corridors as she passed. They were well used to her, but it would not do to attract undue notice. She forced her pace to slow, though she wanted to match it to the racing of her heart. Once inside her bed-chamber, she closed the door and locked it, trembling fingers jangling the key in the lock.

The unicorn was here. She had never expected such fortune in her lifetime, or the chance to serve in so great a manner. She unlocked a drawer at her private writing desk. Sunlight, slanting through a high lancet, gilded the corner of a rosewood box, set afire two long hairs of scintillating red. In a slight breeze, gossamer-fine filaments stirred, curled about her fingers like living things, speaking silent testimony none had disturbed the box or its contents.

She hesitated. What if she was wrong? But Hessarde's wonder-struck face had told the truth of it. He had sensed the power as she had, seen luminous wisps of silver lifting from the horse's body – moonglow, starfire – flowing, whirling around the white stallion. Only adepts could sense such – the power of the Living Sphere – invisible to ordinary mortals.

She opened the box lid, revealing a shard of tourmaline. Her hand closed round the smooth obelisk, a piece of the murdered singing stone of Caerlon. Though lifeless, it still held a connection to stones standing half a league distant on an ocean cliff near Mirador, close enough she could mouth silent words, and call her Mistress to her from a temple hidden from the world of men by glamour upon glamour.

Far, far away on a mountain top, a veil of mist folded over living rocks. Beyond the veil, a white temple lorded it over a fortress cut into marble – a domain of white wherein dwelt the last gifted Ladies of the Grey Sands, and Myrrhye, Mistress of the Living Sphere.

In that domain, the Ladies waited, ever hopeful, for a throwback to that most ancient line of horses: Godsteeds – winged and horned beasts only the Mistress had been sanctified to see. They waited for a horse destined to transform into a unicorn, gods-blessed with power fast draining from the world with the breaking of the singing stone at Caerlon. A unicorn would give them the chance to reverse the ills wrought by the witch-queen Wyndarra.

Gods grant it might restore power enough that one acolyte, bound to the unicorn, could reverse the curses Wyndarra had cast: the plague upon Romondor, the slow death consuming that land and its people inch by murderous inch. One chance, before all singing stones stood forever silent and magic drifted from the world, and immortals died mortal deaths.

But no horse, however Gods-blessed, would bring Myrrhye to Irawan's side. The one acolyte Myrrhye still trusted to be loose within the world, Irawan was also the only woman in the kingdom apart from Myrrhye who could command the singing stones to send warning to Taiere. Few others had ever possessed the gift of portals. The greatest sorceress – Sarrouen – Myrrhye's rival, was a thousand years dead, no threat to any, nothing more than a forgotten memory.

Irawan whispered the incantation to open the portals between the stones of power. Time and space folded. Shadows and colour wove together. From the heart of the wavering light, a grey-cloaked woman appeared in shimmering resplendence before her, black eyes piercing pits of coal in a pale face wreathed in wisps of jet. The passing winters had left no imprint upon porcelain skin stretched over bone, emphasizing the cold curve of lip. But those dark wells of eyes, they held within their depths memories running thousands of lives deep.

It would have cost Myrrhye greatly but she hid her failing strength well, as, without preamble, she snapped, 'You summoned me, Irawan. For what cause? Has something happened to the girl?'

'No, Mistress.'

The girl. It seemed lately all the schemes of men and gods turned upon that gold-haired minx – so close a replica to her accursed mother, in looks and will.

'Has she shown some ability?' demanded Myrrhye, almost-hope in her voice as she stalked around Irawan, long white fingers idly tracing the obelisk that had summoned her.

Irawan shook her head, breathing deep the spikenard-scented air the Mistress had brought with her from the temple. 'No ability in that girl but which batting eyelashes can inspire in weak men. And you'll find precious few of those in this garrison.'

Irawan was glad she could answer with negation. She had lived through the queen's short but apocalyptic reign. She had no desire to live through another. She had come to Mirador at Myrrhye's command, not the king's order, to ascertain if the girl had inherited her mother's gift of wielding magic. But so far – nothing.

Most sorceresses came into their gifts at childhood. In a few, those powers lay dormant. But never as late as this. And Irawan judged this a good thing. As great as their need was, Irawan could not see any good in risking such a brattish, unmanageable wasp of a girl being unleashed upon an unsuspecting world with even a zingar's thumbfull of magic at her disposal.

But for now, there were bigger concerns, tangible.

'I've found the unicorn,' she said.

A lightning strike at Myrrhye's feet could not have produced greater surprise.

'In Mirador?'

'At the horse market. With the keeper of Graycor's son.'

Myrrhye's eyebrows rose. 'Armindras?'

'The very same.'

'Areme knows?'

'I summoned him.'

Myrrhye stood in silence for quite some time before saying, 'What news of the situation between Byerol and Pelan?'

Irawan smiled. Trust Myrrhye to keep abreast of the affairs of the kingdom. 'Close to five hundred horses missing at the last count. I await further reports from my scouts.'

'I don't like it,' said Myrrhye. 'Why this business of missing horses now?'

'Every instinct I have tells me it's more than mere thievery. The two dukes are intractable, throwing blame at one another, and the king makes no show of interceding. Ill feeling makes for poor diplomacy. They all wear the blame for not averting the Great War, for not standing up to the king in Riordehr's defence. And now they take out their frustration on each other.'

'Once I've set matters in Romondor to right, all that will resolve itself.' As rapidly as Myrrhye had turned the conversation, she stole Irawan's face, her form, her dress, with a dismissive flick of her wrist.

The Duchess of Belaron stared at her reflection standing before her, red hair coiffed high upon her head, threaded with moonstone, wisps elegantly coiled to fall like serpents either side of her cheeks, sliding across alabaster skin. 'You wear my visage well, Myrrhye,' she murmured, the words honed to the sharpness of a sword's edge.

Myrrhye's green borrowed eyes glittered like starlit frost as she smoothed emerald brocade across her flat stomach. 'You've lost weight, Irawan. It suits me.'

The duchess did her best to betray no response, schooling her face to stillness. Ever since Wyndarra had flouted every law of the Grey Ladies and released forbidden magic upon the world, Irawan had learned to hold her tongue as well as her powers firmly in check: not that her powers were many. Wyndarra had sucked up the power left in the world and spent it as fast as she could acquire it.

Myrrhye turned toward the door of the bedchamber, gliding over thick rugs scattered across flags. 'Await my return.'

Irawan clutched at her Mistress's hand, noting the ring upon her finger did not match the one on Myrrhye's, the ring of Belaron being green emerald, not crimson fire. 'Best not let Areme see that.'

Myrrhye grimaced a smile, and slid the ring bearing a red firefalcon edged in black from her middle finger. Handing it to Irawan, she said, 'Guard it well.'

At sight of the ring, forged one thousand years before, histories flooded Irawan's mind – the warning of the Horse God, Senfar, to Myrrhye on that fateful day the rings of the Horse Lords were formed.

'Take care to ensure your acolytes cause no more destruction to the Living Sphere; else Shahedur shall send the Spirit Lord to destroy all magic, remove every creature of the gods from your realm.'

Irawan shivered. After Wyndarra's transgression, could such a one already stalk the world? With hesitation at voicing the dreaded thought, she asked, 'The situation in Pelan. Do you think it is linked to the unicorn?'

Myrrhye's brow creased 'Who can say? For now we must proceed on that basis. I'll take no chances. Without magic, without the unicorn, we cannot undo what Wyndarra invoked.'

It was a race, maybe, against forces unknown that might be acting against them. A race for an intact world or a broken one.

Myrrhye placed her hand upon the door handle, slid a glance over her shoulder. 'What will the Duke of Byerol do?'

'He holds no love for the king, as well you know. His country fared worst in the Great War – the first commands launched against Romondor, the first men killed to still their tongues. He'll not ground his weapons, even on a direct order of the king to stand down, nor will he acknowledge his victims as being his brothers in fealty – kingdom men. The king taught him that lesson only too well. Soon he will tear across Pelan with all his men at his back.'

'And Pelan's answer?'

'The same.'

'Well,' said Myrrhye. 'It may provide confusion enough to give us the time we need.' And with that, she disappeared through the door without ever opening it.

Chapter 11

Sword's Kiss

Men converged upon the horse lines, talking and haggling, voices raised to be heard over the terrific din. Riders tried out horses, ran them on leads. Whips cracked. Soldiers shouted. Faces reddened and arguments flared.

Sihan tried to ignore the sea of faces – men ogling Aurion as though he was a sideshow freak. Aurion stamped his hoof, and Sihan laid a hand on the stallion's hot, thin-veined shoulder. His father stood nearby, between the last of the two bay colts he planned on trading. Sihan chewed upon his lower lip, glad of Jaien beside him, but missing Kheran's reassuring presence, and Tejas. He wondered where in all the thick crowds his friends were. Trying to steady his nerves with idle banter, he said, 'What did you call that knight?'

Jaien snorted. 'Shaheden – it's a soldiers curse. It means arrogant lucky prick. It's what we call men deserving to be dead for their recklessness but who have the Gods' own luck in battle.' He smiled, but Sihan, reading his eyes, detected shadows lurking there, and darkness underlying every word.

Jaien caught his appraising stare and said with a sharp edge to his voice, 'Leave it, Sihan. Just remember one thing while you are in Mirador. Stay clear of Areme's men, especially that one. They aren't worth your spit.' He glanced up the horse line. 'Gerhas is coming.' He leaned close. 'Is your father carrying steel? I wouldn't want him to stab Gerhas out of spite.'

'Gods, I hope not,' said Sihan with a tight smile, wondering if Jaien knew about the sword in the cart.

Jaien smiled, 'Let's hope the Gods' luck runs with us.'

Sihan's hand brushed against the pouch at his belt holding his mother's words. He had all the luck he needed right there. She was with him.

As Aurion snuffled at his hand, a lad raced up to Jaien, carrying a large bundle. Sihan was not familiar with all the liveries in the kingdom, but the boy's emblazons were unmistakable, the king's firefalcon stark across his white tabard. A king's emissary. The lad bowed to Jaien and whispered something beneath his breath. The knight's face paled.

'What is it?' Sihan demanded, heart racing, but Jaien was in no mind to answer, staring down at the bundle of white cloth the boy had presented as though holding a nest of spiders. Sihan reached out, folded back stiff brocade hemmed in red.

His heart picked up beat by beat. 'It's not what I think it is, is it?' He searched Jaien's face.

A closed, wary look settled upon the knight's features. 'It seems fate is with us. Strip Aurion,' he commanded.

Sihan obeyed, replacing the Graycor barding with frost-white brocade splashed with four firefalcons. A trumpet cry could not have called more attention to Aurion now.

'I hope you know what you're doing,' whispered Sihan.

'So do I,' answered Jaien, dragging his eyes away.

Horsemaster Gerhas drew nearer, one thumb hooked into the belt encircling his wide girth, king's tabard draped over boots deeply scarred down their length, the other hand stroking his short brown beard as he examined horses. Courtiers hung upon his every word, most, like the horsemaster, dressed in well-worn leather jerkins over woollen tunics and leggings tucked into calf-length boots. Gerhas paused before a group of Emor ponies, eyeing them with disfavour. Thin and scrawny, they were nothing like the well-toned stock of the bloodhorse ranges. Armindras had placed his line right next to them. A trader's ruse, placing quality beside inferior goods to make it look so much the finer.

When Gerhas began to discuss with the Emor keeper the better management of his stock, Sihan clenched his fist, patience wearing to threads. He wanted this over, the decision made, for good or ill.

More knights than he could count stood behind the horsemaster, squires at their heels, all battle-scarred men who had earned rank in the Great War and were held in awe by the nobility and populace alike. If this went bad, there was no escaping his fate.

One knight in particular caught his attention. Areme, champion of the High Princess of Mirador. He stood apart from the others, expression grave as he looked with more interest at the grass tussocks in the field than at anything else.

Gerhas reached the first of the Graycor horses and motioned to Areme, 'Have a look at this horse.'

The knight glanced up, sun shining on the bold, clear outline of his face, long black hair spilling over his white surcoat. The ranks of soldiers opened before him as he covered the ground to the horsemaster's side with long, reaching strides as though claiming possession of the field.

Gerhas waved to one of the bay colts Armindras held. 'The royal line of Graycor, if I'm not mistaken. Worth fifty falcons.'

'One hundred,' Armindras said, teeth set.
Gnarled face creasing into a frown, grey eyes cold, Gerhas regarded Armindras. 'Your pastures have been sound, I see.'

'Yes, Master.' Armindras bowed low, but when he rose, he confronted Gerhas with an equally chilled glare, the thoughts behind those narrowed eyes all too clear.

'Where's that lad of yours?' asked Gerhas, as if with detached interest.

With a look growing colder with every passing moment, Armindras nodded to Sihan who shifted uncomfortably as Gerhas's gaze raked over him.

'He's filled out well,' said the horsemaster, as if examining a horse. 'Looks strong enough to take up a sword. He's of age now, isn't he?'

Armindras answered, 'As well you know, Master.'

Sihan's heart almost stopped at the ice in his father's voice. He pleaded silently for Armindras not to say anything to court disaster.

Smiling at Armindras's black glare, Gerhas untied the bay colt from the tether line and tossed the lead rope to Areme. The knight looped the rope over the horse's neck and tied it to the halter to form a pair of reins. Long, sinuous – grace defined every line as he vaulted onto the horse. In a narrow space cleared of men behind the horse lines, he put it through its paces. With no apparent signals from its rider, the bay cantered, spun, danced to its rider's will.

Sihan's fingernails bit his palm. It was just so between him and Aurion when the white stallion deigned to obey, perfect synchrony of two minds and bodies as though conjoined in thought, action and will. He fought the urge to jump on Aurion's back, before all these men, and prove that day of testing at Yseth a lie.

When Areme returned to the line, the knight slid to the ground and beckoned a squire to step forward. The man presented a purse to Armindras, then led the colt away with the briskness natural to men who served knights. Areme returned to his position in the entourage. His gaze, however, now rested on Aurion.

So did the horsemaster's. Bypassing the other Graycor colt as if it had disappeared, Gerhas strode to the white stallion and threw a pointed glance at Sihan. 'There have been rumours flying all over the fortress that someone brought a white horse to market.' His disapproving eyes raked over the king's barding draped over Aurion. 'Explain the meaning of this.'

Gut churning, Sihan said in a tight voice, 'This is Aurion.'

Gerhas's grey brows tightened above his narrowed eyes. Walking to the stallion's shoulder, he swept back the barding and ran his hands over silken coat whiter than winter snow on the flank of a mountain. 'I see he does not bear the Mirador crest.'

Praying Aurion would not attack the horsemaster, Sihan said, 'He's not of bloodstock, Master.'

'How so?'

Armindras took up the answer. 'He was corpse-born. His dam wandered down from the Graycor Pass, six winters since, and died before giving birth.'

Features stern, Gerhas examined Aurion again. 'He's a fine horse, bloodstock or no. But he's *white*, Armindras. *White!* You know full well only the king may be borne by a white warhorse.'

'No king would be better mounted,' declared Sihan, determined to press his case. 'And Celestion is grey, not white. He was born dark, whereas Aurion was born white.'

Gerhas's face turned to stone, and anger replaced the cold courtesy hitherto exchanged. 'Don't trade words with me, boy. If I want to call Celestion white, then I'll call him white.'

Sihan refused to back down. 'Aurion is *true* white. A Godsteed fit for the king.'

Areme threw him a sharp glance. Shadows deepened the edges of the knight's lips, and for one moment, a subtle curve of a smile seemed to hover and disappear.

Behind the knight, courtiers side-glanced at each other. Not one moved. Not one spoke.

Gerhas impaled Sihan with another glare, then demanded, 'Whose preposterous idea was this?'

Stepping forth from Sihan's side, Jaien grated from between clenched teeth, 'Mine, Sir, actually.'

Gerhas's gaze swept over the knight, then his brow cleared. 'Ah, I see. Had trouble convincing the lad to come with you, heh?' He slapped Jaien on the shoulder. 'Clever ruse. Keep up that inventiveness, and I might even give you back your command.' He turned back to Armindras. 'Geld the animal and sell it to a farmer as a carthorse. And have the boy in barracks by tomorrow night so he can be fitted out.'

Armindras set his lips in a tight line, but Jaien clamped a hand on his shoulder. 'Don't.'

Shaking him off, Armindras growled, 'Get your hand off me!' In less than a heartbeat, fire replaced ice. Grabbing the hilt of Jaien's sword, Armindras brought the blade hissing into the light. He surged toward Gerhas, spinning everyone from his path. 'Oath breaker!' he hurled the curse like a spear straight at Gerhas.

The horsemaster drew his own sword, retreating only a step or two, eyes narrowed upon his accuser, blade raised in challenge. Shocked silence held for a heartbeat, then voices rose in uproar. Armindras lunged. Steel screamed against steel.

As men and horses scurried beyond range of the swords, Aurion reared, ears pinned, dragging Sihan. Flashing a wild look round, heart pounding, Sihan met Jaien's stricken eyes. 'Take Aurion!' he cried.

Before Jaien could move, a hand fell on Sihan's shoulder, pressed hard into his flesh. He half-turned to find Areme looming over him.

'Get that horse out of reach of the blades,' hissed the knight.

'But–'

'Do it.' Areme's quiet words were honed like a dagger and brooked no resistance. He shoved Sihan back, away from the combatants, away from the heaving mob, away from scores of white-and-red-clad guards descending upon the two antagonists, all with swords drawn.

War ran in Aurion's veins. Again he rose into full rear, Sihan only just holding him. If he got loose, no telling what might happen.

Sick to his stomach, Sihan tried to see through the surging mass of bodies following the fight. 'Do something!' he yelled at Jaien, frantic for his father, frantic to keep Aurion from going berserk. Jaien plunged through the ring of soldiers, but, weaponless, could do naught but keep beyond sword range.

Soldiers tried to grab a belt or swirling cloak to haul the assailants apart. Heedless, Gerhas and Armindras both struck with ferocity carrying the full force of their respective bulks behind it.

Areme melted through the ranks of knights. Drawing his sword, he waited calmly on the edge of the conflict, face set in a scowl. Once more Gerhas and Armindras locked swords, steel shrieking. Areme stepped forward and struck Heavenward. The single blow sent both swords flying, one ringing and clattering on the stone fortress road, the other thudding into a patch of thick grass. Unarmed, Armindras still hurled himself at Gerhas.

Jaien and several knights rushed forward and threw themselves upon the two men, prising them apart. Sihan strained to catch a glimpse of his father as more and more soldiers closed around the circle of knights. He loosed Aurion's reins to their full reach, but before he could burrow through the crowd, a reverberating voice rang out. 'Give back! Give back!'

Paralysed silence fell upon everyone, and into it stepped a horse as bright as morning, crest arched, mane a torrent of spun silver flowing in shimmering waves down to a broad chest. On its back rode a man in the white tabard of Mirador emblazoned with the crimson firefalcon edged in gold. The beating of Sihan's heart matched the thundering in his ears. He knew both instantly: Celestion, ridden by the King of Mirador.

The circle of knights gave back, parting for their ruler. The king dismounted, tossing his reins to a squire. Tall, commanding, he advanced, fair hair threaded with grey strands, face burdened and wrathful. He strode to where the two combatants stood with chests heaving, sweat dripping down their sodden brows, Areme standing between them.

'Sheathe your weapon,' the king said to Areme in a low voice, then turned to regard Armindras, severity all supreme in his grey eyes. 'You know full well to bare steel in civil company you imperil your life. To what purpose? Speak, I command you!'

Armindras gasped at breath, face florid and rebellious, eyeing Gerhas and the king equally with accusation. 'I fight for my son, and for justice, and promises broken.'

The king grew pale, but resolve laced his next words. 'You have cast disorder on the celebration of the Living Sphere; you offend the spirits of the earth and sky with this madness.' He nodded to Gerhas. 'This is my second. You know it. If just one drop of his blood had wet the ground, your life would have been forfeit.' He swept his arm around, encompassing all within reach. 'Do well to understand; here you bow to my authority. My rule is law. Accept these terms and put aside your disputes. They will not be entertained where my writ runs.' He stared at Armindras. 'You have broken an edict. You will cool your heels in the dungeon while I consider judgment.'

Sihan gawped, shocked and disbelieving.

Jaien shouldered past him, voice raised to carry full across the field. 'I demand audience!'

The king raised his gloved hand, his chilled order matching the cool, clear emphasis of his words. 'You have neither the right to speak, nor rank to demand my ear. Take care you are not the second to warm the dungeon flags this day.'

The air quivered with rage as Jaien bowed stiffly, then pushed back through the knights to Sihan's side. Anger told in every line of his body. 'Keep silent,' he warned, closing his hand around Sihan's arm.

Knights took hold of Armindras and dragged him, protesting, toward the fortress. The king reclaimed his horse, and Gerhas, his sword, and both men strode away with a retinue of courtiers trailing in their wake. Areme drew aside a little but did not follow the king.

There was wariness in a score of eyes scrutinizing Sihan, to see what he might do. Then, at the bark of soldiers, the remaining crowd dispersed with muted whispers.

Sihan rounded on Jaien. 'I trusted you!' He did not know why, but he had. Something about Jaien had made him believe in possibilities now only shattered dreams. 'You knew they'd never want Aurion.' His hand clenched upon the lead rope. 'And now Father's in the dungeon.'

'The chance was there.'

'Liar!' Hurt slid across wounded pride, extinguished hope. 'I trusted you,' Sihan repeated, choking on a declaration more accusation.

Jaien averted his eyes. 'I'm sorry.'

'Fuck sorry!' Sihan grabbed Aurion's halter. 'And fuck you!'

A hand closed on Sihan's shoulder. 'Leave it, boy,' said Areme. 'It's over. Jaien is not at fault here. The misdeed lies with your father.'

Rage and terror and despair all seething into mindless turmoil within him, Sihan returned Areme's black, chilled stare. Beyond thinking, he spat in the knight's face.

Something struck him, hard, sent him sprawling to the ground in a flurry of dust and pain. His face stung.

Areme stood over him. Nothing flickered in those silver eyes, no muscle moved in his face, but death was written there, nonetheless. With cold calm, Areme wiped the spittle from his cheek. 'You'd best learn courtesy, boy, and fast, else you'll end with a sword in your gut.' And with that, he strode away.

Chapter 12

Favour for a Favour

Hatred lit Sihan's eyes, hostility hitting Jaien like a hammer blow. The lad's clenched fists warned of a future battle, one that would get him killed. Jaien hauled Sihan upright and stood between him and Areme's retreating back. The touch of their hands sparked an unexpected fire that died as quickly.

'Sihan–'

'Don't.' Sihan yanked his hand free and took several steps backward. 'Just . . . don't.' Pushing past Jaien, he grabbed the lead ropes of the abandoned horses, pulling their heads away from trampled patches of grass. In bleak silence, he stalked back to the campsite. Jaien followed, not quite knowing what to do.

I trusted you.

Jaien had misused that trust. He had failed Sihan just as he had failed the boy in the fortress.

Muttering black curses, Sihan tethered the bay colt and stripped the king's barding from Aurion, throwing it on the ground as if it were soiled.

Determined to watch the lad in case he did something stupid, Jaien did his best to make himself useful. He picked up the cast-off barding, folded it and tossed it in the cart. Then he gathered wood for a fire.

For the rest of the day, Jaien and his charge stood apart, wearing time away in uncomfortable, angered silence. Whenever their eyes met, they clashed.

Creaking and grinding, wagons rolled by on the crowded road to the fortress. Men visited the camp to ask for news of Armindras, among them, Kheran and Tejas, and several other youths Jaien recognised from the journey from Yseth. Sihan's gruff manner sent them on their way soon enough.

Tejas stopped beside Jaien momentarily and said quietly, 'I've told Sihan we're all riding tomorrow at the tournament, every Graycor Senfari, every stable lad.' His throat seemed to choke on the words. 'We're all riding for his father. Not ourselves anymore. For Armindras. We've the best horses. One of us will win. That's the boon we're demanding. Armindras to be freed.'

'Ride hard, then,' said Jaien. 'Remember all I told you.'

Tejas's worried eyes met Jaien's. 'We won't fail him.' Then he paused before saying, 'Sihan's still going to ride, isn't he? He's got Spirit, but Aurion's the best we've got, if he behaves.'

Jaien could only shake his head. 'I don't know.'

'Will *you* ride?' Hope was a glowing ember in his eyes. 'You're the best Senfari in the kingdom. You won last year on Falcon.'

The thought had been burning in Jaien's mind also, but all he could offer the lad was: 'We'll see.'

A smile drifted across Tejas's lips, and he clasped Jaien's arm. 'Our thanks, Sir.' Then he followed Kheran from the camp.

When afternoon bled into evening, Jaien cast away discretion and approached Sihan, who sat brooding on a log near the horses. Jaien brought two mead-filled mugs, and dared to sit beside the lad, gaze directed at the ground. When he looked straight at Sihan, braving a face darkly shadowed by anger and distrust, Sihan swiftly turned his head away.

Shifting his body also an inch or two, Sihan said, 'What do you want?'

Gutted, Jaien tried to ignore the widening gulf between them. 'What do I want? Your father set free. You back in Graycor. My commission back.' *Justice. A dead boy living once more. You to trust me.* He held out one mug. 'A host of things I can't have.'

Face empty and ungrateful, Sihan took the mug.

Star-drenched night closed down around them. Hillsides jewelled with the burning raiment of bonfires. A group of young women pushed through the willow fronds, hair braided with snowdrops. 'Come dance!' they cried, running up to Sihan and Jaien, holding out their hands.

'Go away,' snapped Sihan.

Jaien waved them off. They ran through the trees to another nearby campfire where several men smiled at them. The girls joined hands, casting wild shadows as they circled flames in a frenzy of delight. Joining in their merriment, the young men jumped up and stamped around the bonfire, singing boisterously, vying with each other to catch the girls' attention. But Sihan and Jaien just sat, ignoring the revellers.

Sihan's pained voice finally broached the silence between them. 'What's going to happen to Father?'

Jaien stared at his boots. 'I don't know. What he did was madness.'

'Isn't there anything we can do? Speak on his behalf?'

Jaien shrugged. 'Your father drew steel on the horsemaster in full view of a hundred knights. It's not like we can invent a story, claim it didn't happen, or not in the way it did. You can't make the king doubt his own eyes.' He cast a wary glance at Sihan. 'The tournament tomorrow . . . You have to ride.'

'What for? You saw Gerhas. He wants nothing to do with Aurion. And the king didn't spare Aurion a glance.'

'The king didn't get a chance, what with two men on the edge of murdering each other.'

Deep burning hurt lit the depths of Sihan's eyes. 'Surely someone can speak for my father!'

Jaien tensed. A girl flashed into thought. A girl in trouble. No. *More* than a girl. He recalled her words – *A favour for a favour*. He rose swiftly to his feet. 'Not speak. *Command*.' Jaien closed one hand over Sihan's braced, reluctant shoulder. 'Stay here. Do nothing. Await my return.'

Sihan shifted, turning his back once more.

Only one way to bridge this rift.

A plan forming with every step, Jaien hurried through the tangle of camps and tents to his father's campsite, picking up branches along the way. A poor peace offering, but he was unable to think of anything better. He found Cenriin leaning against the wheel of his cart, eyes closed.

With a loud crash, Jaien dropped the wood next to the fire. The old man started from his daydreaming, staring wildly about him, then scowled upon seeing Jaien. Rubbing his eyes, he said, 'I'll have you for that, my lad.' Then he took a ladle and tested the brew boiling in a pot over the fire.

'Smells good,' said Jaien, shoving more wood into the flames. He noted two bowls and two tankards set beside the cartwheel, and bit down a smile.

'What took you so long? I was expecting you at dusk.' Cenriin doled a big helping of helbut stew into one wooden bowl, and shoved it at Jaien. 'Eat. You look too thin. No wonder a man my age was able to steal your sword. Damned sloppy of you. And no wonder you lost your command.'

Jaien quirked an eyebrow. 'You knew?'

The old man threw him an incredulous look. 'With the king and the horsemaster blaring it to the Heavens, how could I not?'

Jaien lowered the bowl, wondering exactly how much his father really knew. Kneeling, he drew a wine pouch from a sack hidden by the cartwheel. Uncorking it, he poured roseberry wine over pale-yellow tubers.

'Hold!' cried his father. 'Helbut is perfect on its own. No need to ruin it.'

Jaien leaned close to his father, pushing the bowl back at him. 'Can you take this to Sihan? The wine will help him sleep.'

His father snorted. 'I might have known the conversation would get round to that lad.'

Jaien did not bother to disguise the desperation in his voice. 'I need your help.'

The old man watched him from beneath lowering brows. 'You're going after Armindras, aren't you?'

'Yes.'

His father's strong hands clamped on his arm. 'Let well enough alone. Armindras can stew in his own pot.'

Jaien shook his head. 'I can't let matters stand as they are. I won't.' He stood, brushing off his leggings. 'I don't know how you can live with yourself. Defending a king who sent a country to war on behalf of a jealous, spiteful woman.'

Anger flared in his father's eyes, and deep pain. 'Would you have me speak my mind and languish in the dungeon, too?' He rubbed the back of his neck. 'The time for speaking of such things is past. Let the past be buried with the dead.'

'What if the dead refuse to keep it buried?'

His father spat. 'Only the living want to dig up ills best left forgotten.'

'Go sit with Sihan, but tell him nothing. You're right. He doesn't need to know what I know. That my father and his were both murderers.'

Jaien started to walk away, when his father called, 'Take your sword, boy.'

The old man grunted to his feet and pulled a sword from the back of his cart. 'Damned sloppy. Losing your sword twice in one day. Twice!' He did not hold up his fingers to reinforce the measure, and Jaien's gut tightened. Always the same, their meetings, this one ended on broken custom and broken hearts and shame. He took the sword and sheathed it, hesitated, asked, 'Have you a rider for Wedge in the trials?'

'Of course.'

Pain dug into Jaien. 'Who?'

A smile touched his father's lips. 'Why, you, of course. Stupid boy. Now be about your errand, and I'll go sort out this lad of yours.' He muttered as he picked up two bowls and a pitcher of ale and tramped off into the darkness.

Jaien wiped at his eyes, then strode toward the fortress, driven by haunting memories of a dead boy, that wasted life never longer than a heartbeat from his mind. He would not let it happen again. Could not.

In Mirador fortress, crowds stood thick around night traders' stalls, a maelstrom of merchants, soldiers, some haggling while drinking mint tea, others watching jongleurs, acrobats, but all the populace wearing the same agonised looks of desperation as bears with rings through their noses dancing for their lives. Everywhere air wafted thick with smoke from bonfires and roasting spits, and tension. Jaien pushed his way through to the forecourt, then across an arched bridge over a canal to the palace.

Beware. Beware. This way lies death. Jaien froze for a heartbeat as that voice called on the wind. He shook it off. Death lay here well enough, without the voice reminding him.

As always after dark, there was a strong watch set, all entrances to the inner palace shut and barred, but the king's guard let him pass, men stiff at attention, faces impassive. He was out of favour, but he had done the deal with Travall who would have spread the word. After his flogging, they would think him cowed, especially with his men and his father virtual hostages.

He entered the first hall through a small door to the side. His bootfalls echoed on flags in the long hall, walls hung with tapestries of horses in flight or grazing in summer pastures. Nothing of war or the dead queen. *Fitting*, thought Jaien. *Pity the king did not banish her from the palace the moment he set eyes on her.* His fist clenched. *Pity no one thought to drown her at birth.* He forced the thought from his mind. No use to think such things when he needed to ask for help from her after-echo.

Before him, guards locked halberds.

'Your business, Sir?' asked one.

'I seek audience with the princess.'

A guard beyond them snapped his fingers. A page, in white tunic and leather breeches, came running. Jaien recognised him as the boy who had delivered the king's barding to the horse lines earlier. His hopes rose.

'Announce Knight Captain Jaien,' said the guard with brisk efficiency.

Jaien winced, unused to his new title. He waited until the page returned. Face flushed, the boy whispered to the guard, who turned to Jaien. 'You're to wait outside the antechamber. You'll be summoned. But before you go, I respectfully request you leave here all arms.'

Jaien gave up his sword and daggers, biting down a grimace at losing his sword a third time in one day. At least this time it went by choice.

The guard stepped aside and Jaien followed the page to the hallway of the princess's apartments. When they reached the end of the hall, the page ran to the princess's door and bowed to the guards before knocking. A maid, hair drawn back and coiffed, peeked out. Low voices exchanged words. The maid's gaze slid over Jaien in a rapid, all-embracing glance, then she disappeared inside the room.

After some little while, the maid peered out once more and whispered again to the boy. He scurried back to Jaien. 'You may enter,' he said, with as much stiff formality as he could muster, nodding his head in salute.

'My thanks for your loyal service.' Jaien gave the boy a pat on the head, then strode to the door. Like the others, the guards at the princess's door stared ahead as though sightless and mute.

The maid stepped aside and Jaien entered the anteroom to the princess's chamber. Thick rugs muffled his boots, his senses immediately swathed in heavy vanilla scent. With her veil in her hands, Orlanda sat on a divan, blonde hair pulled back in a coif set with moonstones. The severe style accentuated her eyes and sunken cheeks. Her dress of white brocade hung loose upon her, though it was cinched at the waist.

Jaien frowned, wondering how he had not noticed her thinness before. But then, he had not cared to notice much in a girl who promised to flower into a replica of her mother – may the dead woman's bones rot in the cursed sea. Shaking off those thoughts, Jaien touched his right knee to the ground.

'Leave us,' said Orlanda, with a dismissive wave of her hand to the waiting maid. When the girl left the room, Orlanda motioned for him to rise. 'You have requested audience. For what business, sir?'

'Not business, Highness. Rather, I've come to ask a favour.'

She motioned to the divan. 'Sit, then, and speak freely.' Everything in her tone and mannerism spoke false, and her eyes flashed warning at him.

Jaien hesitated, only just stopping himself from casting a quick look around. 'Forgive me, Highness.' He coughed. 'My attire . . . I've had no chance to . . .'

Taking up his cue, she motioned to the doors leading to her garden. 'Or perhaps you'd prefer to take the air.'

So stiff, that courtesy, matching the jerking way she rose slowly to her feet, the careful, measured tread. The soft rustle of her dress did not disguise the shift of feet behind a closed door to the right.

'Speak low,' Orlanda whispered, passing close, her utterance a shade above a breath. 'Otherwise without doubt he will hear us.'

Jaien followed her into the garden, boots crunching on the gravel path between withered rose bushes, noting again her unfluid stride, the braced shoulders. He leaned close and spoke low. 'You are wise to be wary of stretched ears.'

The light of torches softened her grave features as she pressed a finger to his lips. 'You think me so frivolous I know nothing of palace intrigues?'

More and more she confused him. The few times he had ever seen her she had been stiff and formal at court. Yet at the horse lines she had been wild and rebellious. Right now it was hard to take her measure. She seemed to be hovering between the two. Perhaps she had been chastised for her escapade at the horse market earlier, and was chastened somewhat as a consequence. There were rumours the king beat her. Again, he examined her closely. Had Callinor discovered it was her that had presented Sihan with king's barding?

'I'm waiting,' she prompted.

Jaien inclined his head, forcing the disturbing image from his mind. 'I'm revising my opinion.'

Suddenly the audaciousness he had seen in the girl at the horse lines returned to her face. 'Good. Now speak your piece. I must attend my father and have little time. Be candid, if it will serve to get us faster to the end you desire.' Even so, every word was strained, and her gaze darted always to the shadowed doors, on the lookout for expected threat.

Sensing the chance might pass as soon as it was offered, Jaien plunged in with all oars. 'I seek the release of a prisoner.'

'A prisoner?' Orlanda's slanted eyes widened. 'Who? Why?'

Jaien averted his gaze. 'It's a private matter. Let us just say he has been treated less than his due.'

'By whom?'

'Your father.'

Her expression became unreadable. 'What you ask is impossible.'

'Not for the woman I see before me.'

The smile touched her lips once more, self-deprecating. 'Spare me your flattery, Jaien. I know well how your tastes fly.'

'I was referring to your rank. Order the king's guards, and they will obey.'

'The king's guards answer only to the king, the horsemaster or the king's champion, Travall.'

'You outrank all men except your father and the horsemaster.'

Her eyes glittered in the light of torches set in braziers among the roses. 'Who is this man, that you seek to flout the king's will?'

'The father of a friend who is sore in need of him.'

'This friend. He's the lad from the market?'

'Yes,' answered Jaien, wondering how she knew.

A hint of coquetry lit her eyes. 'He's your lover?'

'No.' Jaien damped down surprise at her candour, caught off guard as he had been by the wild rebel at the horse lines.

'But still, you love him?' She harried him as a dog would a bone.

Jaien started. Till now his only thoughts of Sihan had been to answer Senfar's call and prevent the lad's death. Then he recalled the deep pain when Sihan had turned away from his hand. Was there more? He was not sure. He met the princess's eyes squarely, recognizing a need within her for an answer to her taste. 'Yes,' he said, surprised at the ease of the lie.

'Without hope of return?'

No need for a lie this time. 'Yes.'

She was silent for a long while, then spoke as if in a dream, 'Of that, I know something.' Walking to the parapet, she stared out over a plain strewn with bonfires resembling myriad flaming stars crashed to the ground. 'Do you know, when I was at the market, your father asked me to try and convince you of the error of your ways. But I don't think love is an error, do you?'

Jaien braced his back. 'No.'

Orlanda tilted her head, studying him. 'How long have you known this lad?'

'Forever.' The word came unbidden, and on his lips the utterance was devotion and somehow, truth.

A softer look entered Orlanda's blue eyes. 'Yes, I know that feeling also.' Suddenly her eyes burned into dazzling brightness, as though they had stolen flames from the bonfires on the plain. 'You'll do anything to save him, even risk another flogging, or death?'

'I will.' He met her eyes directly. 'I think you know something of that, also.'

She stiffened, fire turning to ice. 'All wounds heal,' she said coldly.

The shock of her admission had Jaien hesitating. If the king had beaten her for her escapade, what would he dare if he discovered her complicity in Jaien's plan?

As if reading his thoughts, the princess said, 'Don't fear for me. He couldn't break you. He won't break me. Besides, he needs me for Romondor. Now speak, and hurry. There's more, I know it.'

No longer holding back, he said, 'The heralds proclaim you will take the victorious horse from the tournament as your mount. The plan is for Sihan to ride. On the white stallion.'

Knowing eyes met Jaien's. 'This morning your sights were set on the king.'

'They still are.'

She sniffed. 'You think Callinor so vain he'll claim the horse?'

'If it wins. You must see to it Aurion is allowed to take part in the trials.'

'You ask much.' She was silent for an age, brows knotted in concentration. When she spoke again, her voice was all steel. 'If I do this, it comes with a price.'

Throughout the interview he had sensed something at war within her. Heat and passion suppressed by cold intent. She knew of Jaien's flogging. She knew his request was treason. She knew he had no love for the king. The king had beaten her. Could this impetuous, rebellious girl be plotting some form of revenge? From all he had seen of her that day she was certainly reckless enough to launch into an ill-advised exploit. Suspicion tightened Jaien's voice. 'What price?'

'A favour for a favour.' Her lips curved in the feline smile of a predator. 'A trade.'

'What sort of trade?' Impatient, he waited.

Orlanda walked around him, fingers trailing along the back of a garden seat. 'Oh, nothing very much. Just a man I can trust on the postern gate.' Despite the too casual tone, there was decisiveness and scheming in her eyes.

Jaien hedged. 'You already have them. There's not a soldier in this fortress you cannot trust.'

Orlanda came to a halt before him, and her voice lowered. 'You know well what I mean. I want a man who will ask no questions, tell no secrets, let me pass with no recollection of my passing.'

'You forget; I'm no longer in command.'

Orlanda snorted. 'Don't make the mistake I've convinced everyone else to make. I'm no fool. One thousand men threatened to resign their commissions for you, and all ten of your knight captains stared down Gerhas and told him to go to all seven hells. That sort of loyalty isn't lost by stripping a man of rank. You only have to whisper a word, and your orders will be obeyed.'

Jaien regarded her with increasing interest. 'You seem to have my measure, Highness, and I feel with every moment I have less and less of yours.'

A small smile touched her lips. 'Perhaps that's just as well.' Her blue eyes hardened as she held out her hand. 'Let's not haggle further. You want one man. I want one man. A fair exchange.'

Jaien stared hard at her, trying to fathom her purpose. Unable to, he did the only thing he could. He bowed low, touching his lips to her fingers, and said, 'So it is.'

Chapter 13

Ill Met by Moonlight

Alone, not knowing what else to do, Sihan gathered firewood among the trees, returning to the campfire with arms weighed down. He dropped the timber with a clatter, then just stood, powerless to move or even think, staring down at lifeless pieces of wood.

The moon hung in the sky, a huge ball illuminating branches of willow with silver dust. Distant bonfires blazed through the trunks, and torchlit processions of revellers marched along the main thoroughfare to the fortress. So many strangers, oblivious to his agony. The smell of smoke thickened the air. Shaking his head, clamping down all emotion, Sihan kicked a log onto the fire with his boot. Though the flames heated his face, he shivered.

A gentle breeze touched his cheeks, so soft it might have been a caress. Sihan closed his eyes. He thought of his mother, imagining it was her stroking his hair, dark tranquil eyes watching him without judgment. He thought of her note in the pouch at his belt. He had failed her. And now he had lost his father, too.

He raked his fingers through his hair, pressed them hard to his temples. A band of pain constricted his head, as though he had worn an ill-fitting helm too long. His eyes stung. He blinked. No use crying. No use standing here. He had to find some way to help his father.

What could he do? What he really needed was to undo what had been done. If he had chosen another horse instead of Aurion for the Senfari test. If his father had not drawn sword. If . . . Sihan clenched his fist. There were so many things that might have been done, and none that could be undone.

Twigs snapped to his left. Turning, Sihan found a man approaching, bulk dark against the flames beyond. Joy surged for one fleeting instant. Then firelight caught the man's gnarled face.

Hope disintegrated to dust. Sihan's shoulders slumped, heart bleeding all over again.

'No need to look like that, lad.' Without preamble, the grey-haired man shoved a bowl at Sihan. 'Here. Eat.' He sat by the fire, stretching out stocky legs. When Sihan did nothing but stare at the bowl, the man glanced at him from beneath straggled brows. 'It's not poisoned, lad. Go on. Don't let it go to wasting. Two candle lengths it took to brew. Two!' He held up one hand with two fingers extended.

Sihan sat, loth to eat, but unable to refuse in the face of such courtesy. He choked on the first bite, coughing as fire trickled down his throat.

'My son's doing,' the old man said. 'Jaien always puts to ruin what nature creates well enough plain.'

Sihan shot the man a swift glance. 'You're Jaien's father?'

'The very same. Name's Cenriin. With two i's.' Again he held up two fingers. 'Now eat.'

Sihan obeyed, half-coughing, half-choking.

A soft nicker drifted from the riverbank. Sihan glanced to Aurion. The stallion tossed his head and stood alert, staring intently into the dark. Nearby, the two bay colts did likewise.

'Too much excitement for the young whippersnapper,' said Cenriin. 'Once he's gelded, he'll calm down.' He stopped, staring at Sihan.

Everything inside Sihan wanted to break, the words a final seal on his failure. He forced himself to that dark place of unfeeling detachment. What did it matter if Aurion was gelded? There were more important matters. 'What's going to happen to my father?'

Cenriin patted him on the shoulder. 'Nothing, if my son has his way.'

When Aurion nickered again, Sihan said, 'I–I should check the horses.' Before he could even stand, Aurion's trumpeting neigh split the dark.

Sihan spun to find the stallion rearing in the firelight, straining at his lead rope, a shadow-figure standing before him. Drawing his dagger from its sheath, Sihan jumped up and ran toward the horse. As he did, another grey-cloaked figure emerged from the darkness.

'Get away from him!' Sihan shouted, not sure if he was protecting Aurion from the intruders, or them from what the stallion might do.

'Hold, lad. We are not your enemies.' With long, slender fingers seeming far more suited to handling a foil than the broadsword he wore at his belt, Knight Commander Areme drew back the cowl of his hood. His ensilvered gaze passed over Sihan at leisure, like a sharpened dagger slowly caressing a throat it meant to cut.

Aurion steadied, and bent his head down to the other grey-cowled figure, nuzzling a delicate, outstretched hand. A feminine voice emanated from the hood of Areme's companion. 'What coin for this horse?'

She was no farmer's wife looking for a plough horse or cart dragger. What could she want with Aurion?

Sihan glared at Areme. The knight had struck him earlier. Had he come now to strike a double blow? Take away his only chance to win his father's freedom? Jaien had warned him to stay away from Areme's men. Surely he meant Areme also. Placing a possessive hand on Aurion's neck, Sihan said, 'I'm sorry. This horse is not on the market. I ask with respect you step away.'

Aurion pinned his ears and snapped at the woman, teeth closing on air. Not cowed, she leaned in to the horse, whispered something under her breath. Aurion lowered his head, though his ears remained flat. She fingered the circular whorl of hair in the middle of the stallion's forehead and said, 'If he was any other colour, this would be a star.' Then she turned back to Sihan. 'Tell me, what is the greatest value placed upon a horse selected by the Royal Horsemaster? Name that value, and I will increase it sevenfold.'

Sihan gasped. Seven hundred falcons were beyond the wealth of any but the nobility. The woman had to be of high birth that she could toss out such coin. Still, money would avail him not. Shaking off bewilderment, Sihan responded, 'I'll not see him as a palfrey. Aurion is worthy of a *king*.'

'Worthy or not, that door is closed to you.' A hint of steel edged the soft voice. 'But there are other paths that may lead you to what you seek. The princess will claim the winning horse from the warhorse trials. She is the future queen. The king will not gainsay her if she chooses to be borne by a white horse. Do you accept this fate may yet prove worthy of your steed?'

'Women don't ride warhorses!' Cenriin stepped forward, face suffused with colour. 'And the king made a deathbed vow.'

'All things change,' said the woman.

Still bristling, Cenriin demanded, 'Even if what you say is true, how the blazes are you going to get the horse into the trials? Gerhas has made his feelings quite clear on the matter.'

'My problem, not yours,' said Areme.

Sihan glanced around, half-expecting to see Jaien lurking in the shadows. Perhaps the knight was making good on his promise to help. How else would Areme be here if Jaien had not told him the plan they had concocted in Graycor? And the princess. She was the future queen. The legends of the Godsteeds were that they were bonded to monarchs. Could it be Aurion was meant for the princess? And if Aurion won, Sihan would be able to ask a boon. It was too late for himself, but, like Kheran and Tejas had said, he could save his father. It was one thing he *could* undo. He would beg for his father's release. Desperate not to let the chance slip by, he inclined his head to the woman. 'Seven hundred falcons and I agree to all you ask, providing I claim the king's boon.'

'Then it is settled.' She turned her back to Areme and presented a plump purse of soft leather, chinking with the glittering sharpness of gold. 'A thousand falcons, do with it as you will.'

Sihan stared at her pale hand, the middle finger adorned with a ring bearing the firefalcon edged in black crystal. Sihan's heart drummed. Only members of the royal family were allowed to wear rings bearing the crest of the realm. Could this be the princess herself?

His mind span, turning on all his childhood dreams that might become reality on his father's release. Then he thought of Aurion. Would the horse behave? He had lost a day of work. He would need to prepare now, salt, herbs, water, everything he needed so he had enough time to ride Aurion to obedience on the morrow. He would take him early to the tourney field . . .

The woman turned her attention to Areme. 'You shall ride the horse in the trials.'

Her words cut across Sihan's thoughts like a scythe. 'What? Who?' He stared unbelieving from one to the other.

'Areme will ride the horse,' repeated the woman.

'No,' said Sihan, dumbfounded. 'You don't understand. I'm the only one who can ride him. He won't let anyone else on his back.'

Areme's lips curled in disgust. 'The purse is yours. The deal has been struck. You've lost all right to Aurion.'

'You don't understand,' repeated Sihan. 'He'll kill anyone but me if they try to get on him.'

A sly smile slipped across Areme's lips. 'Be careful in your choice of words, boy. You were trying to sell him to the king this morning. If your words are true, some might accuse you of conspiring to regicide.'

Sihan spluttered, railing at the accusation.

'Enough!' The woman raised her hand, forestalling his protest. 'Areme is the finest rider in the kingdom. There is no horse he cannot ride. He shall not disadvantage your stallion.'

Sihan recalled Areme riding the Graycor colt. Perhaps what she said was true. But when he looked at Aurion he remembered that fateful day in Yseth, and before that, all the Senfari who had failed to tame the beast within. How could a man who had never set eyes on Aurion before this day possibly ride him? Sihan could not risk it. Aurion had to win. For his father's sake. With grim determination, Sihan refused to concede. 'No, this is my task.'

Areme fixed him with a long, hard gaze. 'Your part in this is over.'

Sihan threw the jangling purse to the ground. It sat, sagging and bloated, like an overfilled wineskin. 'If Aurion loses, this is worthless. Only victory will free my father.'

Areme's fingers crept to rest upon his sword hilt. 'I've warned you once already about discourtesy, boy.' He kicked the purse to Sihan's feet. Bursting, it released a slithering stream of gold falcons. 'You made the agreement. I grant no amendment.'

Sihan stood his ground, fingers clamping hard upon his dagger. 'I will ride for my father.'

Areme's hand tightened on the sword hilt; eyes sharp with annoyance. 'Do your best to think of him, then. He'll want you alive, I'll warrant, when all this is over.'

The threat was so real Sihan could taste it like the blood he had tasted when Areme had struck him. But still he could not back away. Driven beyond sense by the need to help his father, he said with force, 'I *do* think of him. He is *my* kin. *Mine*. Not yours. And I'll do all I can to save him.'

In a moment of fraught silence, Areme's eyes barely flickered, the gleam of them ice, but before the knight could respond in word or deed, the woman stepped between them. Inclining her head to Sihan, she said with soft insistence, 'None here doubts your resolve, but I counsel you to wisdom. If you want to achieve your aim, do not deviate from my directions.'

The flat finality of her voice made it clear the conversation was over. Without another word, she took her leave, slipping between more grey-cloaked men emerging from the darkness. Torchlight slid along the blades of drawn swords.

Areme went to shove past Sihan, then paused abruptly, shoulder to shoulder. Granite inflected his voice as he said, 'My second, Hessarde, and my men will guard the horse until the trials are over. Obey their commands as though they were my own.' Then, he turned slowly, clapped his hand on Sihan's shoulder, fingers pressing down with bone-breaking strength. 'Understand this. Your hide or your father's, they're all the same to me. But if one hair of that horse is harmed, I'll flay the skin from both you and Armindras.' Areme released the death grip threatening to cave Sihan's knees. Though he nodded civilly to Cenriin, his final words, laced with perilous calm, were directed squarely at Sihan. 'Until the trials begin, you don't leave that horse's side.'

Nonplussed by this unexpected turn of events, Sihan just stared after Areme as he strode away. A part of him wanted to rail against the knight's arrogance, whatever the cost, but fraying threads of sense stayed his hand and his voice.

He exchanged a glance with Cenriin. There was no going back and undoing the past, but was there now a way forward? He had seen Areme ride, man and horse, one. Nothing for it but to hang on and trust Areme would not betray his hopes, and that Aurion, miraculously, might yield.

Cenriin knelt to gather the scattered coins, and looked hard at Aurion, as though he was trying to measure whether the horse was worth the price paid. 'Do you truly think he can win?'

There was but one answer to that impossible question. Sihan's fingers tangled in Aurion's coarse mane. 'He has to.'

Chapter 14

Shadows of the Past

Orlanda sat beside her father at the high table, hardly eating, drinking little, tasting nothing. On her right, the duchess kept silent, slipping food in tiny slices beneath her veil. The restrained talk of knights and courtiers passed unregarded as Orlanda stared at an empty seat at the long table stretching down the hall.

As on every other occasion lately, Areme was missing. Even after her display at the horse market, he had made no appearance, and no attempt to censure her. Her fingernails dug into her palms. What would spur him to her side?

Her father might have been equally absent for all the attention he paid her, grey eyes trained more upon meat or fowl. He took ale, or spoke quietly to a knight at his left. Never one glance for her, never a word. She wanted to scream, *"Am I a ghost you ignore me so?"* But she had earned a whipping for such not long past, and after the beating for her escapade to the horse lines and stealing a king's barding, she had no wish to add blood to her new-earned weals. Her flesh still burned, the hurt of ten lashes less than wounded pride, dishonour, shame, and lost love. Flesh would knit in scars of pale pink, but not the inner wound. That ran deeper than the strike of a sword.

Abruptly, chair scraping on slate, her father rose from the table. Orlanda stifled a relieved sigh. She wondered what thoughts filled those distant eyes, that lofty brow. His queen, no doubt, dead long winters past.

There were no touches of her mother in the hall. Perhaps because, except for the duchess and Orlanda, the company was male, and the decoration reflected a male domain – warhorses embroidered on wall hangings, tall, rangy beasts with fire in their eyes and arrogance in the arch of their necks. Even the smell was of horses and well-oiled leather, not the perfume of coiffed women. High-backed chairs, the long, plain wood table, but no softness, not even rugs graced the slate floor.

Orlanda closed her eyes, imagining her mother. Just three winters at the queen's death, she recalled only a haze of anger-filled eyes, the slamming of doors, silent, haughty death on alabaster skin, and a man weeping his loss, heart bleeding to ice. Pain. So much pain.

A sense of ease cut among the men following Callinor's departure, but Orlanda sat, braced, abandoned once again. Servants circled with caskets of wine and ale and players plucked at harps and bards sang. Orlanda stabbed at a slice of orange with a knife. A soft shuffling of goatskin boots on the stone floor barely caught her attention, but low whispering caused her to regard a page with lips pressed to the duchess's ear. Nothing stirred in that woman's proud face, but fire glittered behind the dark, thoughtful eyes. The page stepped back, bowed, then walked briskly to a side door.

The duchess turned and touched Orlanda's arm. 'Your Highness, I beg leave to retire.' She stood, her blue velvet gown trimmed with white ermine at the collar and sleeves falling in graceful folds to the floor. Sweeping from the hall via the main doors, she did not deign to meet the approving stares of admirers, face fixed with an air of indifference, lips curved in a vague, derisive smile.

Orlanda arose and slid unnoticed to the side door where the page had left. No guards stood at attention. Orlanda frowned as cold wrapped round her. No night passed without men-at-arms set at every door, especially in the inner palace, where all gates were closed with sunset, barred and bolted. Where were they?

Hushed voices drifted along the hallway. She lifted the hem of her dress and sneaked toward them, taking care to stay in the shadow of pillars. When she reached the arched door of the closed palace courtyard, Orlanda angled for a position in earshot but in cover. Four men stood with heads bent close, all in guards' livery. Orlanda frowned. Areme's men. Why had they left their posts?

The voices stopped, interrupted by the clatter of hooves on cobbles. A rider, clad in a dust-stained tabard of blue and white, cantered into the court. His mount, lathered from poll to flank, checked to a weary, sliding halt. The four men rushed forward. The rider wilted, legs giving way as he dismounted.

'Water!' yelled one man, bracing the rider's weight. 'Someone see to his horse!'

A squire raced for water. Another grabbed the trailing rein and led the horse away to the inner stables. The steed walked, head groundward, sides heaving, steam rising like mist from neck and flank, bloodied foam dripping from its maw.

'What news?' asked a sharp voice, and the duchess appeared from the opposite side of the courtyard.

Slung between two guards, the rider bowed his head in reverence. 'My Lady,' he gasped. 'The Duke of Pelan . . . sends me to bring you word . . . There have been more horses stolen.' His breaths came in heavy huffs.

'How many? Where? How long to carry the news here?'

'Half a moon's cycle,' he gasped, answering the last question first. 'Two score remounts for the couriers, at least . . . and as many men. No better time . . . could we have made.'

'How many stolen?' repeated the duchess.

'A good one hundred . . . on the border with Byerol and Pelan . . . the wood of Calernon.'

A squire arrived with a tankard and held it to the man's greedy lips. 'Slowly, slowly,' the squire muttered as the courier tried to gulp it down.

Water soaking his tabard, the rider closed his eyes. As his breathing quieted, he continued, 'The keeper says he was herding mares through a forest at dusk, a narrow trail, shortcut to the lowland pastures. A mob of rustlers attacked the rear, took off with the wet mares, most still with foals at foot.' He paused, eyes blinking open to the light of the fires in the ironbaskets around the court.

'Calernon is near four Byerol garrisons,' said the duchess. 'Why were more guards not posted?'

'They were sent, but the keeper panicked before they ever reached him. He swore men had been stalking the horses for days. He did not wait for reinforcements.' The courier shrugged. 'Perhaps he was right. If he had waited, the whole herd might have been taken.'

'Was chase given?'

'By some. But the raiders were fresh-mounted; sure of their ground to the point they could gallop in darkness.' The rider's face turned stern.

'What?' prompted the duchess, brows knotted.

'None of the men who pursued came back.'

Silence fell, except for the rider's breaths.

The duchess said, 'Bring this man in and grant him rest.'

As two guards half-carried the messenger to the inner lodgings, the duchess turned to the one guard remaining. 'The men did not return,' she repeated. 'What do you make of that?'

'They were with the raiders.' His voice was quiet, fit for secret exchanges.

The duchess shook her head. 'No. Not bloodhorse keepers. Not the duke's men. They'd never turn coat.'

'Murdered, then.'

'That's my fear.' She placed her hand upon his shoulder. 'That's over five hundred horses taken so far. And now men. If things grow worse, I fear we'll be at war by spring.'

The guard shook his head. 'I don't understand it. The Duke of Byerol has always been a reasonable man, and he denies to the Heavens he's stolen any horses, and has thrown out the same accusation against the Duke of Pelan. This folly seems irregular, ill-thought of him.'

'Indeed. I shall inform the king. He must put an end to this or my hand shall be forced. They are both my allies, but Pelan threw out its grievance first, and has maintained it strongest and loudest.'

The duchess and her man walked down the hall, voices receding to the distance.

Orlanda stood in the shadows, the rider's words flowing through her mind. War between Pelan and Byerol, and now Belaron to toss its weight into the conflict. She walked to her chamber, possibilities tumbling in her mind. The duchess owned men in the palace, that much was certain. She was the most influential of the king's close circle. If she called upon the king for resolution, he would be occupied with this war, and perhaps forget his plans to pursue Orlanda's marriage to Valoren. It was already close to winter, too late for the Duke of Romondor to send a barge for her. No ships sailed from Mirador in winter.

More troubled thoughts came. If the king declared war, or sought to intercede in the conflict, would not Areme be called out also? She clenched her fist. There seemed no solution to her problems.

As she passed the main doors to the hall, two guards there glanced at her in surprise, saluted, arms to chest, then fell into step at her back. She scowled beneath her veil. Hessarde's doing, no doubt, having men dog her every step. They had expected her to leave by the main doors. Something to note for future reference. Well, tonight it played to her favour. She steeled herself to fulfil her promise to Jaien. *Favour for a favour*. Men at her back would only serve her cause.

She strode down a corridor, brocade hissing against slate, then descended a staircase to the level below the palace, along another hall, traversing the myriad paths leading to the dungeons. Cold deepened with every step. Passages narrowed, stone on either side illuminated by small, smoky torches set in sconces. Far above, night crept through far-set windows, tall slits framing a pale dusting of stars.

Orlanda shivered as she halted before a heavy-set man standing before a darkened passage. Brown eyes examined her from beneath a thatch of unruly black hair. He bowed stiffly, face intent and grave as he said, 'Highness?'

'Show me the roll of prisoners,' she demanded.

He turned to a locked door behind him, keys jangling as they struck the bolt. Stepping back, he motioned her to enter a tiny, plain room with a single rushlight sending smoky shadows rippling up the stone walls.

The guard closed the door, then pulled out a strip of vellum from a shelf, longer than a man as he unrolled it. 'This be the most recent prisoners, Highness.'

Orlanda eyed the names. 'Show me those arrested this day.'

A thick coarse hand moved over the vellum, index finger coming to rest above four names.

Orlanda read the first. 'Keeper of Graycor – Armindras – arrested for breaking the king's edict.'

The guard's eyes flashed to hers. 'Your father has just passed on his way to that very prisoner. Have you a wish to join him?'

Choking beneath her veil, Orlanda said, 'No, I do not wish it.' Every instinct told her to run. If her father discovered her here, her cause was lost. But if she ran now, all hope was ash.

She looked around shelves stacked high with scrolls. 'I wish to examine a release order. Freshly drawn.' With time against her and danger close, she waited impatiently while the guard pulled another scroll from a lower shelf and unrolled it.

'This here's the current order – blank – as you can see. Just wanting a name and a seal.'

She picked up the vellum, smooth and cold beneath her fingers. 'I thank you, sir.' Pulling a ring from the little finger of her left hand, she held it out to the guard. 'I was never here. Understand?'

The guard ogled the gemstone and bowed. 'Never.' He rolled tight the leaf of vellum, and rebound the cord and placed it back on the shelf.

While he opened the door, back turned to her, she grabbed the vellum and tucked it within the fold of her dress, taking care lest any of the guards saw. Then, with a sweep of her gown, she strode from the room. When she reached her chamber, she closed the door on Hessarde's guards, dismissed her maids, and sat on a stool at the writing table the duchess had used earlier. With infinite care and precision, she inscribed the vellum with the keeper's name. Then she picked up the duchess's seal, left carelessly on the table, and pressed it to the order. When the wax congealed, she called for the page whose duties would keep him from his cot in the antechamber for half a night yet. The door opened and he ran to her side and bowed.

'Deliver this to the guardroom of the prison at dawn on the morrow.' Orlanda sat back, wiping ink from her fingers with a cloth. As the page strode from the room, a satisfied smile formed upon her lips.

Callinor strode down a narrow passage, pulling his cloak close. Drafts whistled through slitted gaps in the dungeon walls, clearing the dank smell of decay and cloying scent of blood, bringing with them the chill of night. Two men marched at his back, a torchbearer before, boots echoing down the passageway.

A sharp cry rang farther along the dungeon's dark vaults. Far ahead, someone ran with a guttering lantern down the stone passageway, shadows heaving in waves across the wall. Shortly thereafter came a soft thud, a groan, the sound of a body dragged across stone. A door clashed shut. Silence.

Callinor stopped at another door. Tall, narrow, it opened to a key. He stepped inside a stone cell, the span of it no more than a few steps. 'Leave us,' he said quietly to his guards, not bothering to turn to give the order.

'By your will, Majesty,' they muttered, stepping back into darkness.

In the cell, a short brand burned in a sconce on a wall, casting dim light. Moonlight slid through airshafts high in the wall, slanting down the pale stone in a line of silvered grey.

Callinor shifted a little to regard the prisoner lying on a pallet, head pillowed on stone. 'How goes it, old man?' he asked.

'I've known beds harder and colder,' said Armindras in his gruff, familiar tone, voice broken and scraped raw as though from shouting. He sat up, eyes bright with hatred. Though his wrists were chained, iron bands bound his legs, and a thick chain leashed him like a dog to an iron bracket in the wall, the strength of old was there in the challenge, 'Speak your piece. Make all plain.'

Callinor snorted. 'You were once my most prized envoy, yet I noted little diplomacy in your actions at the horse market.'

'Then we are matched, for I've noted nothing kingly in your actions these past years.'

Callinor leaned hard against the door. 'What purpose drove you to defy me?'

'My son. I declared it before all.'

'If you press further, I'll not protect you.'

'If I fail to protect my son, my life is worth nothing, so do with me what you will.'

Callinor drew a heavy breath. 'I caution you to think back on your knightly vows, your faith.'

'I lost all faith during the Great War.' Armindras's words, like his eyes, speared through Callinor.

Tension roiled within the king. The loss of this man's goodwill meant more than he cared to admit. Despair and wrath had left them both betrayed and disillusioned. 'You know the penalty for loose talk is death. None better. You killed enough men to silence their tongues. Why speak now? Why damn yourself?'

'I've given my reason.'

'I cannot give you back your son.' Callinor hesitated on the brink of disclosure, pressed on. 'I need all men with me now.'

'So you can finish what you started?'

Weariness settled over Callinor's heart. 'So I can finish it, yes.'

Armindras's eyes narrowed. 'Why do I hear hidden intent in your words?'

Callinor spread his hands. 'Nothing hidden. I seek only peace, an end to discord. I go to Romondor, with the princess.'

'You'd use her so?' A vulpine smile touched Armindras's lips when Callinor remained silent. 'Ah, I see. You'll throw her to the wolves, unknowing.'

Callinor ignored the barb. 'The aim is true and lasting peace; the cause of all men of good will from both sides.'

Armindras snorted. 'Are there such? It seems goodwill died with honour years ago. On both sides.'

'For the kingdom's sake, there must be.'

'Sihan's a horseman. Better to leave him where he is.'

'I require men to shore up my defences. If things go badly . . .' Callinor stopped, the thought too unpalatable to voice. He drew back toward the door.

'If things go badly,' said Armindras, 'you'll kill eight duchies as well as the one you've already murdered. And no amount of death will silence the voices crying "shame."'

Unable to bear the censure in Armindras's knowing eyes, Callinor inclined his head and opened the door. As he stepped out, Armindras's voice stalked him, chilled. 'Mark well the men who guard your back. More than I will not be much grieved to see you dead.'

Callinor's fist clenched. 'You speak the truth, old man.'

The guards locked the door behind him. If only it were that simple to lock out the recriminations in that voice, those eyes, the eyes of every man who hated him though they knew only half the truths of why they should.

Something bubbled within him. Laughter without mirth. How many men knew the real truth? Of a line of kings ruling without right, without sanction, violating the world and its order long before his error. He climbed the stairs, sought cleansing air, wishing it could purify his soul.

His daughter would set all to rights. Restore legitimacy to the throne. If he could manage to drag her to the altar of the most despised man in the kingdom after himself.

Only when he reached the forecourt, silent pillars awash with cold twilight, did Callinor pause. Every word battered against him, the accusations and warnings of a man who knew only the half of what he spoke.

Callinor crossed the forecourt at a measured walk, the old man's insistent voice in his mind repeating words as much threat as warning. "Guard your back."

Armindras's bitterness expressed outright a deep hatred of the man who had betrayed him. Jaien had been no different, daring to defy his orders.

Callinor would have to move fast, before all was lost. When he started for Romondor, he must ensure he had men about him he could trust. Travall, Balfere. Sound, both. And a company of men who despised the Black Duke – who knew nothing of the truth.

He climbed to a turret and stared out to the ocean. The shore was a distant strip of grey, stark as bone against the dark glitter where sea and river met. Frigid wind buffeted his hair and cloak, salt-thick air scoured his face, clogged his nose, thickened his tongue. Starlit sky gaped above.

He closed his eyes. *Are you here, Wyndarra, my queen, my beloved, my destruction?* Behind darkened lids a vision burned, a flaming barge drifting out to sea.

The voice of memory drifted across water and time. *When I die, I want to join the Heavens reflected in the river*.

And so she had. He had granted her that final wish, as he had granted so many others, to his cost, to the cost of thousands, to the damnation of his reign. Until he discovered her treachery, that she sought to cuckold him with the Black Duke, Riordehr. He knew not which rage cut deeper. That the woman he worshipped beyond life and measure desired another man, or her unfeeling determination to win or destroy that man, to the ruin of his duchy, Romondor.

In dreams, her laughing face still mocked him as she revealed to him secrets hidden for ten thousand years – that the line of kings from which he descended was false.

She felt close now. He tasted her mouth pressed against his, white roses, the sea. He ran his tongue over moist lips, tasted salt. Tears or salt-damp air, there was no way of knowing.

He blinked. Dread filled his gut, hot and heavy. Unbidden, more memories crashed to the fore. Screams around a gag, straining wrists unable to break the bonds tying them, weakening convulsions as life drained.

Callinor recoiled from the memory of his dying wife, the ground beneath him asway like the heaving deck of a ship on high seas. His legs caved, knees striking the ground. Clamping his ears to block out her screaming, tiny, drawn-out moans, small, distant echoes of a voice shattering to silence, he retched.

When he stood, aching, he kicked dirt from a rose bed over his vomit. Night crawled in his eyes, then shimmered, ghost-grey, as he stared between the crenels. Far below, the ghost-memory of a woman glided down the short, sandy path to the narrow beach, past straggling bramble rose and salt scrub.

Callinor's hands white-knuckled on chilled stone. Why did she haunt him still? He had done all she asked until he could do it no longer.

Her voice clotted his ears, soft, pure, stained with blood, tearing at the jagged edges of his heart. *I want the path to the sea sown with white roses. I will walk it every day. I never want to be away from the sound of the sea, away from the ocean air. From you.*

The king turned away. *So be it. If you will not leave, then I must leave you.* As he walked back to his chambers, he wondered if anyone else had noticed since her death every rose along the path to the sea bloomed blood-red.

Chapter 15

Visions from the Past

Areme's soldiers stood in a loose ring around the camp, following Sihan's every move with hunter's eyes. The quiet tension of gloved hands on sword hilts kept passers-by at a respectful distance. Doing his best to ignore them, Sihan poured corn into a bucket for Aurion. The screening curtain of willow leaves flowed over the horse in a waterfall of gold, providing a welcome moment of respite from unrelenting observation. Sihan pulled on a curved ear, earning an annoyed stamp. He laid his cheek against the satin-smoothness of Aurion's neck, ran one hand up to the crest, tangling fingers in the forelock. 'Behave today, you brute.'

The soft black muzzle snuffled chaff in Sihan's hand, snorted a few husks into the wind. They suspended in the air, floating, drifting. Isolation crowded in on Sihan. He saw himself as one of the husks, taken by the will of the air and cast away from all that had once held him bound. If he saved his father, he would lose him in the saving, be forced to take the king's commission, cut all ties to his past, his hopes. Loss dogged whichever path he trod.

He wished for Kheran and Tejas. Even Jaien, to thank him, to apologise, needing support in some small way. But his friends were preparing their horses and the knight was with his own father, helping with the chestnut colt he was to trial. He had returned during the night, pretended surprise at the news spilling from Sihan's lips about Areme, and refused to share his own, though there was assurance in his words, and a thin-veiled promise Sihan's father would soon be free.

Well, if Jaien refused to acknowledge his hand in the night's events, Sihan would work to his own plan. It was better by far, he reasoned, to trust in himself and Aurion. He had trialed horses for two years in Mirador. His father had taught him everything. He knew what to do. Areme would find nothing wanting.

Avoiding Areme's guards, he walked to the cart and rummaged through tack, searching for a pouch of herbs and salt. He found none. His gut tightened once more. Horses pressed hard died fast without salt. It was as important as water.

Visions of staggering horses, eyes sunken in agony, seared Sihan's brain. He shuddered. Running a horse without salt was tantamount to murder. Already sweat rolled down Sihan's back. Today, Aurion would be tested to his limits.

And what if Aurion was injured? He slapped a hand against the buckboard, thinking hard. His father must have the granine in one of the pouches on his belt. The herbs and salt, too.

There was nothing for it. He had to get some. Jaien had salt. Herbs he could buy from merchants. There was money enough with the gold Areme had given him. And though granine was forbidden by king's edict, Kheran would know which Senfari had some and get it for him. He started toward the merchant tents, but before he had gone ten paces, Areme's guards levelled swords at him.

'Where do you think you're going?' growled one.

Sihan scowled. 'I'm getting salt and herbs.'

Hessarde arose from his seat on a log near a fire, picking up a bowl as he did so. In between scoops of porridge, he said, 'Areme gave strict orders you were not to leave the horse.'

'But I need supplies for Aurion.'

'That horse doesn't need any help from you, boy.'

'Do you want him to win or not?' demanded Sihan.

'My master doesn't ride to lose.'

'Then let me go!'

'You can visit your lover later.' Hessarde drew a long thin dagger and slid the flat of the blade along Sihan's smooth cheek. 'I wouldn't want to spoil that pretty face of yours. Jaien would never forgive me.' It was clear that he did not care whether Jaien forgave him or not.

Clenching his fists, Sihan glared at Hessarde. 'He's not my lover!'

'Whatever.'

Anger boiled over within Sihan. 'Do you want Aurion to die? Areme said not one hair on him was to be harmed.' He stared hard at the cordon of soldiers. 'Don't you give salt to your horses?'

No expression at all registered on their closed faces.

Hessarde pushed Sihan back to the fire. 'That beast doesn't need salt, boy, trust me. He doesn't need anything but Areme riding him.'

'But–'

A sharp hiss brought Hessarde's sword to Sihan's throat. 'Areme said nothing about not harming *you*, boy. Nothing at all.' His eyes glittered, hard and chill.

Sihan glared at the knight, not backing down, but unable to argue with cold steel either. 'You're a fucking prick,' he said finally.

'Well,' drawled Hessarde, 'you'd know all about such things, wouldn't you?'

Sihan took one step forward, fists hard as rocks. Only the tip of the sword pressing into his throat stopped him. A self-satisfied smile, more a toothy snarl, lifted the corners of Hessarde's lips; the dare was in his eyes. They both knew who held the upper hand.

Every muscle taut with fury held in check, Sihan stalked back to the cart. Yanking out everything in case he had missed the pouches, he found instead his father's sword. His fingers stroked the scabbard, but he dismissed the thought before it had fully formed. He was no match for these hardened soldiers, and a sword had caused all his current problems in the first place. He could not help free his father if he was dead or in a dungeon himself. Glancing again at Hessarde, he fumed that an experienced cavalryman could dismiss his request so readily.

Cries beyond the camp caught Sihan's attention, vendors' sing-song voices vying with each other in any one of a hundred different dialects. Sihan climbed on the cart. If he could spot Kheran, or one of the Graycor Senfari, catch their attention . . .

More tents had sprouted overnight like mushrooms, filling every patch of dirt. On either side of the bridge, sloping river banks livened with the purple jalabas of Tulitian traders with their brown, kohl-ringed eyes, dark-skinned Andorean blacksmiths, and covered Hyoth women with only their vivid green eyes showing from behind body-length veils. The entire plain before the fortress overflowed with a chaotic floodtide of flocks and men, all carried along like flotsam. There was little hope of seeing anyone he knew. He strained to see past buyers haggling with sellers. With so many stalls, there must be herbalists nearby.

The scent of roasted lamb kebabs on skewers, peppered with cumin and cinnamon, flavoured the air, along with the aroma of goose eggs sizzling in mutton fat. He had not eaten yet and hunger flared. Then all thoughts of food fled.

Along a maze of narrow, sinuous makeshift alleys, swarming with people and tangled with stalls, a black standard wove its way. In its wake a cry went up. 'Vultures! Vultures! Romondor vultures!'

The milling mob jostled, all eyes turning to stare. Carried by a mounted herald, the standard approached the fortress. At the standard bearer's back, black-clad guards rode freely. Lanes opened before them, peasants stepping away as though they feared something obscene might touch them. Even muleteers, stubborn as their beasts, opened a path.

Sihan's stomach knotted as a wave of revulsion washed over him.

Garbed in full armour, black surcoats over black mail, calf-high, black leather boots and black leggings, the troop carried curved oblong shields covering their left sides from shoulder to knee. Long sword scabbards peeked out below. Pennons hissed from the tips of lances. Their horses' coats shimmered. Long, thick manes swept from powerful, crested necks to fall in rivers of night. The Romondor soldiers rode in tight formation with hands on sword hilts.

As well they might, thought Sihan grimly.

'Murderers!' shouted a merchant, raising a clenched fist, loathing in his voice.

Sihan spat. The treacherous turncoats had broken their oaths and murdered innocent folk they were sworn to defend. They were the lowest scum in the kingdom, lower even than zingars. Sihan wondered if these carrion in their jet mail and ebon plumes would make it to the fortress gates alive.

'Shaheden,' Hessarde hissed, moving to stand beside the cart.

Sihan tore his gaze away from the Romondor soldiers. A roughness had caught at the edges of Hessarde's voice, like an uneven blade slid across whetstone. It was the same curse Jaien had used, but somehow on Hessarde's lips it did not convey the meaning Jaien had assigned to it. There was something chilled about it, death-cold. Sihan shuddered, suddenly more afraid of the elite soldiers of Areme's command than the Romondor killers riding past.

The crowd gave back; beggars, traders, flattened themselves against stalls, tripped over tent-ropes. A solitary rider appeared on a horse the like of which Sihan had never seen, a monolith of muscle beneath rippling hide. Night-dark, the stallion marched with proud and arrogant strength toward the fortress, qualities it shared with its master. Feathers fanned about its legs; huge saucered hooves stamped the ground. From head to foot, both man and charger were clad in black: tunic, surcoat, mail, leggings, boots, saddlecloth of leather stretching below the horse's belly and over its rump. On the horse's head, eyeguards bulged from a studded leather chamfron. A black plume fluttered on the breeze. The knight's helm set off his stark olive-hued face. His garments seemed hemmed in shadow, matching the charger he rode.

'Veren,' muttered another of Areme's men, flanking Hessarde, his voice carrying all the weight of history associated with that name.

Shock after shock rilled through Sihan. He knew the name like he knew the names of the gods. Veren. Knight Commander of Romondor.

Hessarde turned to the man beside him. 'Run! Warn Areme!'

As the man took off, the stallion's cry echoed around the stalls, a piercing trumpet challenge raising the hairs on Sihan's neck. A slight breeze brushed Veren's jet-black hair away from his brow, revealing hooded eyes. The knight rode closer, bringing a darkness that drank light. When his shadow fell on Sihan, he shivered.

Dark eyes fastened upon Sihan, the knight's penetrating gaze boring into him, as though looking into the marrow of his bones. Tremors crawled up and down Sihan's spine. He crossed his arms, refused to look away, but the insults he wanted to hurl choked in his throat.

As if he knew, Veren's face tightened in an expression half grim, half amused. Then his gaze slid to Hessarde, who returned it without flinching, lips thinned to a steely line, face twisted awry with more than its usual sneer.

The knight passed along the corridor opening before him, no longer glancing to either side, acknowledging neither insult nor threat. He and his guards rode across the drawbridge to a hollow rumble of hooves and the blaring of horns. The crowd closed behind, hiding them from sight.

It took Sihan some moments to remember why he was on the cart. He looked down at Hessarde. The knight was locked in close conversation with his men clustered about him.

Sihan scanned the camp. He could not see any guards stationed around the perimeter. Casually, he hopped off the cart, picked up a bucket and sauntered to Aurion, sliding in amongst the hanging willow. Sneaking behind the stallion's hindquarters, he turned toward the creek.

'Going somewhere?'

Sihan whipped round to find another of Areme's men lurking in the lee of the willow trunk, sword drawn. The soldier took a step forward, put one hand on Aurion's rump. Squealing, the stallion kicked, landing a solid hoof in the man's groin. With an agonised grunt, the soldier collapsed behind the willow-withy screen.

The way lay open. Sihan scrambled down to the creek. Slipping and sliding across moss-grown rocks, he clambered up the opposite bank, clutching at willow fronds to lever himself up, trying to reach the thick crowd on the fortress road before shouts of "Hold! Hold!" dogged his heels. He hoped the flood of merchants, idlers, peddlers and hagglers jamming the stalls would swallow him whole and hamper pursuit.

He had almost reached the top of the bank when his feet slipped, slid, became as heavy as boots sucked into mud. He fought for purchase, but the more he struggled the more the ground shifted. A whirlpool of shadows spun about him, as though the sun had been drowned by night. His feet ceased moving entirely, as if something had snagged his legs.

A girl took form before him.

No rustle of willow, no crush of leaves, no flutter of scattered birdwing heralded her arrival. She simply misted into reality from air.

He wanted to run, to scream, but dread killed his voice, rooted him to the spot. Memory stirred of a vision in a snowstorm, a girl with flowing midnight hair and burning eyes. Blood drained from his face as a dark gaze locked with his, wolf's eyes. There was no mistaking her.

We will know one another, as long as life and death endures.

Her lips did not move, but he knew she owned that ageless, otherworldly voice; a thing of beauty, of darkness, so pure and true and mysterious it was at once agonizing and enthralling. Her face shone with the radiance of moon glow, voice holding within it the heat of stars. Stricken to the heart by both, Sihan forgot why he had been running, forgot Hessarde, forgot everything but the girl before him.

Time stretched between them, measureless. Slowly, deliberately, she glided toward him, her gown white against willow gold.

Somehow, he found the will to take a step back.

'Don't go.' Her two words bound him like iron.

Sihan fought to gather scattered wits, with a mind slowed to a crawl. 'I saw you,' he whispered. 'When I was a boy. In the snow. In Graycor.'

'You remember.' Close to, the skin of her face was white, smooth as bone, as if the flesh had been drawn tight over the skull. No hanging skin, no dagger, no blood. 'I swore I'd remember *you*. The dark will drain from night, before I break my vow.'

Voice just breath, he stuttered, 'W–What do you want?'

A barren smile slipped across her lips. 'I want to return your gift.'

'G–Gift?'

A breeze kissed Sihan's cheeks with a feather's caress. Branches rattled together like bones. Under that rhythm of wind and wood, small like stardust sighing through the willow, she whispered, 'You saved me. I've come to save you.'

'S–Save me?'

Something touched his cheek like gossamer. The girl trailed a finger along the line of his jaw, traced the outline of his mouth. Soft, so soft . . . In a voice carrying deathly stillness, she said, 'All my death I sought some way to find you.'

Sihan forced his muddled mind to think. 'Your death?'

'I no longer exist in the world of the living. A thousand years I've waited for you.' Wordlessly she floated around him.

Mind spinning, Sihan grasped at random words. 'A thousand years?'

Her finger slipped across Sihan's cheek, down, across his throat, a spider's touch. 'Hatred refuses to wither my flesh.' She smiled, a viper's smile. 'Time crumbles to dust, but one thing never alters; in the black depths of my soul, you alone exist, for all eternity.' She withdrew a silken pouch from the flowing sleeve of her gown, pulled out a thick green tuber. She held it out to him. 'Take this.'

Granine.

She glided around him, a slow circle, voice soft as lamb's fleece. 'You will need it. You must have it.'

He closed his eyes, not wanting to think, to listen. But his fingers clamped on the tuber. It felt so real.

'You must take it,' she whispered.

A weight like a slab lifted from his shoulders. She was right. He had to have it. It was better than salt. Better than anything. He did not wonder how she knew what he needed. She was a ghost, after all. Wasn't she? His eyes blinked open. In a voice barely his, he asked, 'Who are you?'

She held out one hand, tracing images in the air. Mist and sunlight and rainbows wove into a halo of shimmering blue light. The air became eerie still – the uncanny quiet of a graveyard.

Cold air breezed about him as though he stood in a winter field. Another girl walked toward him, between tents, between tall trees, across a meadow shrouded in gloom, next to the battlement, as if the fortress and meadow existed superimposed upon one another. Unlike the ghost girl, there was no brightness in this one, just flat, lifeless shades, the russet and brown of dead leaves.

Were they the same girl? He could not tell.

Her shoulders bent in discouraged wilt. She knelt before Sihan, without meeting his eyes. The deep reverence she made surprised him, more so the shy, quiet words she spoke.

'I know nothing of temples and kings, Anise, but there inside awaits my mother and father and there must I go.' She lifted her hands to his. 'My greatest sorrow is we never lay together.'

She raised her face, eyes pleading and silent. Her hands tightened upon his, trembling and cold. So cold. Her voice came quiet between them, all desperation. 'Ride for me, Anise. Against the Black Prince. Win for me or we are lost.'

His name was not Anise, but he felt compelled to answer her plea. 'I will.'

Her eyes burned with the most unsettling lustre. 'You are more Lord than that other one may be. More Lord, indeed.'

He bent toward her, those blue-tinged lips, wanted to trace that rose-sweet outline. Lilac and white purslane – the scent of her filled him. His fingers trembled upon the smooth, fresh skin of her cheek. Fire coursed through his veins like the sun's melting rays as he opened his arms to fold her within their warmth. He held her, stroking her hair. They held fast to each other, this girl and he, until a distant shout forced him to pull back.

The girl broke away, face pale. 'They come! They come! O wither shall I hide?'

Not knowing why he wanted to help, only that he did, Sihan looked around for a hiding place. But when he turned back, the first girl was there once more, shining with light.

'Wait! Where did she go?' Sihan demanded.

She did not answer, instead raising her arms and whirling in a circle. A whirlwind arose from the willow leaves at her feet, coiling about her. At her back, currawongs wheeled into flight, cries loud, a mournful, drawn-out baby's wailing. Then only empty space remained where she had stood.

Sihan staggered, feet freed of heaviness. Heart hammering, clenching the tuber in his fist, he gasped at air. Shouts thickened in his ears. He turned, reeling into the light beyond the willows and crashed straight into Hessarde.

'You sneaky little cocksucker,' the knight hissed as he grabbed Sihan by the scruff of his tunic.

'Let me go!' spluttered Sihan.

'I should wring your stupid little neck.' White scar stark against his thin, flushed face, Hessarde dragged Sihan back toward the creek, boots squelching in murk at the water's edge. 'How dare you run off to ogle maidens at the revels when there's work to be done.'

'You saw her?' Sihan cried.

'Heed my advice and keep well away from her ilk. The maids of Mirador are pretty as paint. Much prettier than that zingar. No need to chase poisoned fruit.'

A zingar. Was she such? Zingars were rumoured to have strange powers. They stalked villages and fairs, evoking dread and mystery. They were troublemakers who stole, and disappeared without trace. Was she a zingar? She must be. But what did she want with him? He had never owned anything worth stealing. And could she really be the same girl he had seen all those years ago in the mountains the night of Aurion's birth? He shook his head. She could not be.

Sihan clutched at Hessarde's arm. 'You're sure you saw her?'

The knight paused in his stride just long enough to thrust an angry pointed finger in Sihan's face. 'I told you to forget her. She's a zingar. A common, dirty little witch. Filth.' He spat to emphasise the point.

Memory of that other girl flooded Sihan's mind, her eyes lowered, as though in shame. She had called him Anise, and another memory stirred, of a boy denying him his name. Anger coursed through him, deep, urgent, swift. His name was Sihan, not Anise. And zingars were as low as Emor ponies, heathen, obeying no law. But something about the girl's haunted, hurt-filled eyes spurred to his lips words he had never have thought to say. 'She's not filth,' he said, the desire to protect her flowing strong through his veins.

Hessarde spat again at Sihan's feet. 'Dirty zingar lover!'

Sihan met the hard-eyed gaze, fingers playing on the hilt of the dagger at his belt. 'What if I am?'

Hessarde shot him a pitiless look. 'Would you like me to break that news to Jaien?' He did not wait for an answer. 'Come on, you miscreant.' He pulled Sihan through the campsite empty of all but the two bay colts, and kept right on going. Lines of tents and encampments passed in a blur.

'Where are we going?' cried Sihan. 'Where's Aurion?'

'Where do you think? The trials are about to start.'

'Start?' Sihan asked, confused. 'They're not for ages yet.'

Hessarde grimaced. 'You hit your head or something? The morning's half gone.'

Sihan glanced up at the sun tracking half way to its zenith. How was that possible?

Hessarde gave him no time to think, dragging him along through the crowds. Sihan coughed, tongue dry and thick, eyes straining to see through dust kicked up by so many people and animals. Horsemen competing in the day's events had claimed the far right of the tourney field, their tents set up beside long rows of troughs and racks stuffed with hay.

Hessarde reached the edge of the archery field where Aurion stood tethered to four stakes. The stallion plunged from side to side, aiming swift kicks at air. Separate to the long rows of horses, he was surrounded by a multitude of Areme's men in grey cloaks standing just beyond range of the lethal hooves.

'Why isn't that horse saddled?' Hessarde demanded.

'None of us has been able to get near him since the lad took off,' complained one of Areme's men. 'If it wasn't for Knight Captain Jaien, we wouldn't have even got it here! The horse wouldn't listen to no one but him!'

Sihan searched the nearby horse lines for the knight, but amid the frenzied activity of horses being ridden back and forth, Jaien was nowhere to be seen. 'Where is he?'

Sullen faces stared at Sihan as Hessarde pushed him toward Aurion. 'Forget about all your damned lovers! Get Areme's saddle on that horse.' He pointed to a war saddle resting upturned on the ground.

Aurion snapped at Sihan. Sihan's fists clenched and unclenched. Gritting his teeth, he hefted the saddle onto the stallion's back, strained to tighten the girth. Fine though worn leatherwork pressed sun-warmed and smooth against his fingers, the elaborate carved inlay, trademark of a master craftsman. He hoisted the buckle one final notch.

Trumpets blared. Sihan stared across the field to the royal dais. Red tassels fluttered in the breeze from awnings that kept the ever-rising sun at bay. Empty cushions sprawled over a profusion of divans, embroidered covers ablaze with colour. On either side, stood galleries for the nobility. Atop these, a forest of banners and banneroles, stitched cloth dyed a rainbow of hues, hissed and writhed like windborne snakes.

A troop of horsemen rode toward the dais from the battlement gates. The leading knight lifted his mailed arm and the column fanned out and came to a halt in unison across the width of the field, the line marred only by several mounts tossing their heads as they reefed into bits, swinging hindquarters in agitation.

In full armour and spotless surcoat, the King's Champion, Knight Commander Travall, sat astride his bay horse, head held high, flanked by his fellow Knight Commanders, Areme on his iron-grey stallion Seroyen and Balfere upon his massive wall-eyed bay, Dahal.

White surcoats fluttered in the wind. Bright helms jangled against the rings of saddles. Each man carried a shield slung across his left shoulder. Long scabbards held swords against the shoulders of their mounts. The lances the knights held aloft sported red and white pennons.

To a trumpet blast blaring across the field, a big dapple-grey stallion marched onto the tourney ground, trailed by another troop of knights. In ceremonious splendour, the king checked Celestion, dismounted with unhurried grace and strode across the lists, ermine cloak sweeping the ground behind him. A line of courtiers in rich cotte and cloaks fell in behind.

More trumpets pealed. The troop of horsemen drew sword in one flowing motion to salute the king. While nobles took their places in the stand, angling for positions likely to catch the king's notice, Areme dismounted, tossed his reins to a squire, and joined the rearguard of the king's knights, expression dark and brooding.

With all eyes on the royal gallery, Sihan grasped the opportunity to untie the pouch at his belt and shove the granine tuber inside. More nobles rode in, entourages in their wake, richly accoutred, uniforms bearing intricate designs and heraldry. Servants led away steeds while their masters took places determined by rank and wealth.

Sihan scanned the dais, searching for the princess, pressing his lips tight in a frown. All the women wore cowls draped over their faces, or veils, making it impossible to pick out the one he wanted most to see. Something tugged at Sihan's sleeve, and he turned to find Jaien beside him, Wedge's reins looped over his arm.

The knight's eyes narrowed to concern. 'You look like shit.' He reached out a gloved hand to tilt Sihan's chin back. 'Where did you run off to this morning?'

'Nowhere.' Sihan pushed Jaien off firmly to arms length, mindful of Hessarde hovering in earshot.

Jaien refused to stop examining Sihan. 'Where the seven hells did you go?'

Sihan shrugged him off again. 'I needed salt for Aurion.'

Hurt closed Jaien's face, deep like it had been the previous day when Sihan had refused to acknowledge it. 'You could have asked me,' he said, unhooking a pouch at his belt and handing it to Sihan.

'I tried.' Sihan glared at Areme's men. 'They wouldn't let me leave camp.' He carefully avoided mentioning the girl.

Almost-hope sparked in Jaien's eyes, but he damped it down fast. Instead, he nodded at Aurion who now stood still and alert, doing nothing more than eyeing the crowd. 'He's a lot calmer than a while ago, rearing and kicking and trying to maul any of Areme's men who came near.' He flashed Sihan a broad grin. 'If he wasn't white, and Falcon wasn't my pride, I'd buy him myself, just for the company he refuses to keep.' He aimed a sardonic smile straight at Hessarde, not revealing even the thinnest line of teeth. 'Seems Aurion is a great judge of character.'

'Why don't you get on your horse and piss off?' shot back Hessarde.

Jaien's smile sweetened. 'Why don't you go fuck yourself with a sword?' A shrill trumpet blared on the tail of his insult. Jaien turned to the royal stand. 'Has the princess arrived?'

'Can't tell,' said Sihan. 'All the women are wearing veils. What if she's not here?'

'She'll be here.' Jaien's voice was firm, confident.

Sihan shifted his weight from foot to foot, wishing the Fire Rituals did not coincide with the anniversary of the great queen's death. The king had sworn on her deathbed he would never look at another woman. He had proclaimed all women should conceal their faces in order to preserve that vow. Although he had relented after a year and withdrawn the edict, every Fire Ritual the women of the court paid homage to his love for the queen and resumed the custom.

A disturbance in the royal gallery caught Sihan's attention. On the dais, a figure clad in a grey cloak sat beside the king. Drawing a sharp breath, Sihan clasped Jaien's arm, exclaiming as he pointed, 'Is that her?'

Jaien regarded the cloaked figure attentively. 'Must be.'

At that moment, Areme came striding across the field, shrugging off his cloak, flicking his black, leather-bound hair back over his shoulder. His mail glittered over the regulation quilted gambeson, both overlaid by the white surcoat bearing the crest of Mirador. Grey leggings bound long lean muscle.

Ignoring Jaien as if the knight did not exist, Areme stopped before Sihan and glowered, radiating tension like a winched crossbow. 'I hear you've been causing my men no end of trouble.' Without waiting for a reply, he bent down and ran his hands over Aurion's fetlocks, pasterns, tendons, feeling for splints, heat, or swelling, then lifted each hoof, looking for dirt and stones. When he appeared certain nothing was amiss he continued, 'The archery trial's first. Make yourself scarce until afterwards. Give Gerhas a wide berth. He'll be murderous when he realises what's happening and I'd rather not have your blood on my conscience.'

Sihan fought down a retort. Everything about Areme's voice suggested he did not much care if everyone around him fell dead at his feet.

Jaien's hand closed on Sihan's shoulder, the knight flashing him a warning glance before addressing Areme. 'What of you? Surely you're not immune from the horsemaster's displeasure?'

'My problem, not yours.' Areme turned back to Aurion, ran his hand down the stallion's forehead to the soft velvet nose, then his glare intensified. 'Whose stupid idea was it to saddle him?'

Taking an ounce of satisfaction, Sihan pointed at Hessarde.

Hessarde muttered, 'Jousting's bareback, not archery.'

'Get the bridle off, too,' ordered Areme.

Hessarde hurried to obey, trying hard to evade a sharp snap from Aurion's teeth. He untied the leathers, slung the saddle to the ground, then Areme vaulted onto Aurion's back.

Sihan stepped back, waiting for the fireworks, but the white stallion only shook his head and lifted his legs a fraction, eyeing Areme with a long, measuring look. Amazed, Sihan just stared. How was it possible? He stared up at the knight with grudging respect. He surely was the finest rider in the kingdom if he could tame Aurion's willful ways. Hope surged through him.

But despite the fact Aurion seemed perfectly at ease with Areme, Sihan felt bound to offer every ounce of help he could. 'There are things you need to know about Aurion.'

'I know everything I need to know.' A peculiar smile hovered about Areme's lips as he caressed the stallion's neck. 'This horse and I understand each other.' Without another word, he spun Aurion around and cantered away to take his place in the line of mounted archers.

Jaien shook his head, sandy hair falling about his shoulders as he muttered beneath his breath, 'Arrogant prick.'

Sihan set about retying the cord of his pouch. Wedge reached out his nose, snuffling, and grabbed the leather cord between his teeth, yanking hard.

'Hey!' cried Sihan as his mother's note and the granine tuber spilled on the ground.

Jaien blanched white. He dropped to his knees to shove the tuber back in the pouch, then, standing, thrust it at Sihan. 'Put that away and don't let anyone see it.' He half turned away, hesitated, turned back and stared hard at Sihan. 'I prayed for you this morning at the Dawn Prayer.' It was half-confession, half-declaration.

Prepared for neither, Sihan said, half in jest, half discomfited by the other man's too-intent regard, 'You should have prayed for Aurion.'

Once more, pain flecked the knight's green-gold gaze. He turned away and mounted Wedge. Smoothing his gold and black tabard over his cream tunic, his smile at Sihan came somewhat forced. 'Whether you want my good wishes or no, I offer them freely and with good will.' He spurred Wedge away.

Regretting his rebuff, Sihan started to follow, but the moment for amends had slipped away, Jaien lost to sight in a dust cloud of horsemen milling onto the field. Angry at himself, not quite knowing why, Sihan pushed through the crowd toward the dais to watch the mounted ranks of competitors. No point worrying about Jaien, or his own tangled feelings, or even girls who appeared from nowhere only to disappear as mysteriously. Time to worry about Aurion, and the future the horse might deliver or deny. Sihan clenched his fists as he strode toward the archery field. There was now no other path open to him but straight ahead, whether to victory or disaster.

Chapter 16

War Horse

Impatience wove itself around Areme, infused every tense muscle, leached into the horse he rode, making it prance. He flexed his gloved fingers. *Steady. Steady.* He had waited a millennium for this day, and a chance to undo misdeeds of the past. What were another few moments?

Along the battlement walls, his men stood in thin lines of shadow edging the massive marble stones. Waiting, like him, to see what this horse could do.

Areme stared across the tourney field, past new-hewn rails set on upright stakes separating the crowd from the horsemen. The grey battlements of Mirador rose from a sea of dust kicked up by hundreds of horses milling on the field. Slate roofs and blue domed minarets loomed behind them. No one save Areme and his men remembered the fortress as it had once appeared – gleaming white-gold walls and round towers. Certainly not the crowd packed hundreds deep along the peasant side of the field, all straining to find a good vantage point.

Not one of them would recall the river at their back as it had been then, its surface clogged with floating corpses instead of dung. Once, peasants had squatted on rags and bare earth, many without even a yurt to protect them, driven from their land by warlords and corrupt soldiers, forced to live as beggars. Children had lain upon this very ground, looking more like abandoned heaps of rags. Mangy mules had stood in long dispirited lines, with scabs and galls thick upon their rough coats.

Areme scowled, stomach tightening as he recalled the stench – the waste of thousands of nomads littering the roadside, encamped with their sorry flocks, hoping to trade what goods they had for coin. On the first day he had set eyes on Mirador, called Caerlon then, his own men had looked like ruffians, with their scraggly, unshaven beards, worn-out leather boots, patched tunics, twine holding their horses' harness together, their mounts ragged and ordinary.

Areme clenched his fist. Nothing but hard memories in the minds of hard men remained of those days. He tried to confine his attention to the lists in front of the royal gallery, as if that might block out the past. There, more of his men stood guard. Now, in every way, they matched the hundreds of soldiers of the king's guard, clad with mail from which sunsparks danced, swords and daggers in clear view, white surcoats emblazoned with the Mirador firefalcon.

Areme risked a glance at the royal gallery, set on the nobility side of the tourney field, right before the battlement. The field was broad and long, but not so large Areme could not see every detail. Marshalls scraped and fawned as they escorted nobles and their attendants to seats in the royal stand. Callinor had ordered it set high, to grant a grand view of every yard of the tourney. Increasing the range an assassin's arrow had to fly might also have entered his thoughts.

All around the king, men lounged, adorned in flowing silk and brocade, veritable peacocks in display, chaperons sitting like crowns upon their heads. Women, wrapped in cloth threaded with gold and silver, folds so wide and voluptuous the material might have clad three peasants with fabric to spare, moved and swayed like red poppies, flaxen honeyden. Soft wool curved around wrist and forearm, dyed in the deepest shades of indigo and amaranth. Among this rich splendour sat the princess in a plain grey cloak – like a dead tree stump in a flowering meadow.

Areme frowned, wondering if this was yet another of Orlanda's ploys to force his notice. He slid his glance to Knight Commander Travall, standing with his men before the royal stand. Travall's eyes held all the life of granite, every line of him the hard-muscled body of a killer. He stood motionless, face gaunt, mouth tight.

Travall was expecting trouble. Areme bit back a smile. He would get it.

Behind the stands, the battlement wall rose, all twelve fortress gates open, a mark of amnesty and peace in the kingdom. With Veren's arrival, peace was no longer an option.

Trumpets pealed. Heralds shouted, 'Riders! Present to the king!'

Horsemen cleared to one side of the field, sorting

themselves into crowded lines. Standard bearers ran from clusters of tents that filled the flat plain below the fortress. Hessarde ran to Areme's side from the lists, face flushed from dodging through hundreds of horses.

The horsemen began the presentation to the king, advancing in ranks with solemn purposefulness toward the royal stand. Stirrups clanked against stirrups, greaves slid against greaves. From the back, where Areme waited on Aurion, the lines were little more than a wall of rumps striding side by side.

Heralds marched before each horse, holding aloft standards bearing the devices of knights and duchies from all over the kingdom; the white griffin of Belaron against blue, the gold falcon against black of Pelan, amid a rainbow of others.

On the royal dais, the king arose, lofty head unadorned, acknowledging the riders as they rode past with a raised fist. Jaien, as winner the previous year, was accorded the honour of presenting first. He trotted his chestnut stallion clear of the ranks, and stopped before the horsemaster. Jaien's formal reverence reeked an arrogant air of dismissal that could hardly be missed. He compounded the insult by spurring his horse past the king without even sparing him a glance.

Hessarde whistled. 'He'll lose even his captainship if he continues in this vein.'

Areme's lips curved up a little. 'If that happens, Jaien's entire command will mutiny. The king can't afford that. Jaien knows it. But I'll say this for him, after what Callinor did to him, he's got guts.'

The presentations continued, sun climbing higher in the sky, beating down on Areme's back. Warm, lazy puffs of wind carried the hum of expectation and smell of sweat and horseshit. Poor folk leaned against the rails, eyes wide with wonder at the sight of the nobility and the knights barely visible through dust kicked up by fine horses.

'Don't you think you'd better go?' Hessarde's gaze darted between Areme and the stand, as the columns of riders dwindled. 'You're going to run out of cover to hide this white beast.'

'You think a few bays are going to blot out a white horse?' Areme concentrated on the horsemaster, the master of ceremonies, who sat to the king's right. 'The less time Gerhas has to work himself into an uproar, the more chance we have of pulling this off.'

As the last line of riders acknowledged the king, Gerhas arose.

Areme closed his legs and Aurion cantered forward. Light silvered the stallion's coat as they cut through the returning ranks of horsemen like a sword.

The explosion came as Areme expected.

Gerhas thundered, 'What's the meaning of this?'

Ignoring the horsemaster with as much effrontery as Jaien had the king, Areme deliberately urged Aurion to stand directly before the princess. He executed a sweeping salute to the king, who received it with a severe frown and the faintest nod. Before it could be prohibited, Areme fixed Orlanda with his stare and launched the declaration. 'I present this stallion, Aurion, for the favour of her Royal Highness, Princess Orlanda of Mirador.'

Ranks of nobles fell silent and the crowd's hubbub dropped to a murmur. Gerhas's face turned purple. Brushing aside the idea with an impatient sweep of his hand, he turned to the king, but before he could voice one word, a bellowing roar broke across the field. Like a storm breaking on a fair summer's day, a massive black stallion galloped onto the field, ridden by a black-clad knight of Romondor.

Areme wheeled Aurion, and fought hard not to draw sword as he glared at Veren. What the fuck did he think he was doing?

Shouts broke out in the royal galleries. Nobles rose from their seats, faces ablaze with fury. Outrage ran along each row. The words 'traitor' and 'vulture' flashed around the crowd in a continuous sparking of heated anger. As the jeering increased, the latecomer slowed to a canter nearing the dais, black stallion's neck arched, foam spattering its chest from rolled-back lips.

Like Areme, Veren rode without saddle or bridle, completely at ease despite the uproar his arrival caused. He checked his steed before the king, pulled off his raven-plumed helm with one hand. Thick, ebony hair fell straight over Veren's shoulders, merging with his black tabard, mail and tunic. His brows, double strokes of black, were set above eyes of jet. With his other hand he drew his sword in one flowing motion and made deferential obeisance to the king with a bow every bit as elaborate as Areme's.

Areme itched even more to draw sword, that familiar feeling seeping into every nerve, the need to kill, to tear, to rend. He fought it down as one voice rose above the general outcry.

'A beast proposes to match himself against decent kingdom men?' Striding toward the king's stand, his eyes stroking the Romondor knight's flesh with the flagellating caress of a whip master, a hulking Mirador knight bellowed with all the power he could muster, 'How is this animal allowed to enter our demesne? Is he to be given leave to make sport of us?'

Veren stared straight ahead at the king, saying nothing.

Knight Commander Balfere stopped several yards from Veren, as though to ensure he stayed sufficiently clear to avoid the defilement of the Romondor knight's touch. 'What Gods-cursed demon brings you here, to insult all these good people, your peers and your sovereign lord? This effrontery will not go unpunished.' He drew his sword. 'With your permission, Majesty, I'll deal with this dog.'

Areme bit down another smile. The peace might not even last the morning.

To the amazement of the crowd, the king stood and said, 'Your zeal to preserve my honour and that of our people is commended, Balfere. However, this man has come in accordance with my open invitation.' To Veren, he bowed in return, as though the knight was his equal and not a representative of the most despised of enemies. 'Welcome, Veren,' Callinor said. 'My stewards informed me of your arrival. The snows must be heavy – you have arrived with barely time to spare.'

Veren inclined his head. 'Majesty, I trust you'll forgive my tardiness.'

'No matter,' replied Callinor. 'But let us delay the tournament no longer.'

Veren turned to Areme. They eye-fucked each other, long and hard. Rage fired within Areme, growing more heated with every passing heartbeat. Callinor had deliberately invited the Romondor knight to Mirador, to deflect the populace's hatred from himself to those they held in even greater revulsion.

Travall, he noted, did nothing. He must have known Veren had been invited to take part in the tourney. Travall was King's Champion, no doubt privy to Callinor's plans. Interesting he had not informed his fellow Knight Commanders. What else was he hiding?

Veren turned to the princess. 'Romondor presents *this* horse, Belarion, to her most gracious Highness, the High Princess of the Kingdom of Mirador.' Everything about his manner was painstakingly courteous, but still the murmur of the crowd swelled into a howl of protest.

Areme's hand tightened on his sword hilt. What was the Godsfucked prick playing at?

Gerhas appeared to be beside himself, his expression black thunder. Only the king retained his composure, face an impenetrable mask as he raised his hands, signalling quiet before he turned to the princess and whispered something. Her face was hidden behind a veil, but her rigid body betrayed her horror at the black knight's arrival.

Callinor's face remained unreadable, but his gaze was fixed on her, as if he could force her into submission by sheer will.

Don't give in to him. Areme set his own will against the king's. Straining his eyes as if to see through her cowl, he matched his stare with Callinor's. *Come on, come on.* Beneath him, Aurion's hoof dug at the ground, mirroring Areme's agitation.

This was her battle to fight, this girl who gazed at him as if he was her entire world, this girl who could not seem to think of anything except him. He had put her off, constantly, but now, here, he counted on her obsession, and wished suddenly he had given her more than his disdain to hang her hopes upon. He should have gone to her last night, told her what to do, bedded her if necessary. Anything to ensure this horse stayed close. Would she ignore him now out of sheer spite?

A heavy pulse beat in the side of Areme's neck. *Come on, girl.*

Slowly she arose and stepped down from the podium. She paused, turning her head from Areme to the black knight, as if she did not know what to do. Her body shook all over, heaving almost, as if she were battling tears.

Come on, girl. You're better than that. Don't give in to your father.

She stood, unmoving, a statue clad in grey.

Come on, girl. Let's see some of that spirit for which you're infamous. Don't give in to them.

She walked toward Veren. Unreasoning panic swept over Areme. *No!* His heart struck him a blow under his throat. He reeled as though the foundations had been pulled from beneath his boots and he was plunging into an abyss.

Orlanda stopped a pace from Veren.

She pulled back her cowl to reveal hooded eyes beneath long, dark lashes. Her eyes met Areme's, deep wells of cerulean, depths darkened, crying out for help.

He could offer her nothing. This was one battle she must fight alone. But with every ounce of will, he bade her to turn away from the black knight.

She looked up at Veren, tore off her veil. Drawn lips delivered not even a faint tremble of a smile. Her brow furrowed, hard in concentration, as though she were a child trying to recall exactly what she had been told to say.

Don't say it. Don't say it. Areme's body tensed with strain.

Then her eyes became stone. With one hand she drew out the combs holding her hair swept back in a coif. A heavy river of gold glossy hair fell like a waterfall to her waist.

The crowd gasped.

Areme closed his eyes. Here it was. The defiance. Only whores loosed their hair in public. She was delivering a message clearer than words. To Romondor. To her father. If they considered her a whore, she would act like one.

She stepped forward and tied her token around the black knight's arm. In a thin voice, she said, 'Knight Commander Veren of Romondor and this horse may challenge for the warhorse trial.'

The black knight's face never changed as he replaced his helm over his dark hair, and bowed once more to the princess.

Areme stared at Orlanda, heart hammering. What now? Was that as far as she dared take it?

As if in answer to his thoughts, she turned to him. Hollowed cheeks, alabaster skin so pale and drawn it stretched over fine, jutting bones, held the ice pallor of death.

Horrified, Areme stared hard. What had happened to her? Had Callinor beaten her?

She held up her hand, the silk veil fluttering from her trembling fingers. Areme breathed a sigh of relief as, amidst cheers, the princess walked toward him. Clear defiance in her voice, she said, 'This horse may *also* challenge for the warhorse trial.'

Areme bent down to accept her token from shaking hands. Their eyes locked. There was no more pleading within hers, and just three words ground from between her clenched lips. 'Win, damn you.' She turned and strode back to the royal gallery, hair a shimmering banner of mockery.

Areme curbed a smile, veiling his satisfaction in a façade of stony indifference. For the first time since he had known her, she seemed worthy of her title, a princess made of steel. She would need to be, for what the future held.

As she resumed her place on the dais, Veren spurred his black close to Areme. 'The girl has spirit, brother.'

Areme spat. 'Don't soil your mouth with false words of kinship. I have only ever had one true brother, and both you and I know he's a corpse.' He spun Aurion away to the edge of the tourney field. The nonsense had come to an end. Now the war would begin.

Hessarde stepped forward, a broad grin pasted on his lips, and reached out to pat Aurion. Flattening his ears, the white stallion went to bite. Hessarde jumped back and his eyes shot daggers at the horse. 'What in all the hells is wrong with him?'

'Nothing. He answers to only one master, and he'll try to kill anyone else.' Areme's eyes impaled Hessarde. 'Leave him alone unless you're looking forward to another reincarnation.'

Hessarde wiped sweat from his brow with the back of his gloved hand. 'No offence, Lord Master, but I like this life too well to be contemplating another.' He pushed a bow into Areme's gloved hand. 'I hope Aurion chooses the girl, then.

Because if it's not her, we'll all be up for regicide, or whatever it's called when you kill a princess. I still can't understand why the boy can still handle him.'

Areme's gaze swept unerringly to where Sihan stood among peasants, right across from the dais, in full damned view of Gerhas in disobedience of Areme's instructions. The stallion would turn on him, too, sooner or later. Sihan was just lucky Areme had found the horse before it killed him. He kept watching Sihan. What was it about him? There was something there he could not place. Something horribly familiar. Cold swept over Areme. Thoughts of a dead boy filled his mind. A boy who had died a thousand years before at the end of a lance. The only one he would ever acknowledge as his brother. Merien. Areme shook his head. He needed to concentrate.

Just then, Jaien rode past, chestnut frothing foam from its mouth.

'That horse looks good.' Hessarde's voice came as through fog. 'Almost as good as the one he won on last year. Falcon.'

Areme shrugged, forcing his mind back to the present. 'Old news. There's not a horse here that can touch Aurion.' He watched Sihan still, trying to find the cause of the unease he felt.

'What about Veren?' asked Hessarde.

'An annoyance, nothing more.' A lie. And Hessarde knew it.

Hessarde tilted his head in that odd manner of his whenever he was about to make a mocking remark, but held his silence at Areme's warning glance. Areme's fingers tangled in Aurion's mane. Could the white stallion match the black? Was it really the one he had awaited for a millennium? Soon he would know.

Trumpets blared and the crowd cheered as Jaien galloped his stallion onto the tourney field where stewards had set up the archery course. As the winner of the trials the year before, he was accorded the honour of blooding the targets, ten hides draped over hay, a heart circle marked on each. Spaced at uneven intervals, they zigzagged down the tourney field. Five to be shot at from the near side of the horse, five from the off side. Ten arrows. All at a gallop.

Jaien set his chestnut into flight. Smooth, precise, the knight drew each arrow, nocked it, fired. Beneath him, his horse dug deep divots into the ground with each stride, responding to the slightest tilt of its master's body, turning without pause from one target to the next. Arrow after arrow slammed the heart circle. Horse, rider, weapon; one.

Hessarde whistled. 'It's like that horse could do it in his sleep.'

In his sleep . . .

Areme clenched his fist as again a dead boy's face filled his vision, young, alive, arms outstretched, yelling, 'I'm flying!' as he rode a grey stallion across a meadow. Merien *was* flying, united with the animal – bonded that special way only true horsemen could be to a horse. Half-man, half-beast, sharing each other's thoughts, each other's will.

Areme's heart beat with the rhythm of hooves pounding the ground; in his mind he rode with Merien. With Jaien. His body became gossamer. Wind carried him, into the sky, above the clouds, close to the sun, the moon, the stars. Spirits flew with him, stretched out hands. Areme spread his arms, grabbed the hands of the spirits holding him. Let them guide him on invisible wings.

A voice whispered in his ear, low, as though about to reveal a secret. 'You must get out of the tangle of horses and men as quickly as you can.'

And then everywhere there were men on horses, carrying lances, swords, quivers brimming with arrows. But the place was not Mirador – rather a fortress a thousand years distant, and it was his voice he heard, talking to a boy. Merien. His brother.

'Give your horse the reins, trust him, he knows the course, what to do. You have ridden again and again the patterns, he knows the way in his sleep.'

In his sleep . . .

Areme's eyes blinked open in time to see the last of Jaien's arrows edge the heart circle of the final target.

'Nearly a perfect score,' Hessarde said, applauding in spite of himself. 'Jaien only missed one heart.'

Areme gathered his scattered wits, said with anger more for himself, 'He should have marked all ten.' What was it that spurred memories of Merien to come flooding back now? On top of all those others he fought down each day.

Hatred coursed through him – hatred he had thought well behind him. Hatred instilled in him since birth, honed throughout his childhood, his youth, his never-ending life. Areme breathed heavily. Centuries stretched behind him, and a succession of corpses of those he had loved, dead through his fault. His brother. His wife.

He shouldn't be thinking of either, though they were the reason he was here. He forced his attention to Veren as the black horse of Romondor commenced its round. The stallion snorted, mane streaming in the wind like a pennon. Hooves drummed, ramming the ground. Veren drew his arrows in a sweeping arc from the gorytos strapped to his back, nocking them to his bow. Each flew true to its mark. At the end of a perfect round, the crowd hissed.

Areme hawked, spurring Aurion forth as a steward called, 'Knight Commander Areme! Present!'

Blood running fast, Areme drew his recurve bow, a slight touch of his heels sending Aurion to the start of the trial, every step pliant, prancing. Now he would see.

He checked the stallion with just a thought. Aurion stood, ears pricked, listening to the excited murmur of the crowd, flickering back for Areme's instructions, entire body rigid with the tension of an arrow ready for release. He pawed the ground.

Wait. Wait. The steward prepared to give the signal. Muscles bunched and gathered under Areme.

'Go!' shouted the steward, dropping his staff.

Aurion read Areme's mind, plunging from halt to gallop in one bound. Hooves slashed the ground. Faster. Faster. Aurion executed rapid, effortless turns, responding to Areme's body urging him to longer and longer strides till he was flying, barely touching grass or dirt.

Areme's blood quickened. Here it was – the horse he had awaited, the Gods-blessed stallion between his knees. No unicorn yet, but power was there, the promise of supernatural speed. Just a matter of time.

As Aurion galloped down the line of markers, he answered immaculately every command as though Areme's thoughts were his, the least tightening of knees, the feather movement of hand. Wind streamed through Areme's hair, under his tunic, sliding over his skin. He leaned forward, urging the horse faster, harder.

Each arrow hit its mark. Near side, off side. It did not matter.

With only the pressure of his legs to guide the stallion, at full gallop Areme turned his body back to line up the final target. If this one flew home, he would tie the first trial. He nocked the last arrow.

A sense of ease flowed through Areme, of mastery. Beneath him moved a horse of such might and power as he had only dreamed. Glory surged into him, possessed him, racing through his body like quicksilver.

All warhorses possessed rare qualities, spirit and tolerance, speed of arrows in full flight, endurance and tenacity of mules. They could slide to a dead halt from a crazed charge; pass from retreat to attack at the breath of a signal from their rider. Yet no horse he had ever ridden could match this stallion.

A wild thought darted back and forth through Areme's mind uncontrolled. The horse was perfectly obedient to him. No saddle or bridle needed here. Could *he* be the one bonded to the unicorn?

As if responding to the wayward drift of thoughts, Aurion shifted a fraction, and Areme's final arrow slammed a hairsbreadth wide of the heart circle. Areme swore under his breath.

A herald called out the result. 'A win to Knight Commander Veren of Romondor.'

Cursing inwardly, Areme brought Aurion back to his waiting men. He snapped his fingers at Sedor. 'Lance! Helm!'

The bearded soldier ran forward with a lance, spear point tipping the shaft at twelve feet, while Hessarde strapped on Areme's armoured breastplate and another man handed the knight his helm. A herald called the list, pairing riders against each other, then bellowed out the rules of the joust. 'All riders will ride bareback. No one may cast their weapon or aim at the horse. Winners only advance.'

Areme waited, sun hot on his back, breeze so meagre it barely fluttered the skirt of his surcoat. Sweat trickled beneath his gambeson. He had lost the first trial by being unfocused, awestruck by the beast he rode. He would not make that mistake again. He examined his lance, testing the balance.

When he finally entered the list, a narrow strip of trampled earth before the royal gallery marked by ropes and stakes, a storm of cheering broke from the crowd of hundreds packed tight along the line. Areme ignored them, staring instead down the long run, focusing on his first opponent, a young knight from Maroden. He snapped down his visor, closing off all sound.

The herald dropped his staff. Aurion launched into a gallop, flying straight and true like a bolt from a crossbow. The shattering impact of steel on shield jolted Areme's arm back and splintered his lance. His opponent flipped back over his horse's rump to slide to a grunting halt in the dust.

As a circle of squires surrounded the felled knight, Areme rotated his lance in an arc, wondering how many knights he would need to spit before he came to the one that mattered. To the accompaniment of wild cheers, he rode back to where his men waited, then settled in to watch the other knights show their paces.

Raucous jeers met horses shying away as their opposites thundered toward them – an automatic elimination. Cheering met favourites. Shafts cracked and splintered, broken pieces of lances tossed high in the air as men crashed to the ground.

The fierce sun peaked, blazing on armour, striking sparks of light off gleaming coats, and still the bouts went on and on in a blur of colour, of shouting and yelling and spurring of mounts. Hooves beat the ground to the accompaniment of screams and crashes. Squires hauled water buckets for knights and horses soaked in sweat.

Areme lined up against one opponent after another, felling man after man. So did Jaien and Veren, the Pelan knight unhorsing his final victim with a mighty crack full on the helm.

Only three horses remained undefeated. The sun was well past its zenith when Areme was called to meet Jaien. Areme stared hard at him, hand closed on the lance, and once again dreams and memory crashed upon conscious thought.

A scream tore the world apart. A boy lurched forward on his horse's neck, toppled, struck the ground with a thud, shield clattering and rolling till it came to rest in the grass.

Trumpets blared and horns. Shouts thickened the air. But only one scream lingered, a cry of eternity. Areme's cry, 'Merien!' carrying all the horror, despair, grief and fury a brother could feel for causing the death of his brother.

Sweat pearled on Areme's brow, stuck his tunic to his back. He stared at Jaien. Saw Merien – lying on the ground with a lanced spear thrust through his gut.

Stared at Jaien. Saw Merien. Blood pooling in grass.

Who? Who? Who? The question blew across the field.

The lance slid from his hand.

'What are you doing?' demanded Hessarde, stooping to pick it up.

Jaien sat quietly on his horse at the other end of the list. Too quietly. The hum of the crowd died away.

Areme's eyes narrowed as he studied the knight through his visored helm, then he put heels to Aurion and trotted down the list.

Hessarde called out, running after him with the lance, 'What are you doing?'

'He's conceding.' Areme did not know how he knew, but he did. And was glad of it, for as sure as anything, he knew he could never aim a lance at Jaien's chest, not now, not ever. And for the life of him, he did not know why.

Jaien held his lance vertical and set spur to his chestnut. Both men met in the centre and halted. The knight of Pelan tipped his visor up. Sweat poured down his brow, dewed his lashes, but his eyes were keen. 'I'm finished. I concede.'

'Horseshit,' snapped Areme. 'You're not even winded. You're doing this for the lad.'

'Think whatever you like,' said Jaien, wheeling his horse away.

The herald cried, 'Forfeit by Knight Captain Jaien of Pelan. Knight Commander Areme of Mirador advances to the final round.'

Areme returned to the end of the list, hand shaking so much he thought he might lose the lance Hessarde thrust at him.

What was wrong with him? Why did he see his dead brother everywhere he looked this day? Why?

He had to concentrate. He had to win, or all was lost.

The herald called the final pairing. 'Knight Commander Areme of Mirador against Knight Commander Veren of Romondor.'

Areme balanced the heavy lance in his hand. His arm steadied, grew strong once more. This was an adversary whose neck he would have no hesitation in breaking.

Formidable and imposing, Veren waited at the other end of the lists, a dark silhouette of banded mail against the forest of bright pennons snapping in the rising breeze. His face was hidden by his helm, horsehair plume rippling. His mount, Belarion, snorted loudly, as though he was ridding his nostrils of some hated scent.

'Smash that vulture into the dust!' someone screamed.

Then the crowd grew quiet.

Areme pulled down his visor. 'You're not going to flinch, are you?' he whispered to himself, staring at the black stallion he knew of old.

As Aurion pranced to the marker, Areme held the lance in his right hand, angled across the stallion's neck. The steward dropped the staff. Areme set Aurion into a gallop. Belarion thundered at him down the line.

Training the head of his lance at Veren's head, Areme focused on his target, ignoring the vibration of the oncoming horse's hooves and the roar of the crowd. A full hit would snap the vulture's neck, and no one present would care one stitch. It would give him the win he needed, not to mention a great deal of satisfaction. The two horses closed to within striking distance. Lances came down. Areme's eyes slitted. Hot wind flowed through his visor. *Focus. Focus. On the helm.*

He threw his weight forward. Clenched his teeth. Waited for the jolt beneath his armpit.

Suddenly muscles bunched beneath him, the stallion's back rounding so he became one giant curve of flesh. The great neck curled over, head disappearing between the stallion's legs. Then the massive hoofs struck the ground with hammer blows so hard they shook every bone in Areme's body. Aurion transformed into a storm of plunging and rearing. Areme could scarcely believe the speed with which everything fell into chaos. The horse launched so swiftly to maniacal bucking Areme's arm was still extended with the lance – but Veren was no longer there to be impaled.

Something slammed into Areme. He fought for balance, falling forward, clutching at a gaping gash between his ribs. He lost count of how many times the horse whipped about. The world dissolved into an incoherent chaos of fire and dust and hooves and dirt as he smashed into the ground.

Chapter 17

The Speed Trial

Cries of anguish erupted around the field. Stewards raced to the knight lying on the ground, his face contorted in agony. Riderless, Aurion spun and galloped back to Areme, rearing when anyone approached the stricken rider. His neck snaked. Forelegs sliced the air.

Fighting down his own terror, Sihan ducked under the railing, shoving past soldiers in an effort to reach the white stallion before he killed Areme, or anyone else. He could not quite believe what had happened. Aurion had been perfect, and then blown like a volcano. And he had lost two trials. What hope was there now to save his father?

'Someone get a halter!' shouted a soldier as the rampaging stallion struck at him.

Aurion charged and clamped his teeth on another man's shoulder, shaking him mercilessly. The cracking of bone stopped everyone's advance.

'Finish him with a sword!' yelled a voice from the crowd.

Veren circled on Belarion, then dismounted and advanced toward Areme. As the white stallion moved to strike him, he drew his sword, a night-black blade matching everything else about him.

'No!' cried Sihan, trying to worm a way through a hedge of soldiers.

Veren ignored the plea, but as he swung at the white horse, his blade met another in a fierce clash of steel against steel. A knight wearing the Mirador surcoat threw Veren back.

'Get away from him, you black vulture!' Balfere levelled his sword point at Veren's throat. 'I'll not let you shed another drop of the blood of Mirador upon this field.'

'If I don't kill that white demon, Balfere,' answered Veren coldly, 'you'll have the death of your own knight upon your head. Can't you see he needs help?'

'I think you've given him enough help already.' Balfere's face glowed red with fury.

Soldiers encircling him, Aurion plunged, teeth bared, roaring challenge. As a ring of armed men closed around the white stallion, every hand clenched around sword hilts, Jaien forced his way through to Sihan and grabbed his arm. Aurion rushed forward once more, aiming a lethal kick at the nearest man.

'Let me go!' Sihan struggled against Jaien's hands, unable to muster a scrap of strength equal to the knight's iron hold.

Jaien pulled him back. 'It's finished.'

Suddenly a girl rushed into the milling throng of soldiers, grey cloak swirling about her. Blonde hair spilling over her shoulders, she dodged through the cordon of men to stand before Aurion. 'Get out of my way!' she screamed, voice high and strained.

'The princess!' The cry of disbelief came from several horror-struck voices.

Pricking his ears, Aurion came down from a rear. He settled to all four legs, snorted, and stretched out his nose to the girl.

'Get away from me.' She whacked Aurion sharply on the nose and ran past him to Areme's side.

Aurion snorted, throwing his head up, but all the fire extinguished as rapidly as it had ignited.

With an effort, Sihan tore himself free and pushed through the soldiers to Aurion's side. The stallion stood with eyes fixed upon the princess. Sihan ripped off his belt and circled it around the horse's neck, staring down the soldiers who still held swords at the ready.

The princess knelt at the fallen knight's side, grey cloak spilling round her on the trampled grass.

'What happened?' Areme asked, voice weak, eyes glazed.

'Don't talk,' whispered the princess, hand shaking as she stroked his paling cheek.

'Let me through!' commanded Gerhas, cleaving through the mob to where Balfere still had his sword levelled at Veren.

His warning gaze swept over them. 'It was an accident,' he said to Balfere. 'Withdraw.'

'I swear I'll not let this swine leave the field alive,' growled the Mirador knight.

'Then you'll have to fight me to do it.' Gerhas's hand moved to his own sword. 'You both know the edicts. We are met in peace. No arms to be drawn.'

'Horsemaster,' Veren said with civility. 'The horse went mad. I drew only to protect your man.' He returned his blade to its scabbard, then threw a steely glare at Balfere. 'Then this bragabout drew on me.'

'He knows full well why I call him to account,' stormed Balfere. 'Our knights lie dead because of him. I'll not have him draw sword on another while I draw breath.'

'Enough!' said the horsemaster. 'These quarrels are long dead. Sheathe your weapon, Balfere. Draw it not without order. Not for any pretext! I charge all in attendance thus!'

'There will be no more talk of fighting,' declared the king, striding onto the field, his command seconding Gerhas's demand for order. The crowd muttered, parting as he approached. 'There will be no further blood let upon this field,' continued the king. 'Horsemaster Gerhas speaks truth, and any who dispute this will answer to me.'

Balfere sheathed his sword with studied deliberation, but his gaze never left Veren.

The king lifted his hand, motioning for quiet. 'I declare Knight Commander Veren is innocent of wrong-doing.' He glared at Balfere and Veren. 'You, gentlemen, bear it in mind, and see to it you keep your oaths. I'll have no more hot words hurled about.' Ignoring the murmurs of disquiet amongst the crowd, he turned his attention to Areme. Bending down, he pried loose his daughter's fingers still clutching the knight's hand. 'Leave. This is not your place.'

'My place is at his side!'

'Take her back to the dais,' ordered the king.

'No!' cried the princess.

'Go!' roared Callinor.

Convulsing hard with tears, the princess stood, swaying. Soldiers marched back to the dais with her in their midst.

Areme's eyes grew distant. Blood soaked through his gambeson to form a dark stain on the field. He said with effort, 'Sihan . . .'

The king glanced at Gerhas, who motioned Sihan forward. Sihan left Aurion to Jaien and knelt down beside Areme. The knight's face became a paler shade of grey, voice air as he clutched Sihan's arm. 'Ride the horse, boy.' With the last of his strength, he untied the princess's veil and handed it to Sihan. 'Ride the horse and keep it safe.' Then his head fell back and his eyes rolled over white before the eyelids shuttered.

Gerhas knelt over the still body, pressing his hand to brow and throat. He raised one eyelid and stared into an eye blank and expressionless. He looked up to confront Sihan with a bleak glare. 'If this man dies, the fault lies with you.'

Stricken, Sihan stumbled back as Gerhas and Balfere lifted Areme's body and carried him from the field. A red stain fouled the grass where the knight's blood had seeped down under his right side.

The king turned to Sihan and Veren. 'You will continue with the trial.'

Veren inclined his head, pausing to stare long and hard at Sihan as if taking his measure, before walking back to his horse.

The king's glance was equally chilled as he turned to Sihan. 'You ride for Mirador.' He motioned for one of his guards to divest himself of his tabard, then handed it to Sihan, blood staining the soft white wool where his hands held it. 'Hope for your sake and your father's you win and Areme lives.'

Sihan stared down at the blood on his own hands. So much blood. How had it all come to this? His father in a dungeon. Areme dying. And all fault lay squarely at his door just as it had when Yonnad had fallen in Yseth.

Words spun from memory. *Ride for me, Anise. Against the Black Prince. Win for me or we're lost.*

Then the night of Aurion's birth crowded his thoughts and other, darker words. *You are not Sihan*, the boy in the snow had said. *You are not Sihan.*

Who am I, then?
Ride for me, Anise, and win.
I will.

Sihan trembled. It was as if she had known what would happen. That he would ride against Veren. Sihan shook the confusion from his mind. Veren was no prince. And no matter how many ghosts or zingars tried to imply otherwise, Sihan's name was not Anise.

What madness had he promised?

He hardly knew when they got back to the horse lines, or how the saddle got on Aurion's back. He was mad and ghosts were stalking him, and Aurion was madder still, and if Sihan did not overcome all that, his father might rot forever or worse. In a daze, he yanked the girth strap with both hands, coarse palms closed around oiled leather, forcing all his will and concentration to each minute point of saddling the horse. 'It's all my fault,' he muttered, tightening the girth another hole. 'Everything. I should have taken the soldier's commission.'

'Shut up,' snapped Jaien, bridling the stallion and buckling the throat lash. 'Areme's a knight. He knew the risks.'

'I should have trusted you. You said you'd get my father released.' Sihan brushed angrily at stinging eyes. 'I've been blaming you for everything when it was all my idea in the first place.'

'Your father isn't free yet, and you don't know me from squid. You've no reason to trust me, and stop blaming yourself. I could have stopped you, but I didn't. I backed this plan. So I own that fault as much as you.' Jaien's lips pressed together as he tossed a broad leather strap over the saddle and secured it with a flat knot on the underside of the girth strap.

Suddenly Kheran ran up, Tejas in tow, both their faces flushed. 'Have you heard?' he asked excitedly. 'The final joust has been declared a foul. Gerhas ruled Veren violated chivalry by not pulling his lance when Aurion went berserk on Areme.'

'Rot,' said Jaien. 'Anyone could see he didn't have time to pull his lance. Aurion forced Areme onto it.'

Quiet Tejas spoke up. 'Veren's Romondor scum. He deserves no consideration.'

Kheran said to Sihan, 'Aurion and the black horse were both declared joint winners of the joust. Aurion can still tie with Belarion overall if he wins the speed trial. Then it's up to the princess to choose between them, and we all know she won't choose Romondor.'

'Well,' said Jaien. 'That's a bit of hopeful news. Now you two get to your horses.' Jaien pulled roughly on Sihan's sleeve, drawing him to one side. 'I know we've gone over the course a hundred times before, but I've made some changes. The less time it takes, the less time Aurion has to go berserk.'

Drawing a shuddering breath, Sihan nodded.

'You need to be up with the leaders from the outset. Don't take any of the long routes like when you're riding untried horses. Cut every corner, and keep clear of trouble.' Jaien scraped a triangle in the dirt with the heel of one worn boot. 'Here's the course. A straight run to the first marker, the Gallows Tree. After you turn, it's a giant curve to the next marker.'

Sihan frowned. 'You've marked it straight.'

'Short cut,' said Jaien. 'I took it last year on Falcon. Don't follow the trail. Head down the hill. It's rough, but cuts off a half-league. Then you hit the forest. It's one trail going in, splitting fast into three branches. The one to the right is a dead end.'

'I know, I know,' said Sihan. 'It stops at the Death Gorge.'

Jaien half-smiled. 'Just making sure.'

'Of what? That I'm not a complete loon?'

'Desperation can lead to mad decisions.'

'I'm not that desperate.' Or that mad, though Sihan was not quite sure about either.

The gorge had long ago split a hill in half, a river winding through it, the same river flowing past the fortress. Now water flowed around a broken off portion, wearing it away till it resembled a broken off spire. Once, when the gap had been smaller, horsemen had tested the bravery of their horses by daring the leap across the gorge. His own father had won the trials on Celestion by doing so, many years past. But as time wore on, the gorge had become too wide for such folly. After a string of deaths, earning the gorge its ignominious title, the attempt to jump it had been forbidden by king's edict, a ban no sane horseman defied.

Sihan said, 'Go on.'

Jaien continued, 'The track to the left is safe, but long. Don't risk throwing away your lead. Take the middle track. It runs along the edge of the gorge for some way before it heads back down to the plain. Aurion's surefooted enough not to run into trouble.' Jaien patted Sihan's shoulder. 'Stay close to me and Wedge for as long as you can. I'll be trying to set the pace. The rest is up to you.'

Sihan gathered the reins and swung onto Aurion's back. Immediately the stallion wheeled, lunged, propped – charged the few strides to the tourney fence, spun and rushed along it. A blur of faceless bodies leapt back. Aurion baulked, then sped, never going in the same direction for more than a few strides. Swirling dust clouds choked the air. Aurion's back humped, but Sihan was already upright as the stallion launched a fit of bucking. Sihan drove his heels in, forcing the horse's head high.

Nose thrust skyward, Aurion slid to a stop. Sihan jabbed him in the mouth, backing the horse till his quarters smacked the fence. When he tried to take off again, Sihan sat back, curbing the stallion's flight, breaking it to a jerking jog. Amid the thick of the drifting dust he had created, he met Jaien's worried face.

'It's all right,' Sihan called, knowing it was not. It was going to be Yseth all over again.

He shook the thought away. Fingernails bit into palms. His grip tightened on the reins. He could ride this horse. He must.

Jaien mounted Wedge and rode to his side. 'Are you all right?'

'Fine,' muttered Sihan, not bothering to hide the lie.

Jaien slapped him on the knee. 'Belarion might look as though he's built like a siege tower, but he's as fast as a stone from a sling. Don't underestimate him.'

'I won't.'

Jaien stared at him for a long moment with a look half-guarded, half-bold, then slid his gaze away. Sihan decided it was time to amend one error, to apologise. 'I–'

The cry of a horn whipped across the field like a fierce wind, cutting him off.

'What?' asked Jaien.

Seizing the moment, Sihan spun Aurion round and reached out to touch Jaien's arm and said, 'Good fortune.'

Jaien eyed him steadily, no smile in his eyes or on his lips. 'More to you.'

Sihan wheeled Aurion toward the starting markers. Dust and the hot smell of sweating horseflesh filled his nostrils. Stallions bit and kicked at each other, wild with the surging heat of blood. Brassy neighs tore the air. Men shouted insults at their enemies and encouragement to their friends. Graycor Senfari were everywhere, wolf skin caps pulled low over eyebrows. Somewhere in the mess of horses rode Kheran and Tejas and Asher.

Sihan whipped his head from side to side, searching for a clear path. The crowd was nothing but a blur of half-frightened, half-excited faces pressed against the ropes, men kidding the riders, women ogling, children crying. Dogs rushed back and forth, barking and snapping, rolling in smoking mounds of wet dung, yelping when a horse kicked them and sent them sprawling. One stallion let fly with a kick at the horse in front of Sihan, landing a glancing blow on its shoulder.

Sihan wove Aurion in and out of the milling throng, the snaking heads, the plunging bodies. No use Aurion getting injured before they had even started the race. But his mind was spinning. Could he control Aurion long enough to finish the race? Could he even make it to the start? When would Aurion erupt again?

Beneath him, great muscles rippled. Aurion bannered his tail, stepping high, no sign of strain from his countless jousts. Why would there be? Sihan's father always said the mountains of Graycor bred horses with strong lungs, endurance, made them hard.

Sihan wondered at the irony. He was here. In Mirador. Riding Aurion in the trials. Not the way he had dreamed it, or wanted it, or even planned it. He shook his head. He had to concentrate.

Another stallion flattened its ears and leapt high into the air, kicking out behind, its hooves flashing past Aurion's ears.

'Hey!' shouted Sihan. 'Control your piss-arsed horse! This isn't a war zone.'

He almost grinned when the rider turned toward him. Sandy hair falling over his smiling face, Jaien shouted over the din of hooves and yelling men, 'Wedge thinks *every* race start is a war zone.'

Beneath Sihan, Aurion squealed and his body became ramrod-stiff. Belarion appeared at his side, legs moving in a high-kneed trot.

Sihan stole a close look at the Romondor stallion. Its nostrils flared, wide and scarlet; its ears cocked sharply forward. Intent black eyes fringed with dark lashes matched the skirts of hair flaring over massive hooves pounding dirt into submission. Its legs were trunks of solid bone. Its body a mountain of muscle, neck broad and arched. It could not possibly be as fast as Jaien thought. Sihan flicked a glance at the rider, flushed hot as their eyes met and he realised the Romondor knight had been examining him and Aurion with as much intensity as Sihan had been studying them. Knight Commander Veren inclined his head in brief, silent salute, eyes dark and unreadable.

Sihan forced himself to return the courtesy. He still could not believe the king had let a murderer enter the warhorse trials. How a knight of Romondor even dared show his face in Mirador was beyond him.

The two horses danced around each other, belching heavy, snorting breaths from flaring nostrils set in tight-checked, drawn-in muzzles. Aurion pinned his ears, pawed the ground, raking up dust. He lifted one hoof to strike. The black did not even twitch an ear in his direction. Aurion reefed the reins from Sihan's grip, clamped bared teeth into Belarion's rump in passing, drew a crimson stain. Before Sihan could spin Aurion clear, the black's murderous kick of retribution landed with a bone-crushing jar in Aurion's chest. The white stallion reared, plunging after the black.

'Hold! Hold!' cried Sihan, flinging his weight back.

The black stallion swerved to meet Aurion, feinting as if to strike. Sihan knew what was coming. He braced for the shock. Then a blur of chestnut swept between the two stallions. Wedge shouldered Aurion clear of the black. 'Is he all right?' shouted Jaien.

Sihan leaned forward, horrified at the pulsing crimson stream flowing down Aurion's chest.

'Riders! To the start!' the herald bellowed.

'How bad is it?' cried Sihan.

'I can't tell!' called back Jaien.

'Godsfuck! Do I pull out?' He could not pull out.

Jaien snatched at Aurion's bridle, looking down at his chest. 'He's not lame.'

'Riders! Present!'

'Come on!' shouted Jaien, yanking Aurion along by the bridle. 'You'll know if it's bad once we're running. Pull him out then, if you have to.'

'Godshit,' muttered Sihan. There was no time even to apply granine. But he gathered reassurance from each long, springing stride beneath him. His fingers clawed a handful of mane so Aurion could not shoot off and leave him sitting in the dust at the start.

The herald motioned to a man holding a hooded firefalcon. Sihan tensed, waiting for the signal. The falconer pulled off the bird's hood, loosened its harness. Sihan crouched low over Aurion's neck, easing his weight forward. Legs beat swift beneath him, a staccato drumbeat. Aurion champed at the bit, trying to reef the reins through Sihan's fingers. *Wait. Wait.*

The falconer hoisted his arm aloft. A flash of red feathers blazed against the azure sky.

The crowd roared.

Sihan jolted in the saddle as Aurion grabbed the bit and ran. Around them, massed horses surged forward as one, a tumult of horseflesh and screaming riders. Air clogged with dust, the clash of metal, the tremendous confusion of trampling hooves as a hedge of bodies rushed across the open field.

Aurion lengthened stride, white legs racing alongside black, brown, bay and chestnut, hooves drumming the ground, beating wild music, till his hooves barely touched the ground, floating, effortless. Sihan's breath caught in relief. Aurion was not hurt. Not if he could race like this.

Stride for stride, the galloping swell of horses surged across the open field. Sihan slitted his eyes against clods of earth spattering him from hooves of horses in front, the crowd a mere blur on the fringes of vision. Something banged against his leg.

'Move over,' a voice shouted beside him.

'*You* move,' Sihan yelled back, wincing as metal greaves scraped his leg. Shouts and curses filled the air. Riders jostled each other, angling for clear paths into the trees. The Senfari drove their horses ahead, Jaien among them, as if they dared the trees to hit them. Despite Jaien's instructions to stay near the lead, Sihan held Aurion back, gave ground, determined not to run blind into the forest. The Senfari were maddened, by what had happened to Armindras, by what was happening to their sons. They were prepared to risk all. Screams and the sickening thud of flesh against timber tore through Sihan as the tidal mass of horses crashed into the trees.

They dove from bright light into darkness. Trees whipped past, flashes of black. Sihan's breath exploded with a rush. By sheer blind luck Aurion raced along a track. Leaning low against the stallion's neck, Sihan strained to see through gloom. Low branches clawed his back. Heavy canopies of vines cut out the sun. The cloying fragrance of amethyst bellflowers overwhelmed every other scent as hard ground softened to a bed of pink petals on moss.

Shadow horses flickered around him, dodging close-knit trees, hooves thudding. Wet strings of moss slid over Sihan's face. Aurion tore along, pounding, pounding over soft, damp ground.

The forest thinned. The first marker, the Gallows Tree, stood in the middle of a tiny glade. Horses streamed into sunlight, converging on the tree.

The leading riders braced, swinging round it at speed. But others careered straight past, their horse's heads thrown up, fighting stinging steel in their mouths, ignoring their riders' commands to stop. A cry rang out.

Even in the confusion of galloping horses, Sihan recognised Jaien's voice. Wedge, unable to hold the turn, slipped and crashed in a tangle of chestnut legs. The horses following fell straight over the top of the stallion and his rider.

'Jaien!' The name tore from Sihan's throat as he stared at the jumble of bodies and flailing legs writhing in front of him.

He pulled on Aurion's reins, but the stallion refused to abate his whirlwind speed. Sihan jerked to and fro with all his weight. 'Hold! Hold!' he cried, but Aurion never broke stride, flying toward the mess of fallen horses. Bracing for the fall, Sihan seized a handful of mane. His back muscles contracted, his calves clamped in a vice.

Aurion leapt into the air, soared like a bird in flight, and then, in mid-air, seemed to rise higher as if on wings. The stricken men and horses passed by underneath in a blur of entangled flesh. Aurion landed inches in front of the crash. Instantly, the stallion made a sliding haunch turn to Sihan's command, then burst back into full gallop.

'Go! Go! Go!' Jaien's voice, somewhere behind.

Sihan dug his heels into Aurion's sweating flanks, a whirl of rumps and switching tails in front. 'Go, Aurion, go!' cried Sihan, trying to catch the leaders before they entered the next stretch of trees. He leaned low over the stallion's neck, sucked in the hot scent of sweat.

With dizzying speed, Aurion caught horse after horse, racing with the front-runners as they burst into the trees. Sihan ducked, leaves and twigs whipping across his back. Trunks closed together; grazed his legs. All around him, thin afternoon light speared through branches as horses flashed in and out of oblique shafts of sunlight.

They galloped round the flank of a hill. Dark platforms of granite and thick scrubby undergrowth appeared in front. The trail narrowed to a horse-width. Taking a gambler's risk on Jaien's short cut, Sihan turned Aurion and tore headlong downhill, bush-bashing his way toward the bottom of the slope. Branches lashed his head and neck, scratching, tearing. Sweat ran into his eyes. A bough whacked Aurion's shoulder and nearly pried Sihan's knee away from the saddle. Something hard struck Sihan's face and slashed his lip. Stinging tears joined the salty taste of blood. Aurion's hooves scattered stones as he shot through scrub and trees, bounding over logs.

In the space of a stride, Aurion burst into clear grass. Sihan turned him across the face of the trees toward the next marker. A quick glance over his shoulder revealed a line of horses stretched out a long, long way behind.

Aurion tore headlong into a knot of blanket-woods and paperbarks, racing along a cart track. Gang-gangs screamed into the air. Light faded. Creepers crisscrossed the woods. Sihan rode low in the saddle to evade vines hanging in menacing streamers.

Two horses, one light and one dark, galloped in front. Sihan grimaced. What short cut had *they* taken? He clicked Aurion to greater speed. White ears flicked back. Muscles bunched. Aurion raced, faster and faster. The long reaching stride seemed almost slow, followed by the lightning-fast slash of the ground, then the rush of air as he flew once more. Wind whipped Sihan's cheeks and filled his mouth, beat upon his eyeballs, whistled in his ears.

Aurion's stride lengthened; he leveled with the black Romondor horse, then the grey. The track narrowed; thick masses of lantana clumped on either side. Something dark lay on the ground in front of him. Sihan dug in his heels and leaned forward. Aurion sprang into the air, clearing the obstacle, side by side with the other two horses. Sihan's lower legs clamped, upper body swaying in balance with the horse.

The three horses reached the next bend together. There was no room. The big grey crashed against Aurion. The impact lifted the white stallion and threw him sideways, hurling Sihan against a tree. Searing agony tore through him. Aurion floundered, legs trapped in morning glory, bringing him to a halt. Belarion hurtled on.

Gasping for breath, Sihan tried to focus on what had happened. He hunched over. A shaft of wood stuck out through the boot on his left leg.

Something crashed through the trees and a voice echoed amid the ringing of his ears.

'Are you all right?'

'What?' asked Sihan, shaking his head.

'Are you all right?' The worried face of a steward swam into focus.

Sihan sucked in another breath. 'What happened?'

'The grey got caught by a vine. He slammed you into a tree.'

A red mist danced before Sihan's eyes. Groaning came from his left. A grey horse lay sprawled on the ground, unable to rise.

'Is it all right?'

The steward's swarthy face was grim. 'Broken shoulder, I think.'

Ice leached through Sihan's veins. Bending over Aurion, he searched for signs of injury.

The steward ran his hands down Aurion's legs. 'There's blood on his chest, but I think your horse is sound, lucky sod. By rights he should be laid out, too. You better quit and ride him back at a walk. I doubt your leg will take you if you try to lead him.'

'I can't quit,' protested Sihan.

The steward pointed at Sihan's calf. 'You can't ride with that leg. You'll collapse long before you get half-way home.'

Sihan flexed his leg. 'I can't feel it.'

'You will, soon enough. Then you'll be screaming like a stuck boar.' The sound of galloping horses thundered close. 'You'd best move to clear ground,' said the steward, 'otherwise you'll risk being bowled over again.'

'I'll help you with the horse.'

'You won't,' insisted the steward. 'Move your horse over to the side trail on the right, out of the way until the last few stragglers come through. Not much danger of anyone hitting you there.'

Simultaneous waves of nausea and disappointment hit Sihan. He had lost. There was no chance of freeing his father.

As if he sensed Sihan's distress, Aurion tugged at the bit, tossing flecks of foam, eager to be off. Sihan shook his head, trying to clear the strange mist clouding his senses. Any moment now, and he would either fall off or be sick. Maybe both. He did not care.

Suddenly Aurion tensed, became motionless, quivering, steam pouring off his dripping neck. A white ring appeared at the edge of his eyes.

Gods. He was going to blow. Sihan freed his legs from the stirrups, ready to swing out of the saddle. The white ring widened. Spear-pointed ears flicked forward to the forest gloom. Sihan followed the stallion's gaze.

Blood rushed up and down his body as a strange hovering vision of a grey-cloaked figure appeared among the trees. A hand reached out to him, white, beckoning. A voice called, 'Follow. Follow.' Sihan blinked, and the vision melted away into shadow.

The storm broke.

Aurion squealed and reared. Sihan barely had time to clutch at thick wild mane to stop himself slipping off. He grasped at one rein, spinning the stallion round and round. Aurion threw his head down, tearing the rein from Sihan's grasp, then plunged into the forest.

Hanging half off the saddle, Sihan clung like a cat, flailing at leather, trying to get purchase. Aurion sped at a tearing gallop into the trees, crashing through hop scrub, bitter pea and bracken. Sihan's body whipped from side to side, the horse undulating beneath him like a demonic serpent. Sihan only just managed to haul himself back into the saddle as the stallion burst back onto a trail.

Thighs burning, Sihan gripped the saddle, found the stirrups. Not for a heartbeat did Aurion run straight between his knees. 'Hold! Hold!' he cried, trying to gain control of this jagged, warring gallop. He threw his weight against the reins, but still the stallion raced on.

The snaking, twisting ride jerked every muscle in Sihan's body. His head snapped back and forth. Where by all mercy did Aurion think he was going?

Random thoughts ran around Sihan's head like alarmed hornets. What trail were they on? It must be the slow trail, for it remained flat. The trail along the gorge rose along the breasts of hills. Where was Veren? Where were the other riders? The forest swept past. At the speed at which Aurion was travelling, even on the long trail home they could still outpace everyone, catch Veren. If only he could hang on.

But soon wave after nauseous wave rolled over Sihan. Every muscle in his body ached as if it had been trampled. He clung on only because his fists were entangled so tight in Aurion's mane. Tiredness washed over him. He lost all hope of getting any sort of control over the stallion.

A rushing wind came from nowhere, and shimmering blue filled the air. Moments later, a shadow horse galloped through the forest beside them.

'Turn off!' shouted the rider.

Through a blur of pain, Sihan tried to focus.

'Turn *off!*' the rider's voice was insistent.

Through pain and fatigue, Sihan recognised Veren. Where the hells had he come from? Wasn't he way in front?

The black horse galloped at Aurion's side, ears pinned. Veren made a grab for Aurion's bridle. Aurion shied sideways.

Veren tried again. Aurion leapt away in huge cat leap bounds over clumps of scrub.

Sihan's brain muddled. What the hells was Veren doing?

Ground inclined sharply. Sihan grimaced as he put more weight in the stirrups. Pain shot through his injured leg. Why was the trail rising?

Aurion stretched out his neck, powerful haunches propelling him up the difficult steep. Too late did it register in Sihan's mind what the rising ground meant. They reached the summit. A gaping crevasse split the hill. A river snaked at its base. The Death Gorge.

Aurion gathered himself together, muscles knotting and bunching. Sihan did not even have breath to scream.

Aurion sprang into the air, soared across the chasm. Soared, soared. On eagle's wings. Landing with a clattering of hooves on the narrow summit of the spire, he perched between a vertical drop at his back and a steep decline of scree before. Sihan stared with horror at the river far below, water heaving dark with unrestrained force. Not even a heart beat passed before Belarion crashed into Aurion from behind, sending the white stallion lurching forward.

Feet knocked out of the stirrups, Sihan flung sprawling on the horse's bobbing neck. He clamped his arms around thick muscle, pushed, pushed with all his might, back into the saddle. His legs flapped as he bounced. He flung his weight back, gripped hard with his knees. His shoulders jounced against the stallion's haunches.

Side by side, the two stallions crashed down the slope. Rocks gave way beneath their hooves. A roaring cloud of dust and rolling boulders erupted around them. Terror swelled with every stride. The river thundered like booming drums. They slammed into a cauldron of whitewater as if it were granite.

Sihan sank, black swirling behind his eyes, his arms and legs barely able to move against the pressure. One hand smacked hard against straining muscle – solid – moving.

He clutched at neck, at mane, at saddle, at waterflapping leather. His breath burst. Lungs burned. His head broke the surface. He gasped at air, body heaving with racking coughs, hot lungs panting. Every gasp scorched his throat, his chest.

Aurion surfaced nearby, striking out against the current. Sihan grabbed the side of the saddle, trying to stay afloat.

'Turn him!' shouted a muffled voice. 'Head for the sand bank!'

Where? Where? Water sluiced in Sihan's eyes. Wet mane cut into his fingers.

Something dark hit his leg. Belarion's black head bobbed just above the water, nostrils flaring red.

'Stay with me,' called Veren.

Bones aching cold, Sihan squinted, unable to see the steep ridge at his back or the shore ahead.

Reins tangled around Aurion's forelegs. The stallion floundered, submerged, dragging Sihan beneath the surface. When the horse's head cleared the water once more, Sihan choked, spitting water, took another starving breath. Coughed, wheezed.

The more Aurion fought, the tighter the reins ensnared his legs, forcing him beneath the surface once more. With strength born of terror, Sihan pulled himself forward and grabbed onto one thrashing leg. Flailing hooves pummeled his arms. *Bang! Bang*! Like a blacksmith striking an anvil.

Sihan groped for the knife at his belt. He slashed at the reins. Tore them. Aurion surfaced. Catching hold of the stirrup leather, Sihan hung on until Aurion swam to the shore and dragged him out of the water.

Slumped on the sandy bank, Sihan coughed so hard he thought his lungs would burst. Aurion stood beside him, heaving breath as much as Sihan.

'Are you all right, boy?'

Sihan blinked. Light stabbed his eyes. Breathing spiked sharp pain in his lungs. However much he tried, gasping air in and out, he could not get enough.

'Are you all right?'

The deep compelling voice forced Sihan's mind to focus. Veren's intense dark eyes speared through him. 'No,' Sihan gasped through bloodied lips, around the edges of chattering teeth.

Veren knelt down, rubbed his gloved hand through his black hair, shaking water from it. He pulled out a sodden pouch at his belt and untied the leather cord. Forcing something green and foul between Sihan's lips, he said, 'Here, chew on this.'

Sihan obeyed without thinking, mind as numb as his body. A smell like rancid lemon peel filled his nostrils. Gagging, Sihan spat. He twisted his head away, trying to spit out the foul taste. 'Are you trying to poison me?'

Veren's gaunt face cracked into a smile. 'Nice thanks.'

Sihan hawked the residue from his mouth, scrabbling to sit up, every bone in his body aching as though it had been splintered. 'Bloody vulture,' he cursed.

'Even nicer.' Veren hauled Sihan to his feet. 'Now get back on your horse.'

'I can't ride him.'

'Too bad,' said Veren. ''Cause you're on him.' With a heave, he threw Sihan onto Aurion's back. Pointing along the river, he said, 'The way home. I suggest you take it.'

Sihan stared at the knight with guarded eyes, refusing to acknowledge Veren had tried to stop Aurion in his mad flight to the gorge. 'Why are you helping me?'

A lupine smile slipped across Veren's lips. 'Let's just say I'm feeling charitable. Any other day you might not be so lucky.' He knotted the broken reins and closed Sihan's shaking hands around them.

The world swayed once more, Sihan's body feeling like it had been beaten to a pulp. He stole another look at Veren, convinced the man was mad or pulling some trick.

'All right, then,' said Veren. 'It's just you and me. We're a half league in front of the others, thanks to that white demon jumping the Death Gorge.' A full-toothed grin stretched across his sun-browned face. 'I'd say these are the best two horses in the kingdom, wouldn't you? What say we find out which is the better?'

'I–I have to win,' confessed Sihan, not knowing why he felt the sudden need to share his burden. 'The–the king says I ride for Mirador, and Knight Commander Areme. And–And my father's in the dungeon.'

Veren's brows rose in surprise. 'Heavy burdens for a child.'

'I'm not a child.'

Veren's smile vanished. 'When you've reached my age, everyone else is a child. At any rate, you are too young to ride with such a load upon your shoulders. Best ride for yourself.'

'You ride for Romondor.'

'I ride for myself.' Veren gathered up Belarion's reins. 'Come, Sihan, rider of the Firestar stallion, let us be on our way, or it won't really matter who or what we are riding for if someone else steals the victory from under our noses.'

No. It would not.

Sihan did not wait for Veren to mount. Despite all Veren had done, vultures did not deserve courtesy, not under any circumstances. Sihan kicked Aurion into a gallop. The stallion's hooves sprayed up sand along the river's edge. Sihan clung tight to the mane with one hand, guiding the horse with the other. The stallion had returned to his control. Would he remain so to finish this race?

They charged into the last stretch of forest between them and the fortress, Aurion galloping with fleet-footed sureness as if he had trod the path a thousand times. Silver mane flared back into Sihan's face. A field opened before them. They flew across the ground, the world rolling out beneath the stallion's hooves. Elation filled Sihan. Pennons fluttered ahead, the cries of the crowd intensifying with every stride. Behind him the ground shook. Sihan cast a desperate glance over his shoulder. Belarion pounded fiercely in pursuit, black legs ramming the ground, but every stride of the white stallion took Aurion further in front.

They would win.

Sudden agony tore up Sihan's leg. He fell forward, arms hanging like those of a puppet with broken strings around

Aurion's neck. Blood thickened on his tongue, dripping from his mouth to stain Aurion's mane crimson. Sihan could not believe it. The vulture *had* poisoned him.

Belarion's snorting breath filled his ears. Sihan's vision blurred. Thoughts drifted. He imagined he was galloping through darkness with terror at his heels. Hessarde's sword tore his throat. Areme's dagger pierced his chest. Why did everyone want him dead? And then he no longer cared about anything, only for it to be finished.

His grip failed. A heartbeat later he slammed into the ground, face sliding hard against dirt.

Chapter 18

Choices

'Sihan!' screamed Jaien from the edge of the lists, his voice just one of a multitude of anguished cries as Sihan rolled in a flurry of dust and bark, then lay unmoving. Jaien swayed, legs braced, one hand against his injured stallion, staring helplessly to where Sihan sprawled, a broken, inert mass.

Protect the boy! Protect the boy!

That otherworldly voice whipped Jaien mercilessly. He shot one look at Wedge. Blood splattered down the chestnut's swollen foreleg; a flap of skin dangled down its shoulder. It had been a bad fall, but they had walked away from it, making torturous progress back to the tourney field. Some horses had not walked away. Neither had some men. Jaien carried the burden of fault – he had tried to turn too fast round the Gallows Tree. He could bear no more.

Aurion tore past the royal gallery, Belarion on his heels. Then the white horse checked abruptly, skidding to a haunch halt, before doubling back to Sihan.

Protect the boy! Protect the boy!

The voice brought fear with it, more intense than any it had conjured before, red like garnet, filming Jaien's vision. The white horse had tried to kill Sihan and Yonnad at Yseth. It had downed Areme. What would stop it now?

'Go!' shouted Gerein, running from his post among the king's guard, a host of Jaien's former command hard on his heels. The archer tore Wedge's reins from Jaien's grasp. 'We'll see to your horse!'

Jaien needed no further encouragement, had no thought for anything but Sihan. Every muscle and sinew screaming from strain, he sprinted. From all sides of the field, soldiers and stewards ran with him.

Aurion beat them all, rearing over the lad as he had earlier over Areme, roaring challenge. White striking forelegs slashed at soldiers, the stallion a rampaging beast, as Jaien had found him in Sihan's camp that morning. Why had he thought this horse was the answer to all?

Aurion reared, head flung high, striking at air with great hooves that could cleave heads like butter. Jaien ignored the threat, sliding to his knees beside Sihan. The horse had not hurt him before. Would not now. He did not know how he knew, but he did.

The lad lay so still, no sign of life beneath the wet tunic, torn muslin spattered with blood. The chest did not rise. Everything within Jaien became cold and dark. He tore off his gloves, pressed one palm to Sihan's chest. The utter stillness, the ashen hue of eyelids above the battered cheek, all of it tore at him.

Jaien did not know what to do, what to touch that was not broken, or blistered, weeping flesh. He fumbled with trembling fingers, cupped one hand beneath Sihan's sodden hair, drew the lad into his arms and embraced him fiercely. 'Sihan,' he whispered against the bloody brow, voice strangled by pain.

He traced unbroken flesh of eyelid, one edge of a swollen lip. Everywhere else, abrasions, darkening bruises and ground-in dirt marred the lad's face. Tiny lines of sweat slid down brow and cheek. Jaien buried his face in the wild mess of hair, strands tangled with bits of leaves and bark. 'Stay with me,' Jaien breathed the plea, the command. 'I won't let you go. I promised to protect you.'

Footsteps, light, ran up. Jaien raised his head, eyes blurred.

Grey cloak billowing in her wake, the princess, breathing hard, stopped several paces from the white stallion. At her back, soldiers stood. Travall, too, waited just beyond reach of the stallion's stamping hooves.

The princess spun to face them, shouting like she was demented, 'He's mine! Mine! Areme's gift! No one touches him but by my command!'

Aurion calmed, stretched out his nose to butt her gently in the back. She turned, took hold of broken, trailing reins. Head high and defiant, she marched toward the fortress, the stallion following her like a dog. All the soldiers and courtiers gave back, watching her. No one spared a glance for Sihan, ignoring him like he was nothing but trampled dirt.

Jaien held Sihan close, the body from which all life had fled. As though from a distance, a shadow whisper flitted into his ear.

The soul's breath flows from one being into another, newborn.

Jaien tensed.

Breathe his soul into you. Breathe his soul. Bind him within you for eternity. The voice flowed right through Jaien's bones.

Take his soul's breath and join with me. Come . . . Come . . .

Itself a dark thing of ice and nothingness, the voice filled Jaien with an emptiness that made him gasp.

Take his soul's breath. The whisper became stronger, urgency tainting every syllable.

A long shadow stretched lengthwise across Jaien. A firm hand fell on his shoulder.

'It's finished,' said Travall, voice coming as if from far distances. 'There's nothing more you can do.' His fingers pressed harder. 'My men will take his body for burning.'

'No one touches him but me!' Jaien snarled, and the hand fell away.

In the silence following, there was nothing but the voice. *Take his soul's breath*!

It was command, it was entreaty. It was immovable will forcing Jaien's lips to Sihan's. He covered that mouth, knew blood and fear. Knew dread deep within his soul. He breathed. Out. Gave of himself. Did not take as the voice insisted. Breathed out again, forcing breath into that broken body.

Take his soul's breath. The whisper grew to a scream, an onslaught fracturing all thought.

'No!' Jaien's ragged denial railed against the order. 'I promised I'd protect him. I won't let anyone hurt him, not even me.' His words died to sobbing breath, his hand never stopped stroking Sihan's hair, his torn cheek.

An instant passed before he registered the slow rise of Sihan's chest. Jaien just stared, wordless, as if he would choke if he tried to say anything. Another breath.

Jaien staggered to his feet, cradling Sihan in his arms. To Travall he shouted, 'Have Gerein get water ready, bandages.' He saw nothing then, all blurred as he carried Sihan to the barracks. For him, the world was in his arms. The horse might belong to the girl, but this lad, half-destroyed as he was, belonged to Jaien; no one else.

As he entered the barracks, he shouted at milling soldiers, 'Get out! All of you!' Boots thumped against wood as men hurried to obey. With care, Jaien lowered Sihan's wet, limp body onto a hard bunk.

He smoothed the shock of blood-matted hair back from Sihan's face, his heart bleeding. 'You're mine,' he whispered, low and deep in his throat, almost choking on the confession. He pressed his lips to Sihan's brow. 'Always and forever.'

Afternoon light speared through a single window, bringing with it warbling of sparrows and warm autumn breeze. But all was winter within Jaien. He pulled off his tabard and tore it into strips, dabbing blood oozing from a gash on Sihan's pale, swollen lips, trying to clean ground-in dirt and stone-dust from the raw flesh of his cheek. At each of the youth's shallow, gasping breaths, he winced.

He unbuckled Sihan's pouch belt, tossed it aside, untied the leather laces at the collar of the tunic, pulled off the blood-stained garment by degrees, over shoulders and head. Sihan's naked torso was hard and lean, muscles slack beneath torn flesh. Purple, blue and black patches covered the lad's arms and chest. Blood dried in rows of little black beads all over.

Jaien started at the sight of a jagged scar marring Sihan's flat stomach – a scar matching a disfigurement on Jaien's flesh in every detail. It ran in vivid red on white spiderweave across his abdomen. Old, faint.

Jaien traced the outline, fingers trailing across pallid skin and dark hairs. He felt like he was touching his own flesh. How had Sihan come by such a wound? Jaien closed his eyes. *If you live, I swear I'll never let you be hurt again. Upon my honour. My life. My soul. Brother's oath. Whether you want it or not.*

Gerein arrived with a large bucket of water and placed it on the end of the bunk.

Jaien quickly washed his hands. As Gerein hovered nearby, Jaien drew his hunting knife from its sheath and cut the coarse-woven leggings at the thigh, making a long slit down through the top edge of the boot. A wooden shaft stuck out of the calf like a cork stopping a wine casket. There was too much blood. Grimacing, Jaien peeled back dirt-encrusted flaps of skin and flesh.

'Mercy!' Gerein leaned over his shoulder. 'That's almost right through the leg.' His gaze flew to Jaien. 'You can't save it.'

'The hells I can't.' Jaien shook Gerein off. 'Keep watch. Don't let anyone in.' He braced himself, fingers clenched around his dagger, then cut, cut. Cut into flesh, into wood. Blood fountained across his hands, his tabard. Hot, bleeding life.

'Hurry, hurry,' he muttered to himself, probing the squelching mass of flesh and sinew for splinters. Extracting all he could find, he stuffed the hole with a clean wad of cloth. Blood thickened around it.

'Shit. Shit.' He rummaged through Sihan's pouches, found the granine. Green paste slicked his fingers. He pulled out the wad of cloth, pasted the wound with the tuberous slime.

Sihan's face tightened.

'Gerhas is coming,' called Gerein.

'Godsfuck!' Jaien hurriedly bandaged the leg, and shoved the tuber back in the pouch. He drew a shuddering breath and wiped his brow with a bloodied hand, staining his sandy hair to rust.

Gerhas burst into the room, all bluster and fury damped, though his face was red as a firefalcon. 'How is he?'

'I've done all I can.' It was not enough, not nearly enough.

Gerhas stood by the bedside, peering at the boy's grey face. 'How bad?'

'I don't know how he finished the race.' Jaien staggered to his feet, every muscle an agony of hurt. 'By all that is merciful, get his father.'

'Best tend yourself,' said Gerhas. 'You look like hell.'

Jaien strode to the door, casting Gerhas a withering glance. 'Not before I check on my horse. Where's Aurion?'

'The inner stables.' Gerhas's face was just as implacable as he marched outside. 'This was ill-done.'

'Yes,' said Jaien, following the horsemaster. 'Fucking ill-done.' He muttered to Gerein over his shoulder, 'Don't let anyone in here but me or the boy's father.' Then he glared at Gerhas. 'By all that is merciful, go to the king. Get his father released.'

Without waiting for an answer, Jaien continued unsteadily to the stable block where warhorses peered out of box stalls. He was near collapse, but duty demanded he finish the tasks that were his charge. Wedge stood in the stall next to Falcon, one ear drooped, muzzle buried in a nosebag brimming with warm bran. Flesh pushed out from a gash in his shoulder, a loose flap of skin hanging down. When Jaien tried to pat him, the chestnut stamped his hoof and snorted, spraying gobbets of mash all over the stall.

'He's peeved,' grumped Cenriin, rousing from a corner of the stall where he had made his bed.

'I know,' whispered Jaien. 'I failed. On all counts.'

His father's face softened. 'You're hurt. I'll watch over the horse.'

'He's my charge.'

'You've worries enough. I'll bear this burden this night. You tend your lad. How is he?'

Despite his will, tears began to track down Jaien's cheeks. 'Bad.'

'Best go back to him, then.'

Jaien nodded, his father's understanding a sharp pain in his heart. 'I'll check on Aurion first. He'll be asking after him, when he awakens.' *If he awakens* . . . A rush of desolate emptiness coursed through him.

He walked down the line of stalls, wandering without real direction like a rootless tumbleweed tossed by wind. The day had bled away into colourless twilight as bleak as his heart. At last he came to the inner palace stables. In a royal stall, Aurion switched his tail and turned his rump to Jaien. The stallion blew grains of chaff around his trough, then turned again, snuffling through straw for stray lengths of hay. The gash on his chest had been tended, who by, Jaien could not guess.

Jaien leaned on the candlewood half-door, traced his fingers along the intricate designs in the wood. Aurion pinned his ears suddenly, and snaked his neck in threat.

Jaien sighed. *You blame me, too*. He picked up a halter from a hook on the door, twisted the leather aimlessly.

'How fares the boy?' asked a deep voice.

Startled, Jaien spun to find Knight Commander Veren approaching from the palace. He collected his wits, then his manners, and executed a half-bow. 'He's gravely wounded.'

Veren's face clouded. 'It's been a bad day.'

All decorum vanished. Burning words scorched Jaien's lips. 'If this is a bad day for you, I'd hate to see a *good* one.' Despite all he knew – that the queen had been the true cause of the Great War – he found it impossible not to follow long-ingrained impulse to lay blame at the foot of a Romondor soldier. Especially now, with Sihan injured.

'Still your tongue,' said Veren abruptly, as though his word held the weight of law. 'I did not seek you out in order to rub vinegar into an open wound.'

'No?' Jaien's mouth curled in disgust. 'Then why *did* you come?'

Veren drew the token the princess had presented to him from his surcoat. 'I forfeit the race.'

Jaien felt as if he had been hit with the blunt end of a pikestaff. 'Say again?'

Veren's face cracked into a smile like breaking dawn upon a glacier. 'You didn't mishear. Go tell the boy. I can't imagine a better tonic.'

Jaien's fingers closed on the silk ribbon as he shot a suspicious look at the knight. 'Why?'

'My reasons are my own.'

Jaien hesitated, confused, searching for trickery. Sensed none. He met Veren's level gaze – regrouped. Pushing old hatreds – undeserved hatreds many of them – aside, he said with better grace, 'What thanks can I offer?'

Veren's intense jet eyes impaled Jaien as surely as a javelin. 'Swear a vow you'll keep Sihan safe.'

Unbalanced by the request, Jaien fought for stability. 'Why would a Romondor knight care about one of our men?'

'Let's just say he reminds me of my younger brother.'

Unease crept over Jaien at the unflattering comparison. He bristled in Sihan's defense. 'Don't insult him. There's nothing of you in him.'

Veren smiled. 'Perhaps. Perhaps not. It hardly matters. What does matter is you'll do all you can to keep him safe.'

Protect the boy. Keep him safe. Deliver him not unto his enemies. The secret voice had swept around Jaien for so long, like a ripple of memory from a distant past. But that voice had changed this day, had urged Jaien to something darker he did not understand and would not obey.

Jaien raised his chin, in defiance of Veren and his not-so-silent god. 'My oaths are my own; I don't need to swear one to you.' Clutching the silk tight in his hand, he marched away.

Callinor frowned as his daughter stormed into the audience chamber, still looking like a whore with golden hair unloosed and falling about her like a cape.

Scattering attendants with every stride, grey cloak swirling across the slate floor, she yelled, 'I want the white horse!'

Red-filmed mist filled his vision, and then that other voice, sweet, seductive, steel-edged, screaming, 'I want . . . I want . . . I want . . .' What was it Wyndarra had wanted? A white rose, a gemstone, a land filled with rotting corpses. He had given her them all. His fingers tightened to a fist. No more! His imperious roar sheared through the clamour of the court, severing all noise. 'Out! All of you! None but my second, my Champion, and my fool of a daughter, remain.'

Crushing silence fell like a boulder. Everyone froze.

'Out!' Callinor bellowed once more. With a wave of his hand he banished everyone from the room.

Courtiers and attendants moved as one, all shuffling feet and downcast eyes, faces sallow in the brooding light of smoking torches. Liveried footmen closed doors on muted whispers. Only a dozen silent guardsmen remained at their stations around the hall, staring blank-eyed but watchful, fists tight-gripped on grounded halberds. Callinor turned to his daughter. Pale-faced but defiant, she waited in the middle of the hall.

He wanted to seize her by her unbound hair, throw her to the ground, beat her into cowering submission like he should have done her bitch-whore of a mother too many years before. Instead he motioned for Gerhas to hand him a scroll. 'Three times this day you've defied me.' He threw the vellum at her feet. 'A release order for a man I've given orders to rot.'

She half-moved to reach for the scroll, but then forced herself to stillness, veiling her eyes, staring down at the vellum with an equally frozen face.

He dug in the barbs, one by one. 'Even I thought you'd the wit to desist from such rank stupidity. I see I was mistaken. Think carefully in future before you venture to meddle in affairs concerning you not.'

Her face grew paler, as though she finally understood her grim situation, but then she raised her chin, eyes glittering sharp in the torchlight. 'I want the white horse!' There was less strength, but the defiance remained.

'Ah, I see you raise your second indiscretion yourself. It comes as no surprise one who can defy my direct orders, feels also she can defy a king's edict.' He leaned forward, white cloak hanging over his shoulders, and roared, 'None save I may ride a white warhorse! None save I!'

Her fingers clenched at her sides. 'Monarchs ride white horses. I am the future queen. And I was to claim a horse from the warhorse trials. I claim the white horse. I want the white horse.'

'Dare you defy your liege lord?' Callinor's fisted hands betrayed his desire to leap to his feet. He forced himself to relax braced shoulders, slackened his fingers to grip the engraved arms buttressing his throne. And sat. He was king. All lesser beings must stand. He impaled her with his sharpest glare. 'You are willful and ungrateful. I have given my answer, and there lies an end to it!'

Orlanda's eyes widened and filled with equal parts boldness and fear. She trembled as though it took all her strength to face him, to hold herself upright, to not flee. She said again clearly, though her voice stretched thin, 'I demand the white horse!'

'You have no right to demand!' Callinor's fingernails raked the arms of his throne till they bled. Wits shapeless with fury, he saw Orlanda melt into the image of her mother. There was no difference between their eyes, both storm-blue with merciless accusation, or their demanding voices, jagged blades hacking his heart to shreds. He wanted to put out his own eyes so he might not see the horror of beauty desecrated by demonic wrath; he longed to stop his ears to relentless entreaties. *I want. I want. I want.* Wyndarra's presence was so palpable he imagined he smelt the stink of her congealing blood.

He must deny the daughter everything he had failed to deny the mother, to his cost, to hers, to the cost of his kingdom, to the cost of a man he valued as his brother. He drew himself up. 'I'll hear no more of your black ingratitude. None! You dare to dishonour me, behaving like a shameless whore. You respect nothing, not even yourself. I say again, you shall not have that horse!'

Wyndarra's image dissolved back into the girl's shape, unmoving and uncowed despite the hostile words he cast at her that should have sent her whimpering from his sight.

'I want the white horse!' Her mind seemed frozen on those words, eyes fiery pride.

'He didn't win,' muttered Travall from beside the throne, his lean face matching his incisive words. 'The rules say you can only claim the winning horse.'

Orlanda strode to the base of the throne, cloak swishing across slate, clenched hands on hips. 'Aurion crossed the line first. He won. He was tied therefore with Belarion. I claim Aurion.'

Gerhas grimaced, the lines on his craggy face deepening. 'The lad fell off before the finish.'

'I don't want the lad.' The dull thud of her slippered foot had all the impact of her outbursts thus far. 'I want the horse! Where in the rules does it say the horse has to be mounted?'

Gerhas's grey eyes blazed disapproval. 'I think that's a given.'

Orlanda ignored him, glaring at her father. 'You change rules everyday! *You* let the lad ride the white horse, despite your edict.'

With a colossal effort that set his limbs trembling, Callinor only just stopped himself from striking her. All his fury loosed in his voice. 'Only after you publicly defied me by letting Areme ride it first – your third act of treachery this day. You're lucky I didn't have you flogged.' He let the threat register. 'I still might.'

She did not recoil, lips sobering into a tight line of resolve laced with obstinacy. 'You wouldn't dare, so close to trading me to Valoren.'

Callinor's fist crashed down. 'Don't lecture me on what I may or may not dare!' Outrage drove him from his throne, set him stalking across the chamber like a prowling panther. At length he came to a halt where he had started, fists braced on the arms of the throne, entire body tensed.

She stood behind him, her mother's ghost in flesh, taunting him, those brilliant, piercing eyes stripping him bare to the soul. Sweat rolled down between his shoulder blades. Could she see his buried secret, his wickedness, squirming repulsive and undead on the stone before her skewering eyes?

He turned, slowly. Her predatory eyes met his, wary and alert, and somehow knowing. Callinor half-opened his mouth, ready to attack, to continue his tirade, batter down all her attempts to argue. A slight movement to his left stopped him. Travall shot him a warning glance.

She was right. He could not send her to Valoren damaged. Romondor alone would accomplish that. But he would rather be spitted than yield to her.

When he turned his face away, she cried, 'Why won't you look at me, Father? You never look at me! Am I so low in your eyes? So hateful?'

He kept his eyes averted. How could he tell her that her face reminded him of a graveyard?

Her raised voice rang with passionate anger. 'Is that why you entertain thoughts of wedding me to a vulture?' She ran to him, prostrated herself at his feet. Slender, trembling hands clutched at his tunic. 'Give me this horse, and I'll never ask for anything again.'

'I have said no, I'll hear no more from you.'

She opened her mouth.

'One more word,' he threatened, 'and you can be sure you'll never ask for anything again.' He dismissed her with a shove of his boot.

Eyes blank with blind fear, she jumped to her feet, swept the folds of her gown and cloak into one arm and ran from the room.

Callinor stared after her. Was she as empty-headed as she seemed? Perhaps it was better she had no notion of what fate had in store for her. She had lived thus far protected from the world and all its horror, like a passenger aboard a ship that never docked at any port promising strife. When would she realise that ship was sinking fast in a sea seething with sharks?

Travall aimed a glance at Callinor. 'If you give her the horse, she might be more manageable . . . for a time.'

'Time enough to hand her over to Valoren?' Callinor did not waste words in subtlety.

Quick to a fault, Travall took the cue, turning to Gerhas. 'You're the horsemaster. Invent some grounds.'

Gerhas's face darkened rapidly, like a swift incoming storm. 'We all know it's not the horse she wants.'

'It's all she's going to get,' said Callinor. 'She said it herself – she'll not ask for anything again. She damned herself with those words. So be it.'

Gerhas took his time, a deliberate procrastination of obstinate will. When it became clear he would offer nothing, Travall said to Callinor, tone cautious, 'You allowed a change of rider mid course. Why not no rider at all?'

Callinor re-directed the question to his second, 'Well?'

The horsemaster raked knotted fingers through his grey-brown hair. Pitching his tone to grudging acquiescence, he said, 'Veren will not be well pleased.'

'Bother Veren,' said Callinor.

A flare of anger lit Gerhas's eyes. 'If that horse is staying, then so is the lad. That beast is a monster.'

'And if the lad asks a boon?' questioned Travall.

'No need for concern,' said Callinor. 'If he lives, he'll ask for his father, not for himself.'

Travall raised his hand to his mouth, coughed. 'I think we should pre-empt it. We can assume he'll ask. It makes all satisfactory. We keep the lad here; send the father back to Graycor.'

'The lad – he's grievously wounded?' asked Callinor.

'If he lives,' said Gerhas. 'He might never be sound on that leg.'

'I don't like the idea of Armindras loose with that tongue that's taken so to flapping,' said Callinor.

Gerhas shrugged, eyes narrowing to cold calculation. 'If he thinks the lad is safe, he'll argue the less. That's all he wants, I'm thinking – for Sihan not to be commissioned.'

Callinor railed. 'The lad stays here. If I give him dispensation, then I must make the same allowance for all the others. That's over five hundred just from Graycor, when we might need every man.'

Travall stepped forward from beside the throne. 'If I may hazard a suggestion, Majesty. If Sihan lives, give him a rank in the stable.' He paused, forehead creased in concentration. 'Perhaps, the Princess's Groom. An honorary position. Stable boys aren't expected to fight, but many are known to take part in arms drills. We can alleviate the father's concern – and then – when he's gone, if Sihan is sound, push the lad in the right direction. It won't take much.' His lips pressed thin. 'He's young. From the mountains. His friends will all be commissioned. I'm sure he'll go along with them.'

Gerhas nodded consent. 'Admirable idea.'

'It doesn't address the father,' said Callinor. 'I know Armindras. I don't believe it will be quite enough to put a lock on his viperous tongue.'

'Then send men with him to make certain of it. You can say it is to protect the horses.' The horsemaster pulled a scroll from beneath his cloak. The seal, the falcon of Pelan, was broken. 'Another courier arrived a little while ago. More stolen horses in Pelan.'

'How many? Where?' demanded Callinor.

'The forest of Senor. Forty youngstock.'

Callinor's voice exploded into the empty chamber. 'What the devil is Byerol playing at?' He brushed his hand back through grizzled hair. 'He's stymieing our cavalry with this nonsense.'

Travall's advice slid like ice over Callinor's hot voice. 'Sending men to Graycor would be a futile gesture. Why trade men-at-arms for a greenstick? It defeats the whole purpose of keeping the lad.'

'But the horses?'

'Graycor is at our back. Whatever Byerol is doing, he would need to march through Mirador to reach the Graycor bloodhorse ranges. I think we can safely leave those horses with the keeper and his stewards to look after. There's been no report of horses missing there, or Emor.'

'Emor!' Callinor snorted. 'If it was Emor ponies being stolen, I'd send men to help Byerol steal them!'

Gerhas rolled up the vellum. 'I can release Reonor. He's a swordsman, and he's loyal. I was going to offer him first stewardship in Belaron, but Graycor will suit just as well. Yonnad is injured. He can take Yonnad's place.' His eyes narrowed. 'And Reonor can be relied upon to stick a dagger in Armindras if he squawks.' He tucked the vellum beneath his cloak. 'Is your Grace content?'

'I am.'

'Will you give me leave to release his father?'

'No. Go find Veren. Break it to him as well as you can.' Callinor strode to the middle of the hall and picked up the scroll. 'I shall attend to Armindras myself.'

Gerhas bowed, then marched across the chamber to leave by a side door. After he left, Callinor returned to his throne, and slumped as though all his bones had softened. Travall strode to his side.

Callinor fixed him with tired eyes. 'The princess. I should have counselled her on this obsession with Areme. It's the only reason she wants this horse. She would have begged for an Emor pony if he had been riding it.'

Travall shrugged. 'Given what we're about to do to her, it's a small concession.'

Callinor closed his eyes. 'You mean sacrifice, don't you?' *She will not ever forgive me.* He hauled himself to his feet.

Keeping his silent thoughts to himself, Travall bowed low.

Callinor walked slowly to the dungeons, ignoring soldiers who saluted him, waving away the guard falling in at his back. He found Armindras as he had left him – defiant, chained, hair mussed. The flame in the sconce sputtered in a draft, and Callinor pushed the door closed with his boot.

He walked to the lancet, careful to avoid the stinking, shit-caked bucket in the corner. Gulls screamed loud beyond the slitted window. Every now and then, a shadow of wings in flight soared across the light against the far wall. 'They're loud on the seaward side. But at least the sea is calm.'

'I prefer the mountains.' Armindras's walnut-creased face set in a scowl. He followed every move of Callinor's, refusing to break eye contact. 'What is your business?'

'I want you free and out of here.'

'That rests with you.'

'No,' said Callinor. 'It rests with you.' He gave Armindras a long, incisive stare, then said with deliberation, 'I want your solemn word you'll return to Graycor without another outcry or disturbance.'

'Not without my son.'

'Your son has won the warhorse trials. The princess has claimed the white horse. I grant him this boon. Your life.'

'My life is worth nothing!' Armindras jumped up, straining against the chain.

Callinor waited, out of reach. With a small, emotionless smile, and without any alteration in the calmness of his voice, he said, 'You'd like that chain around my neck. Well, I'll not give you that chance. Here is the choice I place before you – you may accept it or gainsay as you please. The lad will stay in Mirador. No commission. He will be promoted to princess's groomsman. No service other than caring for the horse. Upon my word. You will return to Graycor, unharmed. Again, upon my word. Or you will rot in a worse dungeon than you can imagine, and I will press the lad into service. What say you?'

Armindras stared at him, suspicion burning behind his eyes. 'No service?'

'None but that he wills. Are you agreed?'

Mistrust did not abate in Armindras's eyes.

'What say you!' demanded Callinor.

Armindras's fixed stare never wavered. 'If all you say is truth, then I agree to it.' Threat lurked behind the spoken words, unspoken retribution if Armindras discovered Callinor false.

Nevertheless, tension eased from Callinor's muscles. 'I accept your word and grant your release.' He walked to the narrow door, then pulled it ajar and called, 'Send a smith! Strike this man's chains and have a soldier take him to his son.'

Without another glance at Armindras, he marched up the passage to where light, soft, might cleanse the lies upon his lips.

Chapter 19

Lost

Areme drifted on a haze of pain, images floating in and out of his consciousness. Soft gossamer touched his cheek.

From afar, a sweet voice whispered, 'Come to me, my love. Leave this place and ride upon the shores of mystery.'

The world shivered, stars tore across moonlit sky. A woman ghosted to him, white gown flowing about her slender curves, voice a tranquil ocean. 'Come to me, Areme.'

She held out her hand, leading him beneath a sky of shooting stars. The air filled with the song of bellbirds as she led him to that secret place, the pool of the moon on a distant shore. 'Lay down your burden and come with me,' her soft voice beckoned.

'I'm with you,' he whispered.

Silken hair rippled down her back as she drew him down beside her, her eyes the blue of summer sky. 'Remember me, my darling, all promises lost.'

'I've never forgotten you.' A lie, a beautiful lie. Somewhere in the darkness he had lost her face, her name. He searched his mind, its path lit by the flash of swords and bloodied daggers. But the press of her lips, flavour of white roses, the warmth of her fingers upon his skin . . . all that remained.

Areme stroked her face, her body. Magic – she was woven out of magic, eternal, timeless. He traced her flesh, memorising every inch and line, determined to know her so well he could close his eyes and envision every part of her. Never lose her again. He wanted to be able to feel her, even when she was not there.

Because she would not always be there.

Silver-gold hair flared upon the breeze, strands burning in the pale light. Her fingers trembling upon his skin, sending tiny pulses of pleasure through him. His fingers closed upon hers. He longed to keep her in his arms, his heart, his soul, to never let her go. But she slipped away, the air singing with her laughter.

'Don't go,' he cried, too late, as her presence dissolved into another's.

'I am here, my son.'

Fire ripped through his chest.

Areme squeezed his eyes shut. 'I don't want *you*. Go away. Bring her back. If memory is all I have, then let me sleep.'

'Sleep is for the dead, Areme.'

'Then let me die.'

'That is not within my power, my son. I cannot undo the choice you made.'

It was never my choice. A rapid clatter of hooves on cobbles filled his ears. 'Where am I?'

'Your quarters.'

The horse trod steadily across stonework, sharp steps fading to silence. Areme groaned, then opened his eyes. A grey-cowled woman stood before him, shimmering against the bare stone walls of his room like a spectre. There, and not. At her back, clouds drifted across the sky, framed by an arched lancet. He recognised the twisting feeling in his stomach, of life taking root where death refused to dwell. 'Why did you bring me back, Myrrhye?' He refused to call her Mother.

'Your work here is not finished.'

Areme struggled to sit up, scowling as pain set his gut ablaze. His nose wrinkled at the sour citrus smell pervading the room. 'Granine! Snake's piss, Myrrhye.' He spat on the flags, then collapsed against his pallet. Staring at the vaulted ceiling receding into darkness, he willed away visions of ghosts, a woman long dead. His wife.

Cold gusted about him, sharpening his mind as it braced his flesh. His voice was chilled when he spoke again. 'Don't ever use it on me again. I see too much. Remember too much.'

'Shasirre?'

Areme hawked once more, as much to rid the foul taste from his mouth as for emphasis. 'Yes, Shasirre. Always Shasirre. Forever Shasirre.' He tipped his head back and closed his eyes. 'I want to forget her.'

'Would that love could be so easily abandoned.'

Every muscle tensed. 'I didn't abandon her. I killed her. Shoved a dagger into her gut and watched her die at my feet.'

'It was necessary.'

'Like making the horse erupt during the lance trial was necessary?'

Myrrhye raised an eyebrow. 'Not my work, but well done of the horse just the same. You would have harmed Veren. I've forbidden you to raise a hand against him.' She bent and drew him into her arms, her cloak harsh against his cheek. 'You must let the past go.'

Areme pulled away, unwilling to accept her embrace. 'When I dream, all I see is her eyes filled with love. When I wake, all I feel is fear and horror, and all I hear are her last words. "Why, Areme? Why?"'

Behind his eyelids the vision burned. Shasirre. Black tears streaming down her cheeks, eyes filled with the same plea gracing her lips, those lips of rose and music and the song of stars that had trembled not nearly enough against his. 'Why, Areme? Why?'

She slid down him, silver-gold hair slipping through his fingers, the black light of forbidden magic in her eyes extinguished. The taint of death hung upon the air, and wretchedness, despair, loathing for what she had done. As crimson blood seeped through his fingers, Areme could find but one answer. 'For nothing.'

And then she had died.

His head fell forward to his chest. He wanted to curl tight in a corner, press hard against the stones so his knees covered his ears, block out that voice whirling through his room, that face . . . everything.

His mother stroked his hair: her voice, as always, relentless. 'She was too young to understand what happened to her. Too young to control it. And you were not prepared for what happened to you. This time it will be different.' Resolve and certainty laced every word.

Areme pushed her away. 'Will it? Can you really promise that?' He leaned back against the wall. 'Orlanda is even younger. And I'm scared, Myrrhye. Scared I won't be able to protect her and everything will fall apart once more.'

'You are stronger this time, Areme. She will need that strength.'

'If I couldn't save the woman I loved, how can I save Orlanda?'

'With love, Areme.'

'I have no more love in me. It drained away with the last drop of Shasirre's blood.'

Myrrhye pushed back her cowl, bent down and brushed her lips across his forehead, strands of black hair tickling his face. 'There is always love. Perhaps Orlanda's love will be enough for both of you.' Her black eyes shone bright, rushlights reflected in their stone-cold depths. No lines marred flawless skin of which a maiden might boast, but even so, Areme knew the ancient beneath the shell, entrapped, like him, in deathless embrace. How did she bear it, to never age beyond middle years, yet never retain the sense of youth? He thought of Orlanda, young, bright, willful. 'She's a child.'

'Not anymore.'

'She's sixteen winters, Myrrhye, and I'm older than the mountains.'

Myrrhye's eyes grew dark and thoughtful. 'You were twenty-seven winters when eternity claimed you. If she's a sorceress, as her mother, when she comes into her gifts, she may be an acolyte who will know all her past ages as one life. Then she will be your equal.'

What a fate. Try as he might, he could not conceive of Orlanda as a grand, knotted oak trapped forever in the unblemished bark of a sapling.

'I'll never love her,' he said. 'Not like Shasirre. Maybe not at all. What sort of future is that for her?'

'The path of the future is long, my son, and mysterious, even to such as I.' She regarded him steadily. 'Orlanda's love is like dawn's bright rays, but night holds all your heart. I fear for you.'

'Fear for her.'

Myrrhye sighed, her breath a sweet susurration of falling snow. 'Rest now. I must go.'

Areme's eyes glazed over as she faded into the darkness. 'Don't go,' he whispered.

Somehow a grey-cloaked figure still hovered over him and said, 'Never while you need me.'

A name trembled upon his lips. The wrong name. It was not Shasirre, or even his mother. It was the girl. He gathered his scattered wits. 'Your Highness.'

Orlanda's fingers entwined with his. 'Rest, Areme. Your wounds run deep.'

Deeper than you will ever know. Areme forced his mind to focus. 'The race. You've chosen?'

Her fingers tightened. 'There was never a choice, Areme.'

No. Never a choice. Neither for you, nor for me.

Chapter 20

Careful What You Wish For

Pain filled every horizon, trod weary paths leading in all directions, so deep, so enormous it filled the world. Bootfalls echoed in and out of his ears, shouts and curses. Voices blurred together, boots stamped, grew small and distant until he lost all sense of them.

Where was he? What had happened? He could not even remember his name.

Galloping. Hooves. Fast-rushing dirt rising to meet him. He jammed his eyes, not wanting to recall anything more. But threads of memory unravelled in the half-consciousness of shock. A man's hand crushed in the maw of a horse. A dagger with a white-boned hilt. A sword. Pain. Deep, bitter pain.

What were remembrances but reflections of pain? He tried to rearrange them into more pleasing designs, sought escape in thoughts of cool silence, mountain meadows. A stream glittered its winding way to a valley where horses grazed. He lay down in soft clover. The sun, warm against his cheek, arced across the sky, grew hotter, hotter . . . erupted with a furnace blast, a murderous roar, the thunder of the world in one instant. He curled into a ball, hugged his arms about himself, but no matter how small he became, how tight he squeezed his eyes, images tore across his mind, firewind blasted his flesh.

Flames, red-gold, limned with blue-white, spewed scorching spirals of ash. His hair lashed in snaking air. Skin pricked. A spurt of fire sped past, redder than sunset, climbing to the peak of a hill. Against the flame, he beheld a woman – a woman clad in white-robed splendour, proud head thrown up, golden hair streaming in the wind, cast in shining radiance, ringed in fire.

Beautiful.
Terrible.
She sat upon a unicorn that gleamed rose in the burning light.

A man flanked her, glittering eyes reflecting the bleeding sun, sun-gold hair flaring about his shoulders. He lifted a sword, war-red. Blood ran down his white tabard and over tarnished, flesh-splattered mail.

Far below the hill, on a vast plain, men fought on horses, a milling frenzy. The roar of battle battered his ears, bellows of rage and pain, men gutted, torn limb from limb. In the sky, beasts flew, leathern wings outstretched, their speed a scream on the wind. They swooped, spewing flame, incinerating men and horses.

The woman laughed – a bright, desolate sound.

Glorious, horrifying, every line of her body proclaiming power, she raised her hands. A sea of flame washed from them, flowed on down the slope toward distant armies. Wind and fire roared, racing and crackling, leaving no air to breathe. Men exploded into blazing torches. Searing heat shrivelled skin to ash. Birds fluttered in frantic, flame-tossed flight. The world choked with terrified cries and blistering heat, air a stink of burnt flesh and hair.

In a world where everything had gone mad, the fire turned upon him. Terror grabbed him by the throat. Every instinct screamed at him to run, seek cover. Crawling, hands burning on scorched earth, he sought escape.

A voice came as if from great distance, commanding, willing him to obedience. *Empty all thought. Think not of the fire, or it will devour you.*

Whose was that voice? He knew it, somehow. Everything twisted, savage, tangled, frightful. He no longer tried to make sense of his drifting, scattering thoughts, unable to sort them from the flashes of agony scorching his body.

Take your mind to the time when you did not exist.

An impossible thought, non-existence.

His cry of anguish rose along with ash, high into the dirt-coloured smoke.

Fire. So much fire.

Colour fled. The world swirled in pale shades of white, swathed in a haze, elusive and impenetrable.

A boy stood beside him, staring into the distance. The boy from the night a white foal was born.

Lips drawn back from his teeth, eyes blazing, he whispered, *Know what you have done by saving the foal.* He pointed one rigid grey finger to where blood seethed. Shrieking winds whirled across a plain, mountains shook, night burned. Corpses lay thick across scorched ground. One being alone remained standing, spared from the wreckage of a ruined world.

A white unicorn.

He choked. 'What is this nightmare?'

The future. The voice drifted on the breeze. *All this death might be avoided if you join with me. Remember your name. Remember what we were born to do.*

In his fevered mind, the boy stood upon the hill, holding a lanced spear. Threw it. Like a burning snake, the weapon streaked from his hand, straight at the white unicorn with a black falcon brand on its shoulder. The lance struck, plunging deep into flesh. Rearing, the beast screamed. Wavered. Eyes rolling over white, it sunk to its knees. An instant exploded into perpetuity of pain as it lay dying on the ground. The boy walked slowly toward it, silver eyes matching those of the dying beast.

'No.' He clutched at fragments of thought. Somehow, the boy with the spear was him. The unicorn with the black falcon brand had once been a foal born in a snowstorm.

His mind reeled. Who was he? What had he done? What would he do? The need to know drove at him, the unrelenting voice.

Remember, remember who we are and what we were born to do.

He wracked his mind, searching for a name to offer, knowing he must not, but unable to fight that will.

Embers hissed, fiery hail rained from the sky. The firestorm was a scream of fury. Slowly and painfully, gasping, shaking, he tried to crawl away, fingers burning on hot rock.

Speak our name and I will take this fire from you!

Gasping at fleeing life, breath burning his smoke-raw throat, he clawed through ash. 'Gods! Save me!'

The boy turned his wrath upon him, face contorted in a scowl. *Here is salvation*! He spiked the spear into the air. Lightning shot from the clear sky to strike its tip, wove down the shaft, set the boy's body to a white glow. *Mark well this weapon. It will kill any being, even a demon. It holds the unicorn's death.*

A storm of rage welled within, beating, surging. He screamed, 'Who are you. Who am I?'

The boy thrust the spear into the void and the Shadow Realm trembled. *We are one. We were born to destroy the destroyers.* He lowered the spear, arcing energy flowing from it to the void, draining white to grey. He began to dissolve, merging with the drifting dark.

Remember who you are. Remember . . .

The spectral boy vanished, leaving in his wake deep silence. Desolation.

'No.' He refused to listen. None of the shadows were real. The boy who stalked his mind was a phantom of imagination, the world he conjured, a dreamscape of illusion.

'Sihan.'

Another presence, another voice.

'Return, return, from whence you've gone.' Shadows danced around him, ghost shadows, black shadows, blue and red, and the voice drifted in and out of his ears. 'Sihan.'

In that name another world existed, another time. It battered against walls in his mind. Broke them. Remembrance flowed like a stream of birds escaping a cage.

He forced a rasp of breath from his parched throat, 'My name is Sihan.'

A woman ghosted toward him across the firescape. Her eyes were the colour of dreams, and when she spoke, her voice lilted with sorrow. The scent of her teased his nostrils, lilac hovea bushes. Her voice wove a spell around him, held back the firestorm, stopped him from hearing the fire's call. The sun, the fire disappeared. She held out her hand.

Sihan clawed at cobwebs in his mind, trying to make sense of it all, but he was so tired. So tired. He wanted to rest. Sleep.

'Do not sleep,' she said. 'The time for sleep is at an end.'

Slowly, light filled the world, soft. A rushlight? No.

Through slitted eyes he beheld a woman, her pale face wreathed in raven hair. Delicate strands strayed about high cheekbones, wafting like gossamer on a breeze. Long lashes swept down from the mellow curve of her eyelids, closed as if in prayer.

He knew her, lost though she had been to him for so many years. He knew her warmth. Her touch. He reached out his hand. 'Mother?'

Her eyes opened, full dark gems. 'Rest, be calm.' A hand caressed his forehead, and a mist of contentment enveloped him like a shroud.

'Don't leave.'

'Never while you need me.'

Her outline hazed. Light tumbled from the sky and only darkness remained.

Soldiers kept out of Jaien's way, their faces darkened in the encroaching night. Torches, only half-lit around the outer courts, splayed crimson light upon walls streaked with long shadows. Muted horns signalled the barring of the battlement gates.

Wishing he could lock out pain as easily as tower guards barred intruders, Jaien limped to the barracks. His steps firmed as he neared his goal, heart buoyed by the news he longed to share. But as plaintive cries assaulted his ears, dread bottomed Jaien's gut. He quickened his pace to a faltering run, shoving past a host of his own men standing in groups outside the barrack's door. He shouted as he entered the room, 'What's happened?'

Not waiting for Gerein to answer, he rushed to the bunk, placed a hand on Sihan's sweating brow, pushed back the damp fringe of hair. Clammy skin, tinged with grey, shone beneath soft rushlights. The lad lay utterly still except for shallow, rapid breaths hissing between swollen lips.

Kneeling on the other side of the bunk, Gerein shook his head in bewilderment. 'He's been talking in his sleep and keeps screaming, "No . . . No."'

Jaien's gaze raked over Sihan's body and settled on the wounded leg. He pulled apart the bandage to examine the wound. The flesh was closing, binding edge to edge, melding layer by slow layer. Blood no longer seeped.

Jaien pulled a chair close. Gently as a feather's caress, he traced his fingers across the soft line of Sihan's brow, smoothing tangled brown hair back from its wild disorder, stroking the sensitive curves of cheek.

Suddenly Sihan screamed. His trembling lips formed a garbled storm, broken by weeping. Jaien leaned forward, smoothed a hand over the lad's forehead. Tremors escalated to uncontrollable shaking, and Sihan cried out in a voice filled with searing grief. 'I lost . . . I lost . . . I failed . . . Father . . . forgive me . . . Mother . . .'

Jaien took Sihan in his arms, wiped tears away from Sihan's cheeks with the back of his hand. 'You didn't fail.'

Sihan's lips moved soundlessly, the golden flame of a rushlight sending ripples of light across his face. For a moment, his brown eyes slitted. They glowed silver, brighter than the stars. Startled, Jaien recoiled, blinked. He had heard stories about granine, of the glow of madness in men's eyes.

'Aurion! No!' cried Sihan.

'Hush,' Jaien said, bending his head close. 'You must rest.'

'Father . . .' Sihan whispered.

Jaien brushed his fingers through Sihan's sweat-soaked hair. 'Hush, he'll be here shortly.'

Sihan lay still for a moment, then cried out again, 'I lost . . . I failed . . . Aurion! Ghosts! 'ware the ghosts!' He sucked in a ragged breath. 'Don't say that! Don't say that! I am *Sihan*! No one else!'

'It's the edge of a dream,' mumbled Gerein, shadows playing upon his strained face.

'Nightmare, more like.' Jaien tried to make sense of Sihan's wild muttering.

'I don't understand any of it,' said Gerein, lighting a brazier by the bedside.

Sihan's body shook as though racked by violent chills. His lips opened and closed, emitting a long drawn-out groan, but no words came. Then his eyes snapped wide open and stared blankly. Dead of life, they rolled over white.

Jaien wrung out a cloth over a bucket beside the bed. He ran it over Sihan's flushed cheeks, the sweat-beaded forehead.

Boots reverberated on the floorboards at the barrack's door, then Gerhas marched in and strode to the bunk where he bent to examine Sihan closely. 'Still unconscious? Pity. Thought to tell him the princess has claimed Aurion.'

Jaien kept stroking Sihan's forehead. 'Veren told me he forfeited. I didn't quite believe him.'

Gerhas straightened, raising an eyebrow. 'Did he now? Well, that explains his lack of argument when I broke the news.'

Suddenly Sihan thrashed his arms, eyes flaring, pupils tiny pin points, a glaze of white filling the eyes as though they were inflamed by light.

'I lost,' he cried. 'I lost.' He repeated the hopeless phrase over and over.

Jaien took him in his arms. Insistent, he repeated, 'Aurion's been chosen. You've not failed.'

A hard expression set Sihan's face, eyes flashing silver. 'You lie.'

Jaien flinched.

Sihan's shining eyes became distant, then darkened to their normal dark brown. 'All Mirador is a lie . . .'

The door crashed open and Armindras swept across the room. 'My boy, my boy,' he muttered, pushing Jaien aside to envelop Sihan in his arms. His face pressed hard against Sihan's hair. 'What have they done to you?'

Jaien looked away, could not meet the old man's eyes. Seeing Sihan's father brought it all home to him. This was his fault, all of it. He had spared his own father a dagger in the back, just to plunge one as surely into Armindras.

Sihan returned to consciousness with a deep shudder. Heaviness dragged at his body. Why could he not move? Without knowing better, he might have thought lead had been poured into his bones. Realization he was half-naked came slowly.

Then memory rushed forth, unrestrained, the chill and ache of desolation. *Aurion . . . The trials . . . Father.* Agony shot through his jaw. He kept his eyes squeezed shut, not wanting to see, as if that might hold the world at bay.

Somewhere nearby, boots moving restlessly on wooden floorboards. Rowelled spurs jangled harsh. Sihan kept his breathing shallow, tried not to breathe the scent of horses, of bullybeef oil, all the things meaning home. For if he did, surely that home would melt away into illusion.

'Sihan. Wake up.'

He did not want to open his eyes, kept them stuck closed.

'Come on, lad.'

Eyes stinging, he obeyed the command in that voice. Around him, men purled like water blown by a breeze, dissolved and reformed. Was this another dream, an illusion playing havoc with his senses?

A red haze lifted as his eyelids flickered fully open. His father's pale face swam into focus, eyes deep and hollowed with worry. The old man pressed something to Sihan's lips. Cold water dribbled into his mouth, freshening his parched tongue and throat.

His father's hand closed over his, squeezed hard. 'My boy, my boy,' Armindras kept repeating as though he had lost the gift of any other words.

Sihan clutched at him, no voice coming to his call either. His father was here. No illusion. He was free.

Over his father's shoulder, stood Gerhas. A soldier Sihan recognised as Gerein stood nearby, but it was Jaien with whom his eyes locked. They stared at one another, Sihan searching for some hint of smile in those grim features, those green-gold eyes.

'Did I win?'

'Not exactly.'

Hope crushed to dust.

He had lost. His mind doubled and dodged, like a hare fleeing a fox, trying to avoid that fact. But there was no escaping, no hole in which to hide.

'Don't look so dispirited,' Gerhas's loud voice boomed. He leaned over him, smiling through his beard. 'Your horse has been chosen.'

Sihan stared from one face to another. 'Chosen?'

'Yes,' affirmed Gerhas.

Contradictory thoughts chased each other through Sihan's mind, confusing his already befuddled brain. 'I don't understand.'

Gerhas shrugged 'You fell off. Your horse won for you. The princess claimed Aurion.' His expression hardened. 'As soon as you are well, you will have new duties to which to attend.'

'New duties?' Sihan could not think anymore, repeating everything without quite taking it in.

'Tomorrow, you will be assigned new quarters, more fitting for the princess's Royal Groomsman.' Gerhas's voice was laced with vicious satisfaction.

'Royal Groomsman!' Pain coursed through Sihan's leg as he propped himself up in astonishment. His gaze swept to his father.

Armindras nodded. 'I heard it from the king's own lips. No soldier's commission.'

'And you?'

'Free, as you can see,' smiled Armindras.

Gerhas turned to leave, muttering to Gerein, 'Find a room for the lad near the stables.'

Sihan looked straight at Jaien, then, long into his eyes. Silence stretched between them. Shadowed as Jaien's eyes were, a glimmer of smile lit their depths.

'Aurion,' asked Sihan, not able to say anything more, not here, not now. 'Where is he?'

Smile after unrestrained smile rippled across Jaien's lips as he said, 'Stuffing his face in the stables.'

Sihan's head fell back to the pallet. Against all the odds, their plan had worked. His father was free. Sihan would not have to take up the sword. The princess had chosen Aurion.

So why did he suddenly feel more ill than ever?

Chapter 21

A Parting of Ways

Jaien spent the dark of the last morning left to him in Mirador writing a note by candlelight, scratching out the words, cursing, crushing rolled vellum in his fist, discarding it, getting more unmarked vellum, until he finally settled on four lines saying nothing of what he wanted to say, and all he did not. Unsatisfied, out of time, he wiped ink-stained fingers on his leggings, examined the words again, then rolled the vellum and tied it with a leather cord. He snuffed out the candle between finger and thumb, and scraped his chair back from the heavy table in the guardroom.

Beyond the lancet window, low clouds obscured setting stars. There was barely enough disparity between fortification and Heavens to reveal the outline of towered minarets or crenels of the curtain wall. Watch guards were shadows pacing the brattices. In the stable court, silent, grey-cloaked men marched back and forth, all motion a barely visible quivering in the deep murk before dawn.

Jaien drew his cloak close around him and made his way to Travall's quarters. When he entered the room, he braced himself. His former commander, Atiarin, stood beside Travall, gritting his teeth like he was biting back a snarl. He had arrived during the night, sent orders ahead for Jaien to have his men ready to leave first light. Travall took a seat, clear eyes flicking to Jaien's face, resting there, gauging, his bearing so cold it could have turned air into ice.

Eyes flashing in the light from a sconce, Knight Commander Atiarin held out the commission. As Jaien's fingers closed on the scroll, Atiarin growled through his black beard, 'You stupid pup. Throwing away a command for no reason. And after the reports I sent to the duke on your behalf. After Tulit!'

Jaien's jaw hardened. 'I had reason.'

Atiarin crashed his fist upon the table so violently the boards jounced. 'A boy evading commission is no reason!'

'Is a flood of lies, corruption and a king too weak–'

Atiarin hit him. Hard. Jaien had half-expected it, but still he staggered back against the wall.

'I'll break you for even one more word of treason.' Atiarin voice was inflexible as his fist. 'Do you understand?'

'Yes, Sir,' Jaien hissed.

Travall steepled his long fingers on the table and leaned forward. 'Let's keep the war against our enemies, not between ourselves.'

Atiarin stepped away, expression souring into a festering glower.

Balfere strode into the room, beads of sweat rolling down his brow, back soaked. 'Did I hear someone say war?' He sprawled his bulk across a chair. 'Gods! The conscripts aren't nearly ready. Just had two nearly gut themselves in a sword drill.' He slumped further. 'Lucky that vulture Veren wasn't there to see it. Or unlucky. Maybe they could have gutted him and we could have claimed it was an accident like he did after trying to kill Areme.'

'Are you ever going to let that rest?' asked Travall.

'No.'

Atiarin graced Balfere with a brittle smile. 'Just try not to spit him when he comes into the hall to accept the proposal.'

Balfere motioned beyond the door where knights and men-at-arms were saddling horses. 'I see you're leaving before the fun.'

'The Duke of Pelan has declared war on Byerol.'

Jaien's eyes jerked to Atiarin. 'The duke's really going to war over a few horses stolen by Byerol?'

Atiarin raised an eyebrow. 'You're the last man I'd expect that from. Some of them were your father's horses.'

Balfere straightened, massaging his meaty hands together, livening at the prospect of battle. 'Take me with you. Demote me if you have to.'

Atiarin did not smile. 'One unruly ex-knight commander is enough for any command.'

Jaien levelled a glare at Travall. 'You're not really going to follow the king's lead again on this one, are you?' It was more foolish hope than question.

Travall's eyes darkened, contrasting the colour draining from his face. 'I have no choice. I'm in it to the neck. And, as a knight, so are you.'

Atiarin said tightly to Jaien, voice lowered till it became a mere breath of air. 'For the first time there's talk of peace. This marriage of the princess may yet settle old disputes, heal wounds, may bring the king and duke together.'

Jaien ran a hand over his smarting jaw. 'You don't believe that any more than I do.'

'What I believe, is we stand or fall together. A man must hold to his vows. If the duke fails in duty or his word – if he violates safe conduct – it's war, and this thing between Pelan and Byerol will look like little more than a skirmish.' He shrugged into his grey cloak and drew it closed over the golden falcon of Pelan. Eyes, cold as a graveyard, brooked no further dissension. 'You have your orders.'

Jaien stiffened at the curt dismissal, but he had gotten off lightly. He knew it. He started for the barracks where his men were assembling, hesitated, then changed course for the stables where Falcon stood saddled and waiting, next to an empty stall.

Just as Jaien had known he would, his father had resumed their old argument and left in disgust straight after the trials, Wedge walking stiffly behind the cart. The horse had been sore after his fall; the walk would do him more good than standing in a stable. And he was young, rising six, plenty of time to come sound. The real sore point was Jaien's father had spared no time for Jaien to make even an attempt at amends, on any count.

'That's the last horse you'll ruin for me! The last!' Cenriin had thrown his hands into the air as though somehow conveying the measure of 'last'. And he had left, leaving a festering wound in his wake.

Like this other, if Jaien made no attempt to heal it.

He strode briskly along the stables till he found Armindras bundled in a cloak on a bench, snoring the dawn away with heavy grunts. He touched the old man's shoulder, and Armindras started awake, staring about with bleary eyes. 'What? Who?' He focussed on Jaien, then rolled to his feet with an exaggerated groan, rubbing crusted eyelids.

Jaien drew forth the missive he had written, and handed it to the old man. 'My command has been called out. If I could request . . . I'd esteem it . . .'

Armindras's fingers closed on the scroll. 'You'd like me to give this to Sihan?'

Jaien smiled thanks. 'Yes.'

'He'll be about soon. You're not planning on seeing him?'

One fist clenched, fingernails hard to palm, Jaien recalled the voice inciting him to harm Sihan, after first ordering him to protect the lad. He had succumbed to the first demand since it merged with his own desires. But the second . . . In no way would he obey any command to harm Sihan. This call to war was a blessing, almost. Sihan was safe from the king's plans, and from Jaien's demons.

Jaien returned Armindras's probing look. 'I doubt I'll have the chance to see him before we pull out. Pelan's declared war against Byerol. Tell him . . .' Jaien looked away from the man's searching gaze, gut tightening. He drew a heavy breath. 'Tell him I wish him well.' And with that, he walked away.

Sihan stifled a moan as he lay on his pallet, clanging of steel and roar of the blacksmith's bellow making sleep impossible. Beyond his door – always slightly ajar so he could hear any untoward noises from Aurion's stall – light from fresh-lit iron baskets clad the courtyard. Men and horses crowded the court, and stable boys went briskly about their business or running errands for soldiers. A slightly lighter tinge of ebon heralded the new day hidden below the horizon.

Even in the dawn chill, fire tore at Sihan's leg, through his body, heating his face till sweat damped his hair and the back of his neck and dripped between his shoulder blades. His worn tunic scratched at his skin, threadbare as it was, resembling a sack of hemp more than anything else. Crawling from his bed, he limped to a water trough outside his room and splashed water over his face, wishing for the cool peace of a mountain morning in Graycor. His gut clenched at the thought of not returning home. The familiar beat of his father's heavy footsteps upon the stone walkway only added to his woes.

Armindras came to a halt beside him. He smiled but it did not reach his eyes, not at all, neither did he relax an inch in the rigid set of his body. Long, tortured heartbeats passed before he said, 'Well, it's time, lad.' Piercing brown eyes shadowed in his lined, weathered face.

Sihan pressed his lips together. Thoughts darted back and forth like fish in water. Unasked questions flooded his mind, vital things he was sure he needed to know. He wiped his sweating brow with the back of his hand.

'Leg bothering you?' asked Armindras, corners of his eyes crinkling.

'Just a twinge,' lied Sihan, refusing to look down at the baggy leggings covering his wounded leg. His father's – tied with a leather cord about his hips – roomy to avoid rubbing his wound. 'Stop fussing.' He swallowed, hard. In a few moments his father would be gone, and who knew when he would see him again.

As dawn slipped into the new day, they walked to the stable entrance, Sihan forced to measure every stride, think it, pray to the gods to execute it. Daggers of pain thrust through his leg, every step an ordeal. He willed himself to not show any more than he already had, to not add further burden to the gut-aching wretchedness of loss about to claim both him and his father.

Without warning, Armindras turned and enveloped Sihan in a fierce, clumsy bear hug. Sihan ignored the smirks of passersby, returning the embrace with equal strength, if somewhat stiff and awkward.

Sharp tapping hooves beat on cobbles, a heavy rumble in their wake. 'Ho! Armindras! We're all set,' shouted a voice over the creaking of a cart lurching to a standstill beside them. A man with a massive, square face held the mule in check.

Sihan did not hide the question in his eyes.

'Reonor,' said Armindras. 'My new steward. He'll be helping me until you're released from your position.' He paused, running his hand through his greying hair. His mouth opened and closed, unable to find the right words. When he finally spoke, a slight hoarseness caught at the edge of his voice. 'The bay colt. The one you rode here . . .' He paused, coughed. 'I put it next to

Aurion. It's yours, so long as you pledge to keep him safe and return to Graycor on him when you're granted leave.'

Sihan fought not to break. 'I promise, Father.'

Another cough. After some hesitation, Armindras pulled a letter from a pouch at his belt and handed it to Sihan. 'Jaien asked me to give you this. His unit has been recalled to Pelan. The Duke of Pelan has declared war on Byerol.'

A twinge of fear passed through Sihan. 'It's really happening, then?'

'It's a limited conflict between two dukes. You've no need to worry. As the princess's groomsman, you won't be called out.' Armindras's eyes shifted this way and that, never quite meeting Sihan's.

Sihan looked at him hard. His father had been repeating that for days, as though somehow needing the reassurance of the statement on his lips to make it true. So much had happened since the first threat of being called into the army. And despite all they had accomplished, he would still be parted from his father and home.

Armindras's bleak, perturbed countenance hardened to stone through a stretched silence. Then he said, 'Well, take care of yourself. I'll see you before the year is out.' He leaned down for the kiss of kin, touching lips to both Sihan's cheeks. Then his eyes darkened as though a shutter dropped, a blank blind shutting out the world.

Biting the inside of his lip, Sihan blinked hard as Armindras climbed into the over-laden cart, buckboard creaking under his weight. Armindras no longer looked at Sihan, just stared fixedly ahead.

Reonor clicked at the mule, gave a sharp snap of the whip, and the cart lurched forward as the mule picked its way over cobbles. Sihan followed to the stable gates, leaned against the rough stones of the battlement, watching with burning eyes until the cart disappeared round a corner.

A long time passed before he eased himself away from the wall's support to undertake the torturous limp back to the stable. Cast adrift, he felt as though he had been dropped into the middle of an empty ocean. He had seen Kheran and Tejas only once since the tournament. They had been assigned to training quarters and kept busy drilling, along with all the other lads.

In some ways he was glad. Though they had all agreed to ride for his father's release, and seemed pleased that at least Sihan had avoided the conscription, in no way could he shake off the sense of guilt. They would all be gone soon, sent to distant outposts in the kingdom.

Mirador's grey stable walls became a shade colder as Sihan imagined himself walking the alleys with no hope of seeing a familiar face. Not knowing the fate of his friends. Not knowing if he might ever see them again. His leg throbbed unmercifully and for a moment he was glad, not wanting to think.

At the corner of the stable complex, the temple of the god of horses, Senfar, rose before him, cold wash of dawn paling the marble façade to a hue of bluish-white. Soft chanting came from within. A familiar voice pulled Sihan up short like a swift jerk of a rein. Jaien's clear, resonant timbre recited the prayer of Enlightenment.

Sihan slipped inside and secreted himself behind a pillar, knowing full well only knights were allowed within prayer halls. In gloom, a line of grey-cloaked men knelt before an altar. One dropped a handful of chaff before a statue of a rearing horse. 'By all that is merciful,' he said, 'protect Falcon in this time of trouble.'

The others repeated the gesture, a soft chorus of voices naming other horses, then the soldiers stood and filed out, a muffled tramp of boots, leaving the first knight still kneeling. He bent his head and remained silent for a while, then whispered, 'And by all that is merciful, watch over Sihan.'

Sihan drew a quick breath, a harsh sound in the quiet of the chamber. Jaien spun round, the golden falcon against his black tabard catching the dim light. For a long while, neither spoke, then Sihan broke the silence. 'Father said you'd left for Pelan.'

Tension tightened the lines of Jaien's face, emotion damped. 'I'm leaving shortly.' He stood, grey cloak falling to his boots. 'You got my note?'

Sihan had trouble meeting Jaien's eyes. 'I haven't read it.'

Jaien frowned and Sihan almost turned away, so as not to see the dark disappointment in the other man's eyes. Uncomfortable silence stretched the length of the temple between them.

When Jaien spoke again, his voice came strained. 'Will you?'

Sihan could not bear the weight behind the look in those intent grey-green eyes, or the question, and opted for evasion. 'You saved my life after the fall.'

'Not me. Granine.'

'You saved my father.'

'I'm pretty sure I don't own the credit for that either.' Cold dismissal in the tone and a discomfited smile almost hid the hint of a passing look of shame.

'That's not true and I've been a horse's arse, not thanking you.'

A horn blared in the courtyard and Jaien glanced beyond the door where hooves beat sharp on cobbles. 'My company is pulling out.' He walked forward till they were a step apart, eyes glittering with hard resolve mixed with resignation. 'I have to go.' He hesitated. 'Look, I know you're not in the army, but I've asked my friends to look out for you, take you to the sword drills – only if you want. They're good men. You can trust them.' Jaien leaned forward, placing his hands on Sihan's shoulders, the brightness in his eyes igniting to a low-banked fire.

Sihan took a step back, stood Jaien off, hands pressing against the knight's shoulders. 'What are you doing?'

A flush stole across Jaien's cheeks, bringing high colour where before only shadows had moved. His next words came with cautious apprehension, as if he tested each syllable before uttering it. 'The kiss of kin. For good fortune.'

'We're not kin,' said Sihan, suspicious and wary.

Something flickered in the knight's eyes, and a strange sensation coursed through Sihan, a sense of brotherhood, a fleeting feeling of souls linked in common cause. But he made no move to close the distance between them.

Jaien patted Sihan's arm, a swift gesture of cold dismissal. 'No matter.' After another brief pause he said with forced cheer, smiling falsely, 'Truly, Sihan. I'm glad things have worked out for you.'

The naked pain in Jaien's face forced Sihan to relent. When the knight went to push past, Sihan reached out and touched his arm. 'Wait.' He inclined a half-reluctant cheek, breath held. Jaien hesitated, did not smile, though something akin to hope flashed in his eyes. He leaned forward, face so close the heat from his skin radiated against Sihan's cheek. Lips brushed Sihan's skin, warm, hesitant, then Jaien withdrew. Green eyes, gold-irised, gazed stanchly into Sihan's.

Heat flooded Sihan's face, and thoughts his mind. Skin against skin, breath merging with breath. Words, thoughts, awareness threaded through his consciousness.

Jaien's eyes burned high in the darkness when he stepped back. 'Did you mean that, or was it just for show?'

Sihan was glad the muted light in the prayer room hid his discomfort. 'For good fortune.'

A soft laugh escaped Jaien's lips, a short, bitter sound. 'I confess, I was hoping for more.'

Sihan bent his head. 'I'm sorry.'

Jaien reached out, traced the line of Sihan's jaw with one finger, tilting his head up. 'You've nothing for which to be sorry.' He strode out into the dawn light where his squire waited with Falcon and Jaien's sword. The stallion laid back his ears as his master approached.

Raw laughter burst from one of Jaien's men. 'He still hasn't forgiven you for letting his brother crash.'

Jaien sheathed his blade, then vaulted onto the chestnut. 'He'll come round.' He caught Sihan's gaze and held it, then spurred Falcon out the courtyard gate. His company followed in a long double line at his back, grey cloaks fluttering in the breeze over their mounts' swinging hindquarters. Dark steel lance heads silhouetted against the morn-grey of the courtyard walls, torchlight slid over mail and harness and shields.

When the clatter of hooves and ring of brass receded, Sihan unfolded Jaien's letter, and within him a void formed, heavier than lead.

Sihan,

My company is leaving for Pelan, and I might not see you again. I would have liked to have spoken to you in person, but it seemed better not to. You'll find the fortress a hotbed of rumour, and I regret my actions might have caused you grief. I pray you will forgive me, and the day may come when you will not think ill of me.

Jaien.

    Sihan's fingers tightened on the letter. He thought of Hessarde's intimation that he had been Jaien's lover. He thought of pain-filled eyes, of sweat-slicked skin. Of warm lips brushing his cheek. Loss stabbed through him like a sword's thrust, almost deeper than when his father had left.
    Confused, he slipped the letter into the pouch holding his mother's note. He did not think ill of Jaien. He just did not know what he *did* feel. Returning to his room to rest until he was called, he turned and tossed on the pallet, trying to catch a snatch of sleep, unable to dispel the desperate feeling half of himself had been torn away.
    The sun was high in the sky when the stable foreman poked his head in the door. 'Sihan!' he snapped. 'The princess is waiting for you in the arena.'
    Sihan started. 'She is?' He had not seen her since the tournament, sick as he had been.
    The foreman's next words pulled him staggering from his bed. 'She's riding that uncontrollable horse of yours.'
    'She's what?' Sihan stumbled from his room, fighting against pain, following the foreman who strode briskly along the stable walkway. He shot a swift glance at Aurion's empty stall, mind churning in a half-lucid daze. Had he slept? He did not feel as though he had shut his eyes for even a wink. But how else could anyone have spirited Aurion away from under his very nose? And who had saddled him? None of the other stable boys even dared to walk past the stall for fear of Aurion's large, snapping teeth. The only person left in Mirador who had shown

any real ability to handle the horse was Areme, and Sihan had not laid eyes on him since the trials. Rumour had it the knight was recovering, though no one could credit how. If Aurion turned on the princess, and there was no one there to stop him . . . Sihan clenched his fist. He would be dragged to the scaffold faster than the thought had taken form.

Raking his hair into some sort of order, smoothing down his tunic, Sihan struggled after the foreman to the palace quarter, trying to hide the panic within. Sweet scent of spikenard drifted from walkways flanked by marble colonnades enwrapped in ivy. Soldiers stood guard at every doorway, cloaked in purest white, the crimson firefalcon, bright like a splash of newspilt blood, emblazoned on their tabards.

Blood. Sweat slid down Sihan's brow as heat shimmered up from cobbles. He had seen too much blood lately. Jaien was riding toward more. And the princess . . . *Gods!*

'In there.' The foreman nodded at a high-domed building atop which blue tiles glinted in sunhaze. Having delivered Sihan, he marched away.

Not wanting to see what he feared, Sihan limped to a large double door, dark wood inlaid with gold. Guards cleared a path, one pushing the door in a fraction to let him through. It opened upon a high-vaulted hall, walls all stone, wooden galleries at either end for the nobility to watch demonstrations of horsemanship. As the door closed behind Sihan, a soft thud of hooves caught his ear. He peered into gloom, the interior of the hall more stifling than out in the sun.

Sallow sand banked up high against dark wood panels stretching around the riding hall. Priceless gold effigies of horses in myriad postures glowed dully in spaces between high lancet windows. But it was a dull moon-pale shadow that grabbed his attention.

In the far corner, the princess rode Aurion at a walk, one hand on the rein, fanning her face casually with a glove held in the other. Sickness flooded Sihan's stomach as memory flashed through his mind of the stallion galloping madly, dodging thickets of spinifex, hurdling fallen trunks and then an impossible chasm. Of a horse gone mad, a man screaming, of teeth set to tear and rend and hooves to smash flesh to pulp.

Sweat broke out afresh, the reek of it thick in his nostrils. Should he warn the princess of the demon ride the stallion beneath might promise her?

He laboured across the deep beige sand on one side of the ménage, using the wooden railing for support. Rosewood, by its thick, cloying scent, rare and worked to a smoothness the trees had never known in life. His faltering feet, enclosed in short-cut-off boots, slipped amid the soft grains, disturbing fat lazy pigeons which fluttered lethargically to the rafters of the vaulted ceiling.

Aurion stepped into a shaft of light slanting through one of the four slitted windows in the walls. For a moment, a halo of golden hair surrounded the princess, shimmering, flaring over her shoulders. Dazzled, Sihan thought the sun blazed before him, radiant and life giving.

The sun.

From nowhere flames seemed to leap about her, around Aurion, framing them in an inferno. He stared at them both, unable to move, daggers of fear stabbing at him. The narrow light shaft seemed to fling open a tunnel to half-forgotten dreams. A woman astride a white horse, flamewind tugging at her gown, charring everything around her to ash. The stallion's hooves crunched over a field of human bones.

Then Aurion stepped back into darkness, melting back into shadow as black as the brand of a black falcon on his shoulder.

Brand? Full of nameless dread, Sihan stepped back, dazed. Aurion had no brand. Only true bloodhorses were branded. But suddenly no ghost of his childhood appeared so frightful as the young princess or the horse he had sold to gain his father's life. He almost screamed when she stopped Aurion before him. Lurching away, he fell, kicking up a spray of sand with his boots and landing on his backside. Aurion snorted, throwing his head up. A trilling laugh sang above Sihan like a thrush.

'You silly, silly boy! Has someone plucked out your eyes that you didn't see us?'

Robbed of his wits, Sihan just stared up at the princess in stunned disbelief. In the soft light her ivory-white skin shone like morning on a mist-dewed field. Deep pools of cerulean returned his stupefied gaze, empty of malice, or any other ill-intent. And her hair – it was caught in a net at the nape of her neck, not loose at all.

Fighting nausea, he struggled to his feet. Hurriedly, he bowed in reverence. 'Forgive me, Highness.' With his tunic sticking to his back, Sihan was glad of the heavy aroma of vanilla enveloping the princess, masking his stale stink of sweat.

'What do you think of my dress?' she demanded, voice echoing through the cavernous space.

Nonplussed, mind fluttering in every direction like a wind-tossed butterfly, Sihan asked, 'Your dress?'

'Yes. I want a man's opinion, and you're a man, aren't you? Does it suit me?' Right leg hooked over the horn of a sidesaddle, she looked down at him, motioning to her smart white riding costume trimmed with miniatures of the Mirador crest. Its voluminous folds draped over Aurion's hindquarters like a cloak, unmoving in the still, lifeless air, unlike the gown in the vision billowing on gusts of furnace wind. The dress stopped just in front of the saddle, exposing Aurion's shoulder – gleaming white. No brand disfigured the stallion. The vision must have been just some waking nightmare. He was in pain. He was ill. His mind was running wild.

'Well?' demanded the princess. 'I'm awaiting your answer.'

Sihan stared at her helplessly, trying to remember the question – something about her dress. He stumbled over words, 'Oh . . . well . . . yes . . . I suppose.'

Arched eyebrows rose. 'You *suppose*? That's not an answer.' Her brow furrowed. 'Or maybe it is. I'll have another made for tomorrow.' As she waved her glove again, a piece of yellow silk fluttered from her sleeve.

'Tomorrow?' Sihan bent down, glad of a chance not to look at her, and to re-gather his scattered wits. He picked up the ribbon from the sand, and dusted it off.

'For the hunt.' She waved him away when he tried to hand the ribbon back. 'Keep it.'

Even though the vanilla scent was now overpowering, Sihan tied the token to his belt. 'Thank you, Your Highness.'

The princess grimaced. 'Don't call me that. It's so stuffy. My name is Orlanda.'

'But–'

'No buts . . . I'm determined to have at least one person in this fortress who isn't boring, and I've decided you're him. Everyone either bosses me around, or grovels at my feet. I'm sick of both. I'm determined to have fun, and I can't do that if you're going to be so formal.' She picked up Aurion's reins. 'Say it.' It was command.

'Orlanda.' Sihan almost gagged, her name strange and wrong upon his lips. Focussing on something he understood, he took hold of Aurion's bridle with his left hand and led the stallion around the arena, right hand resting on the horse's neck, fingers clutching a fistful of mane, taking weight off his leg. He nodded at patches of light, where sunlight speared through windows to strike the sand. 'Watch out for those changes in light. Aurion might spook and jump the shadows.' It was a lie. He really did not want to see the sunlight catch hold of her again, or Aurion, transfigure them both into a thing of terror.

As if calling him on his lie, the stallion nosed his side hard enough to nearly knock him off his feet. Sihan grimaced as pain lanced through his injured leg.

'What's wrong?' asked the princess.

'Nothing,' lied Sihan once more.

'Silly boy.' She tapped him on the shoulder with her riding crop. 'You're injured. No one expects you to be a martyr. You don't see Knight Commander Areme struggling about, taking part in sword drills. You should follow his example.'

Sihan gazed down at his boots, reminded again that it was his fault Areme lay injured.

The tip of her riding crop pushed under his chin, forcing his face up until his eyes met hers. 'Stop looking at the ground,' she demanded. 'It can't be half as interesting as I am.'

Sihan shuffled his feet, lips twitching as he tried to hide a smile. 'I think you're making sport of me.'

'Of course I'm making sport of you. And stop hiding that smile. Your eyes sparkle like stars when you smile. I saw that the first time I laid eyes on you. I should pass a royal decree forbidding you to frown ever again.'

Her face, at once playful and slightly mocking, set him laughing.

'There,' she said, with a self-satisfied air. 'Much better. I want someone who is fun and not serious. If I wanted serious, I'd be getting stuffy old Gerhas to give me riding lessons.' She paused and looked at him closely. 'Are you really frere?'

'What?' Sihan gulped in air to find a voice to protest, but could utter no other words.

She giggled, putting her hand to her mouth. 'You should see your face.'

Recalling Jaien's letter, Sihan frowned. Was this what he had meant by rumours?

The princess tapped him once more with her crop. 'Now, now. What did I say about frowning?'

'I'm not frere!'

The princess eyed him closely. 'Oh! Poor Jaien. And his heart so set on you. Good thing he's left. I hope you told him. It's better to be open about such things.' Then she smiled. 'You know, I think I'm glad. Frere are boring, too. They all ignore me as though I'm of no more interest than a cow. It's demoralising being ignored by gorgeous men. And even worse when they're plain. What's the point in my paint and my dresses if men won't swoon at my command?'

Again Sihan burst out laughing. 'I'm sure men swoon without a command.'

The princess grinned. 'And quite right, too.' Then she patted Aurion's neck. 'Gerhas is a fool. He asserts Aurion is a dangerous brute.'

Sihan resumed leading the stallion, forcing away the memory of being lashed from side to side as if he rode the tail of a thrashing crocodile, of a man screaming, jaws clamped on his arm, even more so the strange vision of hooves on bones.

'I've heard most of the stable boys refuse to go near him,' continued the princess. 'Even the soldiers think he's dangerous.'

Sihan stole a baffled look at her. 'Then who saddled him this morning?'

'I did.'

'You!' Sihan stared at her incredulously, then his blood froze as he realised the insult he had cast.

Her eyes fired. 'Why shouldn't I know how to saddle a horse? A princess should know everything. And besides, you are injured.'

To Sihan's immense relief, she said nothing more about his tactless breach of etiquette, too busy breaking every rule herself. He guessed a princess could break whatever rules she wanted.

A princess . . .

She was a princess, and would be queen. He shook his head. Could the myths be true? Was Aurion truly a Godsteed? Was it her to whom the stallion had bonded – the future monarch?

Hope was a hard knot in his chest. Aurion had stopped his wildness the moment Orlanda had appeared after Areme had been injured. Just . . . stopped. She had whacked him on the nose, and he had stood like a lamb. Could he truly be a horse of legend?

Orlanda leaned close suddenly and whispered, 'Tell me? How is my speech?'

Shaken out of his thoughts, doubly bewildered by every word she uttered, Sihan said, 'Your speech?'

'Is it passable Common? How the common girls speak? I've been practicing. Lots.' She tapped him again with her whip. 'You're common. Am I doing it right? Would it pass for Common?'

Not knowing whether to be insulted or amused, Sihan spread his hands. 'Well, yes. I suppose.' Why the devil did she want to speak Common?

Her face darkened. '"I suppose" again. Hmm . . . That's not promising.' Leaning down further over Aurion's neck, she dropped her voice to a whisper, 'Tell me of the north, Sihan. That's where you're from, isn't it?'

Reeling, Sihan asked, 'What about it?'

'I hear the mountains are impassable. Is it true?'

'Not entirely. There are passes zingars use.' He said no more, not wanting to recall memories of zingars that came from the north, either.

But the princess continued her relentless questioning, not caring what bruises she rode over in her quest for answers. 'You broke the king's edicts to escape the soldier's commission.'

'I did.' No point in denial. He searched her face for sign she thought him a coward.

'But despite all you efforts, still you are trapped here.' Orlanda's eyes narrowed, countenance grave. She drew a deep breath as if preparing herself to utter hard words. 'We are kindred spirits, Sihan, each trying to avoid fate. Duty binds us, not our hearts.' Her voice became harsh. 'If ever you are offered freedom, embrace it.'

Her gravity spurred Sihan to judge she expected some response, though he knew not what. He touched her fingers with his and said, 'If that is your will, I swear I'll obey.'

His body quivered in involuntary response as her pale fingers, adorned only with the ring of the heir-apparent, a firefalcon edged in white, caressed his hand. Sihan frowned. The night before the trials he was certain it had been edged in black. As he turned his gaze back to those blue eyes, the thought escaped him.

Orlanda straightened and smiled, the dark shadow enveloping her slipping away like a cast-off mask. Then she tapped Aurion with the riding whip. The stallion leapt into a canter, leaving Sihan standing in the middle of the arena. He stared after her. The horror he had felt upon first sight of her distorted into an equally uncomfortable twisting queasiness deep in his gut. In the short space of time he had spoken to her it was difficult to think of her as anything other than frightfully mad. He was not sure which was worse, the reality or the illusion.

After the princess's ride, Sihan led Aurion to the fountain in the centre of the stable courtyard. Giddy from the girl's weirdness, he wondered whether all females in Mirador behaved so strangely. He was hardly in a position to judge. She would think him thrice weird if she knew of his visions, the voices he imagined he heard, and the zingar that stalked him.

Sprays of water arced into a circular trough from the gaping mouths of two ornately carved rearing white horses locked in a fighting stance. Aurion nosed tiny blue and white flowers peeking from crevices at the base of the fountain.

'Hey! Don't let that horse maul the flowers!' A brown-haired young man of middling height strode up to the fountain, lean body moving freely and easily like a prowling cat. Sihan recognised the soldier who had bought the bay colt from his father.

Gerein slowed at the fountain's edge, treading with care, glinting hazel eyes watching the ground as if to avoid stepping in excrement. Despite Aurion's reputation, he showed no fear in grabbing at the stallion's bridle and pulling the great head up.

Aurion laid back his ears and snapped, forcing Gerein to jump back.

'You better watch him,' warned Gerein, pretending composure as he adjusted the gorytos strapped at his belt. 'Gerhas hates him enough already. If he catches him destroying the queen's mistflowers, there's no telling what he'll do.'

Sihan gaped, convinced now everyone in Mirador was quite mad. 'I can't see why you're making such a fuss about a bunch of flowers.'

Gerein's voice edged into faint annoyance. 'Because Jaien told me to watch out for you. So that's what I'm doing. He's made looking after you my penance.'

Sihan stared at the young archer and recalled Jaien's words, 'my friends will look after you' and wondered how close a "friend" Gerein was, mind struggling with the possibilities it opened up. Lifting his chin, he challenged, 'Are you Jaien's lover?'

Gerein laughed. 'Not since I discovered women.' Then he shot back, 'Jealous?'

Sihan crossed his arms, refusing Gerein the satisfaction of a denial.

Gerein's nose wrinkled. 'Phew! What's that smell?' He tugged at the silk tied to Sihan's belt. 'Bit fancy for a farm boy.'

Sihan blushed. 'Orlanda . . . uhh . . . the princess . . . gave it to me.'

A smirk flitted across Gerein's face. 'You're on first-name terms with the princess? Jaien is going to be so pissed his farm boy is making eyes at women not half a day after he left. And the princess, sorry, *Orlanda*, no less.'

Sihan's hackles rose. 'I'm the princess's groomsman.'

Gerein quirked an eyebrow. 'Nice title. But doesn't give you the right to let your horse run roughshod over the *queen's* mistflowers.'

Sihan glared at Gerein. 'What's so special about them a King's Archer feels the need to go on so?'

Gerein sat on the edge of the trough. 'The Lady of Eloin brought them here when she joined the king in formal union. Every royal bride wears a garland of mistflowers. After the ceremony, she sprinkled some petals in this fountain. Don't ask me how, but they grew into plants. When she died, the king ordered them torn out. But they kept growing back, as if the queen refused to be forgotten. Finally, he declared them sacred, and now no one is allowed to touch them.'

'Well, Aurion wasn't running roughshod over *anything*. He's not even shod.' A churlish argument, but in the wake of sparring with both Gerein and the princess, nothing better came to mind.

Gerein's sun-weathered cheeks dimpled. 'You've got balls, boy. I guess that's why Jaien likes you.'

Heat flooded Sihan's face as he caught the grins in the faces of nearby stable boys. Before he could come back with a rejoinder, Gerein said, 'I'd suggest you stop bandying about positions and titles unless you want to look like a prize idiot. You're a glorified stable boy, nothing more. If you want to know who to obey around here – it's simple – if someone shouts at you, obey them.'

A clattering of hooves heralded the arrival of another archer, red hair pulled back in a leather thong, two sets of reins looped over his arms. Sihan recognised one of the horses he led – the bay colt Gerein had bought over-price.

The red-headed archer sniffed the air. 'What's that smell?'

Sihan fumbled to hide the ribbon.

Gerein grinned, pointing. 'You'll never believe it, Camar. The princess herself gave it to him.'

Camar tossed one set of reins to Gerein, then reached out and pulled the ribbon from Sihan's belt. Before it was halfway to his nose, he snorted. 'Whew! You smell like a girl.'

Sihan's fists tightened.

Camar sniffed the air again and examined Sihan closely. 'When was the last time you had a bath?'

Sihan frowned. 'I swam in the river the day before the warhorse trials.'

Rolling his eyes, the archer shoved the ribbon back at Sihan. 'And I suppose you think that drubbing in the trials was another bath?' Camar winked at Gerein as though they were sharing some private joke at Sihan's expense.

Gerein joined in the game. 'You mountain boys think if a tree shakes raindrops in the wind, it's a bath! No wonder she gave you that smelly thing. Without it you smell like a dog's arse hole.'

Camar laughed. 'Go ask the head foreman to show you the baths. While you're in Mirador, you'll bathe every week like the rest of us. Gerhas won't stand for this ribbon-wearing nonsense, on top of the white horse stunt you pulled.' He cast a quick look over Sihan's clothes. 'Wash those, too.'

Gerein laughed. 'One wash will dissolve them!'

Camar, fast to tire of the sport, vaulted on to his horse. 'Come on; let's get this duty over with.'

Gerein straightened his bow and gathered up his colt's reins. Without sparing Sihan even one last glance, he vaulted on his bay and followed the other mounted archer out the stable gates.

Discomposed, Sihan stared after both men, wondering if insanity was prevalent in Mirador. Princesses who wanted to talk Common. King's Archers who cared about flowers and baths. What next?

Beside him, Aurion flapped his lips, playfully splashing water in all directions. Sihan picked up the slack on the lead rope and led the stallion toward the stables. He scowled as he limped, screwing up the princess's token. What was wrong with a swim once a moon's cycle?

The sun poured down from its zenith, as though forgetting winter was around the corner. Sweat poured off Sihan. Perhaps bathing in cold water was not that bad an idea.

'Ho! Sihan!'

Sihan turned to find Gerhas marching across the courtyard, face set in a scowl – the last person Sihan wanted to see. What must he think of Sihan after all that had happened? Glancing back at the mistflowers, Sihan breathed a deep sigh of relief. They were still intact, sparing him adding one more breach of etiquette to an already too long list.

'Follow me,' the old man ordered, without preamble. 'And bring the horse.'

Mystified, Sihan led Aurion across the courtyard, men shrinking back to give the stallion room. Gerhas stopped in a far corner that held a wooden crush. He kicked the chute with his foot, wood resounding with a thump. 'Put the horse in there.'

Aurion sniffed at the chute with suspicion, but walked in at Sihan's bidding. Pushing a holding rail into iron sockets to prevent Aurion backing out, Gerhas threw Sihan a slim piece of wood, the end threaded with cord. 'Twitch him.'

Puzzled, but determined to obey, Sihan wound the cord around Aurion's top lip, then twisted the wood until the cord tightened on the stallion's nose. Gerhas motioned to a soldier who was standing in the shadow of an arch to come forward. In his gloved hand, the man carried a metal shaft glowing white at one end, the brand of Mirador, the firefalcon.

Iced numbness washed over Sihan's body, flooded his veins, consumed all thought. The brand would mean Aurion would be recognised throughout the kingdom as a true bloodhorse. But had not the white stallion in his vision carried the scar of a black falcon brand? This was wrong. Wrong. It had to be stopped. Why, he did not know, but Aurion must not be branded.

With every step the soldier took toward the stallion, whispers of negation forced their way between Sihan's lips. 'You mustn't.'

'Don't tell me my business, boy,' said Gerhas.

Before Sihan could think how to stop them, the soldier struck the burning metal into Aurion's shoulder. A horrific roar blasted the air. Aurion reared, screaming, wrenching the twitch from Sihan's hand, sending the block of wood flying as the cord unwound.

Terror struck Sihan like a blow he did not see coming, almost driving him to his knees. He had heard that sound before, like a scream through his soul. 'No,' he whispered. 'No.'

'Get clear!' yelled Gerhas, jumping back.

But Sihan could not move. The horse from his nightmares stood before him, black brand of a falcon on its shoulder.

A vision shimmered behind Sihan's eyes. The stallion with its head up, blinding light transforming its gaunt body to a burnished silver phantasm, mane and tail flowing like a torrent. Gold and purple and ice-blue fire sparked from each tendril. Heavy plumes of vapour poured forth from flaring nostrils. It stood, gleaming, shining, terrible.

A horn protruded from the horse's forehead. It blazed like a bolt of lightning, arcing white-gold. Twisting strands of purple, gold and white spun together, the fire travelling along the stallion's body, burning the white coat till it shone burnished silver. Sihan's blood chilled.

A rough hand pulled Sihan back. 'Get away from it, lad.'

Sihan blinked. Aurion was still in the chute, screaming wrath. He launched his body at the wooden railings, buckling wood. Rails flew through the air.

Bursting free, Aurion careered around the courtyard. Gerhas hauled Sihan behind a colonnade. Stable boys and soldiers scattered to safety. Only when Aurion stood pawing on the other side of the courtyard, did Gerhas release Sihan.

'Bastard horse,' muttered the horsemaster. 'Catch the damned beast and tend any injuries that brute has inflicted upon itself. Then clean up the mess. I want that animal ready and saddled at dawn tomorrow for the hunt.'

Forever passed as Sihan clawed at sense, the will to move. He edged toward Aurion, staring at the head sporting no gleaming horn, the eye, though white-ringed, showing no malevolence, only wild distrust. Even so, somehow he knew they were the same.

His eyes dragged unerringly to the brand, a raised weal of burnt, stinking flesh and hair. He wanted to scrape it off, but it was done and no way could he erase it now.

In the deep, shattered breath Sihan drew, there was the emptiness of the world. He tried to convince himself it was desperate loneliness, the hell of the last few weeks dragging him into its maw.

But he knew in his heart it was something far worse.

Chapter 22

Of Schemes and Dresses

Orlanda shifted beneath the tailor's measuring stare. He had been working all day on her hunting attire and had not yet finished. When he stood back, she scowled at the mirror. White brocade swirled to the floor from a tight waist, pale swirls of cream ornamenting the hem of the riding dress. Framed against the backdrop of heavy woollen wall hangings, tasselled cushions and rich blankets strewn across her bed, the dress was a white sail against a rainbow sea and sky.

She pushed her hair back over her shoulder, decided the high collar suited her, perhaps better if her hair was coiffed. She piled her hair up into a fist-sized knot at the nape of her neck with one hand, fiddling with stray wisps of gold with the other. It made her look older than her sixteen winters, drew attention to her delicate jaw line, held high and proud – her pale-rose lips also – that Areme had yet to kiss. Yes, much better up, or a braid. She studied the hem again. No, that would not do at all.

'It's not long enough!' she protested, injecting vehemence to make her displeasure crystal.

The tailor sighed. He had been sighing all afternoon. 'It's plenty long enough, Highness. Any longer and the horse will get its legs tangled in it.'

'I want it longer!' demanded Orlanda. 'I want it all the way to the ground when I'm mounted.'

'Gerhas will never allow it.'

'Bother Gerhas. If I say I want it longer, you'll make it longer.'

'Not if it means getting my neck stretched.'

On a bench in the corner of the room near the hearth, two maids twittered, heads bowed over embroideries, ears attentive for orders.

Orlanda fumed. She would get the hem to the ground if she had to sew it herself. While the tailor fussed, her thoughts wandered back to Areme. He had placed men at guard on his door since the trials. She had seen him only once since he had fallen, skin so pale it might have been parchment. Since then, his men told her nothing, brushed her off with vagaries: 'He's resting, recovering, regaining his strength.' How long did it take to recover from a lance wound? Her hands balled into fists. Men did not recover from lance wounds. Perhaps he was mortally wounded and no one would tell her. Perhaps he was dead. She gave a little cry, and the tailor looked up, eyes wide with fear.

'Highness, did I prick you?'

'Yes,' she lied, seizing vantage. She called, 'Page! Send for my page!'

The tailor staggered back. 'Forgive me, Highness. I meant no harm, truly!' He prostrated himself on the carpet, clutching at the hem of her dress.

A smile curved Orlanda's lips. 'Do you know the penalty for harming a Royal Princess?'

'Oh, pardon! Pardon!'

'Make the hem four feet longer, and I'll forget it ever happened.'

'Yes, Highness! Immediately, Highness!' The tailor spilled pins in his eagerness to gather extra cloth. 'Oh! Please don't move, Highness!'

As the tailor scrabbled to pick up the loose pins, a boy ran into the room. He bowed, brown thatch of hair falling over mud-brown eyes and freckled face. 'At your service, Highness.'

'Go to Areme's quarters,' Orlanda commanded him. 'Don't leave till you've seen him. *Actually* seen him. I want a report. Is he well? Why he isn't up and about already? Everything! Go!'

After a bow more hurried than the first, the boy scampered from the room, feet tapping down the hallway.

As she waited, she turned her thoughts to the other problem plaguing her since the trials. Veren. Damn him. Damn Valoren for sending the vulture. Well, soon she would be rid of them both.

She examined the dress again and broached another topic she had been studying as well as common speech. 'I've heard common girls ride astride. I've heard common girls ride in leggings.' She looked down at the tailor. 'You're common. Do you sew for common girls? What do they wear when riding?'

'Common girls,' said the tailor, around the pins in his mouth, 'sew for themselves. Common girls rarely ride. Most can't afford a palfrey.'

'But if they do, what do they wear? Leggings? I've always thought it must be fun riding astride.'

'Common girls are common. They wear what they like. You are a princess. Princesses do not wear leggings. Princesses do not ride astride.'

Orlanda checked her anger to mere thoughts. *Yes, she could, and yes, she would.*

After a long while, a sharp staccato of boot heels against flags signalled the page's return. He ran into the room and touched one knee to the ground before Orlanda. 'I saw Areme,' he gasped. 'He told me to go to all seven hells.'

Orlanda breathed a sigh of relief. 'He's well, then?'

'Well enough to shout, Highness. I didn't wait around to see if he was well enough to gut me with a sword.'

Orlanda snapped her fingers and one of the maids laid aside her embroidery to present the page with a token. Once more Orlanda glanced into the mirror with satisfaction at the hem's growing length. 'Much better.'

And so was Areme, and still avoiding her just as he had before the trials. Well, that would all cease after the morrow. She smiled down at the tailor. 'I want the Mirador crest embroidered around the hem. By morning.'

Behind her, both maids groaned.

Veren stood beside a window, breathing in night-chilled air. Beside him, his mother sat in silence, hands clenched white upon the narrow carven arms of a divan. A draft slapped Veren's cloak against his calves, lifted his dark hair, sent shivers down his neck. But nothing about Myrrhye stirred, not one ebony strand of hair, nor fold in her grey cloak. She might have been a statue carved in rock.

Yet no stone save those holding the power of the world could match the turbulence swirling within her blue-black eyes.

'What do you see?' Veren prompted.

Her voice came as though across a great distance. 'A black void – in Mirador.'

Veren shifted uneasily. 'I sense nothing but the night.'

'And yet it is here, all the same.' Her middle finger, bearing the ring of the firefalcon edged in black, tapped out a beat – half-impatience – half-frustration. The short, sharp sound echoed as in a cavernous space instead of a tiny room. And history, a slithering thing, slid into the room on the eddies of the breeze, reflected in Myrrhye's ageless eyes.

Veren shuddered, remembering a boy struck dead by a lance. Merien, an innocent caught in the dark fury of a woman's vengeance. How had it come to that? He'd had a millennium to ponder that question. The answers came dark and blood-ridden.

His blood. Immortal. Merien's blood. Innocent. The blood of the Gods mixed with the blood of the world, captured now in crystal, the firefalcon rings of the Horse Lords forged by the Lord God Senfar on that fateful day of Merien's death.

But that had not been the beginning. The roots of woe were deeper sown, germinating millennia earlier when the Gods erred by granting kingship of the world to a rake – Veren's father, King Phearin, the first King of Mirador.

Did Myrrhye still think of him, her husband, ten thousand years dead? Did she still feel the betrayal when Phearin cast her aside in favour of a woman who would not wed him unless her future sons inherited the throne? Nothing flickered now behind her eyes; her thoughts might be the cold stone of a tomb for all he could read within them.

Did she despise her own first born son? Veren, God-born, God-blessed, true heir to the Mirador throne. He had thrown away everything, surrendered his birthright for the sake of his father's happiness, swearing to forever defend the throne and whosoever occupied it, and to remain celibate to ensure his half-brother's heirs never had cause to be troubled about their right of succession.

For his vow, the gods had rewarded Veren with immortality and recompensed his mother with powers unknown to men. Myrrhye had been granted the stewardship of Taiere, the Grey Temple of the Ladies, the gifted ones. And long, long life showing no sign of ending.

Veren's fingers tightened on the hilt of his sword. How had a vow of so pure intent become so steeped in blood?

The answer to that question lay in blood also, in Sandor, his sickly half-brother. Destined to rule, Sandor could not even fight for himself in tourney to win a bride. Veren had fought in his stead, swept all opponents from the field. And won a bride – Niameh – who had already pledged herself to another – Anise – a lad Veren killed in the tournament.

Niameh.

Distraught over her lover's death, she had refused the king, humiliating him. Exiled, she sold her soul for a chance to avenge herself on Veren and the kingdom he held so dear, harnessing the powers of darkness, seeking to destroy his world.

Niameh.

Where was she now? Did she still walk the path of reckless vengeance?

'You're thinking of her again,' said Myrrhye. 'I can always tell. You still feel guilt over that little witch.'

Not turning, Veren grated, 'Don't speak of her that way. Was it her fault I won her? Was it her fault she was exiled?' He clenched his fist. 'No such infamy in all the world as what was done to that girl.'

'You dare speak of infamy? That *girl*, as you call her, has brought the world to the edge of ruin.'

'If I hadn't ruined her life, she wouldn't have turned to the gods for help to destroy mine.' He drew a heavy breath, fighting the demons of a history he had no power to change.

'All this conjecture is pointless. We cannot change what is past, but the future is still there to save.' Myrrhye's voice slid like ice between her lips. 'I saw the vision in the pool of the moon all those centuries ago – chaos, destruction, the world in ash. And at its heart stands Niameh. Her quest for vengeance will be the ruin of the world.' Her words struck like daggers in Veren's back. 'I ordered you to put her to death. But you, with your *honour*, refused. See where that choice has brought us?'

Veren held silent. He had been unable to carry out the death of an innocent, and instead had forced Niameh to flee. That decision had ever stood between mother and son, forced

Myrrhye's hand. Made her do the unimaginable, call down a mantra, forge another son. A murderous son.

Areme.

Abandoned at birth to a life of outcast slavery.

Myrrhye wanted Areme merciless, a killer with no conscience and no pity in his heart when set loose upon Niameh. The result had been the death of two innocents. Shasirre, Areme's wife, and a boy, Merien.

It had driven a gulf between mother and son, brother and brother.

Veren dug his fingernails into the palms of his hands. He should have killed Niameh. Who would have thought that one ill-used girl could bring the world to ruin in her quest for retribution? If the choice were his again, the end might be different. Perhaps.

He stared out at a sky devoid of stars. 'What would you have me do?'

'Take Orlanda. Take the horse. Get them out of Mirador.' The orders were sharp, decisive.

'And Areme?'

'I want him here. If anyone can sniff out the threat, it's him.'

Veren pushed away from the wall. 'I think he'll have something to say to that. His intent at the trials was clear – to drive me into the dust.'

'His grudges hold long.'

'A thousand years long, it seems. And no surprise. If it wasn't for me, he would still have Shasirre.' Veren shook his head. If he had done the right thing, Myrrhye would never have felt the need to bring Areme into the world. 'How much longer will Areme fume if I steal the horse and Orlanda from under his nose?'

'It will be done with full sanction; he'll have to hold the king to account as well.'

Veren snorted. 'Areme would not stop at sticking a blade in the king's back if it suited his purpose.'

'Then let us be thankful it does not.'

For now. Veren ran his fingers back through his hair. 'This princess, you've formed an opinion? Is she the one?'

'Areme thinks such.'

'I'm asking what *you* think.'

'I'm thinking she shows no power for one born of a Grey Lady. I'm thinking the power of the world is draining to nothing, and we may never find a way to undo the curses scourging the land. I'm thinking Kosall will fall and join the rest of Romondor in ash, its people all dead to the plague Wyndarra unleashed, if the horse does not turn soon.'

'But you could be wrong?'

'Let us pray it is so. I forged Areme into a weapon to destroy Niameh, never considering he could strike the wrong target. This time I will take my time, make certain the target is true, honed, before I release–'

Veren turned sharply from his indifferent study of the darkness beyond the arched lancet. 'Sihan,' he finished smoothly when she refused.

Myrrhye's black eyes blazed with anger, and perhaps a hint of alarm. 'What do you know of him?'

'Nothing and everything. I know he's my brother. I know he's doomed. And I know you've placed some sort of spell about him I cannot fathom.' His eyes drove into those shining black orbs. 'What have you done to him, Myrrhye? Sihan could barely ride that white beast at the trials, and he's a horseman. I warrant his bowshot will be off by as much again. I don't even want to contemplate what he'll do with a sword.'

Myrrhye waved him away with a careless flick of her wrist. 'A simple spell, easily reversed, though I'll not enlighten you in case you desire to act against my will. I learned that lesson too well when Shasirre deflected Areme from his true course. I thank the gods she is dead and can no longer interfere with my plans. In Sihan, I have forged a weapon that will kill once, and once only, the target of my choice, no other's. I will not release him till I have the target at my knees. Until then, any thought he has shall turn away from death, to peace, goodwill, and any weapon he wields shall fail. Sihan must remain innocent until the last.'

'You play a dangerous game, Myrrhye. In this world men die too easily, men with swords and the ability and will to use them. You put him at great risk.'

'What risk, when I have charged you to protect him, as I will charge Areme to raise no hand against him?'

'Areme knows?'

'No. And I would not have him know. He'll kill Sihan if he suspects what he is. Perhaps even out of care.'

'And if I'm not within reach? Or Areme? What then?'

The tapping of the ring was insistent. 'Fear not. I will place men around Sihan that can be trusted to keep him safe.'

Veren nodded to the ring on her finger. 'It's his ring you carry.'

'Yes.'

'Where's his army?'

'About him. Unknown. Waiting, like him, unknowing, for release.'

'Jaien?'

Surprise glittered in her eyes. 'What of him?'

Veren shrugged. 'He seemed protective of Sihan. I assumed it was your doing.'

Myrrhye brushed the thought aside with a dismissive wave of her hand. 'Jaien is nothing. He is no Shaheden. He's just a man . . . Just a man,' she repeated. 'Nothing more.'

'That's as well considering he's gone back to Pelan. They've declared war on Byerol.'

'So I've heard.' Her rose lips closed over silence.

'These stolen horses–'

'Missing,' Myrrhye corrected.

'Byerol is too smart a man to do something so foolish.'

'I've sent men to his court, his garrisons. No man there knows anything. And they are complaining of missing horses, too.'

'So where are the horses?'

'I know not.'

Veren pressed on, certain she was withholding something. 'You think someone is hunting them?'

The flames in her eyes flared. 'No. They are hunting one only. Aurion. The raiders move in stealth. Silent. Fleet-footed. Even in darkness in forests where it is folly to gallop. They are adepts. But not yours or Areme's, or even Sihan's. There is another faction.'

'Roedan?'

Barely restrained rage glittered in her dark eyes, not quenched even after a millennium. 'He broke fealty to Taiere. He loves me not. He would destroy the Heavens rather than take the risk we are taking in bringing back a unicorn.' She paused, shook her head, wisps of jet quivering and curling about her shoulders. 'Yet I do not sense him in this.'

'Will you give any warning to Byerol, or Pelan? Neither must pay in a war not of their making.'

Myrrhye's face became implacable. 'Once Aurion is safe, in Kosall.'

'Why not Taiere?'

'Roedan knows Taiere. And if it is not Roedan, I cannot judge Taiere safe. Kosall is protected by ward upon ward. Godwards of which Roedan knows naught.'

Veren regarded her for a long moment, pondering her words. 'The raiders will turn to Mirador soon.'

'If they are not here already. I sense danger. Every moment, from the day you arrived in Mirador. Since this whole horse stealing business started.' She clasped her hands and spoke with slow, fierce resolution. 'Let us pray the Romondor ambassador arrives soon. Let us pray the horse turns, that Areme is right about the girl, that the curses her mother cast upon Romondor can be lifted, and I won't have to destroy my youngest son.'

Veren's blood chilled. 'Yes, let us pray.'

Chapter 23

The Royal Hunt

Stars faded into red dawn as the palace forecourt bustled with baying hounds and cursing handlers. Maws a frothing mass of panting, snapping and growling, the rangy beasts clawed dew-slick cobbles, eager to be released. Torches lit riders and grooms preparing for the royal hunt. Lines of stable boys stood in the courtyard, restless and fatigued though the day had barely begun, holding horses tacked up with sidesaddles, which they had worked down in the long dark before dawn. Grim-faced soldiers stood in ivy shadows of marble arches, some of them the princess's guard, rubbing at dark stubbled jaws.

Sihan held Aurion and his bay colt Spirit by the reins, trying to stop both horses slobbering on his new white tabard and grey tunic. He had found the clothes and new boots in his quarters after bathing away the sweat and grime and some of the pain of the trials. Shifting his weight from foot to foot, he failed to ease the tight grip of the leather boots. They pressed against his injured leg, making it throb with dull fire.

The prospect of riding held little appeal. Thoughts of the princess riding Aurion made him feel worse. He could not push the image of her surrounded by flames from his mind. Or the fact Aurion might go berserk at any moment. And if Aurion hurt the princess, Sihan had little doubt where the blame would fall. It preyed on him, shutting out all other thoughts. For the thousandth time he wished he had never made the deal to sell Aurion.

Gerein sauntered past, gorytos slung over his back, eyes bright and alert. Stopping next to Sihan, he sniffed. 'Had a bath, did you? How many times did they have to scrub you to get off that smell?'

Sihan had had enough. On top of his disquiet about the princess and Aurion, the jibes had hardly let up since the day before, from stable boys, from soldiers, all vying with quips regarding baths, and, worse, Jaien, as though Sihan was an Emor pony of which to make sport. Between set teeth, he said, 'Just once. How about you?'

Gerein smiled and swatted a late autumn fly from Sihan's tabard. 'How do you like your new clothes?'

Fingering the wool, soft and luxurious against his skin, Sihan replied with better grace, hoping Gerein had finished amusing himself at his expense, 'I like them fine. But I can't fathom where they came from. They just appeared in a box inside my door.'

Crossing his arms, Gerein raised an eyebrow. 'Try.' He laughed in the face of Sihan's black stare, then bowed, low and half-mocking. 'For the Princess's Royal Groomsman, courtesy of the King's Archer.' Gerein's smile broadened to a full-toothed grin. Patting a purse at his belt, he said, 'At Jaien's expense, of course. It was the least he could do for you after he destroyed all your clothes. Kind of ironic, considering he would probably rather get you out of them.'

'He needn't have bothered,' grated Sihan. 'I've gold enough since I sold Aurion.'

'And no sense to spend it,' said Gerein. 'You're comely enough once you're cleaned up. Flash a bit of gold around and you'd have girls trailing at your feet.' His lips twisted slyly. 'Unless you really are saving yourself for Jaien.'

Before Sihan could say anything, trumpets blared. Liveried footmen hauled open the great candlewood doors of the palace. Sihan straightened, and the soldiers shook off their weariness, standing attentively.

As the sky lightened to steel, dulling the bleached marble façade of the palace walls, courtiers and their ladies streamed out of the hall. Instead of cloaks and cowls, the women wore voluminous riding dresses of embroidered brocade, red, yellow or white, their revealed faces stripped of one mystery, to be replaced by another, painted masks of milk-white chalk with eyes accented by kohl, hair coiffed and strung with pearls. Straight backed, chins high, they glided in a swathe of colour down the grand flight of stairs like disdainful goddesses from a temple on high.

Stallions laid back their ears while stern-faced guards lifted the women onto the horses' backs. The scent of rich perfumes warred with the stink of fresh, steaming dumps of dung. Tight-lipped soldiers adjusted leathers beneath the stirrup-length folds of brocade, chastising mounts dancing at the hiss and swish of silken pantaloons and skirts billowing back over the stallions' rumps.

Then the princess appeared. Dressed in a flowing white habit that trailed the ground, she paused at the head of the steps, ranks of noblemen and women at her back. Her eyes raked over the assembly, touching everyone in one long, sweeping glance.

Sihan stared at her: the coiffed hair, moonstones gleaming in the predawn light, the figure-formed dress, the pert bulge of her breasts, her lips, plush and tinted cherry-fresh red. Though the sun hid below the horizon, the very air about her appeared to flare and quiver with invisible fire. In that instant, Sihan felt he might be the only sighted man in a world gone blind. Try as he might, he could not shift the image. Knowing it could only worsen if she got on Aurion, Sihan turned to Gerein, clutching at the first thing that came to mind. 'She can't possibly mean to ride in that dress.'

The archer muttered low under his breath. 'You're on first name terms. Go tell her.'

The demons were in Sihan's brain, driving him to madness. He clenched his fist and said with vehemence, 'She's not getting on Aurion in that dress.'

Gerein flashed Sihan a look of intense interest. 'You really *do* have balls, don't you? But you'd best watch your tongue, else you'll find yourself tossed in the dungeon yourself. And who's going to save *you*?'

'Enough!' warned Sihan, amazing both himself and Gerein, whose eyes widened fractionally. 'Can you be serious for just one moment?'

Gerein eased his back against a pillar. 'She outranks everyone but Gerhas and her father. I doubt she's going to listen to a Royal Groomsman, no matter how fancy the title.'

'Who will she listen to?'

Gerein kept watching him, attention unflagging now. As if joining in whatever game Sihan was playing, he said, 'I've a good idea who. Hold her off till I return.' Without another word, he dashed off in the direction of the royal stables.

Sihan bit his lip as the Princess approached, the train of her dress sweeping along the cobbles, missing mounds of manure by inches. Vanilla scent enveloped him as she paused at Aurion's head. The mad thought of accidentally treading on her dress and ripping it flashed through his mind. He steadied himself. That was as crazy an idea as the illusions of her and Aurion surrounded by flames. He must forget it, or make a total arse of himself.

'How is Aurion this fine morning?' she asked, reaching out to stroke the stallion's nose.

'Better than he's going to be if you ride him in that,' Sihan replied in a mere thread of a voice, but delivering each word with clarity.

Faces turned to him, soldiers and courtiers giving him swift, probing looks. But Orlanda's laughter rippled across his protest like clear running water. 'Don't be such a bore. Help me mount.'

Standing back, Sihan crossed his arms, daring her disapproval. He told himself the mad, whimsical girl of the day before who wanted him to call her Orlanda would not mind. 'No,' he said. 'I'm not letting you on him in that dress. One misstep and he'll tangle his legs. That will bring both him down, and you.'

Stark silence descended over the entire courtyard. He knew immediately he had erred. The mirth in Orlanda's eyes shuttered, an iron door slammed in his face.

'Dare you tell me what I may and may not do, boy?' The fire of her scorn scorched him. 'You are nothing more than a groom. I am the Royal Princess of Mirador. Obey, or suffer the consequences.'

Sihan shrank back, churning thoughts halted in mid-air, suspended precariously like a pigeon caught in the talons of a falcon. All around him, men whispered, shaking their heads. Just as he was wondering if he would ever be able to piece together the shards of his shattered dignity, Hessarde strode through the arches from the stables, Gerein at his heels. The knight's voice boomed around the forecourt. 'What's this rubbish I hear about long dresses?'

All eyes turned to the princess.

Without hesitation, Hessarde strode toward her, drawing a dagger from the sheath at his belt.

She backed away, toward the hall, white brocade flaring about the stone steps. 'I forbid you to touch even one stitch of my dress!'

Hessarde glowered. '*I* forbid you to ride that horse in that ridiculous excuse for riding attire!'

'He's *my* horse, not yours. I'll wear whatever I like on him.' Lifting the hem of her skirt, Orlanda changed tactics and strode toward the knight. 'And how *dare* you speak to me in such a tone. I am the High Princess of Mirador!'

Disdain lacing his voice, Hessarde shot back, 'Remind me sometime to be impressed.' The incivility of his dismissal raised a flush in Orlanda's rose-smooth cheeks. Hessarde turned to a knight captain who stood nearby watching the altercation with wide-awake interest. 'I want you to find the tailor who designed that ill-advised costume and arrest him. No one puts that horse at risk and gets away with it.' The soldier smirked and strode away. Hessarde turned to the rest of the men. 'No one leaves the forecourt until I give the command.'

'I insist you make your men stand down,' said the princess, her nose barely reaching the knight's chin.

'I'll order my men to stand down when *you* take your dress *up.*'

'That's ridiculous. By the time I change, the morning dew will have burnt off.'

'How tragic,' said Hessarde. 'But I can speed you on your way a lot faster.' He waved his knife.

'Who are you to give me orders?'

'Areme's second, as well you know.' A smile slid across his lips as he poured pitch on a conflagration. 'Try your best to imagine I'm him and my words are his.'

Orlanda appeared to teeter on the sword edge of another sally, then her scowl dissolved into a smile of mocking triumph. She gathered her skirt and ripped it off at mid-waist in one smooth gesture of defiance. Brocade fell to the ground in a puddle of white, exposing long shapely legs ensconced in tight white leggings. She spread her hands across her slim hips, as if to frame them for all to admire. 'There,' she declared, 'do you find *this* more appropriate attire?'

Breath shot out of Sihan. Around him, women howled with consternation and disbelief. All the soldiers' tired faces showed new keenness.

Hessarde's expression turned blacker than thunderclouds. 'You get dressed right now!'

The princess jutted her chin. 'You just told me to get *un*dressed. When you've made up your mind, let me know.' She strode past the knight and winked at Sihan, vanilla wafting from her in an invisible cloud. 'Change saddles on my horse,' she ordered. 'I'm riding astride.'

'The seven hells you are!' growled Hessarde.

Sihan stared from one to the other, unable to obey or refuse.

'Go!' she said, taking Aurion's reins.

'Stay!' roared Hessarde. 'Or I swear you'll regret it.'

Sihan stood motionless, mind bounding erratically from order to order like a cornered hare. He shot a pleading glance to Gerein. The archer just grinned broadly as though Sihan's dilemma was a show put on for his personal entertainment. That made up Sihan's mind. Hessarde might be shouting loudly, but the Princess outranked him. He hurried to do her bidding. He stripped the sidesaddle from Aurion and ran to the stable to fetch a war saddle. When he returned, Hessarde and the princess were still facing off. Everyone else gaped as Sihan saddled Aurion, more so when the princess vaulted onto the white stallion's back.

'Come on, Sihan,' she cried. 'Let's have some fun!' She drove her heels into Aurion's flanks, and he plunged through the ranks of riders and out the courtyard gate.

Hessarde swore, tearing the reins from a waiting soldier of the princess's guard. His muttered orders rang clear. 'I want a cordon round that white horse at all times.'

Sihan's eyes narrowed. While Areme was injured, Hessarde was head of the princess's guard, but why did he have the curious feeling the order was to protect the horse and not the princess? He recalled Areme's strange words before the trials, to keep the white horse safe. And what was it that Hessarde had said? 'No one puts that horse at risk and gets away with it'

The wandering thought slipped away as Gerein slapped him hard on the back. 'That was some show! By all that is merciful, that was worth staying up all night for.' He swung aboard his bay colt, smile stretching wide across his face. 'Come on! I want to catch another eyeful of royal rump!'

In disapproving silence, Sihan scrambled to mount Spirit, pain spiking through his leg as he put all his weight on it, every nerve screaming no. The agony hardly lessened when he was up, but he gritted his teeth. He had trained to be Senfari. One accident could not change that. He would not let it. He was a rider, and this day was a lark. He would survive it.

The colt danced, glad to be on the move in the brisk morning air. They caught the princess soon enough, Aurion's speed checked to a prancing walk in the main thoroughfare to the battlement gate. Brow furrowed but eyes shining, Orlanda wove the stallion between peasants and overladen, creaking carts, sliding between rumps and heaving shoulders of horned beasts, hands light on the reins as if she rode the stallion on a thread. Knots of merchants and fortress folk, clustered round bakeries, turned to gape.

'Come on,' muttered Gerein, urging his horse forward. 'Flank her before someone gets killed.'

'Killed?'

Gerein nodded over his shoulder. 'The princess's guard. They'll kill anyone who touches her, even if it's her fault.'

Sihan glanced back. Hessarde and his men were fast catching up. Faces cold, they stared death at every peasant who ventured within a pace of the princess, leaving little doubt Gerein was right. With Sihan on his heels, the archer maneuvered his bay between peasants, till they were abreast of the white stallion.

Sihan had never seen the streets so clogged. Everywhere, the sound of laughter mingled with the smell of saffron and rare cedar wood. Buyers searched out wares only available at festival, sifting through hycat skins from Pelan, baskets from Guider, silk from Andorea. Alternating patches of shade and light deepened and brightened worn items to richer hues. Motley assumed the lustre of brocade. Bronze pots shone gold in the rising light.

The princess ignored it all, leading the cavalcade across the bridge and out into fields beyond the fortress. At the first open stretch of country, she spurred Aurion into a gallop, stood in the stirrups, and displayed her small but nicely rounded arse for all to see. Sihan rode after her, not wanting to look at her on Aurion, but unable to tear his eyes away from that bobbing backside.

Beside him, Gerein shouted, 'That arse looks good enough to cork. If she keeps it up in the air like that I won't be able to sit in my saddle for a week.'

Sihan forced a laugh, and seized the chance to throw off the label of frere, yelling back, 'Me, neither.'

The princess led her guards and the hunt field of courtiers in a gallop beside the winding road leading south, a hundred or more horses sweeping in a thunderous roar across a plain of short grass hidden under a veil of soft white mist.

The drum of hooves recalled to Sihan the last time he had ridden, and the ache in his leg spiked as if sharing the memory. He settled back in the saddle, easing his weight from stirrup to seat, slowing Spirit a fraction, but slivers of pain impaled Sihan's leg hard and often.

Determined to block out the discomfort, he eyed the passing countryside speckled white with sheep among fat tethered cows whose large brown eyes followed the charge with disinterest. Riders passed him, but he did not care. This was no race, and now there was no danger of unwary peasants touching the princess he was not duty bound to keep the lead.

Racing past the riders, the hounds surrounded a copse blazing gold and brown with pea bushes. A sharp horn blast signalled a halt and the hunt field checked their horses in a steaming, sweating mass. Hessarde's men formed a close ring around the princess, eyeing her with the concentration of hungry puppies at a bitch's nipple. She returned their stares with cold contempt before focusing on the hounds zigzagging, noses to ground.

Breathing heavily, Sihan deliberately avoided her gaze, willing the sun out of the sky before it lit her in flames once more. He turned his attention to Gerein who reined his stallion alongside. 'Do you think they've found something already?'

'We'll see,' came Gerein's non-committal reply.

Despite the ache in his leg and shortness of breath, Sihan was suddenly disappointed his first ride since his accident might end before it had even really begun. He enjoyed the colt between his legs, one he had trained himself. One that never caused half the trouble Aurion did. As hounds ranged to and fro, Sihan patted Spirit's wet neck, fingers sliding along a coat sleek and dark like an otter's, sensing the horse's eagerness for another swift gallop. He noticed the horses of Hessarde's men were not even damp, neither was Aurion, but this colt was not as fit, he reasoned, rising only four as it was, and only lightly ridden up to the trials when all he had been concentrating on was Aurion.

Other riders closed round him, young women with smiles all teeth, watching him with as much intensity as the princess's guard kept watch on her. Discomfited, Sihan tried to focus on the hounds. Bushes ahead of the hunt pack moved as though a line of wind marched across them. A dark shadow flashed between lilac hovea. A brace of hounds bounded forth, bugling predatory cries.

A song of bones and blood, it pricked Sihan's skin, made him want to avoid looking at the princess on Aurion even more. He blew out a deep breath, trying to steady his thoughts, not wanting to think of everything around her in terms of blood and fire and death, but the chaotic wailing of hounds signalling with all their souls their will to rend and tear made that impossible.

Another horn blared a longer note. With a squeal, the princess charged through the cordon of men surrounding her, setting Aurion to a flying gallop. Within a heartbeat, the entire field was in pursuit. Aurion stretched to racing speed, devouring ground with every stride, heedless of ditch or boulder.

Sihan knew the feel of that ride, even though he was only following the horse. And knowledge and memory combined to increase the ache stabbing at his calf. He soon regretted his wish for another run, breath pounding his ribs, reins slick as his mount's hide. Not soon enough did the hounds chase the boar into a copse splashed with lilac. Once more everyone drew rein.

Soldiers swept out in a fan. Huntsmen dismounted, stalking the undergrowth, encouraging the hounds to flush out their quarry. Riders milled about, others still riding up, soldiers mixing with courtiers. Sihan slumped in the saddle, head down, gasping for breath, sweat dripping off him.

'You look exhausted,' commented Gerein, sitting still but alert on his horse nearby.

Sihan looked at him from lowered eyelids. All morning the archer had stayed glued to him like a shadow, seemingly taking Jaien's request to look out for Sihan far too seriously. Still, he was likeable, after a fashion, and almost good company.

'I haven't ridden since the trials,' huffed Sihan. 'And I haven't been doing much else except lying about in bed.'

'Some people have all the luck,' laughed Gerein. 'I hope you didn't waste the opportunity.'

'Opportunity?'

'Girls everywhere have been asking after you.' Gerein ran an appraising eye over Sihan. 'Though I can't see why, myself. You seem to have made quite an impression for a stable boy, bath or no.'

'Asking after me?' said Sihan, stupefied.

'Honestly, you can't be that naive. It's the season of the Fire Rituals, and girls are doing everything they can to try to catch a husband or a lover. It's the best time of the year in Mirador, finding a companion to warm your bed for the winter. Haven't you noticed all the women ogling you this morning?'

'I can't imagine why they would be interested in me.' Heat rose in his face. It was the wrong thing to say if he wanted to dispel the rumours about him and Jaien.

'Can't you?' inquired a sweet voice.

Sihan spun to find the princess looking at him with dancing eyes. He had somehow, thankfully, forgotten her in the fury of the last gallop. Now she was right there, close, watching him with as much intensity as he had been avoiding looking at her. Hessarde's men moved into a ring about them, eyes fixed outward in search of threat, though Sihan could not imagine any threat so close to the fortress.

Neither could the princess, apparently, prattling on without a care of the audience of soldiers listening. 'I will get you a looking glass. Though I fear you lack sufficient vanity to appreciate what you see.'

'And what is that?' asked Sihan, surprised for the second time that day into unaccustomed boldness.

'A handsome, courageous young man who rode the Death Gorge. All the ladies of the court are still talking about it. My maids have even asked for introductions. You are quite the hero in Mirador.'

'But I fell off,' said Sihan, embarrassed beyond measure she might be mocking him yet again with everyone in earshot.

'You were injured. To ride as long as you did showed the height of courage.'

Sihan twisted the reins in his fingers, trying to hide his confusion at her abrupt transition from censure to mischievousness, like a cat purring after a swift claw slash. Not to be trusted.

Thankfully, a horn sounded, signalling the boar breaking cover. Hounds clambered over rocks bordering the copse and took off in pursuit. The princess flashed Sihan a smile like an opening flower, then turned Aurion to force a path through her protectors.

Sihan found Gerein staring at him in astonishment.

'What?' demanded Sihan.

'In very truth, Sihan. First a token, now she's singing your praises. If they haven't already, now every female in Mirador will have you in her bow-sights if the princess has given you her favour! You lucky sod.'

Sihan scowled. He did not want *any* woman in Mirador. They were more trouble than they were worth. Of the women he had met so far, the princess was mad and when she was not humiliating him, she caused waking nightmares, and the only other woman he had met was a zingar masquerading as a ghost. Either was enough to put him off women for life. But if he did not want a woman, that left only one path. Sihan clenched his fist, trying to drive away thoughts of Jaien. Anger spurred him to dig his heels hard into his colt's sides, setting it after the hunt field.

They galloped a shorter stretch, into countryside studded with trees. The rising sun silvered the highest leaves, leaving the shaded grass below still tinged with frost. As the hunt field drew rein, a wind blew out of the north and a strange noise came with it. Black cockatoos wheeled overhead, screeching wildly, red tail feathers flaring. The warning cries made Sihan shiver as though snow had fallen on his back.

'What's wrong?' asked Gerein, shadowing him as always, riding not a half-stride away.

'The birds. They're acting oddly.'

Gerein followed the flight of the circling birds. For a long time he said nothing, but a hint of darkness shadowed his eyes, so swift Sihan half-thought he imagined it. Then the archer beamed and said in a voice so jovial Sihan knew it fake, 'They're saying we're going to be eating boar's meat tonight, Sihan.'

On the tail of the lie, two of Hessarde's soldiers rode up and fell in beside Gerein. One leaned over and whispered something. Sihan edged his colt nearer. The glance Gerein shot him warned him off.

After the two riders rode away, Gerein said, 'Stay with the field. I'm going to see if I can duck around and get a clear shot at the boar from the other side of the wood.' Gerein patted his bow. 'King's Archer, remember. I get all the fun duty.' The sincerity behind the forced curve the archer pasted to his lips shrunk the more he spoke. He waved a hand at the knots of women in the hunt field, many of them stripped of their poise, painted faces streaked with sweat, hair escaping in wild tangles from their pins. 'The women get annoyed when the hunt goes too long and they start to look real.' With a swift jab to his horse's sides, he spurred his mount into a gallop toward the edge of the wood. Other archers veered off from the hunt field as well, making for either side of the trees, giving the lie to Gerein's words he was the favoured bowman. Hessarde traded sharp words with his men, motioning them to hold the women back, moving his horse to flank the princess, while still more soldiers rode into the wood.

Sihan knew there was something afoot, more than just a boar. But what?

'Where are they going?' demanded Orlanda, riding up close.

With no real idea of what to answer to a question mirroring his own, and with Hessarde glaring a more obvious warning to keep silent than even Gerein had managed, Sihan offered the obvious. 'They're off to mark the boar.'

A moue slipped across her lips. 'I wish I could shoot. It's so boring never being at the kill.'

Again Sihan wished her back in the palace. That she wished to be present for the kill, even a beast's, twisted his stomach.

The princess drew him away from his darkening thoughts. Throwing away her frown and smiling, she tore a shred of tattered skirt still dangling at her waist and handed it to Sihan. 'Go mark the boar and claim it for me.'

'P–Pardon?'

Though she spoke to Sihan, she speared Hessarde with a sharp glare. 'Areme has forsworn my company, so I want the best rider in Mirador to be my champion this day.'

Whatever was going on, Gerein had made it certain Sihan had no part to play, and Hessarde's glare was now so sharp it shredded him. He grappled for an excuse to disobey. 'I don't have a spear.'

'Oh, tish tosh. Stop spoiling my fun.' She turned to another of Hessarde's men who hovered in close attendance. 'Give Sihan a spear.'

The man scowled, but obeyed the royal command, edging his horse beside Sihan's bay. 'A word of advice, boy,' he said, leaning in, spear in hand. 'Go softly. Stay in the trees. She'll not know different. And if by chance you see the boar, turn tail. It'll be wary before you get near enough to spear it. Let the archers deal with it.'

Everything in his tone told Sihan the man was not referring to the boar. He nodded his thanks as he tied the princess's token to the spear. 'I understand.' Though he didn't, not really.

Touching his heels to the bay, he wheeled it in the direction Gerein had gone. He gripped the spear hard, all too aware that the last time he had handled such a weapon the day had ended in disaster. It might have been fun to be out riding if danger did not prick at the skin of his neck and his leg did not hurt so.

He turned Spirit into the trees. Eyes focussed on the ground, he followed a worn cattle track – deep imprints of cloven hooves dried and crusted with dark pats of manure. Not far distant, trilled strident calls of frogs, signalling a stream perhaps, or a watering hole for the horned beasts.

He came to a bank where pockets of dew lay thick on grass and water purled over shingles. To waste time, Sihan offered his mount a drink. On the opposite shore, old, pillared trees blocked all beyond. Upstream, dense stands of wattle clad in thick golden balls also bounded Sihan's sight. Fresh hoof marks led along the bank downstream where water seeped into a marsh covered in grey mist and ringed by trees. Thinking to get into better cover, Sihan urged the colt down to the mist.

Forest silence wrapped everything with an impenetrable veil, long, sucking draws of water over greedy lips the only unusual sound. Weeds rippled like eels beneath the water, willows wept golden tears.

Suddenly the colt threw up its head. Ears pricked, muscles tense, Spirit stared into trees beyond the mist. Unsettled, Sihan peered also, clenching the spear. Nearby, a currawong called a warning, a harsh spike of sound. Sihan imagined the bird sitting high in a tree, staring at everything below with intelligence in those yellow-ringed black eyes. What could it see? A snake? The boar? The hunters?

Mist wisped along the stream, long fingers stretching toward them, pooling round the colt's feet, rising inexorably. Spirit bowed his neck tight, nose to chest, fighting Sihan's tightening hold with snorts of fear, patches of foam white against the sheen of its bay coat. Sihan closed his legs, unnerved. What was out there? Did something dark lurk beyond the tendrils of mist?

Knots in oaks stared at him like watching eyes, ancient spirits trapped in wood. Every way Sihan turned, he imagined trees moving, closing in, real eyes and real faces materializing just at the edge of sight, but when faced directly, they disappeared.

Black wings flashed between branches. The colt reared and spun.

'Steady, steady,' soothed Sihan, just as anxious to get away from this place. A shadow rippled between trunks. Sihan tensed, half-expecting a ghost to spring from the forest. Instead, a man appeared, gliding serpent-silent from the edge of the wood into the mist, tunic grey-green with dirt so it did not show clearly. Sihan's breath rushed out in relief. A huntsman, he guessed, sent ahead to flush the boar.

Not long after, muffled hoofbeats eddied within the mist, stopped, moved again, as though the rider was uncertain how to proceed. Sihan angled his own horse into the edge of the forest, not knowing what to do except follow instructions and stay in cover.

That same man appeared from mist not ten paces from him, glancing around as though searching for something. He backed up, step by slow, measured step, so cautiously, he might have been trying to tip toe out of a nest of vipers. Then he disappeared in the enveloping shroud of swirling white. Sihan waited, skin crawling as if spiders were running all over him.

Air whistled past his ear. Spirit leapt forward. Another hiss. A hard thump of steel into wood behind his shoulder left Sihan in no doubt about what was happening. The bay leapt, keeping out of the line of fire. Sihan leaned low over its neck, trying to avoid being scraped from its back by branches. Clenching the spear shaft hard, he tried to peer into forest gloom. Who in all hells was shooting at him?

Fog cleared for an instant, revealing the man standing with hands on hips, a sword slung at his waist. A thin smile etched across his ruddy face as he stared at Sihan, then mist flowed over him once more.

Bow shafts creaked. Not waiting for the next onslaught of arrows, Sihan dropped hard to the ground, agony spearing up his injured leg. With the spear, he whacked his horse on the rump, sending it careering into the mist. Another flurry of arrows whizzed past. One tore through his hair, a second grazed his brow, a third slashed his arm, pinning the sleeve to an oak. He pulled, hard, but the bolt refused to give.

'Shit!' he cursed. 'Come on, come on.' The cloth tore. Freed, he fell to a crouch. A volley of arrows slammed the trunk to which he had been pinned, turning it into a mass of quills. Gut twisting, Sihan flattened to the ground. With his damaged leg, he could not have run if he had wanted to.

'I think we got him,' a tentative voice called from the mist.

'He fell from his horse,' offered another.

'What do you mean fell from a horse?' shouted still another voice, strangely muffled, yet somehow familiar. 'He wasn't *on* a horse! Hold! Don't fire.'

Shadowy shapes of men on horseback approached, pale light glinting on triple-barbed arrowheads nocked to their bows. Some carried naked swords. All wore the Mirador tabard.

Wary, Sihan half rose, spear ready, blood dripping down his brow. A laboured grunt came from his left. He spun to find a huge black boar eyeing him, ivory tusks lowered.

Terror locked every muscle.

The boar charged.

Sihan tried to hoist the spear, but it dragged at his arm as though the entire length was weighted. Black eyes. A flash of white. Time fled. Why couldn't he throw the spear?

An arrow purred, crashing the boar to the ground at Sihan's feet. He stared at the quivering wood, the spasming beast, a shaft buried half way to the feathers.

A heart shot. Impossible.

Sihan sank to his knees as if his legs could no longer support his body. The spear fell from his grasp.

More riders materialised from the mist. Gerein, face a curious mix of half-relief, half-annoyance, jumped from his horse. He snatched up Sihan's spear, then plunged it into the hide of the dead boar. As another soldier rode up with Sihan's horse, shouts and more hoof beats drew near. Bracing one foot on the boar's flank, Gerein broke off the arrow shaft, and tossed it carelessly into a nearby bush. Then he hauled Sihan to his feet.

'Say nothing about what happened,' he warned. 'Or anything you thought you saw or heard. If anyone asks, *you* killed the boar.' He mounted his horse and rode off with the others, leaving Sihan stunned and alone, and trembling like a storm-frozen dog.

A single baying howl pierced the silence. Within moments, the forest was frantic with cries of hounds, shouting men and horn blasts. Growls presaged hounds crashing through underbrush from all around. Streaking blurs of brown fur mixed with Sihan's confusion as hounds swarmed over the boar. Tails whipped. Blood foamed from tearing mouths. Teeth slashed at black hide.

A multitude of riders broke through the trees, surrounding Sihan, Gerein among them, and also the other soldiers who he had seen in the mist.

'Well done, Sihan!' cried the princess, riding up on Aurion, face alight with triumph at sight of her token marking the boar. 'We'll have to promote you to Royal Huntsman! I wondered where you had disappeared. How did you know it would come out here?'

Blushing at the undue praise, Sihan glanced at Gerein. The archer shot him a hard look.

'Lucky guess,' Sihan said.

Gerein nodded imperceptibly.

The princess smiled at Sihan. 'You can add modesty to your list of qualities.'

Sihan quailed. His list of qualities now included brazen lying. To royalty, no less.

While the hunt master disembowelled the boar, slitting it open to reveal the heart leaking dark angry blood, Sihan took the congratulations of courtiers with as much grace as he could muster, trying to ignore the half-concealed black stares of Hessarde's men, the adoring gazes of the women, and the fact he had failed so utterly at casting a spear, something at which he normally excelled. The princess he tried to look at least, but found it impossible when she personally decided to tend his bleeding brow, untying the token from the spear and winding it round Sihan's head in a makeshift bandage.

The hunt master cut out the boar's heart, then offered it to her. Orlanda's wide blue eyes revealed no disgust as she pulled off a glove, and reached to rake her fingers across the organ like a wolf clawing at a carcass. Something akin to terror gripped Sihan when she held her hand out to him, blood dripping from her extended fingers. He backed away, staring at her hand as if it were one of the hounds ready to bite, but his leg almost gave way and he had to stop.

'Stand still,' she ordered. 'This is part of the Fire Rituals. First kill, first blood. You must wear the mark of the game.'

Blood trickled down Sihan's cheeks as the princess ran a finger down either side of his face. His nostrils filled with the sickly odour. And in his mind he saw her standing on a mountain of corpses, blood flowing from her hands in rivers.

The princess wiped her fingers on a cloth the hunt master offered. 'I wish I could bear the mark. But Father won't even let me carry a knife, let alone a sword or bow.'

For an instant, Sihan caught the predatory gleam of a huntress blazing in her eyes, then she blinked, and it was gone. Involuntary shudders ran through him as she mounted Aurion and rode off.

Forcing the image away, Sihan glanced instead back at the marsh. Pools of water caught the first rays of day, reflecting the sun like a red ball. Mist burnt off, seemingly taking all sign of the man with it. Sihan waited till Gerein brought his horse alongside, then whispered, 'Why were you hunting that man?'

'Sihan, I'm going to give you a few words of advice.' Gerein's voice was quiet and composed, but stiff with anger. 'Next time someone tells you to do something, do it. You're lucky it wasn't me shooting, or we wouldn't be having this conversation.'

'I don't understand.'

'We're King's soldiers, sworn to protect our liege, his daughter, and the people of Mirador. And that's what we've been trying to do, until you decided to blunder in and mess it up for us.'

'Protect them from whom?'

'None of your business, Sihan. Just thank Jaien I'm looking out for you. Next time, do as you're told. And say nothing to anyone about what happened today. Is that clear?'

In fraught silence, Sihan struggled back into the saddle. During the ride back to the fortress, he tried not to meet anyone eye to eye. Not only had he been humiliated before everyone by the princess, he had been caught up in some ambush, the failure for which he now wore the blame. While the women stared at him with admiration, the soldiers all regarded him with the truth of knowing in their eyes. Both made him squirm.

No point telling Gerein that Orlanda had ordered him into the swamp, an order backed by Hessarde's man. No point at all.

Sihan caught a smile from the princess, and his unease increased tenfold. Had the man been after her? He shivered and wondered of whom he was more afraid? The hunters or the hunted?

Chapter 24

The Trouble with Brothers

Veren strode along a gallery above the stable courtyard, black cloak swishing against wooden slats. In the ward below, stable boys hurried between stalls and storerooms, hauling hay or straw, or buckets of water from the troughs. Light from the forge spilled like blood on the cobbles.

Weaponless, Veren wondered if Areme would even notice the gesture. He had left this far too long, this feud he had never intended. At his approach, Hessarde and Sedor blocked the way, gloved hands on sword hilts. Veren raised an eyebrow, lips curling into a smile at the empty threat. Only Sedor had the grace to blush.

'What do you want?' Hessarde demanded, reinforcing his anger with the flash of blue eyes.

'To see my brother.'

'You've no right to that title.'

'I've as much right as you have to your title, Shaheden.' Veren shoved his formidable bulk past the two men, and flung open the door on a small room. A thin triangle of light stole inward, illuminating Areme's pale face as he pressed his back against the rough stone wall. He rested his hand close to the hilt of his naked sword, the blade lying alongside him on the bed like a chill, heartless lover. Injured, bootless, dressed only in grey tunic and leggings, every long, lean line of him still exuded power.

'Come to see your handiwork?' Areme made no attempt to hide his smouldering anger. 'Or have you come to finish what you started?'

The barb was launched with intent, and hit the mark, but Veren kept his face closed, masking his own bitter rage at his failure to prevent all that had befallen his brother and the world. Leaning against the door jamb, he took his time answering, examining Areme's quarters for some hint of the man Shasirre had loved.

It revealed nothing not austere, dark, hard, and cold, like the dead heart of the man it housed. One smoky torch rippled shadows across the bed, barely lighting the chest at the foot, or the bed pot beneath. A writing desk stood shoved in a dark corner with two high-backed chairs set near a solitary night-darkened window. A line of lances leaned along one wall; daggers sat on a solitary shelf. Even the Mirador tabard, slung carelessly over a long cloak on the back of one chair, added no softness to a room speaking of war.

Veren regarded Areme with the keenness of a hawk – the set lips, the stony expression mirroring his own. 'It seems we're always meeting at tournaments, with one or the other of us ending up on the sharp end of a lance. For what it's worth, I never meant to hurt you.' Even to his ears, the protest was weak.

Areme shifted uneasily on his bed, grimacing. Random wisps of hair loosed from an untidy black braid snaking over his shoulder. 'Like you never meant to hurt Merien. Hurt Shasirre.' He drove the sword's thrust of a millennium's worth of anger deep.

Veren drew a long breath, inhaling the lingering citrus tang of granine upon the air. As if he had tasted the foul paste, memories struck at him and pain spiked through his gut. He eyed the bandages bulked around Areme's chest, ran a hand involuntarily across his own black-clad torso. 'I still feel it, you know. The lance you stuck in me a thousand years ago.'

Areme looked away. 'I'm glad.'

Glad. Veren stepped forward, leant over Areme, spilt over his brother a judging shadow. 'Glad you pinned me to a singing stone, shattered the world?'

Stillness and silence met his fury. Then, for a moment only, the guard dropped, just once, and a boy's hurt stared out from a man's eyes. Areme sat there, a helpless child. No longer a man. No longer a Horse Lord. No longer strong and invincible, born to protect the world. The whisper, when it came, was more fraught than a scream of pain. 'I miss her, damn you, I miss her. And all you've done by coming here is bring it back to me. I'll never see her again, never hold her, never . . .' Areme drew a long, hard breath, and emptiness, bleak and bitter, filled his averted eyes. 'I'm glad you feel pain.'

Veren unclenched his sword hand, stepped away. It had not been the face he had wanted to see; perhaps the face he sought had never existed, except in a brother in name and soul only. Still there was a chance to reach him, perhaps . . . Veren nodded to the Mirador tabard, took the chance. 'Legitimacy suits you.'

'I'd give it back in a heartbeat.' Areme's words were frosty as gusts of early winter breeze.

'I gave it to you in less.'

'You? Or our sorceress mother?' Areme's lips twisted. 'You think I don't know how she schemed to bring me to the king's tournament to take your mantle as King's Champion? How she set me up?' He slammed his fist on the wooden planks of the bed. 'She *knew* Niameh would come for you. She *knew* it!' Every fluent line of Areme's face betrayed pain, like he had been betrayed so long ago. 'And I fell for it.' He ran one hand through his long hair. 'I fell for it. And Merien paid the cost. And Shasirre.'

'You weren't to know Merien would go off and buy spirit horses from Niameh.'

'I knew the price. He told me – he promised her I would kill you at the tournament. I should have killed you then, like I still want to now.'

Veren crossed his arms, counted the hoof beats of a horse being led across the court outside before he answered. 'What's the point? Assuming you could.'

'No point, you God-born bastard. Other than it would make me feel good.'

'Don't blaspheme. You're God-born, too.'

Areme spat. 'I never asked for that privilege. And what did I get for it? A dead wife. A dead brother. The gods don't answer my prayers to bring them back, not then, not now, not ever. And thanks to you, that Gods-blighted witch is still running around somewhere, for all we know, waiting to cast more unsuspecting souls into hell.'

'Not more. Just one. Me.' Veren closed his eyes, recalled the dark-haired girl striding across the tourney field a thousand years past, gliding almost, in that otherworldly way of witches. Her voice, all darkness and power, demanded Areme keep the pledge Merien had made on his behalf, rising to a windhowl of rage when he had refused. She had cast the curse in the middle of the lance trial – "*If the promise was a lie, the man who spoke the words shall die.*"

And Merien. Poor Merien. Young, inexperienced, riding a spirit horse, paid the price. With a thought more destructive than a blade, Niameh had sent his horse out of control, and in the melee of lances, one had driven straight into his gut, killing him.

Areme's anguished scream echoed over the tracks of time, his grief-wracked voice swearing to fulfil the promise, if only Niameh would let Merien live.

But it was too late.

'Merien made one mistake,' said Veren. 'Just one.'

'One was all it took.' Areme's voice was as unforgiving as his eyes, punching out accusation to the beat of the smith's anvil in the court below. 'You should know.'

'You forgave him his.'

'His was unwitting. Yours . . . Yours was deliberate.'

The thrust of his attack impaled Veren, shattered his heart as fully as the lance that had killed the singing stone of Caerlon. Bled his soul like the Living Sphere bled its lifeblood into the earth. 'What are you going to do?' he asked, hand running involuntarily to his chest, as though the lance still pierced his flesh.

Areme glared daggers at him. 'Among other things, what I should have done a long time ago. Find that bitch, Niameh, and kill her.'

'Don't be a fool,' Veren said. 'No one has seen her since Shasirre died.'

'I saw her, back then. Roedan was protecting her, hiding her in that otherworldly plane he misted to after he walked through fire to become Shaheden.'

The word shivered through Veren. Shaheden. Martyrs of the fire. Sons of Shahedur, Lord-God of the World. Sons of Senfar, Lord-God of Horses. Godwords filled his mind, demanding a sacrifice to staunch the mortal wound the world had suffered.

And such a sacrifice as the world had never seen. One thousand men willingly walking into fire. Burning. Burning. Like the hate in Areme's eyes.

'Take care, brother,' said Veren, 'that your rage does not call forth the creatures of the underworld.'

'I wish it would. They could do my job for me. I wish it could dredge up every dark force in the land. I'd like to see a saraghar rip your head off, scorch you with its breath. Or one of those fire-tongued snakes from the caves of Miarrmer. Maybe a steel-clawed vulture.' He looked Veren full in the face for the first time, eyes too bright. 'You wouldn't be able to hide behind a glamour like that bitch.' He stretched a tense leg. 'Yes, I'd like that very much.'

Ice and times past slithered between them, pushing them further apart than ever. Veren almost wished for a cloak of non-being, to stave off that burning gaze, the hidden agony fuelling the surface blaze.

Niameh had drawn a glamour of non-being about her, when Shasirre had rushed to protect Areme from Niameh's wrath. Veren wanted to close his ears to the voice in his head as much as he wished to block Areme's accusing face from his eyes. Shasirre's voice – invoking the curse haunting every Shaheden and acolyte. Words designed to draw the dark powers of the world to her, meant to hunt Niameh from her lair.

"You can't hide forever. I will surround the world with a vast net. Set the spirit beasts loose, free those of the underworld. However far you run you shall not escape them. I'll send snakes into the darkest pits of all the hells after you. Do you feel their breath, witch? Hot, breathing fire. The saraghar will never rest till they feast on your flesh. Spiders shall weave nets of silk to trap you."

Too young to control them, Shasirre had called more and more creatures of the underworld into existence. They had wreaked destruction upon the world. She had tried to help Areme, and instead forced him to kill her.

Veren grated, 'Do you think this is what she wanted? That you live like this, in hate, in pain, in darkness.'

'I was born in hate, in pain, in darkness. And I killed the only two bright things I ever knew.' Areme's laughter was ash. 'I saved the world by killing my wife. And my brother died for nothing. My chosen brother. More real than you ever were, or ever will be. And for what? For nothing. Myrrhye planned so well. Honed her weapon to a sword's edge. And I killed the wrong target. I'll find the right one, though. If it takes eternity.'

'Niameh has never reappeared, not in a thousand years,' said Veren.

'She's out there, I know it. I'll find her, if it takes the rest of my unnatural life. Once Orlanda comes into her powers, I'll have her strip all glamours from the world, all forbidden magic. I'll find that bitch and I'll kill her.' His voice was cold, deliberate.

'Let it go,' said Veren. 'I'll deal with Niameh.'

Areme's eyes burned with fury, but his voice was quiet as he spoke. 'Like you dealt with her before?'

While the ordinary sounds of the world drifted up from the stable court, the whinny of a horse, the shouts of stable boys, the gulf stretched between them, and Veren knew now it might never be broached. He answered with studied calm, meeting the knowing eyes of Areme's men. 'It is my task to undo all that was done. I've come to take the burden from you. Put aside your sword.'

In less than a heartbeat, Areme threw himself at Veren. Hessarde launched himself from the door to block Areme's path. With Sedor's help, he only just managed to hold Areme back. 'He's not worth it,' grated Hessarde.

Areme swore. 'I'll kill him. I swear it before the Heavens.'

Veren's voice quieted with menace. 'Take back your vow before it destroys you.'

Areme spat in Veren's face. 'I won't. When you've stood on a mountain of corpses, killed that number again with your bare hands, murdered your own wife and brother, then you'll have the right to tell me to put aside my sword. Not before.'

Veren's lips tightened to a line. 'You're my brother.'

'Don't scorch your tongue with that word.' Areme spat once more. Shrugging off the others, he stalked from the room.

Veren started after him, but Sedor placed his hand upon his shoulder. 'Leave him.'

'He wished you dead,' said Hessarde, blunt as always. 'He meant it.'

Veren looked at the empty doorway, bitterness twisting in his gut like a double-edged knife. 'I know.'

Chapter 25

Oath of Love

Orlanda pressed her left heel into Aurion's side, signalling a half-pass across the riding arena. Crossing legs in front of each other, the stallion cantered in a smooth diagonal from one corner of the ménage to the opposite wall. Hooves muffled on sand, hardly raising an echo in the cavernous area. Aurion's gentle snorting was the only clear sound.

High above, galleries at either end sat empty of spectators – no one to witness Hessarde's retribution but pigeons fluttering in the rafters of the domed ceiling. Small comfort. Despite her antics at the hunt, Areme had once more failed to put in an appearance, failed to censure her, failed her entirely.

Maybe she should have stripped naked? What would it take to rouse him, make him come to her side? Orlanda cast a hopeful glance beyond the end doors, opened to let air in. About the ward and in the stable court men came and went, the hubbub of voices a constant drone like bees buzzing around a hive.

But no Areme.

Sweat dripped between Orlanda's shoulder blades, damped her riding habit, dripped off her brow. The unseasonal autumn weather had persisted long past its welcome. The white stallion performed immaculately as usual, but she took little pleasure in his work. He was Areme's gift, but without Areme, any gift was worthless.

When she turned Aurion down the centre line, she brought him to a halt before Sihan, who stood with his arms crossed over a cream woollen tunic, brown eyes in a pale face focused on every movement the stallion made. With his hair tied back in a leather thong, and lips curved down, he resembled Areme more than ever, adding insult to her already injured pride.

'I didn't tell you to stop,' said Sihan, voice strained as he took a stride back, limping markedly. He wiped sweat from his glistening brow.

'I'm tired of this,' she protested, determined to lash out. 'Why do we have to do figures all the time?'

'Because Hessarde told me to make you do figures until you drop.' Sihan's voice hardened in disapproval as though he was Hessarde's mouthpiece. 'I think he called it "settling accounts."'

'Silly old goat.' Orlanda scowled, pulling off a glove to fan her face. 'Never could take a joke.'

Sihan reached out to stroke Aurion's nose, hand trembling slightly. 'No. I don't think he thought it was funny at all.' When the stallion tossed his head, the skin of Sihan's face shaded further to grey.

'You don't look well,' said Orlanda. 'Is your leg still bothering you?'

'It's fine.' Despite his attempt at brushing off his condition, when Aurion shoved Sihan with his nose the young man staggered back and winced, becoming paler by the moment.

'I think it's a lot worse than you're letting on,' Orlanda chided, looking at him in concern. Sensing another opportunity, she said, 'I think you should go and rest.'

'I'm all right.'

She wrinkled her nose, deciding she did not like him much either. In addition to resembling Areme, he looked at her oddly, when he looked at her at all, as though he was not quite seeing her, but something foul and disgusting he would rather scrape off his boots. It reminded her of how her father looked at her. And yesterday, Sihan had dared to reprimand her about her dress. A stable boy!

She gritted her teeth and forced a smile, as she had done the day before when she had poured sweet compliments upon him. All with a purpose – another spur to prick Areme. She had hoped word of her dalliance with a stable boy would prompt some reaction, on top of the escapade with the dress. But so far, both ruses had come to naught.

It was too much to take on top of everything else, this youth who reminded her of both her failures: her father's loathing avoidance, and Areme's indifference. It was time for another attempt to set at least one thing right. She said to Sihan,

'I don't think you are well at all.' Kicking Aurion to the entrance, she cried, 'Help! Help!'

Within moments, bootfalls beat against the cobbled walkway of the stables and several men appeared, Gerhas among them.

'What's wrong?' the horsemaster asked, brown eyes glittering.

'Sihan is not well,' Orlanda announced, determined to scrape back the dignity everyone sought to crush. 'I've ordered him to go rest.'

The horsemaster took his time examining Sihan who limped heavily on his left leg across the ménage, but even he could not deny she was right. 'Off to your bed, lad,' he said. 'I'll have someone else tend the white horse.'

'Who?' protested Sihan as soldiers and stable boys backed away from Aurion, all cringing. 'No one else can handle him.'

Orlanda bit her tongue, the urge to argue that point dancing on her tongue. Sihan had saddled the stallion by the time she had arrived at the stable that morning as if he was doing his best not to let her near Aurion if he could possibly help it. She had the feeling Sihan regretted losing the horse to her, despite the advantageous trade he had made. But, for now, his assertion played to her advantage. He had not let on she could handle the horse without assistance.

Gerhas turned to a stable boy. 'Get Areme down here.'

Orlanda dug her fingernails into her palms. Would he really come?

As the boy rushed off, relief broke out on the faces of the other men. Orlanda waited impatiently. A lifetime passed before Areme came striding down the arched passage bordering the courtyard, no sign of lingering injury marring his gait. Rather, he moved with the lethal fluidity of a sword dancer.

Orlanda forced back a triumphant smile, taking in every sinuous inch of him with a devouring gaze – black hair pulled back and tied with a leather cord, contrasting his grey tunic and grey leather leggings. *At last! At last!* She wondered how best to swoon into his arms.

'What?' Areme demanded, the moment he came within earshot.

'The princess is under instruction,' said Gerhas. 'Sihan is ill. And that horse is a menace.'

Areme sent Orlanda an irritated look, then turned briefly to speak to the horsemaster. 'The Keeper of Mirador has just arrived with mares from the Byerol border. He's waiting for you at the main fortress gate.'

'Hmm.' Gerhas's scowl intensified. 'I don't know what we're going to do with so many mares. The stallions will be rioting if they get one whiff of a mare in heat.' He flashed a withering look at Orlanda before stalking off, ushering Sihan in front of him, stable boys parting to give them passage.

With one hand to the bridle, Areme led Aurion back to the centre of the ménage.

Orlanda broke the swift silence. 'Your injury? It ails you still?'

Hard eyed and hard voiced, Areme replied, 'As you can see, I'm quite recovered.'

Despite the dismissal, Orlanda asked breathlessly, 'What do you want me to do?'

'Exactly what Hessarde ordered. Figures. I haven't seen this horse since I rode him at the trials, and I haven't seen you ride him. Though by all accounts, you've been doing rather well on him.' Despite the compliment every tone bespoke reproach.

Orlanda fought back a retort. Was it her fault he had not seen her or the horse? All he had to do was get out of bed, or, better still, let her join him in his. Then hope flared. He had been getting reports of her. That meant he had not been oblivious to her existence. Spurred by this thought, she said, 'He's a good horse.'

'Too good to have his life put in danger.' Areme's face remained disdainfully handsome, but hardened swiftly to a chilled mask as he looked up at her. 'I heard all about yesterday. I expected better from you.'

The brilliance of his silver-grey eyes boring into hers became so unbearable Orlanda's gaze sunk. She kicked Aurion into a canter, blinking away tears suddenly springing to her eyes, Areme's reprimand more cutting than the scolding her father and

Gerhas had given her. Despite the heat, cold slid over her skin, as though a bucket of iced water had been flung at her.

Until mid-sun she rode in grim inflexible silence that settled like an impenetrable obstacle between them except for a series of sharp commands from Areme. When she could stand no more, she brought Aurion to a halt.

'I didn't tell you to stop.' Areme's clear voice rang out across the arena. Even motionless, he radiated grace.

'I feel like I'm in a sweatbox,' Orlanda complained, horse sweat filling her nostrils. 'If I ride any longer, I'll faint.'

She followed every movement of Areme's narrow hips and long legs as he walked toward her. When he stopped and ran his fingers through Aurion's mane, envy stabbed at her. Why could he not touch her with such affection?

She absently tangled her fingers in Aurion's mane while Areme stroked the horse's head. His lips curved. That smile was worth more than gold; what she would not do to posses it, possess him. When his eyes locked on hers, Orlanda's pulse quickened. She yearned to throw herself into his arms, to beg his forgiveness . . . and more.

Half-trembling, half-braced for peril, she waited for him to hand her down, even though it was her usual custom to slide off. Areme's hands closed securely about her waist, and she almost swooned at the male scent of him – horses, sweat, leather. Her weakness had the desired effect of him holding her more tightly, and she played upon the moment for all it was worth, holding him close for as long as possible without casting all decorum to the wind. His ensilvered eyes looked at her searchingly, but his smile soured. Beyond all doubt, he had read the passion behind the intensity of her gaze, and cared naught for it. But still, he held her. Wild clashing thoughts assailed her as she pondered whether his reaction was encouragement or mockery.

'I'm sorry,' she whispered.

'No, you're not.' Areme's hold tightened. He drew her closer, till only a hand's breadth parted their faces, then his lips brushed against her ear as he murmured, 'You play dangerous games.'

Heat rushed through her, and she weakened further, revelling in the feel of his arm clamped round her, an iron band she never wanted to break. 'It's so warm,' she whispered, keeping her voice low and husky. If only he would untie the laces to her bodice, carry her to his bed.

'I hope that doesn't mean you're planning on taking your clothes off again.'

Orlanda's gaze trailed from the smooth line of his cheek to his thin, well-formed lips. 'I would if you asked.' It was half-hope, half-challenge.

His eyes glinted to shards of winter ice as he put her from him. 'What were you thinking yesterday?'

Her heart bled like a burst wineskin, all hope of kindling some answering flame in him draining away. Bereft, angry, Orlanda straightened, fighting to keep her countenance calm. 'I wanted some sport.'

'You call exposing yourself to ridicule sport? All I've heard this morning are descriptions of how perfect your arse is.'

Orlanda flared, 'Father's giving my arse, and every other bit of me, to Valoren. You think I haven't heard *those* comments? That the Black Duke is going to fuck me, and then hand me around to all his men? The lewdest comment from one Mirador soldier is nothing compared to what Valoren is actually going to *do* to me.'

'That's not going to happen.'

'Are you going to prevent it?'

Areme looked down at the sand, lashes sweeping his pale cheeks. She reached to brush aside a wisp of hair falling over his solemn eyes.

He caught her hand. 'Don't.' His voice was guarded and still.

Her fingers tightened around his. 'Can't you see I'm burning for you?'

'You're a child trapped by a marriage you don't want. What you're burning for is freedom.'

With a jutting lip, she said, 'I'm not a child!'

'Prove it. Talk to your father. Make him see sense.'

Hope dashed itself against his cliff of ice. 'He's beyond reason. And if you won't help me–' Orlanda went to pull away, muttering, 'I'm sorry I spoke.'

His fingers closed around hers. At length, he broke the prolonged hush. 'There may not be cause for sorrow. We'll speak again tonight.'

'It's not words I want from you, Areme.'

Another long silence passed while she stewed in impatience, then he said in a voice stone-chilled: 'You must forget me. My heart is ash.' Without another word, he led Aurion away.

Orlanda stared after him, heart ripped by his swift, stark rejection. If he did not want her, would not love her, then so was her heart ash.

Areme stalked back to his quarters, brushing stable boys and soldiers aside as though they were bothersome flies. His second and Sedor stepped away from his doorway, faces grim. Both men were fully armed, swords and daggers sheathed, quivers stuffed with arrows on their backs.

Without preamble Areme asked, 'You've found him?'

'Not exactly,' Hessarde replied, blue eyes glinting in the soft rushlight. 'He's turning out to be a slippery little sucker.'

Areme slumped in one of the two chairs in the room, not bothering to keep up the act he was recovered. His wound ached, deep, burning. Debilitating. A fight now, and even a squire might best him. And every sense screamed a war was in the offing.

Since Myrrhye had given him word of what had happened in Pelan, all his men had been put on alert to watch for intruders, men behaving strangely, skulking in corners they had no right to skulk. The incident at the hunt had frozen the blood in his veins, more so than the princess's antics. Could that man have been stalking Aurion? Areme leaned across the heavy table. 'You've sent out scouts?'

'Everywhere. No one knows anything.'

'Someone must know of him. There will be traces, leads to follow. Speak to the villagers. Peasant folk keep a close eye on the doings of strangers.'

Hessarde shrugged, shifting his gorytos on his back. 'Hereabouts there aren't too many men with loose mouths.'

'Do your best to loosen them. This man has evaded us too long.'

Sedor ran a hand through his short, black beard, eyes fixed on the goings on beyond the door, keeping guard to ensure they were not disturbed. 'You'd almost think he was an adept the way he's managed to elude our traps.'

The same uneasy thought had been playing around the edges of Areme's mind for days.

Adepts, Shaheden. He did not care what name was used for the martyrs of the fire, each chilled his soul. Armies of men bound to the rings of the Horse Lords. Men, who had walked into flames of their own accord, burned their bodies to set their souls free to return in an endless cycle of reincarnation. Men bound to one master, unstoppable when ordered to fight, eyes glowing silver with killing lust.

Only Senfar knew how many rings had been forged. Areme knew of three. One, he wore. His brother owned one other. And Roedan, prime Horse Lord, the third.

How many more? What if there was another ring? Another Horse Lord? Or worse? With another army?

It did not bear thinking about. Adepts could destroy an army ten times their number without breaking a sweat. He had seen it during the Great War, when the queen had activated the killing lust in his men. It had taken all his strength to stop her, destroyed half his men. Men, who had disappeared upon their deaths, sending ordinary soldiers to madness at the sight.

He had ordered their deaths, the deaths of thousands to keep the secret. But now, what if there was another army? Searching for the unicorn? Areme looked at Hessarde. 'Did Travall's men notice anything? Gerein?'

Hessarde spat. 'I'm not sure Gerein can be trusted.'
'Not trusted? How?'

'He was more interested in protecting that idiot boy. You know, the one who the unicorn should have turned on by now.'

Areme ignored the jibe. 'Why is Gerein protecting him?'

'Something to do with his former commander, perhaps? From what I can gather, Jaien gave orders for those of his men remaining here to look after the lad. Jaien and Gerein were lovers. That'll be a tough loyalty to budge.'

'I want Gerein here. Now. I'll put an end to his conflicted loyalties once and for all.'

The two men left, and Areme held his head between his hands, fixing his eyes on the table.

My heart is ash. He had spoken the words, knowing them a lie. Knowing to his cost his heart bled every moment of every day. How had the world not drowned in his blood before now?

He had murdered Shasirre, the woman he had sworn to love till his dying day. And now this girl, spoilt, petulant, bereft of any redeeming features, sought to usurp Shasirre in his mind, his heart, his soul, his bed. Sought to have him break a vow inviolate, sworn in blood, honour, faith, despair. Would he have the courage to break his vow of eternal fidelity? Could he tear the last gossamer thread holding Shasirre to him?

He had to have Orlanda pliant to his will, but how to without bedding her, lying to her? How could he convince Orlanda he loved her when he did not?

He cast the question to silent gods who had long abandoned the world of men. The gods the knights prayed to every morning not knowing their prayers were empty, and would go unheard and unanswered. Like his.

Soundless, Myrrhye materialised from the shadows before him.

'I wondered when you'd come,' he said, unsurprised at his mother's entrance.

She pushed back her cowl. Red hair spilled around her shoulders as she smiled. 'Gracious, as always, my son. I think perhaps I liked you better when you were at death's door.'

Areme spat. 'I'm always at death's door. That's my problem. Always at it, never allowed to pass through.'

'I see Orlanda has upset you again.'

'Orlanda. The world. Veren. *You.*' He waved at her red hair and face set with green eyes, a mirror copy of the Duchess of Belaron. 'What's that for?'

Myrrhye shrugged. 'A glamour, nothing more. One of the few I can manage without drawing on the lines of power too much.'

'I hope the duchess approves of you borrowing her form.'

'The duchess is an acolyte of Taiere. It is not for her to approve – rather, to obey.' Myrrhye passed a pale hand over her face and red hair transformed into coiling ebony tresses, green eyes to deepest black. 'Do you like this better?'

Areme spread his hands on the table. 'I'd like it better if you'd leave.'

Anger flared in her eyes and the large candle on the table blazed to life between them causing Myrrhye's ivory skin to glow, softening the faint lines at the corners of her eyes.

Areme raised a hand to pinch away the wick between finger and thumb. 'Losing control?' he taunted. 'Or do you think you can frighten me with parlour tricks?'

Myrrhye failed to rise to either taunt. 'I've come to give you warning. The number of missing horses has increased. The circle is widening. A courier has arrived from Belaron with news of more stolen horses.'

Areme slammed his fist on the table. 'Pelan, Byerol, Belaron. And that fool of a keeper has brought all the bloodhorse mares of Mirador here when there are reports of strangers stalking the fortress.'

His mother maintained her composure. 'I see you perceive the urgency of matters. We must make plans to move the horse, and the girl. They are no longer safe in Mirador.'

Areme glared at her. 'That's the real reason Veren is here. You want her in Kosall.' It was not a question.

'If you cannot break the threat to her and the horse, then, yes, that is what I want.'

Areme's hands clenched into fists. 'I'll break it.'

Myrrhye faded into the shadows. 'Be certain, Areme. Be certain.'

A moment later Hessarde and Sedor burst into the room with Gerein in tow. The archer's eyes shot daggers through Areme. 'What the hells do you want?'

Areme stood and began to pace. 'Your orders were to protect the princess. Your orders were to capture or take out any strangers acting suspiciously in Mirador.' He stopped and stared at Gerein, his immobility as taut as his pacing. 'What part do you fail to understand?'

Gerein crossed his arms and leaned against the doorjamb. 'What part of "I'm under Travall's command" do *you* fail to understand . . . *sir*?'

Only just resisting the urge to flatten the archer, Areme replied, 'You're a soldier. You obey whatever knight commander gives you orders.'

'Not under the terms of Jaien's agreement with Travall. I'm Travall's man, not yours. And if word gets out to Jaien to the contrary, he'll be back in arms, with a thousand very pissed off men at his back.'

Areme sat, fighting back a glower. 'Well, we'll just have to make certain word doesn't get out.' Eye contact and the thin-veiled threat were all he needed to spur Hessarde and Sedor into motion. Before Gerein could even form the thought to move, Areme's men gripped the archer's wrists and twisted both arms behind his back. Hessarde gagged him with one hand, then thrust him down on the other chair at the table. Muffled moans and incoherent curses filled the air.

Shaking his head, Areme sighed. 'You'd better hope you are what I think you are, or this room and my face will be the last things you ever see.' He unlaced a pouch at his belt, and pulled out a green tuber, squat, and rank with the scent of spoilt citrus. He drew his index finger along the edge, puncturing the granine, smearing green paste upon the tip of his finger.

Gerein's eyes, wild rage, glinted almost gold-green as he struggled with his two captors.

'Hold him still,' ordered Areme. He pried the corner of Gerein's lips back and daubed the paste inside the archer's mouth, only just avoiding Gerein's attempt to bite. A moment later, the archer stilled and his eyes rolled over white.

Areme straightened, his words escaping like the breath of a sigh. 'I knew it.'

Hessarde released his grip, letting Gerein fall forward, his cheek pressed flat against the table. 'Who'd have thought it? I never picked him for an adept.'

'His skill with a bow should have alerted us long ago.'

'Is he one of ours?' asked Sedor, knowing well how reincarnation could change a man beyond recognition.

Areme pulled the glove off his right hand. A ring with the seal of the firefalcon edged in black circled one finger, sharp-cut facets catching the fire of the rushlights. 'Sit him up, and we'll find out.'

Hessarde and Sedor hauled Gerein upright in his chair.

Taking care to modulate his voice, Areme intoned, 'Awaken.'

'Let me sleep.' Gerein's head lolled to the side, face slack-jawed, drool dribbling from the corner of his mouth.

'Sleep is for the dead,' said Areme, repeating the mantra he had spoken to thousands of men over the past millennium.

'Then let me die.'

Areme stiffened. He had made the same plea to no avail not one moon's cycle past. And, like his mother, he was in no mind to yield. 'Not yet in this lifetime. Awaken and tell me what you see.'

Gerein's eyes blinked open. For a moment he was motionless, eyes wide and wondering. Then his gaze lengthened as if he stared into far horizons. Face contorting, he began to scream. 'Get it off me! Get it off me! By all that is merciful, get it off me!'

'What?'

Gerein's head thrashed from side to side. 'Oh, hells! Hells!'

'What do you see?' pressed Areme, ignoring the anguish and dread cracking Gerein's voice.

The archer stilled. 'A great beast. Black. Leather wings. Eating a rotting corpse.'

'Whose corpse?'

'Mine.' The single word hung upon the air.

'Which life?' Areme asked, almost without sound.

'My first.'

'Of how many?'

'Seven.'

Areme slipped the ring onto his middle finger and held it before Gerein's unfocused eyes. 'Whom do you serve?'

'My Lord Master.' The answer came without hesitation, without guile.

348

With a satisfied grunt, Areme sat back in his chair, regarding Gerein across the table. 'Now we understand each other, I want some answers. Why didn't you follow Travall's orders?'

Gerein replied in a monotone drawl. 'My orders were to protect Sihan.'

Areme leaned forward. 'Let me make your duty clear. Sihan is nothing. *Less* than nothing. Aurion and the princess are everything. You'll do all in your power to protect them, and if that means putting an arrow shaft through Sihan's back, then so be it. Understand?'

'I understand my duty,' repeated Gerein dully.

'From here on, I want you scouting every night. Hunt down that intruder and either take him, or kill him. Do you understand?'

'I understand my duty.'

'Very well.' Areme stood and walked round the table to Gerein's side. 'Other than the will to carry out my orders, you'll remember nothing of this encounter.' With a quick, rough gesture, he brushed both the archer's eyelids closed. When Hessarde lifted one upper eyelid and examined the eye, it showed no reaction to light or dark.

Satisfied, Areme waved Hessarde and Sedor away. 'Put him back in his bunk. Let him sleep it off.'

With a grunting heave, the two men dragged Gerein from the room.

Areme stared at empty air for a long while. If he waited, Veren would spirit Orlanda and the horse beyond his reach. He could not allow it.

Mind set, he took up two keys from the chest at the foot of his bed and walked out onto the gallery, slinging his cloak over one shoulder. In the inner ward, soldiers milled and smiths still laboured over anvils, hammering steel. There were fewer soldiers than usual, due to the forthcoming right of fealty by the young knights. Most had been redeployed to the perimeter of the fortress, reinforcing the outer guard.

Areme made his way to the tower at the south-eastern corner of the curtain wall, avoiding alleys choked with revellers and merchants. Overhead, evening sky hung clear and chill, faint stars blinking points of light.

As he came to the massive bulk of the battlemented curtain wall, he stood in the shadow of two gate towers fronting the bridge. Around the walls, torches burned through deepening twilight. Watchmen on walls paced the guardwalk, alert, enveloped in cloaks though the night was mild.

Travall's men, efficient as always, already had the great double doors of the gate closed, with just the wicket open to reveal bonfires sparking in the plain and on hills surrounding the fortress.

Areme strode to the postern farther down the eastern wall. Beneath the gate's vaulted arch, a man waited, eyes alert. He stepped forward at Areme's approach, smiling narrowly.

'How goes the watch?' Areme asked.

The soldier's lips downturned. 'I'd rather be out and about bedding women, sir.'

Areme walked on, mind turning on a trap. There was a way to sniff out the intruder. It was dangerous, and it could cost them dear if it failed.

He reached the foot of the southern tower. After the slightest hesitation, he turned one key in the lock of a slim door at the base. The door opened in silken silence. Stepping into darkness, he paused at the foot of a curved staircase. Cold, sharp air flowed from airshafts slanted through thick granite walls. A firebasket wavered light down the stairwell. Areme turned and left, pressing the door closed without locking it.

Falling leaves covered the cobblestones of the torchlit palace courtyard in a tapestry of gold, red and orange, more beautiful and intricate than any master weaver could create. From the battlements, the Mirador standard fluttered. Twilight hung in hues of pearlescence over marble pillars lining the palace.

Soldiers paced the length of the guardwalks as nobles and courtiers stood in galleries on either side of the forecourt, looking down upon lines of grey-cloaked knights assembling in ritual procession before a large crowd of men wearing the tabard of Mirador over their grey tunics. Slowly, the forecourt filled and the host of men knelt before the king who sat on a throne at the top of the grand flight of marble stairs.

Ignored again, Orlanda sat beside her father, refusing to look at him, hands gripping the carven arms of her seat, knuckles white as her flowing gown of brocade. Shutting off all feeling, she performed the ritual ceremony, knowing full well he cared more for these men than her.

One cloaked knight arose and stepped forward to begin the ceremony to consecrate the new knights of the realm. Travall's voice, dark and solemn, invoked the prayer for the dead.

'We call to you, our brothers, as stars fall in the deepening darkness.
'Lay down your swords and walk toward the light.
'Let the candle and the stars guide you,
'And by all that is merciful, may you find eternal peace.'

The kneeling men repeated the chant, then Travall continued the prayer.

'Let others take up your burden and answer the call to arms.
'Mark these, our brothers, valiant and true,
'Bearing the badge of courage and unfailing loyalty,
'To follow hereafter in your stead.'

Travall climbed the steps, grey cloak flaring in the breeze. When he reached the king, he bowed his head, wind ruffling his salted-black hair. He touched the slate with his right knee, placing his hands within those of the king and said,

'We offer our Lord our allegiance.
'May we prove worthy and not falter upon the field of honour.
'Consecrate these, our band of brothers,
'By the Heavens, Great Lord, hear our plea.'

Areme arose from the throng and ascended the steps to stand before Orlanda. He knelt and placed his hands within hers, every tendon, every vein apparent through the skin. Orlanda looked down at them in surprise, for his hands were trembling. He spoke quiet words that fell into the silence like petals at dawn.

> 'I offer my allegiance, most worthy daughter of Mirador.
> 'May I hold you in all honour and remain true to my vow.
> 'I pledge my life and my sword to your service.
> 'Worthy daughter, hear my plea.'

Orlanda stared at him. He had not changed the vow, but somehow it was different, as though he had woven a new meaning into his words. Her fingers tightened upon his as she responded with the ritualistic convention. And for the first time, she also sought to inflect new meaning into the age-old words.

> 'Arise, Knight of Mirador, sacred son of the Kingdom.
> 'I accept you with all honour and hold you to your vow.
> 'Your life I hold, your sword I claim.
> 'Worthy son, I accept all you offer.'

Areme stood and his eyes held hers. Trembling also, Orlanda raised her face to his so he could kiss her upon the right cheek. Then he kissed her left cheek, but as he did so, his lips moved, and he whispered death-quiet, 'I am yours. Will you accept me?'

There was a short silence during which neither moved. His face remained close to hers, waiting for her response. Orlanda drew back, stray tendrils of hair curling against her cheek. Uncertainty flickered in his eyes, and it occurred to her he was as unsure of her as she was of him. He bent his head further, so she could complete the ritual. Orlanda brushed her lips across his forehead. 'I have said so,' she replied in a hushed whisper, 'with a heart that burns.'

He took her hand once more and carried it so respectfully to his lips he might have deposited a sigh upon it rather than a kiss. Then he stood and stepped back, his eyes never leaving hers, and Orlanda's heart hammered.

As though nothing untoward had occurred, the king motioned to the young men before him.

'In truth, I consecrate all here who kneel and offer allegiance.
'Rise and be counted among our sacred sons,
'O knights of Mirador.'

Dusk turned to evening, and Orlanda waited impatiently for an end to the solemnities. Torches flared, dancing light and shadow on long rows of marble pillars around the courtyard. Each knight accepted his sword, mail, surcoat and spurs. Gerhas and the knight commanders did the honours while the king looked on. Finally a bard and a singer completed the ritual with a recounting of battles of ages past.

At the ceremony's conclusion, Orlanda followed her father's lead, mingling among the knights and common soldiers before they dispersed to their various stations, and the young knights to celebrations. Areme stood to one side. His eyes did not meet hers, yet she knew he watched her.

Tension mounted in her, every moment apart from him a torment. *Look at me. Look at me*, she willed, but his attention was diverted as Gerhas introduced him to some men now in his command. Orlanda swore under her breath as she made her way across the courtyard. Heads inclined in acknowledgment as she passed.

As evening aged, Areme remained aloof, talking to Travall, his men, everyone, it seemed, but her. Had his words during the ceremony been some cruel jest? She would not stand to be mocked. Orlanda paused to congratulate several young knights, then swept past Areme, continuing down a pillared walkway until she reached the gates to torch-lit gardens.

Night tides rose with the last autumn moon. Myriad stars reflected in fountains, shimmered in elongated ripples in slow-moving water, meandering down watercourses lining garden paths.

Orlanda wandered aimlessly, regretting her impulsive act. Why did she trade the opportunity to gaze upon the man who held her heart in exchange for silent, empty garden paths? Whether he mocked her or not, he was the only bright thing in her world of night.

A gentle breeze wafted the warm aroma of fresh-baked naan, carried the high-pitched clang of shaped steel from the forges. She walked on, trying to escape the blend of voices from the courtyard intruding on her solitude. She longed for only one; Areme's quiet, sombre voice . . . music to her.

'The dark is a lonely place for such beauty,' said someone from the darkness.

Jumping as though stung by a wasp, Orlanda whirled to find a dark shadow of a man looming nearby. He stepped closer.

Veren.

Ice slid down her back.

He regarded her, brows drawn over deep black eyes. Foreboding washed over her. Night cloaked him. Even the torches appeared to dim in his presence.

She schooled her features to the bored expression of a diplomat and inclined her head. 'Knight Commander Veren.'

The knight's lips curled into a faint smile. 'I apologise for startling you, Highness.' He paused, then added, 'You seem troubled.'

On top of Areme's abandonment, to receive empathy from the man sent to drag her to her doom was too much. Bristling, she said, 'My state of mind is not your concern. I came out here to be alone.'

Veren's smile thinned as his gaze shifted from her to the gates leading to the gardens where Areme stood framed in torchlight. His dark eyes flared into amusement. 'Somehow, I doubt that.'

Areme approached, hand resting conspicuously on the hilt of his sword. 'I see you're making a nuisance of yourself as usual, Veren. I respectfully suggest you withdraw. The lady wishes to be left alone.'

Veren flashed the most charming of smiles, and in the serenest voice said, '*I* respectfully suggest if you believe that, you are a fool.'

Lethal flames flared in Areme's eyes. 'Tact and diplomacy were never your strongest suits.'

'Tact and diplomacy are crutches for the weak,' drawled Veren, voice coolly level. 'I prefer honesty, something noticeably lacking in Mirador. Honest men accept the truth, however brutal.' He turned to Orlanda. 'I regret my presence distresses you, Highness. I sincerely hope such will not always be the case, but for now I shall take my leave.' He made a deep reverence, then walked back to the great hall.

Charged stillness filled the air. Orlanda's heart thundered. Strained silence followed Veren's departure.

'Your Highness.' Areme broke the quiet. 'May I ask a favour?'

Her breath escaped in a rush. 'Anything.'

'Grant me leave to withdraw.'

'*Withdraw*?' Orlanda stared at him in bewilderment. How could he want to go? Had she imagined his words, his promises? Had he truly spoken in mockery? She turned away, willing herself not to show her distress. 'You may retire.' When there came no sound of him leaving, she repeated her command in a voice filled with rising anger. 'I said I give you leave.'

Hot breath ran along her throat, against her ear. Lips brushed her cheek.

Orlanda's heart stilled.

Areme slid something cold into her hand, then whispered, 'Come to the singing stones and pray with me.'

Before she could answer, he turned and strode away.

She opened her fingers to find a key. Understanding came on wings. It was the key to the hidden passage from her room, held only by the knight commanders and her champion. A lifetime seemed to pass before she could trust herself to move, the horizon rocking like a boat on water. Then she was running, running. Breathless, mind afire with his words, she vowed – tonight she would make him forget duty and honour. She would make him forget everything except her.

Chapter 26

Fire Rituals

Sihan threaded his way through the fortress, a slow, torturous progress with his gimp leg, uneven cobbles, and the shoving, crowding hordes of festival revelers clogging every walkway and alley between the stable and the battlement gates. Candlewood benches stretched along courtyard walls, burdened with casks of mead, slabs of white goat cheese, and platters of flat naan bread stacked in high columns. Dogs lurked beneath tables, skulking in wait for scraps, shrinking from kicking boots, yelps mixing with the occasional deep bark or growl.

Sihan traded a quarter falcon for a mug of mead and a feasting plate, then struggled on, feeling like hot irons were being thrust through the muscle of his leg. Blisters had also ripened and burst in his new boots, leaving a squelching of raw flesh to chafe against hard leather.

'Sihan! Sihan!' Familiar voices jostled against laughter, children's shrieks, never-ending drumbeats and the lyric strum of lyres. Through the throng, Sihan caught sight of a line of youths, Tejas among them, weaving and dancing in drunken rhythm to the driving, pulsing, heart-quickening thump of skin drums, so frequently colliding with every maiden passing the chances of accident were rendered negligible. Tejas called to him, waving him over to join them, before being lost to view.

A stab of wintry emptiness pierced Sihan and his mead lost all taste. Soon his friends would be gone. Their companies had been called out for duty on border outposts skirting the kingdom. He did not feel up to celebrating that. Nor anything else. The festival celebrated rebirth – a call to the gods to return the land to life after the forthcoming killing sleep of winter. But everything he knew of the impending future promised death. What remnants he had dredged up of the old comfortable joy of the Fire Rituals drained from him.

In a brief gap in the crowd, he sighted Kheran downing a tankard of unknown brew, a maiden laughing merrily up at him.

Too great a distance to call and be heard, and Kheran's grin and encircling arm about the girl's waist made Sihan doubt his friend would foreswear the pretty girl's company for his.

He decided to go far enough to sit in thought by himself. He could not dance with his bad leg, not that he wished to anyway, and the last thing he wanted was to sour his friends' celebration with his dark mood. Without his father, a feeling of abandonment coursed over him, followed by aching yearning, for Graycor, for everything he had lost.

He reached the fortress gates and passed beneath the grim bulwarks. Beyond the battlements, shouts of revellers resounded across the valley, thousands drawn to the festival. Bonfires blazed on slopes and crowned every rise, bright and glittering, as if stars had fallen from the Heavens to litter the ground in burning light.

Booming drumbeats matched the exuberant dancing of youths and maidens circling flames. Several girls skipped past Sihan as he wandered out the postern. Throwing petals at him, they giggled before racing down the hill to the river.

'I hope those aren't mistflowers they're wasting on you.' Gerein stepped from the shadowed battlement into the light of a torch, yawning, white teeth gleaming in his sun-browned face. He brushed the petals from Sihan's hair and shoulders.

Sihan nodded at the gorytos strapped to Gerein's back. 'Isn't it a bit late to be shooting anything? Or is that just for show?'

The archer's face grew grave and preoccupied where a moment before he had been his usual teasing self. 'I'm on duty.'

'At night?'

Gerein stared through Sihan. 'Evil doesn't sleep.'

Sihan arched an eyebrow and burst out laughing. 'Evil doesn't sleep?'

Gerein's eyes snapped back into focus. 'Did I say that?' He yawned once more. 'My brain must be addled.'

'Are you still after that man? The one in the marsh?'

The archer's expression closed down once more. 'That's none of your concern, Sihan. Now be a good boy, and go fuck a maid.' He flicked his brown hair back over his shoulder and smoothed down his white tabard as another group of girls giggled past. Grabbing Sihan by the arm, Gerein steered him down the hill. 'This is the last night of the Fire Rituals. A *log* could get bedded tonight.'

As if to confirm Gerein's assertion, another girl sauntered past, swaying her hips. Her intent gaze fixed upon the archer before she joined a bevy of maidens dancing around a nearby bonfire. Gerein winked at Sihan and strode toward the girls.

With no intention of following Gerein's advice, Sihan continued toward the river. Several maidens gathered in a group near the causeway, laughing and chatting. At his approach, they fell silent, eyeing him closely. When they spoke once more, their voices were low and soft, and their swift half-hidden glances in his direction indicated their sharp interest. Sihan wanted to turn tail. Instead he folded his arms across his chest as if that barrier might ward them off. A group of young men spared his dignity by running up to the girls and grabbing them round their waists, hauling them to a fire to dance.

Careful to avoid catching the eye of any other females, Sihan hurried on, hoping to lose himself in the darkness of stands of sallees between bonfires. The cloying, dank scent of rotting leaves and rough bark comforted him, but even there peace and solace eluded him, with loose children screaming as they raced and dodged around tree trunks, adults singing bawdy peasant ditties as they searched for fuel. Sihan stopped at the edge of the stand of trees.

Nearby, a group of youths kicked glowing coals from a fire into a shallow trench with their boots, then egged on another who had pulled off his boots and stockings to dance screaming across them. He staggered and fell in heap at Sihan's feet, blonde hair falling over his face. 'Oh, Gods, oh, Gods,' he cried, clutching at his soles. 'That hurt!'

Sihan could not suppress a faint curving of his lips. 'Why did you do it, then?'

The youth stared up at him. 'If a man can make it from one side to the other across the coals without burning his feet, then he will have long life.' He examined his feet. 'I'm totally screwed.'

Sihan grinned, the youth's burning feet calling his attention away from his own hurt. 'That's just a folk tale.'

His mother had told him the story when he was young, though embellished as he had come to realise her stories often were. She had said men had once walked willingly into flame, given up their lives, burned, and as a reward, the gods had given them eternal life.

The youth grinned back and took bread from Sihan's plate. 'I'm Maiet.'

'My name's–'

'Sihan, I know. Your reputation precedes you. But that's way too many syllables for a humble soul like me to cope with, so I'll just call you Sih.'

Taking an instant liking to the grinning youth, Sihan asked, 'What reputation?'

Maiet's brow creased in a frown of concentration. 'Which should I start with?'

'How many are there?'

'Lots!' Maiet stuffed a lump of goat cheese in his mouth and spoke around it. 'You're famous . . . or infamous . . . I never can figure out which is the right word.'

'For what?' Sihan regretted the question before it was half out his mouth, hoping Maiet would not mention Jaien.

'Well, for starters . . . riding the Death Gorge.'

Relieved, Sihan admitted, 'That was Aurion, not me.'

Maiet took a swig from a flask he unhooked from his belt. 'Best wine in Mirador,' he boasted. 'Guaranteed to knock you out flat.' He barely paused for breath before continuing, 'The thing you're most famous for is thumbing your nose at Gerhas and the king and getting away with it.'

The smile faded from Sihan's face. 'I think they found a way to settle that score.'

'What? Being forced to stay in Mirador?' Maiet took another swig. 'Trust me; it's better than being commissioned.'

'Are you in the army?'

Maiet upturned the flask completely, draining every last drop. 'King's Command, under Travall.'

Sihan raised an eyebrow. 'You look too young for that sort of duty.' In truth, Maiet looked barely nineteen winters.

Maiet laughed. 'No one's too young any more.'

And that was true enough. Sihan cocked his head to one side. 'Your accent, I don't recognise it.'

'I'm from Maroden.'

'Maroden? That's a way off. How did you come to be here?'

'It's a good tale. You've probably heard it – how they decided who was going to be Duke of Maroden, after the incumbent duke and his entire family got sunk off Crase?'

'Sunk?'

Maiet warmed to his rapt audience, reaching for Sihan's mug and downing the dregs in one gulp. 'Ship went down with all hands. Fast way to end a dynasty. After that, all seven tribes of Maroden put forward their leaders to be the next duke. You'll appreciate this, being a horseman. They decided to let their horses make the choice. They agreed they would ride their stallions into the middle of the square at the fortress of Maroden on midwinter's eve, and whichever horse neighed first, its rider would be the next duke. I was squire to Knight Commander Darog, one of the seven leaders. When I found out about the plan, I snuck off down to the square with his stallion. Then I got one of the in season bloodhorse mares. I introduced them and they just went at it. The next day, when Darog rode the stallion into the square, it recognised the site and got all excited, and was the first to neigh. All the other contenders for the title immediately appointed Darog, Duke of Maroden. When he found out what I'd done, he promoted me to serve in Mirador.' Maiet erupted in laughter.

Sihan felt an instant camaraderie he had not felt except for Tejas and Kheran. Maiet was the only truly happy soul he had met since coming to Mirador, almost joyous in his disregard of the darkness seeming to cloak everyone else.

But only a heartbeat later Maiet keeled over, drunk to the eyeballs. Sihan sat down his plate and set Maiet against a log, then picked up a bough of jarrah and another of sallee and threw them on the closest bonfire, following with a sprinkling of agaric from a pouch at his belt which stretched the flames skyward. His contribution earned him the right to sit by the flames, and he settled on soft turf beside the stand of trees, eating what Maiet had left him of his meal, staring into the conflagration, wondering how long it would be before Maiet regained consciousness.

The youth's carefree abandon and his stories, reminded Sihan of his mother, her stories, his rapture in her tales. Lost in thoughts of childhood, he recalled her dark eyes afire as she wove fine legends. The smell of baking dough merging with the smoky scent of burning wood brought to mind the oatmeal bannocks she had baked. Girls spinning, long hair braided with chains of snowdrops, reminded him of the pale ribbons his mother braided into midnight hair that twirled as she danced.

Shrieks echoed across the valley. Several girls raced down the slope from the fortress. In their wake a line of drummers filed from the main fortress gates, pounding a deep, driving sound from skin drums. A procession of torch-bearing soldiers, all wearing full dress regalia beneath the Mirador surcoat, wound their way to the river like a long white serpent.

Sihan stood, as did everyone in eyeshot. The pageant wove down to the riverbank, drummers never ceasing their dark, deliberate beat, a slow, weighted pulse aligning every heart to its measure. Drummers across the valley took up the rhythm, a booming cadence seeming to emanate from the ground itself. It struck Sihan to the core, reverberating through him like the kick of a colt in its dam's womb, the interminable crash of waves against rock, life beat of the Living Sphere.

In the torchlight, a solitary rider on a pale horse walked toward the oil-black river, the man clad in a moon-blanched surcoat.

The king.

Crowds gathered along the riverbanks and girls cast garlands of flowers into dark water lapping the edges of a wooden barge piled high with wood. One girl stepped apart from the others and strode toward the vessel. She climbed a boarding plank before it was withdrawn by soldiers.

With long poles, men shoved the barge away from the bank. It slowly drifted off with the current. When it reached midstream, an archer, standing on the bank – Sihan knew at once it was Gerein – drew an arrow and dipped the tip into burning oil. He fired it into the timber on the barge, igniting it in a rush of flame.

Sihan wanted to scream a warning. Did they not see the girl upon the barge? But all sound choked in his throat as a silken whisper caressed his ears.

Fret not for her, beloved. She is neither real nor in any mortal danger, not in this world.

He turned, not wanting to, gaze trapped by a shimmer of motion in the tangle of sallee trunks. Clad in a robe spectral pale, the girl of his nightmares glided, keeping cover between him and clear sight of her. At the edges of thought, notes hung upon the air, the resonant brush of air through bone, overlaid on the screaming, screaming, screaming as another girl burned. The spectre clad in flesh beckoned him to follow, and he, wanting to resist, but will mired in sludge, did her bidding. Clear of the nearest peasants, she stepped free from the shield wall of trees to stand before him. No one looked her way as if she did not exist. She smiled at Sihan and said as if reading his very thoughts, 'I make myself known only to you, beloved.'

He recoiled. 'Don't call me that.'

Her lips curved into a barren smile. 'What would you have me call you?'

'Nothing, you zingar witch!' Sihan tore his mind and gaze away, toward the blazing barge where a girl burned and screamed to the beat of drum and roar of fire. Every muscle, every fibre, urged him to run to her, to stop her pain and the screaming that froze thought.

With one ghost-pale hand the zingar beckoned to the withering form of the girl incinerating to ash on the burning barge. 'No pain she suffers can ever match that she inflicted on the Living Sphere. Behold the spirit-form of the false queen, burned to cinders as she so burned the world.'

Spirit-form? Sihan stared at the barge. Was the burning girl nothing but a ghost conjured by the zingar? Was she real? She looked real to him. Sounded real.

The barge sailed on down the river, winding its way to the mouth, then out to the sea. No one moved, nor seemed to see the horror Sihan witnessed, not even the king, a stark, silent sentinel on the riverbank. Only when the barge faded from view, did Callinor dismount and walk alone back to the fortress, leading his grey stallion. Somewhere from the darkness came the mournful cry of a currawong.

The zingar's unwanted voice curled into Sihan's ears like a coil of smoke. 'Heed me, beloved of my heart.'

He could not shut her out, but he could fight her now he knew what she was. 'Don't try your zingar tricks on me.'

Her lips curled in disdain. 'Whatever I may be, I am no zingar.'

'Others can see you.' Derision coated his voice, though with every word he uttered he felt he walked on fire. 'Hessarde saw you, and that's what he called you.'

'Hessarde!' she hissed. 'An errand boy for a man turned blind.'

She could mean one man only. Tension coursed through Sihan's muscles. 'Say that to Areme's face.'

Something flashed in the deep dark depths of her eyes, something wild. Quick damped, but he sensed it still, lurking in cover, like an animal trapped. Beyond doubt, she feared Areme. The knowledge emboldened him. With all the authority he could cobble together, he said, 'Get off from me!'

She braced her spine. 'I cannot, now I have found you. Know you not we are bonded for eternity? Are you also blind? None shall part us no matter how they might try.' The words, harsh, raw, strangled in her throat as if abrading a wound with a scourer doused in salt.

Laughter and gaiety mocked them through the trees, children and revelers oblivious to this fraught battle of word and mind. The zingar waved a hand at a camp in the distance where maidens danced. 'You wonder not why you turn from all these women who claw for your attention?'

'I don't wonder at all. I don't want them. I want–' He stopped, baffled to silence, his mind, his thoughts, his every fibre locking to half-formed images. The world shivered. Shadows and stars wove around him, around her, whispering memories.

The girl in a snowstorm with flowing midnight hair and burning eyes, disappeared.

As through a veil, that lifeless girl he had seen once before, stripped of all colour, replaced the zingar. A shadow image, yet somehow more real. Not one muscle moved, but she seemed to curl into a ball, shoulders drawn, eyes cast down, her entire body folding into itself as if she expected a whipping. Every breath shortened, gasped and bolted down as if she stole air from those more deserving. Beneath straggling hair that fell across her eyes, he spied tears fringing her dark lashes, cleaving tracks through streaks of dirt down gaunt cheeks. When she caught him staring at her, her features crumbled into desolation and loss, her eyes those of a flayed dog begging mercy. Her voice trailed out from trembling lips in the frailest of whispers. 'Don't despise me.'

Everything within Sihan became cold and heavy as a singing stone. 'Why would I?'

Behind her eyes, something jerked. In that instant, for the space between heartbeats, he saw her in brightness, in colours not sepia and the fall of leaves. He knew her in a world before the fall from grace, before tears. A moment, so full it held a lifetime within its narrow bonds, stretched between them.

'I–I know you.' What was he saying? He did not know her. Yet somehow . . .

Her gaze fled from his uncertain eyes, her voice softening to the pale shade of doves. 'Not yet, my love. But I am trapped within your heart as you are caught within mine. You will come to know me as I have always known you.'

Loneliness stabbed him like a blade, the world stripped bare of solace, and he knew it was her heart he felt, her aching solitude coursing through his veins. He stared hard at her, trying to remember, to know all she needed him to recall. But the colours had faded and all he could see was gangling arms shrouded by an ill-fitting moth-worn kirtle of plain wool girdled by thready rope. And her eyes. Her eyes. The deep hurt locked beneath the surface sorrowing, her face the visage of a creature abandoned.

A tempest fermented in his chest. 'How have they hurt you?' The words came from lifetimes distant, but he knew them his.

'Sorrow not for me, Anise. I live only by death's grace. Naught can touch me now but your pain and I would spare you such.' The words were truth upon her lips.

Breath stopped in his throat. She was here, so close he could feel her heat, not death's cold pallor. But the hollows circling her eyes, the worthlessness emanating from every part of her somehow gave her claim truth. Everything within him a void, he folded his arms around her, drew her into a wordless embrace. He needed her, her warmth, against the cold shivering across his skin and into his heart.

Her hands trembled beneath his, quivering like the string of an archer's bow after an arrow's release. A swift glance up. Their gazes caught and held. 'You have only ever spoken truth to me.' She reached out and touched fingertips to his cheek in the barest whisper of a caress. 'Your eyes are the truest things I ever saw.' She drew him down, down, into ageless depths and a desolate, aching, desperate kiss.

At her back, a currawong screeched from the sallees, arced up to blend into the night sky. With a jerk like a trapped beast stuck with a spear point, she broke loose of Sihan's arms. An intense expression of concentration warred with bewilderment in her eyes. Her tone shifted to warning. 'The shadows are stealing me away. There is no time, Anise, for all I must say, all you must know.'

Sihan's gut lurched. A haze enveloped his senses, dizziness as though he had sat up too fast. A thin treble of a flute wove between the branches of sallees. Light – faint and blue – shone through the darkness. A breeze picked up, slapping the hem of his cloak against his leggings, rattling dead branches together like bones.

She grabbed his hand, pressing his palm to her lips, then she released him. Before he could gather his addled wits, she backed away, dissolved back into the form of the zingar.

The dark girl observed him like a predator, a wolf, dark eyes suspicious and watchful.

Mind muddled, he took a stumbling step back, hissing, 'Remove your phantom life from me.'

'I bid you stay.' Her voice was a noose pulling him up short.

'Who are you?' he demanded. 'Where did the other girl go? What do you want of me?'

'I have come to give sight to one who refuses to see.' Transfixing him with a hard, unyielding stare, she motioned to the trees. 'Behold your future and your past.'

Hoof falls, halting. Crack of fallen twigs. Between the trees, gleaming in the pale light of a ring of candles, a white mare emerged, eyes blazing cold blue fire, an apparition composed of winding mist.

Fear knifed in; the nightmare night of wolves and horned demons returned. This was the mare who had died. A living ghost. Panic gripped him. He tensed to run. But every move, every thought, was wrapped in congealing mire, trapping him in this world of unreality.

The zingar's voice eviscerated him like a sword. 'You try to flee but have you not seen already, blind one, wherever you fly, you cannot escape.' She glided toward the white mare, wind tugging at the cloth of her robe. 'You know her, as you know her get. Like her son, she was born in death.' Her face became lifeless as a corpse; empty eyes glittered black. She stared right through him to his bones. In a voice more doleful dirge, she whispered, 'Your past is death. Your future the same – littered with corpse flesh of your making. Your future is a sword gored by blood.'

He fought against the lies in her words. 'I've refused the sword.'

Mockery curved the edges of her disdainful smile. 'The sword has not refused you. It awaits the day you will know yourself.'

Sihan shivered. 'I know myself.' But hard on the heels of his assertion, he envisaged Jaien so clearly he imagined the knight there, before him.

Knowing eyes probed him. 'I think not. So let me give you eyes to see what you refuse to see. The white stallion does not harm you the way it harms others. It is a sign, whether you choose to see it or not. You are Senfaren.'

Winter cold chilled him. She meant Senfari, and all roads to that title had slammed shut in his face.

The smile soured further on her lips. 'That was never your path, blind one. Behold your true path.' Unmoving, she stood, skin luminescent in the moonlight. Then black mist, white mist wreathed about Sihan.

A wasteland unfolded before him, grey wind kicked up eddies of ash. Barren twilight lit earth strewn with corpses. And on a knoll above a field of death stood a white stallion with a horn. Horror twisted Sihan's stomach. He knew this. He had seen this. He wanted to clench his eyes shut, to not see what he knew was to come.

Hot breath touched Sihan's cheek, something grabbed at his arm. He blinked, saw the zingar standing close. Stared beyond her. Saw nothing but darkness in the trees. Heard nothing but the sigh of wind through withered leaves.

Sihan shuddered, hugged his arms around his body. The heat of the bonfire could not ward off the ice in his veins, as if his soul had been torn from his body and death had shrouded him in its wintry mantle.

Fingers traced warmth back into his skin. 'Now you start to see as I see.'

Sihan stared at her, dazed. At her touch, her voice – all thought, all dreams, all visions, fled.

'Tell me your name.' Regret, and a deep sense of foreboding washed over him before the words were half out of his mouth.

She hesitated, then her voice came out as a whisper. 'Niameh.' Without another word, she glided deep into the trees and disappeared into the night.

Sihan stared after her, rolled the name unspoken on his tongue. *Niameh*. Unease clawed at him, half-remembered images of . . . what?

Night breeze touched his burning cheeks, like whispered breath. Like death. Cold, so cold.

He turned toward the fortress. Began to run as fast as his damaged leg would allow. Faster. Faster. As though running for his life. He barged past revelers, ran to his room, slammed the door behind.

In the darkness, his breath came loud, harsh. But not loud enough to drown out a distant whisper upon the night.

You are not Sihan.

He slid down the door, huddled on the stone floor with his arms around his knees, shaking. He rocked back and forth. Clenched his fist. 'My name is Sihan.' The words grated through clenched teeth. 'I am Sihan, son of Armindras.'

His father's name dragged warmth back to him – life – though his hands still shook. *I am Sihan*. But then why had the girl called him Anise? And why had he let her?

Chapter 27

Moon Pool

Key in hand, Orlanda pulled her cloak close and hurried to the eastern wall of her chamber. The starkness of the grey-black stone was masked by woollen rugs draped from ceiling to floor. She slid back the heavy folds curtaining a hidden door.

Her father had ordered it locked after she had been found wandering among the common folk once too often. It had been years since she had possessed the key to freedom. Her hand trembled. Now her goal was in reach, fear washed over her. What folly was this? Was she prepared to give herself to a man who had rejected her till now? And he might still deny her – he had only asked her to pray. What then?

Her hand balled into a fist. She must cut him off, proceed alone, fight her own way to freedom.

Heartbeats passed. She pressed her eyelids closed, recalling his voice, the almost-promise of freedom on his lips. He would save her. He must.

She slid the key into the lock. The bolt clicked smoothly as she turned it. A slight push, and the scent of old stone greeted her on a counter-draft along the passage.

She removed the key and closed the door behind her, pausing long enough to let her eyes adjust to the dark. Creeping cautiously along the narrow passage, she scuffed uneven stonework with felt shoes, doing her best to keep silent. Sconces lit the way, thickening air at intervals with smoke. The passage twisted and turned, following the outer walls of the inner ward, then branched toward the outer ward of the fortress, to the eastern tower that emptied upon a little used area near the curtain wall.

The key grew warm in her sweating palm, and she slid it into a pocket in the fold of her cloak. When she reached the stairwell to the eastern tower, she hesitated, breathing in dust-still air. Was she mad? Was Areme toying with her? Perhaps the door at the foot of the tower would be locked.

She started down the curving stairs, descending three flights, air stone-cold. Midway, a torch flared, testament to the thoroughness of the castle servants in their duty. When she reached the door, she paused, listening. Hearing naught but silence beyond, Orlanda pushed against the wood. The door swung open with nary a sound. Breathing a sigh of relief, she pulled the cowl over her head and peeked outside.

The area stood deserted. She crept out, caution marking every step. Even though the distance was short, untoward haste would like as not catch unwanted attention. Watchmen patrolling the guardwalk might notice and sound an alarm. She forced herself to break concealment and cross the ground at a steady walk. Once against the outer wall, she flattened her back to it and took her bearings.

Men and women crossed from the ward to the wicket farther along the curtain wall, some walking rapidly, some slow. Orlanda hugged the shadows, seeking a point where she could merge into the stream of traffic entering and leaving the fortress. When a detail of soldiers approached, she melted into the dark beneath the guardwalk. Men marched up the steps, then took up the positions of the guard they replaced, leaning in embrasures between the merlons. Certain she had evaded notice, Orlanda edged along, then stepped in line behind a man hefting a sack over his shoulder, raising one hand to ward away light falling on her face from any one of a myriad of torches.

She reached the wicket. In front of her, the man with the sack went through without challenge, but as she went to pass, a red-haired guard placed his boot up on the wall, blocking her path.

'Whither bound, sister?' he asked, glinting eyes raking her up and down.

A year's worth of practised Common fled from Orlanda's mind in a heartbeat. She grasped at a reason, 'I–I–'

The guard laughed. 'No need for shyness.' Not shifting his obstructing leg, he regarded her. 'I'm off duty soon. Why don't you wait here till I'm free? I can wheedle a room at the inn. No need to roll around on damp grass, though I'll do that too if you're keen.'

Affronted, but at a loss what to do without giving herself away, Orlanda backed away, but the man was too quick. He grabbed her arm. Before Orlanda could stop him, he flicked back her cowl, and froze.

Discovered, she fell back on years of training. 'How dare you touch me!'

Abruptly, the guard pressed Orlanda back into the shadows of the wicket. 'Shh.' He leaned out from the archway of the gate, looked left and right, then back to her. For a moment they both stood still, staring at each other. Then he gripped her wrist, and pulled her along the passage to the outer gateway.

'What are you doing?' she demanded.

'Shh. Keep your voice down.' He looked beyond the wicket, standing tense, listening, watching. Then he turned to her, pulling her cowl back into place. 'Tread softly, Highness. And don't hesitate to raise an alarm in event of trouble.'

It took her several heartbeats to master her surprise. 'Why are you doing this?'

The guard smiled at her. 'I have orders, Highness. I was told if ever you came to my gate seeking passage I was to say, "Favour for a favour", and speed you on your way.'

Orlanda almost kissed him with relief. 'You're Jaien's man.'

'Yes.' With a slight bow, he said, 'Camar, if it pleases.' He hesitated as he released her wrist. 'You'll forget what I said?'

Orlanda flashed him a quick smile. 'If you'll forget I passed. Favour for a favour.'

He inclined his head, then turned to the next person scuttling through the wicket. 'Hold! What's in that sack! Empty it, right now!'

Protests and curses filling the air behind her, Orlanda scurried away. When she was certain no one followed, she breathed deeply. The fragrance of burning candlewood hung on the air, sweet and pungent. She peered toward the sprinkled sparkle of fires on the plain, on the valley inclines, among the trees. Figures danced against flames, swirls of frenzied movement. Torch fires bobbed and swayed between gaps in trunks.

Avoiding revellers, Orlanda made her way to the cliffs above the ocean. Black clouds skirted the sky, shrouding the moon for extended intervals. She shivered, feeling as though she was moving through weird, living shadows. Then a gradual radiance sifted through the clouds as the moon appeared, a massive silver ball.

Exposed, even under the veil of night, Orlanda hurried up the trail, leaving behind the festivities, listening all the while in case she was followed. Moonbar and gloom bathed the path as it wound between salt scrub, curving toward a precipice overlooking the ocean. A bleak place, graced only by tall stones, the ocean stretched to one side, the valley of bonfires the other.

Sea tang was strong in her nostrils, salt-spray damp against her cheeks. Balmy wind moaned around the singing stones, making wild music, gusting around black slabs of tourmaline. A long way below, moon-whitened waves crashed against the shore.

Orlanda drew her cloak closer and stood in the windbreak of the largest stone, wisps of gold hair flaring around her face. Alone, unprotected, she stood beneath piercing stars. Blood pounded fiercely in her veins. As her eyes became attuned to the dark, a solitary figure emerged from the shade of a tall stone.

Moonbeams fell between dense cloudbanks, lighting Areme afire, whetting every sharp contour of his face, casting cobalt shadows into the depressions beneath smooth cheekbones. His eyes shone, unnerving in their brightness. Long black hair rippled over his shoulders, flaring with silver shafts of moonfire.

Her legs leadened, refusing to move. What madness had brought her here?

Wind tore at her cloak, lashing it back and forth, as if urging her to action. She pulled open the cloak, revealing her nightdress. Keeping her eyes locked on Areme's, she untied the laces, and drew apart the diaphanous fabric. Current flowed about her, making her aware of her whole body, nervous . . . but also wildly alive. Heart thumping, she twisted the silver clasp pinning her hair, loosed a mane of gold to shudder down past her shoulders. Then she scraped the slippers from her feet leaving her feet cold upon rough cliff stone.

He studied her in silence. When he made no move, she trembled, sensing all her dreams, all her plans striking against the wall of his indifference. She dug her nails into her palms. She would not beg.

Heedless of her will, her knees gave way. She fell to the granite, hot tears sliding down her cheeks, the loss of hope bitter, shame coiling round her heart, a constricting, killing python.

Areme approached, warily, as though toward a deer that might startle to flight. He settled to one knee. 'Don't cry,' he whispered, picking up her cloak and drawing it about her shoulders.

Orlanda bit the inside of her cheek, tasted salt. 'You asked me here. Why? If not to–' Grief-roughened words died in her throat.

Areme touched her cheek, palm warm against her skin. 'I shouldn't have. You're just a child.'

Breath hot and painful, she grasped his hand, pulling it to her chest. 'Is this the breast of a child? You shouldn't have asked. I shouldn't have come. But we're here now.'

He swore, hesitated, leaned in to enfold her in his arms, rough wool of his cloak harsh against her skin. As he silently stroked her hair, Orlanda buried herself in the scent of him – horses, leather. He was warm, so warm. How could he be so cold?

As if reading her thoughts, he drew back, stubbled jaw grazing her skin. 'I swore an oath,' he rasped as though the words scraped raw his throat. 'I thought I could break it. I can't.'

There was only one oath he could mean. Hope fought through a mire of misery. If a knight's oath was all that stood between them, she would remove it. She clutched at the edges of his cloak. 'I absolve you of your oath.'

His fingers tightened on her arms, force enough to bruise. 'You can't.'

'I can. I do.'

He cast his eyes down. 'You misunderstand. *I* can't do this.'

Voice taut with rising anger, she stiffened her back, demanding, 'Can't or won't? If you won't, then I'll find someone who will.'

Long anguished moments stretched between them, the only sound his measured breathing. Then his hands weighed even heavier upon her. 'Don't court foolishness. No man in Mirador will touch you. They're all sworn to the king and won't break their oaths, however great you make the temptation.' Every word was a sword thrust, brutal, deliberate, meant to hurt her to submission.

Orlanda struggled against his grip, her father's will of stone melding with her own urgent need to hurt, to punish, to plead. There had to be a man who cared naught for the king's edicts, who she could bend to her will. Unbidden, Sihan's image formed in her mind. Reckless, courageous, defiant. He had risked death by riding the white stallion. What else might he not risk with some encouragement? And he was comely, in an unfinished way, so much like Areme that if she closed her eyes and mind, she might fool herself he was the man she wanted. She ground out the provocation, 'Sihan has taken no oaths.'

'Sihan!' The name exploded from Areme's mouth like a curse.

She had scored off him. Keeping her eyes upon him, she matched his wounding words with her own more subtle poisoned barbs. 'I'll make certain he doesn't refuse me.' Jutting her chin, she taunted, 'He's handsome, and I daresay more than willing.'

'You'd lie with frere?'

'He's not frere. I've seen the way he looks at me. And I've heard he was one of the men who called my arse perfect. He won't say no. I won't let him.' She met Areme's flint-hard gaze. 'If the man I love won't have me, what else can I do?'

'You can do better than a stable boy.'

'The lowest man in Mirador is worth more than Valoren.'

Once more, Areme's fingers closed around her arms like iron bands, merciless. 'You're not lying with that boy.' His lips claimed hers, savage, bruising.

Orlanda stifled a whimper. She had driven him past his indifference, but she did not want it to be like this. Never like this. She forced words against the punishing kiss. 'Forgive me, Areme. Don't hurt me!'

Areme recoiled as though she had struck him. Eyes, silvered and haunted, he stared at her as if he were seeing her for the first time. Words tore from his throat. 'Who are you?'

A world of hurt layered the question, lay exposed to view in his eyes before they shuttered. She had hurt him, hard, somehow, and though she had wanted to, needed to, this was wrong, everything was wrong. Rubbing her bruised arms, she said, 'You know who I am.'

Stars turned as they stared at each other, his eyes masked and unreadable. She trembled all over when again he leaned close to her, brow resting against hers, strands of black hair brushing against her face. 'You're sixteen winters,' he said. 'When you give yourself to a man, it should be for love, not out of desperation.'

'And if desperation is all I have?' Her voice broke once more. 'Areme, please. I–I don't want Valoren to be the first. I don't want him. Ever.' She bit her bottom lip, then tentatively trailed her lips along his cheek. 'I want you. Only you. For all time. But if this night is all I can have, then show me love. Just once. I could bear any storm if I felt someone could love me, even for one night.'

His eyes darkened. 'What has Callinor done to you?'

Her only answer was a whisper. 'Love me.'

'You ask the impossible.'

She fought the flat finality in his voice. 'Nothing is impossible.'

Areme drew a ragged breath. 'I swore to my wife an oath I cannot break.'

A door slammed in her face could not have shut her out more completely. Vision blurred against agony. She dragged air into lungs closed down as if a tonne of rock had crushed her.

Wife.

With one word the bright vision of love requited and freedom gained evaporated. Her hands dropped away from him, lifeless lumps of clay. 'You–You're bonded. I–I didn't know.' Inside, she screamed, a wordless cry of pain. How could she not have known?

Shame swallowed her like darkness. Her fault, all of it. He was bonded, and she had not known. Had everyone known but her? What sort of fool was she? And Areme. Why had he not just said so?

She looked at him, really looked, but there was nothing in his eyes anymore, his face a bleak landscape. Cold ate at her, deep into her bones. She had hurt him. Must have hurt him every time she had tried to tempt him. Mocked vows inviolate.

How blind she had been. She must amend her fault. It was her task to right it. Steeling herself, ice spreading through her veins, she said, 'You've not dishonoured your vow. Go, now. Go to her.'

'I can't.' In the quiet, his jagged breath caught her ear, grief held tight in check.

Everything told her the path to knowledge held desolation, but she strode into that dark abyss. 'Why not?'

Shuddering, he whispered devastation. 'She's dead.'

Orlanda dared not even breathe. How many wrongs had she tried to visit upon him, and all for her own foolish caprice? Unable to find words, she trailed her fingers through his hair.

Forehead resting against hers, he turned his face until his lips brushed lightly against her skin, warm and moist. 'You're so like her.' The words trembled against her mouth.

Orlanda did not move, but within she pulled away. She had thought to use Sihan in such a manner. And now Areme was overlaying his wife's image over one he cared for not. Perhaps she deserved this, but she did not want it. 'I'm not her.'

Heated breath came against her throat. 'Shasirre . . .'

Shasirre. Your wife. In his voice there was nothing but anguish, and she felt no presence but his loneliness and the despair engulfing him.

He needed this . . . pretence, this sweet, anguished lie. And she? Certainty filled her. If this was all she would have of him, so be it. For one night then, let them pretend they were what each of them needed the other to be. One night to last her until the end of her days.

She slid her arm round his neck, in no way confident of anything she did, knowing only the burning heat within as she touched him, the intense warmth in her loins. Eyes locked on eyes, his, black wells in the darkness. Deep enough in which to drown. And she wanted to drown. Needed it. Just for tonight. A night of forever.

Stillness settled over them both. Despair's sharp edges softened. Slowly, so very slowly, she moved her mouth over his, tasting, exploring, discovering him. And as she did, a feeling welled within her that it was not so much discovery, but more a sense of getting to know him again, as if it had been too long, a lifetime since they had kissed. Yet they had never kissed, not like this.

Her fingers trembled upon the laces of his tunic. He discarded his cloak, laid it behind her, let her lift his tunic over his head. Dark eyes stared into hers as he unbuckled his belt with slow deliberation, then tossed it aside. Eyes, all shadowed black, stared into hers. He breathed harder as she undid the laces on his leggings, opened the fine wool, eased it down to his knees. His manhood stood, erect and proud, a sculpted summons.

He trailed his fingers along her collar bone, a feather's kiss.

Her heated gaze raked over his body, but her fingers bespoke the lie as they trembled from his jaw to his throat, then down the line of fine hair on his chest to where it thickened in a mat of black curls. Before her hand closed to its goal, Areme caught it within his, stared hard at her. His other hand brushed her arm, raising hairs upon it as gooseflesh erupted on her skin.

He drew her down with him, unresisting as he gently lowered her upon his cloak. He pushed up the fluttering folds of her nightdress, stretched his body over her, covered her, every movement a whisper as their bodies closed. His weight pressed down, her breasts cushioning his hard chest, her smooth cheek resting against his, black nest of curls brushing against gold as their hips met. The hard unyielding granite below the cloak pricked her back, buttocks and thighs, but she did not care. Areme was with her. Her beautiful Areme. Everything she had dreamed, and none of it.

Hesitation marked every foray of her fingers down his naked back. Taut, smooth muscles strained beneath her touch. He lifted his face and they stared at each other; their concentration so total upon each other nothing else existed.

Her breath caught.

Everything about him was different, this stranger who stroked her breasts, who did not seem to know her. He caressed the quivering flesh down to her stomach, with such zealous worship her body might have been an altar to Shahedur. His face stripped bare of all the protective masks he wore. Nothing passive there. Nothing indifferent. Just raw, raw need and want.

He pushed one knee to splay her legs, eased himself between slick folds, stroking, stroking, a slow, burning, torturous teasing. His breathing ragged, his face contorted in concentration. Ebony hair spilled around her face like a veil.

Their bodies locked in one convulsive motion. Orlanda gasped, bit down on her lip, just enough to feel it, stifling the moan. Muscles straining; two as one, bound; flesh to flesh, skin to skin. She wound her ankles around his waist and pushed her hips to greet every stroke, begging, pleading.

She wanted to tell him, with her body, with her very being – how right it felt, how perfect. But her voice came only in a wordless, broken moan. She loved him, sought to drive away his pain, and hers, as long as flesh and blood could endure it.

'Shasirre,' Areme gasped, eyes closed, perfect lips forming another woman's name. 'Shasirre . . .'

'Yes,' she breathed, holding him tight, needing him, needing to feel as he did, to know this all-consuming love holding him bound to the memory of a corpse. 'Yes.' *Believe it. Want her. Take me.*

He swept her away on a surging, cresting riptide of feeling, no gulf between his reality and hers, his need and hers.

'Shasirre . . . Shasirre,' a gasp around disjointed words. His rhythm sped to rapid staccato. Every lean muscle of him clenched and tightened. He jerked with the force of sweet, irresistible release, sending rushing heat deep inside her. She threw back her head as her own pleasure spiked.

His face softened. She listened to their beating hearts, feeling the rhythmic thickening and ebbing of him within her.

They eased apart, lay in each others arms, panting and trembling. Windsong, stone-song washed over them as they stilled to languid exhaustion. His face pillowed upon her breast, she touched his cheek. A child's plea slipped past her unguarded tongue. 'Promise you'll never leave me.'

Areme caught her fingers with his lips, eyes opening to glitter in the moonlight. 'I promise.'

She shivered. It was not her to whom he made that vow. But she would not think about that. Silently, she made her own solemn oath. Part of him was hers now, if not the whole, whether he willed it in the cold light of day or no. She would never let him go.

Beneath the thin light of the moon his skin glowed pale. A thin white scar lined his chest – the lance wound from the tournament. When she traced its outline with her fingers, Areme gasped.

She asked, 'Does it hurt still?'

'For eternity.' He gazed deep into her eyes as though searching for something, then pulled her hard against him once more.

The night grew deeper.

At length, Areme eased himself from her embracing arms, rolled to his feet, slowly dressed, then drew his cloak around him. She regarded him silently, certain he knew his error now, watched for recrimination, accusation.

None came. Instead, he held out his hand, eyes dark and measuring. 'Come.'

Uncertain, she placed her hand within his. As she did, a current of living energy seemed to pass between them. She stared at him, startled, but all he said once more was, 'Come.'

'Where?'

'To pray.' He wrapped her in her cloak, kept one arm about her shoulders as she walked beside him to a ring of singing stones. Within the circle lay a small indentation into which the moon appeared to have sunk.

Areme pressed his finger to her lips, bidding her to silence. Releasing her, he knelt and placed his hand into the tiny pool. He cupped the water and drank. After a moment, he said, 'Drink, and make a wish.'

Orlanda hesitated, wondering at the gravity in his tone.

'There's nothing to fear.' He clasped her hand, drew her to the edge. 'Drink.' His face held an expression so profound it compelled her to do his bidding.

She knelt and touched the pool. Endless rippling reflections of the moon scattered to the edges. The water passed her lips, chilled, aflame, trickling down her throat, cascading through her veins, flooding to the end of her fingers and toes. Raising her eyes to Areme's, she opened her mouth to speak her desire, but the thought of him slipped away, replaced by something else, something deeper.

Freedom.

Bewildered, she glanced at him.

'No,' he said sharply. 'Don't tell me.'

'But it wasn't what I meant it to be . . . what I wanted . . .' She reached back to the water. 'I'll make another wish.'

Areme caught her hand before she had a chance to immerse it again. 'No,' he commanded. 'You cannot undo what is done. Your wish is your heart's true desire.'

'*You* are my heart's desire.'

Areme smiled, pulling her close. 'Why wish for what is yours already?'

Desire and confusion rose in her. Did he mean her or Shasirre? No way of knowing, so she murmured against his lips, 'I wanted to consecrate our union.'

'Our union has already been consecrated by the celestial spirits. It needs no other blessing.' He regarded her gravely. 'Remember, if you ever need me, you have but to call my name and I will come for you.'

She tried to speak, but Areme silenced her. 'Just . . . remember.' The soft-spoken word held all the qualities of a prayer, a plea . . . a wish.

As black dawn turned to dark shades of grey, the mystery of the Living Sphere flowed around them. Areme stroked Orlanda's face, her body. Every silken strand of hair radiated her very essence. Magic wove about her, a quality of the future and of the past, of having lived an eternity, yet timeless. Like Shasirre, yet not.

He closed his eyes. Those were Shasirre's words Orlanda had spoken. And when she had touched the scar, for one maddened moment he had thought it was Shasirre with him, Shasirre whose caresses burned his skin. He ran his fingers along the scar on his chest. The wound would never heal, not while the memory of Shasirre lived in his heart, the memory of her pleading face as she fought for her life and lost. He sighed. They had both lost.

A shadow passed over him as a flight of silver cranes circled overhead. They landed on the granite platform before the singing stones, stood facing each other and bowed their pale heads. Slowly they stretched and closed ash-coloured wings, dancing, grey wings sparking radiance in the lucent light. Leaping and bowing, stepping high with their long legs, they trumpeted before arcing into the night sky, gliding over the whitened waves, then rising higher and higher.

Calling of loss, dark shadows silhouetted against the moon, they flew toward the horizon. Areme's skin crawled, then a surge coursed through him, a sensation he was recklessly trying to outrace a hurricane.

He looked back at Orlanda. What was it about her that had suddenly driven him to madness, filled him with an aching need to possess her, hold her, to never let her go? She had awoken something he had thought long dead, feelings belonging to another. She had made him swear an oath vowed to another. What power did she possess over him?

He stroked the silken strands of her flaxen hair, whispered against skin wet and slick and scented with their lovemaking. 'I swear I'll not hurt you like I did her. By all that is merciful, I swear it.'

Chapter 28

An Enemy Revisited

Sihan oiled Aurion's bridle for the second time that morning. The princess had sent a note saying she would be riding after mid-sun, leaving him at liberty till then, but with just two horses to care for, and two stalls to clean, he was fast running out of chores to keep himself occupied. And he needed to keep busy, to ward off thoughts whispering madness.

As he hung the bridle on a hook outside Aurion's stall, short, sharp beats of hooves on cobbles signalled the arrival of several couriers into the stable courtyard. One rider threw off his cloak to reveal the black and gold tabard of Pelan.

Boys ran forward to put hands to bridles. 'What news?' they cried, all eager for any scrap of the war.

Cautiously, Sihan edged near, not wanting to appear too eager. All four couriers wore grim expressions and said nothing, striding to the palace, leaving the boys to lead foam-flecked mounts away. Fear gnawed at Sihan. He spied Gerein leaving the soldiers' barracks, and hurried to intercept him, his injured leg only hindering his pace a little. 'Why didn't they tell us anything?' he asked.

Gerein strapped his sword belt round narrow hips, mouth tightening in a pensive face. 'They're carrying death lists.'

Ice slithered down Sihan's spine. 'Have you news of Jaien?'

The archer regarded him without the usual mocking glint in his eyes. 'No. Have you?'

Sihan averted his gaze, worry pooling like acid in his gut.

Gerein slapped him on the shoulder. 'No news is best. Jaien can look after himself. You should worry more about yourself.' He patted his sword hilt. 'The offer's there if you want it. Come to the sword drill with me.'

With nothing else to do, Sihan fell in beside him. He saw no need to invite further disdain by telling Gerein of his mother's wish he not take up the sword. He was skilled at swordplay, just as every lad in training to be Senfari. It was not like he was breaking her wish. He was not a soldier.

They passed through the door to the ménage. At the far end, Knight Commander Balfere stood next to an ugly brute of a horse, surrounded by a group of lads no older than Sihan.

'I've brought you another victim,' called Gerein.

The big knight frowned and said to Sihan, 'I thought you had a gammy leg.'

Forcing himself to walk evenly, Sihan said, 'Not any more, sir.'

'Excellent!' The knight turned toward the other youths and shouted, 'The hero of the warhorse trials! Just the man we need to demonstrate.'

Sihan cringed at the accolade as lads surrounded him, faint grins on their faces. Balfere dusted his hands, then unsheathed his sword and held it out to Sihan. Its lethal length glinted in rays of light spearing through the shafted windows.

As Sihan took the hilt, memories pressed upon him. He stared at the sword, recalled his mother's letter. Against it warred the winter of reality; Jaien fighting somewhere in a distant land; a princess in danger. As he balanced one against the other, there came a whispered hiss, as faint as breath against his ear.

Touch it not! For this you were not meant!

He set his jaw and closed his fingers firmly about the hilt, then slid his other hand along the flat of the blade, its cool touch sending a shiver down his spine. Only gradually did the horror of defying his mother's wish ebb from him, replaced by the ease of being his own man, unfettered. With new determination, he closed his mind to the voice and turned his attention to the task assigned.

'No! No! *No!*' bellowed Balfere, battleground roar cutting through the guffaws of soldiers standing around the edge of the ménage. 'How many times do I have to tell you, boy? Never, and I mean *never*, let go of your sword.'

Sihan lay on the ground, pain spiking up his arm. Balfere's sword lay nearby, once more wrenched from his grip. Bolting around the arena, Balfere's wall-eyed bay jumped over patches of light falling through high slitted windows, kicking up sand while it dodged men grabbing at its reins.

Trying to ignore the laughter from the other lads taking part in the exercise, Sihan sat up. At the far end of the ménage, Gerein rolled his eyes and smirked.

Balfere, face redder than usual in the heat of the indoor arena, caught the horse and thrust the reins at Gerein. 'Wipe that stupid grin off your face and show him how it's done.'

Scowling, Gerein stalked past Sihan. 'Heavens, Sihan, a horseman like you should be able to manage something as simple as this.'

Sihan brushed the sand off his leggings, glad at least these latest aches and bruises had not made his leg worse. 'When you said I was going to learn how to use a sword in these drills, I didn't think I'd be spending all morning flinging myself off a horse.'

'Not much use teaching you to use something you can't even keep hold of,' retorted Gerein. 'Perhaps instead of the broadsword, you'd like a dagger.'

Sihan fumed. Why could he not manage this task? Everything had gone wrong since he had picked up Balfere's sword. Despite his best efforts, he could not wield it, even when he could hold onto it. The weapon weighed too heavy in his hands and handled like a cudgel. And all the lads whispered, "the hero of the warhorse trials!" in mocking tones.

Gerein rode the horse to the end of the ménage, turned, drew his sword and set the horse into a gallop. As he passed Sihan, he flung himself into the sand, rolled neatly, and sprang to his feet, sword in hand.

Balfere strode forward, huffing, beads of sweat on his brow. 'Now do it again, Sihan. And this time, do it right. What's the rule?'

'Release all but your sword,' Sihan repeated the words.

'Sihan!' a strident voice called.

The princess stood at the edge of the arena, lifting the hem of her pale blue riding habit above the sand. Sihan hurriedly straightened his tunic.

'Hurry up, Sihan!' The princess stamped a grey boot.

Sihan's face flamed as he turned to Balfere. 'I forgot she wanted to ride after mid-sun.'

'Go,' said the knight, 'but mind you come back tomorrow. I'll finish what I've started, even if it kills you.' He held out a half-sword. 'Practice with this in the meantime.'

Sihan sheathed the sword in the scabbard at his belt, thankful for the small mercy that at least it was not quite as humiliating as a dagger.

Gerein said in a low voice, 'What's it like being rescued by a woman?'

'Shut up,' snapped Sihan. 'Or I'll wipe that smirk off your face.'

'Bet you any odds it won't be with a sword.'

With only a slight limp, Sihan hurried toward Orlanda. She pushed him toward the inner stables, face glowing, blue eyes sparkling. When she skipped along the alleyway, the gold fringe of her dress trailed wisps of hay in its wake. She glanced over her shoulder and grinned, the edges of her almond-shaped eyes crinkling. More carefree than he had ever seen her, she almost made him forget the morning's embarrassment as he tacked up Aurion and the bay colt, then legged the princess into the sidesaddle before mounting his own horse.

A stable foreman approached, holding two cloaks. 'You'd best take these. There's a storm coming.'

Sihan shifted in his saddle, sweat dripping down his back, and glanced between pillars at the sky where silver gulls glided against the blue. 'Are you sure?'

The princess muttered, 'I want to gallop, not argue about weather.' She spurred Aurion toward the stable exit.

Shrugging apology to the foreman, Sihan urged his bay after her. They rode through the fortress to the battlement gate. A cavalcade of grim-faced soldiers, fully mailed and armed and led by Hessarde's second, Sedor, waited on the other side of the river.

The princess scowled. 'How tiresome, like a score of sour-faced Hessarde's trailing my heels.' She kicked Aurion into a canter the moment they came abreast of her guards, not giving Sihan any choice but to follow.

Their horses pounded through fallow fields surrounding the fortress, then across grass . . . uphill . . . downhill . . . high into the foothills. At their back, the mounted soldiers kept a discreet distance.

Sun struck flame from mottled leaves of sprinkled clumps of candlewood. When they reached clear going, Sihan encouraged Spirit to greater speed, and for a few moments, the bay galloped shoulder to shoulder with Aurion. Sunlight flooded down on them, shimmering to crimson the bay's dark hair, rippling across Aurion's coat in silver waves. Then Aurion shot ahead.

Wind rose, whipping Sihan's skin. Massing clouds obliterated the brightness of the day. A leaf hit him in the face as the sky clouded over. They came to hills threaded with streams, iron-grey against withering brown autumn grass. Scattered rocks, piled on top of each other, dotted the landscape. Icy wind wailed among granite tors.

Orlanda reined in Aurion, waiting for Sihan to catch up. High overhead a flight of gang-gangs swooped, red crests stark against grey-green plumage, cries wild and shrill.

Sihan's skin broke into gooseflesh, breath coming in white clouds of steam mingling with that rising off the horses. He turned in the saddle. Snowflakes drifted down, all around, whispering as they fell. The escort was a grey shadow in the distance. Sihan frowned. The princess and he had not galloped particularly fast. Why was the escort lagging so far behind?

'Snow!' Orlanda exclaimed as ice crystals fell, bejewelling her ears, nose and hair.

Shivering, Sihan said, 'I can't believe it's become so cold so fast.'

Orlanda shrugged. 'Last year we had two freak storms much earlier than this, and much closer to the fortress. Didn't the stable foreman warn you to bring cloaks?'

Sihan smothered a retort.

Flashing him a bright smile, Orlanda said, 'Do you want to see something special?'

'Shouldn't we wait for the escort?' Sihan rubbed his hands, the skin on his knuckles turning white.

Her face twisted into a grimace. 'Bother them. We're in Mirador. Why on earth should I be hounded by a bunch of ill-mannered men every time I turn around?' She took off, not waiting for the answer threatening to slide from Sihan's tongue. Snow spray flew out from Aurion's hooves.

Wet reins slipping through his hands, Sihan followed the princess down a well-worn track into a deep gully. Arching tree ferns brushed against his legs and snow blossoms adorned the leafless tea tree bushes. They stopped at a sandy clearing next to a pool, where sweet wattle fragrance rose faintly on the air. Cascades sparkled down from a series of ledges like lace veils. Bellbirds sang all around them, liquid calls a counterpoint to the water's burble.

'This is the Bridal Falls,' Orlanda said, sliding from her sidesaddle, leather boots crunching on snow-dusted sand. She looped Aurion's reins over a stump. 'Don't you think the waterfalls resemble the veils women wear when they marry?'

Sihan quirked an eyebrow, surprised by her talk of marriage when it was a well known fact she despised her intended, Valoren.

Orlanda put her fingers to her lips, motioning him to silence, then pointed toward the lowest waterfall. A lirifen emerged from behind it, tail feathers showing in display. It started to dance, fanned tail swishing gracefully, swaying to the music and rhythm of whispering snowflakes.

There came the sudden call of a mopoke owl.

A sharp needle of fear stabbed at Sihan. He swung his horse around and peered into the bushes.

'What is it?' asked Orlanda.

'I don't know.'

'My guards, no doubt.'

'I don't think so.'

The mopoke called repeatedly. Sihan tried to see through lurking blocks of dark underneath trees around the sandy grove. A movement among the ferns caught his eye. A thickset man emerged from the bushes, clothed in a cloak of rough-spun wool, narrowed eyes glinting as he fingered the hilt of the heavy sword at his belt – the man from the marsh Gerein had been hunting.

Drawing his half-sword, Sihan spurred his horse forward, shouting at Orlanda, 'Get behind me.'

'Is that any way to greet an old friend?' growled the stranger. 'And here I was thinking you had arrived specially to pay me a visit.'

'You're no friend of mine,' said Sihan.

'Why don't you introduce me to your lady?' The stranger advanced to within a few yards.

Aurion squealed, pulling back on the reins holding him captive.

'Withdraw.' Sihan tried to inflect as much confidence and authority into his voice as possible, levelling his sword at the man. Within a heartbeat, a voice crashed against his ear, no longer a whisper, but a clamorous warning.

For this you were not meant! Your hands are meant for one death only! Share not in death before your time.

The sword trembled in Sihan's hand.

The stranger sneered. 'Get out of my way, little boy. Let a real man teach that whore how to ride.'

Fury surged through Sihan. Ignoring the voice calling for inaction, he clenched the sword hilt, slashed at the man, barely grazing him across one cheek. Seeing Orlanda had no way of remounting Aurion without assistance, Sihan leapt from his horse, knocking the man backward. He drove one knee into the man's gut, forcing the wind out of him.

For a moment they grappled hand to hand, then the man rolled him. Sihan hit the sand hard, cracking his elbow against rock. Grimacing, he scrabbled to his feet. His sword lay where it had fallen.

The man kicked it away, drew his own weapon. 'Nasty temper for a little brat.' He turned to Orlanda. 'I hope *you're* as headstrong. I *like* breaking in nice fillies before I ride them.'

Sihan sprang between them, swung his fist. The man blocked the blow with his forearm, then swung at Sihan with the sword. Naked steel coming for his face, Sihan ducked below it. Younger and faster, he dodged another strike as he angled the fight to get back to his sword. The man came after him, muttering obscenities.

Slipping beneath another sword thrust, Sihan yelled at Orlanda. 'Take my horse!'

Orlanda ran, but before she could reach it, the man struck the bay on the rump. It leapt away into the undergrowth. Distracted by the fleeing horse, Sihan never saw the fist crash into his eye. The man's meaty fingers clawed at his tunic. Sihan staggered back. Fists pummelled him again, slamming him against the ground.

Another blow smashed his cheek, buffeting his head violently to one side. Pain exploded through his jaw, then his chest. A boot struck Sihan's face. Breath rasping, ribs on fire, he lay on the sand, cold snow against his bloodied mouth, waiting for the sword thrust that would take his life.

'Leave him be!' Orlanda lunged, clutching at the man's arm. He grasped her by the hair, jerking her head back. As she screamed in pain and fury, he flung her to the sand. Grey steel gleamed on the ground before her. Without hesitation, she grabbed Sihan's half-sword, leapt to her feet, and slashed at the stranger.

Stepping away, the man leered, licking his lips like a slavering wolf. 'I've got a much nicer sword for you to play with.'

'Shut your mouth, you uncouth rat!' she shouted.

A thin smile hovered about his lips. 'Only if you open yours and suck my–'

'Shut your piss-filled mouth!' Orlanda swiped at him, blade hissing through the air.

Anger rippled across his face. 'You've got a common tongue about you for a princess.' He struck the half-sword from her grip with a single blow, sending it spinning into the pool. 'But all tongues are the same, I'm thinking, when they're wrapped around a shaft.' He stalked toward her.

Head spinning, Sihan tried to rise, but shaking limbs refused to support him. Helpless, he could only watch as Orlanda stared at the oncoming man as though mesmerised by a cobra. The stranger jumped forward and grabbed at her hand. She leapt back, fingers sliding through his closing grip, leaving him with an empty glove. Dodging behind Aurion, she thumped the stallion's rump and yelled, 'Attack him!'

With a violent toss of his head, Aurion tore the reins free. The man leapt forward once more, and this time managed to grab her hand. Twisting Orlanda's arm behind her back, he forced her down and dropped astride her, heavy thighs pinning her down.

'Areme!' she screamed. 'Areme!'

With a squeal of rage, Aurion launched himself at the man, raising a flurry of swirling sand. He reared, striking out. Eyes wide with shock, the man fell back and let go of Orlanda. She scurried back out of range of the stallion's hooves.

As the stranger slashed at Aurion with his broadsword, an ear-shattering roar filled the grove and blue light shimmered all around. Hooves thundered, and another horse, coat glimmering silver like moonlight on snowbark, plunged into the sandy clearing.

A rider jumped from the horse and advanced upon the marsh man. Tall, lithe, black braid swinging like a rope at his back, eyes glowing silver rage, Areme drew his sword and lunged.

Areme hammered the man, filling the afternoon air with the sound of striking steel. Although both he and the stranger were tall, the other man easily outweighed Areme, but that gave him no advantage. As each of the stranger's blows crashed in, they became a flurry of wasted force, Areme barely shifting an inch of ground to meet them, not ceding one pace.

He glanced around for Orlanda, relief coursing through him when he found her standing, unhurt, by the edge of the pool. The fool boy lay on the ground still, blood dripping down his face to stain snow crimson. Areme yelled at him, 'Get her on Aurion. Hurry!'

As Sihan peeled himself from the ground, Orlanda drew back only far enough to be safe out of reach, her worshipping gaze never leaving Areme.

Areme cursed, swinging his sword in a vicious arc. The stranger twisted to one side, the blade hissing past his shoulder. Pivoting, the man countered, aiming at the knight's head, but there was no moving Areme who allowed the sword to swish past his ear, then thrust forward, sword stretched to the man's jugular, forcing him back. Perspiration dripped down the stranger's face, his breathing harsh and loud, while Areme remained as calm as if he were handling a foil.

Areme edged his adversary to the rim of the pool, the stranger flailing at him, wasting his strength. Finally, Areme retreated a step, parried four fierce thrusts, then caught the sword of his opponent with his own and sent it flying to the other side of the pool. Seizing the man by the collar and belt, Areme hurled him into the pool.

Crashing and the shriek of steel filtered through the surrounding forest. Areme spun round. The stranger splashed about, regained his feet, leathers stained dark with water. He sputtered for a moment, then smiled a half-sneer without parting his lips. 'Did you think I was alone?'

Areme strode to the horses just as Sihan hoisted Orlanda into the saddle. Before Sihan could take even a step back, Areme grabbed hold of him and threw him onto his grey stallion. 'Go!'

'But there're more of them coming–'

Areme clenched his teeth as he spat, 'If you don't get the princess out of here, I'll kill you myself. You can't use a sword to save your life, so don't pretend you can watch my back.'

Sihan blushed, but started to dismount anyway.

'I'm staying, too,' said Orlanda, defiance in the set of her mouth.

Areme glared at both of them, then walked up to Aurion's head and whispered into the stallion's ear. A moment later, the white stallion reared and spun away, a blur of white sweeping down the bed of the creek.

Areme shoved Sihan back into the saddle, then took hold of the grey's bridle and yelled, 'Seroyen, go!' The grey took off after Orlanda.

As riders hurtled into the clearing, Areme hauled the stranger out of the water, holding him with one hand and pressing a dagger to the man's throat with the other. Cold disdain laced his voice as he motioned to struggling captives strung over the hindquarters of his soldier's horses. 'Behold, your men.'

He pushed the marsh man toward Hessarde. 'Tie this dolt up.' To Sedor he asked, 'Did any get away?'

Sedor, dark hair messy with congealed blood, said, 'No, Lord Master.'

Areme regarded the struggling prisoners, their rough garb and leathers stained with blood. 'Have any talked?'

'None, Lord Master.' Sedor paused. 'We'd better get back after the princess.'

Shaking his head, Areme said, 'She's my charge. I'll follow after we take care of business here.' Even as he said the words his gut twisted. This trap had come too close to costing Orlanda or the horse, perhaps both. How many more intruders might be stalking Aurion and the princess before long? He should spirit her and the horse away like she wanted. But how to do that without plunging the kingdom into war?

Anger and frustration coursing through him, Areme sliced through the bonds of one prisoner before pulling him from the back of a horse. 'So we all understand each other, I shall now demonstrate mercy.' He drew his sword and skewered the man's stomach. The prisoner's eyes bulged, then light faded from them as he slipped to the ground, a lifeless bundle of tattered rags.

Areme wiped the blade on his leggings before sheathing it. 'Be certain, the interrogator of Mirador is not so merciful. Remember that when I next ask you a question.' He turned to the man he had just fought, his slow smile carrying the promise of carnage as he pulled off his glove to reveal the ring of the Horse Lords. 'You're too stupid to have planned all this by yourself. Whom do you serve?'

The stranger choked, swallowed, then shook his head.

Hessarde ripped open the man's tunic, and pointed at a viper tattoo on the stranger's chest. 'Mark of the guild assassins. He won't break that oath without help.'

Shrugging, Areme said, 'Take them to the interrogator.'

Hessarde finished binding the struggling man. With the help of another soldier, he hefted him onto the back of his horse, then mounted. Hessarde urged his horse onward, and preceded the other riders up the trail leading to the fortress. The drumbeat of hooves faded, and then blue light shimmered in the clearing and a vision of a grey-cloaked figure rose in the air in front of Areme.

Myrrhye traced the air with a hand, pale fingers in thick folds of grey. Beside her appeared an outline of a horse, breaking up and merging with the mist before finally coalescing into a blue-roan stallion.

Areme clenched his fists. For a thousand years he had held to one thought, one vow – made to a dead woman, his dead wife – to rid the world of the curses Shasirre had unleashed in her desperate bid to save him and the world from the dark sorceress, Niameh. And with the two things he needed to reverse the imprecations upon the world – a sorceress bound to a unicorn – finally acquired, his mother had almost caused the death of both.

Areme struck the branch of a tree with his gauntleted fist. 'He could have killed Orlanda and the horse. Why did you wait to summon me?'

His mother pushed back her cowl, a tight smile hovering about her lips. 'Neither was in danger in my presence.'

His rage vented in hot words. 'The *plan* was to portal me to the scene the moment you were certain we had our man. The *plan*–'

Sparks blazed in the cauldrons of Myrrhye's black eyes, and a tempest of wind threw Areme back against the solid trunk of a candlewood. 'Do not presume to lecture me on strategy! I am the Lady of the Grey Sands, charged with the guardianship of the Living Sphere. Do not dare to presume upon my good favour because you are my son. As I gave you life, so will I be your ruin if I choose. Because of *your* folly, *your* disobedience, *your* pride and *your* arrogance, chaos now threatens the world.'

Areme staggered in the wake of her rage. He closed his eyes, shutting out the snow swirling about him, wishing he could shut out the words striking a discordant beat against his soul. Every word she spoke was truth.

Through his error a thousand years past – he had broken the singing stone at Caerlon – he had torn a breach in the lines of power running like invisible threads through the world, and all the power remaining was now slowly leaching into the earth.

As suddenly as it had flamed, Myrrhye's fury died. She slumped to the sand, ivory face white as the snow around them, her hand trembling as the reins of the horse slid through her fingers.

Areme stared at her. 'What's wrong?'

Her breath came harsh from her throat. 'I have not the strength I once held. My power is failing. The power of the world is failing. Soon there will be nothing left upon which to call. Even the dark creatures of the underworld no longer stalk the world as once they did. Everything is dying. The wards around Kosall will fall. The curse the queen laid on Romondor will destroy the last of that country, reducing it to death spanning eternity. And every other curse cast by forbidden magic plaguing the world, destroying it inch by deadly inch, will continue unabated, unchecked.'

'Then portal Aurion from danger while you can.'

'I cannot. He is power itself. Ancient when this land was new. The magic of the world will wash over him like water across a rock, leaving him untouched, or worse – broken. The texts of Deranen speak of the destruction of waiting unicorns – their unborn power shattered by forces of the world. I will not take that risk.'

Areme knelt by her side, taking her cold hands in his. 'Once Aurion takes on his true form, power will return. Enough to reverse the curses. Restore the world to rights. Undo the wrongs of sorceresses past.'

'Only if Orlanda is a true sorceress, like her mother.' Myrrhye hesitated a moment. 'But not too much like her mother. We must be able to control her, bend her to our will – prevent her from calling upon the dark arts. That way lies ruin.'

Areme's hand tightened upon his mother's as he remembered Shasirre's fall from grace. 'Orlanda won't fall. I won't let her. I've bound her to me. As long as I'm with her, she won't abuse her powers.'

Myrrhye snorted, colour returning to her face. 'If she lives long enough to acquire some. Perhaps you should teach her fighting skills instead of–'

Refusing to let her finish, Areme pulled his mother to her feet. He glanced in the direction Hessarde had ridden. 'That man was a guild assassin. But his intent was to rape her, not kill her.'

Myrrhye frowned. 'I feel strange forces at work here.'

Areme kicked the sand. 'He wasn't an adept. I gave him every opportunity; he took none. He fought only with the brute strength of an ordinary man. The others, too, I'll wager.' He turned on Myrrhye. 'There's something more going on than we know. These men were not after the horse, but every sense I have tells me someone is.' Anger blazed once more. 'Why *did* you leave it so late to summon me?'

Myrrhye shrugged. 'I wanted to see the girl's mettle, this one you proclaim sorceress. I wonder if you are mistaken. I saw no sign of power in her. With her life at stake, she should have turned to her gifts, impaled him with a lightning strike – something. At her age, her mother was casting every spell she could as rapidly as she could acquire them. But Orlanda . . . nothing. Perhaps she does not take after her mother.'

Areme bit back the words that that could only be a blessing. 'She's the daughter of a sorceress, and the horse acknowledges her. That's enough for me.' He was not ready to admit he had sensed the power lying dormant within Orlanda while he had held her in his arms.

Myrrhye observed him steadily. 'Aurion also acknowledges Sihan.'

Areme grimaced. 'Only because he raised the horse. The boy is nothing. *Less* than nothing. If he was one of us, he would have fought to protect the horse.'

'He tried his best.'

'His best is pathetic. And in such close proximity to the horse, he's a liability.' Areme's hand clenched upon his sword hilt. 'I should have taken the opportunity to kill him myself.'

Myrrhye's eyes pooled black. 'I forbid you to harm him.'

Shrugging, Areme said, 'The horse will do him the kindness itself when it turns.'

Irritation flared in Myrrhye's eyes. She tossed him the reins of the stallion, and with a haze and shimmer, disappeared.

Sihan rode after the princess, every muscle burning and aching, iron taste of blood strong upon his tongue. Snow swirled about them, blasting off branches as the horses turned up a steep track bringing them out of the gully onto a ridge. He lifted his hand to feel out the damage the man's fists had done to his face. Even the lightest brush from his fingertips sent a thousand agonies coursing through every nerve. He rubbed his eyes with the back of his hand, grimaced as hot pain struck, fingers coming away with more blood over them.

Orlanda tugged at the reins but Aurion strode purposefully onward. 'What did Areme do to Aurion? He won't listen to me.' Her voice tightened. 'We shouldn't have left him.'

Shifting uncomfortably in the saddle, Sihan wiped snow from his lashes with a trembling hand. 'He left us no choice.'

'If only I knew how to fight.' Orlanda balled her hands into fists. 'If Areme is hurt, I'll kill that man. I'll kill him, his family, his friends . . . everyone.'

A rush of water dislodged from a bunch of leaves as Sihan rode past. It trickled down his neck and made an uncomfortable wet patch on his chest, making him shiver even more, but all he could think of was her words – of killing everyone, and that was enough to recall the vision of fire and corpses.

Not wanting to look at her, he brushed his sodden hair from his brow, then winced as pain stabbed through his shoulder.

At his sharp intake of breath, Orlanda's brow creased in concern. 'You're badly hurt.'

Shivering even more, Sihan replied through chattering teeth, 'It's nothing.'

Orlanda reined Aurion closer. 'That's a lie. He beat you to a pulp. You should see your face.'

Shamed even further, Sihan muttered, 'I'd rather not, if it's all the same to you.' He had failed in duty. He had failed to protect the princess, should not have let her ride off when he knew someone was stalking her, should have fought harder. Tried harder. Something. The fact she had not made one complaint at his ineptitude, made him feel worse.

They reached a wide cobbled road. At its crest, the fortress appeared in the distance, grey bulk rising from mist like a place of enchantment. Dark figures paced back and forth on the guardwalk. Distant shouts emanated from behind the curtain wall, the faint clang of metal on metal.

Orlanda glanced at Sihan. 'Home,' she murmured.

At the sound of that single word, a flood of warmth coursed through him, but all his thoughts were of Graycor. He forced a guilty smile, echoing without enthusiasm, 'Home.' He refused to admit his home and hers were worlds apart.

Her sudden gasp had Sihan reaching involuntarily for the sword he no longer carried. 'What is it?' he cried, wheeling his horse, staring into every shadow as though it augured treachery.

But Orlanda was staring to the shoreline. Sihan followed her gaze to where a large ship sailed up the coast, black standards fluttering in the darkening sky.

'Romondor,' she whispered, and the word hung upon the air like death.

Chapter 29

The Proposal

Hooves clattered on the cobbled road at their back, urgent, purposeful.

'Ride on,' said Sihan, battered face pensive.

Orlanda's fingers clenched the reins. Glancing behind, she tried to identify the rider galloping toward them through the drizzling rain. A horseman clad in a white tabard appeared through the gloom.

'Areme!' she cried with joy, then fear spiked through her at the blood spattered over his face and chest. As he reined in a blue-roan stallion beside Aurion, she cried, 'You're hurt!'

He dismounted and strode to her, gloved hand closing on hers, warm. 'Be calm, I'm well.'

'But–' She motioned to his tabard.

'It's not my blood, and that brigand is no longer a threat to any.' Turning to Sihan, he said in harsher tones, 'Get off my horse.'

Without question, Sihan obeyed, handing the knight Seroyen's reins. Carelessly, Areme tossed him the reins of the roan.

Heart thumping, Orlanda motioned to the vessel sailing up the coast. 'They've come for me.'

Areme remounted. After a long examination of the ship, he said, 'There's nothing to fear. The rigging shows they have passed through heavy weather, and our scouts report Pelan is already snowbound. There will be no ships moving south before spring.'

Orlanda shivered in the darkening gloom. Despite his words, trepidation settled like a black pit in her gut.

Areme moved his horse closer, shook off his cloak, and placed it about her shoulders. With Sihan and Areme at her back, she rode down the valley, pacing the ship, past the fortress and on to the harbour crowded with shipping. Out in the bay, transport ships moored bow to bow, while broad cargo boats bobbed on the incoming tide at the quays. Along the dock, chains of men unloaded crates under torchlight.

She ignored the dockers, sailors and traders who bowed their heads as she passed. She ignored everything but the black vessel heaving to. With a groan of wood against wood, the Romondor ship dropped anchor alongside the king's barge, dwarfing all of the vessels save the king's warship.

Orlanda reined Aurion to a halt, wrinkling her nose at the stink of rotten fish, tar and salt spray. The stallion snorted at gulls shrieking and squabbling over a spilt bucket of pink squid bait sliming the walkway. Running to haul massive lengths of plaited and tarred bamboo, dockers set crowds of seagulls flashing into the air, birds screeching and fighting around the piers for scraps of fish.

On the Romondor ship's deck, black-clad soldiers stood with hands on sword hilts. A man waited near the railing, garbed in a black tunic, calf-high, black leather boots and black leggings, barking orders.

'Who is that?' asked Orlanda.

'Emissary Vaill,' said Areme. 'The duke's ambassador.'

Bitterness choked Orlanda's throat. Her gaze swept over the ship, sleek and narrow in beam, light and high out of the water. 'That's not a merchant vessel.'

Areme made no pretence at denial. 'It's a troop ship, carrying men and horses.'

Orlanda's hands trembled under her cloak. Horses. They meant to race winter and take her over the mountains to Kosall. She rode Aurion down a cobbled walkway to the head of the vessel, sat there, proud and defiant, fighting back tears with raging hatred.

On board, the ambassador executed a formal bow, face as cold and hard as Veren's, dark eyes set in ivory skin. Gritting her teeth, Orlanda inclined her head, then wheeled Aurion away through the dock gate, into the fortress forecourt. Soldiers outnumbered courtiers, full-armoured and carrying steel. An arch of torches lit the pale stone of the palace. Guards patrolled the stairway to the western doors, a clear sign the entire wing had been assigned to the Romondor ambassador and his entourage.

Her father had known of the arrival in advance and told her naught. Orlanda kicked Aurion on. In the stable courtyard, Sihan dismounted and held the stallion while Orlanda slid off. Areme threw his reins to a stable boy and made to follow her.

'Areme!' Gerhas's sharp voice rang out across the courtyard.

Behind Gerhas, Travall and Balfere motioned for him to attend them. Areme hesitated.

'Go,' said Orlanda, striding toward the palace. 'You can't help me now.' No one could.

Gerhas sat at the candlewood table that stretched the length of his room. Rippling light from sconces set around the walls illuminated the three grim-faced knights sitting opposite. Without preamble, he said, 'Trav, I want you to assemble a company of men, the best you've got. You will lead the escort.'

'What escort?' Areme's voice held a sharp edge.

Gerhas barely flicked him a glance. 'The king is taking the princess to Romondor.'

'When?' demanded Areme, features frozen despite the warmth of the flickering light.

'Tomorrow.'

Areme slammed the flat of his hand on the table. 'Impossible! Pelan is snowbound.'

Now Gerhas fully returned Areme's daggered gaze. 'Byerol is not.'

'Byerol!' Balfere cried out in amazement, ruddy face growing redder by the moment. 'By all the Heavens, Byerol is at war with Pelan!'

Leaning back in his chair, Travall locked hands behind his head. 'He's taking a mighty risk, travelling with only one company, and at least half a company of vultures.'

'How did you know that?' Gerhas demanded.

'I have eyes, the same as everyone else.'

Areme rounded on Travall. 'That ship only just arrived. How did you know what it was carrying?'

'Scouts from Pelan saw it dock a moon's cycle past at Tulit.' Travall pulled a sheet of vellum with scratchy writing on it from beneath his cloak, and flung it across the table at Gerhas. 'Look familiar?'

Gerhas glared at Travall. 'This is for the king's eyes only. Where did you come by it?'

'We are Knight Commanders of the Realm. You think we sit around waiting for a bunch of fops and dandies to give us information? If we did, we'd be dead by now.'

'Interfering with king's mail–'

'Is a hanging offence,' finished Travall with a bored drawl. 'With the amount of broken edicts around here lately . . .' He left the sentence unfinished.

'You didn't think to share this information with us?' Even Balfere's usual jovial voice was low and cold.

'You've been too blind-drunk to notice, and you . . .' Travall said to Areme, 'well, you've been otherwise engaged.'

Areme's eyes became glacial.

Gerhas stood, chair scraping the slate floor. 'Get your men together. Byerol shouldn't give too much trouble. You'll probably pass through their territory without them even knowing you've been there.' He paused a moment, then said, 'And make sure you take the boy, Sihan.'

Areme's head snapped up. 'What?'

Gerhas forced himself to hold Areme's furious gaze, to give no hint of the layered lies beneath his next words. 'Veren requested the princess be allowed to take the white horse, as a courtesy to her. After all the fuss she made to get hold of it, I doubt she'll leave it behind. That means someone who can handle that beast must accompany it. That's either you or the boy. He's expendable; you're not.' Gerhas turned to Travall and Balfere. 'You two are dismissed.'

Areme waited until the pair left the room, then rounded on Gerhas. 'This has nothing to do with being expendable.'

'No,' affirmed Gerhas, glad the next untruths to spill from his lips at least held a measure of credibility. 'The king is well aware of the princess's infatuation with you. So he's making sure to keep temptation out of her way. His express orders are that you remain here at Mirador until he returns.'

For a long while Areme said nothing, features rigid stone. Finally, he said, 'Am I dismissed?'

Gerhas eyed him sternly, reading the rage kept barely in check behind those dark eyes. 'I must warn you; you're treading on dangerous ground. Nothing is more important than this union between Mirador and Romondor, and I won't let you do anything to jeopardise it.'

Areme glared at him. 'It's not me jeopardising the future of the kingdom, but the man charged with protecting it with his life.' And with that he stalked from the room without waiting for leave.

Orlanda raced through the palace, ignoring startled looks of soldiers and nobility alike. She came to the doorway of the king's audience chamber, but the king's guard crossed halberds in front of her, barring her entrance.

'Let me through!' she demanded, trying to push past the heavily armed soldiers.

A firm grip on her shoulder by one guard held her off. 'The king is in audience, Highness. He has given orders.'

Her voice rose, 'I'm countermanding them!'

'Pardon, Highness, but–' The guard stopped as the carved door opened and a man peeked around the edge, sun-washed blue eyes in a thin face taking in everything at once.

Orlanda sighed with relief. 'Castellan Maraid, please tell these buffoons to let me through.'

Maraid stepped into the antechamber. Pale hands fluttering in the air, he pushed down the halberds. 'Yes. Yes. You may enter, child. But a word of warning . . .' One cold spidery hand clutched hers, grip firm despite its frail appearance. 'Knight Commander Veren is within. Say nothing to offend.'

Orlanda raised her chin. 'I'll be as offensive as I like. I didn't ask for this marriage proposal, and he had no right to bring it!'

Maraid's grip tightened. 'There is no fault in him. Do not blame him for carrying out his duty.'

Fuming, Orlanda shouted, 'Was it his duty to slaughter thousands of our kinsmen?' Her gaze trailed up and down the castellan's skeletal frame, taking note of his dark grey robes. 'Why do you wear these sombre hues? Any darker, and they would be black. Are you a vulture in disguise?'

The castellan shook his head, flaxen hair wafting about his shoulders. 'You know not of what you speak.' He stepped aside. 'Enter, and be done with it.'

Orlanda pushed past him into the audience chamber. It was empty and dark. No rushlights lit the wall hangings, the gilded throne, or the slate floor.

Voices trembled on the air. Moving toward the balcony, she recognised her father's deep tones.

'It's best she leaves now,' said the king. 'I fear she is becoming too headstrong. Too much like her mother.'

'That may be no bad thing,' said a dark voice that filled her with dread. 'She'll need to be strong once she gets to Romondor. It's a hard decision you've made.'

'I've made harder.'

'Yes.'

Orlanda gasped as a shadow fell across her. Veren walked into the room, filling the entrance to the main chamber. He inclined his head. 'I bid you welcome, Your Highness.'

Recovering her wits, she grated, 'I bid you to piss off.' Glaring at Veren, she moved to confront her father. 'Why do you consort with this murderer?'

The king, mantled in his white cloak, drew a heavy breath. 'He has killed men who did not deserve to die. Like any soldier. That doesn't make him any more a murderer than other men.' His voice was granite, like his face.

Orlanda clutched at the sleeve of his surcoat. 'Don't send me away. Not to Valoren. I'll marry anyone else you choose, I swear it, as long as it's someone from Mirador.'

A smile, pressed too thin, marred her father's face. 'And as long as they're called Areme, I suppose.' He marched past her through the audience chamber, cloak swirling in his wake, not even looking at her. 'Don't bother to deny it.' His voice was clipped. 'I've given orders. The ceremony is tomorrow at dawn. We leave straight after for Romondor. You won't be allowed to escape from the fortress, so don't bother trying. I'll throw Areme in the dungeon if you do.'

'You can't!' Unable to fathom this abrupt turn in fortune, Orlanda fell to her knees. 'Father, please!'

'Do not dare to tell me what I can and cannot do. And trouble me no further this night, for you shall hear no words I have not spoken before your betrothed's representative.' He strode from the room.

A hand fell upon her shoulder. 'He's doing what he thinks is best,' said Veren.

She shuddered, scrabbling away from him. 'Don't touch me. Don't speak to me. I hate you!' Stumbling to her feet, she spat at him.

Veren calmly wiped the spittle from his face, then bowed low. 'Please excuse me till the morrow.' He straightened and strode to the door of the audience chamber, where Maraid stood, face ashen.

'She didn't mean it,' the castellan whispered to Veren. 'She's overwrought.'

'I meant every word, you misfit little vulture's accomplice!' Tears scalded Orlanda's cheeks as she ran out into the hall and on down the corridor. Maids scattered as she raced into her room. 'Get out! Get out!' she shouted. Everyone bustled out, whispering behind their hands; all except the tall, red-haired woman who rose quietly from a divan next to a hearth. 'I gather you've seen the ship,' the Duchess of Belaron murmured.

'The ship. The king. The vulture. I hate them all!' Orlanda stalked across the room, kicking tasselled cushions aside. 'He wouldn't even look me in the eye. He's never looked at me since Mother died. Is that why he's sending me away? I remind him of her?'

'That answer you know already. Your father loved her deeply.'

'Too deeply. He's obsessed with her memory. He should have taken another wife by now.'

'For some men there can only be one woman.'

Like Areme. Orlanda tore aside the canopy overhanging her bed and flung herself upon the blankets. 'What do I do?' she wailed.

The duchess sat next to Orlanda and stroked her hair. 'What you were born to do.'

Chapter 30

Duty and Honour

Myrrhye watched the king from the Duchess of Belaron's borrowed eyes. Green eyes. Some would say stolen, but she had no intention of keeping them. She much preferred her own, black pools of night darkening to deepest ebony when she called power to her.

No such power this night, as a king sat in his private study, scratching out orders in black ink. And power became more elusive by the day, as the singing stones grew silent.

She cast an eye about the room. No others stood attendance upon their liege, not his second, neither his castellan. A sore point. She had wanted to examine Maraid more closely, but he had taken ill, laid up in his bedchamber. And her strength was failing – only enough now for one last glamour, and to portal home.

She would leave soon, and the duchess not far after. Things were running out of control between Byerol and Pelan, and Belaron had been called upon by both rival dukes to intercede. Irawan must act, but for the moment the only player on this stage of kingdom politics was Myrrhye.

Clearing her throat to announce her summoned presence, she waved an idle hand at a blank stone wall where a portrait had once hung of the queen. 'I see you've not kept even one token of her.'

Everything of Wyndarra had been removed from sight since the queen's death. It was unnerving, as if he knew the truth of her, but how could that be? It was a long-forgotten custom, that no image or representation of a witch must be made, else she might return to the land, or cast spells through lifeless painted eyes. It was a foolish custom. Magic wielders were born, not made.

Myrrhye pushed aside the horrifying prospect that Wyndarra had told her husband her secrets, that she was a sorceress. Surely no acolyte, no matter how fallen, would have revealed the secrets of the Grey Ladies, that Horse Lords and Shaheden strode the land, that magic had been wilfully used to strike a land to ruin.

Determined to press for all he knew, she advanced from the door where she had stood unobserved before she had spoken, and traced a finger across a worn leather-bound tome upon the king's writing desk: a detailed account of the Great War by the court historians, Kersus and Tetachian. It noted only facts ordinary men knew, and omitted a plethora of truths, including the reality that a witch had walked among men.

The king sat back, pain and loss etched deep into his craggy face, and something more . . . lost hope? He forced a smile to stretch his lips, pushed words past. 'What need have I of paint, Duchess? Her image is burned upon my soul. You think one moment passes into the next when her face does not haunt me?'

'You do her honour.'

He slammed his fist upon the book. 'Not by intent! *Never* by intent!'

Myrrhye took an involuntary step back. 'Sire?'

The king closed his eyes, waved her to a chair opposite. 'Forgive me. I called you here for a purpose, Irawan. This war is of concern. What communiqués have you from the duke?'

'Pleas and entreaties to come to his aid. The same from Pelan.'

'Byerol has requested no intercession from me.'

Myrrhye tilted her head back, weighed the king's words and expression. Both were heavy with grief and guilt. 'Did you expect such? After Romondor?'

'I expected better than silence. Even recrimination would please me.' He stood, began to pace. 'How do you battle silence, or reason with it?'

Myrrhye waited, guessing the thoughts running through his mind. Byerol had been the first to answer the call to war all those years ago, and held the line even now, forced to maintain its boundaries, prevent the unfortunates of that catastrophe in Romondor from entering the kingdom. But there was more to Byerol's animosity toward his king. He had been one of a chorus who had spoken against the Lady of Eloin, counselled caution in the king's choice of bride before she had been made queen.

Had he seen Wyndarra plot and scheme, lusting after the dark Lord of Romondor, Riordehr, even while she had promised her hand to the King of Mirador? Had Byerol seen lust contort to rage when the Black Duke had cut her down cold, declared his love before all for a woman Wyndarra had sought to grind to dust beneath her boot heel? Myrrhye had seen the unfolding of that rage in a thousand conceits, culminating in the destruction of an entire land stretching from one coast of the kingdom to the other, and the death of thousands.

If she did not know any better, she would have laid odds Wyndarra had caused the eruption of the volcano on her home island of Eloin that had forced the king to offer her people sanctuary. No acolyte held such power, not since the death of the singing stone at Caerlon. But she *did* know Wyndarra owned the blame when on every parcel of land her people were given, crops failed, and hunger ruled.

And then that Gods-blighted witch had prevailed upon her husband to do more. Had suggested the eastern plains of Romondor be granted to her people, to which the Duke of Romondor had acceded as a loyal subject of the king. But when crops there failed also, followed by the unending plague sweeping across the land, Myrrhye knew. The queen had done what was forbidden, turned gifts bestowed upon her by gods to a blight upon the Living Sphere, all for vengeance against the man who had spurned her.

And Riordehr, to his damnation, had returned her spite with interest. Killed her countrymen, forced the king to declare war upon him, resulting in a kingdom drowned in innocent blood. Mirador's commands had returned home, ranks torn, to a kingdom never knowing the real cause of the war.

And Byerol wore the cost, even now, his border garrisons forced to turn back the plague victims whose numbers would never end till Romondor itself ceased to exist. Romondor's destruction must never come to pass. Somehow the spell seeking to destroy Romondor must be reversed. Then the Duke of Byerol would be able to call his men back from their dismal duty. Once more Myrrhye's finger drifted across the worn leather tome.

Strange, the force of history; that it could hold a people in bondage for ten thousand years.

Real truth – in all its sordid detail – was now only to be found in the histories held in the vaulted libraries of Taiere. Myrrhye held the king's chilled gaze. Wondered at the thoughts running through that hidden mind.

'I mean to travel through Byerol,' he said at length.

'Without his leave, that is not advisable. With tensions so fraught in that quarter, if you come with men in arms, unannounced, Byerol will just as likely treat it as a declaration of intent to back Pelan.'

'If I ask leave, as you know I must – even a king is not above the law of the land – he'll deny it, especially when he knows with whom I am travelling.'

Myrrhye did not bother saying he owned the fault for that.

'I am in need of peace there.'

'Your men and mine crossed Byerol's borders not too many years past to invade Romondor, and what we did there made certain peace on Byerol's borders would never be secure.'

The king ceased pacing, stood with drawn brows and unseeing eyes before the empty space the painting had hung. 'What a waste the world is, if all the good a man might do in his life cannot outweigh the measure of one vile act.' Heavy silence weighed upon the night, then the king fixed his gaze upon Myrrhye. 'What say you, Duchess?'

'I want no more deaths, if possible. One anguished land is more than the world can stand. A second will be a mortal wound.'

With forbidding quietness, Callinor said, 'I will make use of Byerol if I must, and make reparation later.'

'You are the king. You must serve justice and show mercy.'

'Yes.' His response was short and forbidding as he turned and left the room.

Myrrhye stared after him, shiver after shiver coursing over her. He *knew*, by all that was merciful, he *knew*.

Travall stripped. Splashing cold water from a bucket over skin marred and puckered by scars, he scowled as his second pulled out fresh clothing from a chest at the foot of his bed. Once he had wiped away the worst of the grime and sweat, Travall shrugged into his quilted gambeson.

Giermont sniffed as he held out the hauberk. 'I don't know what good this is going to do you. Make a nice burial shroud I suppose.'

A scowl twitched the corners of Travall's mouth. 'Cut the doom-mongering, Monty. We're not going to war. This is just an escort.' He wondered at the calm in his voice. With every word, visions of two dead women haunted him; one, Wyndarra, the Lady of Eloin, the anointed queen, dead at his hands; the other, the former Duke of Romondor's wife, Ahnvieh, Lady of Anjour, dead by the queen's blade.

'An escort to *Romondor*, sir!' Giermont's voice grew strident. 'Black bleeding vultures itching to tear the hide off your back.'

'Enough!' Travall's voice was equally sharp.

Giermont fitted the banded mail. It fell from shoulder to knees, thin leather snug against the padded undergarment. Travall donned a leather skullcap, took the coif his second offered him, and waited while Giermont buckled the strap behind his head.

Balfere strode into the room, bulk dressed in mail covered by the white tabard with the firefalcon blazon. He ripped his sword from its sheath.

Travall rolled his eyes. 'You're not going to sharpen it again, are you?'

'Can never be too sharp.' Balfere inspected the weapon under a rushlight, running his finger alongside the razored edge.

When Giermont had adjusted the straps around his chausses and wrists, Travall bent his arms and tested the range of movement in his legs. Giermont picked up a white surcoat from a chest. At a nod from Travall, he drew it over the knight's head, the garment falling to his master's knees. Then he hefted a broad, leather sword-belt from the narrow bed, and buckled it around the knight's waist, fastening the heavy leather sheath.

Travall strapped on a dagger, eyeing Balfere as he sat on the edge of the bunk greasing his sword. Ignoring both men, Giermont bustled about, stuffing packs, laying out a bow and a gorytos crammed with arrows on Travall's bunk, then placing five lances against the wall.

'What are you *doing*, Monty?' roared Travall, patience at an end. 'There're only a handful of knights in this party, not counting Veren. Do you really think we're going to be charging anyone?'

'Can't be too careful.' Giermont picked up the high-cantled saddle from the floor, and headed off to the stables.

'He's right,' said Balfere. 'Take the lances. We can always charge Veren for practice.'

'Thank the Heavens we're leaving our seconds at home. I've never had one that shoots his mouth off so badly.' Travall picked up his helm and put it on the chest. 'He's worse than you, and that's not a compliment.'

Balfere ignored the jibe. 'A moon's cycle free of Monty. Might almost be worth a war.'

Travall smiled and walked outside. The chosen men stood assembled in the stable court, fully mailed and armoured, waiting for him to make his inspection before standing down for the night.

'Did you find Gerein?' Travall threw the question over his shoulder.

'No,' Balfere replied. 'Camar and Maiet are out searching for him now.'

'Night stalking?'

'That'd be my guess. Gerein's taking your orders rather to heart. I didn't think he would be quite so amenable considering his loyalty to Jaien.'

'Neither did I. And I don't remember telling him to scout all night. Maiet's my best scout. If I was going to tell anyone to do that, it would have been him.'

'Gerein's got sharp eyes, and he's the best archer in the kingdom. Whatever orders he thinks he's following, he'll be with us by morning.'

'Have you broken the news to the lad?'

Balfere let out a raucous laugh. 'Ever seen someone with their eyes set out on stalks?'

Travall snorted. 'I don't like taking out greensticks on errands like this. I heard he's hopeless with a sword.'

Balfere tossed the grease rag aside and moved to stand next to Travall. 'Some lads take time to warm to it. At any rate, he's a pretty game whippersnapper, riding the Death Gorge and all.'

'The horse bolted. He wasn't riding it, he was holding onto it for grim death.'

'Hardly his fault. You saw his leg. Only a Senfari could have kept horsed after that.'

'A Senfari would have chosen a better mount. I heard it also dumped him in the Senfari trial at Yseth. A true horseman knows his horse. He didn't. Twice.'

'Neither did Areme. I'd like to see you tell him to his face he's no horseman.'

A movement on the gallery above caught Travall's eye. He looked up to where Areme leant on the railing outside Gerhas's room, face drawn in a dark scowl.

'Poor sod,' said Balfere, following his gaze.

Travall shrugged. Areme was not in love with Orlanda, and perhaps that was the only good thing that could be said about this entire business, if she turned out to be anything like her mother . . .

Wyndarra's face filled Travall's mind. Even in death, beauty haunted her corpse, clinging at the edges of cold, alabaster skin, the soft curve of lash, the bloodless rose of full lips. And beside her, a man on his knees, tears of anguish staining his cheeks as he held the broken body of his wife – a little thing in tattered rags. And that voice, screaming, "How can she be dead, and I still live? How can she be dead?"

Shaking off memory, Travall strode to the inner stables where he found Sihan standing over a neat pile of saddle-packs next to the smithy. Waves of heat roared from the furnace. Travall raised his voice over the clang of anvils. 'Are you ready, boy?'

'I think so, sir,' said Sihan, lifting his battered face.

'What happened to you?'

'I was in a fight, sir.'

'Really?' Travall quirked an eyebrow. 'Looks like you lost. Where's your sword?'

Sihan dropped his gaze, mumbling through swollen, black-blooded lips, 'I lost it.'

Travall spat his disgust. 'What is it with you and swords? First you can't hold one in the sword drills, and now you lose it. *Nobody* is that inept. I've seen you handle a bow and a lance well enough. Are you being deliberately pathetic?' He relented at the lad's mortified expression. No point demoralising him into dust. 'Go to the sword smith and get a new sword. Tell him I sent you.' Out of temper, Travall turned and strode to the waiting soldiers. Nothing augured well for this expedition. But then again, nothing had been well for close on twenty winters.

Areme stalked to his quarters where Hessarde waited. 'Have any talked?' Areme demanded.

Hessarde allowed his cloak to fall open, revealing a blood-spattered tunic. 'Not yet, and the interrogator has killed two already.'

'Keep at them,' muttered Areme. 'I want them broken. I want them talking. We're running out of time.'

Hessarde tilted an eyebrow. 'I'd say we've run out of time.' He lowered his voice. 'Sedor brought in another dozen men, stalking the bloodhorse mares.'

The news struck Areme hard. The enemy was closing in. Resolution set him on a course of action he suspected he would fast regret. But what was one more regret against so many?

He sat at the small writing table in one corner of his room. Myrrhye was right. The girl had to leave Mirador, but he would make certain of her first. Make sure he was the only one she looked to for aid. Hurriedly, he pulled out two rolls of vellum from a drawer and scrawled two notes. After tying one with red ribbon, he went back to the door and handed both to Hessarde. 'Give these to Sihan. The tied one is for the princess. The other will get him past the guards.'

Hessarde shook his head. 'I'll take them myself.'

'Travall's guards won't let any of my men within arrow's range of her tonight.' Areme shoved Hessarde along the gallery.

412

'Get Sihan to make a garland of mistflowers as well, and take it with him. Now go!' King's edicts be damned. They had all fallen by the wayside of late, and if he was going to break one, he might as well break them all.

Sihan waited at the forge, pounding of hammers mirroring the drumming of his heart. Heat flowed over him, and he could no longer tell how much the sweat dripping from his forehead was from pain, and how much was from the heat of the furnace and molten steel.

The sword smith, a heavyset man of over fifty winters, ran the back of his hand across his brow. 'This'll take some time, lad. Best go pack your belongings.'

'I already have.' Sihan cast a glance at the stable temple. 'Do you think I could go pray?'

'Why not?' The sword smith waved him away. 'No one will be standing on ceremony tonight.'

Armed with permission, Sihan entered the candlelit temple, thoughts tumbling over each other – of flailing fists, a hastily scrawled letter to his father, packing an assortment of odds and ends. Kneeling on the flags before the white horse effigy, he whispered, 'Forgive me, Father. Forgive me, Mother.' And, while remaining on his knees with closed eyes, he cast a thought to Jaien, who had risked all to stop him from taking this path. 'Please understand, this isn't my choice, but I won't shirk my duty.' He bowed his head on his arms, breathing hard as though he had been running, then touched his head to the chill stone of the altar.

Sharp bootfalls echoed through the temple, and a harsh voice said, 'There you are!'

Hessarde marched up to Sihan and hauled him to his feet, then shoved two scrolls at him. 'Go make a garland of mist flowers, then give that, and the note with the red ribbon, to the princess. Use the other note to get past the guards. Don't get the two confused, and don't say anything to anybody.'

Sihan gaped at Hessarde. 'Mist flowers?'

'Is there something wrong with your hearing?'

Sihan's bewilderment settled into a measuring stare. He did not like Hessarde, nor his master, nor any of Areme's men.

At any other time he would have concluded Hessarde was setting him up for a fall. But on this night, with so many men on tenterhooks at being called out, the chill dread of an impending confrontation with Romondor, it seemed Hessarde would have better things to do than bait Sihan. So what was the knight's true purpose? Sihan crossed his arms. 'Pick your own damned flowers. I've already got orders and no time for your games.'

Hessarde leaned over him and hissed, 'I gave you an order, boy. Get those flowers. Get them *now*!'

'Travall's orders outrank yours.'

Hessarde's eyes took on a dead tone, as though deprived of light. He said, voice tight and controlled as he shot Sihan a killing glare, 'These orders are Areme's. The man who saved your miserable little life today.' He grasped Sihan's hand in his, unheeding of the tiny clotting wounds in the rough, cracked skin, and pressed the scrolls into his palm. 'Now get going while you can still walk.' Murder and intent mixed equally in Hessarde's face before he strode away.

Nonplussed, Sihan stared after the retreating knight. Not knowing quite what to make of it all, he glanced at the scrolls. One was a pass, just as Hessarde had stated. The other, sealed... he could not imagine what it might contain. But Areme was the princess's champion. So him sending her a scroll was nothing out of the ordinary. Was it? And Sihan was the princess's groomsman, so ranked low enough to be used as a delivery boy. Tonight it was not Sihan's place to question. He had let Orlanda down badly enough already with his incompetence. And her face when she had seen the ship from Romondor had held such dread. Whatever was afoot, he would deliver the message.

Sihan hurried to the fountain, wishing the black pelt of night might drape over him, but torchlight lit the sable darkness, flames rippling in the fountain water, lengthening into swaying golden spires dancing wild shadows along the walls. Amid all the activity of stable boys leading horses, he prayed no one would notice him stealing the flowers, or worse, tying the flowers together by their stems like some maid. He cast an anxious glance over the fountain rim. If Gerhas caught him, he would die of embarrassment. When he stood, agony from the thrashing speared through every nerve in his body. Maybe death was not a bad thing. Fighting the torment, he tucked the garland under his tunic, then hurried to the palace.

Lost in the myriad halls, he sought directions from liveried guards at every turn, showing them Hessarde's note. When he finally arrived outside the princess's door, Sihan handed the note to the last in a long sequence of guards. The soldier scrutinised it, then, like all the others before him, stood aside.

Heart pounding, Sihan knocked on the door. When it was opened by a maid, he gagged at the heavy aroma of vanilla. Further in the room, a red-haired woman in a green damask gown approached. Sihan gulped as he recognised the Duchess of Belaron.

'Yes, young man?'

Her dulcet voice did not soothe his nerves. 'I–I have to give these to the princess.' He held out the letter and the flowers.

'Indeed.' Brow creased, she examined Sihan closely. 'And do you know what you are holding?'

'Yes, Your Grace. Mistflowers.'

Her eyebrows rose in an elegant arc. 'Who asked you to bring these here?'

Sihan squirmed. 'I can't say.'

The duchess smiled. 'You may enter, young man.'

Sihan walked into the room. Orlanda turned from a blazing hearth, white dress stark against the backdrop of silken hangings adorning the grey stone walls in radiant splashes of summer hues.

Sihan blushed as his gaze wandered to the bed overhung with a billowing gauze canopy. The duchess sat on a divan, pushing aside a tasselled cushion.

'What do you want?' asked Orlanda, voice a husky rasp, eyes red-rimmed.

Sihan held out the note and the garland. 'I was told to bring you these.'

Hesitating, Orlanda stepped forward, eyes wide. Her fingers strayed over the tiny blue flowers. Trembling, she took the note and untied the ribbon. Shock flashed across her face, then a whirlwind of other emotions too quick to read. When she finished scanning the letter, she crumpled it in her hand.

Clutching it with white-knuckled urgency, she ran to the divan to pick up a cloak, before turning to the duchess. 'If anyone comes, tell them I am not well.'

With a curt nod, the duchess said, 'You had best be back by the time your father calls for you in the morning, or those words will hold some truth.'

Orlanda scowled, then flashed a quick smile at Sihan before disappearing at a run into her antechamber.

Orlanda hurried to an alcove at the other end of the room, the words of the note emblazoned upon her mind. "*Meet me in the rose garden – Areme.*" Fumbling with the key in her hand, she pushed aside a wall hanging. He was coming for her! And she was not dressed properly for travel, or even ready, but what did it matter? Areme was going to save her.

The narrow door behind the hanging opened without so much as a creak. She ran along a passage, dress swishing against stone, shadows rippling and flaring ahead. When she reached a turn, she pushed open another door leading to a narrow winding staircase descending two flights. She leapt down the steps two at a time, praying she would not fall over her dress, footfalls reverberating madly about her. Bursting through a door into a tiny rose garden overlooking the fortress, she gasped as a sword point levelled at her throat.

'Gods' blood, are you mad!' Areme swore, lowering his sword. The flickering torchlight from a sconce set in a nearby wall did not disguise his scowl.

Orlanda backed away, noting a group of armed men at Areme's back. 'What are you doing?' she demanded.

'Defending my life, as it happens,' said Areme. 'With all that stomping, I thought you were the king's guard.' He turned to his men. 'No one comes near here.' As the heavily armed soldiers marched away, he turned back to Orlanda. 'Did you bring the garland?'

'Yes.'

He placed his hands on her shoulders and said with forced calm. 'Get on your knees.'

Orlanda backed away from him. There was no love in his voice, no sweet endearments. Nothing she wanted or needed.

Nothing of the man from the night before, as if that had all been a dream. Her fingers crushed vellum and petals in her hand.

Areme's eyes shone silvered shards of light. There was a stillness about him, like a cobra about to strike. He pulled the garland from her hands, and shoved it on her head. 'This is what you wanted. So get on your knees so we can get this over with.'

Orlanda met his cold-metal stare. Ever since they had made love, she had forced away the thought he had loved her in error, against his will. She had wanted to believe in the chimera of love, however ephemeral. But now, here, faced with his steely aloofness once more, she railed against it. She wanted more, deserved more than his disdain, his martyred love that was no love at all. She would not settle for the crumbs off a dead woman's plate.

Beyond the merlons, frigid wind roared, carrying the briny smell and mist of the ocean. Wishing its ice could turn her heart as cold as his, Orlanda said, 'This sham of a ceremony isn't necessary. More, it's a waste of time. If we are going to escape we have to do it now. Tonight's our only chance.'

'We're not escaping.'

'But . . . I thought . . .'

Relenting his harshness, Areme pulled her into his embrace. 'I know what you thought. You must forget it. I've left it too late to get you out.' Then, taking her by the hand, he led her to a fountain in the middle of a circle of withered rose bushes. Old pain etched deeply the lines of his hard face as he said, 'Marry me.'

She pulled back, watching him uncertainly. 'I won't come second to a ghost.'

His head snapped back. 'What did you say?'

'You heard me well enough. You think because I'm so young I don't know my heart. But I do. I've known since the day I first saw you.' She lifted her chin. 'But you've never looked at me that way. Even last night, it was Shasirre to whom you made love. Not me.' She forced her voice not to break. 'But that's all right, because at least in doing so you took from Valoren something he can never get back.'

'Is that really all you think last night was to me?' His eyes glittered in his still face.

A precarious silence hung between them.

'How could I not, when every whisper of your voice was, "Shasirre"?'

He stared at her, hard, as if measuring whether her words were truth. Then he drew a long breath. 'I said that?'

'Never Orlanda. Not once.'

One of his hands tightened on hers, while the other touched the garland of mistflowers adorning her golden hair. 'Then I'm a fool.' He pulled her to him, stubbled jaw grazing her cheek as he whispered against her ear, 'If you believe nothing else, believe this. If you marry me, I'll banish all ghosts, all shadows. There will be only you in my heart. And I'll get you back, even if it means setting the country ablaze. I swear it.'

Did he mean it? Did he really want her, not Shasirre? His eyes gave no clue how to value his words.

'I won't make you break your vow.'

'I already have.' Then he was kissing her, like he had in the shadows of the singing stones, all fire.

Everything broke within her. She flung her arms around his neck, kissing him back. Nothing mattered but his lips, the roughness of his jaw, the smell and feel of him. Black and gold hair flared about them. Then she fell to her knees, tears scalding her cheeks, praying all he promised was truth.

Areme knelt before her and took her tear-stained face in his hands. He turned to Hessarde. 'Bear witness to our union.' He fixed his gaze upon Orlanda. 'By the sacred laws of Mirador, I do solemnly pledge to honour this woman as my life companion.' He pulled seven petals from the garland and scattered them into the fountain.

Orlanda pulled more petals from the garland and scattered them in the water and repeated, 'By the sacred laws of Mirador, I do solemnly pledge to honour this man as my life companion.'

She closed her eyes, hardly hearing Hessarde's part of the ritual, fear and joy fighting for dominance in her heart.

'By the sacred laws of Mirador,' finished the knight, 'I do solemnly avow to bear witness to the sacred union between this man and this woman.' Hessarde took the crown of flowers and placed it on the water, letting it float, concentric circles rippling to the edge of the fountain. 'We are all bound, now and hereafter by this deed. Let not one of us forget our duty and our honour.'

Eyes and thoughts filled only with Areme, Orlanda no longer cared if he lied or not. His lies were better than the abysmal truth of a future with Valoren.

Chapter 31

Sacrifice

The king sat on his throne. Before him, the assembled court filled the great hall to overflowing. Slivers of dawn streamed through tall slitted windows, cutting through the gloom of the walled chamber to light the grey slate floor. Hundreds of nobles and soldiers stood shoulder to shoulder, air reeking of perfume and incense. His daughter sat beside him, gold hair framing her clear, pallid face. In silence, she turned toward him, eyes deep cerulean – too like her mother's.

His heart clenched. No, he would not think of *her*. He must bury the past and look to the future. He motioned to Maraid, who struck the ground three times with his staff. Blows resonated throughout the hall.

'Who claims our daughter of Mirador?' The castellan's voice rang out.

From the front of the assemblage, Emissary Vaill and Knight Commander Veren strode forth, black-plumed helms setting off black tunics, leggings and boots. A line of black-clad men, fully armed, formed up at their back.

'Romondor claims the hand of the daughter of Mirador,' replied Vaill. Veren and his men touched their right knees to the ground, heads bowed, while he waited for her response.

The king shifted uncomfortably upon his throne. They looked more like a flock of carrion crows than vultures. He cast a quick glance about the hall, knowing too well archers held arrows nocked to bowstring in the high cupolas, weighing risk, measuring intent in every one of the massed courtiers staring toward the dais in expectation.

He took Orlanda's hand in his, ignoring her trembling and the icy feel of her skin. One day, she would understand this was for the best.

A hush fell over the crowd. Only muted brushing of brocade and thud of shuffling boots against flagstones disturbed the silence.

Orlanda remained seated, making one last, deliberate act of protest; the final spasm of an animal before death. Callinor contemplated her bleak face through a long silence, noted dark stains beneath her eyes, and steel within them. Finally, he leaned close. 'If you think to wait long enough for the snows to cover my grave . . .'

She did not let him finish, rising with resolute dignity, white gown falling in folds to the floor. For a moment, the court seemed to be caught in a golden haze of distant memory, where his queen was once again amongst them. Orlanda descended to the base of the staircase, then sank to her knees before the emissary.

Throughout the antechamber, gasps of woe mingled with those of relief. At least a few held fast to the slim hope a union between Romondor and Mirador might banish the chance of war between the two lands forever.

For his part, Vaill maintained a haughty but dignified countenance as he, too, bent his knee before the princess. No words were necessary, the act of mutual supplication more binding than anything either might have uttered. Then shouts permeated the solemnity of the ritual, until the entire antechamber rang with forced cheers and applause. The king rose to declare an end to the proceedings, relieved it had passed without incident. His thoughts turned to Romondor. Now the hard part would begin.

Flanked by Travall and Balfere, Areme stood on one side of the hall with the other knights. Upon conclusion of the ceremony, he forced his way outside, striding to a secluded garden where he leaned against the rough stone wall of the outer battlement. In a shimmer of blue light, a cowled woman appeared at his side.

'Everything's gone to hell, Myrrhye,' he said. 'I've lost her. And the horse, too. The king has forbidden me to leave Mirador. How do I protect either of them from here?'

Myrrhye answered, 'There is danger here in Mirador. Long have I felt it in my bones. For now, the horse will be safer where your brother can watch over him. Romondor is the last place anyone would search for him.'

'The horse belongs to me. I hope you made him understand that.' Areme glared at her, determined to get at a truth he had also begun to suspect she was denying him. 'I want to know about Sihan. He's being sent with the horse.'

Myrrhye's lips thinned to a line. 'The boy is not your concern.'

'He is if he gets the horse killed. He's somehow suddenly become the worst fighter I've ever seen. I've seen him at other tournaments – he wasn't hopeless then. Armindras would never have allowed him to undertake a Senfari trial if he wasn't ready.'

Myrrhye's hand snaked out and gripped Areme's arm. 'You'll not defy me. Sihan will fight if I feel there is need. Not before.'

Areme shrugged her off. 'You've put a charm on him. Why?'

Myrrhye's expression gave away nothing. 'My business, not yours.'

'He's a danger to the horse.'

'He is not your enemy, and I forbid you to raise a hand against him.'

'I swore an oath, and I mean to keep it. This madness must end. It's all I have left. I'll kill anyone getting in my way.'

'That is well, because for now, I need you here, sword at the ready. My powers fade, and we must root out the enemy before it is too late.'

Trumpets blared over the battlements, heralding the new day. Myrrhye pulled her cowl over her head. 'Let us see what the future brings.'

'There is no future without Shasirre. Just an endless age of nothing.' Areme pushed past his mother and bounded up a set of stairs to the top of the battlement. The words rang false to his own ears. Somehow Orlanda had made them false. He had forced her into a union for his own ends. Bound her to him to ensure her obedience when he came to claim her for the destiny awaiting her. He had broken the vow he had made to his wife when she had lived, in order to keep one he had made to her after she had died. Strange irony. But was there more? Why did the breaking of the oath of love not weigh heavier upon his soul? Could the girl really have ensnared him, or was it merely the magic held checked within her that reminded him of Shasirre?

    Wind burned against his skin. Salt spray stung his eyes as he stared over the ocean. He placed his hands on the stone and stood in silence, gazing unseeing into the distance, then finally lowered his head to rest on his folded arms. Tears stained the battlement like morning dew, droplets glinting in dull morning light. A fitting epitaph for the death of his soul.

Chapter 32

Sea of Eagles

Black currawongs flew high above the battlements of Mirador, white-tipped wings outstretched. Grey curtains of rain drifted across grass fields, showering the company of leather-armoured soldiers stationed before the fortress, and forming puddles around their horses' muddy hooves.

Sihan shifted in his saddle, droplets sliding down his face like frozen snakes, the unseasonal autumn heat broken well and truly. He was stiff and cold, but pain distanced itself as though somehow his body had resigned itself to the constancy of hurt. Beside Sihan, Gerein looked bored but resolute, and the red-haired youth Sihan had met early in Mirador – Camar – just yawned.

Gerhas's fingers clenched and unclenched his horse's reins, a sour grimace deepening the lines on his weathered face. Grey dusted his grizzled brown hair and short beard, sprinkled to silver by drops of rain.

Nearby, Balfere patted his wall-eyed horse, then mounted, settling his bulk into the saddle. A trumpet blared on the battlements. Travall, surcoat and armoured finery hidden beneath a long grey cloak, rode down from the fortress and drew rein before the horsemaster. The king and the princess, both grey-cloaked, rode out the fortress gates with the half company of black-clad riders of the Romondor escort at their backs.

Meant as a symbol of trust and unity. The men around Sihan muttered less charitable interpretations. It did not augur well for good relations on the journey. Sihan huddled deeper into his cloak.

The escort formed up, outriders on either side of the king and the princess. At the van rode Balfere and Veren, as unlikely a pairing as Sihan could have imagined. Balfere wore an expression of disgust, as did his stallion, the bay's ears flattened, head snaking at Veren's black.

The king rode beside Vaill, cloak sweeping over Celestion's rump like a blanket. Aurion pranced, bearing the princess. Her cloak hung limp over her white riding habit, a match for her wan, lifeless face, a mask cast in frost, blue eyes cold as she pushed a strand of wet, gold hair behind her ear and drew her hood further over her head.

Gerhas's gnarled face twitched as he turned to Sihan. 'You keep that white horse under control. If he gets out of hand, he might start a war all by himself, and this whole marriage business will have gone for naught.'

Sihan opened his mouth, hesitated, hand fluttering nervously beneath his cloak. 'I wrote a note for my father.' He pulled out a piece of vellum. 'Would you see he gets it?'

'Yes, lad.' Gerhas took the scroll. His gravelly voice lowered. 'If it were any other horse–'

'I know.' Sihan's throat constricted as he cut Gerhas off. If it were any other horse but Aurion, he would not be going to Romondor. But it *was* Aurion, and all of his dreams of returning to Graycor and becoming Senfari were ash.

Gerhas said, 'For what it is worth, your service ends upon the death of the white horse.'

A chill coursed down Sihan's spine, a remembrance of the night the foal was born, of a dream, a voice claiming he would be Aurion's death. And now here was the horsemaster saying Aurion's death would buy his freedom, as if urging him to the task.

He shook off the words, if not the distaste. Words were only words, and dreams just dreams. In no way would he ever again make the decision to take a horse's life except in mercy. In no way would he defy Senfar's law.

He took his place on the fringe of the escort. As they turned south to Romondor, he cast a glance northward, to Graycor, imagined his father and the Senfari bringing in the mares from Yseth, pitching hay into barn lofts. Every stride south, the cord binding him to all he once knew unwound.

Echoing his mood, the overcast sky lowered slowly until it settled in a film of grey mist over land blanched of colour. The escort rode at a steady trot through harrowed brown fields until late afternoon, moist scent of sodden earth filling the air. As day wore into evening, fewer travellers hailed them, most farmers and their stock already bundled up against the cold in the shelter of cottages, barns and folds.

It was an odd cavalcade, fifty-odd Romondor soldiers massed together; with over a hundred grey-cloaked men from Mirador in their own separate group; all of them mute, as though one word would spark a war. It was all ill-omened. Even Travall, bringing up the rear, constantly turned to look behind as if expecting attack, despite scouts and sentries riding ahead and at their back.

Though Sihan rode in the most exalted company anyone could wish, taking part in the forging of a new destiny for Mirador – a permanent, indisputable peace with Romondor – cold foreboding filled him. Perhaps it was the desperate cost of that peace – Orlanda.

Sihan glanced at her, could see nothing but misery in her face and downcast eyes. Perhaps it was something closer at hand than the dark fate awaiting her. Areme had caught the marsh man, but were there others after the princess? Perhaps it was the thought he could not shake, that they were riding toward war, not against it, as his father had claimed.

He closed his eyes, trying to focus. He should have written a note for Jaien as well. Let him know what had happened. Why hadn't he? Would Jaien even care?

'Rider! Incoming!' shouted the rearward sentry, jolting Sihan to alert.

The escort closed around the king and princess. Steel flashed as swords hissed from scabbards. One rider flew down the fortress road, then slid to a frenetic halt, and performed a haphazard bow from his saddle to the king. His grey cloak swept back, revealing leather armour and a sword, and a dagger at his belt. He leaned forward and held out a scroll to Travall. The knight gave a cursory glance at the missive, then waved the rider away. 'Sheathe swords,' he ordered.

The young man drove his chestnut stallion into the mix of soldiers and fell in beside Sihan, earning scowls from the men of Romondor and recriminations from those of Mirador. He maneuvered his horse to flank Sihan, green eyes glittering from beneath shoulder-length hair flicked rakishly over his forehead. 'Greetings, again,' he said.

Recognizing Maiet, the mad drunken youth from the Fire Rituals, Sihan smiled. 'You were riding fast as a courier.'

'King's Scout, actually.' Maiet patted his chestnut. 'Warwind here – he can outrace anything going, except maybe Aurion.' Maiet deliberately angled his chestnut to bump Sihan's bay away from the others. 'You've no idea how glad everyone is that Aurion's going to Romondor.' Maiet lowered his voice a fraction. 'We . . . all the soldiers of Mirador . . . think the white stallion is our new secret weapon. I'll bet you anything you'll get a note from Gerhas soon after you reach Romondor, telling you to get the hells out of there and to leave that white beast to run amok. We think he'll wipe out the entire Romondor army within a moon's cycle.'

Sihan burst out laughing. 'Not even Aurion could do that.'

Maiet grinned. 'I wouldn't be game to bet on that. And at least he would save us a battle or two.' Maiet waved a hand at the flat plain of cropped fields stretching into the distance to low, blue hills. Bare of trees, only granite tors speared into the sky. 'At least there's scant chance of an ambush here. Reminds me of the flatlands in Maroden. I was in a party trying to clean out a nest of raiders. They turned out to be a bunch of superstitious fools who worshipped goats. All we had to do was round up a flock of those hair-brains and run them in front of us. Their archers stopped shooting at us in case they shot a goaty god!'

'Will you two shut your traps!' bellowed Balfere.

Maiet winked at Sihan, uncorked his water pouch, took a swig, wiped his mouth on the sleeve of his thick leather coat, before hooking the pouch back to the front saddle horn, next to his helm. Sihan prayed it did not contain wine. The last thing they needed was for Maiet to fall off his horse or run his mouth off even more.

The evening wore down. Sihan smothered a yawn and rolled his shoulders inside his leather jerkin, trying to relieve knotted muscles in his neck and back. To while away the monotony of endless trotting all day, he had put his horse through its paces, schooling it to rein back, leg yield, pay him respectful attention – Senfari skills, glad there was something he knew how to do right in this world where everything had gone wrong. He wondered if he would be allowed to train horses in Romondor. He clenched his teeth. He must.

Dusk brought with it an iced breeze. Brown land gave way to fields of yellow stubble, then purpling hills studded with trees to which thin withered leaves clung. The escort traversed a narrow track, winding upward through a sward of saltbush. As the going steepened, the horses slowed, hooves biting into packed, grey-white sand.

At the summit, the king called a halt. The hill dropped away to the edge of a lake, bloodstained from the dying light of the settling sun. Sihan squinted but could not see the opposite shore. Soft, crimson billows lapped against trunks of dead, white trees protruding from the surface.

Without warning, an eagle swooped overhead, dipping its mighty wings as if to salute the King of Mirador.

'This is the Sea of Eagles.' The king waved his arm expansively, speaking to Vaill who stopped his horse beside him. 'Salt-ridden now. We will camp a league or so further on, at a freshwater stream.'

Vaill's mouth twitched. Gaunt face as bleak as the princess's, the emissary spurred his horse down the slope.

Spellbound, Sihan rode toward the shining water. A flight of butcherbirds swooped to land on a bleached branch of a dead tree near the shore, adorning it like black and white flowers.

Veren dropped back to ride next to him. 'What do you think of the dead sea?'

Sihan glanced at the knight, surprised by the question, and the fact Veren was talking to him at all. Especially him, the lowest ranking member of the Mirador party. 'I'm not sure I think anything of it.'

'You don't find it appeals to you? The desolation? The mystic beauty in death?'

Cold flowed over Sihan. A sense of timelessness filled the knight's tone, his dark eyes. Sihan examined the knight closely, trying to fathom the meaning behind his words. Discomfited, he feigned disinterest. 'Death's death. There's not much beauty in it. And I don't see what it has to do with this sea.'

Veren waved a hand toward the lake. 'Nothing grows here. Behold the trees. Stark, white monuments to loss. Beckoning. Calling.'

An eerie silence rose like chilled mist from the lake. And then a whisper. *Come, join with me. Death is not the end.*

Sihan whirled around, but there was no one behind him. He forced himself not to listen, turned to Veren and said, 'I can't say I think about death much, in seas, trees or otherwise.'

Veren's black eyes bored into his. 'You are very fortunate. I think about it constantly. It haunts my dreams.'

'I'm sorry,' said Sihan, trying to find any response to this bizarre comment.

'So am I, Sihan. So am I.' Veren spurred his horse to the head of the column.

Sihan pulled his cloak close, staring after the knight, wondering at his strange words that almost filled him with dread. Then he glanced round once more, glad when no more voices touched his ears with ghostly breath.

Before dusk dissolved into night, Balfere and Travall stopped their horses at a clearing surrounded by scrubby wood where a stream meandered along one side. The princess slid off Aurion, grey travelling cloak rumpled. Sihan gave her a tight-lipped smile, then led Aurion away to tether him to a tree next to Spirit. He helped Maiet erect tents, then gathered kindling, lit a fire, and prepared the evening meal, forcing his injured muscles to work. Comfortably tired, he took pleasure in the heat suffusing his face as he sat on the ground, close to the flames, smell of baking damper thick in his nostrils.

Maiet's face became pensive. 'Oh hells, here comes trouble.'

Balfere strode toward a group of Mirador soldiers who sat demarcated from the Romondor men. 'You four take first watch.' Then he approached Maiet. 'You take second watch with Sihan.'

Sihan started in surprise at being included.

Maiet groaned. 'He can't even fight.' He shot a quick glance at Sihan. 'No offence.'

Sihan blushed. Was there anyone in Mirador who did not know about the beating he had received?

Balfere looked hard at Sihan. 'Are you going to use your gammy leg as an excuse?'

'No,' snapped Sihan.

Gerein slapped him on the back. 'Good lad.'

Sihan stared after Balfere as the knight walked away, recalling his failure at the sword drill. He touched the hilt of his new sword, wondering again how his skills had somehow evaporated since coming to Mirador, and determined to give a better accounting of himself than he had heretofore.

As they ate their meal, Maiet motioned to the Romondor soldiers, hunkered in tight groups around their own fires. 'They certainly know how to keep a quiet tongue in their heads.' He stood and walked to a knot of black-clad men who sat in front of black leather tents, offering one a piece of damper.

'I'm right,' replied the soldier, turning away.

Maiet ignored the icy rebuff. 'What's your name?'

The soldier shot the scout a dirty sideways look and said in short, clipped words, 'My name is for my friends.'

Face closed, Maiet returned to Sihan's side. 'Nasty little vultures,' he muttered. 'No wonder the princess looks like someone's ripped her guts out.'

Sihan glanced at the princess. She sat in front of a fire set outside her tent, picking at a wastel loaf. Flickering firelight accented the downward set of her lips.

'In very truth,' continued Maiet. 'I've never seen someone look so depressed.'

Poking more kindling into the fire, Sihan said, 'She's got every right to be. Fancy being forced to marry the Black Duke. Sends shudders down my spine just thinking about it.'

'Me, too.' Maiet kicked a log. 'Get some rest. I'll wake you when it's time.'

Pulling a coarse woollen blanket over his shoulders, Sihan turned his back to the fire. He did not know when or if he drifted to sleep, but it seemed no time at all before Maiet tugged on his arm and hissed, 'Get your blades and follow me.'

Sihan sucked in a ragged breath and rolled to his feet. Running his tongue across his bottom lip, he tasted blood where a wound had re-opened.

Adjusting dagger and sword, he cast a wary glance about the camp. Empty saddle rolls next to the dying fire told that others were already out scouting.

At camp's edge, Maiet strode into undergrowth, lean body clad in brown leather armour, leggings and tunic indistinguishable from the forest. Sihan followed, predator-silent despite the limp he suppressed.

Soft breezes sighed through trees, gently swaying strips of bark. Every muscle tense, Sihan strove to see or hear anything unusual.

A possum quarked among thick coachwood leaves; bush rustled with night creatures. Maiet crept through a tangle of shrubbery, leaves swishing.

Black clouds covered the moon, the night smelling of rain to come. Dark enfolded them as they moved farther from the camp. At their backs, sharp pinpricks of red light glowed from embers of spent fires.

After a while, they emerged at a point overlooking the stream. Maiet hunkered low. He tugged Sihan down by the sleeve, and placed his hand on the earth. 'Feel it?'

Sihan concentrated on the smooth imprint of a half-circle in the soft ground, edges soft and yielding, not dried and crumbling like old spoor. 'A shod horse passed here not long past.'

'The other scouts said they picked up signs we're being followed.'

'By whom?' asked Sihan, rubbing sweating palms against his leggings.

'My bet is vultures. If I'm right, we want them alive. We need them to talk and give us evidence Romondor has broken the truce, sending spies or assassins to Mirador.' Light drops of rain began to fall as Maiet stood. 'Let's find them before the rain really gets going.'

They stalked through the dark, rain pattering on leaves. Maiet halted at odd intervals, sniffing the air, then dropped to one knee once more, feeling wet ground. Something moved in a low tree limb next to Sihan's shoulder. Hot, feral breath warmed his damp skin. A pair of blazing blue eyes flashed. Sihan shout-whispered a warning, 'Maiet! Down!'

Maiet rolled too late. A small black lonyx fell upon him with a high-pitched screech. Lunging blindly, Sihan grabbed at the heavy pelt, tore at the predator. In a heartbeat, the beast twisted, latching on to Sihan's throat. Skin split, fangs raked.

'Shit! Shit!' he cursed.

'I've got it!' Maiet swore as he yanked at the creature. Claws slashed like blades across Sihan's open wounds. Sihan clawed for his dagger, panting. It slipped through blood-wet fingers.

Holding the furry assailant aloft with one hand, the animal slashing at the scout's leather gloves, Maiet pulled a pouch from his belt with his other hand. He struggled to stuff the head of the spitting beast into it, then drew the leather cord tight.

Sihan fell to one knee, groping for his dagger. Instead, he found ridged indentations, deep, half-moons. Keeping his voice low, he called out, 'Maiet! Over here! Tracks.'

Maiet knelt. 'Hmm,' he muttered. 'Hooves wrapped in leather boots. They're trying to hide their trail.' He straightened. Turning the lonyx on its back, he rubbed the exposed stomach, cursing softly as the beast's claws scratched his arms. Slowly the lonyx stiffened into a trance, a foot of limp fur. 'Just like a chicken,' said Maiet.

'What are you *doing*? Kill it!' urged Sihan.

'No.' Maiet kept one hand on the animal's belly. 'I've got a better idea.'

'The bloody thing will rip your throat out if it gets loose.'

Ignoring Sihan, Maiet stuffed the lonyx inside his tunic. 'I wish I had Trav's gambeson. If this thing wakes up, I'll be screaming like nobody's business.'

'What are you doing with it?'

'Ever seen what a lonyx will do to a horse?' Not waiting for an answer, Maiet hunkered low, and followed the trail of the leather-bound hooves. At length, he paused, and sat on his haunches behind some bushes near the bank of the stream. He pointed across ink-black water at several dark forms lying on the opposite shore. 'There they are.'

Sihan looked up and downstream. 'They haven't set scouts.'

'Might be further down.' Flattening to the ground, Maiet groped along the rocks to the edge of the stream, slipping over the side of the bank. He waded into the water, waist deep. Sihan grimaced as night-chilled water filled his boots, biting into his skin. His teeth were chattering long before they reached the opposite shore. They slithered out on the bank and scrabbled toward the horses.

Maiet paused as wind picked up and rustled leaves of nearby trees. When no one stirred, he crawled on. They came to a tether-line, down wind from the horses and not thirty yards from the sleeping men. Sihan arose slowly. Squinting in the darkness, he moved slowly so as not to frighten the horses. Stroking one on the shoulder, he whispered to Maiet, 'They aren't black.'

'Vultures wouldn't use black horses if they're spying. Grab two. I'll take care of the other.'

Sihan cut the tethers and tugged on the lead ropes, urging the horses to follow.

'Get them down to the river's edge,' whispered Maiet. 'I don't want them spooking when I pull the lonyx out.' But not moments later, fierce spitting and a muffled curse blew Maiet's plan apart as the lonyx tore the makeshift muzzle from its face.

The two horses Sihan held, reared and swung away, yanking the lead ties out of his hands. They crashed away into the darkness. Maiet threw the lonyx at the remaining horse. The beast thumped against the horse's rump, then latched on with its claws. The stallion recoiled, then bucked furiously, trying to dislodge the beast tearing into its flesh.

Shouts filled the darkness.

'Hells! Run!' urged Maiet.

Sihan ran as fast as his injured leg would let him, to the stream, feet squelching inside waterlogged boots. Somewhere at their back, came shouts and the scream of a horse in agony. Arrows hissed past Sihan's head, striking the stream. He launched himself into the water and swam for the other bank, then clambered out on the other side, doubly numb as when he had first crossed. Maiet struggled out after him, and they struck out at a run, Sihan's injured leg dead and unfeeling with cold. As they careered through the bush, a thunderous crack exploded from the darkness. Lightning illuminated the surrounding area.

'Great,' said Maiet, breath harsh.

Footfalls and shouts neared. An arrow slammed a tree next to Sihan, buried inches deep. Maiet dodged into thick hop scrub and bracken. They clambered through undergrowth, trying to keep as much cover between themselves and enemy arrows as possible. High above the treetops, rivers of light flooded the sky. At their back, cursing men smashed through branches and bushes.

Sihan stumbled, his leg warmed to the point pain returned with a deadly rush. 'Go on,' he pushed Maiet onward when the scout slowed to help.

Instead, Maiet grabbed Sihan and pulled him tumbling down a slope into a tangle of brambles. Sihan's heart beat fierce as shadow figures crashed past above.

'We'll backtrack around them,' whispered Maiet.

When the sound of footfalls ebbed, they struggled out of the thicket, sharp thorns tearing at skin and clothing. They angled away from the direction their pursuers had taken. Lightning flashed and Maiet stopped, dropping to one knee. He brushed his hand over the ground. 'Hells! Those vultures are circling for us.'

Dread coiled in Sihan's gut. 'I can't run with this leg.'

'Sit tight. The others will come for us when we don't return.'

'That's a piss-poor plan.'

'Only one I've got.'

Branches broke nearby. Sihan froze. Flashes of lightning followed rolls of thunder. Footsteps drew nearer. A blaze of light lit up the bush around them, revealing the predators to the prey.

Before the archers could nock arrows, Maiet took off, pounding through the bush, dragging Sihan beside him, three men in close pursuit. Heavy drops spattered from the sky, closing round like a grey cage. They raced out of the bushes onto the pebbled edge of the inland sea. Behind them, three men appeared.

Armed only with swords and daggers, Sihan and Maiet backed away, step by step. There was nowhere to hide, nowhere left to run, only the dark bulk of a large stone standing alone like a sentinel on the shore – closer to the hunters than Maiet and Sihan.

The men armed their bows. Again the whole world blazed. The massive stone glimmered violet and indigo, three men silhouetted against it. Lightning crashed, illuminating them. As they approached, an immense roar filled the air.

Sihan blinked, senses addled, staring beyond the enemy. In the trees, stood a grey-cloaked woman, arms raised, next to a rider on a black horse lit bright by a shimmering of sheet lightning.

A blinding flash seared Sihan's eyes. Serpents of light slithered from the dark, winding above the ground to explode over the stone. Sihan recoiled, fell, breath knocked out of him. Pain shot through his ears, and a cacophony of sound, like voices screaming.

An age passed before he recovered enough to struggle to his knees. Rubbing his eyes, he tried to erase the bright lights streaking across them. Another bolt of lightning set the sky aflame, exposing a tangle of bodies in front of him. Gagging at the appalling smell of scorched flesh and hair, he stumbled to a dark heap on the ground. 'Maiet!' he cried. 'Maiet!'

The scout lay stretched out on his side, cheek against sand, sword by his side.

'Maiet!' shouted Sihan over the ringing in his ears. A hand clasped him on the shoulder. Whirling, he wildly swung his sword.

'Hold!' cried a familiar voice, the shadowed figure dodging out of the way.

'Gerein!' Sihan stared at the archer, uncomprehending. Then, relieved, cried, 'Thank the Heavens.' Dropping his sword, he fell on his knees beside Maiet.

Someone shouted nearby, and men from the Mirador watch ran toward them.

'In very truth, my ears are killing me!' exclaimed Camar, running up from further along the sea, shaking his head. He kicked one of the bodies. 'Damn! All dead. Now we'll never know who they were or what they were up to. Trav'll kill us.'

'Better Trav than them,' said Gerein.

'What's wrong with Maiet?' asked Camar, while the others poked around the dead bodies.

'Lightning flash,' said Gerein. 'Bolt struck right in the middle of those vultures. If Maiet had been any closer, he would have been crisped, too. Let's get him up.'

While the other men pulled the dead men into the trees, Sihan and Camar helped Gerein lift Maiet to his feet. Maiet staggered. Another loud rumble sent them all cowering beneath the shelter of trees.

'Let the storm abate a little,' said Gerein.

Sihan looked around, scanning the trees. Had he really seen a woman, or a rider?

His cloak, tunic, and leggings clung to him like wet rags, and runnels of water slid down his forehead and cheeks. The pale light of dawn had drawn over the sky by the time they arrived back to the camp. Thin wisps of smoke threaded the air with the scent of burning wattle. Most of the escort were already mounted, having broken camp and doused the embers of dead fires.

The king mounted his horse, flicking his grey cloak over Celestion's rump. He inspected the scouts silently, gaze fixed on their dishevelled, sodden tabards, then turned a stony, rain-streaked face to Travall. 'See to the princess.'

After lifting the princess onto her horse, Travall vaulted onto his own, eyes glacial as he raked a gaze over Maiet and his companions. To Balfere he said, 'Take as long as you need.'

Balfere stood in silence, clenching and unclenching his gauntleted fists. Veren and his soldiers mounted, then formed into two lines at Vaill's back, faces grim. But Veren kept his eyes fixed on Sihan.

Sihan returned the stare, and a strange sensation washed across him that somehow the rider on the shore had been Veren. But how was that possible? He pushed the wild thought aside. There could not have been a woman out there in a storm either. He had been seeing things.

When the escort disappeared behind a stand of acacias, Sihan lowered Maiet to the ground and pushed the scout's bedraggled blonde hair out of his face. 'Maiet!'

'Let me die,' the scout groaned.

'What happened?' Balfere demanded.

Gerein grabbed a water pouch from the saddle of his horse and offered it to Maiet. 'The men tracking us, sir. We found them.' He dribbled water across Maiet's pale face, then dabbed at it with a strip of cloth torn from his under tunic.

'Where are they?' asked Balfere.

'Lightning strike killed the lot.'

Balfere grimaced. 'Hells. I would've loved to wipe the smirk off Veren's face. Did you search the bodies?'

Gerein picked up his travelling cloak from his bedroll and wrapped it around his shoulders. 'Nothing on them. They could be zingars for all the evidence we have.'

'What's your gut feeling?'

Without hesitation, Gerein said, 'Vultures.'

'What now?' asked Camar.

Balfere motioned to the scouts from the last shift, 'Stay with Maiet till he regains his senses.'

Maiet sat up and stared dazedly around. 'My head hurts.'

Balfere walked to his horse. 'Follow soon as you can. Pairs, either side of the road. There'll be more of them out there. I'll stake my life on it.'

As Balfere mounted his wall-eyed bay and rode after the escort, Gerein exchanged a look with Camar, then spat. 'He's staking *our* lives on it, actually.'

Sihan stared after Balfere, thought of the marsh man, and the others Areme had fought the day before. He wished suddenly Areme was with them, and Hessarde and all his cutthroat command. If the past few days had taught him anything, the king and the princess were in danger and it was going to take more than Travall and Balfere, Gerein and one hundred of the king's elite command to protect them.

Chapter 33

The Road to Romondor

Travall rode alongside the king, well ahead of the others. Low clouds filled the late afternoon sky, making the forest around them dark and oppressive. Only the jangle of bits and stirrup irons and the muffled thud of hooves striking leaf-strewn earth disturbed the stillness.

The lines around the king's eyes worried Travall, and the dead look within the grey depths. In too short a time, vulnerability and desperation had replaced strength. Grief had worn Callinor to a shadow, refusing him rest from pain, or guilt.

'What is the feeling among the men?' Callinor's words dripped slowly into the silence like the first spattering of rain.

Replying with reservation, Travall said, 'You have a death wish.'

'Indeed.' Callinor focused on the trail ahead, back ramrod-stiff. 'And what do *you* think?'

'I don't think. I follow orders.'

'A dog's response!'

'Well then, sire. I rather think your secrets are your own. I'll not reveal them, just as no man before me who served in the Great War and valued his life has ever revealed them.' Travall ran a gloved hand through his close-cropped hair, the horror of killing men with whom he had served coursing through him.

A fine pair, the king and he, murderers both, and liars. Would the people of Mirador ever know the truth? That Travall had strangled a queen, and his monarch had killed a country? There was no forgiveness in the world that would remove those crimes from their hearts.

A currawong called its first drowsy song from among tall trees lining the track. Travall drew a heavy sigh, voicing once more the arguments so many had laid at the king's door of late. 'I know what's at stake. But this is no simple call of courtesy. Turn back for Mirador with me. Let the duke come to us.'

Callinor shook his head, grave certainty in his voice as he said, 'Valoren would have equal cause – no – *more* – to envisage the same fate for himself if he came to Mirador. No, I will carry this through, at whatever cost.'

'At least hand over Orlanda at the border.'

'And brand myself coward as well as tyrant?'

Travall leaned close and kept his voice low. 'Consider what you are doing. If you believe handing yourself over to Valoren will grant you absolution, you're mistaken. Your daughter – that's symbolic – but yourself? It's long past time for such gestures.'

'You speak your mind, Travall, and you know when to keep silent. I've always admired you for both.' Again weariness passed across Callinor's craggy face. 'Set your heart at rest. Every day death draws nearer, but I do not feel it will be by Valoren's hand.'

'No. He's got so many men wanting to kill you it's unlikely he will have to sully his own hands with blood.' Travall gazed through the trees at gathering winter dusk, blue and luminous, turning away from a distress he could neither prevent nor help.

Callinor's lips curved into a sad smile. 'You're a hard man, Travall. I hope when the time comes, you'll have enough grace to shake Valoren's hand.'

'I will do whatever my king commands.'

The king's back braced in the saddle as though he was preparing to receive a blow. 'Yes, Travall, I know.'

Orlanda rode in silence, gaze fixed on the grey-cloaked backs of her father and Knight Commander Travall. With Emissary Vaill on her right and Veren on her left, every nerve screamed at her to set heels to Aurion and flee.

She had fought her father's resolve for more than a year, but now, here she was, riding toward a hateful future. She balled spit on her tongue, longing to make her displeasure known. Even if her father turned back now, begged her forgiveness, left her everything he had to leave, she would scorn it all. Her mind had turned to hate when love had left her nothing but pain.

'My lady is curiously silent,' said Vaill, brown eyes glittering in his thin face.

Orlanda shuddered as he brought his horse close. If she had been riding astride, his leg would surely have brushed hers.

'I was informed your wit matched your beauty,' continued Vaill. 'But perhaps the journey tires you?'

Glaring at him, she snarled a parody of the words she had heard his men utter the night before. 'My wit is for my friends.'

'Ah . . .' A soft half-smile formed on Vaill's lips. 'You must forgive my men. Old habits break hard. When you get to know them–'

Diplomacy vanished with the dissolving mist. 'I have no intention of getting to know them. What do you think I am; a common whore?'

'No, my lady,' said Vaill with resigned tolerance. 'That is not what I think.'

Orlanda snapped. 'I accepted the proposal. When I get to Romondor I intend to tell Valoren exactly what I think of him and his murderous country. Other than that I will not acknowledge any of you vultures. Now leave me alone.'

'Those remarks are unworthy of a woman charged with such great destiny,' the emissary answered with the studied calm of a veteran well practiced in dealing with awkward episodes.

'Let her be.' Veren moved his black horse closer to Aurion, who flattened his ears. He regarded her steadily with narrowed black eyes filled with shrewdness.

Orlanda clenched her jaw, and tapped Aurion into a canter, sending him surging forth from between her tormentors. 'Barbarous brutes,' she sniffed as she brought Aurion to a walk next to her father.

The king did not even look at her. 'Calm your heart. They are men, nothing more or less.'

Orlanda flashed into further vexation. 'I have no heart to calm. It belongs to another.'

'You have given what was not yours to give, as I once took what was not mine to take.' His tone was dull and heavy, like a great weight had settled about his shoulders.

She shot him a swift glance. 'What do you mean? What did you take that was not yours by right?'

The king stared ahead, all expression veiled. 'It matters not. Trust this course is wise and will bring, in time, a greater joy than any you may have dreamed elsewhere.'

Orlanda spat. 'Joy with a man I despise?'

Her father reached across and grasped her arm in a fierce grip. Anger flared, clear and strong, across his face, burned in his eyes, chilling her to silence. 'Judge no man unless you have walked his steps. There is not one of us who cannot lay claim to some flaw or frailty.' His hand dropped away. He clicked at Celestion, and the grey stallion bounded forward.

Startled and disquieted, Orlanda raised her crop to send Aurion in pursuit, but Travall closed his hand on the white stallion's rein.

'Let him go,' he said quietly.

She rounded on him. 'What ails him?'

The knight grew pale.

'What do you know?' she demanded, her father's words weighing like an anchor upon her soul.

Travall released his hold on the rein. 'Everything, Your Highness. And when you meet Valoren, you will, also.' Without another word, he spurred his horse after the king.

Orlanda stared after him, puzzled.

Balfere, riding up by her side, pointed to the distance where blue shadows bulked against the sky. 'The Byerol Ranges.'

Devastation struck her like a sword blow. 'You mean we're at the border?'

'The ranges extend into Mirador, but we'll be at the border within the next day or so.'

Orlanda exhaled sharply. Soon she would not even be in the same country as Areme.

The hills became longer and steeper, grassland pastures replaced by dense forests of stringy bark and blue ash. Dusk gathered around them, greenish light of the forest growing deep. Travall gave the order to make camp.

While Sihan tended Aurion, Orlanda stood near, waiting for the men to erect her tent, tired and aching in every muscle of her legs, back, and shoulders.

The white stallion shone under the distant light of the stars, a pale marble statue. Areme's gift, yet she took no pleasure in him. She had planned to escape on him, but here she was, every beat of his hooves bearing her further away from hope, toward doom. Her hand clenched his mane. Exhausted, faith draining from her soul, she stared into the dark. Where was Areme? When would he come for her?

Chapter 34

Blood for Blood

Dank air, tinged with the sickly odour of congealing blood, filled the interrogation chamber. Areme leaned against the wall while the interrogator sharpened a knife – short, sharp echoing rasps. Rivulets of water streamed down rough rock, following the coarse paths of inter-woven granite – cold against his skin. Only four of the latest dozen men his soldiers had captured still drew breath. Each bore the mark of guild assassins.

The interrogator approached his next victim. Shackled, the prisoner croaked, 'Have you no mercy?'

The curve of the interrogator's smile pushed through his neat, pointed beard as he caressed the thin blade. He ran the steel edge across the man's throat, breaking skin, drawing a trickle of blood. 'Tell us what you know and I'll spare you. A quick death, or . . .'

The man gulped, staring at dismembered corpses littering the chamber. His face paled to a shade of jaundice. 'I don't know anything.'

Areme stepped forward. 'Your friends targeted the princess. What were you planning on doing with her? Besides rape.'

The man shuddered and shook his head, wisps of hair sticking to his bleeding scalp.

Areme pulled the glove from his right hand. The ring with the red firefalcon edged in black glittered in flickering torchlight. To date, it had born no fruit to ask the question, failing to unearth adepts. Strange incongruity, that the guild of assassins contained no men sworn to the rings of blood. He focused on the man. 'Whom do you serve?'

A sharp intake of breath broke the silence following the question. Areme whirled, following the ripple of movement that went round the room, as all heads turned in one direction, all eyes fastening on a small man with a whippet-thin face who had just been brought in. Little flesh hung between skin and bone, his face grey as lavender, shrunken into deep lines.

Without another thought, Areme plunged the dagger into the throat of the prisoner at his feet. A gurgling cry split the dark gloom.

Then Areme faced the chained man who had gasped, demanding, 'What do you know?'

The prisoner's face was impenetrable as he answered, 'I knows thy ring, Warden of the Living Sphere.'

At last. Areme drew a ragged breath. 'Whom do you serve?'

The man's bright eyes clung to Areme's. 'You, Lord Master.'

'You bear the mark of guild assassins.'

The man snorted. 'I was bound to this ring five lifetimes ago. What allegiance can outweigh that owed to a Senfaren Lord?'

Areme said to the interrogator. 'Finish the others. I only need this one.'

Amid screams and pleading and agonising death cries, Areme released the adept from his bonds. 'Tell me what you know.'

'Little, Lord Master.' The adept motioned to the dead men lying in pools of spreading blood around the chamber, his hand so thin, the light shone through it when raised. 'Like them.'

'A little may be enough.'

'Many moons past, a dark man came to our camp, dressed like death.'

Areme knelt before the prisoner and gripped his shoulders, their faces eye to eye. 'What man?'

'A cowl covered his face. But I'll never forget that voice; daggers through your soul.'

'What did he want?'

'Nothing that made sense. He spoke mostly to others, guild leaders. But I caught some of the gaggling. Something about the dark man wanting a horse of power.'

Areme's head snapped back.

The adept placed his hands within Areme's like a begging dog. 'My dead friend here . . . wily fellow. Always thinking how to cut the greater chance. He said the dark man was willing to pay a king's ransom for the horse. Horse of power. King's ransom. Could only mean one thing. The king's horse, Celestion.'

Celestion? Areme shook baffled bewilderment impatiently from him. They were after the wrong horse. He let out a slow breath.

The adept continued. 'There was no way of reaching the king's stallion. Not while he's stabled in the fortress. So the Guild Master planned to capture the princess and hold her for ransom.'

'The ransom being Celestion.'

A tentative smile bowed the adept's mouth. 'You are wise, Lord Master.'

Areme's thoughts raced. They knew about the horse. But not which one. And not about Orlanda. His fist clenched. It made no difference. If they were after Celestion, Aurion was in danger. He should never have let them go. He ruffled the adept's dirty hair. 'You've served me well.'

The man's eyes blazed with fanaticism. 'I live to serve my Lord Master.' He sank down to the flagstones, eyes faded to dark pits in the scrawny face, his part done.

Areme waved a hand at the body. 'Bind his wounds and look after him.'

The interrogator eyed the adept without interest. 'What's to be done? We both know which horse the dark man *really* wanted. And it's marching straight to Romondor in company of the horse everyone is targeting.'

Areme spat. 'Not for long.'

'You'll never catch them in time.'

Areme strode toward the door of the chamber. 'You forget who I'm riding. The escort won't be travelling at more than a trot, and Seroyen can fly like the wind. Once I get to Taiere, Myrrhye will send me the rest of the way. Send word to Hessarde. If this country is about to drown in blood, I want my men ready to march.'

The interrogator's eyes burned steadily as he asked the question they both feared. 'And if the king interferes?'

Areme's fingers clenched on his sword hilt. 'I won't give him the chance.'

Chapter 35

Ruined Castle

As the camp roused to another bitter dawn, Sihan wrapped his thick travelling cloak closer and belted the folds securely about his waist. Trees reached for the pink and gold sky, and an immense silence pervaded the forest, not a branch moving in lifeless air.

Nearby, Camar stumbled from his tent, rubbing the crust from the corners of his eyes, then stamped his feet and clapped his hands. Gerein, on his knees holding a staked, roasting rabbit before a fire, laughed. 'Is that the latest dance?'

Camar squatted beside him and grimaced. 'Have I ever told you I hate the cold?'

'Frequently,' answered Gerein, tearing off pieces of rabbit and handing it to Camar and Sihan.

In between bites, Sihan helped Maiet break camp.

'Saddle up!' Balfere's order shattered the stillness.

Soldiers jumped to their feet, stuffing damper into mouths, and kicked dirt over fires. Some rushed to relieve themselves, while others saddled horses. Sihan tossed the bones of his rabbit into ash, then waited next to the horses until Orlanda was ready to mount. When his hands closed about her slender waist, he hesitated. There was more dress than body, bone than flesh. He shuddered. She seemed to be withering to nothing. Leaning close, he whispered, 'You've got to eat.'

Sorrow touched her lips. 'I haven't the will.'

Her breath came warm against his cheek and the scent of mint merged with the trace of vanilla still lingering about her dress. Sihan lifted her onto Aurion, then mounted his own horse. Despite Sihan's best efforts to ignore the princess's haggard face beneath limp yellow hair, he found it almost impossible to drag his gaze away from her to focus on the landscape, with its rugged hills.

He was glad when Balfere ordered him to scout with Maiet. They rode along a narrow stream that curved and glimmered in the sunlight. The bank rose, sandy and steep, undercut in places by the current, levelling off into a plain of grass with a rising ridge of wattle and thorn bushes, a filigree screen of sallees beyond.

The meadow gently steamed as sun drew off the morning mist and dew. Black and white willy wagtails, mottled wattlebirds, and bright-plumed finches skimmed the bushes of the headland and flickered among tree branches.

Sihan's bay brushed through flowering acacia bushes lining a narrow, overgrown track. Balls of fluff flew into the air, a myriad of golden swirling suns. The sweet itch of pollen blew on the breeze as blossoms danced in the sunlight. Maiet swatted an insect, his unwashed blond hair hanging in tangles around his shoulders. Sihan brushed the pollen dust from his leggings.

'Leave it,' said Maiet. 'It pretties you up a little.' He pointed at a red bloom, larger than his fist, crowning a tall leafy stem. 'That's a blood lily. There's a legend that once all lilies were white, then one day the Lady of Eloin went out hawking with a hunting party. Her hawk caught a white dove, but it escaped, badly injured. It hid among a sward of white lilies, dripping blood on them, staining them red. Ever since, there have been red lilies.'

Sihan examined the flower, thinking how much it did look like the colour of blood. 'Where do you get all these stories?'

Laughing, green eyes bright, Maiet said, 'In truth, I wanted to be a bard when I was young.'

'My mother would have loved to meet you. She was always telling stories.' Sihan's mind formed memories of sweet-smelling herbs dangling in bunches from the rafters of the cottage, his mother standing on the kitchen table to reach up long pale arms to tie them in place. 'I'll bet she would have found a use for these plants.'

'Was she a healer?'

Sihan shrugged. 'Mother often helped Father with the horses, made poultices and such. Father said it was amazing how much she knew just by instinct, not being raised around horses.'

Maiet cocked an eyebrow. 'Where was she raised?'

'She was a weaver's daughter. From Hermas. Father said she wove a spell around his heart the first moment he set eyes on her.'

Maiet laughed. 'He sounds like a bard.'

Sihan peered through the bush around them, taking his duty as rearguard scout a touch more seriously than Maiet ever appeared to do. But not even a shadow flickered through the trees. For days they had seen no sign of pursuit, and fewer and fewer settlements. Apart from king's couriers, and soldiers of outlying garrisons, there had been few riders or travellers making their way along the high road.

Maiet stopped to let Warwind drink from the stream, stroking the chestnut's mane with his gloved hand. Currawongs called from black sallee branches, harsh cries mingling with piping tree creepers.

Sihan's throat itched. He pulled aside the collar of his tunic to scratch at his wounds.

'Will you stop doing that?' chided Maiet. 'It'll never heal if you keep pawing at it.'

'I can't help it,' complained Sihan.

'Leave it alone.' Maiet cast a considering glance at Sihan. 'Or at least put some granine on it.'

Staring at the scout in surprise, Sihan said, 'How did you know I had that?'

Maiet threw him a lop-sided grin. 'It's my job to know everything. Just don't let anyone else know.'

Sihan scowled, pulled the collar of his tunic closed, and forced his mind elsewhere. 'Do you really think there're more vultures stalking us?'

Maiet shrugged.

Pressing the issue, Sihan said, 'I wonder what happened to those men's horses?'

'The way they were running, probably bolted back to Romondor. Nothing like a good lonyx.'

'Probably bolted to the nearest bloodhorse range. There's one hereabouts, isn't there?'

'Not any more. This is horse desert, right up to Byerol. The Mirador keeper was ordered to bring the entire herd in due to the fighting between Byerol and Pelan.'

Sihan contemplated the unreaped meadow, measuring it with narrowed eyes – grey-green grass bleached into winter pallor, ripened and seeded half a moon earlier – good forage, almost as good as the Yseth plains in spring.

Skin warmed by the sun, Sihan rode along in silence, glad to be out riding under clear skies. If only he did not need to listen for strange noises and guard his back against strangers.

They rode away another day before meeting up with the escort in late afternoon. The king stopped within the depths of a forest to peer down an avenue of grass between immense candlewood trunks dappled in cold blue light. He turned to Veren, lines deepening in his face as he smiled. 'This ancient forest makes me feel young again.'

The knight patted his black stallion. 'It makes me feel old.'

They rode along the edge of the trees until they reached a cleared ridge. Balfere led the escort up a narrow trail.

The king pulled his horse aside and dismounted. 'Ride on. I would gaze a while upon the last of Mirador.' He nodded to Sihan. 'Leave the lad.' The king's stern tone brooked no argument.

'By your command.' Travall turned to Sihan. 'Stay with the king.' Then he rode after the others.

'Come,' said the king. 'Let us see what there is to see.' He led Celestion along the ridge to the far side.

Nonplussed, Sihan dismounted and followed.

Endless blue mountains stretched away, each separated from the next by cavernous clefts. Snowbound slopes beyond them glittered.

The king pointed to a jumbled crag of rocks jutting out at the summit of a distant ridge. 'What do you make of that, lad?'

Sihan screwed up his eyes against the sun's glare. The range, with snow-covered granite boulders crowning it, shone like white satin. 'It looks like a ruined castle.'

The king smiled. 'I've often thought so, though who would build a castle high atop a mountain surrounded by impenetrable forests has always eluded me. I've long had a mind to journey there and discover its secrets, but that adventure is for younger men.' As the king continued to stare into the distance, he said, 'Tell me. Do you know why you are being sent to Romondor?'

Sihan's heart beat loud in his ears. 'To look after Aurion.'

'That is not the greater half of it.' The king turned to Sihan, eyes matching the grey stone on which he stood. 'You are being sent there for her protection.'

Sihan stared at the king, black foreboding spreading within him, choking thought. 'Sire?'

'You would be Senfari were it not for my will. A Senfari is what the princess may need unless I am much mistaken.'

Sihan tried to still his spinning mind.

'No Mirador soldier would be allowed to stay within Romondor's border. But a stable lad will not be an affront to them, will be more readily accepted, more readily ignored.' He placed his hand on Sihan's shoulder. 'I charge you thus. If things go . . . badly . . . If the princess is in danger, you are to use all your skills as a horseman. Take her and ride for Mirador with all speed. Do you understand?'

'Yes, sire,' whispered Sihan, holding the grey gaze, too awed to muster real voice.

'If your service is true, I'll grant you the title of Senfari myself.' The king resumed his inspection of the mountains.

Far and wide the mountains stretched, coming together below them to form a wide valley, rimmed by forest. Sihan tensed. On the edge of the trees, camped a group of five men, less than a league down the valley.

'Byerol soldiers, by the green of their tabards.' The king turned his horse, and walked back from the edge of the ridge. 'Best we avoid them. A battle now will not serve us well. Say nothing, lad. A misplaced word at this point could start a war.' Without haste, he mounted Celestion and rode after the others.

Sihan followed, stomach set in a tight knot, heart hammering. He had been of no use to the princess when the marsh man attacked. How would he ever be able to help her in the heart of Romondor, surrounded by vultures?

Chapter 36

Stingers

Sihan rode through the forest with Maiet, trotting between white-trunked ribbonbarks intertwined with dark sallee copses. Wet black soil squelched beneath their horses' hooves, The air reeked of steaming mould and rotting ferns. Stagnant green moss draped from branches, thick and heavy.

A soft drone caught Sihan's ear. His bay skittered sideways, shaking its neck, ears flattening. A white-and-black-striped bee alighted on Spirit's mane. Sihan swatted hard, then glanced around uneasily. He knew these bees from the mountains, filthy things that took over unattended hives. A shudder ran through him. They stung more than once and were vicious when aroused. A swarm could kill a horse.

'What's wrong?' asked Maiet.

'Stinger,' said Sihan, eyeing the trees. A king parrot sat unperturbed on a branch overhead, breast a red gash between green wings.

Maiet frowned, brow creasing beneath his blond hair. 'We must be close to the border. It's marked by bee boxes.'

They rode on. Sure enough, the ribbonbarks thinned, revealing a line of wooden boxes extending the length of a shallow valley.

Maiet pointed across the valley to a stand of trees. 'That's the Byerol-Mirador border.'

Sihan looked to the Byerol forest, recalling the Byerol soldiers he had seen with the king the day before. 'What if we're caught in their territory?'

Maiet shrugged. 'Depends on how big a grudge the Duke of Byerol holds against the king. There's bad blood between them since the Great War.' Maiet rode through the undergrowth. A little farther along, he checked his horse.

Sihan examined churned earth – black, friable soil ground into withered winter grass. 'Cavalry, two score at least.'

Maiet followed the trail. Everywhere horses had trampled grass among the sallees. He pointed at a path where bushes hung broken and torn as riders had crashed through. 'Riding north at speed. Let's report back.'

Sihan turned up the collar on his tunic as they trotted up a shallow watercourse, unable to shake the feeling of being watched. He recalled the king's words about wanting to avoid a conflict with Byerol, and wondered how marching unannounced into the country of a man who already held him in ill favour, would achieve that. When they reached the escort on the high road, they both drew rein.

Balfere rode forward. 'Well?'

'Trouble,' said Maiet.

A scowl crossed Balfere's ruddy face. 'Gerein said the same thing.'

Hoofbeats approached, and Camar arrived at a trot through the trees. 'I think there's a skirmishing party from Byerol lurking on our side of the border,' he said.

Wrinkles deepened around Balfere's eyes as he grinned. Rubbing his gauntleted hands together, he said, 'If they chase us over their border, we can claim aggrieved status.'

Maiet returned the predatory smile. 'If we keep moving, they won't be able to help themselves but attack.'

'About time I tested my sword.' Balfere turned his horse and trotted back to the king, grey cloak flapping against his horse's flanks.

Sihan's eyes widened. 'He *wants* us to get attacked?'

'Politics,' said Maiet, clapping him on the shoulder.

Romondor and Mirador soldiers alike stuffed their cloaks into their packs, leaving ready access to weapons. Gerein fell in next to Sihan, four pheasants strung to his saddle. Eyes alert, he deftly pulled an arrow from the gorytos at his belt and twirled it between his fingers.

Something purred through the air and struck the Romondor soldier riding in front of Sihan. The man tipped from his saddle and fell to the ground, a lifeless black lump against pale yellow grass, an arrow buried in his neck. Not a heartbeat later, Gerein nocked arrow to bow and fired.

Horses snorted and reared. All archers in the escort unshouldered bows. Amid shouting and the metallic hiss of swords, Balfere and Veren spun their horses and galloped down either side of the escort. 'Move forward!' they yelled in unison at the hundred and fifty soldiers of Romondor and Mirador. 'Into the trees!'

The escort raced into the forest, grey and black-clad riders flashing through mottled undergrowth, horses leaping rotten logs and tree ferns, forcing a path through tangled brush. Aurion surged past Sihan, the princess's grey cloak billowing.

'Flank her!' shouted Gerein, kicking his bay to protect her right, Maiet on her left.

Setting his bay in pursuit, Sihan fought the urge to crouch as arrows whizzed past, determined to give the princess as much cover as possible. Sticks and branches broke against him, beneath the bay's legs. Then riders galloped from every direction, hooves drumming, drumming. On either side, air choked with crashing horses through scrub, shouts and curses, shadow riders dodging between trunks. In the blur of leaves and forest, he could not tell friend from foe.

Aurion's rump disappeared in the trees ahead, the white stallion easily outracing both protectors and pursuers. Sihan's bay, best of the Graycor bloodhorses, obedient to leg and spur, dodged and leapt, racing, racing, somehow keeping his feet in the jumble of logs, fern trunks, criss-crossing creeks. Something slapped Sihan across the face, clutched him around the throat before tearing – hanging moss streamers. He shook his head, trying to rid himself of them, rot of deadwood thick in his nostrils.

An arrow struck his bay's leather breastplate. A rider clad in mail topped with a green tabard, burst from the trees to his right, ranged alongside, swiping at Sihan with a sword. Then he spurred his horse ahead, after the princess at reckless speed, his mount's hooves clattering, stumbling across a rubble of rock.

'Orlanda!' Sihan shouted, unsheathing his half-sword. 'Stay in the trees!' He knew better than anyone how good Aurion was at dodging in woods. Following her, he plunged his bay into thick snowbark suckers, matching the enemy rider's perilous pace, trying to outrace him, leaves and boughs stinging as he swept by. Ahead, Aurion leapt and swung, scorning the traps of interlacing branches set to entangle unwary hooves.

Too soon they ran out of trunks. Enemy riders bore down on Orlanda. Sihan swung his stallion sideways. The bay crashed shoulder first into the closest of the pursuing horses. Steel crashed against steel. Sihan knew immediately he was no match. But horsemanship was on his side, the cunning of Senfari in the testing. He threw his sword between the enemy horse's legs, bringing it to its knees. The rider lurched forward as his horse fell, crashing to the ground in a confusion of arms and legs.

The other Byerol soldier attacked, sword raised. Scrabbling frantically at his belt, Sihan drew his dagger from its sheath. As the rider lunged, he threw it, hard. Steel buried into throat flesh. Blood spurted. The rider tipped backwards out of the saddle.

Light and pain flashed behind Sihan's eyes. An image formed of a girl in snow. Her bleeding face with a dagger embedded.

Sihan shook his head, clutching at fragments of thought among tumbling chaos. A feeling like he had broken a covenant tore at every fibre of his being.

Riders raced past, shouting, 'Go! Go!'

Heart pounding, breath nothing more than a series of gasps, Sihan spurred his horse into a dead gallop after the princess. They raced into the valley of hives, joining the escort hurtling toward the border. Soldiers flanked the king and the princess, horses sweating, straining, eyes wild, the beat of hooves rolling thunder. Then a line of archers emerged from the opposite tree line, hunkered down and thrust arrows into the ground.

'Ambush!' shouted Balfere, from the van. The cry ripped back through the ranks. 'Ambush! Ambush!' Everyone slid their horses to a halt, whirling in confusion. From the forest behind came the fierce clash of steel on steel where soldiers fought hand to hand. Travall and twenty-odd riders burst into the clearing. 'Go on! Go on!' he shouted.

'Ambush!' yelled back Balfere.

Then suddenly the king was shouting, 'To me! To me!' and spurring his horse, galloped toward the archers. 'To me! To me!' he cried, sword drawn, strong voice cutting through the melee. It was a battle cry, a war cry, a cry to arms and fealty no one could resist.

'Go! Go!' shouted Travall to Balfere. 'We'll hold those at your back!'

Then a dark voice was shouting, 'Line! Line!' Romondor soldiers formed a battle line, swords ready. Veren bellowed at Travall, 'To your king!' and Travall obeyed as if his own liege had roared the order, flying through the Romondor soldiers after Callinor. Everyone spurred their horses and raced across the clearing. Sihan clenched his teeth. Weaponless, he still had Spirit. His stallion would charge a shield wall if he so willed.

Clods of dirt struck Sihan in the face as he rode next to Gerein. An arrow strike would hardly be noticed. Then, suddenly, the Mirador archer stood in his stirrups, checking his horse a fraction. His cry went up, 'Hold! Hold! Pelan! Pelan!'

Sihan squinted, caught the flash of gold on the tabards of the archers in front of them. Breath emptied his lungs in a rush. The archers forming the line before them were not the enemy.

Cries were all around now. 'Pelan! Pelan! Hold! Hold!'

As if by command, the escort split, fanning right and left to either side of the Pelanese archers. Sihan, grabbing the princess's rein, checked Aurion in cover of trees. Across the field behind them, a flood of riders surged from the forest, the remainder of the broken escort and a horde of the enemy, still fighting, sword to sword – black-clad riders of Romondor, grey-cloaked soldiers of Mirador – and a swarm of green-tabarded riders of Byerol. Then more Byerol cavalry raced from the trees.

'We're not going to be able to hold them!' cried the captain of the Pelanese archers.

The king spurred Celestion toward the thickset man wearing a black tabard with a gold falcon emblazoned across it. 'Bring them all down!' he bellowed.

Orlanda swung round, stared in horror at Sihan. 'There are Mirador soldiers out there!'

Maiet, face awash with blood, said from nearby, 'If those bastards get across the field, we're all dead.'

Pelanese archers shot flight after flight of arrows. In the field, men and horses screamed. Mirador and Romondor soldiers toppled from their horses to be ridden down by Byerol horsemen. Maiet swore.

Orlanda clenched her hand on Sihan's arm. 'Do something!'

There was nothing he could do. Nothing. Save charge into a losing battle. But her eyes were begging him. And the king had charged him to protect her. And she was in trouble and it was his task. Not knowing what he was doing, he kicked his bay out into the field.

Panicked voices cried at his back, but he was galloping now, unheeding of anything but the urgency of pleading eyes, of fealty, of duty. Flying, flying, hooves drumming. Then a fragment of a vision returned of the bleeding girl in snow, and her voice screamed, '*Stop! Stop!*'

His eyes snapped into focus. He was half way across the valley, a melee of riders thick before him, bee boxes either side. He checked Spirit in a sliding haunch halt. Duty, battle, voices screaming blurred in his mind. He leapt from his horse, grabbed hold of the nearest box wedged hard into the ground. 'Come on! Come on!' he grunted, heaving, hoping, praying, dreading, all at once.

A shadow fell over Sihan. He spun to find Veren on Belarion towering over him, black eyes burning. The Romondor knight leaned over his horse's wither, shouting, 'Have you gone mad?'

The wooden box gave all at once, and a fierce drone filled the air as the sky above the box thickened with bees rising in swarm.

'Stingers!' shouted Sihan, and he did not need to shout more.

As the swarm rose higher and higher, swirling into a murderous white tornado, Veren hauled Sihan up by his arm and threw him on the bay, whacked its rump, setting it into flight. But Sihan was not finished. He yelled to Veren as he galloped down the line of hives. 'Go! Light fires!' He kicked over the next box with his boot, on down the line. At his back Veren bellowed to his men, 'To me! To me!' with all the authority of command. To a few he yelled, 'Get to the king. Get the archers to fire these boxes.'

They raced toward the line of Pelanese archers, skidded to a halt, shouted Veren's orders.

Gerein was with the bowmen, shouting, 'Fires, fires!' The cry raced up the line, Camar and Maiet and a score of archers joining their voices to the chorus. Men fell to their knees sparking flints, archers wrapping oil-soaked rags to arrows. They thrust the cloth into the fires. Raised their bows. Released in quick succession, arrows soared into the air like a flight of red falcons. They struck the line of hives and torched the ground between.

Lungs on fire, breath rasping, Sihan urged Spirit to fly faster than the colt had ever galloped, tearing down the meadow. The stingers were chasing him; the fires were between him and safety.

Tears ran down Sihan's cheeks from the acrid smoke. He set his bay at the fire. 'Go! Go!' he urged with hand and heel. The colt answered, flying toward the flames. Leapt. Leapt high. Heat and flame clutched at Sihan, then they were through and bolting across open ground to safety. Sihan halted in the trees, bent over, checking Spirit for burns, swatting at stingers that had caught hold. He barely noticed the princess riding up beside him, her face pale and frightened.

In the battlefield, Veren's men turned from the fight, rushed through the flames, raced to the Pelanese line and halted, swords bloody and ready for a final assault. Beyond the flames, plunging horses bucked as bees stung and enemy riders fell to the ground, howling in agony while their horses bolted. Struggling through the smoke, they jerked and convulsed, spinning like tops when arrows struck, crimson staining their tunics as they dropped.

Maiet strode up, blinking and rubbing his red-rimmed eyes, and said to Sihan, 'You complete and utter madman.'

Sihan said nothing. Just stared at men thrashing upon the ground, faces and arms swollen to twice the size they should have been, tearing at their clothes until all they could do was kick or twitch feebly, grunting and groaning as they died.

That night the soldiers of Pelan who were not busy guarding prisoners or preparing pyres for the dead, sat with the escort, tending wounded. Nearby, a young Mirador archer lay groaning while Gerein tore the tunic away from his wound. When he finished dressing the gash, Gerein sat the lad up. The archer's arm hung limp and useless at his side.

'They might have at least got my bow arm,' he said, pale face wincing.

'No drawing until next spring, lad,' said Gerein. 'You're for the garrison at Senor. Nice, friendly girls at Senor.'

The archer grimaced a smile.

Sihan hung his head, wrapped his arms around his legs. For the first night in twenty, Travall had taken him off the roster for night stalking. Over the cook fire, Camar recounted Sihan's exploits in the forest battle – protecting the princess's back, taking out two soldiers. They had called him "hero" for what he had done with the stingers, but the title sat false upon his shoulders and he refused to own it, not with so much blood upon his hands, so much death.

Even Maiet could offer no words, so said nothing. Camar walked over and held out a roasted pheasant leg. Sihan took it out of courtesy, tore off a piece of meat, but the flesh tasted like grit in his mouth, the smell of roasting flesh reminding him of the stink that would soon be coming from the pyres.

Sitting down, Gerein sighed. 'Not the most pleasant way to get blooded.'

'You mean there's a pleasant way?' asked Maiet, weariness lacing his voice.

Gerein did not answer.

The princess emerged from her tent, and walked to where Sihan sat. In the darkness, blonde hair straggled in limp threads over her cloak. Silent, she sat on the log beside Sihan, folds of her travelling cloak spilling across the ground in a grey pool.

Maiet and Gerein stood and walked away.

For a long time she remained soundless, then quietly began to hum an aimless tune. Tiny sparks from the fire spiralled upward into the night sky. Sihan's breath caught as memories of burning arrows flying through the air flooded his mind. The tune ended.

Sihan stared at her. Anguish deeper than anything he had ever seen filled her eyes. And something within them called to him, whispered of promises long past, hidden, never forgotten or set aside. She took his hand, her smooth fingers tracing the calluses, scars, cuts. With her other hand she stroked his tangled hair with her fingers. Fires burned around them, but her fingers felt cold as death.

Sihan entwined his fingers in hers, and both of them gazed into darkness.

Chapter 37

Romondor

Sihan's hands tightened on the reins as his horse snorted and shied from a pile of bloated bodies lying next to the Romondor road. Everywhere, acrid smoke belched from pyres, obscuring charred landscape like soiled mist. Sihan wiped at stinging, watering eyes, wishing he could blow the stink from his nostrils, or better still, return to Byerol, a quarter of a moon's cycle behind, green and too far away.

Gazing ahead, the Romondor soldiers ignored the funereal wasteland of rotting corpses, closed expressions as dead as the countryside around them.

On the edges of the road, old men leant on picks and shovels, unsmiling and silent as the escort passed. A woman, face livid clay, wrinkled like the tattered strips of cloth hanging from her gaunt body, tugged at a carcass lying on a cart. It slid, falling limp to the ground. Farther on, two men, clothing barely covering their twisted bodies, dragged another corpse to a mound of skeletal cadavers.

Sihan turned away, skin crawling, only to confront the sight of more pyres. On the other side of the flames, a boy stood, staring at him with dull, flat eyes. His skin sagged, like the old woman's. He held out a hand to Sihan, and cried, 'Help me. I'm lost. Please, take me home.' He moved forward, feet barely seeming to touch the ground.

A breath of wind whispered against Sihan's ear. *At last you see the world for what it is.*

The boy from his nightmares materialised from the shadows, glided across the flames, then motioned to grey figures wreathing like mist around the pyres. *Behold the world of spirits, of lost souls, forgotten, left behind. Lost.*

All around, between the pyres, men and women drifted, silent, shadowed, clothes in tatters, faces grey, sunken. The rustle of leaves turned into the murmuring of shadow voices, of men long dead, of women, of children.

Sihan stared wildly around him, at the other riders, wondered how they heard nothing, saw nothing.

Only you can see them, like you see me. Your eyes are opening. Soon you will see all the world. Because you are lost, like them. Like me. The boy became corporeal and held out his hand. *Come, speak my name. Join with me. Help me. Help them. Save them from sorrow, grief, guilt, shame. Speak my name.*

'No,' whispered Sihan.

One by one, the ghosts faded, dissolved, disappeared.

Sihan shook his head. He wanted so hard to believe there was nothing there. That he was seeing things.

The boy hissed in his ear. *This is no delusion. This world is as real as yours, where souls wander in eternity.* He leaned forward, voice a breath against Sihan's face. *Do not deny you see the despair. Come, join with me and release them from this bondage. Come, my brother, myself. I have wandered in shadow too long. You must recall me to the world. Join with me.*

'No,' croaked Sihan.

The boy became inert grey, yet his chilled fingers still touched Sihan. *Do not resist me.* He slid his fingers across Sihan's eyes. *Refuse me at your peril.*

Then darkness shadowed all.

Sihan shivered. Fighting to recover his senses, he glanced around, found Veren regarding him with an intense gaze.

'What?' Sihan challenged, throat raw and voice half-choked on smoke and fear.

Veren said nothing, a grim expression across his ash-streaked face.

The bleak surrounds never altered as the day wore on, and Sihan wondered if all Romondor was like this. Who would not have waking nightmares in such a land? How he longed for the emerald valleys of Graycor, his lungs aching to breathe fresh mountain air. Moving his horse close to Maiet, he asked in a hushed whisper, 'What is all this?'

Maiet answered in a dead voice, 'The plague.'

'From the Great War?' Sihan stared at the scout incredulously. 'How can it have lasted this long?'

'No idea. But who *has* any idea about this place?' Maiet kept his voice low. 'My uncle talked on his deathbed about burning and corpses in Romondor. I don't remember much of what he said. I asked my mother about it once, when I was older, and she got upset and told me never to ask again.'

Sihan thought of his own father and the way no one who had lived through it spoke of the war. What had Armindras known? Sihan whispered once more to Maiet. 'If there is still plague, it can't be safe for us to be here, can it?'

'Quite safe,' said Veren, low, dark voice matching the surrounds. 'At least for kingdom men. Not one Mirador man has died in all these years from plague.'

'No,' shot back Gerein. 'You vultures finished them with steel long before the plague killed them.'

A warning look from Travall silenced the archer.

Veren continued, 'Healers surmise it is something specific in the constitution of the Romondor populace that ails us and not others. So fear not. We do not willfully lure men to their deaths.'

Maiet coughed, shooting Sihan a meaningful glance, but thankfully held his tongue.

Despite Veren's assurance, Sihan sensed something beneath the words, something false. '*You* look healthy enough.'

'Some of us are blessed, though all live in fear. And we do all we can to remain untouched by this curse upon our land.' Veren's words once more held unfathomable depths, setting Sihan's teeth on edge. He recalled Jaien sounding just the same when he had arrived in Yseth.

Everyone rode in fraught silence, no doubt contemplating what manner of death would claim them in this harsh, bleak land.

A lifeless breeze picked up flurries of powdered ash and flung them about like snow. Grey ash clung to the horses' legs. Sihan glanced across at Aurion, grimacing at the prospect of having to continuously wash the white stallion's legs, only to find they were pristine white. No ash stuck to them at all, though Aurion ploughed through it the same as every other horse.

It was not natural, like Sihan's visions were not natural. He recalled the visions of the stallion surrounded by fire, the land charred around him. Like Romondor. Is this what he had seen? Orlanda was riding Aurion, the land was burned to ash, corpses surrounded them. Had what he had seen been a prescient vision of Romondor? He almost hoped so, for, bad as this was, the horrors in his vision had been worse.

The sun lowered in the sky, orange and pale, warmth stifled by haze. As it descended to the skyline, Veren motioned to a point in the distance. 'Our lodgings this night.'

A huddle of buildings, crumbling and deserted, loomed out of the veil of smoke; remnants of a fence, a twisted skeleton of shattered wood. Tangled weeds contended for root in doorless doorways. Half-shuttered windows tried to turn back the grey light. Detritus of lives long gone clung feebly to the place, chill, indifferent, melancholy.

Frigid wind swept over Sihan, carrying a forlorn whisper. *Save us*. And in its wake came sorrow and despair.

'In all truth,' whispered Maiet. 'I don't envy you one bit having to stay in this forsaken land.'

Chilled to bone depth, Sihan replied, 'Neither do I.'

As they rode into the deserted farmyard, Orlanda stared at a gap between two buildings where some structure had been torn down to its foundations and left abandoned and rotting like a sawn-off stump. Like her.

Veren jumped from his horse and tied the reins to a railing in the courtyard. He pointed to a long, low-roofed building. 'There are fresh provisions in the stables for the horses, and bunks along the walls for your men.'

Orlanda glanced at her father who made no move to dismount. He looked grim and thoughtful, his men weary. The faces of the vultures of Romondor were as harsh and unrelenting as the landscape through which they had travelled.

'The duke awaits me,' said Vaill, also remaining seated on his horse, grey face matching his grey hair. 'I will travel on and inform him of your arrival.' He waved a hand to the two-storey farmhouse. 'There are rooms upstairs for yourself and your daughter.'

'My daughter will rest here awhile,' said the king, sitting easily on his grey stallion, though his face looked drawn. 'I will go with you and speak with your lord.'

'By your will.' Vaill inclined his head.

At the end of hope, Orlanda mustered strength for one final protest, voice raised to cut through the thick air, rough with pain. 'I'm not staying here! It's a hovel!' She glared at Vaill. 'Is this the way you treat the king and heir-apparent?'

Without a word, her father swung from his horse. Pulling her from Aurion's back, he took her by the wrist and hauled her to the side of a building, out of sight of the others.

Orlanda squirmed, dress grey and streaked, tangled blonde hair hanging limp around her face, shame warring with resentment. 'You drag me before them like a common whore; you let them see me in this state!'

His voice hissed in her ear. 'You will not insult Vaill again. He is an honourable man.'

'Honourable!' Orlanda spat. 'There's not a man of honour in Romondor.'

She waited for the hard, too-well-known strike of fist, but instead her father pulled his gauntlet from his hand and then the ruling signet ring from his finger. His grey eyes, dull as the ashen twilight, held hers as he handed it to her. 'This is the seal of Mirador. This signifies the right to rule. I charge you thus. When you meet Valoren, and have spent one day in his company, you will decide which man owns that right.'

Orlanda's mind reeled. 'What fool's words are these?'

'I'll say no more.' The lines on his craggy face deepened as he grimaced. 'The decision is yours. You alone will choose the ruler of the kingdom.'

He released her wrist, strode back to Celestion. With a hand to the reins, foot in the stirrup, he sprang lightly into the saddle. 'Travall, stay with the princess.' Motioning Balfere to come alongside, he said, 'Ride with me.' His face darkened as he glanced at Orlanda, a flicker of life returning to his haggard visage. 'I will return with the duke.'

Orlanda backed away, clutching the ring.

The king drove spurred heels into Celestion's dappled flanks, ranks parting to let him through. Surrounded by black-clad vultures of Romondor, he rode with his back braced straight as a javelin. For a moment, his silhouette was clear against a grim sky, then he was gone, without looking back.

Ice slithered down Orlanda's spine. Her gloved fingers tightened on the signet ring. He had gone quite mad. Why had she not seen it before?

Travall lit a torch, and preceded her into the decayed building, lighting rushlights mounted on the walls. Except for a few rushes on one side, the room was bare, hearthstone silent and cold, soiled with remnants of ash. Brittle grey leaves lay in corners, silted into nesting-places for rats. Long coils of bramble trailed in at a vacant window. Nettle and groundsel sprouted from crevices in the flooring. Everything bespoke of a land at war to seal over the traces of man.

Orlanda's nose wrinkled at the must, a poor improvement on the foul stench of the air outside.

Travall disappeared up a creaking flight of stairs.

Orlanda paced, boots scuffling the wooden floorboards. What could she do if Areme did not come? Her heart jolted. Her father had commanded her to choose a ruler. But what if he fell? Who would lead Mirador? What if she fell also? Questions spun in her mind with dizzying rapidity.

Travall returned, then set about blocking the open doorway with a broken door lying propped against the wall. 'You will sleep in the second room at the head of the stairs. I've lit a rushlight on the wall in the hallway. There's a bed of sorts. Nothing grandiose.'

'Do you expect anything in Romondor might fit that description?' Orlanda asked with a tight-lipped smile.

The corners of Travall's mouth twitched, face matching the salt-and-pepper grey of his close-cropped hair. 'We can but live in hope, Your Highness.'

'Hope is for fools, Travall.'

'I'll check on the men, then I'll return to keep guard in here.'

Orlanda forestalled him, placing a hand on his arm. Warily, she peered beyond the door into the courtyard, but spied only dark shapes of soldiers tending horses. She turned her full attention to Travall. 'Tell me. Who was the man who triumphed in the most battles in the Great War?'

Travall's blue eyes turned glacial. 'No one triumphs in war.'

'Answer the question.'

The knight tensed. 'Knight Commander Farran.'

'The Duke of Omrah?'

'The same, Highness.'

'What sort of man is he?'

Travall shrugged. 'A strong leader. And a fair one. Why do you ask?'

She pulled off her glove and tugged the ring of the heir-apparent from her finger, then handed it to the knight. 'I name the Duke of Omrah my successor.'

Travall's eyes in their darkened hollows showed astonishment. 'What are you saying?'

'You have ears.'

One rapid glance took her measure. 'What did Callinor say to you?'

'He gave me the right to choose the next ruler of Mirador. I'm doing it. If things go badly here, I'll not forsake the kingdom by leaving it without a ruler.' No matter what, she would not give Valoren a scrap of the kingdom. For a moment, she considered giving Travall the ruling ring also, but decided she could dispose of it easily enough if necessary – drop it in the ruined land where it would never be found.

'Why not the Duchess of Belaron? By rights, Belaron is the second ruling house in the kingdom.'

'The passes to the north are closed. You'll never make it to Belaron.'

Travall placed the ring in a pouch at his belt. 'Do I ride for Omrah now?'

'If things go badly . . .' She heaved a ragged breath. 'Tell Farran the king and his heir are fallen.' Orlanda started to place the ruling signet on her finger, but Travall stopped her. Grey face conveying a mixture of surprise and horror, he said, 'Are you wearing a chain?' His voice choked on the question.

'Yes, why?'

'Don't wear it openly unless duty demands.' Travall turned and left the room.

In the courtyard, Sihan held Spirit and Aurion while they drank from a trough filled with dark, brackish water.

Travall strode across the courtyard and said curtly to the Mirador soldiers, 'Take the horses into the stable to be brushed and fed.' He dropped his voice low and said to Sihan, 'Put your saddle on the princess's horse. Then get a saddle from one of the remounts. Make sure no one sees. Both horses stay saddled.'

Without a word, Sihan led Aurion into the mud-brick stable, tying him in a stall at the far end. He glanced at Gerein and Maiet, wanting to ask what was going on, but they were busy with their own horses and ignored him.

Everything smelled of disuse, low rafters festooned with dust-coated cobwebs that looked like they had not seen a spider in years. He removed the ash-caked saddle and placed it to one side, then twined some hay into a wisp. Strapping Aurion, he dried dark patches of sweat, then unsaddled Spirit, rubbing him down also, removing encrusted grime and dirt from legs and belly. Following Travall's orders, he placed his saddle on Aurion, cinching the girth loosely.

A soldier strode past and thrust a saddle at him, then walked straight on. Sihan took it, and saddled his horse. He tossed both horses some hay, then wandered past the rickety truckle beds into the courtyard. Along hitching rails running the length of the courtyard, the remaining Romondor soldiers tended their horses as meticulously as the soldiers of Mirador had theirs.

Maiet joined Sihan. 'So, the princess is planning on riding astride into Romondor?'

'Wouldn't surprise me.' Sihan spoke out of the side of his mouth. In truth, he felt nothing could surprise him anymore.

Chapter 38

Burned to Ash

In oppressive silence the escort rode with the dead sun at their backs, their horses' sweat-streaked coats grey with ash and dust. Riders merged with the shadows that obscured lifeless villages. Stink of pyres, and cold, congealing blood on corpse-flesh, poisoned the thick stagnant air. Ribbed dogs stood watch in empty doorways, too weak to raise hackles or even growl. Few other living beasts marred the tortured landscape.

Light ebbed below horizon's edge, dusk mixing with smoke to smother a wasteland of despair – Romondor's ruin of ash, charred bone, and twisted, broken men. Callinor's fingers gripped the reins so hard, bones paled through flesh. To either side of the beaten track, figures shivered in the twilight, rags of children, eyes and bellies hollowed out with famine, men doubled over like stunted, windbent trees, all slaves trapped in the chains of impending death.

An old man stooped to pick up a rock to toss at a vulture feasting on a corpse. The vulture hopped two steps, shook its feathers, but refused to leave. Strength gone, the man slumped to the ground like an empty sack and waited his turn.

Too many years of war had hardened Callinor to death. But this . . . This he could not bear. Fixing his gaze to the stony ground, heart beating loud in his ears, he rubbed his face, long cragged lines of care, rough beneath his callused palm. Dirt and ash flaked away. He wiped his hand against leggings grimed with filth. Even his cloak, stinking of horse sweat, lay stiff with traces of old dried blood. He must look like some vagrant – not a king at all. Fitting.

After all, he was no king.

Bones creaked, muscles ached. He longed to melt his old, old bones in stone-heated water. But not this day. This day he would not wash the dirt from his body. Neither would he sleep. No amount of water could wash away his guilt. No bed could ease his conscience.

He must come before Valoren shattered and stinking, like the beast they thought he was. He must abase himself before the son of the man he had wronged, the man whose land he had reduced to a scar, the inhabitants to withered flesh.

Riordehr.

Duke of Romondor.

His enemy.

His friend.

As it had so many years before, and so many times since, his heart wrenched and twisted and tore. Riordehr and he had been brothers, not of blood but of heart, so alike, their thoughts and actions moved in tandem, like twins born of the same womb. He had trusted Riordehr with his life, granted him his armies to the south. He had made him his second, sworn a blood oath, named him closer than kin.

And then Wyndarra had come, slithering into his heart like a viper.

His eyes drifted closed and memories flickered behind his eyelids. Wyndarra smiling, eyes cast down, demure, chaste. And when she raised her eyes to him, he lost himself to her, fell without resistance into eyes of sapphire, starved to know every intimate curve of her body, loved her beyond reason, beyond all.

Sharp, hard memories blooded his mind.

Riordehr's stern, cold voice mouthing black words – 'By all the Gods, by Shahedur and Senfar, I beg you. Turn your back on this woman. She is unworthy of your heart. She covets naught but your crown. My words cut, I know. It grieves me to utter them. But I cannot stay silent. I am your friend. I hurt you out of love and duty.'

His disapproval cut deeper than a sword thrust.

But Callinor chose to stay deaf to all Riordehr's entreaties, and blind to the shadows behind Wyndarra's eyes. He heard only her soft words coiling round his heart, squeezing out all else – 'I am yours, Callinor. The gods will it, so shall it be. We are bound until the end of the world.'

How could he deny her? His heart beat only for her, his eyes feasted on her.

And then the cruel day came when she ceased to haunt his steps. Every day he waited for her. Empty days of pining,

pining. Then Riordehr announced a banquet, unexpected, for austerity was his want. Callinor graced the duke's left hand as honoured guest. And then, there she was, gliding through the arched doors of the banquet hall like a queen, resplendent in all the jewels Callinor had bestowed upon her. She stopped before the head table. She did not look at Callinor. Not at all. Her eyes knew only Riordehr. Just for that, he could have killed her.

Betrayal came as a dagger strike, sharp, cutting steel thrust deep into his heart. A double blow, because had Riordehr not used the words, 'I hurt you out of love.'

Love.

All Wyndarra's love had flown, her voice stone if she addressed Callinor at all. Now Riordehr owned all her soft words.

Callinor's heart shrivelled. He no longer knew Riordehr, this man who could betray him so cruelly. And he would fight him, his brother, his friend. Wyndarra was his, until the end of all. Whether Riordehr willed it or no.

Here then two hearts no longer ran in sync. Here then began the rift that would never be breached.

Ice ran through Callinor's veins.

How much more mistaken could he have been?

Even when Riordehr took to wife Ahnvieh, Lady of Anjour, scorning Wyndarra, Callinor could not fail to see the want in Wyndarra's eyes. And for that he blamed Riordehr. Even when Wyndarra accepted Callinor's proposal and swore undying devotion, he knew she lied. To please her, to win again her lost love he gave her people land when their own died below a volcano's smiting wrath. To please her more, he forced Riordehr to cede part of his duchy.

He ignored it when her countrymens' greed outstripped the land they were granted, their grasping hands stealing more and more. He ignored that they overburdened the lands they had been gifted.

Riordehr had come to him, begged him. 'Her people are laying waste to our land and when they have blighted it they take what is not theirs. If you do not put an end to this, they will strip the flesh from Romondor and leave naught but a carcass.'

'I can do nothing,' Callinor had answered, voice cold stone. 'I have given my queen my word.'

Riordehr's knee bent to the floor before him for the last time ever in this world, 'She loves you not, Callinor. She loves not even her own people. You know why she does this. You know it. Cast her down, Callinor, before Romondor is reduced to bones. Cast her down before she comes for you. You are the king, Callinor. Remember that. Remember our friendship. Remember all she is grinding into dust.'

Perhaps Riordehr had truly thought Callinor would listen, that he would forswear Wyndarra, understand at last every word from her lips was poison. But Callinor did not. He loved her. Loved her from the first heartbeat he beheld her. He said only, 'My word has been given, it shall not be altered.'

Black rage met his words, and threat. 'If you do nothing, Romondor will die. I will not allow it. If you will not act, then you force my hand.'

And so it began. The Great War between friends turned enemies.

And Wyndarra, Wyndarra. She used Callinor's jealousy of Riordehr, used the cruel power of her sought-for love. She knew he would destroy anything, anyone, to gain one scrap of her affection. She set his hand against Riordehr, the brother of his heart. He forgot the past, the bonds of brotherhood, over twenty winters of fighting side by side, of laughter shared. He forgot everything until there was nothing left but blood, terror and death.

Corpses filled the land, followed by black swarms of vultures. Everything once green, withered. Naught that moved between earth and sky survived – crops rotted, horses, beeves, goats, lambs, all starved to death. And the people, the people . . . Wyndarra's people, Romondor's, Mirador's – soldiers from every duchy in the kingdom – died beneath the yoke of war.

And then plague gripped the land. Black plague annihilating all that was left. Babies rotted in their cradles. Women and men haemorrhaged from eyes and ears. And Wyndarra laughed, laughed.

Too late did Callinor know the full horror of what she had done; what his wife truly was. He had been blind. He had chosen to be deaf. Too late did he learn the truth of her – that she was accursed, a witch, and she had cast a curse upon the ground on which her people died. Cursed Romondor, laid the land low with her witch tongue, reducing all to bones.

    All would die there until the end of the world.

    Unless . . .

    Orlanda.

    He had ridden from her, left her surrounded by soldiers, seen her heart tear and bleed as it had every time he had denied her. All his life he had banished her to a shadow life, chilled her with cold hard eyes. She was all he had left of Wyndarra, but he could not even bear to look at her, so like her cursed mother was she. Wily, manipulative, she wanted her own way in everything, and so, unlike her mother, he had cut her down with every heartbeat. But now, this day, he had given her everything, the ruling ring, to bestow how she saw fit. And perhaps, perhaps she had it in her to end this.

    His heart beat hard with foreboding.

    What would come of this venture? To what cruel fate had he condemned his daughter?

    Like breeze upon water, questions rippled across the surface of his mind, splashing against muddy banks of disquiet at the edges. No man knew the secrets he held in his heart. He had wed a witch. His kingship was false.

    He must amend it. All of it. He must remove all blame from Riordehr. Riordehr was Wyndarra's victim, like Callinor. Like Valoren, like Orlanda.

    Too many dark, dark, memories. The stench of them fused with smoke from the pyres, choking him. Orlanda as a child, weeping, calling for a mother who would come no longer. Wyndarra's hissing breath as Travall strangled the life from her. Riordehr on his knees, his murdered wife Ahnvieh in his arms, crying, 'How can she be dead and I still live?'

    Pain stabbed Callinor's heart. Riordehr too had lost his Lady that dark, dark night too many winters past. His child also wore the passing years, breathing, crying, heart wounded, his mother a scattering of ash.

    Long, long years had passed with Callinor trying to heal the rift, between countries, between men. But no word of forgiveness ever came. The darkness of time took Riordehr with it, until he was little more than a memory.

And then arrived the offer of marriage from Valoren, a faceless, unknown man.

Did Riordehr live still? Surely not, since Valoren had assumed the title, Duke of Romondor. Callinor did not know whether to feel relief or pain. Relief he did not need to look into those aggrieved, condemning eyes. Pain there also, but the greater part in knowing Riordehr had taken with him the last hope Callinor had had in this world, a chance for reconciliation, redemption. He would need to settle for the slim hope of reparation instead.

Callinor slid a glance sideways. Beside him Balfere's face soured in a frown. Nothing would please the knight more than to be quit of this dead, dying land. Vaill, on his right, kept silent, staring straight ahead, no anger marring his stone visage, no outward sign of grief, face smooth of care.

They had not spoken of Riordehr, only Valoren. Valoren, five winters in advance of Orlanda in years. What truths did he know, or even Riordehr?

Callinor braced his shoulders. Valoren would know all soon enough.

Chapter 39

Fall of Kings

Vaill's face slowly merged with oncoming night, but once, he turned, eyes cold and grave, to meet Callinor's searching gaze. Callinor forced himself to hold contact, measured the shadows flitting across Vaill's visage. Even though Vaill showed nothing, to Callinor it seemed those dark eyes shouted, 'Murderer!'

The men of Romondor rode close. Unease filled Callinor, a feeling vultures flanked him, shadowing a dying beast.

To what end were they riding? To what end?

Darkness stretched around them, vast and deep, only pinpoints of pyres marring the veil of black. Silence wrapped all except for the muffled thud of hooves and sporadic jangle of bits. Then, just at the edge of hearing, a small sound, faint.

Vaill searched a night shivering with shadows, dark eyes filled with caution.

To one side, a flicker of motion caught Callinor's eye. More sound, still undiscernible but growing louder.

Balfere stopped his warhorse dead in the road; his sword hissed from its scabbard. 'You!' he shouted with a battleground roar. 'Retreat, or fall where you stand!'

And then it came clear: voices shouting, tramping feet striking ground hard.

'Ride on! Ride on!' urged Vaill, his own sword drawn.

Shadows formed into flesh, men in dark and mottled gear, swords and daggers and spear points catching the light of pyres.

'Ride on!' shouted Balfere, setting spur to his mount as all around them men seethed and teemed, more and more falling out of darkness into the eerie light. Screams rang in Callinor's ears.

His breath came short; his mind a storm of incredulity. Was this treason? Was this a trap set by Valoren to lure him to his death? The disbelief in Vaill's eyes told him no, but Vaill was just one man, a man Callinor knew could be trusted, Riordehr's castellan from years long past. Valoren could use such a man to such a purpose.

All the same, Callinor drew his sword. He deserved this but his mind fought. Time stopped and once more he was caught in enmity forged in a past that refused to release it.

Hooves pounded as horses wheeled and lurched into a nightmare terror of flashing blades. War cries pierced the dark, harsh shrieks of death, a tumult of screaming. Men on foot surrounded Callinor on all sides, running, running, swords flailing.

Celestion roared, hooves savaging forearm and thigh as he plunged to meet the clash of arms. Strength of old filled his ancient bones as he reared and struck, eyes wild with a storm of rage. Arrows struck his flesh, spear points dug deep into his chest.

A dagger slashed Callinor's thigh, an arrow tore across his cheek, splitting flesh. Exhaustion had him reeling, but he was not ready to die. Not yet. Not like this. He ran his sword into one attacker, spun Celestion and severed the arm of another. Blood fountained into the air, spraying the battlefield.

Another blow struck him but pain was a thing apart, more real the taste of warm blood upon the tongue. Who were these men? Were they Romondor soldiers? Were they the dying rags of people he had left to rot? He did not know. Pyre light glanced off steel, night and smoke engulfing all else in a murderous convulsing mass. Only voices half-heard told him enemy from friend.

Sword thrusts punctured flesh, savage stabs gutting. A slash ended in a scream. Again and again until this cycle was all he knew. Every muscle in Callinor's body tore and shrieked, every sinew over-stretched, begging mercy. Breath seared his lungs, blood drained from his lacerated body.

A thudding of hoof beats. A ragged cry tearing the air. 'To me! To me! To the king!' Balfere forced his way through the chaos, face a mask of blood, wielding his sword like a cleaver. Blood sprayed the dark. A spear point struck the knight in the upper leg. He wheeled Dahal, brought his sword down hard, a mighty crack breaking the attacker's shoulder.

Callinor could not see the faces of the other knights who fought for him, the archers who bled, the men who died. The night was a blur of motion and smoke and confusion and screaming. He shattered the head of an enemy striking for Balfere's back, registered somewhere the man wore no helm, just rag tag leather armour on his torso. What sort of soldiers were these, fighting unarmoured like savage beasts? Valoren's soldiers were armoured, those he had seen. It hardly mattered. Whoever they were, they had come for him.

Callinor heaved at air, fighting to breathe. He forced just enough life into his starved lungs to bellow to Balfere, just half a stride away, 'Orlanda! Get her out! Warn Travall!'

He did not know if Balfere heard. Foot soldiers swarmed about them, forcing them apart. Steel slashed him across the back. Sobbing for air, vision a blur of crimson, Callinor hefted his sword and struck blind. Iron tainted his lips.

The air shrilled with shouts and screeching, stank of fresh blood and spilled entrails. Callinor rode the carnage, slashing, stabbing, sword arm heavy as he cored the guts from enemy soldiers, his blade, his arm, crimson to hilt and shoulder.

Celestion slipped in ash churned wet with gore, and then they were upon him. A sword thrust pierced the stallion's throat. With a strangled groan the big grey staggered. A second strike laid the stallion's shoulder open to the bone. Daggers, steel, so much steel, slashing, flaying, tearing, ripping, shredding muscle and sinew to ribbons of flesh, severing tendons, laying open veins. Celestion's knees buckled and he crashed to the blood-sludged ground.

His warhorse's fall into the reeking stew of mud and blood sent Callinor flying. Every joint jarred. Breath tore from enflamed lungs as he struck the ground. He hacked with his sword, cut legs out from formless beings he could barely see through blood running into his eyes. He hit out once more, rolled, staggered to his feet, sucked in putrid drafts of air.

Corpses and dying men and horses packed the ground around him, but no enemy sought to strike him down. Callinor swayed, head spinning. He pulled on Celestion's reins, willing the stallion to rise. The horse grunted, scrabbled with one leg, tried to lift his noble head. He lay at Callinor's feet, body spent, all strength fled. The great heart pumped blood, feeding the quagmire in which he lay. Callinor's face twisted, his body heaved; he crumpled to the ground.

Each juddering beat spewed life from the horse. They had cut the stallion to ribbons, but they had not finished Callinor. Why?

Somewhere at Callinor's back the screaming never stopped, raw in the throats of his knights, Balfere's bellowing louder than the rest, urging his men to slaughter. But all he heard was Celestion's tortured breathing as his life bled out. The stallion's chest rose shallower each effort, heaving air into failing lungs. One last time the horse breathed air out in a long drawn sigh. The ribcage did not lift again.

Callinor tried to rise, but his legs were water. Air rattled in and out of his chest. He was dying; he knew it. He pressed his face into blood-smeared hands. Had Valoren betrayed him? He would never know.

His breathing faltered. His eyelids weighed heavy. He could not keep them open. He clawed to Celestion's mane, sprawled across the hulk of the dead stallion. Corpses lay strewn across the ground, but all his thoughts turned to the dead horse, the only gift Wyndarra had given he did not regret – noble, beautiful and without a single flaw.

Callinor sunk into shadow. Would Wyndarra find him there?

Stillness filled him. Then, above the fading noise of battle, a whisper like fetid breeze, a voice.

Is that you, my love?

He forced apart leaden eyelids. She glided across the battlefield, hair a mane of spun gold like a crown upon her head. One with the shadows, she wore night like a mantle. Coming to a halt before him, she smiled, a snake's baring of fangs. *Why did you come back, Callinor?*

Every breath a gasping wheeze, he said, 'Speak not my name with your viper's tongue. It is poison on your lips.'

Stone cold, no pity marred that perfect face. She was putrefaction, the embodiment of corruption.

And still he loved her.

She knelt beside him, soaking herself in blood, in gore. Framing his face between her hands, she hissed, *Your forebears broke the king's line. Riordehr was the true king. His line is the true line. You seek to rectify this by marrying Orlanda to the rightful king? Your hopes are ash. She will rule over naught but corpse flesh.*

His breath shuddered. 'No.'

She will know naught but blood and fire until the sun dies in its birth.

Her chilled breath iced his skin, but her words, her words . . . daggers piercing him, conjuring a whirlwind of flame, a roaring furnace, scorching the world.

'No. No.' He must deny her, must deny this prophecy of woe. Must deny her in death all he could never deny her in life. She used words like men used weapons, to hurt, to kill, to leave her victims bleeding.

He was sinking into shadow, his vision clouding. He reached for her, but she was fading, her spirit merging with smoke and night. No chance to tell her the things he knew, the other secrets she had hidden from him. Perhaps that was just as well.

Pale blue radiance of a portal glimmered around Areme, stark against dark of night. Twenty Shaheden rode forth with him from the light, horses prancing beside a singing stone that hummed until the luminescence faded to black. The portal closed. It would not open again till Myrrhye regained her shattered strength. Areme's last image of her was the sorceress collapsing to her knees. No way home this way.

Hessarde raised the visor of his helm and peered into the darkness. In the distance, red stained the night. Sniffing at the stench of smoke and rotting corpses, he said, 'How in all the hells are we going to find the horse in all this.'

'He's near,' said Areme. 'Myrrhye sensed the stallion's growing power through these stones.'

Shouts carried on the foul night air, the clash of steel. A scream rose in Areme's throat. Was he already too late? He drew his sword, slammed heels into Seroyen's flank. The stallion reared, then launched into a gallop, flying across ash, hoofbeats muffled on dead ground. Fires glowed ahead, red and orange, shadows dancing against their light.

'To me! To me!' Balfere's familiar bellow hung upon the air, above the din of cursing and shouting and agonised death cries. 'To me! To me!'

Seroyen galloped across ground clogged with dead men and horses, their blood pouring out upon ash-caked ground, turning it into a mire. Men clad in black fought sword to sword with the men of Mirador. But there were other figures also, closing for the kill, crossbows aimed only at the horses. The killers sent to destroy Aurion.

Areme's eyes raked the battlefield. No sign of the white stallion.

'What do we do?' asked Hessarde, galloping alongside. 'Romondor will get blamed for this.'

Areme yelled back, 'Portal to Myrrhye soon as you can. Tell her Kosall is not safe. I'll take Orlanda and the horse and ride for Byerol and meet up with the rest of my men. Tell her I'm bringing the horse and the girl to Taiere, whether she wills it or not. Go! Go! Go!'

Hessarde wheeled away.

Areme's eyes narrowed on the soldiers hacking at each other, steel shrieking against steel. He could not see Travall, or Veren. He could not see much of anything in the mad melee. Veren would not have abandoned Orlanda and Aurion. Had he got them free? Areme did not know.

Rage devoured him. He shouted to Sedor and the others, 'Kill them! Kill them all!'

There would be no quarter. The mercenaries, Romondor's men, the king's. Areme did not have time to care. He would kill them all to save Orlanda and the horse.

Every face closed down to a dead look of mercilessness. As one voracious beast, Areme's men launched themselves into the fight, galloping across churned earth.

Seroyen charged the fray, knocking down soldiers and mercenaries alike, hooves smashing them to pulp. Areme swung his sword, took off an assassin's arm, opened another's throat. A single swipe cleaved two heads wide. He wheeled Seroyen and buried his sword to the hilt in an attacker to his right.

Hatred powering every straining muscle, Areme struck holes through chests, split bodies from shoulder to hip. Guts gaped, spurting innards into the muck beneath sliding hooves. Screams filled the night, grunts of pain, wet slap of spilled entrails.

All about Areme, men wore masks of gore, eyes livened with fear. Soon they would be dead, stares unseeing. Areme's world reduced to blood, sundered flesh on steel. He breathed the stink of corpses, shit and piss. Everything that moved, he killed, mind lost in an orgy of death. For this he had been bred. He knew no other purpose.

Maddened, Seroyen took flight after prey, an assassin aiming at Sedor with a spear. Ten strides shortened to one in a heartbeat, the big grey flying. Areme's blade caught the man across the neck, sent the head rolling, the body lurching in its wake in a sliding fall across blood-slick ground.

Areme spun Seroyen back to the tumult, but at the edge of the carnage, a groan caught his ear. A pale shadow lay on the ground. A dead horse.

Everything within Areme became ice. He tore Seroyen about. Steel gleamed, a sword in the hand of a man who lay across the carcass. Somehow Areme cobbled together a face beneath the straggling, bloodied hair. Callinor. Relief surged. The horse was not Aurion, but Celestion.

Areme stared hard at the unmoving man lying atop the grey carcass. Callinor had finally received his deserved judgment. To die, fall unheralded, alone in the dark in the country he had murdered.

With the noise of the battle at his back, Areme swung from the saddle. Kneeling, he stared into Callinor's tired, worn face. He wanted to shout, to scream – *Where is she*? But his voice instead came quiet, 'How goes it, old man?'

The king's eyes fluttered open and focused, surprise glittering in the grey depths. 'How did *you* get here?' Every word came out in a wheeze.

'Too long a story.'

Callinor's hand clenched the mane of the dead stallion, his words slurred, 'He was her gift to me. Now I've lost everything.'

481

Areme said in a low, judging voice, 'There's still your daughter.' *Where is she? Where is she?*

A spluttering cough brought blood to the king's lips. 'I betrayed her.'

'Perhaps not.'

Something flickered in the king's eyes and his voice carried knowledge no mortal should have. 'You're one of them, aren't you? A Horse Lord.'

Areme started. How in all the hells did Callinor know that? No time to find out. Instead he answered, 'Yes.'

Callinor's eyes dimmed, voice thinned like stretched cobweb thread. 'I always knew you would come.' He coughed once more, then fear echoed in the remnants of voice as he asked, 'Is she her mother's daughter?'

He knew; the gods only knew how. Areme said, 'Now, and always. And more.' She would have to be if she was to save the world.

'Can she undo the curse?'

The words were so strained and quiet, Areme had to lean close to hear. 'Only with my help.' May the gods grant him the strength not to fail her like he had failed Shasirre. 'Where is she?'

'Lodgings a half-league back, with Travall.'

Areme released a harsh breath. Veren would be with her.

The spark of life diminished, but the voice lingered, weighed down with grief, love and guilt. 'Have you ever . . . loved a woman . . . so much you would put the world to war to bring one smile to her lips?'

Areme's voice was level and firm. 'Yes.'

'I would not live through another war.'

No chance of that, but Areme wanted certainty. He raised his sword. A soft curve touched Callinor's lips as cold steel fell.

Chapter 40

The Curse

The last fragments of sun had long since slipped below the horizon, yet an eerie glow prevailed over the landscape, feeble light from fires that littered the countryside. Beyond the rundown barn, indistinct figures continued grisly work beyond sunfall. Sihan and Maiet sat pensive in the stables, chewing tasteless crumbs of day-old damper. As night closed round, they lay on makeshift pallets, leaving bedrolls still packed behind saddlebags, but no one slept. Not really.

It took an age before Sihan's eyes drooped. In the grey zone between reality and wakefulness, a girl, comely, walked barefoot across a spring field, lips curved in a smile. Black tresses, the length of a man's forearm, coiled around her face. Poppies and everlastings rustled around her white ankles in drawn out, rhythmic sighs. She held out her hand to a man dressed in plain, dark garments.

The small colours of meadow flowers deadened, and the warmth of a morning, filled with blown apple blossoms, turned to sullen winter chill in a heartbeat.

The man knelt upon ash, before him a body, swathed head to foot in rotting cloth. When he pulled the folds of wool back, trembling hands revealed a skeletal face, hung only with traces of dried and shrunken flesh. The fingers emerging from the long sleeves were bone. His cry of "How can she be dead, and I still live?" shattered sleep.

Sihan's eyes snapped open. Skin clammy with sweat, he looked around. Bridled heads clinked against the wood of stalls as horses sought relief from bits in mouths. Over the soft snuffling of the horses' noses in feed bins, a distant rumble brought all the soldiers of Mirador to their feet, weapons drawn as they strode to the door.

Maiet hissed to Sihan, 'Get the horses into the yard by the back entrance.'

Heart jolting, Sihan hurried to the end of the stable and untied the first two horses. Peering through a slit in the wall, he just made out men moving in the courtyard, Veren and the Romondor soldiers who had remained behind, all looking toward the courtyard entrance. The soldiers of Mirador walked out of the stable, slowly, too casually.

A roar of hoofbeats filled the air as horses raced into the courtyard. Led by Balfere, they galloped straight at the Romondor soldiers, the Mirador riders cutting down the men in their path. Gerein and the others hesitated only a moment before they hacked at the black-clad men who had escaped the charge. Shouts and screams and clashing steel filled the air.

In shock, Sihan recognised Areme among the incoming riders. The knight leapt off his horse, and advanced toward Veren, the only Romondor soldier left alive. Areme levelled his sword at Veren's throat. 'Where is she?' he demanded, voice harsh.

Veren answered quickly, pointing at the ramshackle farmhouse. 'Upstairs.'

Balfere, limping, covered in gore, advanced upon Veren with murder in his eyes.

Areme stopped him. 'Don't kill him. Not yet.'

Balfere pressed his sword point to Veren's throat. 'Just tell me when.'

Areme kicked in the door of the farmhouse with a crash and pushed his way past Travall, who was barely able to stop himself from impaling his fellow knight.

Sihan hurried into the courtyard with the horses, handed them to their riders, and ran back for the rest. Camar, who had ridden out with the king's escort, rushed in and grabbed two more. His face was a mess of blood, one open flap of skin peeled back like a skinned nectarine.

'What happened?' cried Sihan.

'Those bleeding vultures killed the king,' hissed Camar.

Sihan's breath came in short, sharp pants. 'What are we going to do?'

Camar did not stop as he said, 'Run for our lives.'

Disturbed by muffled sounds from beyond the shuttered window, Orlanda rolled over on her pallet and shuddered. Between the slats, the sky outside bathed in an eerie red glow as though the sun refused to relinquish its sovereignty.

'By all that is merciful,' she whispered, 'where has fate brought me?'

Something rustled near the window. She turned to where a shadow crept toward her.

A rat. Orlanda clenched her fist. Did her father really expect her to live out her life in such a place?

The clear sound of clashing steel cut across her anger. She hurried to the window, rubbed at smeared glass. Soldiers milled in the courtyard; screams filled the air as red-hued steel flashed in the dim light of torches.

Dazed and bewildered, Orlanda ran for the door, struggled to find the handle. Flinging it open, she ran headlong into a cloaked man in the hallway. A scream tore from her throat, shrill and loud.

'Shut up!' said a voice, longed for and familiar, and harsh.

Areme shoved her brutally toward the stairs. 'Get out. Get out now!'

Orlanda stared at him without understanding. Then something wet and sticky beneath her fingers made her recoil. Blood, thick and congealing, covered her gloveless hands. Before her mind could come to terms with that, Areme pushed her stumbling down the stairs.

On the ground floor, the room filled with blood-soaked soldiers. Orlanda kept her hand on the banister for support. 'Where's my father?' she demanded, voice high and thin.

'Dead.' Areme pushed past her, leaving by the doorway to the courtyard to shout at the men beyond, 'Mount up! Mount up! Leave the baggage. Everyone ready to ride!'

Balfere, thick veins bursting from his neck, red face filled with fury, dragged Veren inside the room. His sword, blood-soiled from hilt to point, pressed at Veren's throat. Beneath its layer of thick blood, Balfere's face was hard with rage, telling her more than she wanted to know. In that moment of recognition, something snapped inside – her heart, her mind,

485

perhaps both. She waved a trembling hand at Veren. 'Is he the only vulture left alive?' To her ears her voice sounded calm, detached.

'Yes, Majesty.'

Majesty. It was true, then.

'Don't kill him. I want him alive.' She closed her eyes, trying to concentrate, trying to block out pain and grief.

Travall waited, mind spinning. Callinor was dead, released from the horror of all he had done, but Travall was still trapped. Envy warred with regret. And anger. If only Callinor had never married that bitch in the guise of a goddess, they would all have been spared this demonic conflict no one seemed able to end.

Orlanda's eyes opened, burning with a universe of hate. She stalked toward Veren, hissed breath in his face. 'Go. Tell Valoren. I will live with just one aim. From now until my dying breath, dawn to dawn. I will bring this curse upon him. I will raze Romondor and its allies to a pile of ash, and then I will come for him.'

Veren's face paled, but his voice came calm, low, filled with force. 'This was not our doing.'

Balfere roared, 'You lie through your teeth!' As an ominous growl rippled among the Mirador men, Balfere struck Veren hard with his fist.

Orlanda rounded on the Mirador knight. 'Don't touch him! He's dead. They're all dead. I want them to know.' She backed away and snarled, 'Get that vulture from my sight!'

Balfere grabbed Veren by his black tabard, and shoved him toward the door. Areme entered, long black hair dishevelled and matted. He shot a sharp glance at the Romondor knight and demanded of Balfere, 'What are you doing with him?'

'Sending him to Valoren with a message from the queen.'

Areme shot a look at Orlanda. 'What message?'

Orlanda leaned against the wall, breathing hard as if all the wind had been knocked out of her.

'Leave her alone.' Travall interposed himself between Areme and the new queen. He pushed Veren out the door and ordered the men outside, 'Get him out of here.' To Sihan, who was standing next to Maiet with other pale-faced, blood-spattered soldiers. 'You. Get your horse for the queen.'

'No!' Areme's voice came, sharp, decisive. 'She rides the white horse.'

Travall spat. 'So everyone can mark her?'

'The white horse will bear the queen. No other.' Areme's words dripped out in measured tones, each one punctuated with menace.

No time to argue. 'Get the horse.' To Maiet, Travall said, 'Get a cloak for the queen and take her outside.'

When the room stood empty of everyone but the knight commanders, Travall demanded of Balfere, 'What in all the hells happened out there?'

Balfere shook his head, running a gauntlet over his unkempt hair. 'They fell upon us. A horde of vultures. Hit the king first . . .' He rubbed his face, streaking blood and ash across it like paint. 'After that . . . It was dark. Confused. They took out so many horses, took them out first. Gods . . .' Balfere shuddered. 'If Areme hadn't turned up when he did–'

'How many got away?'

'Hard to tell. Those bastards are so dark they melt into the night. Enough to warn Valoren that some of us escaped. We've not got much of a start, less if we run into anyone between here and the border. And our horses have travelled hard.'

'We've got to get out of here, fast,' said Travall. 'Get the men mounted, and take the Romondor blacks.' As Balfere left, Travall rounded on Areme. 'What are *you* doing here? You had strict orders to remain in Mirador.'

Areme's lips formed a bloodless line. 'Those orders lost all value when we interrogated the men we caught.'

Travall snapped, 'What did they say?'

'They had orders to take out the king and the princess.'

'Orders from whom?'

'They died before spilling that. But I think it's obvious now, don't you?'

Travall's gaze remained on Areme, sensing evasiveness with every word sliding off the knight's tongue. 'If I find out you had something to do with this–'

Areme's hand settled on his sword hilt. 'What are you implying?'

His own fingers closing around his sword hilt, Travall said, 'It won't be the first time an aggrieved lover has killed those standing between him and his love.'

A chilled smile fixed upon Areme's lips. 'You really think I could take on the entire army of Mirador by myself?'

'With your entire command of cutthroats at your back. You've arrived here just at the right time. It wouldn't be hard for you to make it look like Romondor did this to throw us off the scent.'

Glaring, Areme drew his sword. 'I'll kill you for that.'

Travall held his ground, but did not draw. Areme was hot for a fight, and that did not accord with what he knew of the man. If Areme had been guilty of treason, he would have done it cold, calculated, efficiently, finished everyone with a dagger to the back. He would not have brought back Balfere as witness.

Travall took his hand from his sword. 'Don't bother. The Romondor soldiers will finish us both soon enough. We won't get to Byerol on tired horses before they catch us. Where's your command?'

Areme never stopped glowering. 'Byerol.'

'Mine?'

'Gerhas deployed your command and Balfere's to the southern borders. He's taken command himself. After your skirmish, we've got free rein through Byerol.'

'And a war on two fronts. Who is Regent?'

'Maraid.'

'How many men did you leave him?'

'Enough. The danger's not in Mirador.'

'Godsfuck,' swore Travall. 'The danger is everywhere.'

Maiet poked his head through the shattered doorway. 'Sir, we're ready.'

Travall followed Areme into the courtyard. He mounted his horse and rode down the line of grim-faced soldiers before taking his position at the van next to Areme, who flanked the queen. 'Right. Let's go. Heavens help us if the vultures catch us.'

Chapter 41

Flight

Colourless shadows galloped in a grey-black landscape, an exhausted, desperate flight, men and horses at breaking point. Not until they approached the Pelan border did Travall give the order to slow pace. In fading darkness, all ears strained for sound of pursuit.

Pre-dawn light showed the inhospitable land of Romondor giving grudging way to the pale green smear of the valleys of Pelan, frost furring grass stems. A flock of white cockatoos screeched across the pallid sweep of sky, then a cold, bloodstained sun rose above the eastern horizon. Westward, the Heavens graded from mist-grey depths to blue-black heights where stars still pricked sharp.

Travall rode next to Balfere and Areme, while two soldiers galloped ahead to the crest of a ridge, scouting. Together, the knights watched the signals the men made with their arms.

'Full company of vultures, not far behind,' interpreted Balfere. 'And they'll be on fresh horses.'

Travall rode back to the queen. Dirty gold hair trailed down her ash-streaked dress. 'I'm going to split the party, Majesty,' he told her. 'That's the only chance to get you back to Mirador alive.'

'You have your orders,' she said, voice laced with hidden meaning, face brooding.

Travall gave a swift nod, whirling his horse around as Areme approached.

'What orders?' demanded Areme, eyes slitted.

Caution had made Travall hold his tongue to Areme about his plans, but now he had no choice but to spill his intent. 'We'll head for the Korin Pass. The vultures are less likely to suspect we'll try that route.'

Areme's counter argument came fast. 'If the pass is closed we'll be trapped. Better to make a run through Byerol and meet up with my command.'

'With these?' Travall waved a hand at the soldiers' mounts plodding with heads hung low, flanks heaving. Ash-white foam lined the edges of harness and saddlecloths.

For some moments, Areme sat his horse in black and frowning stillness, then said with iced resolve, 'The queen comes with me to Byerol.'

Travall's face hardened. With Orlanda's words flowing through his mind, he braced his back, but it was Orlanda that answered. 'Travall has my orders. We make for the Korin Pass.'

Areme threw her a furious glare, and Travall quickly interceded. 'The Korin Pass is going to be unreachable unless we split the party. We need some riders to set a false trail through Byerol, the rest stay with us to Pelan.'

All the soldiers exchanged knowing glances.

Drawing a deep breath, Travall rode through the escort and stopped before a bearded soldier. Areme's man. 'Sedor. You're in charge of the party to Byerol. Pick the ten weakest horses to take with you.'

After shooting a quick glance at Areme, Sedor shouted ten names, then smiled grimly at Travall. 'We'll see you in Mirador in the spring.'

Travall watched them as they rode away. He was sending them to certain death; they all knew it.

The queen's escort rode until sunlight withdrew behind veils of thick, dark clouds swelling above candlewood crowns. In the distance, thunder rumbled over the ranges. It was not long before the rain came. Dispirited more with every stride, the riders wound their way single file along a narrow trail up a mountain, huge tree ferns brushing against their legs.

Sihan turned up the collar of his cloak. Heavy drops of rain ran down the soft wool to splash in mud puddles churned by the horse's hooves. He patted his bay. Spirit trotted along, tired but willing, thudding soft on ground deep in leaf mould.

The pace slowed to a slithering walk as the trail inclined sharply and turned to clay. Sihan's horse slipped and skidded, grunting in effort, hindquarters straining. Wrapping his fingers around the black mane, Sihan leaned forward over its neck, and muttered, 'Steady, steady.'

Through a gap in the trees, a crescent-shaped cliff line rose to the sky directly above. Camar slicked back his sodden red locks with his gloved hand, careful of the bandage covering his cheek. 'By the Heavens, that can't be the way.'

From the van, Travall forced his horse down the line of riders. He stopped in front of Maiet and said, 'Get up front and mark the trail.'

Maiet dismounted and tore off his cloak, bundling it into a pack on his saddle. Leading Warwind, he scrabbled up a narrow track up the cliff face, and disappeared among the trees. A short time later he shouted down, 'Everyone will need to dismount.'

Travall turned to Gerein. 'If those vultures are going to catch us, this is where it's going to happen. You and Camar to bring up the rear. Hold them off.'

Faces grim, Gerein and Camar held their horses as the rest of the riders filed past. Sihan jumped off his bay and unhooked the outside rein from the bit, leaving one long rein attached to the bay's left bit-ring. He threaded it back through the left stirrup iron, patting the horse on the rump.

Areme helped Orlanda do the same, voice low as he gave her instructions. 'Let Aurion go first, you follow. Hold on to his tail; let him pull you up after him. Don't pull on the rein except to stop him.' She nodded, face drawn and pensive.

Areme yelled back down the line. 'Two horse lengths between each horse. Watch the horse in front, and don't let your horse proceed until you have a clear space above you.'

One at a time, the escort started up the faint track zigzagging up the cliff face. Hooves skidded across rock and greasy clay. Balfere favoured his wounded thigh, relying on his warhorse to pull him along.

Sihan gritted his teeth. He had done this sort of thing often in the mountains, but knew one instant of miscalculation could mean death. Feeling like a bug in the shade of the cliff, he kicked his boot against a boulder to dislodge clay as he leaned against a tree until it was his turn to move. Rain came in gusts against his back. Though he hunched against the wind, cold air still found its way to the sweat on his skin. He froze as a panicked shout came from above.

'Stop! Stop!' shouted Orlanda.

Sihan stared up through the trees. Orlanda huddled against a trunk as a loose brown horse surged up the trail and passed her.

Sihan forced down a mad impulse to rush up and stop it. The horse pushed past Aurion, and only stopped its uncontrolled ascent when Areme whacked it on the face with the flat of his sword. The knight glared down at the horse's rider, who was struggling in pursuit of his wayward mount. The man reached the horse and grabbed it by the rein, breathing heavily.

Sihan didn't hear what Areme said to the man. He didn't need to.

He patted Spirit on the nose, breath forming a misty vapour matching volleys of steam pouring from his mount's nostrils. 'You're well-named, Spirit,' he said. 'You're going to need it to get us to the top.' As the trail cleared ahead of him, Sihan crept on, muscles burning.

Large tree roots broke the trail into steps. Spirit jumped up each one, dragging Sihan along by his tail as he lurched upward. Then the stallion stopped, refusing to move.

'What's the hold up?' called Gercin from behind.

Sihan pushed past Spirit, and found a rock blocking the path, at least three feet tall. He patted Spirit's neck. 'Come on, boy. It's just another jump. Everyone ahead of you has done it.' He tugged at the reins, but the stallion only made a half-hearted effort to raise a leg, head drooped, panting. The horse was young, not seasoned like the others. Sihan cast an anxious glance behind, to where Gerein and Camar waited. His breath caught in his throat.

Far below, tiny figures moved through the trees.

'Gerein!' he called, pointing.

'I see them,' replied the archer.

Then Balfere's bellow came from above. 'Move that horse or push it off the cliff!'

Sihan braced himself. There was no way he would shove any horse off the side of the cliff. He pulled on Spirit's rein, trying to keep desperation from his voice as he begged, 'Come on! Come on!' Making another feeble attempt, Spirit raised one foreleg and struck at the rock.

Scrambling up behind, Gerein shouted, 'Will you shift your great arse!' He drew his sword and brought the flat down on Spirit's rump with a mighty thump. Ears pinned, the bay surged onto the boulder, almost bowling Sihan off the trail. Sihan made a swift grab at the tail, flashing a grateful smile at Gerein over his shoulder.

'Hurry up!' shouted Travall, urging everyone to the summit.

Rock replaced clay as the trail wound between huge boulders. Sihan crested the top, and collapsed among the others huddled in a sodden heap in the middle of a clearing.

Horses walked around the boulders, drinking from pools of water on the ground, sweat and heavy breathing filling the air.

Maiet strode to Travall's side. 'There's only one path down to the west. Bad going, steep, clay.'

Travall motioned Gerein over. He pointed back at the trail up which they had just climbed. 'What do you think?'

Gerein leaned over a boulder at the crest. 'Perfect defensive position. One archer could hold off an army from here. They'll have to come up that path one horse at a time, just like us. And the cliff is impossible to climb any other way from this side, so they can't send unmounted men to try and get behind anyone defending this position.'

'You're going to get the chance to prove that theory.'

Gerein unshouldered his bow.

The soldier who had lost his horse walked forward, brown hair straggling over his tired face matching the mud on his boots. 'I'm not a bad shot with a bow.'

'You wouldn't be in this party if you were,' said Travall, rubbing his neck. 'What's your point?'

'You need Gerein more than you need me. I'll stay and hold them off.'

'If this has to do with what happened before–'

'No, sir, it doesn't.' The soldier cut him off, brown eyes wary. 'Well. Maybe it does.' He drew aside his cloak, revealing a deep slit in his thigh. 'I caught a sword when the king fell. That's why I couldn't hold the horse, sir. I won't be able to hold him going down neither. But I can hold a bow, and those vultures off long enough.'

Travall pulled his gorytos from his back and emptied arrows onto the ground. 'You're going to need these.'

All the men placed half their arrows in a pile next to the soldier. Maiet tore off a piece of his tunic, and bound the soldier's leg.

The man handed his reins to Maiet. 'Take my horse. He's a good one. If you lose Warwind, you'll do worse than taking him as your second mount.'

Maiet's gloved fingers closed on the bay's reins. 'I'd be honoured. What's his name?'

'Karfen.'

Orlanda arose from a boulder on which she had been resting and walked over to give the soldier her water pouch. 'What's *your* name?'

'Mendet, Majesty.'

Orlanda's hand closed upon his. 'Thank you, Mendet.' Everything, from the wide fear in her eyes, to the troubled tone of her voice, told of her deep concern at his sacrifice.

The soldier bent his head, long hair falling over her leather gloves. 'My life is yours, Majesty.'

Travall waited until she walked away. 'Is there anything you'd like me to tell your family?'

Mendet straightened, eyes bright. 'Tell them I did my duty.' Face set, he turned, and found a position overlooking the trail, then nocked an arrow.

'Let's move!' ordered Travall.

Sihan got to his feet, determined to show no complaint no matter how bad he felt. With the rest of the escort, he walked to the other side of the ridge and waited his turn to start the long climb down.

Maiet looked at the trail, red and orange clay interspersed with streaks of yellow. 'I'm going to send Karfen down first.'

'No,' said another soldier. 'He'll foul the whole trail and turn it into a quagmire for the rest of us. Send him down last.'

With a sharp twist of his head, Maiet flicked his wet blond hair out of his eyes. 'You saw what he did going up. He'll bolt going down, and who knows how many of us he'll bowl off the track as he hurtles past.'

'Maiet's right,' said Travall. 'Besides, the track's going to be a nightmare once any of us gets on it. There's not going to be an advantage whether you go down first or last.'

Decision made, Maiet slapped Karfen on the rump, sending the horse skittering down the trail. Karfen slipped and slid, then disappeared, hidden by the smattering of trees and thick wattle saplings lining the path.

When it came to his turn, Sihan slithered down the slope, grabbing at tree trunks and bushes in a vain attempt to stop sliding uncontrollably, boots sucking on clay. Legs straight, Spirit braced against the unstable terrain, rocks giving way beneath his hooves.

Slowly, clay gave way to solid granite ledges, twisting down in a spiral pattern as though a giant had carved a staircase to the base of the slope. Sihan led Spirit from ledge to ledge until the slope ended abruptly in a shallow creek.

While Spirit sucked at the clear mountain stream, Sihan shivered and pulled his cloak close. Wind cut through the clay-encrusted garment, deep into his exhausted body. Nearby, Gerein wound a new strip of torn tunic across Camar's wounded cheek, while Balfere tightened a bandage wrapped round his own injured thigh.

After a close inspection of the horses, Travall ordered two to be unsaddled and turned loose, both with strained tendons. One rider claimed Karfen, and the other rode double.

With everyone mounted, Maiet took the lead, following a trail along the creek. Dappled light filtered through towering crowns of swampwoods, cliffs producing an artificial dusk long before the sun set.

Sihan shifted uneasily in his saddle, skin chafing from his sodden garments. Large boulders rose like islands among a sea of ferns, ground alternating between rock and mud. They edged around a large jutting rock to where a massive overhang cast the track into darkness.

Travall called a halt. 'We'll rest here till morning. Cold camp.'

Everyone dismounted. Maiet and Sihan tethered the horses while the soldiers searched out defensive positions.

To Camar, Travall said, 'Look around.'

Camar stalked quietly into the undergrowth. Sihan gathered thistles for Spirit and Aurion, then searched for a dry place to sit. Cold rock offered no comfort. The men ate, but cautiously watched the area around them, alert, listening.

Everyone jumped to their feet and drew swords when a sound like metal striking metal rang out. Gerein nocked his bow and aimed in the direction from which the noise had come. His fingers twitched on the string when Travall knocked his bow away. 'Don't. It's a bird.'

'Good.' Gerein raised his bow. 'We can eat it.'

Once more forcing the archer's bow down, Travall said, 'It's a lirifen.'

Gerein's mouth twisted. 'You're going to let a perfectly good dinner run away because of superstition?'

'That's right.'

Shouldering his bow in disgust, Gerein stalked to his horse.

'What was that all about?' asked Sihan, turning to Maiet.

Maiet pulled out a dagger to scour half-dry mud from his cloak and boots. 'There's a myth a lirifen is the spirit of a warrior disarmed in battle, searching for his lost weapon. You don't shoot an unarmed man, so you don't shoot lirifens.'

A cold wind blew whispers through the trees. *They lie.* The ghost boy's voice drifted on the wind. *They've all shot unarmed men.*

Sihan shivered, wondering whether he should be more afraid of the Romondor soldiers pursuing them, the Mirador soldiers, or his own ghosts.

Hunched and rigid with cold, Orlanda huddled under the overhang. Areme sat beside her, holding her close, all sense of propriety giving way to the necessity of keeping warm. She took little comfort in his presence, the price too high.

The faces of the men under her command were stern. They had to be exhausted, but not one of them showed the strain. She wished she could match them. Her thoughts turned to her father, memories corroding all her reflections on their anguished relationship. All hope of reconciliation was lost. Maybe it was better she was too tired to even cry. She would do that later, when she could bear it.

She nestled herself into the hollow of Areme's shoulder and whispered, 'Are we going to make it?'

His arm tightened about her; warm breath caressed her cheek. 'Yes. And don't ask that question again.'

'Why?'

'It shows you're afraid.'

Pulling away, she gazed at him through wide eyes. 'Of course I'm afraid. Do you think I'm some sort of rock?'

Areme hushed her outburst. 'You're queen now. You must set the example for the men. Like it or not, you have to be the rock holding them steady.'

She stiffened against him. 'They're experienced soldiers.'

'That is a statement that has undone many a leader. Don't overestimate anyone. If they see you afraid, seeds of doubt will take root and grow. If they think you don't have faith in them, then they'll lose faith in themselves. Even the best of them.'

Orlanda gnawed her lip, brows drawn together. 'What can I inspire, when they have you, and Travall, and Balfere to follow?'

His fingers closed on hers. 'Courage and faith. If they can see a girl showing fortitude in adversity, how can they not follow her example?'

Orlanda placed her head against his shoulder. 'You expect much.'

'What I expect is no more than you can deliver. Grief and fear are private affairs for monarchs, to be expressed only behind closed doors.'

Orlanda buried her face against his chest, trying to draw his strength into her. 'Like love.'

Areme remained silent for a long while, then quietly whispered against her hair, 'Yes. Like love.'

Chapter 42

The Korin Pass

Mist rose from the forest as the first rays of sunlight heralded an icy dawn. Sihan lifted his head from its tough pillow of saddle-leather to cast bleary eyes about the camp. Soldiers crawled from bedrolls, stretching muscles cramped from cold and the tense sleep of fear. Rough moss-draped rocks added no comfort to hard muscles. Sihan stood and stamped about to force some warmth into his body: cloak, tunic, and leggings still sodden. The men wrapped themselves in cloaks, warding off the biting wind.

Sharp orders came to mount. Orlanda approached, eyes red-rimmed, face drawn. Without a word, she took Aurion's reins and numbly pulled herself into the saddle.

The refreshed horses traversed the flat winding trail at a harried trot, riders nervous, twisting in their saddles, heads jerking from side to side at the least flutter of birdwing brushing leaf. From time to time, Sihan glanced behind but saw and heard nothing amiss, thick copses of trees offering nothing more dangerous than a scurrying fox. By the time the sun ascended mid-Heavens, the trees opened on a valley to the left, running parallel to the trail.

Travall held up his hand, his stallion jog-trotting on the spot. The knight scanned the ground, then turned his mount from the trail, following the deep imprints of Warwind's hooves into the valley below. With the others, Sihan set Spirit downward also, longing to bathe in the ripening sunrays. Travall checked his stallion in the edge of the trees, looking out for danger. Long moments stretched while all the men strained their eyes. A series of rolling snowgrass pastures, carpeted in snow daisies, poppies and centaury, stretched into the distance, coming to an end at the base of the first of a succession of mountains. Snow-capped peaks rose like spires, disappearing in a haze of clouds.

At Travall's nod, they broke cover. The knight set the pace, a loping canter across the grass, only bringing the escort back to a trot as the plain met the lower slopes of the mountains. When they came to a clear stream, he allowed the riders to let their horses drink and graze.

Gerein glanced behind as he reined in his horse. 'Still nothing.'

'Do you think Mendet's still alive?' asked Sihan.

Gerein shrugged. 'He'll hold out for as long as possible, but in the end he'll fall. No man can stay awake for more than a few nights and days. And he was injured. That'll take a toll. Not to mention he'll probably run out of arrows before he succumbs to the wound.'

'Typical, Gerein,' muttered Camar, gingerly fingering the bandage across his face. 'Always the optimist.'

The escort resumed the trek. Snowgrass valleys gave way to rock as they reached the trail running around the base of the mountains. They found Maiet encamped halfway up the first incline with the welcome news the snow did not look impassable at the level of the Korin Pass.

They climbed the serpentine mountain trail to the snowline. Nothing moved but wind among the treetops, and a windhover hanging in the air above them, circling on the currents. Twisted snowbarks filled the slopes, jagged bark in shades of green and grey, or tints of red, yellow and orange.

As the sun set for another night, Travall called a halt. Iced wind drove down from the mountains, gnawing at flesh and bone. Another cold camp promised no sleep, and as the clear night sky deepened, weighed down with huge stars, everyone pressed together for warmth.

Maiet pulled his cloak over his head, shivering beneath it. Too cold to even attempt sleep, Sihan got up and went to Aurion. As he ran his fingers through the long mane, combing out tangles, light sparked from the tendrils. Sihan stepped back in surprise. A strangle glow outlined the stallion like a silver-edged cloud.

He left the horse's warm body, and sat on a slab of granite, staring at Aurion. He was imagining things again. It was surely a trick of moonlight. He rocked back on his haunches and tilted his head to the sky. Stars blazed brightly, some scorching across the Heavens, fiery tails streaming behind them. He sat breathless, staring, wondering if they were the flight of gods.

'Can't sleep?'

Startled, Sihan spun round. Areme stepped out of shadow into a shaft of moonlight that set his long black hair ablaze with ice fire. Sihan shivered. There was something different, intangible, about him, a quality whispering of ages past.

'Have you seen the fire trails before?' asked Areme, breath ribbon threads of mist in the iced air.

For a long while they regarded each other mutely, then Sihan looked back at the shooting stars. 'In Graycor. But they were never like this. Here I feel I can reach out and touch them.'

Areme favoured him with a small and private smile. 'I feel the same way. They are so close, and at the same time so distant.' He sat on the rock, but his gaze remained fixed on Sihan. 'Tell me about your mother.'

Sharp surprise fixed Sihan's eyes to the dark face so close above his own. 'My mother?'

Areme's gaze never left his. 'What do you remember of her?' Everything about his voice bespoke casual curiosity, as if he cared not one jot about any answer, but something in the brilliance of the knight's eyes spoke otherwise.

Nonplussed, Sihan took a moment to gather his thoughts. 'She was beautiful. Dark hair, like the night.'

The knight remained silent for a time, his profile against the moon piercingly clear, shadows making sharp edges of his cheekbones. 'What else?'

'She taught me letters and numbers.' Recalling his mother's words forbidding him to take up the sword, the page from her book still safe in a pouch at his belt, he said, 'I think she would have liked me to be a healer – she taught me herbs and healing arts.' He finished with a vague shrug. 'I don't know what you want to hear.'

Voice neutral, Areme asked, 'Did she ever give you any gifts – a token – a ring, perhaps?' He watched Sihan intently, with a suspicious watchfulness reminding Sihan of a hawk about to swoop. Areme's fingers tapped the hilt of his dagger.

Ice crawled over Sihan's skin. Sensing danger, he chose his next words with care. 'All she gave me, I carry in my heart.'

Areme regarded him with a frown, as if judging the weight of his words, then let out a slow sigh and moved his hand away from the dagger. His teeth gleamed in a half-formed smile and he shifted the conversation. 'Tell me, did your mother talk about the stars when she was alive?' His tone was neutral, but his eyes never strayed from Sihan's face.

Sihan was quick to note the strangeness of the chosen words, yet somehow he felt compelled to answer. 'Sometimes.' Again, he thought of her letter, the words about the Firestar.

'Have you seen her since her death?' The question came fast, calculated, measured for effect.

Sihan choked. 'What?'

Areme's voice was hard. 'You heard me.'

Standing up, Sihan bristled. 'That's not funny.'

Areme joined him on his feet. 'I wasn't trying to be funny.' His voice was demanding as he took a quick, silent stride toward Sihan, grasping Sihan's wrists in lean, strong hands. 'Have you seen her in dreams or visions?'

There was some trickery here. Why was Areme asking these questions? What did he know of the visions? Sihan thought of the girl in the snow, the boy whose touch was ice, the grey-cloaked woman in the trees on the shore of the Sea of Eagles. None of these were visions of his mother, yet he felt Areme wanted all his secrets when he had asked that question. Staring into Areme's eyes, Sihan encountered nothing but darkness.

'No,' he said, foreboding settling around him like a mantle. Forcing himself to ease into submission, he waited for Areme's grip to relax. When it did, Sihan seized the opportunity and pulled away. 'What do you want from me?' he demanded.

'The truth,' said Areme.

'I owe you nothing.' Before Areme could waylay him further, Sihan returned to his place beside Maiet.

Areme remained near the rock. As the moon reached it zenith, lucent flames seemed to spark around him. Then, slowly, while the shimmering light diminished, he became a shadow. Sihan shivered once more, as though snow slithered down his back.

Before dawn, hoarfrost shone in the half-light of the stars, silver and glistening on snowgrass. The escort continued up the mountain trail, roseate wisps of cloud streaking across the sky as morning bloomed.

Sihan's skin prickled. He found Areme staring at him without any attempt at concealment.

'What's wrong?' asked Maiet. 'You look like someone is pissing on your funeral pyre.'

Keeping his voice low, Sihan said, 'Areme keeps looking at me in a funny way.'

Maiet shrugged. 'That's funny. I get a weird feeling whenever I look at *him*.'

'Why?'

Pulling up the collar on his cloak, Maiet said, 'There's something strange about him. A lot of things really. Maybe you haven't been around long enough to notice, but Areme never seems to age. I've known him for eight winters, the same as Bal and Trav. But he doesn't show any signs of wear and tear. Bal and Trav both have a lot of scars and lines and all sorts of things you'd expect from men who have been around since the last Great War. But Areme, he looks like a man who's known less than thirty winters, and not harsh ones. By my reckoning he should be over forty. And I still can't understand how he recovered from what Veren did to him at the warhorse trial. It's not natural.'

Thoughts churned in Sihan's mind, but then who was he to question what was unnatural? Trying to push aside disturbing images, he asked, 'Do you think we'll get to the pass today?'

Maiet glanced up at the mountain. 'Yes. And if the pass is clear, we'll be in Pelan by tomorrow.'

'Then what?'

'We hole up there till spring, and then we launch war on Romondor.'

Travall rode up and said, 'You two take the van.'

They rode to the front, much to Sihan's chagrin. The last thing he needed was the uncomfortable feeling of Areme's eyes boring into his back.

Day wore on. Wind shredded black clouds speeding across the mountains, leaving scattered pennons of azure in their wake. Cold bit sharper into Sihan's skin. Beside him, the scout gnawed at his lip, then sniffed. 'I smell rain, maybe something a lot worse.' Maiet wheeled Warwind around and rode back to the escort. He yelled to Travall as soon as he was within earshot, 'Snow's coming! We're going to have to make a run for it!'

Travall waved him on. 'Ride up to the pass and let us know if it's clear.'

While Maiet raced back up the track on Warwind, Sihan fell back to the rest of the party. They came to a gap between two towering granite cliff-faces studded with trees. Sihan pulled his cloak tight against the wind buffeting and tearing at him, at the same time struggling to keep Spirit from veering sideways as the horse sought to keep its rear end to the wind.

Storm-twisted candlewoods lashed back and forth. Rain came as predicted, icing into sleet, causing the horses to curl their heads to their chests. It was all the riders could do to force them into the face of the storm.

The escort passed through the cleft, hugging the side of the mountain. Wind brought stinging flakes of snow which thickened swiftly till they obliterated ground and groaning trees. Above the clamour came the breaking and snapping of limbs.

Sihan strained to see ahead, cold stinging his nostrils with every breath. Suddenly Spirit stopped.

'Keep going!' yelled Gerein behind him, voice barely audible above the howling wind.

Sihan tapped Spirit's sides with his boots but the stallion refused to move. A huge roar set Spirit rearing. A massive tree uprooted on the mountain and thundered down.

'Get back! Get back!' Balfere rode up and grabbed at Spirit's bridle, pulling him backwards just before the tree tore across the space Sihan and Spirit had just occupied.

'By the Heavens!' cried Camar, eyes wide. 'That was too close.'

Blood pounded in Sihan's temples.

'Ride on!' yelled Balfere.

Snow struck Sihan's eyes and hit his legs, chest, and arms as Spirit floundered over rocks brought down by the tree. He rode to where riders huddled in the shelter of a rock overhang.

'We have to go now, if we're going to go at all,' yelled Travall. 'This storm will cut the trail.'

'It's slippery and narrow ahead.' Maiet's voice was raw with fear. 'One horse at a time.'

Balfere bellowed, 'Spread the word.'

Maiet pushed past and rode down the line of riders.

Travall turned to Orlanda. 'Stay close to the wall. There's a thousand-foot drop on the right.'

Orlanda nodded, face pale and frightened. Areme pushed his horse up alongside and reached out to touch her on the arm. 'Don't worry.'

'Who's worried?' She pressed her lips to a thin smile.

Travall took the lead along a narrow ledge, followed by two soldiers, then Sihan. The overhang receded to half its width as the storm caught the riders.

Sihan's left leg scraped against the cliff-side. His face stung and his eyes burned. Halfway across, an ear-shattering blast reverberated from above, slamming hard against his eardrums, surpassing even the roar of the blizzard. A torrent of rocks and ice crashed down.

Screaming filled Sihan's ears as the rider directly in front of him caught the brunt of the avalanche and fell with his horse into the abyss below. Another scream came from behind. Sihan turned, and his blood froze.

Orlanda hung off Aurion's side, arms clamped around his neck. While the white stallion scrabbled furiously to remain on the trail, her slender body whip-lashed back and forth as ground gave way beneath the horse's hooves. Orlanda clutched at the reins, tried to crawl back onto the saddle.

'Let go of the reins!' cried Areme, 'Don't pull him over!'

Reins slipped from Orlanda's grasp as her body tipped backwards. She grabbed at the stallion's mane, screaming, 'Areme!'

The knight spurred his horse forward and grabbed at the stallion's bridle, pulling Aurion along by the head. Then he reached across the horse's neck. 'Grab my hand!'

Orlanda's fingers touched his. Aurion kicked furiously at the cliff edge with his hind legs. Her hand slipped away.

Sihan jumped from Spirit. He grabbed at the breastplate and hauled.

Orlanda lost her grip on the mane. As she slid down Aurion's vertical body, she clutched at the saddle, fingers clawing at leather.

Camar, following at Areme's back, jumped off Warwind, caught the flap of Aurion's saddle. He thrust his back against the wall, levering his legs against the rocks. Another roar erupted above.

'Pull!' yelled Areme.

All three dragged the white stallion back onto the track as snow and ice smashed down. A mass of white swirled in front of Sihan, a whirlwind of twisting snow. Ice slammed at him. Pain speared his body, chest and ribs aching as though someone had hit him with the blunt end of an axe.

Camar leaned back under what was left of the overhang, shaking, plumes of white fog obscuring him as Aurion's breath spewed out through dilated nostrils. The avalanche subsided.

Areme held the white stallion's reins.

There was no sign of Orlanda.

End Part 1

Thank you for reading my book. If you enjoyed it, won't you please take a moment to leave me a review at your favourite retailer?

Thanks!

BJ Hobbsen

Continued in Godsteed

Book 2

Darkness Before Death

Other books by BJ Hobbsen

Prequels to the Godsteed series:

Watchnight (Veren's story) (release 2017)
Horse Lords of Senfar (Areme's story) (release 2015)
Godsteed - The Great War (release 2017)

Godsteed series:

Godsteed Book 1 Night of Wolves
Godsteed Book 2 Darkness Before Death
Godsteed Book 3 Ascension
Godsteed Book 4 Dead Man's Race (release 2015)
Godsteed Book 5 Riders of the Mist (release 2015)
Godsteed Book 6 Redemption (release 2015)

Connect with BJ Hobbsen

Friend me on Facebook:

https://www.facebook.com/profile.php?id=100005210629349

Printed in Great Britain
by Amazon.co.uk, Ltd.,
Marston Gate.